WARNING: MATURE CONTENT—ADULTS ONLY

This dark fantasy, paranormal romance contains explicit content including detailed intimate encounters, graphic violence, visceral combat sequences, and intense scenes of a sexual nature. Reader discretion is strongly advised. This work is intended for mature audiences only.

This is a work of fiction. All characters, names, places, businesses, and incidents are either products of the author's imagination or used fictitiously. Any resemblance to actual persons, living or dead, events, or locales is purely coincidental

A.L. Hampton asserts the moral right to be identified as the author of this work.

The author and publisher assume no responsibility for errors, inaccuracies, omissions, or any other inconsistencies herein, including the persistence or accuracy of URLs for external or third-party Internet Websites referenced in this publication.

Dark Skies

First Edition, 2025

Paperback ISBN—979-8-9892342-8-8

Ebook ISBN—979-89892342-7-1

CONTENT WARNING

WELL HELLO AGAIN, LOVELY READERS!

Let's be real—if you've made it this far into the series, you're practically family at this point. I'm assuming you're well acquainted with how I roll when it comes to steamy encounters, spicy scenes, and those knock-down-drag-out fights that leave everyone breathless (and not always in the fun way). But for those who need a refresher (and because my lawyer insists), let's break down what you're diving into...

The Spicy Stuff—

By now you know I don't always fade to black. These pages contain the same explicit, detailed encounters you've come to expect from me. We're talking about all the good stuff: *dominance play, edge-of-your-seat tension—Spanking, breath play, edging, degradation, domination, explicit sex, anal sex, oral play, public sex, choking, spitting, cum play, rough sex, power play, face-fucking,* and those deliciously detailed scenes that make you check twice to ensure no one's reading over your shoulder.

Battle and Brutality—

If you've been here since book one, you're nodding along because you know—our characters fight dirty, fight often, and sometimes fight pretty. Blood will be spilled, bones might be broken, and yeah, some people are going to have really, really bad days. Just like the previous books, expect battles that'll make you wince and consequences that'll make you gasp.

The Emotional Rollercoaster—

Three books in, and our characters are still unpacking their emotional baggage like they're moving into a mansion of trauma. We're keeping it real with mental health struggles, past wounds, and the kind of emotional depth that might have you reaching for both chocolate and tissues.

Sensitive Content—

This book contains references to and descriptions of sexual assault and abuse perpetrated by antagonists. While these scenes are not gratuitous, they are integral to the plot and character development. None of these acts are committed by our main characters, but they do deal with the aftermath and consequences. These topics are handled with care but may be triggering for some readers.

Listen, if you've made it this far, you know exactly what you're signing up for. If you're new here... well, honey, you might want to start with book one (or at least grab a stiff drink first).

XOXO and Let's Get Back to the Chaos,

A.L. Hampton

P.S.—If this warning made you nervous, you should probably stop here. If it made you grin... welcome to the dark side, we have cookies!

DARK SKIES

THE CROWN OF THE SEVEN REALMS SERIES

BOOK IV

PRONUNCIATION GUIDE

ÁSGARD------AHZ-GAHRD

BRAXOS------BRAH-KHOS

DRAUGER------DROU-GUR

EINHERJAR-----AINE-HAHR-YAR

HEIMDALL-----HAME-DAHL

LUCIAN-----LOO-SHIN

RHYLAND-----RYE-LAND

SKADI-----SKA-DEE

SLEIPNIR-----SLAYP-NEAR

VIDAR-----VEE-DAHR

RHYLAND

1

Ásgard?

A bitter laugh tears from my throat. Un-fucking-believable. The golden realm of the gods spreads before me in all its mythical glory, mocking everything I thought I knew. For centuries, I'd dismissed it as nothing but horseshit stories—tales we Vikings swallowed with our mead, promises of glory in death.

"Well, isn't this a mindfuck?" I growl under my breath, my hands clenching into fists. The same legends my mother beat into my head as a child now stand before me. Not some fairytale paradise waiting for warriors who died with sword in hand.

Restless and raw, my power ripples beneath my skin as reality bends around me. Every instinct screams that I shouldn't be here—that no vampire, not even one with Viking blood, belongs in this realm of gods and legends.

But here I fucking stand.

And somewhere in this golden cage, someone will give me answers whether they want to or not.

My legs nearly give out as reality warps around me. My predatory instinct roars to life, fangs dropping as I face the towering figure before me. Those green eyes bore into me like acid, stripping away every defense I've built over centuries.

"Rhyland of Midgard." His voice crashes like a thousand thunderbolts. "We've been waiting."

This hulking bastard towers over me, a mountain of rippling muscle and ancient power. His dark skin looks like it was carved from granite, and his eyes burn an unnatural green that feels like it could strip the flesh from my bones.

Dark braids fall down his back, adorned with glinting gold, and his armor looks like it was forged in the heart of a star. The sword at his hip thrums with a power that sets my teeth on edge, a silent warning that he's not to be fucked with.

He carries himself with the confidence of a god, and every movement is precise and calculated. But I don't give a damn about his power or his posturing. I want answers, and I want them now.

Gold metal walls stretch up into darkness, covered in weird-ass symbols that seem to move when I'm not looking directly at them. Colossal gears and shit I can't even begin to understand spin overhead like some twisted cosmic machinery.

The floor under my boots pulses with light like it's alive, and steam—or whatever the hell it is—hisses from vents with an electric charge that makes my fangs throb. Nothing about this place makes sense to my predatory instincts. One minute I'm about to tear Azrael apart, the next I'm standing in... wherever the hell this is.

This has to be some kind of hallucination. But the raw power crackling through the air feels too real, setting every nerve ending on fire.

The beast inside me snarls, clawing to get out. "Who the *fuck* is waiting?" I growl. "I'm not some goddamn lapdog to be summoned at will."

The bastard dares to smirk. The air is tense as he steps closer, power rolling off him in suffocating waves. Every muscle in my body coils tight, ready to strike despite knowing I'm outmatched.

"You dare question the will of Ásgard?" His voice drops dangerously low. "Your arrogance blinds you, vampire. You are here because forces beyond your comprehension demand it."

"I don't give a shit about forces or demands," I snarl, baring my fangs. "Tell me who the hell you are and what game you're playing."

"I am Heimdall," the words echo with ancient power. "I am Guardian of the Bifrost, Watcher of Realms. And you, Rhyland Eriksson, are testing my patience."

My ancestors' stories flood back—tales of this very being who stands before me. But none of that matters. I can only focus on the severed connection to my mate, the hollow emptiness where Dani should be. I reach desperately through our bond again, my chest constricting when I find nothing but silence.

"What the *hell* is this about?" Every muscle in my immortal body is coiled tight, ready to tear through anyone stupid enough to keep me here. "I don't give a damn what you gods want—send me back to my mate *now*, or I'll paint these halls red."

I'm a live wire ready to snap at any moment. It's different here—stronger, more intense like someone cranked the dial up to max and ripped off the knob. I can feel it crackling through my veins, an electric current that flows through me.

It's a rush like nothing I've ever felt before, and it's all I can do to keep it contained. I feel like I'm a grenade with the pin pulled, just waiting for the right moment to explode.

I don't know what the hell is causing this surge, but I do know one thing—if anyone tries to fuck with me now, they're going to find out exactly how dangerous I can be. And maybe, just maybe, that includes the high and mighty Heimdall himself.

Heimdall's hulking form towers closer, his green eyes blazing. I stand my ground, fangs bared. I might be outmatched, but I'm no one's puppet.

"Watch your tongue, *Godborn*." His voice thunders through the space between us. A warning. "Your Viking blood may grant you privilege, but even that has limits. Follow me—*now*—or discover how merciful I've been."

A savage snarl rips from my chest.

Godborn?

Another fucking riddle when all I want is to get back to Dani. The bond screams in my chest, the hollow ache where our bond should be drives me insane. Every second I waste in here is another second she's alone, vulnerable.

Heimdall turns on his heel and strides away, leaving me no fucking choice but to follow. A door opens, and the sight that greets me knocks the wind out of my lungs. Ásgard, in all its goddamn glory, stretches out before me like a fever dream.

The bitter cold bites at my skin, ice and snow blanketing everything in sight. Frigid winds howl around me like hungry wolves, carrying the bite of ancient winters in their teeth.

Through the swirling white, a mountain pierces the sky like a titan's spear. At its peak, a palace gleams like it was torn from the fabric of the cosmos itself—all crystalline spires and impossible architecture that puts every mortal wonder to shame. The whole thing sparkles in the otherworldly light, each facet throwing off rainbows that mock the northern lights. It's a middle finger to reality itself, screaming to all creation that the gods can build whatever the hell they want, physics be damned.

But it's the bridge that really catches my eye. The damn thing looks like it's made of pure glass, pulsing with an inner light, that shifts and dance. It stretches out towards the mountain like some celestial pathway, daring me to step onto it and see where it leads.

Am I dead? Did that piece of shit, Azrael actually manage to kill me, and this is some twisted version of the afterlife? If this is supposed to be Valhalla, then someone's got a really fucked up sense of humor.

My head's pounding with a thousand questions, each one more maddening than the last. And the constant whispers from this goddamn Soul Stone aren't helping. They claw at the edges of my mind, a never-ending chorus of voices that makes me want to rip my own skull apart.

I clench my jaw, focusing every ounce of my willpower on shutting them out. It takes a moment, but finally, the whispers fade into blessed silence. My eyes snap open, and I stare ahead, my muscles tight with tension.

This is some grade-A bullshit. I should be holding Dani right now, her sweet scent in my lungs instead of this frigid mountain air, my hands covered in Azrael's blood—not standing here with my dick in my hand. I'm stuck in this mythological mindfuck, dancing to the tune of some holier-than-thou cosmic bouncer.

Heimdall glances back at me, his eyes flashing with impatience. "Follow me," he commands.

I bite back a snarl, every instinct screaming at me to tell him exactly where he can shove his orders. But I need answers, and if playing along is the only way to get them, then that's what I'll do.

For now.

We finally reach the giant structure sitting center—"the Elemental Spire," Heimdall tells me. And I can't help but stare at the monumental tower stretching up into the sky. This thing is a fucking beast, its base wide enough to swallow Manhattan whole and a peak that vanishes into the clouds like it's trying to stab heaven itself.

Ice crystals form in my beard and hair, the brutal cold biting deep enough to make even my vampire ass feel it. The wind howls around us, carrying snowflakes sharp as razor blades, but the Spire stands untouched, like winter itself bows before its might.

As we approach the base of the spire, I can make out intricate carvings etched into the surface, pulsing with an otherworldly light. Runes and symbols that seem to shift before my eyes, their meanings just beyond my grasp.

The entire structure throbs with power, each pulse sending waves of energy through the air that make my fangs ache. It's like standing next to the heart of the world, feeling each massive beat shake the ground beneath my feet.

I bite the inside of my cheek, trying to shake off the feeling of being a mouse in the presence of a lion. But as we step through the vast archway and into the heart of the spire, I know with a bone-deep certainty that I'm in way over my head.

The doors groan open like the maw of some ancient beast, revealing a hall so extensive it makes me feel like a fucking ant. The whole place looks like some giant carved it straight from the planet's skeleton—all gleaming stone and impossible architecture.

Heimdall swaggers through like he's got a golden stick up his ass, every step radiating 'I'm better than you' energy. My boots ring out against the polished floor behind him, each echo a reminder that I don't belong in this realm of myths and legends. The air itself feels heavy with power, pressing down on my shoulders like a physical weight.

Carved columns stretch up into shadows so deep even my vampire eyes can't pierce them, and every surface is etched with stories of gods and monsters. Funny how I used to think those were just fairy tales my mother told me. Now I'm walking through their fucking palace like some twisted tourist attraction.

But it's the three figures seated at the far end of the hall that really catch my eye—seated on thrones that look like they were forged from the bones of the earth itself. I swallow hard, my heart pounding as I try to make sense of what I'm seeing.

There is a Zeus-looking son of a bitch, all bulging muscles and crackling energy. His hair and beard sit perfectly, and his eyes—fuck me, those eyes. They flash like polished brass in firelight, searing into my soul with an intensity that makes me want to drop to my knees and pledge my goddamn allegiance.

There's something familiar about him, like a half-remembered dream scratching at the back of my mind. But I can't quite put my finger on it. All I know is that this fucker radiates power like a supernova, and every cell in my body is screaming at me to bow down and worship at his feet.

But I'll be damned if I'm going to let some muscle-bound prick with a god complex make me his bitch. I clench my jaw, meeting his gaze with a defiant stare of my own. If he wants my respect, he's going to have to earn it.

And then it hits me—that sweet scent that can only be described as heaven. It's like a siren call, tugging at something deep inside me. The same intoxicating aroma that clings to Dani, driving me to the brink of madness every time.

I close my eyes, fighting to control the surge of thirst that wells up inside me. My throat burns, my fangs itch, but I swallow it down, forcing myself to stay focused. This isn't the time or place to lose my head.

But fuck, it's hard.

"Welcome, Rhyland." My eyes snap open at the woman sitting on the right, who really steals my breath. She's a vision of divine beauty, with hair like spun gold cascading down her back. Her eyes are a piercing blue, and her skin seems to glow with an inner light. She carries herself with grace and poise that speak of great wisdom.

I nod, and the man in the center draws my gaze like a magnet. He's a hulking figure with a beard that falls like a cloud of silver down his chest. His armor is adorned with runes that seem to dance in the light, and the spear at his side thrums with a power that makes my blood run cold. But it's his eye that really sends a chill down my spine. A single, piercing orb that seems to see straight through me, weighing and measuring every inch of my soul.

Recognition slams into me. I've heard the stories and seen the carvings. But nothing could have prepared me for the reality of standing before him.

Odin. The AllFather himself.

I swallow hard, my mouth suddenly dry. This can't be real. I must be dreaming, or maybe I really did die, and this is some fucked up version of the afterlife. But as I stand there, staring at the gods of my ancestors, I can't deny the power radiating from them. It's ancient and primal, the kind of power that could reshape worlds with a thought.

And right now, all that power is focused on me.

DANICA

2

Agony explodes as Damon's fangs tear into my flesh. Each pull steals more of my life force, my blood flowing freely as darkness creeps at the edges of my vision. I push against his chest, but my strength is fading fast.

"D-Damon..." The plea catches in my throat, replaced by a wet gurgle. This can't be happening. Not like this.

Azrael. That sadistic bastard must have turned my brother—fed him vampire blood before snapping his neck. A final, twisted gift designed to destroy us both. He's transformed my protective little brother into the very monster Damon despises.

The newborn hunger consumes him completely. My brother is lost in a frenzy of bloodlust he can't control. Each desperate swallow drives him deeper into darkness, stealing more of his humanity. The pain of watching him transform is worse than the physical agony of his feeding.

"Damon, please..." I beg, voice a weak, terrified whisper. "This isn't you. Fight it! Don't let this control you!"

My consciousness flickers like a dying flame. Through our bond, I reach desperately for Rhyland, but find only a terrifying void where his presence should be. He's gone—taken somewhere beyond my reach. The emptiness feels like a knife twisting in my soul.

Who has taken him?

What fresh hell awaits us both?

If I die here, Rhyland will be lost to the Darkness forever. All our nightmares, all our fears of his descent into shadow, will become reality without me to anchor him to the light. We're bound together—two halves of one whole. I can't abandon him to that fate.

Tears mix with blood as I beat weakly against Damon's shoulders. "Please... stop..." The words dissolve into wet, choking sounds. My own brother will drain me dry—kill me if I can't break free.

Suddenly, Damon's weight vanishes. Through my blurred vision, a woman materializes—fiery red hair framing a face of cruel beauty. Her emerald eyes glitter with malicious triumph as she stares down at me.

"Well, well, look what I've finally found."

Who the hell is this?

Terror turns my blood to ice. I press a trembling hand against my ravaged neck, feeling my life pump between my fingers. "Who—?"

"Introductions can wait," she purrs, yanking me up like a ragdoll. The world spins violently. "Let's get somewhere more private. Can't have you dying before I'm done with you."

I thrash against her iron grip, but Damon's feeding has left me drained and broken. My body, already battered from the earlier battle, betrays me. Panic claws at my chest as the helplessness of my situation crashes over me.

Through the haze of pain and encroaching darkness, I hear Seraphina and Emily calling for me desperately. Their voices sound distorted, as if reaching me through deep water. I try to scream back, but my ravaged throat produces only a wet wheeze.

The forest blurs around us as my captor moves with supernatural speed. Shadows and moonlight swirl together in a nauseating dance. Questions thunder through my fading consciousness:

Where is she taking me?

What horrors await?

Will I ever see Rhyland again?

But the darkness is relentless, dragging me under despite my desperate fight to stay aware. As consciousness slips away, I'm swallowed by the void, lost in an abyss of uncertainty and terror.

The last thing I register is the woman's cold laugh, promising torments yet to come.

Darkness engulfs me as I slowly regain consciousness, my mind struggling to make sense of my surroundings. A solitary lamp casts a feeble light, barely illuminating the room. As my eyes flutter open, I realize I'm lying on a bed, the softness beneath me a stark contrast to the confusion and fear swirling within.

Blinking away the lingering haze, I take in the room around me. It's clearly not a hospital but a lavish bedroom that exudes opulence and sophistication. The furnishings are pristine, and the decor is tasteful and expensive. It's like I've woken up in some ritzy place, but the sterile, chemical scent that permeates the air reminds me that not all is as it seems.

A barn owl perches near the window, its heart-shaped face ghostly white in the dim light. Those black eyes track my every move with unsettling intelligence, like it's reporting my status to whoever orchestrated my current predicament. The creature's pristine feathers ripple as it cocks its head, studying me with that eerie supernatural awareness that screams 'magical spy camera.'

Questions flood my mind as I decipher how I ended up here. The last thing I remember is the horrifying attack, Damon feeding on me, the searing pain as my life drained away, and that...*woman*. Panic rises in my chest at the memory, my heart pounding against my ribs.

Gritting my teeth, I attempt to sit up, only to be roughly yanked back down. Confusion and panic surge through me as I glance at my wrists, my heart plummeting when I see the glint of metal shackles binding me to the bed.

Goddamnit!

I yank against the metal shackles until my wrists are raw, fighting with every ounce of strength I have. But it's pointless—my body, still ravaged from Damon's attack, betrays me.

Defeated, I sink back into the pillow, my chest heaving. *Focus, Dani.* I close my eyes and reach deep within, searching for the familiar warmth of my light, that core of power that's always been there.

Nothing. Where my power should burn bright, there's only emptiness.

What the hell did they do to me?

The realization hits like a meteor strike—they've found a way to cut me off from my own essence. I'm not just physically trapped, I'm magically neutered. Helpless in every way that matters.

The vulnerability of my situation crashes over me in waves of pure terror, and anger.

I'm so goddamn tired of this, of constantly being a pawn in someone else's twisted game. How many times do I have to be angel-napped by these self-righteous assholes who think they can just do as they please? It's infuriating!

But as much as I want to scream and rage against the injustice of it all, I know I can't afford to lose my cool. Not now, not when Damon needs me. My brother is out there somewhere, lost and confused, a newly turned vampire struggling to accept his fate. If I don't find a way to get to him, to help him, he could end up hurting someone. Or worse.

The thought of losing Damon forever chokes me, the pain almost unbearable. No, I won't let that happen. I can't. He's my brother, my family, and I'll be damned if I let him face this nightmare alone.

When I saw Damon lying there, lifeless and still, I thought my world had shattered. The pain of losing my brother was a gaping wound in my heart, a void that could never be filled. But then, in a twisted turn of fate, he hadn't truly died. No, instead, he had been reborn as a vampire, cursed to walk the earth as one of the undead.

Part of me wants to see this as a blessing, a second chance for Damon, for our relationship. After all, I haven't lost him forever, not in the way I had feared. But I know the road ahead will be far from easy. Becoming a vampire isn't a fairytale. It's a brutal, unforgiving reality.

Rhyland, Erik, and Lucian have taught me so much about the struggles of newly turned vampires. The hunger that burns in their veins, the insatiable thirst for blood that consumes their every thought—it's a constant battle that can take years, even decades, to master. And the consequences of losing that battle, even for a moment, can be devastating.

The door crashes open, harsh light from the hallway spearing into the darkness. I flinch, momentarily blinded. As my vision clears, my heart stops—it's her. The red-haired bitch who stole me away from everything I love stalks into the room like a predator, each step a deliberate display of power.

Her movements remind me of a cobra preparing to strike—graceful yet deadly, beautiful but lethal.

The way she prowls toward me makes my skin crawl. This woman didn't just take me by chance—she's been hunting me, and now she's savoring her victory.

"Well, well, look who decided to join the land of the living," she sneers, with disdain. She saunters over to the side of the bed, her emerald eyes raking over me like I'm a piece of meat, a plaything for her amusement.

She reaches for me, and I can't help but flinch, my nerves frayed and raw from the ordeal I've endured. "Oh, don't be such a baby," she scoffs, rolling her eyes. "I'm just checking your neck."

With a rough yank, she peels back the bandage that I now feel, the sticky sound of dried blood peeling away from my skin, making my stomach churn. Suddenly, her fangs slide out, gleaming and sharp, and she licks her lips in a gesture that's both hungry and predatory. I scuttle back against the headboard, a gasp of fear escaping my lips.

She's a vampire.

"Hmm, not bad," she remarks, her tone bored and unimpressed. "I suppose I'll have Morgan come and clean you up. Can't have you bleeding all over my expensive sheets, now can we?" She smirks at me, those soulless green eyes glinting with a malevolent light that chills me to the bone. "And don't even think about trying to escape or calling for help. You're on a magical leash, sweetheart. A little cocktail that was whipped up just for you."

Whatever cocktail of drugs they've pumped into my system is working perfectly—my powers are completely muted, locked away behind an impenetrable wall. The familiar warmth of my magic, usually thrumming just beneath my skin, is gone. Even my connection to Lucian, that constant reassuring presence in the back of my mind, has been silenced.

These bastards knew exactly what they were doing. They've stripped away every defense, every advantage I might have had. The violation goes beyond physical restraints-they've reached inside and stolen a fundamental part of who I am.

Rage burns in my chest, but it's tainted by crushing helplessness. I'm completely at their mercy.

The drugs feel like liquid ice in my veins, a constant reminder that these monsters have thought of everything. They're not just containing me—they're erasing everything that makes me *me.*

I frown at her, my eyes narrowing in defiance as I find my voice, the words rasping out of my throat like sandpaper. "Who the hell are you? And what the hell do you want?"

She laughs then, a mocking sound. "Oh, where are my manners? I'm Lilith, darling. And you, my dear, are the key to getting what I want—or rather, *who* I want."

What the hell? I don't know this bitch from Eve, and yet here she is, claiming that I'm some sort of pawn in her twisted game. Anger surges through my veins, hot and potent. "And what the *hell* is that supposed to mean?"

She looks at me like I'm a particularly slow child, her lips curling into a sneer. "Rhyland, you stupid girl. I'm talking about Rhyland."

My heart stops, then kicks into overdrive, pounding against my ribs like a caged animal. "What about him?" I ask, my voice trembling despite my efforts to keep it steady.

"Oh, please," she scoffs, waving a dismissive hand. "Don't play dumb. It's unbecoming. Rhyland is mine, always has been, and always will be. And you, my dear, are nothing more than a temporary distraction. An obstacle to be removed."

Rage boils up inside me, so hot and fierce that it nearly chokes me. "Listen up, you arrogant bitch," I snarl, my hands curling into fists in my restraints. "I don't know who the hell you think you are, but Rhyland is *not* yours. He's mine, and I'll be damned if I let some delusional, entitled psycho like you think to take him away from me."

She throws her head back and laughs, the sound grating and cruel. "Oh, you poor, naive little thing. You really have no idea who you're dealing with, do you?" She leans in close, her breath hot and fetid against my face. "I am his Maker, you insignificant bitch. And I will take back what is rightfully mine, no matter who I have to crush beneath my heel to do it."

ERIK

3

I rise to my feet, my jaw clenched as I brush the dirt and debris from my black leather jacket. The vortex hit like a battering ram from hell, sending Lucian and me flying like ragdolls. My head throbs, but I push the pain aside, my eyes scanning the dense forest surrounding us.

Lucian lies motionless on the ground nearby, still knocked out cold from the blast. The eerie silence of the woods is broken by the distant calls of Seraphina and Emily, their voices laced with desperation as they search for Danica. They're undoubtedly getting closer, guided by Seraphina's blood bond with my brother.

I square my shoulders, my voice cutting through the air like a knife. "Over here!"

We need to regroup, assess the situation, and figure out what the hell just happened.

I watch Seraphina and Emily burst through the brush, their faces etched with worry and exhaustion. Blood and dirt cling to their skin, a testament to the chaos that just unfolded.

"Lucian!" Seraphina's melodic voice rings out, laced with concern, as she rushes to my brother's side. Her delicate hands push back his hair, checking for any signs of injury.

Emily's piercing gaze locks onto me, her tone sarcastic. "Well, isn't this just fucking great? Mind telling us what the hell just happened, Mr. Stoic?"

That blasted vortex, or portal, or whatever the hell it was, absconded with Rhyland, leaving me standing here with a myriad of unanswered questions.

I meet her gaze, my own eyes narrowing slightly. "I was about to inquire the same of you, Emily, though perhaps with a touch less sass, if you'd be so kind."

Emily's eyes widen, realization dawning on her face. "Wait, where's Dani?" She whips her head from side to side, her rainbow-colored hair flying as she searches for any sign of her friend.

I sheath my sword, the metal sliding against the leather with a soft hiss. "I don't know," I admit. "I lost track of her after the blast."

Seraphina looks up from Lucian, her honey-colored eyes filled with worry. "This isn't good. We must find her quickly! I can't sense her presence nearby."

Okay, new priority—Danica and ensure she's safe. I'll be damned if I let anything happen to her on my watch.

Emily throws her hands up in exasperation. "Great, just great. Rhyland gets sucked into a vortex, and Dani's missing. Could this day get any worse?"

I clench my jaw, my mind racing as I try to piece together what happened—the vortex, the blast, and now Dani's disappearance. Something's not right, and I'll be damned if I don't get to the bottom of it.

The hairs on the back of my neck stand up as a figure emerges from the shadows, stumbling towards us. In a flash, my sword is in my hand, the blade gleaming in the dim light. I push Emily behind me, my body shielding her and the potential threat. "Stay back," I growl, my voice low and dangerous. "I'll handle this." I take a step forward, ready to confront the bloodlust vampire, one of the bastards who brought this hell upon us. He must have slipped through the cracks during the battle.

Emily's hand shoots out, grabbing my jacket and yanking me to a halt. "No!" she hisses, her eyes wide with recognition. "That's Damon. Dani's little brother. You can't kill him."

I pause, reassessing the situation. Damon staggers closer, his face a mask of confusion and fear. "Help... me," he pleads, his voice barely above a whisper. "Please. I don't... know... what's—"

Emily steps out from behind me, her voice soft and reassuring. "Damon, hey. It's going to be okay. We'll explain everything."

Realization dawns on me. Azrael. That twisted son of a bitch must have turned Damon before he killed him. It's the only explanation for why Dani's brother is now a fledgling vampire. I sheathe my sword as Emily approaches him, but my instincts scream at me to stop her. I reach out, grabbing her arm and pulling her back firmly. "Don't," I warn, my voice stern. "He's new, and his impulses are—"

Before I can finish my sentence, Damon lunges at Emily, his eyes wild with hunger. I react on pure instinct, my hand closing around his throat in an iron grip.

"Don't kill him!" Emily shouts, her voice laced with panic.

I almost want to laugh at the absurdity of her plea, as if I would ever hurt Dani by taking away the last of her family. I hold Damon steady, my gaze boring into his. "Not today, little vampire," I snarl. "Where is your sister?"

The scent of her blood lingers on his lips and courses through his veins, igniting a primal urge within me to rend him limb from limb.

Damon gasps as I loosen my grip on his throat, tears streaming down his face. "I-I attacked her," he sobs, his body shaking uncontrollably. "I-I couldn't stop myself." He takes a shuddering breath, his words tumbling out in a rush. "She-she was taken by some... woman. I don't know. What the hell is wrong with me? Am I—"

I release the fledgling with a firm shove, my mind churning with the revelation that someone has taken Dani. White-hot rage surges through my veins, but I force it down, focusing. "Indeed, you are a vampire now," I state, my tone as unyielding as bedrock. "And I strongly advise that you refrain from sinking your fangs into anyone, lest you find yourself on the wrong end of my blade."

I turn back to face Damon, my gaze intense and unwavering. "Describe her appearance to me," I insist, my voice carrying an undercurrent of barely restrained fury. I stand ready to unleash the very fires of hell upon those who dare to harm the Little Huntress.

The sound of Lucian's groan reaches my ears as he starts to regain consciousness, a stark reminder of the turmoil that engulfs us. Time is of the essence, and we must obtain the information we seek post-haste. Dani's very existence is at stake, and I'll be damned before I allow her to be taken from us without moving heaven and earth to bring her back. She's become my sister, and it is my solemn duty to safeguard her as such, come what may.

"I-I don't know, it was dark," Damon stammers, his eyes darting around as he tries to recall the details. "She was... strong." He swallows hard, his voice dropping to a whisper. "So strong."

I clench my fists, my mind racing with possibilities. Who is this mysterious woman, and what does she want with Dani?

Lucian's voice cuts through my thoughts as he staggers to his feet, Seraphina fussing over him like a mother hen. "Well, that was a wild fucking ride," he quips, rubbing his head. He saunters over to me, a grin on his face despite the gravity of the situation. "How's it hanging, bro? Still got all your bits and pieces?"

I inhale deeply, trying to keep my cool in the face of Lucian's incessant bullshit. "Lucian, now's not the time for your wisecracks," I rumble, my patience growing thinner by the second. "Dani and Rhyland's whereabouts are unknown, and it is imperative that we locate them with all due haste."

Lucian holds up his hands in mock surrender, a smirk on his lips. "Alright, alright. Don't get your leather panties in a twist, Erik." He turns his attention to Damon, snapping his fingers in the fledgling's face. "Hey, baby vamp! Focus up. The woman who took your sister—I need deets, and I need 'em now. And don't give me that 'it was dark' crap. You're a vampire now, kid. Your eyesight's better than a fucking eagle on steroids."

Damon blinks, taken aback by Lucian's intensity. "I... I don't know. It all happened so fast."

Lucian leans in closer, his eyes narrowing. "C'mon, kid. Dig deep. You're telling me you didn't catch a single glimpse of this chick's face? Not even a passing glance? A fleeting moment of eye contact before she went all Xena: Warrior Princess on your ass?"

Seraphina clears her throat. Her angelic presence starkly contrasts Lucian's chaotic energy. "Perhaps a gentler approach might help gain better results," she suggests, her voice soothing like a lullaby.

Lucian scoffs, waving her off. "Please, Cupcake. We don't have time for hand-holding and kumbaya. We need answers, and we need them yesterday."

I pinch the bridge of my nose, feeling a headache brewing behind my eyes. "Lucian, enough. Let the kid think."

"She had long fire-red hair and, she... she had green eyes. Piercing green eyes that seemed to glow in the dark. And her face... it was like porcelain. Flawless and pale."

The description slams into me like a battering ram, stealing the breath from my lungs. Beside me, Lucian goes rigid, his eyes wide with a horror I've never seen in him before. Seraphina, ever attuned to his emotions, rushes to his side, her angelic face etched with concern.

"What? What is it?" she asks, her voice barely above a whisper.

Lucian remains silent, his mind no doubt reeling with the same terrible realization that grips my own. Seraphina turns to me, her golden eyes searching mine for answers, but I have none to give.

It can't be.

Not her.

Not our Maker, the one who brought us into this cursed existence only to harm us with her sick and twisted ways.

Memories of her flood my mind, each one a searing reminder of the vileness, the evil, and the utter lack of humanity that defines her very being. I feel myself sway, the weight of the past threatening to crush me where I stand.

Emily's patience snaps like a twig underfoot. "Oh, for fuck's sake, you two!" she explodes, "Just spit it out already!"

Lucian meets my gaze, and in that moment, we both know. The name falls from our lips in perfect unison, a whisper that carries the weight of a thousand nightmares.

"Lilith."

Rhyland and I had dealt with her presence eons ago. What in the seven hells is she doing here now? And more importantly, how did she manage to escape?

The atmosphere grows heavy with tension as if the very fabric of reality is holding its breath in anticipation. Seraphina's eyes widen, and her delicate hand flies to her mouth in a gesture of profound horror. Emily looks between us, confusion and fear warring on her face.

"Who the hell is Lilith?" she demands, her voice shaking.

The thought sends a chill through my veins, colder than the grave. If Lilith has taken Dani, then there is no telling what horrors await her. What twisted games our Maker will play, what unspeakable torments she will inflict.

Lucian's voice, hard and sharp as a blade, breaks the silence. "We have to find her. Now."

There is no room for argument, no space for doubt. We have a name, a target. And now, we have a mission.

RHYLAND

4

"Rhyland of Midgard." Odin's voice booms through the hall, his one eye fixing me with a stare that feels like it could strip the flesh from my bones. "A grave error has been made. It is only now that we realize the necessity of enlightening you."

An error? What kind of fucking game are they playing here?

The Zeus-looking bastard clears his throat, and my gaze snaps to him. "It seems we have all been deceived regarding your... existence. Upon this realization, we convened and summoned you here."

I clench my fists, my confusion and frustration boiling over. I don't give a flying fuck about their mistakes. All I want is to get back to Dani.

"Cut the crap and get to the point. I don't have time for this bullshit or whatever grand revelation you gods need to drop on me." I snarl, my patience wearing thin.

Odin gestures to the hulking man beside him, "Rhyland, meet Elysium. He is here to rectify the situation."

My eyes nearly bug out of my skull as I stare at the man who's supposedly Dani's father. Elysium? Here, in the flesh? What the everloving fuck is going on? And why in the world is he in Ásgard, of all places?

The questions swirl in my mind, but before I can voice them, Elysium speaks, his voice ringing with an otherworldly power that sets my teeth on edge.

"Rhyland Eriksson," he begins, his golden eyes boring into mine with an intensity that makes me want to look away. But I hold his gaze, refusing to back down. "You have been misled about your true nature. It is time for you to learn the truth of your heritage."

For fuck's sake, here we go. I couldn't give two shits about this nonsense.

"We believed you perished centuries ago," Odin interjects, his voice grating on my nerves. "But we now understand our error. You were, in fact, resurrected—as a vampire. Thus, retaining your heritage, power, and role in this prophecy."

"Why now? Why the fuck are you just now telling me this shit?" I can't help but ask.

Elysium lets out a sigh that drips with frustration as if he's not thrilled with Odin's little revelation. "It was only when you unleashed your lightning that we recognized our grave oversight," he growls, his eyes flashing angrily.

Heimdall turns to me, his expression serious. "I couldn't pinpoint your location after I found out," he says, sounding like he's trying to explain how our little portal-skiing escapades through the realms fucked things up.

I shrug, unfazed by their little display. "Listen, I don't know what kind of games you all play up here in your fucking ivory tower, but I really couldn't care less about whatever bullshit you're spouting," I snap. "I have one mission, and that's protecting *your* daughter." I fix Elysium with a cold, hard stare, daring him to challenge me. I can see it in his eyes, those golden orbs that are so much like Dani's—he despises the fact that I've bonded with her, claimed her as my mate—tough shit.

"Make no mistake, boy! I still don't trust you around my daughter—your kind is tied to darkness."

"You may not like it, but Dani is *mine*," I continue, my voice low and dangerous. "And I'll be damned if I let anyone, god or otherwise, stand in the way of keeping her safe. So, whatever grand plan you have for me, you can shove it up your divine ass. I'm not playing your games."

The air is tense as I stare down the gods before me. I don't care who they are or what they want from me. All that matters is returning to Dani and fulfilling my vow to protect and love her, no matter the cost.

Elysium takes a deep breath, visibly struggling to maintain his composure. "I am well aware of that, vampire, which is precisely why I am permitting this union. You were destined to play a role in this prophecy—two saviors are needed to exist: mates of different worlds, one born of mortal and divine blood, and the other born of the gods."

Two saviors? The prophecy never mentioned two—only that finding one's mate would awaken their powers. Did I misinterpret it? Could the fucking puddle in Aquaria have been right when it spoke of *'saviors'*?

But it still doesn't add up. Dani and I are two halves of a whole, two souls torn from different eras.

I stare at him, stunned. "If that's the case, wouldn't Dani had to have been born in my time if you hadn't assumed I was dead?"

Odin sighs, "Indeed. We had a mate chosen for you..." He glances at Elysium. "Do you wish to reveal the truth to him?"

My gaze darts between the two, my mind reeling. Heimdall stands beside me, still as a statue, but he can't even hide the unease radiating from him at this bombshell.

What the ever-loving fuck is going on?

"Enough with the cryptic bullshit," I growl. "If there's something I need to know, then spit it out."

Elysium and Odin exchange a loaded glance, and I can feel the weight of centuries of secrets hanging in the air between them. Whatever they're about to reveal, I know it will change everything. And I'm not sure I'm ready for it.

"Brynhildr," Odin's voice rings out, echoing through the hall.

From behind their thrones, a woman emerges—no, not just a woman, a goddamn Valkyrie. She's a vision of fierce beauty, with one eye Noric blue and the other honey gold. Her long, platinum blonde hair flows like silver, and her body is toned and firm, the physique of a seasoned warrior. She finds a seat next to Elysium and sits with a huff. "It's Bryn," she snaps at the old man.

Elysium's lips curve into a smile at her audacity, and then he turns to me, his expression sobering. "This is Bryn, whom we initially intended for you. However, her light proved insufficient. Her power did not align with what the prophecy demanded." His words have a profound sadness and a heavy sense of regret in the air. "Bryn cannot wield fire. But Danica—"

"What about Danica?" I snarl, cutting him off mid-sentence. "Your precious little girl that you couldn't be bothered to save when she was on the brink of death? The one whose guardian angel you fucking banished from Atheria because she had the balls to defy you and keep her alive?" I can barely keep my rage in check as I spit out the words, the truth burning like acid on my tongue.

Odin leans back, looking at me like I grew a second head. Bryn sucks in a sharp breath turning to Elsyium, "Father, you didn't..."

"You talk a big game about prophecies and destinies," I growl. "But when it comes down to it, you're just a bunch of self-righteous pricks who don't give a damn about the people you claim to protect."

Elysium's voice booms, "My judgment was clouded, formed in ignorance of your true nature. I believed Danica's association with you would lead her down the path of darkness—to death itself."

"So you were just gonna leave her to die?" I shout. "You thought wrong," I growl. "Dani's stronger than you give her credit for. She's a fighter, a survivor."

Elysium's eyes flash with anger. "Watch your tongue, boy. I am still your elder, and your better."

I laugh harshly. "Elder and better? That's rich, coming from a god who can't admit when he's fucked up."

Elysium shouts, "An oversight! And one I am rectifying! Danica is the *rightful* savior from *my* blood."

Bryn scoffs at his proclamation, and Elysium turns to her, his voice softening. "Bryn, you remain an extraordinary woman—my daughter—you have brought me immense pride."

I stand here, my jaw hanging open, as I am just now piecing things together. "Hold the fuck up," I manage to get out, my mind spinning. "You're telling me that she"—I point to Bryn—"is your daughter? Dani's half-sister? And you banished her here as punishment because she didn't meet your standards?"

Odin interjects, "Bryn was brought here for her protection, as she failed the requirements for the prophecy. I gave Elysium my word that I would keep her safe. She is of Viking blood."

I shake my head, trying to wrap my mind around this twisted revelation. "So, let me get this straight. You had her," I point to Bryn, "and when she didn't become the *savior* you wanted, you just tossed her aside and started over with Dani's mom?" I can feel the rage building inside me, my power crackling beneath my skin. "What kind of fucked-up game are you playing, Elysium?"

I can't believe what I'm hearing. The gods, playing with lives like they're nothing more than pawns on a chessboard. Anger surges through me, white-hot and all-consuming.

They gawk at me like I just took a piss in their divine punch bowl. These almighty fuckers probably aren't used to anyone having the balls to call them out on their bullshit, especially not some vampire with an attitude problem. Well, tough shit. I'm not here to stroke their celestial egos or play nice with the powers that be.

"I don't give a fuck about your prophecies or grand plans. I care about Dani, and I'll be damned if I let you use her as some kind of sacrificial lamb in your war against Moretemis."

Bryn's eyes flash angrily, and I see the hurt beneath the surface. Although I may not know her, I feel a sense of kinship with her. We're both pawns in this cosmic chess match, our lives dictated by the whims of gods who see us as nothing more than means to an end.

I can feel their eyes boring into me. But I don't back down. I won't let them manipulate Dani the way they did, Bryn. I'll fight tooth and nail to keep her safe, even if it means going against the gods themselves.

Elysium clears his throat. "No, that is not my intention with Danica. I know her role in this prophecy and the power she wields with...her true mate, by her side." He runs a hand down his face, frustration etched into every line. "We just didn't see...this—you two—together. When you fell on that battlefield, I had no choice but to seal the realms—the Darkness was closing in, consuming everything in its path. I did what I had to do!" His shout echoes through the hall, raw and desperate. "I had no idea you were turned into the *creature* you are today." he spits the word creature like I'm disgusting to him.

The memories of that day come rushing back—the Darkness swallowing the world whole. I lay there, bleeding out, knowing it was the end. Never in my wildest dreams did I imagine I was a piece of some cosmic prophecy, a pawn in a game played by gods and monsters.

And then, to have that demonic whore Lilith sink her claws into me, twisting and corrupting my very essence until I was reborn as something else entirely—a fucking creature of the night, a monster in my own right. The irony is not lost on me.

But that bitch got what was coming to her, and I don't regret making her pay for what she did to me—my brothers, not for a single goddamn second. She thought she could break me—break us, mold us into her perfect little pet monsters, but she underestimated the fury that burns in my veins.

"So, I died. Your only option was to seal the realms and start over—with Dani's mom? What about me?" I demand. "If I'm a crucial piece in this cosmic puzzle, Dani's other half—a savior in my own right—then who's the divine bastard responsible for my creation?"

Odin begins, "Rhyland, your lineage is...complicated."

I laugh bitterly. "Complicated? That's the understatement of the fucking century. You're telling me I'm the other half of this chosen one shit, a savior born of gods. But you still haven't answered my question. Who. Made. Me?"

Odin leans forward. "Rhyland, you are a child of the gods, born of both Ásgardian and Olympian blood. Your father was a great warrior, a hero who fought alongside us. And your mother...your mother was a goddess in her own right, a being of immense power and beauty."

I stare at him, my mind reeling—a demigod born of two pantheons, two worlds that should never have crossed paths.

I shake my head. "No. My mother was mortal. Freya. What kind of bullshit are you trying to feed me?"

Odin sighs. "No, my son. We concealed your true heritage, placing you among the mortals until you came of age to embrace your destiny."

The words hit me like a gut punch. My entire existence...a lie? A carefully crafted illusion to hide the truth of my blood?

My memories of my mother's chants and whispered prayers to the gods for the gift of a child take on a whole new meaning now. The words twist and warp like a hall of shattered mirrors.

I can hear her voice, soft and reverent, thanking the deities for the blessing of my life. But now, knowing the truth of my heritage, those gentle murmurs become a twisted mockery, a cruel joke played by the very gods she so faithfully served.

She had no idea, no inkling of the divine blood that flowed through my veins, the legacy of power and tragedy that I was born to bear. To her, I was a miracle, a gift from the heavens. But in reality, I was a pawn, a chess piece in a game played by immortals. My fate decided before I ever drew breath.

I clench my fists. "Then tell me," I growl, my voice low and dangerous. "Who were they? My real parents, the ones who brought me into this world only to abandon me to the fates?"

Odin meets my gaze. "Your father was Magni, son of Thor, a warrior of unparalleled strength and courage. And your mother was Nyx, the primordial goddess of the night, a being of ancient power and mystery."

The names echo through my mind: Magni, Nyx, demigod, and primordial goddess, united in a forbidden love that brought forth a child of two worlds.

Fuck. My. Life.

DANICA

5

ait. Rewind. Did she just say she's Rhyland's Maker? Well, isn't that just fucking peachy. My Viking vampire beefcake somehow forgot to mention this particular skeleton in his closet. Sure, he gave me the Cliff Notes version of his turning, but skipped the chapter about the psycho ex-maker with abandonment issues.

And wait—if she made Rhyland, that means... oh, *fantastic*. She's Vampire Mommy Dearest to all my guys. Erik, Lucian—they're all her immortal offspring. Though clearly, the "how to not be a complete psycho" gene skipped a generation.

I eye Miss Thing standing before me, taking in the waves of jealousy and obsession rolling off her like cheap perfume. The way she's looking at me, you'd think I'd stolen her favorite Gucci bag instead of her centuries-old boy toy.

That's some grade-A obsessive ex-girlfriend energy right there.

Well, if this delusional vampire bitch thinks she can waltz in here with her "I made him" bullshit and stake a claim on my man, she's got another thing coming. Time to channel my inner bad bitch and show her exactly who she's dealing with.

I plaster my best 'bless your heart' smile and decide to go for the jugular. "Listen here, *sweetheart*," I drawl. "I don't give two shits about who you claim to be or what ancient history you're trying to dig up. But let me paint you a picture—while you've been off doing whatever it is bitter ex-makers do, Rhyland's been pretty busy. And by busy, I mean buried so deep inside me that he can't even remember his own name, let alone yours."

I lean forward as much as I can in this position. "Face it, honey. You're not even a footnote in his story anymore. You're just a bad memory he didn't even bother to mention. So why don't we cut the territorial vampire queen act and call this what it really is—pathetic."

The look on her face? Priceless. Sometimes the truth hurts, especially when it's served with a side of sass and a garnish of 'go fuck yourself.' Though something tells me, this particular truth bomb might come back to bite me in the ass. Literally.

She's in my face faster than I can blink, fangs out, gleaming and sharp. "Watch that pretty little mouth of yours," she hisses. "You're playing with forces far beyond your pathetic mortal comprehension."

Oh, so that's how we're doing this? I may be chained up, but my attitude is still locked and loaded. I strain against the restraints, getting right back in her face. Because if this bougie bloodsucking bitch thinks I'm going to cower like some helpless damsel, she's got another thing coming.

"Or what?" I spit back, channeling every ounce of defiance I can muster. "You'll do your worst? I've faced scarier things than a desperate ex with daddy issues. So go ahead, show me what you've got. But know this—Rhyland is *mine*, and no amount of vampire mean girl bullshit is going to change that."

Her eyes flash dangerously, like emerald lightning. "You insignificant little harlot," she seethes, her perfectly manicured hands curling into claws. "How *dare* you speak to me that way. I am his *Maker*. I *own* him!"

"News flash, bitch," I sneer, even as my heart pounds against my ribs. "This isn't the dark ages anymore. You can't just stamp 'property of psycho vampire' on someone and call it a day. So why don't you take your entitled ass back to whatever crypt you crawled out of and leave my man alone?"

She reels back as if I slapped her. Good.

I might be scared shitless on the inside, but I'll be damned if I let this immortal Regina George see it. Rhyland is worth fighting for, and if that means going toe-to-toe with his Maker? Well, bring it on, bitch.

One second, I'm running my mouth; the next, this psychotic snatch has her fangs buried in my throat. The pain is excruciating, nothing like Rhyland's gentle bites. I scream as she violates me, stealing what isn't hers to take, her grip tightening like a vice as she gulps down my blood with perverted pleasure. I thrash against her, but it's like fighting a steel beam—utterly useless.

The door crashes open, the sound barely registering over my screams and thundering heartbeat. "LILITH!" A commanding voice cuts through the chaos. "Enough! You can't kill her. Yet. Control yourself, for fuck's sake!"

Lilith detaches herself from my neck with an obscene pop, making a show of delicately wiping my blood from her lips like it's fine wine. "Morgan, darling, so nice of you to join our little party," she purrs, all fake refinement and smug satisfaction. "I was merely sampling the merchandise. And my, my... she really does taste divine. Like nothing of this world." Her eyes gleam with predatory hunger. "I think I've found my new favorite snack."

I glare at her through the pain and terror, trembling with equal parts fear and rage. If looks could kill, this bloodsucking bitch would be a pile of designer ashes right now.

Morgan shoves past Lilith like she's swatting aside an annoying fly, settling beside me on the bed. She's young, with rich mahogany skin gleaming in the dim light. Her straight dark hair falls just past her shoulders in a sleek curtain, the ends perfectly trimmed and not a strand out of place despite the drama unfolding. Her hands, elegant and sure, reach for my ravaged neck, and I flinch away instinctively.

"Girl, stop being difficult," Morgan says, her no-nonsense tone. "Unless you're eager to bleed out and die right here?" She glares at me sternly, her light brown eyes assessing me. "Let me stop the bleeding. Trust me, you don't want to check out just yet—the show's barely started."

Great. Just what I need—another cryptic warning from a bitchy mean girl. But damn it, as much as it grates on me, she's right. I can't meet my end here, not like this. Rhyland needs me. My brother and my family all need me.

Please, let Lucian, Erik, Emily, and Seraphina be okay. Let them find Damon and help him through this nightmare.

So, I grit my teeth and let Morgan work her magic, all the while plotting exactly how I'm going to make Lilith pay for this little vampiric violation.

Morgan's hands hover over my ravaged throat, her eyes drifting closed as she murmurs incantations under her breath. The language is foreign, ancient-sounding, and practically drips with power. Well, that answers one question—we've got ourselves a witch. Fantastic. Because this situation wasn't complicated enough already.

I feel the magic working, a warm tingle spreading across my skin as the bleeding finally slows. Morgan reaches into what looks like Mary Poppins' bag of magical remedies and pulls out fresh bandages.

"Interesting," she muses, applying the dressing with clinical precision. "Seems like that fancy rock of yours isn't too fond of vampire bites. Some serious limitations on that healing power you've got there."

My blood turns to ice. They know about my crown and its stones. Wonderful. What else do these psychos know about me?

"Yeah, well," I manage to croak out, shooting Lilith my best 'eat shit' glare, "the stones are pretty discriminating. They know trash when they see it."

And like a light bulb flickering to life, it hits me. No wonder I couldn't save Damon. This damn rock clearly has a personal vendetta against vampires and their bites.

Like when Lucian bit me, his bite only healed because he gave me his blood.

Lilith's perfectly shaped eyebrows arch in amusement, but I catch the dangerous flash in her emerald eyes. Good. Let her be pissed. At least that makes two of us.

Morgan's hands still against my neck, her touch a silent warning to behave. But honestly? When have I ever done what I'm told? Especially when I'm being held captive by Vampire Barbie and her witchy sidekick.

"There. All patched up," Morgan announces, packing away her magical first-aid kit. "Time for your medicine. Be right back." She heads for the door before spinning around like some hall monitor. "And Lilith? Keep your fangs to yourself."

Lilith responds with a dramatic eye roll that probably strains something. She waves Morgan off like a queen, dismissing a peasant.

Medicine? That can't be good. "What medicine?" I call after Morgan, alarm bells ringing in my head.

"Just a special little cocktail to keep those savior powers of yours in check," Morgan throws over her shoulder with a wink that's anything but reassuring. The door clicks shut behind her with an ominous finality.

I'm not taking anything they give me. They can fuck right off.

Lilith glides over to her feathered spy, offering it a treat with all the smug satisfaction of a Bond villain petting their cat. The owl accepts its reward while those black eyes continue their creepy surveillance routine.

Then Little Miss Vampire Princess sashays over to a corner table, pouring herself a generous glass of Grey Goose vodka like she's starring in some twisted Real Housewives of the Seven Realms episode.

She settles into the chair with all the practiced grace of someone who's spent lifetimes perfecting their "I'm better than you" pose, crossing her endless pale legs.

Now that I'm not actively being used as a snack, I finally get a good look at my captor. She's tall and model-thin, with fire-red hair cascading dramatically to her waist like some gothic Rapunzel. Those gravity-defying breasts? Definitely aftermarket additions. And that skin-tight red dress? Pure vampire hooker chic.

Honestly, she looks like she raided the "Desperate Immortal Seeking Attention" section at Vampires R Us. But hey, when you've had hundreds of years to perfect your look, and you still end up looking like a blood-sucking streetwalker, that's on you, honey.

"Now then," Lilith purrs, swirling her vodka. "Let's cut to the chase, shall we? Where's *my* Rhyland?" Her emerald eyes start doing this weird hypnotic dance like a snake trying to charm its prey. "And please, spare me any creative fiction. I haven't even broken out my favorite party tricks yet."

I resist the urge to get lost in that green vortex of crazy and straighten against the headboard, trying to channel my inner badass despite these stupid cuffs, turning my arms into a torture experiment. "Here's a thought—why don't you go fuck yourself?"

The way she addresses Rhyland as hers pisses me off to no end.

She laughs, and it's about as warm as a morgue in December. "Now, now, darling. No need to be crude. I'm asking such a simple question." Her perfectly painted lips curve into a predatory smile. "Don't make me compel it out of you."

Compulsion? Because, of course, this walking fashion disaster has that particular trick up her sleeve. I can block Lucian's mind games, no problem, but this bitch? She's old. Like, probably-watched-the-pyramids-being-built old. And with age comes power—Vampire 101.

Her smile widens like she's reading the panic right off my face. "Oh yes, sweetheart. That pretty little mental shield of yours? About as effective as tissue paper against me. Call it a special talent." She downs the rest of her vodka like it's water and sashays back for a refill, her hips swaying with eons of practiced seduction.

"He's not here," I snap, gathering my inner 'done with this shit' attitude. "So why don't you take your fancy fangs and fuck right off? And don't bother asking where—I'm as clueless as you are about his whereabouts."

Lilith's stare is so intense it could strip paint, making me feel like a lab specimen under her microscope. "Hmm," she hums, taking another prissy sip of vodka. "No idea where that vortex whisked him away to?" I stare at her, not giving her anything. "Then let's discuss something else—the Soul Stone, perhaps? I caught that little performance with Azrael. Quite the show, darling. Though now it seems to have... disappeared."

Just perfect. Another immortal nut-job with a hard-on for that cursed paperweight. I pull out my best 'bored-out-of-my-mind' face. "Gone. Vanished. Did the whole Houdini thing. And before you waste your expensive breath asking—no, I don't have a clue where it went."

Her emerald eyes drill into me like she's trying to perform supernatural brain surgery. My heart's pounding against my ribs because, yeah, I know precisely where that damn stone is—with Rhyland. And that thought scares me more than this wannabe vampire queen could ever hope to.

God, I hope my poker face is better than my thundering pulse would suggest. Judging by the predatory glint in her eyes, I'm about as convincing as a toddler covered in cookie crumbs swearing they didn't raid the cookie jar.

Time to flip the script. "What's your damage anyway?" I sneer, going on the offensive. "Can't take a hint that he wants nothing to do with your ancient ass? Or is the concept of him finding a real woman too complicated for your centuries-old brain to process?"

Anger flashes in those emerald eyes before her face settles back into its usual 'entitled bitch' default setting. "He and I have a score to settle," she says, all prim and proper like she's announcing tea time. "An old debt that needs... collecting."

Oh, it looks like I found a nerve. Time to dance on it.

"Aww, what happened? Did he finally put your crazy ass in check? Or could he just not stand looking at your face for another century?" I smirk.

She throws back her vodka like it's holy water, and she's trying to cleanse herself. "He locked me in a tomb for close to two hundred years," she spits with enough venom to kill a horse. "But what we had... what we shared... it's beyond your pathetic mortal comprehension. Rhyland loves me, and I will get him back. Mark my words, you insignificant little bitch."

I can't help but laugh. Like, actually laugh. "Oh sweetie, let me explain something in terms your delusional mind might understand—when a man locks you in a tomb for two-hundred years, that's not exactly sending 'I love you' vibes. That's more like 'please die and never come back' energy. Though clearly, subtlety isn't your strong suit."

I lean forward as much as my restraints allow, dropping my voice. "While you were taking your two-hundred-year beauty nap—which, by the way, clearly didn't help—Rhyland was busy forgetting you existed. He never even mentioned you. Not once. Guess you weren't as memorable as you thought."

Her face contorts with rage, and honestly? Worth it. Because if this discount vampire dominatrix thinks she can just waltz in and claim what's mine, she's about to learn exactly why they call me feisty.

She rises from her chair, murder in her eyes, when Morgan swoops in like some arcane referee. "Down, girl. Back away from the prisoner. We need her alive for the ritual, remember?"

Hold up. *Record scratch.* "I'm sorry—the *what* now?" My head whips toward Morgan so fast I nearly give myself whiplash.

Lilith's lips curl into a smirk that belongs in a horror movie. "Oh yes, darling. Since you so kindly disposed of that pompous ass Azrael—thanks for that, by the way, he was becoming quite the thorn in my heels—you get to be our star player." She click-clacks back to her vodka station in those 'trying too hard' red heels. "All we need now is my Rhyland and that pretty little Soul Stone."

I roll my eyes so hard they might get stuck. "First of all, he's not *your* Rhyland. And second, if your grand master plan involves me playing along with whatever twisted ritual you've cooked up in that two-thousand-year-old brain of yours, you might want to pour yourself another drink. Because that's about as likely as those breasts being real."

Morgan laughs, "Damn, girl, you've got fire. Almost makes me sad we have to sacrifice you."

My stomach does a violent flip as the pieces click into place. The same ritual. The same goddamn sacrifice Azrael wanted to use Rhyland for—to drag Moretemis into our world like some twisted demonic DoorDash.

Only now. I'm the main course.

I force out a laugh that sounds brittle, even to my own ears. "Wow, you two really are scraping the bottom of the evil villain barrel, aren't you? Recycling Azrael's greatest hits?" My hands tremble against the restraints, but I keep my chin up, gathering every ounce of sass I can muster to mask the terror clawing at my throat. "What's next—gonna start wearing his hand-me-down robes and chanting his old catchphrases?"

The words come out strong, but my heart's pounding pure panic against my ribs. This isn't just about some vampire's twisted revenge fantasy anymore; this is about bringing literal darkness into the world. I've just been cast as the unwilling star of their apocalyptic production.

But even as I throw sass-like armor, ice crawls through my veins. Because if they succeed where Azrael failed... if they actually manage to bring Moretemis through... God help us all.

"Mmm, there's a certain poetry to it all," Lilith muses, twirling her vodka like she's at a wine tasting rather than plotting murder. Her emerald eyes glitter with malicious delight. "Just imagine—watching your feisty golden eyes dim, knowing I'm destroying the little mortal who dared to touch what belongs to me." Her perfect lips curl back, fangs gleaming in the low light. "Consider it spring cleaning—taking out the trash—cluttering my future." She laughs, " And then I'll be there to wipe Rhyland's tears and erase you from his memory."

RHYLAND

6

Well, shit, that explains the lightning crackling through my veins, the electric power that dances at my fingertips, begging to be unleashed.

Lucian's gonna have a goddamn field day with this. I can already hear the asshole cracking Thor jokes left and right.

But Nyx? In all my fucking centuries of existence, I can't recall ever hearing about this Greek goddess.

"Who the hell is Nyx?" The question rips from my throat, my curiosity getting the better of me.

The woman beside Odin, who's been quiet as the grave until now, finally speaks up. "Your mother wielded powers beyond mortal comprehension, Rhyland. Nyx, goddess of night, could bend shadows to her will, manipulate the very fabric of darkness itself. Every whisper in the dark, every spirit that haunts the shadows—they all answered to her."

Something in my expression must give away my confusion because she softens slightly.

"I am Frigg, wife of Odin and Seeress of Ásgard," she says, her tone gentler but no less powerful. Her golden hair catches the light like spun metal, and those piercing blue eyes seem to look straight through my soul, reading secrets I didn't even know I had.

Realization hits me like a goddamn freight train. All these centuries of moving shit with my mind, of reaching out and bending reality to my will—it wasn't just some vampire quirk. It was my mother's blood, her power running through my veins.

"Nyx was ancient even by our standards," Frigg continues, her voice taking on an edge of reverence and fear. "She emerged from Chaos itself, wielding power that could reshape reality. The night wasn't just her domain—it was her very essence."

I listen intently, my mind racing with the implications of her words. My mother, a fucking goddess of darkness and nightmares. It's almost too much to wrap my head around.

"Nyx was feared and revered in equal measure," Frigg's voice rings out with divine authority, her eyes distant as if peering through the veils of time itself. "She commanded the night, casting her shadow across existence, plunging worlds into darkness. And with that darkness came the nightmares, the primal terrors that lurked in the depths of mortal minds, waiting to be unleashed."

"Hold up," I cut in, my mind reeling from this cosmic bombshell. "Are you telling me my mother created the very Darkness we're fighting against?"

The irony of this shit is almost too much to handle.

Frigg's expression softens, her celestial aura pulsing with gentle reassurance. "Not precisely, Rhyland. Your mother was far more complex than that. Nyx wielded her power for the greater good," her voice takes on a note of respect that makes my skin tingle. "She possessed the ability to transform the darkest nightmares into the most brilliant of dreams. She was a force of healing rather than destruction."

Then Frigg's expression darkens, and I can tell she's about to drop some heavy shit on me. "That is...until Moretemis coveted her power..."

"Fuck me." The words tumble from my lips, a half-whispered curse that echoes through the chamber. My throat feels like it's been scoured with razor blades, and my pulse is pounding so hard I swear my veins are about to burst. "So you're telling me this power, this darkness...it's inside me? Flowing through my fucking blood?" My voice is raw, jagged, torn between mind-numbing fear and a twisted sort of wonder.

Odin's voice cuts through the chaos in my head, his tone steady and sure. "Not entirely, Rhyland. From what we can discern, your abilities seem to align more closely with your father's lineage. However, the full extent of your powers remains to be seen."

I barely have time to process this before Frigg continues. "The blood of Nyx flows through your veins, Rhyland. Granting you a portion of her immense power—it is a heavy burden to bear but one you were born to carry."

I take a deep breath, trying to steady myself against the weight of her words. A burden...that's putting it fucking mildly. The idea that I could have that kind of power, that kind of influence over the minds and hearts of others...it's both exhilarating and terrifying at the same time.

"But you must be careful," Frigg warns. "The power of Nyx is not to be trifled with. It can consume you if you let it. It can twist your mind and soul until you become what you seek to destroy."

I clench my fists so hard my knuckles turn white, fighting like hell to keep my shit together as the truth hits me like a goddamn sledgehammer. "No fucking shit," I spit out. "The Soul Stone—that's her power, isn't it? My mother's legacy wrapped up in this piece of cosmic jewelry?"

"Watch your tongue, boy." Odin's voice cracks like thunder across the chamber, his single eye blazing with divine fury. "And yes. That very power forged the Soul Stone—the artifact Moretemis hungers for to fulfill his twisted destiny."

Holy shit.

The stone in my pocket suddenly feels like it weighs a thousand pounds, its presence burning against my thigh like a brand. Its whispers start creeping into my mind, seductive and dark, promising power beyond my wildest dreams. I squeeze my eyes shut, trying to block out the voices, fighting against the pull of its ancient magic.

I can't let this thing get its hooks in me. Not now. Not when there's so much at stake. But Jesus fucking Christ—as if things weren't already fucked up beyond repair enough, now I find out I'm carrying around a piece of my mother's power, and in my veins, the very thing our enemy wants to use to tear the realms apart.

The irony of it all makes me want to laugh or punch something—preferably both.

This explains why Azrael wanted me for his fucked up ritual.

What does Moretemis know?

"What happened to them?" I demand, the words tearing from my throat like they're being ripped out. "Where the hell are they now?"

Odin's gaze drops to the floor, and I swear I see a flicker of pain in his ancient eye. "They fell in battle against the forces of Moretemis, fighting side by side until the very end. Magni was struck down first, his body broken and bleeding, but still, he fought on, determined to protect your mother and the realms they both held dear."

The Valley of Ancients...those goddamn walls. I relive the memories and the visions we saw dancing off those ancient stones as we watched that battle play out. And I had no fucking clue those warriors were my parents.

"In Magni's final moments, Nyx cradled him in her arms, her heart shattering as his life slipped away. But even in the depths of her despair, her fury knew no bounds."

He pauses, his single eye distant, as if lost in the memories of that fateful day. "She rose like a vengeful goddess, a maelstrom of shadow and darkness that consumed all in its path. She attempted to use her power against Moretemis, channeling every ounce of darkness and nightmare she possessed. But that sadistic bastard..." His voice falters, divine authority cracking under the strain of remembered horror. "He turned her own power against her, ripped it from her very soul. The process destroyed her immortal form, tearing her essence apart until nothing was left but scattered fragments of what she once was. The Soul Stone, born of her sacrifice, became his prize, even as her immortal body crumbled to dust."

"And her power?" The words come out as more of a growl.

"Absorbed. Corrupted." Odin's eye gleams with a mixture of sorrow and anger. "Moretemis twisted her abilities into something perverse. Something never meant to exist. He reversed her gift for transforming nightmares into dreams, creating a weapon of pure terror and darkness."

Well, isn't that just fucking perfect. Not only did this asshole kill my mother, but he's also running around with her stolen powers, using them to terrorize the realms. The rage inside me burns hotter, threatening to consume everything in its path.

I'm going to find him. And when I do, I'm going to make him pay for every single fucking thing he's done. That's a promise.

ERIK

7

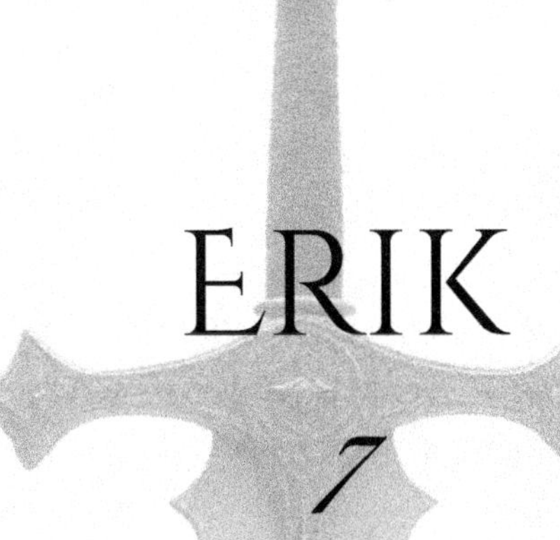

From my position at the kitchen counter, I hear Lucian's voice echoing from the basement."Chill out, baby vamp! You'll be fine down here!" A pause, followed by his characteristic irreverence. "I'll bring you some O-negative happy meals. Premium stuff, none of that bargain basement blood!"

The fledgling's sobs reverberate through the floor. While confining Dani's brother is far from ideal—and would undoubtedly earn us her considerable wrath—current circumstances leave us with no alternative. His safety, and that of others, must take precedence until we can properly address his transformation.

I maintain my rigid posture as Lucian storms back into the kitchen, his usual sardonic demeanor twisted with rage. "Well, isn't this just a fucking party favor wrapped in barbed wire?" He yanks at his golden hair, pacing like a caged animal. "Our psycho mommy dearest decides to crash back into our lives after playing hide and seek for centuries? Should we send her a welcome back fruit basket? Maybe some artisanal blood truffles?"

I resist the urge to pinch the bridge of my nose at his theatrical display, though I understand the sentiment behind it. My brother's ability to transform every crisis into a one-man Broadway production never ceases to amaze me.

We've retreated to the mansion to formulate a strategy—I recall the aftermath of our recent disaster with practiced detachment. Alaric and Vivienne departed an hour ago, their expressions grim as they headed back to the UK. Our powerful allies need to be informed of this catastrophic shift in power—Lilith's return poses a threat that extends far beyond our immediate circle. Political chess pieces need to be moved, alliances reinforced.

Brandon's return to New York presents its own complications. With Azrael's death, the wolf packs have lost their primary blood supplier. Years of drinking vampire blood have turned them into addicts—a strategic disaster waiting to explode. The wolves' dependency on vampire blood was always a tactical vulnerability, but now, with Lilith controlling the game board, their desperation could make them dangerous wild cards.

"Brother," I state, my voice carrying the weight of decades of dealing with his dramatic bullshit, "you must compose yourself. This situation requires tactical precision, not your usual chaos and prayer approach."

"Compose myself?" Lucian whirls on me, his face inches from mine. "Our batshit crazy Maker has Dani, and you want me to keep my cool?" He resumes his relentless pacing, brushing off Seraphina's attempts to calm him. The angel's honey-colored eyes follow his movement with growing concern.

I observe his mounting distress, remembering the fragments of horror he's shared about his time under Lilith's control. His current anguish is more than justified if his experiences mirror my own torments.

"The evidence suggests a Hawthorne witch still walks among us," I declare, my mind returning to that fateful day when Rhyland and I sealed Lilith away with the help of their ancient magic. "Only one of their bloodline could have broken the enchantment binding her."

Lucian freezes mid-stride, his dark brown eyes boring into mine. "Come again? In my ears this time."

I fight the urge to snap back at Lucian's biting remarks."Rhyland and I decided to entomb Lilith to protect anyone else from further torment," I explain. "We believed it was in your best interest not to burden you with knowing her fate. By telling you she left, we hoped this would help you."

That day is seared in my brain.

London, England 1866

Wind lashes against my face as I stand beside Rhyland in the ancient cavern. Grave Warden, firmly in my grip. The Hawthorne witch, Elizabeth, chants behind us, her voice echoing off the cave walls.

"Brother," Rhyland's commanding voice cuts through the howling wind that whips through the entrance, his ocean-blue eyes blazing with determination. "Any fucking second now."

The very air trembles as Lilith approaches. Her green eyes glow with otherworldly malice, porcelain features twisted into a cruel smile.

I watch as she stalks through the cavern entrance, her white dress stained crimson with evidence of her latest atrocity. The memory of St. Catherine's Orphanage threatens to crack my careful control—twenty-three small bodies, arranged like broken dolls in their beds. Her "tribute to innocence," as she called such displays.

In all my years of existence, I have witnessed mankind's capacity for cruelty, yet Lilith's systematic targeting of children—her perverse obsession with their "pure souls"—represents a darkness that exceeds even my considerable experience with horror.

My grip tightens on Grave Warden's hilt, centuries of disciplined restraint warring with the urge to separate her head from her shoulders. But we must maintain our positions. The witch's spell requires precise timing.

This ends tonight. It must.

"Well, well... if it isn't my two favorite disappointments," she sneers, with aristocratic disdain. "Summoning me here to beg forgiveness for your atrocious manners? Or are you here about that pathetic waste of immortality you call a brother?"

The memory of Lucian's suffering grinds my teeth—decades of psychological torture that drove him to press a stake against his own heart, demanding his freedom. Even now, the scars of her "motherly affection" haven't fully healed.

"You sick bitch. The only groveling will be you begging for mercy," Rhyland snarls, his massive frame tensed for battle. "Your reign of terror ends tonight."

I grip my sword tighter, watching as Elizabeth continues her incantation. The ancient runes we'd carved into the stone walls begin to pulse with an eerie light. Just a few more moments...

Lilith's laughter echoes through the cavern. "You dare challenge me? I made you what you are!" She blurs quickly attacking Rhyland, but Rhyland stands firm, his own abilities matching hers.

"Now, Erik!" Rhyland roars.

I move with unnatural speed, my blade singing through the air. Lilith deflects my first strike, but it's merely a distraction. Rhyland's attack comes from behind, driving her deeper into the cave.

Elizabeth's voice rises to a crescendo, the Hawthorne magic crackling through the air like lightning. "By blood and bone, by ancient stone, I bind thee!"

Lilith's screams of rage turn to horror as she's magically sealed inside—a barrier she cannot even break. "You cannot do this to me! I am your Maker!"

"You are nothing but a monster," I state coldly, watching as the enchanted stone tomb seals her fate. "And monsters belong in the dark."

Rhyland's power combines with the witch's spell, forcing the stone door closed. "You will never harm another soul," he declares, his voice resonating with authority.

The last thing we see is Lilith's face contorted in fury before the stone door seals shut, Elizabeth's magic binding it with ancient Hawthorne symbols.

Rhyland places a heavy hand on my shoulder, "It's done, brother."

I nod solemnly, knowing we can never tell Lucian of this night. The trauma Lilith inflicted upon him runs too deep. "What of the witch?" I ask, turning to where Elizabeth stands, exhausted but proud.

"Her bloodline will guard this secret," Rhyland responds. "The Hawthorne's have sworn it."

We believed it would hold her for eternity. We were wrong.

Destroying one's Maker requires power beyond conventional means. The bond between Maker and progeny creates a nearly impenetrable defense—a fact Lilith exploited with calculated cruelty. Even with our combined strength and combat experience, Rhyland and I could only manage to imprison her. The witch's ancient magic, combined with our abilities, barely proved sufficient to seal her in that stone tomb.

The fact that she has now broken free... *troubling* would be a gross understatement.

I blink away the memory, jaw clenched tight. Our...final solution...to ensure Lilith's imprisonment—one that still haunts me centuries later—should have made this impossible. Unless—

"You fucking did what?" Lucian's voice rises to a roar. "You trapped that psychopath and never thought to mention it?"

I meet his furious gaze steadily. "We made a conscious decision to spare you further trauma. Rhyland believed it would be... kinder. By allowing you to believe she had simply left, you could heal, knowing she had relinquished her hold over you."

A bitter laugh erupts from Lucian, sharp and caustic. "Oh, that's just fucking perfect. *Really* stellar brotherly bonding moment here. Thanks for keeping me in the dark about entombing our psycho mom. Really appreciate that tidbit of info being kept—"

"—Hey, Captain Man-Pain!" Emily's voice cuts through the tension like a sharp blade. "How about we shelf your dramatic feelings for later? Instead of crying about being excluded from the Super Secret Vampire Club. Maybe we focus on Erik's intel about the psycho bitch who has my best friend?"

The corner of my mouth twitches at Emily's brazen outburst. Lucian responds with an exaggerated eye roll before dragging himself to the nearest stool. Seraphina immediately gravitates to his side, her gentle presence tempering his volatile emotions. He whispers soft apologies to her, his earlier fury dissipating under her touch.

Emily arches an eyebrow. "Don't you have some vampire blood hotline thing going with Dani? Maybe try using that?"

"Oh, Em—gee, why didn't I think of that?" Lucian gasps dramatically, smacking his forehead like an idiot. "It's almost like I haven't been trying to reach our favorite feisty savior for the past few hours. Spoiler alert: the connection's about as dead as your Friday nights with your Netflix subscription and that sad pint of Ben & Jerry's. But please, continue giving me vampire advice, Professor Single-and-Salty."

"Well, try harder, Count Snarkula!" Emily snaps, as she throws her hands up in exasperation.

Lucian releases an exaggerated groan before closing his eyes in concentration. "Yo, firecracker, throw me a bone here," he mutters, fingers pressed to his temples. "Even just one tiny 'fuck you' would do. Hell, I'd settle for a mental eye-roll at this point."

The silence that follows is... concerning.

"Someone's blocking the connection," I state, my voice measured despite the implications. "Likely through arcane means."

"No shit, Mr. "I'll Save You (But First, Let Me Frown)," Lucian snaps, his frustration manifesting in typical crude fashion. "What was your first clue? The radio silence, or the fact that our batshit crazy maker's witch friend is having a magical fucking field day."

I maintain my impassive expression, though internally, I calculate the growing complications of our situation. The ability to suppress a blood bond requires considerable magical prowess—power that could prove... problematic.

I clear my throat, adjusting my posture. "I need my computer." As if summoned by thought alone, Sable appears from the living room with my laptop. "Much obliged."

My fingers fly across the keyboard, executing a series of complex algorithms I developed during the dot-com boom. Back in '95, I recognized the digital revolution as a new frontier of warfare. While Rhyland focused on traditional combat and Lucian built his nightclub empire, I immersed myself in the emerging cyber realm.

Lucian can hack, but not like I can.

I breach the first firewall of the local real estate database, a ghost of a smirk playing at my lips as I remember the months I spent as a "security consultant" for various Fortune 500 companies. Those arrogant tech bros never suspected the apathetic freelancer testing their systems was actually a vampire gathering intelligence. I made a fortune finding vulnerabilities in their networks—officially, of course, through their "bug bounty" programs. Unofficially... well, certain offshore accounts grew quite healthy during those years.

Their knowledge, combined with my pattern recognition and an impressive portfolio of zero-day exploits I've collected, made me a formidable force in the digital underground. There's a certain poetry in how corporations will pay millions to protect themselves from exactly the kind of attacks I perfect in my spare time.

"What exactly are you doing?" Emily peers over my shoulder, her tone heavy with curiosity.

"Creating a Boolean search algorithm to cross-reference recent high-end property acquisitions with specific parameters that match Lilith's... particular tastes," I explain, my fingers never pausing. "The pretentious bitch hasn't changed—she still favors expensive architecture, private grounds, and ostentatious displays of wealth."

Multiple windows populate the screen as I breach various databases—property records, utility activations, and shell company registrations. Each piece of data flows through my custom-built tracking program, which I developed during a particularly enlightening stint with a black hat collective in Moscow in 2010.

I smirk as my customized program flags a hit. "There you are, you sneaky cunt." A recently purchased estate appears on screen, registered to a corporation named 'Inanna Holdings'— the Babylonian goddess of love and war.

"Got her," I announce, my voice carrying the weight of certainty. "Twenty thousand square feet of overcompensation, complete with underground wine cellar and private grounds. Purchased six weeks ago through a shell company that practically screams 'Look at how clever I am.'"

Lucian peers at the screen, his eyebrows rising. "Damn, bro. Remind me never to piss you off enough to hack my browser history."

I cast him a withering glance. "Your browser history is disturbing enough without my interference, brother."

"Location?" Emily demands, her impatience evident.

I verify the coordinates. "Vancouver BC. Nestled right along water."

"Oh, for fuck's sake," Emily groans, throwing her hands up. "That's a four-hour drive from here, assuming traffic doesn't completely fuck us."

I shut the laptop with a decisive click, meeting Lucian's gaze. His usual smirk has been replaced by something darker, more predatory. "Then I suggest we cease this idle chatter and depart immediately."

"Uh, hello? Did you forget we have a literal jet at our disposal?" Lucian interjects. "We could be strutting down the tarmac in thirty, landing in BC before Erik's expression changes—in Maple Leaf territory, ready to kick some bitchy ass."

I grunt my acknowledgment, despite my distinct aversion to air travel. The efficiency cannot be denied.

"Road trip from hell it is," Lucian quips, but there's steel beneath his sarcasm. "I call shotgun and DJ privileges."

I suppress the urge to roll my eyes. "Touch the radio, brother, and you'll find yourself running alongside the vehicle."

"I'll stay here and watch over Damon," Sable states with quiet confidence. Though she possesses minor witch abilities, her intelligence and technological expertise make her a valuable asset—qualities I've come to appreciate in our operations.

"Listen here, Witchy Wonder," Lucian waves his hands dramatically, like a deranged traffic conductor. "That reinforced door stays locked tighter than Erik's ass cheeks during a pole dancing competition. Blood bags are in the mini-fridge—one per hour, like some twisted vampire McDonald's drive-thru. No supersizing or I swear to whatever unholy deity is listening, I will come back and personally kick your magical behind into next Tuesday."

He points an accusing finger, "And for fuck's sake, do *not* go all Mother Teresa on his bitey ass. Getting within fang distance of a baby vamp is like trying to diet at an all-you-can-eat buffet—somebody's getting hurt, and it'll be the menu—aka—you. Capisce?"

I observe their exchange with measured attention, noting that despite Lucian's theatrical delivery, his instructions are fundamentally sound.

"I think I can handle Vampire Daycare." Sable fires back. "Or did you forget the weeks we spent making sure *you* didn't go full Walking Dead on us during your convenient case of paranormal amnesia?"

"First of all, *rude*," Lucian clutches his chest in mock offense. "Second of all... okay, yeah, you've got me there. But in my defense, I was a *fabulous* disaster to babysit. Like, we're talking five-star Yelp reviews of chaos. 'Would definitely recommend this vampire's amnesic ass again, great entertainment value, minimal civilian casualties.'"

Internally I question, not for the first time, how I'm related to this theatrical imbecile. Sable's experience managing Lucian's... condition... does qualify her for this task.

Emily rushes about gathering a few supplies while Lucian snatches the keys. I mentally catalog our weapons and necessities—grabbing a few viles of Dani's blood she keeps stashed and stocked in the fridge—when Seraphina's melodic voice cuts through our hasty preparations.

"Wait." Though gentle, her command carries an unmistakable authority that stops us in our tracks.

"What's troubling you, Cupcake?" Lucian's voice softens as he wraps his arms around her waist, his usual snark momentarily subdued.

Seraphina cradles his face in her delicate hands, her honey-colored eyes swimming with celestial worry. "Are you truly prepared to confront her, Sparky?" The angel's intuition, as always, proves sharp—she senses the turmoil roiling beneath Lucian's carefully constructed facade. The psychological warfare Lilith waged against him took decades to overcome.

"Hell fucking yes," Lucian declares, though I detect a slight tremor in his voice. "I've got you now, Phina-baby. My own personal angel therapist who fixed my broken ass." His signature grin returns, though tinged with genuine emotion. "Ready to go show that psychotic bitch what happens when you mess with a reformed bad boy with his heavenly honey."

Seraphina tucks a strand of golden hair behind her ear. "Okay, but maybe we could, you know, come up with an actual plan first?" Her melodic voice remains gentle as a summer breeze. "Instead of our usual 'run in guns blazing and hope we don't die' approach? Because that's been working out *super* great for us."

The weeks among us have clearly left their mark on heaven's messenger.

"Holy shit, would you listen to that sass!" Lucian practically bounces with delight. "I've created a monster—a totally adorable, celestial monster. Should I be worried you're gonna smite my ass now, Cupcake?"

"Someone must be the voice of reason among our little family," she counters. "Since you're all ready to charge in like vengeful warriors without divine guidance—"

"A strategy will be devised during transit," I interject, checking my watch. "The journey provides ample time for planning."

DANICA

8

After a battle royale of trying to force-feed me their witch's brew, the terrible twosome decided to take a more direct approach—jamming a needle in my arm. My muscles scream in protest as Lilith's iron grip pins me to the mattress, her perfectly manicured nails digging crescents into my skin. Morgan looms over me, syringe gleaming menacingly in the dim light. Despite my thrashing and cursing, the needle finds its mark, and liquid fire courses through my veins.

"There we go. That wasn't so terrible, now was it?" Morgan's voice drips with false sweetness as she caps the empty syringe, like she's just given a child their annual flu shot instead of injecting me with their bullshit poison.

"Fuck you. Fuck both of you straight to hell!" The words tear from me, raw and furious. Already the drug seeps through my system like a cold sludge, numbing everything. Leaving me hollow and defenseless. The emptiness where my magic should be aches like a phantom limb.

Fucking witches and their supernatural roofies.

Lilith rises like some twisted Disney villain, smoothing imaginary wrinkles from her skin-tight dress that looks like Jessica Rabbit went through a goth phase. "Well then, dinner awaits." Those emerald eyes flash with predatory anticipation. "Our guests are getting restless downstairs, and I've wasted enough time playing with the likes of *you*. Come, Ishtar."

Her creepy feathered surveillance camera glides from its perch with silent grace, settling on her shoulder like the world's most judgmental accessory.

She spins on her fuck-me heels and click-clacks towards the door, pausing to toss a final command over her shoulder."Morgan, dress her up. Make her look..."Her lips curl into a cruel smile. "Presentable." The door closes with an ominous click, leaving me alone with Witch Bitch and the sinking realization that 'dinner' probably isn't referring to a nice pot roast. Something tells me I'm about to star in the world's worst vampire dinner theater, and I'm not going to like my role.

I glare at Morgan. "Let me guess—it's a black-tie affair in the torture dungeon?"

But even as I spit sass like armor, fear claws at my insides. Dinner guests? Lilith's twisted idea of presentable? I have a sinking feeling this isn't going to be a pleasant evening of small talk and canapés.

Morgan's smile spreads across her face like poison, all sugar-coated malice. "Impressive—you'll see."

The second the cuffs click open, I launch into action like a caged animal finally freed. My fist flies toward her face—and then nothing. My body freezes mid-swing, muscles locked in place like I've been turned to stone.

What the hell?

"Cute," Morgan drawls, circling my paralyzed form. "But let's get one thing straight—I can turn you into a living statue with less effort than it takes to blink." She taps my frozen chin with her finger. "So maybe we skip the heroics?"

Ice slides down my spine as the reality of my situation sinks in. This isn't some bargain-basement witch playing at dark magic. The power rolling off her in waves makes my skin crawl—ancient, dangerous, and absolutely lethal. And here I am, powerless as a kitten thanks to their magical cocktail, at the mercy of a witch who can apparently turn people into human mannequins with a thought.

"Mm-hmm," I manage through gritted teeth, because what else can I do? Morgan finally releases me from her magical straitjacket, I massage my wrists, trying to get feeling back into my tingling fingers while my mind races through escape scenarios—each one more impossible than the last.

"Perfect. Time to play dress-up," Morgan chirps like we're having a goddamn slumber party, disappearing into what I assume is the closet from Hell.

I'm left sitting here, my heart beating out of my chest, wondering how the hell I'm going to MacGyver my way out of this one.

After hours with a beauty SWAT team—enough makeup to stock a Sephora and enduring hair-yanking torture sessions—I'm trussed up like a Thanksgiving turkey in expensive silk. Morgan painted, plucked, and polished every inch of me, probably using products that cost more than my car payment.

Given my recent greatest hits—featuring my brother's attempt at vampire murder—fighting every supernatural on the planet—getting kidnapped by Vampire Barbie, and being drugged into magical submission—I must have looked like something dragged backward through hell's gift shop.

Now I'm being paraded through what has to be Bruce Wayne's evil twin's summer home—if Bruce Wayne was a bloodsucking sociopath with a thing for dramatic real estate. The place is a monument to "fuck you" money, perched on its cliff like a glass and steel predator watching the waves below. Floor-to-ceiling windows stretch toward the star-studded sky, framing a view of the ocean that's gone midnight-black, that would be breathtaking if I wasn't, you know, being held hostage.

City lights twinkle in the distance across the water, close enough to taunt me with freedom but too far to offer any hope of rescue.

The mansion itself is some unholy union of modern architecture and supervillain chic—all sleek lines and polished surfaces.

Where the hell am I?

The grand staircase sweeps down into a two-story great room where wall-to-wall windows frame the churning sea like nature's own IMAX screen. Crystal chandeliers drip from elaborate coffered ceilings, throwing prismatic light across marble floors so polished I can see my reflection in them.

The sound of violins drifts up as we descend, and I nearly wipe out in these medieval torture devices masquerading as designer heels.

The place is teeming with the vampire elites, all decked out in black-tie attire like this is some twisted immortal prom night. Everyone's sporting masquerade masks, only adding to the eerie vibe.

What's the deal with vampires and masquerade balls, anyway?

"Move it," Morgan commands, like I'm her personal show pony.

I plant my feet, summoning my inner stubborn mule, but suddenly my body jerks forward like I'm a marionette on invisible strings. I stumble, barely avoiding a face-first introduction to the marble floor.

"Jesus, do you have to be such a Grade-A bitch?" I snarl under my breath, burning holes in the back of her head.

Morgan glances back, her smile sharp as a razor. "Behave, and I won't have to be. Simple as that. Now, be a good girl and put on your pretty smile. We wouldn't want to disappoint our hostess, would we?"

Great. I'm trapped in some twisted fucked-up soirée, being paraded around like a prized poodle by Witch Bitch while Vampire Regina George probably plots my demise over chilled blood champagne.

The crowd parts like the Red Sea as Morgan drags me through, but it's not respect moving them—it's hunger. Heads snap toward me, nostrils flaring as they catch my scent. My heart hammers against my ribs like it's trying to escape, and based on the way these vampires are looking at me, it has the right idea.

Their eyes track my every movement, pupils blown wide with bloodlust. High-priced suits and couture gowns can't hide the predators beneath—if anything, they make them more terrifying. These aren't your average street vamps; these are apex predators in Armani.

"Mmm... such a delectable little morsel," purrs a woman in a red dress, her tongue sliding across pearl-white fangs.

A silver-haired vampire in a tux inhales deeply, his eyes rolling back. "I simply must have a taste. The aroma is... intoxicating."

"So this was Azrael's obsession," another whispers, voice thick with anticipation. "I understand now—she smells divine."

Cold fear slides down my spine as their words sink in. My fingers tremble against the silk of my dress as realization hits—this doesn't feel like a normal party. It feels like this is a fucking tasting menu, and I'm the main course. These trust fund bloodsuckers are looking at me like I'm a vintage wine at a sampling event.

Bile rises, as Morgan continues to drag me through this gauntlet of gleaming fangs and hungry eyes. Every cell in my body screams to run, but between Morgan's magical leash and my power-dampening cocktail, I might as well try to sprout wings and fly.

I smooth trembling hands over the dress they've poured me into—a white silk number that screams "virgin bride." The fabric whispers against my skin, hugging every curve like it was painted on. It's the kind of dress that would cost three months' rent, and here I am wearing it to what's probably going to be my last supper.

The neckline plunges into a deep V—my breasts on full display, while the rest of the dress flows like liquid moonlight to the floor. It's elegant in its simplicity—no beading, no lace, just pure white silk that practically glows under the chandelier light.

Could this be it? The moment where they serve me up to Moretemis like some gift-wrapped offering—the ritual? Everything I know about the shadow god floods my mind—his hunger for power, his taste for innocent blood, his ability to corrupt souls.

The sick irony of wearing pure white to what might be my own funeral isn't lost on me, while surrounded by bloodthirsty vampires in a mansion that probably has more secret passages than the Winchester Mystery House.

"Ah, there's our guest of honor." Lilith's voice slices through the crowd. She sashays toward me, her own mask barely hiding the malevolent glint in her eyes, a pack of balenciaga-clad vampires following her like obedient pets. "Morgan, darling, escort our little star to the stage."

My stomach drops as I spot the setup—a single chair and microphone standing in the spotlight like some twisted American Idol from hell. What fresh nightmare is this? Are they seriously expecting me to perform like some circus animal?

Lilith's feathered spy—Ishtar—lurks in the shadows above the stage, those black eyes drinking in every detail of this twisted bullshit. The owl's heart-shaped face seems to glow in the dim light, a silent witness to my personal nightmare. Perfect—even the wildlife is in on this sick show. At least someone's enjoying the performance.

Morgan's invisible leash yanks me forward again, and the crowd of vampires parts, their fangs gleaming as I pass. They snap their jaws at me like rabid dogs testing their chains, making my skin crawl with each click of teeth.

Suddenly, a blur of movement and expensive cologne—a vampire materializes beside me, fangs aimed for my throat. Before I can scream, Lilith appears, her manicured hand locked around his neck. "Do. Not. Touch. Her." Her voice carries the weight of centuries and promises violence.

For a split second, relief floods my system—until she continues, and my blood turns to ice in my veins.

"Not until you bid. Is that clear?" Her perfectly painted lips curl into a cruel smile.

The vampire struggles against her grip, testosterone and pride warring with self-preservation. Lilith merely tightens her hold, eyebrow raised in challenge. Finally, he yields with a jerky nod.

"Good boy." Lilith pats his cheek like he's a misbehaving puppy. "Now, get in line. The show's about to begin."

Bid?

My God. My knees threaten to buckle as the reality of my situation sinks in.

Morgan drags me onto the stage, my legs trembling so violently I'm shocked I'm still upright. The click of Lilith's heels behind me sounds like a countdown to execution, each step echoing through the suddenly hushed room. She grabs the microphone, her blood-red lips curved in a smile.

"Welcome, distinguished guests." Her voice slithers through the room. "Thank you all for attending tonight's... special event." The crowd raises their glasses in unison, the dark liquid inside definitely not wine. The sight of all those crystal flutes filled with blood makes my stomach lurch.

"I know you're all eager to begin. And I promise, you won't be disappointed. We have quite the prize tonight—a genuine angel." Her gaze slides to me, sharp as a blade. "One whose blood grants the greatest gift of all—the ability to walk in daylight."

The crowd erupts in excited whispers, their hungry eyes fixed on me like I'm the last meal they'll ever have. Jesus fucking Christ. That bastard Azrael actually did it—he broadcast my secret to every bloodsucker with a pulse. Or, well, without one. The thought makes me want to vomit—I've become the vampire equivalent of a winning Powerball ticket.

"Bullshit!" A voice cuts through the murmurs like a knife. Some vampire in the back, clearly skeptical of Lilith's claims, stands up. "No blood exists with that kind of power. This is a scam!"

For a brief, beautiful moment, hope flutters in my chest as the crowd starts muttering in agreement. Maybe they'll call this whole sick auction off. Maybe—

"Oh, trust me, darling." Lilith says with smug satisfaction as she runs her tongue over her fangs. "I've already sampled the merchandise myself. She's the real deal."

My mouth goes dry as the crowd's skepticism evaporates instantly. They're nodding now, completely convinced by Lilith's firsthand testimony. Because of course they are—why would the powerful, ancient vampire lie about something like this?

"But before we proceed with the bidding," Lilith's voice takes on a dangerous edge, "there are rules. And let me be perfectly clear—anyone who breaks these rules will answer to me personally."

The temperature in the room seems to drop ten degrees as the gathered vampires lower their eyes, their earlier bloodlust temporarily dampened by fear. Even these powerful immortals know better than to cross Lilith. The way they shrink from her gaze tells me everything I need to know about her age and power—and none of it's good news for me.

"Rule number one. The winner gets one night with the angel. No extensions, no negotiations. She returns to me immediately after." My breath hitches, terror clawing at my chest.

No. No. Fuck NO.

"Rule number two. She is not to be killed. You will be monitored at all times—and yes, that includes during any...*intimate* activities. Consider it mandatory audience participation."

Rage explodes through me, hot and bright enough to momentarily override my fear. "Like hell you will, you psychotic bitch!" I scream, my voice raw with fury and terror. "No one is going to fucking touch me!"

Lilith's mouth twists into something cruel and predatory. "Morgan," she breathes, the word barely audible.

In an instant, my scream dissolves into nothingness, silenced by magic. Morgan's dark power slithers around me like arctic chains, binding me in an invisible prison. I'm frozen, reduced to nothing but a spectator in my own violation. Hot tears of fury and terror streak down my cheeks as I'm forced to watch this horror show play out.

The utter helplessness is suffocating. I'm trapped inside my own body, every muscle locked in place by Morgan's supernatural grip. My voice—my last weapon—has been stolen away, leaving me mute and powerless. My rage has nowhere to go, burning uselessly beneath my skin while these monsters toy with me.

Lilith continues as if I'm nothing more than a minor interruption, examining her blood-red nails with casual indifference. "Rule number three. Payment must be made in full before you claim your prize. Are we all clear?"

The crowd murmurs their agreement like well-trained pets, hungry eyes fixed on me.

"Excellent!" Lilith chirps. "Now, who would like a little sample of our angel before the bidding begins?"

The room erupts in a frenzy of raised hands and eager voices, every vampire desperate for a taste of my blood, for the promise of sunlight it carries. I've never felt more like a piece of meat being dangled before starving wolves.

God, Rhyland, where are you?

"Ah, Silas." Lilith's voice drips with cruel anticipation. "Please," she gestures toward me like I'm an appetizer being served. "Give her a taste. I promise you won't be disappointed."

Panic explodes through me as I struggle against Morgan's invisible bonds. But it's useless—I'm trapped, forced to stand here like a statue while this monster approaches. My heart slams against my ribs so hard it hurts.

Silas stalks toward me, his huge frame blocking out the chandelier light. He's built like a concrete wall, all rippling muscle and brutal strength, and the hungry look in his eyes makes me want to vomit. Even behind his ornate mask, I can see the savage anticipation written across his features.

He towers over me, lowering his face to my neck, and inhales deeply. His hot breath against my skin makes my flesh crawl. "Mmm... you do smell delicious." His voice is rough with desire. "I bet you taste even better."

Without warning, his monstrous hands seize my waist, yanking me against his chest with bruising force. I feel his arousal pressing against my stomach, and I feel utterly sick. Every cell in my body screams in revulsion. This is wrong, so fucking wrong. I want to fight, to claw his eyes out, to scream until my lungs burst—but I can't move a single muscle.

"Don't keep us waiting, Silas." Lilith's impatient command cuts through my panic. "We don't have all night."

Silas strikes like a cobra, his fangs ripping into my neck without hesitation. The pain is excruciating. It's violation, pure and simple, and though Morgan's magic mutes my physical screams, my mind howls in agony.

"RHYLAND!!" I scream through our bond with everything I have, hurling my terror and pain and desperate need across whatever distance separates us.

Please hear me. Please find me.

But only silence answers my mental plea, and Silas continues to drink deeply, each pull of his mouth draining away not just my blood, but my hope of rescue. The crowd watches with ravenous eyes, waiting for their turn, and the reality of my situation crashes over me like a tsunami—this is just the beginning of my nightmare.

RHYLAND

9

I've had it with this shit. "Send me back. I'm done listening to this," I snarl, my patience completely shot. "I have a job to do—keeping *your* daughter safe." I fix Elysium with a glare. "You're keeping me from my goddamn job."

My thoughts drift to Dani, and my chest tightens. She better be safe at the mansion, though knowing my stubborn angel, she's probably trying to tear open reality itself to find me. Which brings up a good point—why hasn't she managed it yet?

Suddenly, a wave of fear hits me like a fucking semi-truck, nearly bringing me to my knees. I clutch at my chest, my heart feeling like it's being ripped out of my ribcage.

"Dani." Her name is a strangled sob on my lips.

"Are you alright?" Heimdall's voice comes from somewhere above me, his hand steadying my shoulder.

I must have collapsed under the weight of the terror coursing through my veins. I struggle to stand on shaky legs, the need to get to Dani is like a physical force crushing my chest—she needs me, NOW.

I've never felt anything like this from her before—this raw, primal fear that's clawing its way through our connection. Whatever or whoever is causing my mate this kind of pain is going to die by my hand. Tonight.

I'm going to find them, and I'm going to rip them apart piece by bloody piece. Death will be too kind for anyone who dares to hurt her.

"Get me the fuck out of here!" I roar. "It's Dani—" I can't even finish the sentence. My lungs feel like they're being squeezed in a vice.

Elysium's eyes widen, his heavenly composure cracking. "What? What is it? What's happened to my daughter?" he demands, his voice booming through the hall.

The mighty god of light doesn't sound so high and mighty now—he sounds like what he is: a father terrified for his child—for Dani. Welcome to the fucking club, pal.

"I don't know—she needs me. Send me back, NOW!" The words tear from me, raw and desperate. These pricks and their questions can go straight to hell.

"Heimdall, move!" Odin's command cracks like thunder through the hall.

We bolt from the chamber, the bitter wind and stinging snow whipping at our faces as we race toward the bridge. My boots pound against the crystal surface of the Bifrost—my only fucking ticket out of this place. Heimdall reaches the control chamber first, ramming his sword into the mechanism.

"Til Valhalla," he growls, and before I can process what the fuck he's talking about or what's happening, the bastard shoves me forward.

The floor disappears beneath my feet, and I'm falling, my body feeling like it's being ripped apart at an atomic level. The sensation lasts for an eternity and no time at all before I slam into solid ground, the impact driving every ounce of air from my lungs.

As I lay here gasping like a landed fish, trying to get my lungs to function—the scents quickly hit me—rich earth, scorched flesh, and rotting forest debris. My eyes snap open, taking in the dense canopy above. Back in the forest. Finally.

Now to find out what the fuck is happening to my girl.

I slam my eyes shut, reaching for that familiar golden thread that ties us together. Her signature pulses like a beacon, but it's distant—too fucking distant.

What the actual fuck? She's nowhere near Lucian's place.

"Baby? I'm here. What's going on?" I push through our mental bond, desperate to reach her. But all I get back is that same black void, that emptiness that pisses me off to no end. A growl rips from my throat, primal and raw.

I blur through the trees to where we left the cars, only to find empty spaces and tire tracks in the dirt. Goddamnit! How long was I stuck in that divine circus?

My fangs descend, razor-sharp points pricking my lower lip as I catch her scent heading north. I launch myself forward, pushing my vampiric speed to its limits. The forest becomes a green blur around me, branches whipping past my face and leaving stinging cuts in their wake as I tear through the wilderness like a man possessed. But even at full throttle, I'm burning through energy like a motherfucker. I need wheels, and I need them now, or I'll flame out long before I reach her.

The distance between us feels like a physical wound, each mile another knife in my heart. *"Hold on, baby,"* I send through the bond, praying that she can hear me. *"I'm coming for you. Just hold on."*

Whatever's keeping me from reaching her is going to regret the day they were born.

I hit the city limits and force myself to slow down, my predator's gaze already scanning for a car. A sleek black Mercedes catches my eye—perfect timing as some suit-wearing bastard is just climbing in. I blur across the street, faster than any human eye can track, and wrap my fingers around his throat. The guy lets out a strangled gasp as I yank him out of the driver's seat.

His eyes go wide with terror as I lean in close, my fangs visible as I snarl, "I'm gonna need to borrow your car." The stench of his piss soaked pants and fear fills my nostrils as I snatch the keys from his trembling hand.

With a dismissive shove, I send him stumbling back, not even sparing him a second glance as I slide behind the wheel. The engine roars to life under my touch, and I slam the door with enough force to rattle the frame.

Tires screech against asphalt as I punch the gas, the Mercedes leaping forward like a beast unleashed. I weave through traffic with reckless abandon, the speedometer climbing higher and higher as I push the machine to its limits.

Hold on, baby. Just fucking hold on.

"Brother. You return." Erik's voice cuts through my mind, precise and controlled as ever.

Fuck, why didn't I think to contact them? My brain's been so laser-focused on Dani that I've been operating on pure instinct. *"Yes. What the fuck is going on?"* I fire back through our mental bond.

Erik's hesitation bleeds through our connection like a freezing mist, his usual stoic demeanor wavering. That alone makes my blood run cold. *"Erik. Answer me, goddammit!"* My grip on the steering wheel tightens until the leather creaks.

"It's Lilith." Two words, delivered with Erik's characteristic restraint, but they hit me like a lightning strike.

My lungs seize up, and for a moment, I forget how to breathe. That name—that fucking name—tells me everything I need to know. The thought of that sadistic bitch anywhere near Dani makes my stomach lurch. Hot tears burn behind my eyes, but I blink them away. No. We locked that psychotic cunt away. We made damn sure of it.

I force myself to swallow past the knot. *"Where? Where the* fuck *is she?"* The words come out as more of a growl.

"We're here, brother. But the situation is...delicate. We have a plan—"

I slam my hand against the steering wheel, pissed off. *"Fucking where Erik?!"* I cut him off with a shout. I know what he's doing—trying to protect me from our maker like he always has, but I don't have time for his strategic bullshit right now.

Erik finally relents, giving me an address in that clipped, efficient way of his. *"Be careful, Rhyland. Don't let your anger cloud your judgment."*

The warning in his tone is crystal clear. We both know the fucked-up hierarchy of vampire creation—we can't overpower our maker. It's like some cosmic joke, a glitch in the supernatural matrix. But I've got an ace up my sleeve.

I pull out the ring from my pocket—the Soul Stone drinks in what little light there is. My mother's power pulses within it, dark and ancient and hungry.

If she could wield it, why can't I?

ERIK

10

From my concealed vantage point, I observe the scene with deliberate restraint, my jaw clenching at Lilith's imperious command. "Don't keep us waiting, Silas. We don't have all night."

The assembled garbage—society's elite vampires draped in designer wear and manufactured superiority—mill about like vultures circling their prey. Their collective greed and depravity fill the air as thick as the scent of aged blood. My infiltration among them proves almost insultingly simple; wealth breeds complacency, and complacency breeds weakness.

Dani, forcibly restrained while that worthless piece of shit follows Lilith's depraved orders. My fingers itch for Grave Warden's familiar weight—one clean stroke would demonstrate precisely why my blade earned its reputation. Yet strategic necessity dictates patience.

My intelligence network revealed Lilith's masquerade ball and its true nature—an auction where these entitled bastards intend to bid on Dani like some rare artifact. The mansion blueprints, acquired through my more... sophisticated methods, revealed several promising infiltration points. The wealthy's predictable obsession with secret passages proves consistently useful.

I located a worthless excuse for a vampire lurking on the mansion's periphery. Eliminating him and appropriating his formal attire proved efficient—his mask and invitation providing the perfect cover. While I harbor no moral reservations about dispatching our own kind when necessary, I maintain certain principles regarding humans. Call it nobility or weakness, but centuries of existence have taught me the value of maintaining some ethical boundaries, even in our darker nature.

Rhyland's rage pulses through our bond like a gathering storm. His primal need to protect his mate threatens to shatter what little remains of his reasoning. My attempts to moderate his fury prove about as effective as reasoning with a goddamn hurricane. We must execute our extraction plan before his arrival inevitably transforms this operation into what Lucian would term a "supernatural shit show."

Lucian and Emily maintain their positions outside—a decision made upon our arrival. My brother, for once displaying sound judgment, convinced Seraphina to remain at the house with Sable. Having a pure angel in this den of predators would be like igniting dynamite in a powder keg.

My gaze catches the owl perched atop the crystal chandelier—another of Lilith's surveillance tools. Her obsession with the species makes this one's purpose obvious. No doubt it serves as her newest familiar, watching our every move.

The scene before me makes me sick. This worthless excuse for a vampire gorges himself on Dani's blood, her tears cutting deeper than any blade. The violation transcends mere physical trauma—forced feeding while bonded to Rhyland represents a particularly cruel torture. Her body cries out for her mate while this pathetic piece of shit forces his attention upon her.

"That's quite enough, Silas darling," Lilith demands. The evil bitch hasn't changed at all.

Yet this scumbag appears to have developed a death wish. Rather than heeding his hierarchy command, Silas tightens his grip, drawing more deeply from Dani's veins. I watch her strength falter, knees beginning to give way.

"For fuck's sake, can we move this along?" I project my irritation across the room. "Some of us have other engagements this evening."

The assembled parasites murmur their assent, their own impatience feeding into my fabricated persona. Yet this worthless bastard continues to defy her, each passing second fueling my growing rage. My fingers flex instinctively. One clean stroke would—

"You absolute imbecile!" Lilith's hand shoots out, yanking Silas away with such force that Dani collapses into the chair. Her green eyes flash with rage. "When I give an order, I expect it to be followed *immediately.*"

Silas cowers, Dani's blood staining his unworthy mouth. "Forgive me, Mistress. Her taste... it's beyond anything—"

The words die in his throat—literally. Lilith moves with lethal grace, her fingers tearing through muscle and bone like tissue paper. Silas's head separates with a wet crack, his final expression frozen in eternal surprise as his body crumples. Dark blood paints the marble floors while his head rolls to a stop at Dani's feet.

Dani's sharp intake of breath draws my attention. Her eyes wide with terror, skin pale beneath her tan complexion as she presses herself further into the chair. The scent of her fear permeates the air, mixing with copper and death.

Lilith delicately wipes her hands, not a hair out of place. Her casual display of brutality serves as a stark reminder of why it took both Rhyland and myself, plus ancient Hawthorne magic, to merely imprison her. Her power radiates through the room like a physical force, millennia of accumulated strength making the air heavy with malevolent energy.

"Now then," her voice maintains its cultured refinement. "Let's be perfectly clear about the rules of engagement. This exquisite creature is merely on loan. Damage my property, defy my wishes, and well..." She nudges Silas's head with her Louboutin heel. "I trust I've made myself clear?"

The assembled crowd shifts nervously, their earlier bloodlust tempered by healthy fear. Even these shit stains recognize an apex predator when they see one.

"Consider yourselves privileged," Lilith continues. "Her blood is simply *divine*—something none of you pathetic peasants will ever experience again. Now, shall we proceed with our little auction?"

The assembled elite stir with renewed interest, their earlier fear of Lilith's display quickly overshadowed by base desire. Their muttered speculations and thinly veiled hunger fill the air like decay. My jaw clenches hard enough to crack marble as I catalog every exit and potential threat.

"Morgan, dear," Lilith beckons the witch forward. "Do be a love and attend to our merchandise. We can't have damaged goods at auction, now can we?"

The witch's familiar features nag at my memory as she weaves her healing incantation over Dani's wounds.

Where do I know her?

The bleeding from Silas's feeding begins to slow, though the damage—both physical and psychological—has already been done.

Rhyland's fury pulses stronger now—he's getting closer. Time becomes a critical factor.

"Let's begin." She gestures to Dani, displayed like a macabre artwork in that blood-stained white gown—an intended visual designed to entice these assholes' basest instincts.

"Five million dollars seems a reasonable starting point for such a... unique specimen."

The room erupts in a flurry of raised bidding cards. These vultures, so eager to part with their fortunes for a taste of power they don't deserve. Pathetic.

"Oh my," Lilith's laugh rings with false delight, though I detect the underlying cruelty. "Such enthusiasm. Perhaps we're being too modest. Let's start at twenty million, shall we?"

Several cards lower—apparently, some of these worthless assholes have limits to their depravity. I maintain my position, raising my card with indifference, playing the role of wealthy collector.

The numbers climb higher: thirty million, forty, fifty—each bid accompanied by Lilith's performative excitement, like some demented auction house hostess. I counter each offer, watching these fools deplete their fortunes in pursuit of power they'll never possess—assuming they live long enough to regret their choices.

The bidding has devolved into a two-person war—myself and some arrogant bastard across the room. We assess each other through our respective masks, this theatrical facade of anonymity serving both our purposes. Based on his posture and tailoring, his bearing suggests old money, probably European. Irrelevant details, but years of observation, become a habit.

Dani's labored breathing draws my attention momentarily. Her chest rises and falls, her golden eyes wide with panic as they treat her like a prized thoroughbred.

This arrogant bastard across the room won't claim her—not while I draw breath. Though I maintain my dispassionate expression, my fingers tighten imperceptibly on the bidding card. Rhyland would tear through these walls like an enraged berserker, but this situation requires patience, not brute force.

Hold on, Little Huntress. I think, watching her struggle to maintain composure.

Your mate's more controlled brother has this situation well in hand.

My enhanced senses register the threat a fraction of a second too late—an inexcusable tactical error. Powerful arms, cold with death, lock around my head and neck.

I drive my elbow back, aiming for solar plexus—careful, controlled, nothing to draw attention from the auction. The bastard absorbs the blow like concrete. My fingers claw at his arms, trying to break his death grip, but his arms might as well be steel bands crushing my neck. This isn't some fledgling enforcer; this is an executioner, one old enough to match my strength.

The wealthy never play fair.

We struggle in near silence, a deadly dance disguised as a casual embrace to any observing eyes. My boots slide across marble as he forces me back, each movement precise to avoid disrupting Lilith's little show. I attempt to shift my weight to gain any fucking leverage, but his grip only tightens—professional, methodical.

The pressure increases with surgical precision. No rushed amateur move. I feel my vertebrae protest under the growing force—C1 and C2 screaming in warning. Even for a vampire of my considerable age, a cervical fracture of this magnitude would incapacitate long enough for them to win Dani and claim her as their prize.

One final, desperate attempt to break free—my fingers finding his face, digging for eyes—but it's too late. The sharp, wet crack of vertebrae shattering echoes through my skull like a gunshot, though I know only supernatural hearing could detect it over the auction's din. White-hot agony explodes from my neck, racing down my spine like molten steel. My body betrays me instantly, limbs becoming useless weights as neural pathways sever.

As my face meets marble, my last coherent thought is of the inevitable chaos. Rhyland will come crashing through these walls like an enraged Viking god, probably getting Dani—every fucking one of us—killed in his rage.

Then blessed darkness claims me, and I know nothing more.

DANICA

11

My chest constricts painfully, heart thundering against my ribs as two vampires wage a bidding war over me—my blood, my body, my existence. I'm being auctioned off like some rare vintage wine, the price climbing to obscene heights.

Silas's corpse lies at my feet, a grotesque reminder of his final act. His poison courses through my veins like liquid fire, forcing unwanted heat through my body until I want to claw my skin off. This invasion runs deeper than the bite—my flesh betrays me, responding to his toxic gift while my mind recoils in horror.

I battle against the sensation, but it's futile. His dark magic sends waves of unwanted pleasure crashing through me. I want to scream, to kill, to tear this whole fucking place apart with my bare hands. This is assault at its most primal level—my body forced to dance while my mind howls in rebellion.

Hot tears of rage and shame streak down my face as I struggle against Morgan's magical bonds and this chemical prison. It's a desecration beyond words, and I'm powerless to stop it. Even in death, this bastard torments me, his poison commanding responses I never consented to.

With Rhyland, each bite was sacred—pure love, trust, and passion merged into one perfect moment. His fangs pierced my skin because I craved it, needed it, welcomed it. Even Lucian's unexpected bite held a measure of understanding between us.

But this? Feels like the ultimate betrayal—my flesh singing while my spirit screams. I'm trapped in my own body, forced to perform in this hellish puppet show while my mind rages against every sensation.

The bidder stands before me, power draped in expensive clothes. His predatory gaze marks me as conquered prey. His eyes never waver as he casually tosses another bid—eighty million dollars. The auctioneer's voice scrapes against my nerves like broken glass, each call making me flinch.

"Eighty million going once..."

My gaze darts desperately to the back of the room, searching for the other bidder. Nothing. Just silence. He's abandoned the game. Apparently, that's my price tag—eighty million for one night of horror. One night where some ancient monster gets free rein over my body, all because my blood holds the key to daylight.

Nausea claws at my throat as Lilith's words echo in my head—how the winner claims me until sunrise, how "nothing is off limits." My stomach heaves as I imagine what awaits me. The thought of being used, not just for blood but for... everything else? Makes me want to scream until I shatter.

"Eighty million going twice..."

The vampire before me lets his victory smile spread, already savoring his prize. His gaze strips me bare, calculating exactly how he'll break his new toy. I've never felt so raw, so reduced to mere merchandise. To these monsters, I'm nothing but property to be traded.

The crowd drifts away, bored now that the entertainment's ending. They mingle through the ballroom like they're at a charity gala, not watching someone's life being sold. Their casual chatter floats up to my display platform, where I sit waiting to learn which sicko buys the right to destroy me.

They sip blood-laced champagne, gossiping about the evening's prices like they're discussing art pieces. The surreal disconnect makes my head spin—how can they stand there, socializing while participating in supernatural sex trafficking?

My insides twist as I await the final blow.

"SOLD! To Mr. Leighton!" The announcer's enthusiasm makes me sick. Lilith claps and smiles, gliding toward her customer. I squeeze my eyes shut, feeling hot tears escape despite my resolve.

Morgan's magic binds me like steel chains as she drags me from the ballroom. Behind us, Lilith and my "buyer" negotiate terms as if discussing a business merger. My struggles against her spell might as well be a kitten batting at iron bars.

She hurls me into my prison chamber—the same room where this nightmare began. Poetic, really.

"Wait here while the winner claims his prize," Morgan announces, clinical as a mortician reading a toe tag.

The casual cruelty of it all makes my blood boil. This woman—this witch—is supposed to represent balance and nature. Instead, she's playing enforcer for Lilith's sadistic games. What happened to all that bullshit about cosmic harmony?

"Why?" I demand, fury giving me courage. "Why are you helping that psychotic bitch? What's in it for you?" The words come out sharp enough to cut.

Morgan pauses at the doorway, turning back with eyes like frozen amber. "It's simple, really," she says, hatred lacing her words. "I have my own score to settle with your little vampire family. Consider this payback for what they did to mine, back when we served them."

Wait—what? My mind races through possibilities. Rhyland? Erik? Lucian? This could be useful. If I keep her talking, maybe she'll reveal something I can use.

"Who?" I soften my tone, letting curiosity mask my intent. "What happened to your family?"

Come on, spill your tragic backstory, you vindictive witch. Give me something I can work with.

"Ever heard of the Hawthorne witches?" Morgan seethes with generational venom. My blank look draws a bitter laugh. "Of course you haven't. Well, here's your history lesson, princess. Your precious vampires used my fourth-great grandmother, then threatened her into some bullshit treaty. We Hawthornes don't bow to anyone—especially not fucking vampires."

Raw hatred radiates from her, dropping the room's temperature several degrees—old wounds festering through generations.

I piece together this warped puzzle, choosing my words carefully. "Let me get this straight—you're throwing a tantrum over some ancient contract, and somehow that justifies using me as your revenge prop?" I arch an eyebrow. "And out of all possible allies, you picked the poster child for vampire daddy issues? Why Lilith?"

Morgan's smile turns vicious, triumphant. "Because Lilith *was* the treaty, you idiot. I freed her—breaking the chains your precious vampires put on her. You have no idea the depth of their sins. She's their Maker, the oldest, the strongest. And to get what I want?" Her eyes gleam with malicious satisfaction. "She's exactly the weapon I need."

Well, holy fucking plot twist.

The pieces click together with sickening clarity. The treaty wasn't just paper and promises—it was a magical prison for Lilith herself. Now, this vindictive witch has unleashed her, all to settle a centuries-old blood feud.

Perfect. I'm caught in the crossfire of a revenge plot that's been brewing since before I was born, complete with a crazy vampire queen and her pet witch with an ancestral axe to grind.

"So you see," Morgan says with vindictive promise, "I'm done letting vampire assholes control my family legacy. Lilith and I have an... arrangement. One that works quite nicely for both of us."

My mind spins from Morgan's revelation, but before I can respond, she vanishes. The door seals shut with the finality of a tomb.

Oh, hell no. Pure adrenaline launches me at the door. I wrench the handle with enough force to send pain shooting through my shoulder. Locked. Because, of course, it fucking is.

Desperation sends me flying to the windows. My fingers skate across flawless glass, searching for any weakness, any escape route. Nothing. Just an endless expanse of smooth, impenetrable barrier between me and freedom.

"Goddammit!"

The bathroom becomes my last hope. There must be a vent, a window, any possible exit. But no, it's just another gilded cage, all marble, and luxury masking its true purpose as a prison.

The bedroom door hinges creak...

My heart stutters, then freezes. Lilith glides in like death-wearing couture, flanked by my "buyer" and Morgan. My own personal tribunal of nightmares, here to begin their show.

I retreat until my back hits the far wall, instinct screaming for an escape route that doesn't exist. One look at the buyer's hunger tells me exactly what kind of performance they're expecting.

Rhyland, where the fuck are you?

"Come out, come out, wherever you are, darling." Lilith's sing-song voice slides through the air. "We promise not to bite... much." Her laughter shatters the silence, sharp as broken mirrors. Morgan's spell coils around me, serpentine and cold, dragging me from my corner.

Silas's dried blood still maps my skin and dress, a crimson testament to earlier horrors. The buyer's gaze dissects me inch by inch, reducing me to meat at the market. His tongue sweeps across his lips—a predator's tell—and bile burns my throat. Power rolls off him in arctic waves, ancient and corrupt. Those aristocratic features might belong in a Renaissance painting if they weren't twisted by such raw hunger.

"Release the magical bindings," he commands. "I want her unrestrained. I didn't pay eighty million for a fucking docile doll." Another slow lick of his lips. "I want every scream, every struggle."

Lilith flicks her wrist as if shooing a fly. "As you wish." Her casual permission lands like a death sentence.

Morgan's chains dissolve, leaving me unbound. I face my triumvirate of tormentors—Lilith's serpentine smile, Morgan's glacial indifference, and the buyer's ravenous anticipation. This newfound freedom is just another move in their game. They don't want a passive victim; they want the thrill of the hunt.

My muscles coil tight, every instinct screaming to run, to fight, even knowing both options lead nowhere. The buyer tracks my movements with practiced patience, a spider watching its web tremble.

His eyes promise torments that make my blood freeze. I've seen that look before in human monsters, but this is infinitely worse—this is a predator with immortal strength and centuries to perfect his craft.

"Wait outside," the buyer orders, his voice rough with anticipation. "I promise to keep her breathing."

My lungs seize as Lilith and Morgan share a silent exchange. They discuss my fate through looks alone while I stand here, a lamb watching butchers debate knife techniques. Rage and terror war in my chest, each fighting to escape in a scream.

"Very well." Lilith purrs. "I'll remain within earshot." She studies her manicure with theatrical boredom. "You have until dawn. Then your... entertainment ends." Emerald eyes flash with lethal promise. "And remember—damage my property permanently, and your existence ends. Understood?"

He offers an elaborate bow, a mockery of courtly manners. "Crystal clear, my queen."

Their casual exchange about my impending torture might as well be a discussion about borrowing a designer handbag. *Property. Entertainment. Understood.* Each word strips away another layer of my humanity. To them, I'm nothing but a toy passed between immortal hands.

The sounds of destruction erupt from below—glass shattering, wood splintering, primal roars of combat—my pulse spikes.

Lilith's eyes flutter closed, pleasure painting her features. "Ah, he comes. Right on time." She turns to Morgan, satisfaction curling her lips. "Let's go greet my love."

Hope detonates in my chest like a supernova. *Rhyland.*

"R-Rhyland—RHYLAND!!!" His name tears from my throat.

Stars explode behind my eyes as the buyer's hand cracks across my face. Copper floods my mouth. His glacial breath ghosts my ear, promising nightmares.

"Hush now," he purrs. "Can't let my eighty million go to waste." Those soulless eyes dismiss Lilith with imperial arrogance. "Leave us!"

His casual brutality, his way of reducing me to a price tag—it sets my blood boiling even as my cheek throbs. The bruise spreads like spilled ink beneath my skin, but I lock my spine straight. Terror claws up my throat, but I'll be damned if I let this monster see me break.

The sounds of chaos from below grow louder, and I cling to that hope like a lifeline. Rhyland's coming. I just have to survive whatever this psychopath has planned until then.

"With pleasure," Lilith purrs, sashaying away while death stares at me through immortal eyes.

Survival instinct kicks in—my knee rockets upward with desperate force. Instead of pain, his pleased growl fills the air. Ice floods my veins as his eyes slide shut in ecstasy—my resistance feeds his perversion. Dear god.

"Such spirit," he breathes, satisfaction with each word. "We're going to create such beautiful music together."

Time fractures. In one heartbeat, my dress becomes confetti. The next, iron bands masquerading as fingers lock around my wrists. My back slams against the wall, breath deserting my lungs. His frame becomes a cage of muscle and malice, supernatural strength rendering my struggles meaningless. Still, I fight—spitting defiance, screaming rage. His answering smile belongs in hell's darkest corner.

His free hand claims my breast, ice-cold fingers bringing waves of revulsion. Nausea rises as his touch brands me. "Exquisite," he growls, malice gleaming in bottomless eyes. "I'll savor breaking every inch."

His head strikes like a cobra. Fangs pierce delicate flesh, and agony explodes through my chest. My screams shred the air until my throat feels raw. I thrash against his grip but might as well fight a mountain. He pins me like a specimen under glass, drinking in my terror as greedily as my blood.

The battle rages below, but it's a lifetime away. Each second stretches into infinity as this monster feeds, his grip painting bruises across my skin. My struggles only fuel his frenzy.

Rhyland, please. The prayer echoes in my mind. *I don't know how much longer I can hold on.*

RHYLAND

12

I explode through the doors like a force of fucking nature, my rage a living thing that turns the opulent ballroom into ground zero. These privileged bloodsuckers scatter like vermin, their champagne glasses shattering as they realize death just crashed their party.

Lucian and Emily tried to hold me back, begging me to stick to their precious fucking plan. But the moment I heard these bastards were auctioning off my girl like cattle, any chance of restraint went straight to hell. Erik's gone dark, which means shit's already hit the fan, and I'm done playing nice.

The stench of their corruption fills my nostrils—sex traffickers, murderers, bloodthirsty fucks thinking they own the world. My hand punches through silk Armani, past the ribcage with a wet crack, and emerges clutching a dead, shriveled heart. Blood sprays across their pretentious-ass artwork as I crush it, arterial red painting abstract patterns on gilt frames.

A diamond-dripping bitch in Chanel tries to run, her heels click-clacking across marble like a wounded deer. I grab her by her jeweled neck, feeling vertebrae snap under my fingers before ripping her head clean off, her pearls scattering across the floor like dropped teeth—her body twitches, painting the floor red.

A fat fuck in a tuxedo pisses himself as I approach. His scream gargles into silence as I tear out his throat, strings of muscle and tissue dangling from my claws. I drive my fist through his chest cavity, feeling ribs splinter and organs rupture before yanking out his dead heart.

I lose myself in a symphony of violence, baptizing the walls in their corruption. Their screams are fucking music as I deliver the justice these arrogant shit-stains deserve. One by one, they fall, their blood turning the polished floor into a crimson lake.

My entire world narrows to a single point—Dani. Every other thought burns away in the inferno of my rage. These undead fuckers dared to look at her, to think they could own her. Their lives are forfeit.

"RHYLAND!!"

Her scream knocks the wind out of me, her terror and panic slamming through our bond hard enough to make my knees buckle—she's upstairs. I rip the heart from the worthless cocksucker in my grip, letting his corpse drop into the growing pool of blood at my feet.

I blur toward the stairs, ready to tear through anything between me and my mate. But before I can cross half the distance, an iron grip crushes my windpipe, slamming me against the wall hard enough to crack the marble. The touch is like arctic ice, familiar in the worst possible way.

Lilith.

The sadistic bitch who made me stares back with eyes like frozen hell, her fingers tightening around my neck with centuries of power behind them. My maker. My fucking nightmare.

"Well, well, well," her voice slithers like a snake, those emerald eyes gleaming like a predator toying with its meal. "If it isn't my favorite little creation. Have you been pining for me, darling? Like I've pined for you?" Her nails slice into my flesh.

"Get your fucking hands off me, you psychotic cunt!" I snarl, thrashing against her hold like a rabid wolf.

My mind latches onto a marble monstrosity behind her—some overpriced piece of shit these assholes probably worship. It launches at her skull like a missile, but the ancient hell-bitch moves with that infuriating speed of hers. She drops low, and the statue screams past us both, exploding through the wall in a shower of plaster and shattered dreams. Debris rains down inches from my head because the universe just loves to fuck with me.

"Oh darling," Lilith purrs, with that sadistic glee I remember all too well. "Still trying to use those cute little powers against me? Have you forgotten?" Her grip tightens painfully. "I'm older, stronger, and so much better at this game than you'll ever be."

The smug satisfaction in her voice makes me want to rip her throat out with my teeth. If I could just reach her...

Dani's screams pierce through me from above, each terrified cry driving me closer to losing my shit. Some undead bastard is up there, touching what's mine, hurting her, and this immortal psycho-whore is standing in my way.

I swing at her face with everything I've got, but she catches my fist like it's nothing, crushing my hand beneath her grip. The crack of breaking bones mingles with my roar of pain as she spins me around, slamming me face-first into the wall hard enough to shower us both in marble dust.

"Oh, sweetheart," she purrs against my ear, with false sympathy. "Does it burn you up inside, hearing your little pet crying out like that? Such a pathetic replacement for what we had together." She presses closer, her designer perfume choking me worse than her grip. "Remember how perfect we were, my dark prince? The blood we spilled together?"

Her words make my skin crawl, but Dani's next scream hits me like a kick to the balls. I'm going to tear this fucking building apart brick by bloody brick if that's what it takes to get to her.

"You still love me, darling. We both know it," she breathes against my ear, words slithering like venomous snakes. "I've forgiven your little tantrum. Locking me away like that? Naughty boy." Her blood-red lips curve into a predatory smile. This twisted bitch wouldn't know love if it staked her through her dead fucking heart.

"Go fuck yourself!" I spit the words through gritted teeth, fighting against her grip like a feral beast.

Dani's next scream tears through the air, weaker this time, and something inside me shatters. My girl, my fucking heart, is being broken piece by piece while I'm pinned here by this monster who made me. The sound of her pain rips me apart, knowing what kind of damage they're inflicting. How the fuck am I supposed to put her back together after this? How do I heal wounds that cut this deep?

"Mmm... that dirty mouth," Lilith purrs, running one nail down my cheek. "Remember how you used to eat my pussy like a starving man? All those nights of you fucking me raw..." She pouts like a spoiled child denied her favorite toy. "My cunt's been aching for your big cock, lover. No one fills me up quite like you do."

My stomach clenches at the memory of those nights—when she'd use her maker's command to force herself on me, compelling me to perform like her personal fuck puppet. I couldn't say no, couldn't fight back, could only hate myself as she took what she wanted. And the sick bitch got off on my disgust, fed on my helpless rage like it was the finest fucking wine.

Another weak cry from Dani ignites my fury anew. I'm going to find a way to end this bitch, Maker's rules or not.

No choice left. If this power consumes me, I know Dani will drag me back from the darkness. She always does.

I reach into my pocket and slide the ring onto my finger. The effect is instant and overwhelming—black magic explodes through my veins like liquid nitrogen, the air around us turning thick with shadows. I reach into the Soul Stone's power with a savage growl, and holy fuck—the darkness responds like a starving beast, eager to be unleashed.

I dissolve into shadow, leaving Lilith grasping at empty air, her perfect features twisting in confusion. Before she can process what's happening, I materialize behind her, commanding the darkness to wrap around her, choking her—like ethereal pythons. The power surges through me, intoxicating and dangerous as hell—each tendril of shadow answering my will sends a heady rush. I squeeze harder, watching her perfectly made-up face turn an interesting shade of purple.

The darkness whispers promises of more power, control, and everything. It would be so easy to lose myself in it, to let it consume me completely. But I hold onto Dani's presence in my mind as it anchors me and keeps me from drowning in the endless black.

Lucian shows up out of nowhere, a blur of lethal intent. Before I register his presence, he's already hefted the massive marble statue and is repeatedly smashing it into Lilith's head. Each impact is a symphony of brutal, bone-crunching satisfaction.

Our maker crumples to the floor like a broken porcelain doll, her exquisite dress pooling around her in a morbid tableau of stillness.

The shadows around me writhe and whisper, hungry for more violence. It takes every shred of my willpower not to unleash them.

"How's that for family therapy, you ugly bitch?" Lucian snarls, his usual smart-ass demeanor stripped away to reveal years of raw hatred. "Go get our girl, bro. I'll make sure this waste of immortality stays down. Maybe rearrange her face a bit more—you know, for old times' sake."

His trademark smirk doesn't quite hide the murderous gleam in his eyes. Some wounds run too deep for even his jokes to cover.

I don't need to be told twice. I blur up the stairs, following Dani's scent like a guided missile. The door splinters under my assault, and what I find on the other side—

My world stops. Then explodes.

The scene before me ignites something primal, something so fucking dark that the shadows still writhing around me seem bright in comparison. In this moment, burning the world to ash doesn't seem like enough. No, this calls for something much, much worse.

"Rhyland..." Dani's soft whimper of hope and relief floods through me.

I lunge ahead, but Lilith appears out of fucking nowhere like death. My arm snaps with a sound like a rifle shot as she twists it behind my back—savage strength behind that delicate grip. She slams my face into the hardwood with enough force to send splinters flying. Her talons rip the Soul Stone from my finger.

What the fuck? She should be down, her skull crushed to pieces by Lucian's assault.

"Now, now, my dark prince," she coos. "Can't have you using Mommy's little trinket against me." The ring disappears into the shadows with a flick of her wrist, accompanied by that smug, aristocratic laugh I've always hated. "We're going to do this the old-fashioned way—just like old times, darling."

The power that had been surging through my veins vanishes, leaving me trapped beneath her. The bitch has me pinned like an insect, all that power bearing down on me with sadistic precision. Every move I make just results in more bones snapping under her grip. My maker always loved playing with her food before she devoured it.

"Oh, sweetie, is that any way to treat me? After everything I've done for you?" She tightens her grip, grinding my face harder into the splintered floor. "And poor, pathetic Lucian—always trying to play hero. I never did like that mouthy little shit. But don't worry, darling, I made sure his death was... appropriately unpleasant."

She clicks her tongue like some disapproving socialite at a charity gala. Every word is intended to cut, delivered with that superior, condescending tone that makes her sound like the queen bitch of the universe.

A wet thud beside my head draws my attention. The sight hits me like a sledgehammer—Lucian's heart, still dripping blood, tossed there like some fucked up calling card. My stomach clenches as the reality of what I see punches through my gut.

My brother. My sarcastic, pain-in-the-ass, loyal-to-the-death brother.

"NOOO!" The roar tears from my soul, primal and raw. Not Lucian. Not my wise-cracking brother who's had my back. The same brother who gave me shit about everything, who ran that ridiculous nightclub, who finally found his mate in Seraphina.

The sound that rips from my chest isn't human—it's the howl of a beast watching its pack die.

"Really, this is all so beneath us," she sighs dramatically. "All this fuss over some worthless little tramp? I expected better taste from you, darling. But then again, you always did have a weakness for damaged goods."

Dani's anguished screams tear through me as Lucian's "death" hits her. Our bond amplifies everything, turning our shared grief into a vicious cycle of agony. Her pain becomes my pain—becomes her pain—an endless feedback loop of raw devastation.

The bond we share, usually such a blessing, now feels like a curse—forcing us to experience this loss twice over, each of us drowning in not just our own grief but each other's as well. Her heart shattering for her friend, my rage at losing my brother, all of it spiraling together into a maelstrom of shared suffering.

"Oh yes, lover," she purrs, twirling Lucian's heart between her fingers like some fucked-up trophy. Blood drips onto my cheek as she flaunts her prize. "A souvenir for our little reunion. Isn't it divine?" Her laughter echoes through the room—that same deranged giggle that still haunts my darkest memories. "Your precious brother's heart—the one you so nobly tried to save by offering yours instead. There's something deliciously poetic about it—don't you think? Like a tragic opera, but with more... gore."

The scent of my brother's blood fills my nostrils, making tears burn behind my eyes. That heart in her hand used to tell the worst fucking jokes—used to beat faster whenever Seraphina walked into the room, used to... Christ, I can't even finish that thought without wanting to vomit.

The reality of what I'm seeing crashes over me. This can't be real. This isn't fucking happening.

"And now," Lilith purrs, grinding my face harder into the floor, "you get to watch my friend break your little pet."

I'm helpless, arm shattered, pinned to the floor, as this fucker slams Dani to the ground. She's too weak to fight back as he forces her legs apart.

"NO! I WILL FUCKING KILL YOU!" The scream rips from me as I thrash against Lilith's grip, desperate to reach Dani.

"What's wrong, darling?" Nails dig into my scalp. "Why waste your time on this worthless thing when what we had was so... special?"

Dani's honey-gold eyes find mine across the room, and I watch in helpless agony as that precious light—that fierce spark that makes her who she is—starts to fade. Each brutal violation dims it further, like watching someone slowly extinguish the sun. Her gaze holds mine, silently screaming what her voice can't anymore while that piece of shit grunts and thrusts above her like the animal he is.

Hot tears scald down my face as I'm forced to witness the unthinkable—my mate's spirit breaking piece by precious piece. Each second burns itself into my memory like acid, a testament to my failure to protect her. Our bond amplifies everything, forcing me to feel each fragment of her soul splinter and crack.

This isn't just rape—it's the systematic destruction of everything pure and beautiful in my world. And I'm fucking powerless to stop it.

Some protector I turned out to be. "I'm so sorry, baby. So fucking sorry."

RHYLAND

13

Dani's scream pierces through the fog in my head, yanking me back to—wait. The shadows still writhe around Lilith's throat like living nooses, exactly where they were before that nightmare started. My hands shake as I try to process what the fuck just happened—was any of that real? Cold sweat soaks my shirt, and I can still taste the phantom fear of Dani's screams and pain.

But Lilith's still here, still caught in my shadow grip, her perfect makeup starting to run as she claws at the darkness crushing her—suffocating her. Not lying broken on the floor. Not holding me down while some bastard... The terror and rage from that vision still pulse through my veins, making it hard to separate reality from whatever mind-fuck the Soul Stone just put me through.

The bond throbs with Dani's fear from upstairs—real fear, not the soul-shattering anguish I just witnessed. Or didn't witness. Fuck, my head is spinning, trying to piece together what actually happened and what the stone forced me to see. These memories—these vivid, gut-wrenching scenes—they don't match what's in front of me. But they felt so fucking real: the blood, the screams, the...

What the hell is this stone doing to me?

Jesus fucking Christ. The Soul Stone's power is more twisted than my darkest expectations—forcing me to experience my worst fears in full sensory overload. Not just watching them play out, but living every excruciating detail: Dani's eyes as that bastard—No. That wasn't real.

I scrub at my face, wiping away tears I didn't realize I'd shed. The image of Lucian's heart lying in its own blood refuses to fade from my mind's eye. This stone, this cursed piece of my mother's legacy—it doesn't just destroy bodies. It shatters minds first, leaving the soul in pieces.

Fuck that. My woman needs me intact, not broken by this corrupted power. The stone can keep its twisted nightmares.

My hands shake as I claw at the ring, desperate to get it off my finger. The shadows retreat like smoke in the wind, but Lilith's body slams into me like a missile before I can process it. We crash through wall after fucking wall, plaster dust and chunks of stone raining down as the ring goes flying, forgotten in the chaos.

Each impact feels like being hit by a semi, but it's better than letting that stone turn me into another shadow-drunk monster. My mother's power might be a seductive bitch, but I've got too much to lose to dance with that particular darkness.

My back hits solid stone with bone-crushing force, driving the air from my lungs. Lilith straddles me, her perfect face twisted into something demonic, designer dress now covered in debris and fury.

Copper floods my mouth as my fangs slice through my lip, rage and pain fueling every move. The impacts rattle my bones like artillery strikes, but I catch her with a wild hit. Her perfect face caves under my fist as she flies across the room. I spring up, muscles coiled and ready for her next attack.

Dani's terrified screams pierce through me from above, each one a knife in my fucking chest. I don't have time for this ancient bitch's games—Dani needs me.

"Does it grate on your nerves, Rhyland?" Lilith snarls with sadistic glee, her perfect lipstick smeared with blood. "To hear her scream for you, and there's nothing you can do about it?"

I blur toward the stairs, desperation giving me speed, but she appears like a demon from hell, slamming me back with centuries of power behind her strike. The marble floor spiderwebs beneath me as I crash into it, the impact driving the air from my lungs for a second time.

The sound of Dani's pain is driving me fucking insane, but this sadistic bitch just keeps smiling, enjoying the show.

"Continere malum, protegere bonum, sigillum potentiae!"

Emily stands at the doorway, her hands weaving intricate patterns as she chants.

The air crackles with magic, thick and electric. Blue energy explodes from Emily's fingertips, slamming into Lilith like a tidal wave. The bitches eyes go wide with shock as mystical chains of light wrap around her body, forcing her back against the wall.

"*Carcerem aeternum, vincula immortalia!*" Emily's voice rises, and her eyes blaze with power. A crystalline barrier forms around Lilith, trapping her in a prison of pure magic.

Lilith screams in fury, hurling herself against the barrier, but it holds—each impact sending ripples of blue light across the surface. "You little witch bitch!" she snarls, her perfect features twisted with rage.

"Go!" Emily shouts between incantations, sweat beading on her forehead as she maintains the spell. "Get to Dani! I can't hold this bitch forever!"

I blur toward the stairs, every cell in my body locked onto Dani's scent. Emily's spell holds Lilith in that barrier, but my mind can't shake off that fucked-up nightmare. The similarities are too close, too raw—like the Soul Stone gave me a preview of my personal hell. But I can't let that poison my head. Not now. Not when Dani needs me.

Lilith's rage-filled screams echo behind me, nearly drowning out Emily's steady chanting, but I've got bigger fucking problems ahead. Whatever's waiting for me upstairs, I swear to every god listening—it won't play out like that nightmare. This time, I'm ready.

The taste of Dani's fear in the air drives me faster, harder. Time to remind these pieces of shit you don't fuck with me and mine.

The door explodes inward under my assault, wood and metal shrapnel spraying across the room like deadly confetti. My vision narrows to a crimson tunnel as I take in the scene before me—rage burns through my veins hotter than any bloodlust I've ever known.

The bastard has his filthy fucking hands all over my woman's bare skin, holding her down while she fights with everything she has left. Even weak from blood loss, Dani's clawing and thrashing against him like a wild thing—my fierce little warrior refusing to break.

Her skin is painted with bruises and bitemarks, dried blood tracking down her beautiful neck where he's been feeding from her. The sight of those wounds, of this worthless fuck's hands on my angel, ignites something primal in my chest. Something that makes the vampire in me look fucking tame in comparison.

I'm on this fucker like a demon straight outta hell, crushing his windpipe in my grip before his tiny dick-brain can even register he's fucked. My other hand rips down, tearing off his pathetic excuse for junk—cock, balls, the whole worthless package comes off in a spray of blood and meat. His scream is fucking beautiful, arterial blood painting the fancy-ass wallpaper like abstract art.

Somewhere in my peripheral vision, Dani curls into a ball, screaming—but the red haze of rage has consumed me completely.

I jam my thumbs into his eyes for daring to look at what's mine—they pop like overripe grapes, spraying juice and jelly down his cheeks. But it's not enough—this cocksucker dared to taste what's mine. His screams turn to gurgles as I grab his tongue—still stained with her blood—and rip it out by the root, taking chunks of his throat with it. The wet muscle flops onto the carpet like a dying fish, blood bubbling from the gaping hole where it used to be while he gargles on his blood.

Still not nearly fucking enough for what he's done.

My power surges through me like hot lava in my veins. I lock onto his blood with my telekinesis, feeling every drop flowing through his worthless veins. His body goes tight as his own blood turns against him, choking as blood leaks from every orifice. His hands claw desperately at his skull as if he can somehow stop what's coming.

One savage mental push is all it takes. His head explodes in a grotesque fountain of gore—brain matter and skull fragments spray across the expensive wallpaper. What's left of his face is a mangled crater of bone shards and tissue, his body twitching in its death throes as neural signals misfire.

Dani's broken whimpers slice through my bloodlust like a blade to the heart. I drop to my knees beside her, but she thrashes against my touch, fighting with the last scraps of strength she has left.

"No! No, get the fuck off me!"

Raw terror tears through her voice as she lashes out. Her fists pound my chest, nails raking skin—pure survival instinct driving her. Each blow, each scream, pierces my heart—my mate lost in a nightmare where she can't recognize me.

Her eyes dart wildly, seeing threats in every corner. The scent of her fear chokes me, mixed with blood and the stench of what those bastards did to her.

Each rejection burns deeper than any battle wound, but I'll endure it all until she finds her way back to me. They might have broken her body, but I won't let them shatter her spirit.

"Baby... baby, it's okay. It's me. I'm here." I keep my voice soft and gentle, even as rage burns in my chest at what they've done to her. She's trembling like a wounded bird as I carefully cradle her face between my palms, needing her to look at me, and my heart fucking shatters. Those bastards have turned her beautiful features into a canvas of violence—one eye swollen shut, lip split and bleeding, dark bruises blooming across her cheekbone. Blood matts her hair where they slammed her head down.

"Look at me, Angel. I got you." I pour everything I am into those words. My fierce girl fought like hell, and I swear no one will ever touch her again.

The monster in me howls for more blood and more vengeance, but right now, my mate needs the man, not the beast. Everything else can fucking wait.

"Rhyland..." My name breaks across her fragile, broken lips. Her beautiful eyes, that are like warm as summer sunshine—one swollen and bruised, finally focus on my face. The fog of terror lifts just enough for recognition to spark in those depths I love so much—like a drowning person finally finding solid ground.

The moment she sees me something fractures deep inside. Her gaze holds such pain, such relief; it feels like my heart's being ripped out.

"Yeah, baby. I'm here. I'm...so fucking sorry." The words feel pathetically inadequate as she crumbles against me, her sobs tearing through my soul.

My angel buries her face in my neck, arms wrapping around me like I'm her last anchor to sanity. Her naked body maps their brutality—bite marks ravaging her throat and breasts, bruises painting her skin in violent shades. Her precious blood seeps from countless wounds, each drop, another failure carved into my conscience.

"Shh...Shh...I gotcha, Angel. Come 'ere." My voice cracks as I gather her broken form against me, moving with all the gentleness I possess. She weighs nothing in my arms—too much blood lost, too much pain endured. Her skin is deathly cold, her heartbeat a fragile flutter against my chest. Every shallow, pained breath she takes twists the knife of guilt deeper.

The question burns in my mind like acid: did that piece of shit rape her before I got here? The thought alone makes me want to drag his worthless soul back from hell just to destroy him again and again, make him suffer for eternity for every mark on her skin, every drop of blood stolen, every second of terror she endured.

"It's okay, baby." I breathe into her blood-matted hair, pushing every ounce of love and protection I have through our bond. "Let's get you home. Where I can heal you, keep you safe, make sure nothing ever touches you again."

Her sobs gradually quiet into shuddering breaths as the tension bleeds from her body. Even beaten and broken, she clings to me with surprising strength—those delicate fingers digging into my neck like she's afraid I'll disappear. My fierce little angel—still showing that iron will even after fighting for her life.

The trust she shows, letting her guard down despite the horror she just endured, humbles me to my fucking core. I don't deserve it—not after failing to protect her.

My woman. My everything. The only light pure enough to pull me back from the edge of darkness. I'll spend the rest of eternity making up for failing her tonight.

LUCIAN

14

I watch my brother blur up those stairs like Satan himself lit a fire under his Viking ass—and considering the murder written all over his face, the Devil better take a number. Wherever Rhyland vanished to earlier, it clearly didn't improve his mood. When he's this pissed, even the apocalypse would take one look and say, "Nah, I'll come back later."

Meanwhile, Emily's got our psycho maker trapped in her magical hamster ball, and those emerald eyes bring back every twisted memory I've spent *years* trying to drink away. No way was I letting Emily go all Sabrina the Teenage Badass to face this nightmare alone—though convincing my stubborn angel to sit this one out took every trick in my considerable charm arsenal.

"Please, Cupcake," I'd begged, actually *begged*—and let me tell you, that's not a good look on this handsome face. "Someone needs to keep an eye on Sable while babysitting Baby Vamp downstairs." But we both knew I was really saying, 'I can't watch you get hurt.' My celestial sweetheart's already survived enough of our vampire family drama to fill several heavenly therapy sessions—last thing she needs is a front-row seat to Mommy Dearest's psychotic comeback tour.

My eyes scan for Sir Broods-a-Lot, but Erik's pulled a Houdini on us. That brooding bastard never misses a chance to judge our life choices with his disapproving stare—something's definitely fucky here, and my undead gut's doing backflips.

"Think you can keep me in this sparkly timeout corner, you weak witch?" Lilith sneers through the barrier. Just hearing that voice—that same fucking voice that used to whisper such sweet poison while she broke me piece by piece—makes me shiver.

Emily's got her best "fuck around and find out" face on, hands weaving magic like she's conducting an orchestra of pure sass. "Bitch, I could do this with one hand and still scroll TikTok with the other."

Those emerald eyes lock onto me, and suddenly I'm right back there—forty years as that Fanged Thunder-cunt's favorite fuck toy. Made me slaughter innocent kids with a smile while my soul turned to ash. Finally shoved a stake against my own heart, ready to punch my ticket to hell just to escape her twisted shit show. If Rhyland hadn't fed this Couture Cock-goblin's ego exactly what her psychotic heart wanted that night... well, some nightmares are better left choking on silence.

"Well... if it isn't my greatest failure," she drawls. "Tell me, darling, have you missed Mummy?" Her nails tap against the barrier. "Should have let you end your pathetic existence that night. Forty years trying to mold you into something worthy—what a waste."

The rage bubbling up tastes like copper and children's screams.

I force my best shit-eating grin, even as my hands shake. "Oh, *totally*, Mom! Been meaning to send a card—'Sorry you're a rapist psycho who gets off on mind-fucking people into being murder puppets' wasn't available at Hallmark. But hey, maybe Etsy has something in the 'Go Fuck Yourself' collection?"

One second I'm verbally middle-fingering the Gucci Gutter Slut, the next I'm doing an impromptu flying lesson across the foyer. Fun fact: drywall? Not as soft as it looks in the movies, and trust me, I've been thrown through enough walls to be a fucking expert.

I peel myself off the floor, spitting out plaster and what might be a tooth, to find myself face-to-face with a witch with a vengeance.

"Morgan, kill that little shit—this weak witch, and get me the hell out of here!" Lilith screeches, sounding exactly like she did when she'd ordered her "children" to torture others for her sick amusement.

Morgan—Witch Bitch 2.0—stands over me like some twisted queen, those hate filled eyes screaming, "I snort nightmares and shit curses." Ancient words slip from her lips, each syllable cracking the air violently. "*Mens dominari,*" she hisses, and suddenly my body's not my own anymore—like someone's rewiring my brain with barbed wire.

Emily's counterspell hits like a divine bitch-slap. *"Ignis protego!"* Blue flames erupt between us, shattering Morgan's mind-control spell into a shower of magical sparks.

I stagger through the wreckage of Lilith's dinner party from hell, following a trail of bodies and broken furniture straight to the ballroom. Behind me, Emily and Morgan's magical cage match sounds like Latin for "fuck you" meets reality-bending chaos. But something's wrong—Erik's about as likely to ghost a fight as I am to join a monastery.

I scan the chaos until—ah, fuck. My stomach drops as I spot him crumpled in a dark corner of the ballroom, head twisted at that unique angle that screams, "Someone's been playing chiropractor from hell." I know that look intimately—Rhyland's favorite move during my more "rebellious" phases and Emily's go-to solution when my amnesiac ass got too rowdy for her witch-sitting abilities.

"Well, Silver Sorrowpants, it looks like someone adjusted your attitude," I mutter, kneeling beside him. "Though I gotta say, this is a bit dramatic even for you." I hoist his deadweight over my shoulder, and that's when I see it—karma's middle finger glinting under a broken table.

Azrael's ring, complete with that world-ending Soul Stone, just chilling there like the world's deadliest party favor. I drop Erik (sorry, bro, priorities) and blur toward it, but Morgan's stray spell hits like a metaphysical freight train.

"That is mine!"

The ring goes airborne like a cursed Frisbee because of-fucking-course it does. I scramble after it, dodging Morgan's *"Mens dominari!"* while Emily's counter-curses light up the air like supernatural fireworks.

A blur of feathers and talons dive-bombs for it like some crackhead pigeon on a mission. My hand closes around the ring just as the bird's talons snatch something off the marble. I stuff our apocalyptic jewelry into my pocket like it's plutonium wrapped in dynamite, then blur back to Erik, who's still doing his best impression of a broken action figure.

Just in time to see Rhyland emerge from upstairs with Dani cradled against his chest. Holy shit—she looks like death warmed over, and the rage on my brother's face promises the kind of violence that makes our maker's tantrums look like a toddler's timeout.

Just another family reunion, chez Lilith. At least no one's on fi—

"Inferno circulus maxima!" The mansion erupts in flames as Emily's voice rings like that of a vengeful witch from hell.

Blue flames race along the walls, climbing higher than the roof, turning the whole place into Satan's ass. The heat's so intense it's making my eyebrows crispy even from here.

Well, fuck. Me and my big mouth.

"Move your undead asses! This won't hold forever!" Emily shouts over the roar of her magical inferno.

Rhyland blurs down the stairs with Dani cradled against his chest. We haul ass for the cars, Erik's dead weight still flopped over my shoulder like the world's most expensive gym equipment. Behind us, the mansion's windows explode outward in a shower of glass and chaotic energy. Whatever Emily just pulled from her magical hat, it's big enough to register on the Richter scale.

I dump Erik in the back of the Mercedes with all the grace of a drunk moving company. Emily staggers out of her ring of hellfire, looking like she just went ten rounds with Doctor Strange. I blur over, scoop her up before she face-plants, and zip back to the car. She lands in the backseat with a grunt that promises future revenge.

"Drive!" Rhyland roars from the passenger seat, Dani still clutched to his chest like she might disappear if he loosens his grip.

The Mercedes roars to life, its tires shredding pavement as we tear out of there like bats out of hell. In the rearview mirror, Emily's magical inferno transforms Lilith's pretentious mansion into Vancouver's most expensive light show—it seems Rainbow Brite has a flair for dramatic exits.

Our maker might be a psychotic bitch, but she's like a cockroach—impossible to kill. Still watching her bougie paradise go up in flames? That'll slow her entitled ass down. At least long enough for us to get the hell out of dodge.

"So, you gonna tell us where the *hell* you disappeared to, or are we playing otherworldly charades?" I can't help running my mouth—it's kind of my brand. But Rhyland just keeps that 'I'll murder the universe if it breathes wrong' stare locked on Dani.

"Is she—" The question dies on my tongue as I glance at Rhyland. His face carved from stone—but his eyes? Pure Viking murder.

"Just drive, goddammit." His voice could freeze hell itself.

Right. Driving. I can do that.

I slam the gas pedal to the floor, the Mercedes eating up asphalt like it knows what's at stake—forty-five minutes to the tarmac, where our jet's waiting.

Just forty-five minutes of praying Erik's neck heals, Emily doesn't pass out, and Dani...

I press the pedal harder. Some questions are better left unasked.

I barely make it through the front door before a golden-haired missile slams into me. My angel's arms around my neck, her celestial warmth chasing away the last of Lilith's icy memories. "Lucian, thank god! Are you all okay?"

I crush her against me, breathing in her heavenly scent like it's the only thing that can wash away the stench of tonight's family reunion. "Yeah. I am now." The memory of Lilith's voice still crawls under my skin, but my angel's touch burns it away like holy water.

Rhyland shoulders past us, Dani limp in his arms as he makes a beeline for the stairs. The flight home was like watching the world's most fucked up medical drama—my brother trying to force-feed Dani his blood while she barely clung to life—so much blood loss.

My brother claimed the entire back of the jet like some possessive Viking gargoyle, snarling at anyone who got too close to Dani. Can't blame him—watching Dani try to choke down his blood while dealing with the unholy trinity of trauma, blood loss, and our maker's unique brand of psycho? That's enough to turn anyone into an overprotective asshole.

Our firecracker has a long road ahead between Lilith's twisted games, those bite marks, and whatever other hell she endured. Returning to her usual sass-slinging self will take more than just vampire blood and willpower.

"Dani..." Seraphina's voice cracks and her delicate hand flies to cover her mouth. Her honey-colored eyes fill with tears as her angelic empathy kicks into overdrive. "Is she—?"

"She'll pull through, baby girl." I pull her close, trying to soften the blow of what we both know happened tonight. "Our feisty savior is tougher than she looks. Besides," I attempt a smile that probably looks more like a grimace, "you really think Rhyland will let anything take her from him now?"

On our way home, I gave my angel the cliff notes version—what little we knew about Dani's nightmare. But the real horror show? Whatever happened behind that bedroom door with that sick fuck who "bought" her. That's a darkness only Rhyland will ever know if Dani can even bring herself to tell him.

Erik, our resident master of stealth, finally decided to rejoin the land of the conscious mid-flight. Looked around like someone had replaced his tactical manual with a Dr. Seuss book. He gave me one of his patented "thank you, but I'll never actually say it" nods. Obviously, I had to give him shit about getting his neck snapped during his super-secret spy mission. Can't let The Gloomy Gladiator think I'm going soft.

Meanwhile, Emily ransacks the liquor cabinet as if she were auditioning for "World's Thirstiest Witch." Can't blame her—after spending the entire flight passed out and turning Lilith's mansion into a pile of ash, she's earned a drink. Or ten.

"Come on, Cupcake." I tug Seraphina toward the vault, my pocket feeling heavier than all my of sins combined. Each step closer to that reinforced door adds another layer of 'we're so fucked' to this spectacular disaster of a night.

"Sparky, where are we going?" Her voice carries that perfect blend of heavenly concern and 'what stupid thing did you do now' that only she can manage.

I punch in the vault code with shaking hands—when did I turn into such a bitch? The ring feels like it's burning through my pocket as I pull it out.

"Oh my goodness, where did you find that?" Seraphina's excitement dies faster than my attempt at sobriety when she sees my face. Her golden eyes narrow with that celestial perception that makes lying impossible. "Lucian... what's wrong?"

Somewhere between cloud-hopping and trying not to think about the shit show we'd left behind, I finally checked our apocalyptic party favor. That's when I noticed it—must've been when that witchy bitch Morgan went all magical IED on my ass, and that demonic vulture.

I hold up the ring under the vault's fluorescent buzz—the cosmic equivalent of a broken condom—the broken edge of the stone catches like a guilty secret.

"Our little nuclear bomb just went half-sies. Ten bucks says Hells Favorite Hooker has the other half tucked away in her Gucci handbag by now."

DANICA

15

Our bedroom door nearly flies off its hinges as Rhyland carries me across the threshold like precious cargo. My Viking, ever the dramatic. He lays me on our bed with a tenderness that contradicts the lethal rage still emanating from his powerful frame.

My body trembles—a lovely cocktail of adrenaline crash, vampire blood, and fresh trauma. Tonight wasn't content being a regular nightmare; it had to shoot for the 'worst night ever' championship.

The memories blur together in a kaleidoscope of horror. That monster's fingers forced their way inside me, each brutal thrust tearing through my most intimate places. His uncut nails raked my inner walls as he violated me, drawing blood and screams in equal measure. His fangs marked my breasts, my neck, and my thighs—treating me like his personal chew toy. But then Rhyland appeared—my avenging dark angel.

Strange how a vampire's bite can be both sacred and sacrilege—the most intimate expression of love or the darkest violation imaginable.

"I'm going to start your bath, baby." Rhyland cradles my face in his hands like I'm spun from crystal. I manage a weak nod as he disappears into the bathroom.

His blood may have erased the physical evidence—healing every mark and tear—but it can't wash away the memories that cling to my skin like a shadow. My man tries to piece me together, but some fractures run deeper than flesh.

My strength returns gradually, pain fading to echoes, but my mind keeps replaying tonight's horror show on an endless loop. Beneath the trauma, worry for Damon gnaws at my core. My brother's out there somewhere, lost in his newfound bloodlust, probably drowning in self-loathing for what his hunger made him do.

Perfect. One flavor of PTSD wasn't enough for tonight.

Rhyland returns and lifts me with impossible gentleness. I could probably run a marathon thanks to his blood, but my man needs this. Our bond pulses with his guilt and desperate need to protect and make things right. I feel how tonight's events consume him, how he shoulders blame that isn't his to carry.

Note to self: add "convince stubborn Viking he's not responsible for psychotic vampire drama" to my already overflowing plate.

But we've got some serious conversations ahead, starting with his mysterious vanishing act. Someone powerful enough to yank my mountain of a man through a vortex? And Lilith's apparent obsession with my beefcake?

I guess having a sadistic vampire-maker stalking my man wasn't significant enough to mention over morning coffee.

Rhyland sets me on my feet, peeling away the blanket he wrapped me in like he's handling priceless silk. The bathroom glows like a sanctuary—candlelight dancing off steam, the king-sized tub promising salvation. I sink into hot water with a groan of pure relief, and in one fluid motion, Rhyland strips and slides in behind me.

Rhyland's touch turns reverent as he cleanses tonight's horror from my skin. Warm water cascades over my shoulders as his powerful hands work with impossible gentleness. He takes his time, washing away every trace of blood with tender dedication. His fingers weave through my hair, massaging away the dried crimson stains while his lips brush soft kisses along my temple, my shoulder, anywhere he can reach.

Each caress feels like absolution, transforming this simple act of cleaning into something sacred. Through our bond, I feel his need to erase every mark they left, to restore me to myself again—with this quiet devotion that makes my heart ache.

Those powerful arms band around my waist, drawing me back against the solid wall of his chest. His face burrows into my neck, breathing me in like my scent anchors him to sanity. "I'm sorry," he whispers, voice shattered. "I'm so fucking sorry, Angel."

His guilt crashes through our bond like a tidal wave, stealing my breath. I try to turn to face him, but his arms become steel bands around me, holding me still against his chest.

"I failed you," Rhyland's voice breaks, thick with self-loathing. "When I saw what that bastard did to you—seeing you hurt like that..." His immense frame trembles against me. "It fucking destroyed me, Angel. I should have been there. Should have protected what's mine."

The raw anguish in his voice cuts deeper than any blade. My fierce warrior, my protective alpha, drowning in guilt over something he couldn't control.

"Stop that right now," I order, my voice cracking despite my resolve. "This wasn't your fault, Rhyland—none of it. You literally saved me from—" The words catch in my throat as fresh memories surface. "But you did come. You found me. That's what matters."

He trembles against me, all that lethal power reduced to this by misplaced guilt. I lean deeper into his embrace, pushing comfort through our bond like a lifeline.

"Now, want to tell me where you disappeared to? Because one minute you're there, the next you're getting sucked into some magical vortex like a Viking-sized dust bunny."

A broken laugh rumbles through his chest, but then I hear it—that soft catch of breath that shatters my heart. My fierce warrior, my overprotective alpha-hole, is crying.

Oh, hell no. That's my limit.

I twist in his arms, crushing my mouth to his with desperate intensity, pouring everything I can't say into this kiss.

You saved me. I'm here. We're okay.

He breaks away with a watery laugh. "Still throwing sass even at my fuck-up—when I fail to protect you."

My hands capture his face, forcing those ocean-blues to meet mine. "Listen up, you sexy idiot," I whisper, thumbs catching his tears. "You didn't fail. You *saved* me. Got it? And yes, my sass is immortal—probably why we're perfect for each other." I summon my best smirk. "Can't have your ego getting too big without someone to check you."

Rhyland attempts a smile, but shadows still haunt his features. I brush away his tears, and his answering look could light up the darkest corners of any realm. He draws me down, claiming my mouth with a kiss that curls my toes.

Our bodies align like puzzle pieces carved from starlight, and his arms become steel bands of protection. The kiss deepens and transforms into something more—our tongues dancing a familiar rhythm that speaks of reunion, relief, and desperate need. All our fear and longing pour into this moment, and this connection reminds us both that we're alive, together, and *home*.

My lethal vampire, who tears immortals apart without breaking a sweat, who commands fear with a glance, becomes something else entirely when he holds me. His touch speaks of reverence, of a tenderness that exists only for me beneath that murderous exterior. The same hands that deal death now cradle me like I'm made of spun glass.

The need to reclaim my body, to replace violation with love, burns through me like wildfire. Only Rhyland's touch can burn away the shadows and replace nightmare with sanctuary. His desire echoes through our bond—the desperate urge to mark me as his, to prove I'm safe in his arms.

"Make love to me," I breathe against his lips, each word a caress, a prayer.

Rhyland freezes beneath me, agony flashing across his features as dark thoughts clearly war in his mind. The bond floods with his fury and fear—he's imagining the worst.

"He didn't," I whisper quickly, cupping his face. "That monster didn't get that far. You got to me first."

Relief crashes through our connection as the tension drains from his powerful frame. Those eyes lock with mine, searching for truth. Finding it, he crushes his mouth to mine in a kiss that speaks volumes—gratitude, love, and lingering rage at how close it came.

When he pulls back, those blue eyes blaze with ethereal fire, burning with an intensity that steals my breath. His big hands cradle my face again, his thumbs brushing away tears I didn't know had fallen.

"You are everything to me," his voice cracks with raw emotion. "My heart, my soul, my reason for existing. I love you *so fucking* much it consumes me. I will tear apart anyone who dares lay a finger on you. I will paint the realms red with the blood of those who hurt you." His eyes shimmer with unshed tears, vulnerability cracking his warrior's facade. "But tonight I failed you. Please—I need your forgiveness."

My fierce alpha-man, reduced to this by misplaced guilt. My heart threatens to burst from my chest. How can he not see?

"There's nothing to forgive," I whisper against his lips, pouring all my love into the words. "You came for me. You saved me. I love you so much it hurts to breathe sometimes. And right now, I need you to remind me that I'm yours—only yours. Show me what it feels like to be loved by someone who owns my heart."

His eyes darken with possession and promise. "Then let me worship every inch of you, Angel. Let me remind you what it feels like to be touched by someone who would burn worlds to keep you safe."

The world blurs as Rhyland sweeps me to our bed, his sexy frame pinning me against silk sheets. Droplets glisten on his skin, each point of contact sparking electricity between us. His eyes devour every inch of me—savage need warring with tenderness.

His mouth claims mine, demanding and fierce. One hand tangles in my damp hair while the other blazes a path down my side, each touch replacing pain with passion. A growl rumbles through his chest when I arch into his caress.

"You're mine, Dani" he breathes against my lips, his voice dark velvet. "You hear me? No one else will ever lay hands on you again."

Our bond ignites with shared hunger. His mouth trails fire down my throat as I dig my fingers into his shoulders, desperate for more. He worships every curve with lips and tongue until I'm trembling beneath him.

"Please," I whimper, need making my voice crack. "I need you."

Rhyland locks his gaze on me, his midnight desire darkening it. "Look at me, baby. Keep those beautiful eyes on me—I'll take it away."

He knows without words what I need—to replace every unwanted touch with his claiming—to erase tonight's horror with his love until nothing exists but us.

He enters me with deliberate slowness, watching my expression. There's only completion, only the perfect fusion of our bodies that makes the world fade away. But his careful control isn't what I crave.

"More," I demand, nails raking down his back. "Make me forget everything but you."

"I don't want to hurt you, baby." His voice drops to that dark place that makes me shiver. "After what you've been through—"

"I want *you,*" I cut him off, rolling my hips against his restraint. "Not this careful version. I want my possessive man, who knows exactly who I belong to. Who marks me, claims me, reminds me that my body is only his to touch." My fingers dig into his hair. "Make me forget everything but how it feels when you own me."

Something primal flashes in his eyes. His grip tightens in my hair, exposing my throat to his hungry gaze. "You want a reminder?" The dark promise in his voice sends heat pooling between my thighs.

"Yes," I gasp as his thick cock slides inside me slowly. "Remind me."

A growl tears from his chest as he pulls almost completely out, then he drives into me with devastating force, stretching, filling, claiming. My cry of pleasure echoes off the walls as he sets a punishing rhythm. Each powerful thrust erases another unwanted memory, replacing horror with pure ecstasy.

"This sweet little pussy belongs to me," he growls, skilled fingers finding my clit. "Every sound, every shiver, every drop of pleasure is mine to command." His touch sets my nerves ablaze while he drives deeper. "Tell me who owns you."

"You," I moan. "Only you."

He shifts his angle, hitting spots that make my vision blur. My walls flutter around him as pressure builds, turning my world to static and stars. His powerful body above me, inside me, consuming me—this is what I crave. My man is marking his territory, burning away the darkness with overwhelming ecstasy.

"Please," I beg, exposing my throat—needing his bite, his claim.

A feral sound rumbles from his chest. His pace turns punishing, the bed frame protesting beneath us. "You want my dark kisses, baby, while I'm owning this pussy?" His fingers continue to circle my clit with practiced skill, knowing exactly how to drive me wild. "Want me to mark you while you drench my cock like the greedy girl you are?"

The filthy words, combined with his possessive touch, make me whimper. This is my Rhyland—the perfect balance of degrading desire and protective love. Our bond pulses with shared understanding; he knows exactly what I need.

"Yes—fuck—" My words dissolve into a deep moan as his fangs pierce flesh. The sharp sting, mixed with his relentless pounding, hurls me over the edge. My walls clamp down as I shatter, my release gushing around his thick length.

"Goddamn—there's my girl." he groans, watching my pleasure soak him and the sheets. "I fucking love watching you fall apart around me." His thumb never stops its sweet torture. He licks the fresh marks on my neck, the gesture possessive and tender.

Another climax builds impossibly fast—the love pulsing through our bond creates pure magic. This is salvation—my man claiming every inch of me while his love wraps around my soul like armor.

After sleeping through an entire day—my overprotective Berserker using his body as my own personal shield unless bathroom breaks were required—we're finally facing the music. Rhyland decided on group story time rather than playing twenty questions on repeat. Smart man, even if he's being suspiciously tight-lipped about his vanishing act.

Somewhere between playing my sexy bodyguard and sneaking off to chat with his brothers while I was dead to the world, Rhyland drops another bomb—Apparently, they've got Damon locked up in the basement like some feral pet. And yeah, I get the whole baby-vamp-bloodlust thing, but that's my brother down there. Rhyland can growl all he wants about waiting, but we're definitely revisiting that conversation later.

Between psychotic vampire-makers, extraterrestrial disappearing acts, and my newly-turned brother locked in the basement, my stomach's staging its own rebellion. Pretty sure I'm about five minutes away from committing homicide for a grilled cheese sandwich.

I throw on my comfy armor—well-worn sweats and my favorite pink tank that's probably seen better days—and head downstairs. Not exactly runway ready, but after the night I've had? Fashion can kiss my traumatized ass.

The moment we hit the bottom step, I'm tackled by a crying squad of bestie fury. My guardian angel, rainbow-haired rebel, and sweet Sable—the trifecta of my girls create a group hug that threatens to squeeze the life I just managed to keep.

"Can't breathe," I wheeze, though I'm grinning like an idiot. "Unless the plan is to finish what those psychos started?"

"Don't even joke about that!" Seraphina smacks my arm, her eyes watery.

Emily gives me her patented 'I will hex you if you ever scare me like that again' glare while Sable's doing her best not to ruin her mascara with the tears she's totally failing to hide from her big brown eyes.

"Ladies, if you could avoid crushing my girl?" Rhyland's amused voice rumbles behind me. "I just got her back in one piece."

I shoot him a look over my shoulder. "Please, like you weren't just claiming every inch of me upstairs with that overactive stamina of yours." The scandalized gasp from Seraphina and Sable's knowing smirk is worth the predatory heat blazing in his gaze.

"Seriously?" Emily's eyebrows hit her hairline, her rainbow hair looking like she lost a fight with an F5 tornado. "You just escaped Satan's sugar baby, and you're up there banging your—you know what? Viking dick time is over. This bitch and I have a date with several bottles of very expensive alcohol."

"Food first," I groan, my stomach choosing that moment to growl loud enough to wake the dead. "Unless you want me face-planting in those expensive bottles of yours."

She yanks me toward the kitchen, where Erik and Lucian are holding court on the island. The moment I appear, Erik's stoic facade cracks. He crosses the space in three long strides, wrapping me in an embrace that screams 'protective vampire brother.'

Rhyland told me how Erik tried to outbid my buyer, willing to spend every penny he had to save me. My heart swells with love for my silver protector—beneath that brooding exterior, he's got a heart of gold.

"Little Huntress," his refined voice cracks slightly. "I should have reached you sooner. My failure to—"

"Oh my god, stop writing poetry about your feelings and give her here," Lucian yanks me from Erik's arms. "Jesus Christ, you'd think getting your neck snapped would make you less dramatic." He squeezes me tight, dropping a kiss on my head. "Besides, your whole 'martyr in a tactical vest' routine is seriously harshing my buzz."

Erik's eye roll could win Olympic medals, but I catch the slight upturn of his lips.

"Welcome back to the shit show, princess," he winks, ignoring Erik's death glare. "Better watch out—Erik wrote three haikus about his guilt while you were gone."

"I hardly think—" Erik's dignified protest gets steamrolled by Emily slamming shot glasses onto the counter like she's arming for war.

"Shut it, Mr. Tactical," Emily commands, amber liquid sloshing as she pours with terrifying efficiency. "Next person who opens their mouth before downing four shots gets transformed into the tackiest garden gnome Target's ever seen. Complete with a fishing pole and little red hat."

Lucian, being Lucian, naturally opens his mouth—probably to ask if his gnome transformation would be anatomically correct and well-endowed—but Emily's 'try me, bitch' glare has him snatching his shot glass.

I'm seated at the island, and then, like the food gods have answered my prayers, Rosa drops a mouth-watering plate in front of me—a perfectly grilled steak cooked medium-rare, garlic mashed potatoes drowning in butter, and roasted asparagus that smells like heaven. I beam at her like she's just handed me the keys to paradise.

"Oh my god, thank you, Rosa!"

When Lucian said he had staff on speed dial, I thought he was full of shit. And right now, I could kiss her entire face for knowing exactly what my starving ass needs.

Rosa's been our personal kitchen goddess since she arrived a couple of weeks ago, right before our little dance with the apocalypse—AKA Azrael. Her culinary magic has been blessing our taste buds three times a day, heavy on the Mexican cuisine because apparently Lucian's immortal ass can't function without his daily dose of authentic enchiladas. That man may have decades under his belt, but his devotion to Rosa's cooking borders on religious fervor. Not that I'm complaining—pretty sure she could make a gourmet meal out of a pack of ramen and some pocket lint.

"Eat up, cariña," Rosa says with a knowing smile.

I don't waste time with manners, attacking my steak like I'm auditioning for National Geographic while everyone else throws back shots. Rhyland hovers behind me like my own personal bodyguard as I demolish my plate with zero shame.

Through a mouthful of heaven, I wave my fork at Erik and Lucian before jabbing it over my shoulder at Rhyland. "Alright, spill it. All of you. Starting with why your psycho maker is obsessed with my man and ending with whatever cosmic field trip yanked his brooding ass through that vortex."

RHYLAND

16

I spill the whole shit storm—my part in this prophecy, my seriously fucked-up family tree, how my mother's power—her darkness is tangled up with the Soul Stone, and my surprise father-in-law chat with Mr. Sunshine himself—Elysium.

"Magni?" Erik questions from his chair, methodically sipping from a blood bag—his typical reserved approach to feeding, always maintaining that iron control.

"Thor's son," I confirm, jaw clenching at the memory.

"Holy shit-balls, I knew it!" Lucian cackles like the maniac he is. "You're Thor's buff-as-fuck grandson! No wonder you've got that whole 'God of Brooding' vibe going on. What's the family motto—'With Great Power Comes Great Daddy Issues'? Wait, wait—can I call you Thunder Thighs? Point Break?"

I glare at my brother, seriously considering ripping out his fucking vocal cords. Leave it to Lucian to turn my bloodline revelation into his personal comedy hour. The asshole's probably already planning merchandise with my face on it.

"Oh! I know—Thunder Vamp: The Winter Soldier! Come on, work with me here, guys, this is premium material!"

"You done?" I growl, watching him practically vibrate with glee like a kid who just discovered sugar. "Or should I give you a few more minutes to get all this shit out of your system?"

"Aw, come on, Thunderstruck—don't be such a buzzkill! I'm already designing the family reunion t-shirts. 'My brother went to Ásgard and all I got was this lousy god complex.'" Lucian dodges the empty blood bag I chuck at his head, cackling like the insufferable dick he is.

"Hold up—my father?" Dani arches an eyebrow, pointing her fork at me like a weapon. "You had a divine daddy-daughter talk without me? That's just rude."

I lean on the island, running a hand through my hair. "Yeah, apparently he fucked up or something. I was supposed to be first pick for this prophecy shit, but then I died—so your father sealed the realms. Then tried for round two with you." Christ, even saying it out loud sounds like a bad movie.

"So you got a vampire upgrade courtesy of psycho-Barbie, and that kept you in the game?" Dani asks between demolishing her steak like it personally offended her.

I nod, "That's what they're saying."

"Did he seem sorry for screwing this up so badly?" Seraphina asks softly, her delicate fingers intertwined with Lucian's.

I think back to that self-righteous prick's attitude. "Fuck if I know. He still eyes our kind like we're something stuck to his golden shoe, but yeah—this shit definitely threw a wrench in their perfect sacred plan."

Seraphina's expression falls, that celestial glow dimming like a cloud passing over the sun. I know that haunted look—she's replaying her angelic demotion for doing exactly what a guardian angel should: protecting her charge. Even if it meant saving Dani from my dumbass brother's memory-wiped shenanigans.

"Nuh-uh, Angel Cake, don't you dare go there," Lucian squeezes her hand, his trademark smirk softening. "That celestial dick-wad lost the best guardian angel in the business. His cosmic fuck-up is my jackpot, baby."

A small smile graces Seraphina's lips, but I can still see the shadow of hurt in her eyes. Getting kicked out of her home tends to leave a mark, even on the strongest angels.

"But if you died, how would we have even found each other? I mean, the prophecy says a mate has to awaken my powers and shit. And you're, like, ancient as hell," Dani asks between bites, her analytical mind kicks into high gear. The same fucking question I grilled her father about.

"That's when this shit gets even more complicated."

Dani turns to me, eyebrow raised. "Okaaay...."

"Their original plan," I growl, running a hand down my face. "Already picked out some mate for me—another of Elysium's bloodline. But she didn't measure up to their sanctified standards, so they dumped her ass in Ásgard. Odin's been playing guardian ever since."

Dani's eyes go wide. "Wait—you're telling me I have—"

"A half-sister? Yes." I confirm. "She's a Valkyrie now. Your Father says she didn't have your fire, your power."

Seraphina gasps, "Oh my god. I remember whispers about this centuries ago, but it was never confirmed."

"Wait, wait, wait—" Lucian throws his hands up. "Are you telling me there's a backup baby Jesus running around Ásgard with wings and a sword? Holy shit, it's like finding out Nick Fury's got a secret superhero stashed away! Man, the Avengers ain't got nothing on this family drama!"

Dani groans into her hands. "How is this my life right now?"

"Oh! Oh!" Lucian bounces in his seat. "I've got it—it's like celestial reality TV! 'Keeping Up With The Divines!' One sister gets the brooding vampire-Thor hybrid, and the other becomes Captain Valkyrie as a consolation prize. Quick, someone call Netflix, this shit writes itself!"

I shoot him a look that promises violence, but my brother just grins wider. Asshole never knows when to shut his mouth.

"And this Soul Stone," Emily cuts in, pouring shots like she's arming for war, "is basically your mom's power recycled?" She snorts. "—and I thought my family reunions were fucked up. Drinks are mandatory for this level of dysfunction, people."

"Not recycled," I grumble, running a hand through my hair. "This is pure darkness—the real fucking deal." I break down Odin's story about my parents tag-teaming Moretemis before Mom went full dark side. "I've tasted that power firsthand." The nightmare's memories flash behind my eyes. "And trust me, that shit's not some parlor trick—it's nuclear—it'll eat your soul if you let it."

"Speaking of nuclear..." Lucian exchanges a look with Seraphina that screams, 'We're so screwed.' His usual smartass grin nowhere in sight.

"What did you do?" My tone drops to arctic levels.

"Funny story—more of a whoopsie, really..." Lucian fidgets. "Remember the little witch cage match adventure? Found the fancy ring, thought it might come in handy for Operation Save The World..."

He'd mentioned finding it when I was hell-bent on saving Dani, using it as some twisted pep talk—now sitting downstairs in the vault.

"Spit it out, asshole," I snarl, patience evaporating.

"Well," Seraphina jumps in, trying to save Lucina's ass, "what my eloquent disaster here is trying to say—"

"Oh, for fuck's sake," Emily interrupts, rolling her eyes. "Your idiot brother found mommy's ring of doom and didn't think to mention it until now. Let me guess—you tried it on like it was a clearance rack accessory and found out it's not just a fashion statement?"

Erik's silver eyes narrow slightly. "Only you would treat an ancient artifact of devastating power like a carnival prize, brother."

"The faith you all have in me is truly touching," Lucian clutches his chest dramatically. "I'm wounded. Devastated. Completely—"

"LUCIAN!" We all shout in unison.

"Fine," Lucian drops the bomb, actually serious for once. "That spell Morgan fired at me? Ring went flying, and I didn't notice until I was on the plane that it pulled a disappearing act. Well, half of it did. Pretty sure, Lilith's personal carrier pigeon from Satan's asshole swooped in and snagged the broken piece."

Everyone just stares, silent as the grave until Emily explodes.

"God fucking dammit." slamming her shot glass down. "I should've just fried that witchy bitch when I had the chance instead of playing nice." She whirls on Lucian, eyes blazing. "And you! You've been sitting on this catastrophic bullshit of information this whole time? What, were you waiting for the perfect moment to tell us half of an ancient death stone is in the hands of the psycho squad?"

Dani drops her fork, pinching the bridge of her nose. I feel her frustration building through our bond like a nuclear reactor about to blow. "Jesus. We finally get all the pieces together, and now we're back to a Humpty Dumpty situation—and your certifiably insane 'mom' has the other half? Perfect. This is just...fucking perfect." She stabs at her steak with enough force to make the plate protest.

Erik's expression remains unchanged as he analyzes the situation, his tactical mind already mapping out implications. "This complicates our position significantly. The fractured stone could have unforeseen consequences—if Lilith uses it... we need to consider how this affects the power balance and prepare accordingly."

"No shit, Sherlock," Lucian rolls his eyes at Erik. "Got any other brilliant observations? Maybe warn us that water is wet while you're at it?"

"Can we go back for it?" Emily asks after slamming back a shot of bourbon like it's water. She pours me another, and I knock that fucker back, letting the burn settle my nerves.

"Holy shit, did you suffer brain damage from all that witch-slapping?" Lucian's mouth runs faster than his brain, as usual. "Or did you forget that Morgan makes Bellatrix LeStrange look like a Disney princess? We barely escaped with our perfectly sculpted asses intact!"

"Please. I handled that situation better than you handled your hair care routine, vampire Ken. Or did you miss the part where I was turning that place into a supernatural Fight Club?"

I've got to hand it to the witch—what I saw when I carried Dani out was nothing short of fucking biblical. Emily's powers have definitely leveled up from parlor tricks to apocalyptic shit-show. The kind of force that makes even vampires think twice about pissing her off.

Dani shoves her plate aside, fixing me with that honey-gold stare that sees right through my bullshit. "Alright, babe, spill it. What's the deal with your psychotic Maker? Because after that little reunion, I think we need the full director's cut of that horror story."

The temperature in the room drops ten degrees as Erik, Lucian, and I go rigid. Talking about that sadistic bitch is like voluntarily swallowing broken glass. But with her loose and causing chaos, they deserve to know the whole fucked-up truth—even if we still don't know how she slipped her cage.

Erik's silver eyes darken with eons of carefully contained rage while Lucian's usual smartass grin vanishes completely. Some demons are better left buried, but this one's already clawed its way back to the surface.

DANICA

17

Rhyland takes my hand and leads me to the living room like I'm some sort of delicate flower. I practically face-plant into the plush black couch, burrowing into the cushions. Time for the tea to be spilled, the beans to be dished, and the skeletons to come dancing out of the closet. Storytime, bitches—let's do this.

Lucian plops down in the oversized armchair, pulling Seraphina into his lap like she's his personal angel-sized teddy bear. Rhyland claims his territory at my feet, those huge hands working magic on my tired soles as he drapes my legs across his thighs. Erik, Emily, and Sable claim their spots at the end of this monstrosity of a sectional that's practically the size of a small country. Seriously, this thing could host the UN summit and still have room for a dance party.

"Lilith is..." Rhyland starts. I can feel the tension radiating off him like heat from a furnace as he struggles to find words dark enough to describe his maker's twisted origin story.

I wiggle my toes against his palms, trying to coax the story out of my brooding man. Whatever he's about to drop on us, it's clearly worse than finding out your ex is dating your best friend's cousin's roommate's dog walker.

"Lilith is old. Like, watching-paint-dry-in-the-Paleolithic-era old," Lucian offers. "Rumor has it, she was Adam's first. You know, before Eve got the gig."

My brain does a record scratch. Hold up. Adam's first wife? As in, *the* Adam? From the Bible? No way. No fucking way.

"Are you....?" I ask, but I'm pretty sure I already know the answer, and it's making my head spin. "Nooo. Seriously? As in—"

"The Garden of Eden," Erik confirms, his face somehow even more grave than usual.

"Holy shit!" I nearly choke on my words. "Are you telling me your psycho maker is *the* Lilith? Like, the original 'I don't need no man' badass?"

Lucian grins, but it's all sharp edges. "The one and only. Apparently, she and the Big Guy upstairs had some creative differences, so she peaced out of paradise and went full-on Queen of the Damned."

I blink, trying to process this biblical bombshell. "So, your maker is the OG feminist who told God to shove it, then what? Decided to become the world's scariest cougar?" My brain hurts just trying to wrap itself around this.

Erik nods, his silver eyes distant as if seeing centuries past. "She's one of the most powerful of our kind."

Damn. And here I thought my supernatural drama couldn't get any more epic. Apparently, I need to start brushing up on my Bible studies because this shit just went from zero to Old Testament real quick.

"So she's basically prehistoric? Like, 'I watched the Dead Sea when it was alive' ancient?" The scientist in me is already calculating timelines, probably with a wild look in my eyes. "No wonder she's impossible to kill—she's got more centuries than a history textbook. Wait—does this mean every vampire out there is her demonic offspring? Because that would be one hell of an Ancestry.com update."

"No," Rhyland grumbles, his powerful hands working the tension from my feet. "Only those she's made directly—which has only been us four—" He stops, pain flashing across his features. "Three."

The unspoken name hangs heavy in the air.

Adrian.

The fourth musketeer of their dysfunctional little brotherhood. My heart does a painful little twinge at the memory—the brother who betrayed us, who chose darkness—but then wanted to change and ended up dead in the end. My heart aches as I watch Rhyland wrestle with that particular demon.

My inner nerd suddenly takes over, DNA sequences and genetic markers already dancing through my head. "So not every fang-bearer out there is part of your family tree?"

"If every vamp was rocking Mommy Dearest's premium vintage blood, we'd all be one big happy telepathic family," Lucian snorts, sprawling in his chair. "But nope—it's just us three bromigos sharing the mental party line. There are other ancient bloodsuckers out there, old as Satan's retirement plan."

"The blood bond only connects the three of us," Erik clarifies. "Which suggests multiple progenitors of the vampire species."

My mind drifts back to my time as Lilith's prisoner—her arctic indifference, that superiority complex that could rival Mount Everest. Now I understand why she acted like God's gift to vampires. She literally predates the Bible. Talk about your original mean girl.

"Her obsession started right after she turned me—I was her first," Rhyland's voice pulls me from the memory pit of horror. His jaw clenches. "Said I had a 'unique aura' and that she'd found her perfect counterpart."

The three brothers paint a picture darker than a black hole—how Lilith used her Maker's command like a puppet master, forcing them to perform her twisted desires—sex, murder, stealing innocent lives. According to them, babies are her favorite targets. My stomach does a violent flip at that particular revelation.

Lucian's usual smartass demeanor cracks, showing the trauma beneath. Seraphina wraps herself around him like a celestial security blanket, her angelic presence trying to soothe decades of psychological wounds.

"Found a witch willing to break the Maker's bond," Rhyland continues, his hands stilling on my feet. "She managed to free Erik and me, but Lucian..."

"The witch met an untimely end before Lucian's liberation could be completed," Erik interjects, but I catch the rage simmering beneath his stolid facade.

"So what was Adrian's deal in all this?" I ask, unable to resist poking at that particular hornet's nest.

"Adrian made his choice." Erik's silver eyes turn cold as steel. "He preferred Lilith's leash to freedom."

Well, isn't *that* just a fun little plot twist in this family drama.

The pieces of this puzzle are starting to click into place like some sort of horror story.

"Then my noble Viking brother here went all self-sacrificing hero," Lucian drawls, but the gratitude beneath his snark is evident. "went full martyr mode like some pornographic Jesus. Offered up his body as a sacrificial dick appointment to that Bloodwhore just to save my fabulous ass. After that, these two tactical fuckers pulled off the ultimate 'fuck you.'"

My stomach turns at the implication. The thought of Rhyland forcing himself to sleep with that monster, enduring God knows what kind of twisted games, just to save his brother...The sacrifice makes me want to simultaneously hug him and hunt down Lilith to introduce her face to my fist.

"Don't you ever fucking forget who had your back, dickhead," Rhyland growls at Lucian, his tone lowering with that signature alpha-male authority. But beneath the harsh words, there's an undercurrent of genuine affection—the unbreakable bond of brothers who've been through hell together.

I clear my throat, desperately trying to bleach my brain of any mental images involving Rhyland's dick anywhere near that couture-wearing cockroach. "Yeah, your bat-shit crazy maker gave me the cliff notes version of her tomb vacation during her 'evil villain explains it all' speech. Though she was a bit light on the details while she was busy auctioning me off like some expensive take-out order."

"Indeed. The Hawthorne witch's magic was essential for the binding spell," Erik confirms.

My brain screeches to a halt like someone yanked the emergency brake. "Hold up—Hawthorne?" Every head in the room snaps toward me like I just announced the apocalypse. "That witch working with Lilith—Morgan? She's claiming Hawthorne lineage and apparently has a massive hate-boner for all of you."

Sable's sharp gasp cuts through the tension. Emily whips around to face her. "What's got your witchy senses tingling?"

"The Hawthorne's..." Sable's voice trembles with awe. "Their bloodline traces back to the Salem trials of 1692—they were the real deal, not those poor souls who were wrongly accused. The Hawthornes were some of the most powerful witches in history. Their magic is... legendary. Everyone thought they'd vanished centuries ago."

The temperature in the room plummets like someone cranked the AC to Arctic blast.

"The facial structure, those amber eyes—I should have recognized the Hawthorne traits immediately," Erik states, clearly irritated at missing such a crucial detail.

"We didn't have a fucking choice," Rhyland growls, rage and old guilt warring in his voice. "Couldn't trust they would keep the treaty—they had already threatened to release her. So...we slaughtered every last one of those witches to keep that bitch locked away. Or so we fucking thought..."

Woah. The weight of this revelation settles over the room like a lead blanket. My guys didn't just kill a few witches—they took out magical royalty. Turns out they missed one—and now that oversight has come back to bite us all in the ass with a vengeance.

"Holy shit, bro. That's like supervillain-level evil, even for you," Lucian quips, his eyes wide with genuine shock. Clearly, his internal WTF meter just broke through the ceiling.

"Well, isn't this just a delightful little nugget of 'what the actual fuck?'" Emily snarks, her eyes narrowing at the vampire duo. "You dickwads really went full medieval on an entire line of witches just to shove She-Devil in a supernatural time-out? Gold star for problem-solving there, assholes."

I can't help but cringe at Emily's verbal evisceration. I mean, she's not wrong—the whole 'murder all the witches' plan doesn't exactly scream 'well-adjusted decision-making.' But at the same time, I'm trying to wrap my head around the level of desperation that must have driven them to such extremes. When your choices are 'commit magical genocide' or 'eternal enslavement to a psycho vampire dominatrix,'... well, let's just say I can understand why they chose the nuclear option.

"Dial down the righteous indignation, Rainbow Brite!" Lucian snaps, his usual snark laced with defensive anger. "Was their solution ideal? Was it the most ethical move? Hell no. But it's done, and we can't exactly send a 'sorry we murdered your entire family' fruit basket."

My brain feels like it's running a high-speed obstacle course in the middle of a battlefield. Let's review our current shit show, shall we?

One ancient death stone playing split personality—with the evil twin probably tucked away in Lilith's favorite Coach purse.

Throw in one seriously pissed-off witch channeling eons of family revenge, armed with enough magical firepower to make Hogwarts look like amateur hour, and holding one hell of a grudge over my guys' little witch-massacre adventure.

My brooding man isn't just packing vampire powers—turns out he's basically supernatural nobility on steroids. Grandson of Thor and son of some ancient goddess of darkness? Talk about your complicated family dynamics. I mean, the whole lightning-throwing thing should've been a dead giveaway, but hearing it confirmed takes it to a whole new level of 'are you shitting me?'

And because the universe loves to pile on the crazy, we're still running around collecting magical rocks like some deadly Pokemon game. Two and a half stones to go, and now we're racing against my man's psycho maker.

I need a drink.

"I think it's time for that drink. Or several." I announce, my brain still spinning from the onslaught of revelations.

Emily stomps off to the kitchen, muttering under her breath about idiot vampires and their half-baked plans. She returns with a shot glass and a bottle of something that could probably strip paint. I toss it back without hesitation, welcoming the burn as it scorches a path down my throat. I run my tongue across my lips, savoring the lingering taste of liquid courage. Emily's already pouring a refill before I can even ask.

"Keep 'em coming, babe. I'm gonna need a lot more alcohol to process this."

After negotiations (and some serious pouting on my part), I'm finally cleared to visit Damon in what Lucian dramatically dubbed "The Dungeon." Real original there, buddy. As I descend into the basement, emotions churn in my gut like a bad cocktail—anger at having to treat my brother like a convict, frustration at the whole situation, and a sadness so deep it makes my chest ache.

The sight of his 'cell' makes my blood boil. Sure, Rhyland keeps insisting this is for everyone's protection—including Damon's—but seeing my baby brother locked up like some dangerous criminal feels wrong on every level. I get it, I do. New vampires are about as stable as a nuclear reactor having a meltdown. But understanding the logic doesn't make this any easier to stomach.

I'm trying hard to be mature about this and see it from their perspective. But watching the security cameras flicker and seeing the reinforced steel door? Yeah, that's a reality check I wasn't quite ready for.

After much-needed food and another day of rest, my powers are back online. That witchy roofie Morgan slipped me has finally worked its way out of my system, and I'm feeling more like myself.

I approach the door cautiously, taking in the bars and small window set into the reinforced steel. Peering inside, I spot Damon lying on a cot, his back to me.

"Go away!" he shouts, and I can't help but flinch at the pain in his voice.

Rhyland's arm bands around my waist, trying to guide me back, but I plant my feet and shrug him off. "Not happening, Damon. We need to talk."

Damon squirms on the bed, his voice cracking. "Please...I can't—not after what I did. I don't want to hurt you again."

Rhyland mentioned this door could withstand a nuclear blast, so I stand my ground, confident in its strength. "Damon, listen to me. I'm okay. See? You can't hurt me. What's happened to you..." The words stick in my throat. How do you apologize for a fate he never asked for? "It wasn't fair—but we can fix it. We can help you."

Damon sighs, the sound heavy with despair, as he finally rolls over to face me. The anguish etched into his features hits me hard. "The hunger—it's constant, overwhelming. That bastard turned me into the very thing I hate most. I feel sick!" He spits the words like they're poison on his tongue. "Leave. Please!"

I take a deep breath, trying to find the right words to reassure him. "Damon, this isn't going to be easy, but we're here for you. We'll help you learn to control it, to—"

Before I can finish, Damon lunges at the door with preternatural speed; his fangs bared in a snarl of pure hunger. A yelp tears from my throat as I stumble back, heart pounding against my ribs. In an instant, Rhyland's powerful arms are around me, yanking me against his solid frame. He positions himself between me and the door, every muscle coiled and ready to defend me if Damon somehow breaks through.

Fear claws at my insides as I stare at my brother—or the creature that used to be my brother. Those once-familiar hazel eyes now blaze with an inhuman hunger that sends ice through my veins. Is this what he felt when he attacked me in the woods? This overwhelming terror, this sense that the person you love has been replaced by something...else?

Rhyland's growl rumbles through his chest, warning and promising protection. But even as I lean into his strength, I can't tear my gaze away from Damon's snarling face, from the reality of what he's become.

"Why do you smell so *fucking* delicious?" Damon growls, his words distorted by the fangs crowding his mouth.

And there it is—the question I've been dreading. The one that leads down a rabbit hole of prophecies, celestial destinies, and the whole 'surprise, your sister's not quite human' revelation.

I close my eyes, taking a steadying breath. This conversation was inevitable, but that doesn't make it any easier. How do I explain to my brother that his big sister is some sort of chosen one tasked with saving the world from an ancient evil? That my very blood is vampire catnip?

Rhyland's arms tighten around me, his solid presence a reminder that I'm not alone in this. But even his strength can't chase away the knot of dread in my stomach.

Time to rip off the proverbial Band-Aid and dive headfirst into the shitstorm that is my life. Yay me.

DANICA

18

"I brought both books," Seraphina's melodic voice chimes as she gracefully settles onto the couch, her golden hair catching the light like a halo. "The Norse mythology and everything we have on Zephyria." She arranges the ancient tomes on the coffee table with delicate precision, right next to our steaming mugs of coffee.

I eye the Norse book like it might bite. After finding out my Nordic Nookie is basically supernatural royalty, I'm hoping there might be some juicy additional details about his role in all this cosmic drama. Though honestly, we already know the cliff notes version courtesy of dear old Dad—you know, the same father who'll chat up my mate but can't be bothered to talk to his own daughter?

"Which would you like to start with?" Seraphina asks sweetly. "The 'your boyfriend's a demigod' primer or the 'how not to die in the air realm' guide?"

I can't help but smile at her gentle attempt at sass—my sweet guardian angel's definitely been picking up some attitude since joining our little family. The irony of the situation hits me like a cosmic joke: my father, in all his divine wisdom, kicked this literal angel out of Atheria for saving me from Lucian's memory-wiped brain. And now here we are, finding out my snarky vampire brother-in-law is technically related to the other half of their precious prophecy.

Seriously, for being the God of Light, my father really needs to work on his judgment calls. Maybe we should send him a self-help book: "Godly Parenting for Dummies: How Not to Banish Angels Who Save Your Kid."

It's been three weeks since our little dance with Lilith, and surprisingly, life's finding its own twisted version of normal. Lilith and Morgan have been suspiciously quiet, probably plotting her next psychotic fashion show of doom.

After dropping the whole "surprise, your sister's basically Angelic royalty" bomb on Damon, he took it better than expected. Sure, he laughed it off at first—probably thought I was trying to distract him from his own vampire drama—but eventually accepted that his big sister is some prophesied savior. Because why not? His life already went full Twilight. He might as well add "sister is cosmic chosen one" to the mix.

Meanwhile, Damon's making progress with the whole blood-drinking situation. Lucian's been a godsend (ironic, considering his occupation), taking point on Operation Baby Vamp Training. Makes sense—he's the youngest of my immortal trio and still remembers what it's like to fight that overwhelming hunger. Erik keeps the training structured with his military expertise, while my Thunder Buns brings the muscle when Damon's bloodlust gets a little too frisky.

Who knew vampire rehab could be a family bonding experience?

Emily and Sable still play supernatural recruiters, building their magical army one witch at a time. My colorful-haired rebel, in all her badass glory, started her own coven—and because Emily is Emily, she dubbed it the Rainbow Coven. Lucian, being the walking smartass he is, practically busts a gut every time he hears the name, turning it into his personal comedy routine.

"What's next, Skittles? Gonna make your official motto 'Taste the Magic'?" He'll quip, which usually ends with Emily threatening to hex his balls off.

I try to hide my snickers behind my hand during their verbal sparring matches, but truthfully, the name carries more weight than Lucian's tiny brain can comprehend. It's not just about Emily's technicolor hair—it represents unity, hope, and promise. My bestie and Sable are working their magical asses off to restore balance to this realm, building bridges between covens that haven't spoken in eons.

Watching my formerly nerdy biochemist friend transform into this powerful witch queen? Yeah, that's the kind of glow-up that makes a girl proud.

"Let's focus on our next magical scavenger hunt item—the Zephyrite stone," I announce, trying to inject some enthusiasm into our trinket treasure hunt. Sure, tracking down the other half of Mom's Nightmare Stone of Doom should probably be priority number one. Still, Seraphina's been pretty insistent about collecting the other stones first—something about maintaining magical balance before playing with the world's deadliest mood ring.

After hearing Rhyland's horror story about his dance with the dark side, I'm not exactly eager to take that particular plunge myself. The way he described that nightmare vision still makes my skin crawl. My man may be built like a mountain and have the attitude to match, but hearing how that stone nearly broke him? Yeah, I'll take my guardian angel's advice on this one.

However, I still can't wrap my head around how Calypso managed to rock her piece without going full Dark Side. But then again, she wasn't dealing with the complete package like Rhyland was. Add in the fact that my brooding beefcake's got his mom's power running through his veins like some twisted inheritance, and suddenly, his struggle makes a lot more sense.

"Perfect!" Seraphina's voice chimes with its usual sweetness. "Though I should mention I've already explored the Norse text. The book's details about Ásgard and other geographical locations are quite fascinating." Even discussing ancient texts, she sounds like she's describing a delightful tea party.

"Cool, we can dive into that book report after we tackle this stone situation," I reply, lifting my coffee for a much-needed caffeine boost.

Seraphina launches into her supernatural speed-reading, her delicate fingers flipping pages so fast they create their own personal breeze. I barely get the mug to my lips when Seraphina's delicate gasp catches my attention. In record time, her face has gone from 'angels singing' to 'someone kicked a puppy', and her gold eyes are wide with shock.

"What's wrong? You look like you just caught Lucian reading the Bible."

Instead of answering, my guardian angel attacks the Norse book like it personally offended her, those fingers flying through pages faster than humanly possible. The massive tome hits the table with enough force to make her coffee do a little dance.

"This is... oh my goodness... but that would mean..." She's practically vibrating with whatever bombshell she's discovered. Her cute nose is scrunched up in a way that means her brain is working overtime.

"Okay, you're starting to freak me out here," I set down my coffee before her nervous energy makes me spill it. "What's got your halo in a twist?"

Seraphina finally meets my eyes, those swirling depths of honey and amber are practically glowing. "They're the same."

"Okay, you'll have to give me more than that, Sera. What's the same?"

She lets out that little huff of frustration—the one that screams, 'Why can't mortals keep up?'—before grabbing both books. "These texts describe the same realm, just from different perspectives. The geographical locations match perfectly."

I blink at her like she's speaking in tongues. "You lost me at geographical."

"Look here," she says, her delicate fingers dancing across ancient pages. "See how the Norse text describes Ásgard? The cloud palaces made of solidified clouds infused with celestial light? The way Valhalla stands adorned with gold and silver?" Her voice carries that musical lilt of excitement. "Now look at the Zephyrian text—it describes 'magnificent cloud castles that float gracefully above the landscape, constructed from solidified clouds that blend seamlessly with the surrounding sky.'"

My jaw drops as she continues, her voice taking on that excited teacher tone. "And here—the Norse book mentions the Bifrost, their light bridge, while the Zephyrian text speaks of 'Sky Trails, invisible air-current pathways connecting various floating islands.' They're describing the same celestial highways, just through different cultural lenses."

"Hold up," I lean forward, coffee forgotten. "Are you saying Ásgard is in Zephyria?"

"Precisely!" Seraphina's practically bouncing with enthusiasm now. "The 'Wind Spires' in Zephyria match perfectly with the descriptions of Ásgard's ancient watchtowers. Even their sacred sites align—the 'Elemental Nexus' in Zephyria corresponds with the gathering places in Ásgard. These aren't separate realms—they're different cultures interpreting the same space!"

Well, shit. Looks like our magical scavenger hunt just got a whole lot more interesting.

My brain short-circuits as the implications hit me. If Ásgard and Zephyria are the same realm, then not only did Rhyland take an impromptu trip to the air realm, but somewhere up there, walking on clouds and probably rocking some killer armor, is my half-sister. The sister I never knew existed until Rhyland dropped that particular bombshell.

The possibility of meeting her sends my thoughts spinning. What's she like? What color are her eyes? Are they like mine? Does she also think that our Father is a self-righteous pain in the ass, or did she luck out with the whole father-daughter relationship thing?

I shake myself out of my celestial sister daydream. "So... any chance this magical geography lesson tells us where to find our next shiny rock?"

Seraphina's eyes scan the text. "According to this, the Zephyrite stone resides in the highest Wind Spire, where the Zephyrian's maintain their most sacred temple. It's said to be guarded by ethereal beings who can manipulate air currents and command the winds themselves."

She traces a detailed illustration of a magnificent floating structure. "The spire rises above even the cloud castles, its peak seemingly touching the stars themselves. The stone is kept in what they call the Elemental Nexus—a sacred site where the purest essence of air converges. The text mentions that only those deemed worthy by the winds themselves can approach the stone."

"Great," I mutter, taking another sip of coffee. "So we just need to break into the realm's most sacred site, climb what's essentially a tornado turned sideways, and somehow grab a magical rock without getting blown into the next century. Should be fun."

Seraphina gives me that angelic smile that somehow makes impossible tasks sound like a delightful afternoon activity. "At least we know where to look!"

"Yeah, assuming any of this is still accurate," I snort, remembering our last magical treasure hunt. "These books aren't exactly up to date with current events. Remember Aquaria? That whole 'peaceful underwater paradise' description turned out to be complete bullshit. More like, 'Surprise, here's a smear campaign to overthrow a mermaid queen, force her to wear a corrupted stone, and oh yeah, let's just lie about an entire species to keep people away from the Lyre.'"

I take another sip of coffee, grimacing at the memory. "At this point, I wouldn't be shocked if we get up there and find out the Zephyrian's have turned their sacred temple into a cosmic nightclub or something. These ancient texts have about as much reliability as a weather forecast in Seattle."

"It's a start, Dani." Seraphina's melodic laugh chimes through the room. She nibbles her lower lip thoughtfully, that mind clearly piecing together some puzzle. "Actually, this explains quite a bit."

"Care to share with the class?"

"Well," she begins, her voice carrying that 'I just solved a riddle' tone. "It actually makes perfect sense when you consider the bigger picture. The Norse gods, particularly the Valkyries, have always been associated with wind and flight. Their very essence is tied to the air itself. No wonder they're the guardians of the Zephyrite stone."

"Well, when you put it that way—"

"And your sister!" Seraphina practically bounces in her seat. "She might be able to help us navigate all this!"

The mention of my mysterious sibling reminds me of something that's been nagging at my brain. "Hey, speaking of my long-lost sister—you mentioned hearing something about this centuries ago. What exactly did you overhear?"

A shadow passes over Seraphina's delicate features, her eyes growing distant with memory. "It was right after the realms were sealed. I was stationed near the Hall of Light when I overheard Elysium speaking with Jophiel." She wrings her hands, a very un-angelic gesture of nervousness. "They were discussing the prophecy—about how one savior was dead and the other..." she pauses, choosing her words carefully, "unable to handle the power required. Elysium was insisting a new plan needed to be formed."

"What happened next?"

"Unfortunately, I was immediately called away to my duties," she sighs, clearly frustrated by the memory. "I only caught fragments after that—something about 'trying again' and 'this time it must work.' I never knew what all that meant." She smooths her hair, a nervous habit I've noticed. "But now? it's clear they were talking about you and Rhyland—well, the original plan for him and your sister, at least."

"So you got assigned to me as my guardian angel without knowing what or who I really was?"

Seraphina's delicate features cloud with memory. "Not at first. It wasn't until I was sent to protect your mother before Azrael could..." She trails off, those honey-colored eyes darkening with pain. We both know how that particular chapter ends—or would have ended if she hadn't intervened. "Elysium was furious when Azrael discovered the truth. It meant Moretemis knew about his backup plan." She shakes her head, golden hair catching the light. "That's when everything became clear—who you were, what you were destined to become..."

Well, isn't that just perfect? Even my guardian angel's assignment came with a side of secrecy. At least Seraphina turned out to be more than just my celestial babysitter—she's family now, whether my father likes it or not.

"Your father was... less than pleased, when he found out about Rhyland—his...nature. He thought something had gone terribly wrong, that your powers had been corrupted somehow. But now?" Her face lights up. "Now we all know the truth. Rhyland truly is and was your destined mate. The prophecy wasn't broken; we just didn't have all the pieces—it was fulfilling itself exactly as it should."

Looking back, I can't help but smile. Sure, Rhyland and I didn't exactly have love at first sight—more like lust, sass, and a healthy dose of supernatural drama. But that pull between us? That bone-deep certainty that we belonged together? That was real from the start, even if it took awhile for my brain to catch up with what my heart already knew.

Fate had its plan all along; it just took a few unexpected turns and threw in some plot twists that even the Gods didn't see coming.

Guess sometimes destiny needs a little chaos to get things right.

RHYLAND

19

"When do we leave?"

Dani's curled up on our bed, breaking down everything she and Seraphina discovered about Zephyria. Or should I say fucking Ásgard? Because apparently, they're in the same goddamn realm. Perfect.

"Whenever you're ready," she says calmly, which makes my predator instinct go haywire.

The thought of leaving the mansion ties my guts in knots. That psychotic bitch Lilith is out there somewhere, probably plotting her next twisted move with half of my mother's cursed stone. Yeah, Emily and Sable turned this place into a supernatural fortress—their magic could probably handle an atomic blast. But this is *Lilith* we're talking about. That sadistic cunt will burn the world to get what she wants.

And what she wants is me.

That fucking nightmare still haunts me—watching her rip out Lucian's heart, using Dani like a plaything. The worst part? I wouldn't put any of that shit past her. My maker's got millennia of practice turning people's worst fears into reality.

"Hey..." Dani slides off the bed with that grace that makes my mouth go dry. Her hand finds my chest, trailing up to my neck like she owns every fucking inch—which she does. "Stop brooding, Mr. Growly. You'll give yourself wrinkles, and then what will the other demigods think?"

She forces me to meet her gold eyes swirling with flecks of silver. "The fortress of supernatural sass is locked down tight. Seraphina and the walking smartass will keep the council in line—probably with a healthy mix of wisdom and inappropriate jokes. It's just you, me, and Mr. Stoic on this field trip to Cloud City. We'll grab the shiny rock and be back before you know it.'"

Her confidence makes me fucking melt. After everything she's been through—the assault, the blood violation, the whole fucking nightmare—she's still standing here, stronger than ever. When I think something might finally break her, she comes back swinging with that sass and fire that made me fall for her in the first place.

She's handled every cosmic curveball like a champ—finding out about her sister and dealing with her father's gold-plated indifference when she needed him most. My fierce little warrior just takes it all in stride, turning trauma into armor and pain into power.

I crush her against me, my hands spanning her waist as I yank her flush to my body. Those molten-gold eyes darken instantly, pupils blown wide with desire until only a thin ring of gold remains. "Mr. Growly? The fuck? I don't growl—that much, Angel."

"Oh please," Dani laughs, the sound going straight to my cock as I bury my face in her neck, inhaling her addictive scent that makes my fangs ache with need. She smells like sunshine and sin, a combination that turns my brain to static. Her fingers thread through my hair, nails scratching my scalp in that way that drives me fucking wild. A growl rumbles through my chest before I can stop it.

"You were saying?" she teases, with her signature sass. "Because that definitely sounded like a growl to me. Want to try that denial again, or should I start keeping score?"

I land a sharp smack on that perfect ass, making her yelp. The little minx retaliates by sinking her teeth into my neck, sending a jolt of pleasure straight to my already hardening cock. "Down, boy," she pants, pushing against my chest. "We've got places to be and stones to steal, O' Mighty Dick of the North."

The title startles a laugh from me, but I'm already pulling her closer, dragging my fangs along her ear before licking that sweet spot on her neck that makes her melt. Her moan hits me like lightning, her body going soft and pliant against mine. "You sure about that, Angel?" I grumble, rolling my hips against her. "Pretty sure I can have you screaming my name—any of them—in record time. Want to test that theory?"

Her arousal slams into me, that sweet fucking scent demolishing any self-control I've got left. I haul her up by that delicious ass and throw her onto our bed before she can fire off another smart-ass comment. Her shirt is gone in seconds, revealing those gorgeous tits that drive me fucking insane. My mouth latches onto one dusky pink nipple, sucking hard until it peaks, drawing those desperate little moans from her throat as she clutches me tighter.

That first night after I brought her home, after what those bastards did to her—Christ, I thought I'd lose my mind. Couldn't breathe, couldn't think straight until I saw those sparkly eyes looking at me with pure love and need. I was sure she'd flinch from my touch, that the trauma would create a wall between us. But my fierce little angel surprised me again—demanding I replace every violated memory with pleasure only I can give her, turning horror into healing with every kiss, every touch, every claiming.

I blaze a trail of hot, open-mouthed kisses down her tight stomach, feeling those muscles jump under my tongue. Each nibble and lick draws those sweet little gasps from her throat as I work my way toward paradise. She's already surrendering, spreading those thighs wider, grinding against me like she's dying for it.

"I'm thirsty," I growl against her skin. "And this sweet pussy's the only thing that'll quench it." I grab her yoga pants and tear them off. Her perfect cunt gleams in the light, wet, slick, and ready, making my mouth water.

Dropping to my knees, I drag her to the edge of the bed with one rough pull, drawing a surprised yelp from those perfect lips. "Hold on tight, Angel," I command, my voice dark with hunger. "Because I'm not fucking stopping until you're screaming my name and soaking my tongue."

After Dani flooded my mouth like the angelic fountain she is—Christ, watching her fall apart—those thighs trembling as she soaked my tongue and beard with that perfect pussy—and then taking her until she's a whimpering, well-fucked mess, we finally pull ourselves away from paradise to deal with reality.

The moment my boots hit the living room floor, AC/DC's "Thunderstruck" blasts through the speakers at ear-splitting volume. Because, of fucking course, it does. There's my dipshit brother, planted in the middle of the room with that shit-eating grin plastered across his face, air-guitaring like he's auditioning for a rock god position.

"Na na na na na na na na na naaa..." he belts out, like the attention-whoring asshole he is.

I'm going to murder him. Slowly. Painfully. Right after I figure out how the fuck he rigged the sound system to trigger that specific song the second I walked in.

"THUNDER! *na na na na naaa...*—THUNDER!" Lucian screeches like a tone-deaf banshee, the bass vibrating through the fucking walls. Dani's doubled over, clutching her sides as she loses her shit, while our personal peanut gallery—Emily, Sable, and Seraphina—are sprawled across the couch in various states of hysterics.

"I was caught! In the middle of a railroad track—THUNDER!" The walking, talking smart-ass continues his one-man show, completely ignoring the fact that I'm plotting at least twelve different ways to end him. Trust Lucian to find the most obnoxious possible way to mock my newfound heritage. Fucking typical.

I stalk over to the stereo like a predator hunting prey, searching for whatever button will end this bullshit. Screw it—I reach behind the system and rip the cord straight from the wall. Blessed silence fills the room, though everyone is still cackling like hyenas at a comedy show. Even Erik is failing miserably at hiding his amusement behind his bourbon glass in his corner fortress of solitude.

"You finished with your little performance, dickhead?" I snarl, fighting the urge to throw the stereo at his face.

"What's wrong, Rhy-Rhy?" Lucian grins like the cat that ate the whole damn aviary. "Don't tell me the God of Thunder's grandson can't take a little AC/DC tribute? The song's practically your origin story now! I've got a whole playlist ready—'Electric Avenue' is up next!"

I level my most lethal glare at the smirking prick, but Dani slides between us, still fighting back giggles as she wraps those arms around my neck. "Come on, Thunder Buns," she grins up at me, eyes sparkling with mischief.

I barely have time to roll my eyes, already knowing this is going to be like throwing raw meat to a starving lion. Lucian's going to be all over this shit like—

"Thunder Buns?!" Lucian howls, practically vibrating with glee. "Oh, Dani-girl, you beautiful, sassy genius! I'm *SO* using that from now on. Hey, Rhy-Rhy, can I be Lightning Cheeks? We'll be the Electric Ass Avengers!"

I shoot him a glare, but it just bounces off him like everything else. This asshole's got the self-preservation instincts of a fucking lemming.

"Besides," Dani continues, her fingers playing with the hair at the nape of my neck in a way that makes me want to purr, "now every time I hear that song, I'll think of my sexy demigod Viking—talk about a playlist upgrade."

Fuck. How's a man supposed to stay pissed when my woman's looking at me like that, all sass and sunshine? My anger melts faster than Lucian's brain cells in a crisis, and I can't help but capture those smart-ass lips in a quick kiss, drinking in her laughter.

"You're welcome, Captain Scowls!" Lucian preens like a peacock on steroids. "See? I'm providing a valuable service here—making your woman laugh while roasting your consecrated ass. I should start charging for this serv—."

"Lucian," Erik interjects, his refined tone barely masking his exasperation with our resident pain in the ass, "I would strongly suggest reconsidering your current course of action. Though I must say, your persistent ability to challenge the depths of your own idiocy remains... fascinating."

"Oh, I'm sorry—did I interrupt your morning routine of color-coding your ammunition and practicing your brooding face in the mirror? Don't get your tactical panties in a twist, Sergeant Serious. I've got a whole playlist ready—'Mission Impossible' for when you're skulking around, 'Smooth Criminal' for your fancy ass walk, and 'Ice Ice Baby' for that frozen stick up your ass!"

Erik's eyes roll skyward, his refined features screaming, 'I cannot believe I'm related to this walking disaster' as he gives Lucian that signature arctic glare—the same one he's perfected through years of enduring our brother's verbal diarrhea. Meanwhile, Seraphina's angelic composure shatters completely as she dissolves into very unheavenly snorts of laughter, and Dani vibrates against my chest, desperately trying to contain her own hysterics. Fucking perfect. My dipshit brother managed to corrupt an actual angel and turn my mate into his personal laugh track.

"Alright, enough—playtime's done," I snap, my voice carrying enough authority to cut through the bullshit. "We've got a magical stone to hunt down in Zephyria and shit to sort out here before we leave."

The room's atmosphere changes instantly, like someone flipped a switch. Even Lucian's smart-ass grin fades as everyone straightens up, and the reality of our situation settles over the room like a heavy blanket.

Let's just hope Dani and I can pull this shit off and be back before shit hits the fan here. With my luck lately, that's a pretty fucking tall order.

ZEPHYRIA

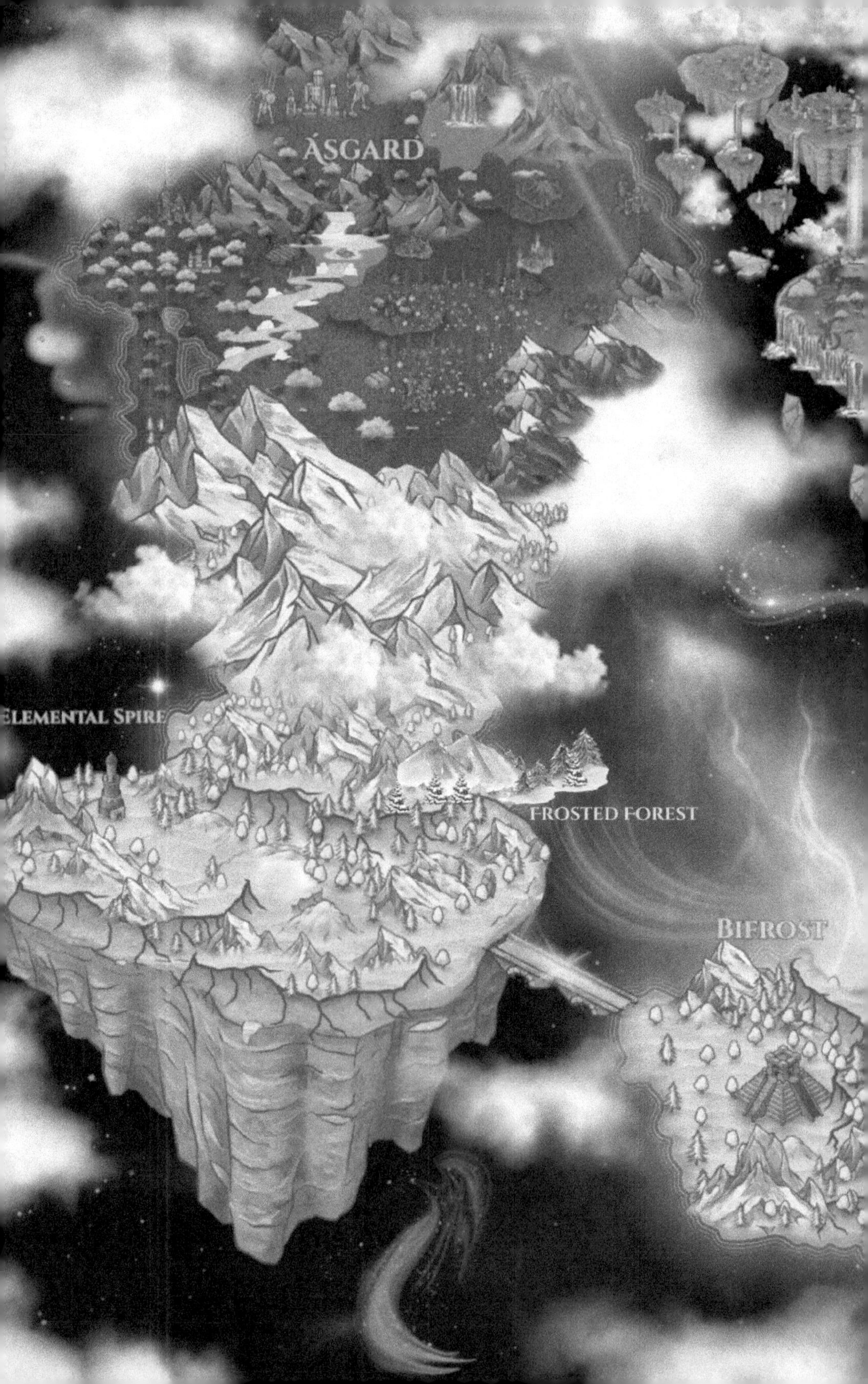

ÁSGARD
ELEMENTAL SPIRE
FROSTED FOREST
BIFROST

ELEMENTAL NEXUS
VALHALLA'S VEIL
ACES
RDS
VALOR'S WATCH
THE HALL OF WINGS
TWILIGHT EYRIE
ZEPHYRIA

DANICA

20

The air here is so frigid, my nipples could probably cut through reinforced steel. They're staging a full-scale rebellion against the cold, turning into icicles beneath my multiple layers of clothing.

I yank my fur-lined hood tighter around my face, trying to create some kind of barrier between my delicate skin and the elements that are clearly trying to murder me.

The landscape stretches out in every direction, an endless expanse of white that makes the Arctic Circle look like a tropical paradise. Everywhere I look, it's just snow, ice, and more fucking snow—like we've stumbled into the world's largest freezer.

I'm bundled up tighter than a burrito thanks to Rhyland's little pre-quest REI adventure (because apparently "hey, it might be chilly" translates to "buy every piece of winter gear known to man"). I've got so many layers on, I'm pretty sure I could survive a nuclear winter—but even that's not enough to keep the chill from seeping into my very soul.

I feel like the Stay Puft Marshmallow Man's more fashionable cousin, waddling through the knee-deep snow in my expensive yeti suit. If I fall over, I'm pretty sure I'll just roll away like a puffy tumbleweed, never to be seen again.

Rhyland and Erik trudge ahead through snow deep enough to swallow a small car, their boots crunching through the frozen crust with each step. I have no clue where precisely in Zephyria we landed, but judging by the way my nose hairs are turning into icicles, I'm guessing we're somewhere in the "holy-shit-that's-cold" region of the realm.

The altitude isn't helping either—each breath feels like I'm trying to suck air through a frozen coffee stirrer. Between the bone-crushing cold and the oxygen-deprived atmosphere, my lungs are probably plotting their resignation as we speak.

Rhyland's recent field trip to Cloud City left him with a mental map of the place—well, if you consider "there's a big pointy thing and a light bridge" a map. Armed with his vague descriptions and Seraphina's geographical Cliffs Notes, I tried to piece together a destination in my mind before opening the portal.

Before our arctic adventure, Lucian pulled his version of responsible adulting—shoving property papers in my face and insisting I sign the deed to his mansion, with vampires unable to cross the threshold without the owner's permission (hello, most obvious vampire rule that we somehow forgot about until now).

It was pretty clever of him—like adding another lock to an already fortress-level security system. With Emily and Sable turning the place into Fort Knox with their witchy protection spells, this deed transfer was just another middle finger to any uninvited guests. And by guests—specifically, one designer-wearing psychopath who thinks a "restraining order" is just a suggestion. Nothing says "stay out " like magical wards and good old-fashioned property law.

The snowflakes swirling around us are so thick that they're practically a white-out curtain, obscuring anything more than a few inches from my face. The wind howls like a pack of rabid wolves, tugging at my clothes with icy claws. Visibility is a joke—I can barely make out my gloved hands, let alone any mystical landmarks.

Just as I'm about to start questioning my life choices, a familiar warmth blooms in my chest. My power unfurls like a miniature sun, chasing away the chill from the inside out. The sudden reprieve makes me sigh in relief—even my magic has had enough of this frozen hellscape.

Rhyland materializes at my side, his strong arms snaking around my waist. He pulls me close, anchoring me against the relentless gusts that threaten to send me tumbling ass over teakettle into the nearest snowbank.

Here's hoping we don't wander off the edge of a cloud or something equally embarrassing. Nothing ruins a heroic quest like plummeting through the sky because you couldn't see where you were going.

After hours of walking in this frigid mess, mountainous silhouette looms out of nowhere, rising from the swirling snow like a giant. It's hard to gauge just how big this thing is, because its peak vanishes somewhere in the cotton-candy mess of clouds above. I'm guessing it's not your average skyscraper.

"There!" Rhyland's voice barely registers over the howling wind, but I catch enough to follow his pointing finger. "The Elemental Spire!"

Oh, good. I'm glad we're headed toward the ominous tower that could double as a supervillain's summer home. I was starting to worry this little adventure might be too easy.

Rhyland, ever attuned to my emotional state (or maybe just sensing my sarcasm), tries to reassure me. "It's okay. I've been in there before."

Well, that's comforting. I feel so much better knowing Rhyland has already braved the mysterious spire of doom. It's not like anything could have changed since his last visit, right? It's just an ancient, magical tower in a realm of literal gods and monsters. What could go wrong?

Erik, deciding that this conversation is beneath his tactical expertise, trudges ahead through the snow like a man on a mission. His silver head bowed against the wind, he forges up the hill with the determination of a soldier charging into battle—or a vampire who's really, really done with this arctic bullshit.

The structure grows larger with each slogging step, its peak vanishing into the swirling white abyss above. It's like Jack's beanstalk on steroids—a vertical monstrosity that probably has a killer view of the entire realm. You know, assuming you can reach the top without becoming a human popsicle.

Rhyland forges ahead with the determination of a man on a mission, his hand never leaving the small of my back as he guides me through the knee-deep snow. I can practically feel the waves of protective energy rolling off him, his inner caveman on high alert in this alien environment.

Guess we're off to see the wizard—or in this case, climb the magic spire and hope we don't die of frostbite before we reach the top.

By the time we finally reach the base of this architectural monstrosity, I feel like I've aged a decade. Every muscle in my body is screaming in protest, and I'm pretty sure my lungs are filing a formal complaint with the union. Erik's perfect posture has started to crack, his silver hair crusted with ice as he glowers at the endless snowfall like it personally offended his sensibilities—his expression replaced by one of pure, unadulterated "done-with-this-shit."

The entrance looms before us—a set of doors that would make Paul Bunyan feel inadequate. They stretch so high I have to crane my neck back just to see where they end. Their surface is carved with glowing runes that pulse with ancient power. The glyphs dance across the metal like ethereal fireflies, casting an otherworldly glow across the snow.

In all his Viking wisdom, Rhyland approaches the doors with his usual subtle diplomacy, which means he tries to muscle them open. When that fails, he switches to Plan B: pounding on them hard enough to wake the dead. The sound is like thunder, making me wince.

Real smooth, babe. Nothing says "we come in peace," quite like trying to break down the front door of a sacred temple.

The ancient doors finally surrender with a groan that echoes through the frigid air, as if the building sighs in resignation. We scramble inside like frozen refugees, and my jaw nearly hits the floor. The interior stretches upward into what seems like infinity, and the ceiling is so far above us that it disappears into shadows.

I push back my snow-crusted hood, sending a mini avalanche of ice crystals cascading around my shoulders as I spin in a slow circle. The space around us could swallow entire city blocks whole—it makes Grand Central Station look like a cozy closet in comparison. Gigantic pillars, each thick enough to wrap a bus around, soar upward into the gloom, their surfaces etched with glowing runes that cast ethereal light across the polished stone floor.

My neck starts to ache from craning back to take it all in. Whoever built this place had a severe edifice complex. Though I've got to admit, they nailed the "awe-inspiring architecture" aesthetic. It's like someone took every description of a magical citadel, cranked it up to eleven, and then decided that it still wasn't impressive enough.

"You've returned."

The voice booms through the vast chamber, making us whirl around like startled cats. Standing there, looking like he just stepped out of a mythological bodybuilding competition, is a mountain of a man. His bronze skin gleams in the ethereal light, and those acid-green eyes seem to strip away every secret I've ever had.

"Heimdall." Rhyland's voice carries a mix of recognition and wariness. "Yes. Where is everyone?"

I try not to gawk at the giant before us, but it's hard when the guy is pushing eight feet tall and wearing armor that looks forged from pure sunlight. The golden metal ripples with intricate designs that pulse with their own inner glow, making him look like a walking constellation.

"Gone." Heimdall's response drops like a stone in a still pond.

Well, isn't that just wonderfully cryptic? These immortal types need to work on their communication skills. Would it kill them to elaborate once in a while?

My heart does a pathetic little flutter at the realization I won't be having any daddy-daughter time today. Not that I should be surprised—apparently, the God of Light is too busy polishing his halo to spare five minutes for his chosen savior. Sure, he'll chat up my man all day long, but his own flesh and blood? Nah, that's not worth his precious immortal time.

The fact that I even care makes me want to punch something. Here I am, getting all emotional over a father who couldn't be bothered to lift a celestial finger when I needed help. It's like having a paper cut that won't heal—this tiny, persistent ache that shouldn't hurt as much as it does.

And then there's my mysterious sister—the original chosen one who didn't make the gig. I'd been secretly hoping to meet her, to find someone who understands what it's like to have the world's most emotionally unavailable deity for a father. But it looks like that particular family reunion will have to wait.

Awesome.

"What do you mean gone?" Rhyland demands, his voice echoing off the ancient walls.

Heimdall glides toward us with the grace of a predator, each step making his armor sing. "As in Elysium returned to his realm, Odin went back to Ásgard, and Bryn returned to the Valors Watch." Those eerie green eyes lock onto me like targeting lasers. "You must be Danica." His gaze slides to Erik. "And who is this?"

Well, I might as well jump right into the deep end of awkward introductions. I peel off my snow-crusted glove and thrust my hand toward him like I'm meeting a new coworker instead of an ancient godly guardian. "Hi, it's Dani. It's nice to meet you."

He stares at my outstretched hand like I'm offering him a live grenade but eventually wraps his massive paw around mine with surprising gentleness. "And this is Erik. My friend and Rhyland's brother," I add, trying to diffuse the tension that's thick enough to cut with a knife.

A ghost of a smirk tugs at Heimdall's lips like he's both amused and baffled by my complete lack of proper divine etiquette. "It's a pleasure to make your acquaintance, lightborn."

My chest tightens. *Lightborn.* I haven't heard that title since Adrian used it on that stone Golem. The memory hits like a sledgehammer, and I physically shake my head to dislodge it. Nope, not going down that particular angst-ridden rabbit hole today. I've got enough on my plate without taking a stroll down traumatic memory lane.

"Just call me Dani." I flash my best 'let's-all-be-friends' smile while Erik starts his typical security sweep, probably cataloging every possible exit and threat like the strategic vampire boy scout he is.

"How do we get to Ásgard from here?" Rhyland demands, his alpha-male energy practically radiating off him. "We need to speak to him, to find the—"

"Stone?" Heimdall interrupts, looking way too pleased with himself.

"Yeah, about that..." Rhyland's voice drops to that dangerous growl that usually means someone's about to have a very bad day. "What the fuck possessed you ancient assholes to skip the part about this being the same goddamn realm as the air stone?"

Heimdall's lips curl into a smirk. "What was more pressing at the time, Godborn? Your cosmic destiny or a geography lesson?"

I have to bite my lip to keep from smiling. Who knew the Norse watchdog had such a sharp wit? Judging by the muscle ticking in Rhyland's jaw, he does not appreciate his answer.

"Besides," Heimdall says condescendingly, "it isn't our responsibility to guide the saviors through their quests. You two are supposed to figure these things out on your own." His precise tone suggests he's explaining basic math to particularly slow students.

I roll my eyes. Oh, for the love of *GOD*. If I have to hear one more person spout this "figure it out yourself" garbage, I will lose it. Who came up with this brilliant rule anyway? Some sadistic deity sitting on their throne thinking, "You know what would be hilarious? Let's make them solve deadly riddles and hunt for magical rocks across multiple realms without any actual guidance!"

Because heaven forbid they give us a straight answer for once. No, that would be too easy. We've got to earn our apocalypse-preventing merit badges the hard way.

"But it seems," Heimdall's voice carries the smug satisfaction of an immortal who's seen it all, "that your mate is quite the clever little thing. Figured it out in no time at all."

Yeah, except it was Seraphina who connected those particular dots. But I'm not about to correct this behemoth of snark.

"You still haven't answered my question." Rhyland's patience evaporates like water on hot coals. "How do we get to Ásgard?" His hands curl into fists, and the air around us dances with electric potential. Through our bond, I feel his power surge like a gathering storm, making the hair on my arms stand on end.

"I suggest you keep those sparks under control, Godborn." Heimdall's tone drops to a deadly warning. "Unless you fancy testing if lightning can bring down a sacred spire."

Rhyland exhales forcefully as if physically wrestling his power back under control. I know that feeling all too well—Luminara's magic had me buzzing like I'd mainlined a dozen magical espressos. And now, it seems this realm is cranking Rhyland's divine mojo up to maximum levels.

"But I'm so pleased you asked," Heimdall says. "Odin, in his infinite wisdom, anticipated your return. He has graciously provided you with a means to traverse the realm." He motions for us to follow, leading us to the rear of the Spire.

With a flourish that's entirely too dramatic for my taste, Heimdall throws open a massive door, revealing a sight that takes my breath away.

What in the actual hell?

RHYLAND

21

We stand here like fucking statues while the arctic wind tears at our clothes and snow falls in chunks the size of my fist. But I barely notice the cold because, holy shit—there in a covered corral—

A stupendous stallion towers before us, its coat gleaming like pure molten gold in the winter light. This isn't just some oversized horse—it's a war mount bred for giants, its muscles rippling with power beneath that metallic hide. Every movement screams raw strength, a reminder that this beast once belonged to creatures who could level mountains with their bare hands.

Its mane and tail flow like liquid sunlight, somehow untouched by the bitter wind and swirling snow. Those eyes, though—Christ, burn with an intelligence that makes my predator instincts stand up and take notice. Deep amber orbs lock onto me with an intensity that makes my skin buzz like this creature recognizes something in my blood.

The horse is decked out in battle gear—ancient Nordic symbols etched into gleaming armor that covers his towering frame. The headpiece alone probably weighs more than Dani, decorated with runes that pulse with old magic. A saddle that looks like it was forged by the gods themselves sits on his back, and ornate armor pieces flow down his powerful legs to hooves that could crush a fucking car. Jesus, each hoof is bigger than my head—it's a beast bred for war, every inch designed to strike fear into the hearts of enemies.

"This is Gullfax," Heimdall announces with reverence. "Your father's steed claimed in battle from the ice giant Hrungnir. Odin deemed it fitting that Magni's son should inherit his mount." His voice carries the weight of prophecy. "Like your father before you, this golden one will carry you across the winds themselves. Water, air, earth—all bow before Gullfax's might."

Fuck me. My father's horse? The same beast that helped him claim victory over a fucking ice giant? I stare at this beast, trying to process this cosmic hand-me-down. The stories said Gullfax could match Odin's mount, Sleipnir—for speed—a creature powerful enough to run across air itself.

"Oh my god," Dani breathes out in awe, her face lighting up with wonder. "He's beautiful—it is a he, right?" The stallion responds to her voice with a deep whinny, that golden head lowering to study her with ancient eyes. Of course, my mate would charm my father's war horse in under five seconds.

"Indeed," Heimdall confirms, approval coloring his usual clipped tone. "It seems Gullfax has taken a liking to you, lightborn. You may approach."

Every protective instinct in my body screams to grab Dani and pull her back—this guy stands taller than any mortal horse, its head level with the second story of a building. But I force myself to stay put, my jaw clenching as she moves closer. Something tells me my father's mount wouldn't take kindly to me questioning its judgment.

My heart damn near stops as Dani approaches the corral's edge, her small hand reaching up toward him like she's greeting an old friend instead of a monumental beast. Gullfax—this giant who could crush her with one wrong move—lowers his enormous head with surprising gentleness. His hot breath creates clouds of steam in the frigid air as he huffs softly, those ancient eyes drifting closed at her touch.

My fierce little angel doesn't hesitate, her fingers finding that sweet spot behind his ears that apparently works on mythological war horses just as well as on regular ones. The sound that rumbles from Gullfax's chest is somewhere between a purr and a whinny—like this battle-hardened mount is turning to putty under my mate's delicate hands. Her giggles echo across the snow as she lavishes attention on him, utterly unfazed by the fact she's petting a piece of my father's legacy.

"Rhyland, come here," Dani beckons, her hand never leaving Gullfax's golden coat. I approach with measured steps, my warrior's instincts keeping me alert despite the beast's apparent gentleness. Those amber eyes snap open as I reach Dani's side, fixing me with a stare that seems to pierce straight through to my soul.

He stretches his neck forward, hot breath ghosting across my face as he huffs softly—that typical horse greeting that somehow feels more significant coming from my father's mount. My hand lifts automatically to stroke his velvet nose.

"He says don't be scared. He knows who you are." Dani's voice carries that otherworldly note that makes me glance down. Sure enough, the Faerite stone pulses with ethereal light in her crown. Of course, my clever mate would use her gift to chat up this magical creature.

"Hey, big guy," I murmur, my hand sliding along his powerful neck. For all his intimidating size and battle-bred strength, Gullfax's coat feels like silk beneath my palm, that metallic sheen somehow soft as velvet despite looking like living armor. Standing here, touching this piece of my father's past, something shifts in my chest—a connection I wasn't expecting to feel.

"You possess the ability to converse with him?" Heimdall's voice cracks with disbelief, his usual godlike composure slipping for the first time since we arrived.

Dani throws him a look over her shoulder, that signature sass dancing in her beautiful eyes. "Yep. Comes with the whole magical stone package deal," she says casually like she's explaining why the sky is blue rather than dropping a cosmic bombshell. "The Faerite stone lets me chat up anything magical—you know, mythological horses, ancient guardians, grumpy Viking vampires." She winks at me with that last one before turning back to scratch behind Gullfax's ears. "Though some are chattier than others."

"Fascinating," Heimdall muses, his godlike voice tinged with genuine curiosity. "Such a gift will undoubtedly prove... advantageous."

"Oh, it's definitely got its perks," Dani agrees, her tone a mix of appreciation and exasperation. "But let me tell you, it can also be a real pain in the ass sometimes."

Heimdall nods sagely. "I can only imagine." He turns his gaze to Gullfax. "The mighty steed will carry you all with ease. He will navigate the realm effortlessly and guard you with his very life."

Erik materializes at my side with his characteristic silent grace, his silver eyes assessing the situation. "It appears, brother, that you've acquired quite the formidable ally." His refined tone carries that hint of dry humor only those who know him well would catch.

Gullfax responds by damn near knocking me on my ass that bulky head butting against my chest with enough force to make me stumble. Dani's laughter rings out across the snow at my graceless recovery.

"What do you think, big guy? Friends?" I ask, steadying myself against his powerful neck.

Gullfax bobs his head in what's clearly an affirmative, and I glance at Dani for translation. Her eyes sparkle with mischief as she listens to whatever he's saying.

"He says, 'Your father's blood runs strong in you, young prince. I would be honored to carry Magni's son as I once carried him.'" Dani's voice softens with the weight of the moment before her sass returns. "He also thinks you're less broody than your dad, which is apparently a good thing. Though I've got to say, considering how much time you spend perfecting that scowl, I'm having a hard time believing your father could out-brood you."

The laugh bursts out of me before I can maintain my composure, and Gullfax's responding whinny sounds exactly like the equine equivalent of a chuckle. Great—my mate's sass is apparently universal enough to amuse even this ancient beast.

"Really, Angel? You're critiquing my brooding when you're the one who called it 'irresistibly sexy' last night?" I smirk down at her, watching that blush creep across her cheeks. "Pretty sure my brooding game is what sealed the deal with you." Gullfax snorts in what sounds suspiciously like agreement, his hot breath creating clouds in the frigid air.

He nudges me again with his head as if backing me up, making Dani roll those honey-gold eyes at both of us. "Great," she mutters, "now I've got two of you ganging up on me. Just what I need—a supernatural powerhouse enabling your smart-ass comments."

I smirk, "What did he say?"

Dani sighs, "Golden Boy here says, 'The prince makes a fair point—your heartbeat tells a different story about his brooding.'" She shoots the stallion a betrayed look. "Seriously? You're taking his side? I thought we were having a moment here, you majestic traitor."

I cross my arms, fixing her with my best brooding stare. "Face it, Angel. You're outnumbered here. My brooding is legendary—even my father's horse agrees. Might as well admit it: you're hopelessly drawn to my dark and mysterious charm."

Dani rolls her eyes, a dramatic sigh escaping her lips.

Erik arches one perfect silver brow. "Your pulse just proved his point, Little Huntress."

"Yeah, yeah," she waves him off, turning to Heimdall with a smile that's just a little too sweet. "It was an absolute pleasure meeting you, Heimdall, but we've got a magical scavenger hunt to get back to. You know how it is—destiny waits for no one."

Heimdall inclines his head, his armor catching the light. "Until we meet again in Ásgard, Lightborn."

Heimdall turns and leaves us with Gullfax, who lowers himself to one knee—a clear invitation for us to mount up. Dani, never one to hesitate, wastes no time unlatching the gate and letting herself into the corral. She runs her gloved hands along his shoulder, admiring his golden coat, before attempting to jump onto his back. Key word: *attempting.* What actually happens is she ends up falling on her ass in the snow, a surprised yelp escaping her lips.

I can't help but chuckle as I head into the corral to help her up. "I think you might need a boost there, Angel. This isn't exactly your average pony."

"No shit," she huffs, "It's this freaking Yeti suit! Can't hardly move in this thing." Brushing snow from her face with a scowl that's more adorable than intimidating.

She positions herself at Gullfax's shoulder once more, and I easily lift her into the saddle, settling her in. Erik enters behind me, his movements as silent and graceful as ever. I jump up and slide in behind Dani, while Erik takes his place behind me.

"Alright, handsome," Dani says, patting Gullfax's neck. "Show us what you've got."

Gullfax takes off across the snow, his hooves barely seeming to touch the ground. Dani grips his reins, a delighted squeal escaping her as I wrap my arms securely around her waist.

It's like riding a fucking roller coaster as Gullfax picks up speed, moving faster than I've ever experienced on horseback. And then, suddenly, we're airborne—the ground falling away beneath us as the stallion takes to the skies, a shimmering rainbow trail stretching out in his wake.

DANICA

22

Holy. Shit.

If you'd told me a few months ago that I'd be riding a magical golden horse through actual air, I would've suggested a good therapist. Yet here I am, playing jockey on a mythological mount while defying every law of physics I learned in college.

The wind whips past us at speeds that should probably terrify me, but I'm too busy being awestruck to care that my face feels like it's being sandblasted by arctic air. Even through my frozen eyelashes, the view below is mind-blowing.

I risk a glance down and—wow. Just... wow. It's like someone draped a giant white blanket over the entire world. The snow stretches out in every direction, broken only by the occasional mountain peak or cluster of trees. From up here, it all looks so peaceful and serene.

It's like some crazy mash-up of Norse mythology and *The Neverending Story*, minus the tragic horse-drowning-in-a-swamp scene (thank god). Though I've got to say, Falkor the luck dragon has nothing on our golden boy here. Gullfax is practically glowing with happiness, his powerful muscles moving beneath us with all the confidence of someone who regularly tells gravity to go screw itself.

Rhyland's arms band around my waist like steel cables, his chest pressed against my back as I grip Gullfax's reins. Gullfax moves with the fluid grace of liquid gold, each stride covering impossible distances as he literally runs on air. Through the Faerite stone, I can feel waves of pure joy radiating from him. He's finally getting to do his job again after who knows how long. There's something adorable about how proud he is to be carrying Rhyland—like he's come full circle, serving the son of his former rider.

I never thought I'd say this, but galloping through the sky on a magical warhorse while my demigod vampire mate holds me close? Yeah, it's definitely going in my top ten most remarkable moments ever.

After what feels like an eternity of arctic torture (but is probably closer to an hour), the endless sea of white suddenly transforms into something that makes my brain short-circuit. The landscape below us explodes into a spectacular vista, and I forget how words work. Gullfax's giant hooves dance across invisible air, and through our connection, he proudly announces, *"Ásgard."*

And my god, if this isn't the most incredible thing I've ever seen. Sorry, Grand Canyon—you've officially been demoted to "mildly interesting hole in the ground" status.

As we soar through the air, he becomes my tour guide, pointing out sights that make my inner science nerd have an existential crisis.

"Those peaks before us," he explains as we glide past mountains that pierce the sky like giants' teeth, *"are older than time itself. Their snow never melts, blessed by the first frost giants."* The mountains gleam with an inner light that is definitely not covered in any National Geographic episode I ever watched.

We bank left (and *fuck,* who knew a horse could corner like an F-16?), giving me a perfect view of what looks like rivers made of liquid crystal. *"The sacred waters,"* Gullfax tells me, *"flow with the essence of life itself. One drop can heal any wound, though few are deemed worthy to drink."*

The forests below us shimmer with leaves that actually sparkle in the light, creating a natural light show that would put Times Square to shame. *"The ancient groves,"* my golden guide explains, *"where the first gods walked. The trees remember their footsteps still."* Well, that explains the bling—these trees are literally older than dirt.

Meadows burst with flowers in colors that probably don't even have names in mortal language, their petals throwing off light like nature's own disco ball. *"The Fields of Forever,"* Gullfax says with what I swear is a mental smirk. *"Where spring never ends and winter dares not tread."*

"This is incredible," I whisper, though the wind probably steals my words. But Gullfax's answering whinny tells me he heard me just fine.

"Just wait," he tells me, his mental voice tinged with mischief. *"You haven't seen anything yet."* And without warning, he does a dive maneuver—like a roller coaster drop—that makes my stomach relocate somewhere near my throat.

Show-off.

I play translator for Rhyland, relaying highlights from Gullfax's guided tour while my Viking drinks in the view of his ancestral realm. Our bond allows me to feel his mix of awe and something more profound—like pieces of his heritage finally clicking into place.

When Gullfax finally touches down on actual solid ground (praise God), my thighs and ass immediately file a formal complaint. Holy hell—apparently, those horseback riding muscles are entirely different from my "running for my life" muscles.

"Ow." I groan, trying to rise with some semblance of grace and failing spectacularly. "I didn't think my ass could hurt this much after such a short trip."

Though considering it feels like we were galloping through Luminara's enchanted forests not long ago, you'd think I'd still have some horseback riding muscles in working order. Clearly, magical realm-hopping does nothing for maintaining one's equestrian fitness level.

Rhyland and Erik hop off like action heroes because, of course, they do. Meanwhile, I'm sitting up here contemplating if breaking both legs would be worth keeping my dignity. Thankfully, Gullfax seems to understand my human limitations and kneels like the gentleman stallion he is.

"Need a hand, shorty?" Rhyland's lips twitch with amusement as he reaches for me.

I shoot him my best death glare. "Not everyone has vampire-enhanced agility and legs that go on for days, Thunder Thighs."

"Indeed," Erik adds dryly from somewhere behind us. "Though your strategy appears to require some practice."

He's not wrong. My dismount attempt quickly turns into an X-rated circus act as I somehow manage to wrap my legs around Rhyland's head. Thirteen feet is a long way down, and my man's giant frame has become my personal fireman's pole—except I'm pretty sure real firefighters don't end up with their thighs accidentally choking their rescuers.

"If you're done using my face as your stripper pole," Rhyland growls from somewhere between my legs (and oh god, this position is definitely not appropriate for divine company), "we can schedule a private performance later."

I flail around like a drunk octopus, trying to untangle myself from my compromising position. My foot catches in his jacket, my other leg is somehow hooked around his neck, and I'm pretty sure I just kneed him in the ear. It's like a game of Twister gone horribly wrong.

"Though I gotta say, Angel," he purrs as I continue to struggle with this damn marshmallow suit that's intended to suffocate me, "I'm enjoying this new dismounting technique of yours."

My face feels hot as I try to salvage what's left of my dignity. I swear I can hear Gullfax laughing his golden ass off at my predicament. Even Erik seems he's trying not to choke on his amusement.

"Not my fault you're built like a redwood tree," I mutter, my face burning hotter than the sun as I try to extract my leg from behind his ear. *How did it even get there?* "A little help here would be nice instead of just enjoying the show!"

His hands finally grip my waist, but I swear he's taking his sweet time helping me down, enjoying every second of my mortification. By the time my feet touch the ground, I've given him a full-body massage with my failed attempts at dismounting.

Gullfax's mental laughter booms through my head while Erik's trying (and failing) to hide his amusement behind his hand. Great. I've just turned this into an erotic comedy show for both immortal and equine audiences.

"Glad my suffering provides quality entertainment," I grumble, trying to massage feeling back into my mutinous legs.

"Don't worry, baby," Rhyland whispers in my ear, his voice pure sin. "I've got some special exercises planned to help with those sore muscles. Lots of stretching involved."

"Odin awaits," Gullfax's voice echoes in my mind before he takes off like a golden meteor. His hooves barely touch the ground as he disappears quickly, leaving us in a cloud of dust.

"Well," I turn to my boys with what I hope is a confident smile, "according to our fancy four-legged Uber, the big man himself is waiting. Guess it's time to meet the god who makes Thor call him daddy."

The joke falls a bit flat as the reality of what we're about to do sinks in. We're about to have a sit-down with the All-Father himself. No pressure or anything—it's just the most powerful god in Norse mythology. The guy who sacrificed his eye for wisdom and hangs out with ravens who spy on the Seven Realms.

Totally normal.

I finally take in our surroundings and holy moly—if I thought the aerial view was impressive, it's nothing compared to seeing this place up close. The palace of Ásgard rises before us—soaring spires of polished gold and gleaming silver pierce the sky, their surfaces etched with runes that pulse with ancient power. Huge columns that look like they were carved from pure starlight frame a courtyard larger than a football field, and fountains that seem to flow with liquid light cast rainbow reflections across walls that weren't built by mortal hands.

"Damn," I whisper, trying to pick my jaw up off the ground. "And I thought Vegas was flashy."

The steps leading up to the entrance are carved from what looks like pure crystal, each wider and glowing with internal light. When we reach the gargantuan double doors, I'm sure my jaw is permanently unhinged. These bad boys look like they were forged by giants—their surfaces etched with scenes of ancient battles and victories that seem to move when you look at them too long.

Talk about making an entrance. The gods didn't skimp on their home improvement budget.

I lean into Rhyland, my voice barely above a whisper. "I feel like we should knock. Or, like, announce ourselves. Do they have a magical doorbell we're supposed to ring?"

Ever the pragmatist, Erik strides forward and places his palm against the gleaming surface. The doors swing open with a groan that shakes the ground beneath our feet, revealing a cavernous hall.

The moment we step inside, I'm gobsmacked. If I thought the outside was impressive, the interior is like someone took every fantasy palace ever imagined and said, "Hold my mead." The ceiling soars so high that it might contain its own weather system, complete with constellations that spin and dance overhead like a living planetarium. Chandeliers that would make the Palace of Versailles look like cheap motel lighting cascade down like frozen waterfalls of crystal and starlight, each one probably worth more than the entire global economy.

Columns that look carved from captured moonbeams rise around us, their surfaces etched with runes that pulse with power. The floor beneath our feet is some otherworldly stone I've never seen before—darker than a midnight ocean but shot through with veins of living gold that seem to shift and flow. It's like walking on a moving river.

Tapestries hang between windows tall enough to park a Boeing 747 vertically, making me question everything I know about textile production. They ripple and move like they're alive, their scenes shifting and changing as we watch—probably telling the entire universe's history.

The whole place screams, "Gods live here," in a way that makes my mortal brain want to curl up in a corner and contemplate its own insignificance. I mean, how do you even dust something like this? Is there a cleaning service? Do they have Roombas?

Great, now I'm imagining tiny Valkyries with feather dust—

"Welcome, dear ones."

I nearly give myself whiplash, spinning at the melodic voice like a kid caught doing something terrible. A woman stands there—though 'woman' seems inadequate to describe her. Her golden hair falls in gentle waves around a face that manages to be both fierce and kind, like a warrior queen who also bakes delicious cookies. Her eyes are summer-sky blue and seem to hold the wisdom of ages within their depths.

"You must be Danica," she says, her voice warm but with steel undertones—the perfect blend of maternal warmth and authority. Her gaze shifts to Rhyland, and a smile curves her perfect lips. "Rhyland, welcome back."

She turns to Erik, extending a hand with the elegant grace of someone who's had millennia to perfect the gesture. Erik, our resident master of stiff composure, looks flustered— like a diplomatic vampire caught without his backup plan.

"My lady," he bows slightly, all proper Victorian manners. "I am Erik, Rhyland's brother."

"Ah yes, the vampire brother." Her eyes sparkle with ancient knowledge. Erik clears his throat—holy shit, is Mr. Stoic nervous? File that away under 'things I never thought I'd see.'

"Yes, madam," Erik manages, his usual refined confidence wavering slightly under her knowing gaze.

She waves away his formality with a gesture that somehow manages to be regal and motherly. "Please, none of that 'madam' business," she laughs, the sound like silver bells. "I am Frigg and any family of Rhyland's is family of mine." Her smile could probably melt glaciers—"even the vampiric ones."

Erik's face softens into one of his rare genuine smiles, and Frigg beams like she just won some achievement for cracking Erik's armor.

"Come," she gestures with ethereal grace. "Let us get you settled. You must be exhausted from your journey, and I'm sure you'd appreciate a chance to refresh yourselves before dinner." Her eyes sparkle with knowing humor. "Odin awaits your company this evening—though perhaps with fewer layers of winter gear."

Oh god, yes. The thought of a hot bath and getting out of my yeti cosplay makes me want to weep with joy. Don't get me wrong, this expensive snowsuit probably saved me from becoming a frozen statue, but I'm pretty sure I'm sweating in places I didn't even know could sweat.

"Thank you," I manage to say with what I hope is appropriate gratitude, though I keep getting distracted by the Herculean statues lining the halls. Each one depicts some ancient Norse deity looking appropriately badass and immortal, and I'm pretty sure I should know who they are. However, my brain is too busy dancing about the promised bath to remember my mythology lessons.

"Heimdall has informed us of your arrival," Frigg's melodic voice drifts back to us as she leads our little group through hallways that could probably fund a small country. "We have prepared a feast in your honor, and eagerly await the pleasure of your company this evening."

I can practically hear my stomach doing a happy dance at the mention of food. Apparently, trudging through the arctic tundra and riding magical horses really revs up the old appetite. Though considering this is Ásgard, I'm guessing the menu isn't exactly burger and fries. Probably more like roasted bilgesnipe and mead served in golden chalices.

"That sounds wonderful," I manage to say with a smile that hopefully doesn't scream 'I'm hangry enough to eat my own arm.' "We're looking forward to it." And by 'it,' I mean stuffing my face with whatever delicacies they place in front of me. Manners are great and all, but at this point, I'd wrestle a Valkyrie for a dinner roll.

Rhyland's arm snakes around my waist, pulling me against his side like I'm his personal teddy bear. I glance up at my beefcake, and my heart does a little flip—his ocean-blue eyes practically glow with joy, like a kid who just discovered he inherited Disneyland. Can't blame him though—this is literally his ancestral home turf. The power radiating through our bond feels like pure electricity, hot and wild as a lightning storm.

Let's hope my sexy demigod can keep a lid on all that power before he accidentally turns someone into a S'more.

LUCIAN

23

"L ucian," Seraphina's angelic voice drops to that sweet-but-dangerous tone that makes my dick twitch. "If you don't put down that phone, I will have to get creative with my heavenly persuasion." She bends down, her golden hair brushing my cheek while her honey-warm breath teases my ear. I'm trying to text Alaric about our psychotic maker, but holy fuck—having a literal angel whispering in your ear is one hell of a distraction.

"Cupcake, if you're looking for some quality time with this walking disaster, all you gotta do is ask," I groan, already fighting a losing battle with my self-control. I've been spamming every vampire contact on my phone like a teenager with an Instagram addiction, trying to get any intel about that Psycho Dick-Tator. It's been quiet as fuck these past few weeks, and I know Lilith—that crazy cunt's got a few screws loose in her pretty little head. When she's this quiet? It means she's plotting something that'll make Lucifer's ass clench.

With Team Thunder Buns, Mr. Stiff Upper Lip and our resident scientist are off playing tourists in Cloud City (and no, not the cool Star Wars one), I'm stuck here holding down the fort like some supernatural building manager. Because, being the fun brother also means being the responsible one when everyone else decides to go dimension-hopping. Go figure.

"Just let me finish up with this, I know she's planning something, and I can't—"

Seraphina's lips find my neck, trailing soft kisses that make me groan with need. The phone slips from my fingers, forgotten. "I know. But you've been driving yourself insane since Lilith returned." Her breath whispers against my ear, sending shivers down my spine. "She's not getting in here, Lucian. We've taken every precaution—Emily and Sable's magic, Dani holding the deed..." Her tongue traces a sinful path along my throat, and my cock practically salutes. "It's time to unwind."

Christ on a cracker. A fucking meteor could be hurtling toward Earth, and I wouldn't give a single shit—not with my angel working her heavenly mojo to drag me back from the edge of this anxiety-fueled hellscape I've been trapped in. I've been losing my mind since Lilith strutted back into our lives as some demonic fashion show reject.

Finding out my brothers went full supernatural genocide on the Hawthornes to keep Satan's Side Piece locked up? That was one hell of a plot twist—killed an entire witch bloodline because they couldn't trust them to keep their magical mouth shut. Fuck a lot of good that did—now we've got their pissed-off descendant playing tag team with our maker.

Seraphina rises like sin in silk, sliding those mile-long legs between my knees as I sprawl in my favorite chair. Her fingers toy with the belt of her robe, and Mother of Merc with a mouth—that glacial smirk promises heaven beneath that flimsy fabric. My mouth goes desert-dry.

Please let her be naked. For the love of all things holy, let there be nothing but angel under that silk.

Emily dragged Sable out for some "witch gone wild" dive bar and Damon's downstairs in Vamp Kindergarten class, probably angsting his way through a few blood bags.

So it's just me and my celestial snack cake, and she seems determined to make me forget my own name. Not that I'm complaining—I'll take any distraction from the shitstorm brewing outside these walls.

"Don't be a tease, Angel Face. Give me a peek at the goods." I shoot her my patented panty-melting wink and reach for her, but she twirls away like a ballerina, that silk robe staying firmly in place.

I collapse back into my chair, grinning like the lovesick fool I am. This heavenly minx is playing coy, and it's adorable as hell. She toys with the robe's edge, drawing out the suspense until I'm ready to beg. Then, with a flutter of silk, my world detonates.

Sweet merciful fuck.

I swear I hear a choir of R-rated angels singing Hallelujah.

"See something you like, Sparky?" she purrs, and hot damn if that voice doesn't go straight to my already straining zipper. The robe slides off one shoulder, giving me a peek show that would make a saint commit felonies.

She's rocking a white lace teddy that should be illegal. The sheer fabric clings to every delicious curve like the gods themselves painted on it. Intricate patterns swirl across her breasts, drawing the eye to where pebbled nipples strain against delicate lace. The neckline plunges to her navel, held together by a single satin bow begging to be tugged loose.

The lingerie lovingly cups her ass, framing perfection in floral lace. A matching garter belt hugs her hips, clipped to sheer stockings that make her legs look like they were carved by Aphrodite herself.

My cock goes from interested to diamond-cutting hard so fast I nearly pass out. Seraphina smirks, fully aware of the effect she's having on me. She could ask me to recite the alphabet backwards, and all I'd manage is a caveman grunt.

"Holy shit..." I drag a hand down my face, brain cells committing mass suicide at the sight before me. "Like is the understatement of the fucking century, Cupcake." My hands itch to touch, to claim, to worship every inch of that heavenly body.

"You're trying to kill me, aren't you?" I groan, drinking in every lacy detail like a man dying of thirst. "This is revenge for that time I used your halo as a frisbee, isn't it?"

She laughs, the sound of pure sin wrapped in angel wings. "Maybe I just wanted to give my favorite disaster a surprise. I used that magical plastic rectangle again—I hoped you'd approve." Her smile makes my dick throb.

My credit card. She's talking about my damn credit card. And approve? Christ, I want to build a fucking shrine to whatever genius designed this scrap of lace and temptation. "Angel face, you've got 'til the count of 'I'm too fucking horny to count' to shimmy that delectable ass over here before I channel my inner caveman. And trust me, there will be grunting."

Her eyes dilate at my less-than-subtle threat, eclipsing honey-gold with 'fuck me' black. My kinky Cupcake gets off on this—the thrill of the chase, the promise of being caught and thoroughly debauched.

"Catch me if you can." She dances back with a smile.

"Oh, it's on like Donkey Kong, baby girl." I launch from the chair like a heat-seeking missile with a hard-on.

She bolts with a laugh that's purely erotic in surround sound, darting behind our couch like it's base in some X-rated game of tag.

"Playing hard to get? That's adorable. Like hiding behind furniture will save that sweet ass from what's coming." I stalk around the leather behemoth, channeling my inner predator—if predators had raging boners and zero chill.

"Maybe I'll just stay here all night," she teases, matching my movements with grace. "Safe behind my leather fortress."

"Newsflash, Cupcake—this isn't Fort Knox, and I'm about to stage a hostile takeover." I fake left, then vault over the couch like some sexually frustrated ninja. She squeals a sound that goes straight to my already aching cock.

The chase is on—like some twisted version of Cops but with more sexual tension and less tasering. Though I'm not ruling that out for later. My angelic cocktease is quick, but I'm the fucking Flash of fuck. I snatch her around the waist, hauling her back against the rock-hard evidence of how much I want her.

"Gotcha, baby girl. Now, what am I going to do with you..." I nip her ear, grinding against that perfect ass. "I'm thinking something biblical. Really put the 'sin' in sinful."

She melts into me, her ass grinding back in a way that makes me moan. "Oh, I'm sure you'll think of something," she purrs, exposing the length of her throat like an all-you-can-eat buffet.

Holy hand grenades and hot sauce. This angel's gonna be the death of my dick, and I'm 169% on board.

"Mm, you're damn right I will." I drag my teeth along her racing pulse, savoring how her breath hitches. "But first things first..." I walk us back to the couch, spinning her around and plopping down so she's straddling my lap.

She settles against me with a little shimmy, her pretty pussy pressing into my painfully hard dick. I fist my hand in her hair, tugging until she mewls. "You're not playing fair, Cupcake," I growl against her lips, my free hand sliding under that delicate lace to grab a handful of angel cake. "Strutting around in this 'make Lucian lose his mind' ensemble? That's like waving a red cape at a very horny bull with excellent taste in lingerie."

"Maybe I like playing dangerous games," she purrs, grinding down on my dick that makes my brain cells wave little white flags of surrender.

"Oh, we're way past games, Angel Face." I nip at her lower lip, enjoying her sharp intake of breath. "This is more like nuclear warfare, and baby? I've got my finger on the button."

Her laugh is pure temptation wrapped in honey. "Then what are you waiting for, Sparky? Launch the missiles."

"Fuuuck," I groan, my hand finding her hip as she rocks against me. "You're gonna make me spontaneously combust, you know that? They'll find me here, nothing but ash and a happy smile, with 'Worth It' carved into the coffee table."

"What a way to go though," rolling her hips, making my vision blur. "Death by angel—I'm sure that'll look interesting on your obituary."

"Fuck yeah, it will. 'Here lies Lucian—died doing what he loved: corrupting his angel and loving every damn second of it.'" I grab two handfuls of her perfect ass like it's my own personal slice of heaven. "Though if you keep moving like that, we might need to add 'died of extreme blue balls' to the epitaph."

She giggles before trailing those perfect lips down my neck. "We can't have that, can we? What kind of guardian angel would I be if I let you suffer?"

"A very, very cruel one." I tug at the bow, holding her teddy together, watching it fall open like the world's sexiest Christmas present. "Though I gotta say, this whole 'innocent angel gone bad' routine? Solid fucking gold. The Academy Awards of seduction."

Her fingers find my shirt buttons, popping them open. "I learned from the best," she purrs, scraping her nails down my chest. "You've been quite the... thorough teacher."

"Oh baby, class is definitely in session." I claim her mouth like I'm the fucking pope of pussy, all tongue and teeth, and 'I'll eat you alive.' She opens for me, pliant and perfect. I plunder every inch of that sweet mouth. "And tonight's lesson? 'Advanced Anatomy: The Hands-On Edition.'"

I kiss her again and focus on these delicious tits. I palm the soft weight, rolling pebbled nipples between my fingers until she's writhing in my lap.

"Lucian, please..." Her head falls back on a moan as I pinch and tug, her hips finding a desperate rhythm against my straining cock.

"Please, what, Cupcake?" I dip my head, drawing one aching nipple into my mouth like the world's most delicious lollipop. She cries out, her fingers clawing at my shoulders as I lavish her sensitive bud with my tongue. "Gotta be specific, Angel Face. Use your words, or I'll be forced to punish you. And by punished, I mean to tease you until you're begging for mercy in every language known to man and a few I just invented."

"You," she gasps, arching into my touch like a woman possessed. "I need you, Lucian. Inside me, filling me. Please, I—"

Her broken begging shatters my last thread of control. I shred the lace like wet tissue, leaving her naked and glorious. She's bare, slick, and ready for me. Knowing she's been wet this whole time, that flimsy lace is the only thing between us, and it nearly ends me.

"Time to make you see stars, Cupcake," I vow, two fingers delving into her soaked heat. She clamps down, pulling me deeper. "You gonna sing for me?"

She rides my hand with wild abandon—head tossed back in rapture as I stroke her velvet walls. I crook my fingers just right, nail that magic button, and she shatters with a silent scream. Her cunt spasms around me, gushing her release all over my hand.

I bring my fingers to my lips, savoring her taste like the finest champagne. "Goddamn," I groan, chasing every drop of heaven. "You taste like everything good in this world, baby girl. Could feast on you for days."

She watches me through heavy-lidded eyes, chest heaving. "More," she breathes, voice wrecked with need.

What can I say? I'm addicted to making my angel fall from grace. And holy hell, does she fall beautifully.

Her fingers scrabble at my zipper, desperation making her clumsy as I claim her mouth, hot and hard. Finally, she frees my straining cock, the cool air a shock against fevered skin.

I shimmy my pants down just far enough to free the beast, and she rises above me like the Queen of All Things Naughty. I stare, slack-jawed and drooling, as she lines up my throbbing cock with her dripping entrance. The first teasing brush of her silky kitty against my swollen head makes me see stars, stripes, and a whole fucking fireworks display.

"Je-*zus*, Phina," I groan, my hands gripping her hips. "Sink down on my dick, baby girl. Ride me hard, like you're gunning for the gold in the Erotic Olympics."

She gives me a smile that's pure filthy promises before lowering herself onto my aching shaft with agonizing slowness. Her sweet pussy grips me tight.

"Holy *shit*, you feel incredible," I pant, my eyes practically crossing from the sheer bliss of being buried balls-deep in her. "Gonna ruin me, Cupcake. Gonna make me forget my own name and just become a babbling puddle of Seraphina-worshipping goo."

She lets out a throaty laugh before starting to move, undulating her hips in a rhythm that should be illegal in all fifty states and at least a dozen intergalactic realms. Each roll of her body drives me deeper, and I'm pretty sure I'm seconds away from ascending to a higher plane of existence.

"That's it, Angel Face," I encourage, my fingers digging into the plush flesh of her ass. "Bounce on my cock like it's your divine purpose. Wanna feel you soaking my balls as you ride me into sweet oblivion."

Her eyes lock with mine, molten gold swirling with love, lust, and pure fucking need. It's a look that could bring mightiest warriors to their knees, and damn if I'm not ready to pledge my eternal allegiance to the Church of Seraphina's Naughty Hips.

"You feel so good," she breathes, bouncing on my cock. "Stretching me, filling me... gods, Lucian."

I give a sharp thrust upward, reveling in the way her breath hitches. "Damn right I do, Cupcake. Now take what you need from me. Ride my cock like it's the last dick on earth, and you're on a mission to save the human race."

Jesus, in a jetpack, does she deliver. She rises and falls on my shaft like it's her sole reason for existing, each downward slide taking me deeper into her heavenly pie.

I could die a happy man, buried balls-deep in my sexy seraph, but I've got plans for this pussy. Time to rock her world harder than a magnitude 10 earthquake and make her forget everything but my name and the word—

The front door crashes open like a SWAT raid. "Everyone on deck! We've got a situation that—*oh my fucking God!*" Emily's voice cuts through our passion fog like a bucket of ice water.

I let my head thunk back against the couch, staring at the ceiling like it holds the universe's secrets. Fucking fuck. Nothing kills the mood quite like a surprise visit from the Rainbow Brigade.

Seraphina tries to bolt off my lap, but I lock my arms around her waist. Like hell am I letting this perfect ass out of my grip.

Emily slaps a hand over her eyes while Sable squeaks and ducks behind her. "There are like fifty rooms in this mansion! But no—you had to defile my favorite spot. I WATCH TV THERE!"

I fumble one-handed with my zipper, the other arm still banded around Seraphina. "Aren't you two supposed to be out getting shitfaced?" I snap, finally managing to wrangle my dick back into my pants. "You know, painting the town red? Raising hell? Generally being anywhere but here?"

I blur over to her robe and quickly place it around Seraphina, yanking her back into my lap.

Seraphina's embarrassment floods our bond, her face buried in my neck. *"Don't, Cupcake,"* I soothe through our mental link. *"This is our house. We'll fuck on any surface we damn well please."*

Emily groans, peeking through her fingers like she's watching a train wreck in slow motion. "What is this, the supernatural edition of OnlyFans? Some of us actually SIT on that couch, you horny disasters." Her eyes flick to Seraphina with a mix of sympathy and amusement. "Honey, if Count Hornula here is making you fulfill his exhibitionist fantasies, just give me the signal. I've got a spell that'll Hex his dick off."

"Okay, first of all, rude," I gasp, clutching my chest in mock offense. "I would never pressure my angel to do anything she didn't enthusiastically beg for. And second..." I turn to Seraphina with a wicked grin. "Baby, tell Rainbow Brite over there how much you love when I rail you on the couch."

Seraphina's face flames brighter than the sun. "Lucian!" She smacks my chest, but I catch the hint of a smile playing on her lips.

"You're both nasty," Emily declares, throwing her hands up in defeat. "Just nasty. I hope you know you're steam-cleaning every inch of that couch. Twice."

"Only twice? That's cute." I waggle my eyebrows. "Challenge accep—OW! Cupcake!"

Seraphina cuts off my retort with a sharp elbow to the ribs. "We promise to be more discreet in the future," she assures Emily, ever the polite one even with a raging blush.

Emily drops onto the nearest chair, rubbing her temples like she's nursing the mother of all magical migraines. "As much as I'd love to keep roasting your public displays of passion, we've got bigger problems." Her voice carries the weight of an oncoming apocalypse. "We've got a Category five shitstorm brewing."

My internal alarm goes from "mild concern" to "holy fucking catastrophe" in zero seconds flat. Even Seraphina's earlier blush vanishes.

"What now?" I demand, already knowing this is gonna be worse than that time I tried to teach Erik how to use Twitter.

"It's Lilith." Emily's face hardens, her eyes gleaming with panic. "She and Morgan opened a rift. But that's not the worst part—" She swallows hard, looking between us with genuine fear. "Something came through. Something big."

RHYLAND

24

Fucking surreal doesn't even begin to cover this shit.

This is beyond anything I could have imagined. One minute, I'm dealing with vampire drama; the next, I'm soaring through the clouds on my father's battle-bred stallion. Life's got one hell of a sense of humor.

My fierce little angel amazes me by chattering up Gullfax like they're old friends. The beast practically preened when she translated his pride at carrying me, telling me how honored he is to serve. That kind of legacy hits harder than any battle wound.

They've set us up in quarters that would make mortal kings weep with envy. Everything gleams like polished moonstone and ancient power. After washing off the realm-hopping grime in a bath that could double as a small lake, we're dressed and seated at the table.

And by dressed, I mean holy fucking shit. My woman's gown looks crafted from pure sin and warrior's dreams. The silvery fabric hugs every curve, Norse runes tracing paths I want to follow with my tongue, gold armbands wrapped delicately around her biceps. That neckline dips just low enough to make my fangs ache, and the slit up her thigh is going to drive me fucking insane all night. Not that it matters what she wears—Dani could be dressed in a garbage bag, and I'd still want to bend her over the nearest surface—but seeing this much of her skin on display? Makes me want to wrap her in my jacket and snarl at anyone who dares to look too long.

Her hair cascades down her back like a waterfall of chocolate, intricate braids woven with precious beads that catch the light with every movement. The style screams warrior princess, but all I can think about is how much I want to wrap those silken strands around my fist and—yeah, better keep those thoughts in check. Not the time or place to let my inner beast show how much my mate's beauty affects me.

They've got me in some fancy warrior get-up—black leather pants, a midnight blue tunic with silver runes, and a vest that probably costs more than most kingdoms. At least the boots are made for combat—if anyone's eyes linger too long on my mate tonight, they might find out exactly how well they're crafted for ass-kicking.

This table is a fucking behemoth, groaning under the weight of a feast that could feed an army of warriors. We're talking a whole roasted boar that could gore a man, mountains of potatoes, and piles of fruits and veggies I can't even name.

I lean into Dani, my lips brushing her ear as I mentally connect, *"Try to keep those sexy table manners in check, Angel. Don't need these gods knowing what that mouth can really do."* I smirk, remembering how her enthusiasm for a meal gets me rock-hard and ready. The way she devours everything with gusto, all satisfied moans and licking her fingers clean? Fucking hot as hell. But maybe not the best look in front of the Gods.

"Oh, you are so going to regret that later, mister," Dani's mental voice is pure sass, that dangerous, sweet tone promising retribution. *"Keep it up, and I might just have to get creative with my... appreciation of the cuisine if you catch my drift."*

The promise in her words sends a bolt of heat straight to my cock. My girl never backs down from a challenge, and I fucking love her for it. But as much as I'd like to take her up on that offer right here and now, I'm pretty sure Odin wouldn't appreciate me defiling his dining table.

"I trust your chambers are to your satisfaction." Odin's voice rolls like distant thunder across the table.

"Yes, they're beautiful. Though I'm a bit lost on the proper etiquette for addressing the king of gods," Dani quips, her smile bright despite the nervousness I feel through our bond. "Do I curtsy? Bow? Sacrifice a goat?"

A rumbling laugh escapes the All-Father. "Odin will suffice, child. Such formalities have no place among those destined to reshape the realms." He raises his goblet, studying her with that penetrating gaze. "It brings me great pleasure to finally meet you, Lightborn."

Dani's cheeks flush as she raises her glass, some of her usual sass returning. "Right back at you. Love what you've done with the place."

"The architectural magnificence is truly remarkable," Erik says from my left, his refined tone conveying measured appreciation. "One could spend centuries studying its intricacies."

"You're too kind," Frigg's voice flows like liquid silver, her smile radiant. But something shadows her ethereal features as she adds, "We've worked tirelessly to preserve its glory... though I fear for how long we can maintain such splendor."

"What do you mean?" Dani's brow furrows that analytical mind of hers already working overtime.

Heimdall's acid-green eyes sweep across the table like searchlights. "She speaks of the Dark Prophecy. We've already witnessed this realm's destruction once during Ragnarök—rebuilt it from ashes and—"

"—And we pray fervently that Moretemis shall not succeed where others failed," Frigg interjects, her tone tight with concern. "Your victory is crucial, both of you."

The memories slam into me like a battle axe—nights spent in smoky longhouses, drinking mead while village elders spun tales of Ragnarök. That apocalyptic clusterfuck tore through the realms like a hurricane, leaving dead gods in its wake. Thor, that mighty bastard, went out like a true warrior, taking down that world serpent even as its venom killed him. Tyr lost his final battle, and Freya fell in flames—one by one, those immortal powerhouses dropped like flies. Only a handful crawled out of that cosmic shitstorm alive Odin, Heimdall, and that chaos-loving prick Loki, who probably orchestrated half the carnage himself.

And my father... Magni. However, finding out his fate is a whole different kind of gut punch. Guess fighting ancient darkness runs in the fucking family.

Next to Frigg sits some pretty boy who looks like he's never seen a day of actual combat—all golden hair and perfect features, decked out in pristine white and gold armor that's probably never tasted blood. Everything about him screams privileged prince, from his perfectly styled hair to the way he carries himself like he owns the fucking place. The kind of immortal who's probably never had to fight for a damn thing in his life.

"Forgive my manners," Frigg gestures to the golden-haired boy. "May I present our son, Baldr. He shall accompany you on your quest."

"The fuck he will," I growl before I can stop myself. The last thing we need is some pampered prince tagging along.

"Rhyland..." Dani hisses, gripping my arm in warning.

"Baldr's wisdom, earned in the halls of Valhalla itself, shall light your path," Odin's voice crashes like storm waves. "The secrets of our realm flow through his veins as surely as the waters of Urðarbrunnr. His knowledge shall prove as vital as Mímir's counsel in the trials ahead."

The pretty boy has the nerve to look smug like he's just been handed the keys to the kingdom. Great. Just fucking great. Another immortal complication we need to add to this shit.

Dinner drags on like a fucking funeral march, the silence broken only by Odin's sporadic interrogation of Dani. He's grilling her like she's on trial—her take on this cosmic shit-show, and how much she looks like Bryn. That name alone sends Dani's emotions ricocheting through our bond like a pinball.

"So, any chance I could get a face-to-face with this long-lost sister of mine?" Dani asks, her casual tone barely masking the hunger for answers.

"Indeed. Bryn commands Valor's Watch, training our Valkyrie warriors," Odin rumbles. "That should be your next destination."

I can practically taste Dani's anxiety through our link, and the unspoken questions about her father clawing at her insides. But my girl's too bright to poke that hornet's nest now. Instead, she focuses on the issue hanging over us like a guillotine.

"Okay, I have to ask. The Soul Stone," she says, her voice steady as a sniper's aim. "Rhyland told me of its origins—how it was made. But how did it end up broken?"

Damn, good question. One I should've thought to ask when they dropped that bomb about my mother's power.

"An excellent question, indeed, Little Huntress," Erik nods, his tone as stiff as his posture.

Frigg sets her silver fork down, her voice soft. "Loki," she breathes, like the name itself is poison. "That trickster shattered the stone, scattering its pieces across the Seven Realms like seeds of chaos."

Of fucking course. Leave it to that trouble-loving prick to turn a simple task into a realm-wide scavenger hunt.

"I'm assuming he had a reason—"

"He sought to thwart our victory over the Shadow Lord!" Odin's fist crashes against the ancient table with thunderous force, making the vessels dance. His single eye blazes with the fury of a thousand burning worlds. "Once again, the Trickster's poisoned words and serpent's schemes wound the halls of Ásgard deeper than any giant's blade. The prophecies were known to him, carved in the roots of Yggdrasil itself!" His voice drops to a rumble. "Yet he chose the path of Chaos, betraying not just his kin but all Seven Realms. Even now, his treachery echoes through Ginnungagap's depths."

The pieces click into place like a jigsaw puzzle made of pure fuckery. Leave it to Loki to turn a weapon of mass destruction into his personal game of hide and seek. That sneaky son of a bitch probably sat back and laughed his immortal ass off while watching everyone scramble to find them.

"Well, on the bright side, we've managed to snag all three pieces," Dani offers, but I can feel her nerves fraying through our bond. "Well, sort of..." She lays out the truth that might blow this feast to Hell.

"This outcome was foreseen," Frigg intones. "The path to reclaiming what was lost shall be fraught with peril. I have witnessed it in the threads of fate—a great battle, an enemy reborn, and a sacrifice that shall shake the very foundations of the realms."

Yeah, no fucking shit. When has anything in our lives been simple? At this point, I'd be more surprised if the universe didn't try to bend us over and—

"You must tread carefully," Frigg warns. "The forces you face will test you in ways you cannot imagine. But remember, even in the darkest of times, hope remains. You two are the key to salvation—never forget that."

I watch Dani swallow hard, plastering on that fierce smile I know too damn well. But I feel her terror spike at Frigg's words.

"What of the Zephyrite stone?" Erik inquires, his refined tone cutting through the doom and gloom like a blade. Trust Mr. Stoic to keep us focused on the mission.

"The Elemental Nexus," pretty boy Baldr finally decides to grace us with his voice, speaking like he's announcing the second coming. His perfect face lights up with excitement. "Getting there isn't exactly a casual stroll through Zephyria's elements and beasts. You'll need warriors—*real* warriors—to reach it."

The way he emphasizes "real warriors" makes my teeth itch like this pampered prince would know jack shit about actual combat. However, something in his tone suggests he knows more than he's letting on like he's been waiting all night to drop this particular bomb.

"Beasts? What kind of beasts are we talking about here?" Dani asks.

"Oh, you didn't think our realm would be all rainbow bridges and golden halls, did you?" Baldr's lips curl into a knowing smirk, and I fight the urge to introduce his face to the table. "There are... dangers."

"Gee, thanks for *that* detailed intel." Dani fires back, her warm amber eyes sparking. "Any chance you could be a bit more specific about these 'dangers,' or should I just assume everything is trying to kill us?"

"Frost giants, for one," Heimdall interjects. "But they are far from the only threat you may encounter, lightborn." He leans forward, ancient eyes gleaming. "Draugr—the undead—roam the icy wastes of Valhalla's Veil, their hunger for living flesh insatiable. Trolls lurk in the surrounding areas, their strength rivaling even the mightiest warriors. And the great eagles of Hræsvelgr..." He shakes his head, golden armor glinting. "Pray you do not draw the attention of those mammoth, sky-darkening terrors."

Fuck. Sounds like this little field trip is gonna be a real walk in the park—if that park was filled with undead assholes, angry giants, and oversized pigeons from hell.

"The likeness you bear to your sister strikes deep," Odin's voice rumbles, his single eye blazing with ancient pride. "You both possess the same fire in your spirits, that warrior's tongue that fears no god nor giant." His piercing gaze shifts to me, a weight of centuries behind it. "And you, heir of Magni—by the Norns themselves, it is as if my grandson stands before me once more. The same fire burns in your eyes, ready to shake the very foundations of the Seven Worlds."

He rises like a mountain stirring to life, power radiating from him. "Rest well this night, for when Sól's golden chariot breaks the veil of darkness, Baldr, Heimdall, and Bryn shall guide you through the paths of Yggdrasil. The road ahead demands strength that only sleep can restore."

Without another word, he strides from the great hall, each step echoing with authority. Even after his departure, the weight of his presence hangs in the air like the aftermath of a storm.

"Where the hell is Loki now?" I demand, focusing on Frigg.

God knows I'd love to run into that slippery bastard on our quest.

"The Trickster vanished like morning mist after his betrayal," Frigg conveys, ancient wisdom dancing in her summer-sky eyes. "Odin's fury shook the very roots of Yggdrasil itself when he discovered his treachery." Her delicate fingers trace patterns on the ancient table as if reading the threads of fate itself. "With the realms sealed by Elysium's power, Loki's path became hidden even from my sight..." She pauses, knowledge and concern mingling in her ethereal features. "Yet whispers reach us still, carried on winds as old as time—tales of the Serpent's Child weaving his schemes from shadows where even Heimdall's gaze cannot pierce."

Shit.

LUCIAN

25

"**H**old up, time out, flag on the play," I interrupt, my brain doing mental parkour to keep up with this fuckery. "A rift? Like the universe just split its cosmic pants?"

Sable, our resident ray of sunshine, breaks it down for me. "A rift is essentially a break in the barriers between realms," she explains patiently. "If Lilith used the Soul Stone, she could have forced an opening to the Shadow Realm."

I feel my balls trying to climb back into my body at the mere mention of that unholy shithole. "The Shadow Realm? Are you saying Lilith just rang the Devil's doorbell? Because if Moretemis is out for a leisurely stroll, we're all majorly boned."

"We're still trying to piece together the specifics of what or *who* slipped through the rift," Sable says. "But we—the witches feel it. Whatever it is, it's...something we can't ignore."

"Wait, I thought Dani was our only reality-ripper extraordinaire. When did we start handing out interdimensional scissors to the new kids on the block?"

"Well, it appears that Morgan has quite a bit of power," Sable explains, her voice soft and knowing, like a wise old owl with a PhD in witchy bullshit. "And with their half of the stone..."

Emily, perched on her throne of judgment like the queen of snark, looks torn between suiting up for battle and having a full-on meltdown. "Should we phone home to E.T.? You know, get our favorite feisty savior back here before shit hits the supernatural fan?"

Sable's eyes widen, her head shaking faster than a drunk bobblehead. "I don't think that's a good idea. Remember how upset Dani was the last time we pulled her away? She's dealing with a lot right now. Letting her focus on her quest might be best while we handle things here."

"Okay, new game plan," Emily declares, her eyes glinting with that 'done with this bullshit' look. "Sable, dig through your spell book and find us a way to text Dani without, you know, actual phones." After Sable's quick nod, Emily turns to us with her patented 'why is this my life' expression. "As for right now, pack up the Scooby Gang. We're heading to ground zero and see if we can stitch reality back together before anything else decides to crash our realm."

Fresh from his stint in Baby Vamp Bootcamp, Damon saunters into the kitchen and plops down in a chair. He's got a blood bag dangling from his hand and a look on his face that screams, "I'm one crisis away from a full-blown emo phase." But hey, credit where it's due—the kid's been handling this whole vampire gig like a champ. As long as he keeps suckling on that crimson Capri Sun, he's... well, not a total liability.

Still, I'm not taking any chances with my angel cake. I tug Seraphina into my lap, putting a good stretch of marble countertop between her and the baby fang.

"What's got you guys all riled up?" Damon asks, with all the enthusiasm of a DMV employee on a Monday morning.

"How's the bloodsucking business treating you, Damon?" Emily asks, her tone softening a fraction when addressing Dani's brother.

"Getting better. The urges aren't as—"

"Yeah, that's fascinating and all," I cut in, turning to Emily and completely steamrolling over Damon's brooding vampire diary moment. "but can we focus on the more pressing issue? Where exactly is this cosmic tear in reality's pants? You got some magical Google Maps that can point us toward certain doom? Because I'm not in the mood to play Marco Polo with a portal to Satan's basement."

Sable leans forward, her expression grave. "You remember Thornewood Castle, right?"

I feel my left eye twitch at the mention of that godforsaken place. The same castle where Azrael and his witchy sidekick played Operation on my brain and held me captive. The site of our first epic showdown with this shit show.

"You've gotta be kidding me," I groan, my head falling in exasperation. "The rift is there? In the same place, we went nuclear on a coven of crazy to stop this shit the first time around?"

Sable nods solemnly. "The catacombs beneath the castle, to be precise. Given the history of past attempts, it's the only spot where the veil between realms is thin enough."

"Well, fuck me gently with a chainsaw," I mutter, channeling my inner Ash Williams. "Looks like we're heading back to the crime scene, kids."

"What if it's a trap?" Seraphina's gentle voice carries a hint of steel as her fingers dig into my arm. "What if *she's* there? I won't let you anywhere near her, Lucian." The fierce protectiveness in her tone goes straight to my dick. There is nothing hotter than my angel getting all commanding.

"It's alright, Sera," Emily soothes. "Sable and I were able to track her. Our intel confirms Lilith is far from here. She took whatever she managed to grab through the rift with her."

"Hold the fucking phone!" I explode. "You're telling me you've got some magical LoJack on that psychotic bitch? And you're just mentioning this *now*? After weeks of me losing my shit trying to figure out where she slithered off to?"

"Oh, I'm sorry," Emily's eyes roll so hard they probably get frequent flyer miles. "I didn't realize I needed to submit my magical activities for your approval, Count Dramatic. And for your information, we only figured out we could track her prehistoric ass a few hours ago."

"Alya helped us," Sable explains softly. "She has...unique tracking abilities."

"Define 'unique,'" I press.

"Let's just say she's got a knack for tracking sup's signatures like a bloodhound," Emily drawls, examining her nails like she's bored with my questions.

When I just stare at her like a concussed puppy, she rolls her eyes again. "Not that I expect your last two brain cells to grasp the finer points of witchcraft, but Alya can taste the residual magic in the air— literally. She can pick up magical traces like they're different flavors of evil. Word is, our favorite psycho-witch's magic tastes like rotten cherries and desperation. In Oregon.

Well, excuse me for not being up to date on the Food Network: Witch Edition.

Oregon? At least that bloodsucking fashion disaster is out of our state. Though knowing our luck, she's probably turning Portland into her personal vampire speakeasy.

The Bentley purrs to a stop, and I take a moment to appreciate the sheer creeptastic vibes this place is giving off. Thornewood Castle looms in the distance like a rejected Hogwarts, all gothic spires and "abandon all hope" energy.

The night sky is pulling a full-on emo phase, with stars playing hide-and-seek behind these thick-ass trees, practically wearing signs saying, "Only idiots proceed beyond this point." And guess what? We're today's winning idiots!

I lace my fingers with Seraphina's, our hands becoming a knot of 'oh shit, we're really doing this.' We're pulling a classic horror flick move, traipsing across this lawn that's so overgrown, I swear the grass is hissing, "You dumb fucks are gonna die" with every step. And get a load of that lake, would you? Shimmering in the moonlight like a giant obsidian mirror, still as a corpse at a wake. Which, let's be real, with our track record of epically bad decisions, it's probably where the bodies are buried. Just add water and stir for an instant nightmare cocktail.

The entrance to the catacombs yawns open like Satan's personal glory hole, all dank stone and "welcome to your worst nightmare" ambiance. The whole setup is screaming "horror movie cliché" louder than a sorority girl in a slasher film.

If mist starts rolling out of there, I'm officially submitting my resignation from this shit.

I mean, look at this place. It's like someone watched every B-grade horror flick on Netflix, took notes, and then decided to build the ultimate "fuck around and find out" tourist trap. All we need now is some creepy Latin chanting and maybe a virgin sacrifice to complete the "about to die horribly" aesthetic.

Though finding a virgin in this group would be harder than finding a vegetarian at a vampire convention.

Emily and Sable better not be blowing smoke up my ass about this. It's one thing to square off against an interdimensional glory hole to Satan's asscrack—it's another to go poking at it with the Soul Stone. I mean, seriously, would it kill the universe to provide a damn instruction manual for these things? I was skeptical as fuck when the Witchy Wonder twins suggested using our half of the stone to seal this rift. If we somehow fumble this cursed rock, let's just say Dani will roast my undead nuts over an open flame. And that's if I'm lucky.

I take a deep, unnecessary breath, the scent of ancient evil and probable regret filling my lungs. "Alright, ladies," I say, my voice echoing through the night like a douchebag in a canyon. "In and out. No fucking around."

When we step inside the catacombs, it's like walking into a mausoleum's moldy armpit. The air is thick and heavy, reeking of centuries-old dust and stale secrets. And because this place wasn't creepy enough, there's a whole Pinterest board of bones decorating the walls, with skulls giving us their best "you're gonna die" grins from every possible angle. Our footsteps echo through the narrow passageways, the sound bouncing off the damp stone like a mocking chorus of the damned.

"Do you feel that?" Seraphina goes rigid beside me, her hand clutching mine like a lifeline. A wave of fear crashes through our bond, hitting me like a kick to the nuts. I pull her closer, wrapping my arm around her waist like I can physically shield her from the impending shitstorm. I'm starting to regret bringing her along, but my stubborn angel insisted on being here. Apparently, the phrase "self-preservation" isn't in her celestial vocabulary.

"It's pure evil, Lucian," Seraphina's voice trembles through my mind. *"I've never felt anything like this before."*

"Oh, I feel it alright," Emily mutters, her eyes darting around the gloom like she's expecting some eldritch horror to leap out. "Whatever it is, it's bad news bears."

We see it as we venture deeper into this subterranean house of horrors. It's like someone took a sledgehammer to reality itself, leaving a gaping wound in the fabric of the universe. The edges of the rift shimmer and writhe, tendrils of inky smoke curling out like grasping fingers. The rift pulses eerie light, casting sickly shadows across the stone walls. The air around it feels wrong like it's been tainted by something that shouldn't exist in this or any other realm.

Really brings down the property value of the whole "reality" neighborhood, if you ask me.

"Fuck, fuck, fuck," I mutter under my breath, my eyes darting between the cosmic tear and the two witches who are our only hope of unfucking this situation. "Alright, no more screwing around. It's time to put your magical money where your mouth is and seal this blow hole before something really nasty decides to come a-knocking."

Emily fixes me with a glare that's one part steely resolve, two parts 'I will curse your dick into a cactus if you push me.' She holds out her hand, fingers snapping like an impatient diva. "Cough up the magic pebble, jackass. And start making offerings to whatever twisted gods you worship because if this goes sideways, we're all screwed."

"Wow, way to sugarcoat it, *Glinda*," I snark, fishing the Soul Stone out of my pocket like a used tissue. "Why don't you just tell me to bend over and kiss my ass goodbye while you're at it?"

I drop the stone into her waiting palm, trying to ignore how it pulses with malevolent energy. "Just don't go all Dark Phoenix on us, yeah? I'd rather not have to explain to my sister-in-law why her best friend went nuclear and turned us all into demonic kibble."

Emily rolls her eyes. "Gee, thanks for the pep talk, Coach. Really feeling the confidence here." She closes her fingers around the stone, taking a deep breath like she's about to dive into the deep end of a cursed pool. "Alright, let's see if all those late-night Latin study sessions were worth the crippling student debt."

Emily's eyes drift shut as she begins to chant. The words are ancient and guttural, the kind of language that could unravel the very fabric of the universe if spoken just right. Or just wrong, depending on your perspective.

"Claudere portam, et signa fractum, restituo velum inter mundos!"

Seraphina presses close to my back, her fingers curling into my shirt like a lifeline. I can feel her trembling, the fear rolling off her in waves. I reach back, gripping her hip in silent reassurance. I'll be damned if I let anything happen to my angel cake, even if I have to personally punch every eldritch abomination in the face to keep her safe.

Sable steps up behind Emily, placing her hands on her shoulders like she's jump-starting a car battery. She joins in the chanting, her voice rising perfectly with Emily's.

"Ex umbra in lucem, ex nocte in diem, ex inferis ad vitam!"

The air around us begins to crackle with power—the fine hairs on the back of my neck standing at attention. Emily's brow furrows—sweat beading on her forehead as she pours every ounce of her considerable magical mojo into the spell. The rift pulses and writhes like a living thing, tendrils of inky smoke lashing out as if in defiance of the witches' attempts to close it.

But Emily is a fucking force of nature, her power bolstered by the strength of a hundred witches. She grits her teeth, her hand shaking to channel the stone's energy into the rift. Emily's closed hand begins to glow an eerie purple, pulsing in time with the tear in reality.

"Sigillum fractum, clausus portam, finem tenebris!" Emily's voice rises to a fever pitch, the words tearing from her throat like they're being ripped out by force.

The rift shudders and convulses, the edges beginning to seal shut like a gruesome wound knitting itself back together. The air is filled with the sound of reality itself screaming in protest, a high-pitched whine that sets my teeth on edge and makes my brain feel like it's about to leak out of my ears.

Just as the rift is about to close completely—

"Oh, *shiiiit*" I breathe, instinctively pushing Seraphina further behind me. "That's not good. That's so *very, very* not good!"

The creature that just slipped through the rapidly closing rift is the stuff of nightmares. It's tall, easily towering over all of us, with a body that looks carved from the darkest shadows. Its skin is mottled black like it's been scorched by the fires of hell, and wicked-looking spikes protrude from its shoulders and spine like some demonic porcupine.

But the face seals the deal on the whole 'unholy abomination' vibe. Its features are twisted and grotesque, with a maw full of razor-sharp teeth that look like they could shred flesh from bone with ease. Horns curl back from its skull like a crown of thorns and its eyes... Christ, its eyes are like pits of pure, malevolent flame, burning with an intelligence that makes my skin crawl.

Seraphina whimpers behind me, trembling.

Emily and Sable exchange a look of 'oh shit,' but to their credit, they don't stop chanting. If anything, they redouble their efforts, their voices rising to a desperate crescendo as they pour every last ounce of power into sealing the rift.

"Finem! Finem! FINEM!" Emily screams, her hand clenched so tightly around the Soul Stone that I'm pretty sure it's gonna leave a permanent impression.

With a final, gut-wrenching howl, the rift slams shut, the edges sealing together like a zipper being pulled closed by the hand of God himself. The sudden absence of sound is almost deafening, the only noise the ragged breathing of four people who just stared down the barrel of the apocalypse and lived to tell the tale.

But we're not out of the woods yet. Not by a long shot. Because now we've got a pissed-off demon from the depths of hell itself stalking towards us, its clawed feet gouging deep furrows into the stone with each step.

"Alright, new plan," I announce, my voice only shaking slightly. "So far, we've checked off 'seal gaping asshole' and 'prevent the universe from going kaboom' from our to-do list. Gold stars all around! But now we've got this walking Hot Topic mascot. Anyone got a demon-sized rolled-up newspaper we can smack it with?"

Emily and Sable look at each other, then back at the demon, then back at each other. I can practically see the gears turning in their heads, the calculations of 'Can we magic this thing back to the abyss before it rips our faces off?' running at lightning speed.

"I'm open to suggestions," Emily begins to back up, her voice strained with exhaustion and panic. "Because I'm running on empty here, and I don't think asking it nicely to pretty please go back to whatever circle of hell it crawled out of is gonna cut it!"

I take a deep breath, squaring my shoulders as I step forward. "Well, then. Guess it's time for Plan B."

Seraphina's hand shoots out, gripping my arm. "Lucian, no. You can't—"

"*Maga.*" The demon's voice is like gravel being dragged over a cheese grater, low and menacing. Its burning gaze locks onto Emily like she's the only thing in the room worth noticing.

Emily, to her eternal credit, doesn't even flinch. She thrusts out her hand like a magical crossing guard. "*Daemonium, ego praecipio tibi! Flectere genua et oboedire!*"

And then, in a twist that makes my brain do a record scratch, the big evil demon drops to one knee like a fucking medieval knight pledging fealty. "*Ego ad mandatum tuum, venefica,*" it rumbles, its head bowed in submission.

I blink. Once. Twice. Nope, still see a creature straight outta Satan's asshole kneeling at the feet of my sister-in-law's bestie. "Well, then," I mutter, my jaw hanging open like a broken puppet.

Seraphina's grip on my arm tightens, her nails digging into my skin like she's trying to anchor herself to reality. I don't blame her. I'm half-convinced I'm hallucinating this whole thing, and any second now, I'm gonna wake up in a padded room with a straitjacket and a daily dose of the good drugs. But nope, this is happening.

Emily, our resident witch queen, just made a fucking demon her bitch. And I thought I'd seen everything.

"Uh, Em?" I venture, taking a cautious step forward. "Not that I'm not impressed by your sudden foray into demon taming, but what the actual fuck just happened?"

Emily glances back at me, her eyes wide with shock and dawning realization. "I... I think I just bound him to my will," she says slowly like she's testing out the words as she says them. "Holy shit, I didn't even know I could do that."

"That makes two of us," I mutter, eyeing the kneeling demon warily.

Now we have to figure out what the hell to do with our new pet hellspawn. Because something tells me this isn't the kind of stray you can take home and feed table scraps.

"*Ego ad mandatum tuum, domine mi.*" it says to Emily, voice like gravel in a blender. "*Potestatem deae habes et ego apud te miserere.*"

"What the hell is it saying?"

"He said, 'I'm at your command, My Lady. You possess the powers of a goddess. I am at your mercy.'" Emily conveys.

"Wow, laying it on thick there, aren't we, edgelord?"

Emily's eyes go wide, then smirks. "Is that so?"

Oh *shit*—I know that look. That's Emily's patented "I'm about to be a magnificent asshole" face.

Emily's lips curl into a shit-eating grin. "*Oh,* this is gonna be good. Okay, big guy. Do your best chicken impression!"

Big, dark, and demonic just stares at her like she's lost her mind. "Right—maybe your new pet only speaks the language of dead people and Catholic guilt."

"*Click sicut pullum,*" Emily tries again, because apparently demon-taming isn't entertaining enough.

The demon's flaming eyes narrow like someone just insulted his mother. "*Non sum spectaculum aliquod entertainment.*"

Emily snorts like a teenager who just found their parent's browser history.

"Translation for those of us who didn't take 'Speaking in Tongues 101'?"

"He said 'I am not some entertainment show.'" Emily repeats, looking way too amused. "Our demon's got *sass!*"

Great. Just what we needed. A demon with attitude.

"Uh, guys?' Sable interjects, looking two seconds away from shitting her pants, "Not to rain on this weird little parade, but can we continue this discussion somewhere that's not a creepy catacomb full of unspeakable evil? Just a thought."

I clap my hands together, echoing through the chamber like a gunshot. "Alright, kids, mission accomplished! We've sealed the butt hole, acquired a pet demon, and I'm missing my favorite TV show. Time to blow this popsicle stand before something else decides to crash our party."

I turn to Emily, gesturing grandly to her new pet. "After you, O Mistress of the Damned. Lead the way."

Emily rolls her eyes, but I can see the hint of a smile playing at the corners of her lips. She snaps her fingers, pointing towards the exit. *"Audisti hominem. Movere eam."*

The demon rises, towering over us like a living shadow. It inclines its head towards Emily, a gesture of respect that looks utterly bizarre coming from a creature that probably eats souls for breakfast. *"Ut iubes, hera."*

And with that, our little party of misfits and monsters makes its way out of the catacombs, one apocalypse averted, and one demon tamed.

All in a day's work for the fucking Scooby Gang from hell.

DANICA

26

After a flight that made my inner thighs scream for mercy, Gullfax finally touches down outside a towering ice gate that looks like it was built by the abominable snowman. Our golden boy takes a knee, while Rhyland helps me navigate the dismount without turning it into another unintentional pole dance.

Don't get me wrong—galloping through actual clouds for four hours straight on a magical stallion is exactly as epic as it sounds, but nobody warns you about the saddle soreness of straddling a horse at a thousand feet.

The view was insane, though—like being in first class if the airplane was made of pure muscle and golden fur, and the windows were replaced with face-numbing wind and cotton candy clouds. We'd burst through cloud banks that felt like cool mist against my skin, then emerge into patches of pure sunlight—then turning everything into a wintery starry night. Watching the landscape below shift from Ásgard's gleaming spires to Zephyria's snow-capped peaks was like witnessing geography on fast-forward.

I'm rocking some serious shieldmaiden chic—a white fur-lined cloak, leather bracers, and buckskin pants that are cozy and badass. And, of course, my trusty daggers are strapped to my hips because a girl's gotta accessorize. Rhyland and Erik look like they just stepped off the "Viking Vogue" cover, all rugged furs and dangerous charm.

"My lady, welcome to Valor's Watch," Gullfax announces as I slide down Rhyland's chest, trying not to get distracted by the feel of his abs through his tunic.

Speaking of distractions, can we talk about Baldr's ride? Gullfax isn't the only equine overachiever in this realm. Baldr's mount is none other than Sleipnir, Odin's steed. And get this—the horse has eight legs. Eight. As in, two times the normal amount.

What, were four legs just not enough for the All-Father? Did he look at regular horses and go, "Nah, needs more limbs"?

"Thanks for not dropping me from the stratosphere, buddy," I murmur to Gullfax, reaching up to give our charger an appreciative scratch. He dips his big head with all the grace of a gentleman, though I swear I catch a glimmer of amusement in those otherworldly eyes.

The wind is biting enough to make a polar bear think twice about going outside, but between my fancy Viking fur coat (which is totally going in my permanent wardrobe rotation) and my own personal power heater, I'm managing not to turn into a Dani-sickle.

A stable hand appears—because even divine warrior compounds need horse wranglers—and leads Gullfax away toward what looks like the Ritz-Carlton of horse accommodations.

"I will await for you both," Gullfax says as he follows with his usual majestic swagger, probably looking forward to whatever passes for premium hay in this realm.

We crunch our way through the ankle-deep snow towards a gate that looks like it was carved out of a glacier by a giant with anger issues. Seriously, this thing is massive. And guarding it? A bunch of Viking dudes who look like they go tree tipping for fun. They stand there, still as statues, their armor and weapons glinting in the frosty light.

Baldr takes the lead, strutting to the gate like he owns the place. Which, I guess, technically, he does, being Odin's son and all. He has a quick chat with one of the guards, and then, with a groan that sounds like a giant waking up, the gates begin to swing open.

We follow Baldr inside, and the moment I cross the threshold, it feels like someone just pulled the plug on my mojo. I gasp, stumbling a step as a wave of exhaustion hits me. Erik and Rhyland freeze mid-stride, looking as confused as I feel.

"What the hell? Did someone turn off our magic?" I ask, trying to shake off the sudden drain.

Baldr glances back, a smug little smile on his perfect face. "Ah, yes. Forgive me, I forgot to mention. These ancient runes—" he gestures to the glowing symbols carved into the archway, "—they equalize all who enter. Powers, enhanced abilities, magical advantages... all temporarily suppressed."

He spreads his hands with theatrical flair. "Can't have a fair training ground if some warriors can throw lightning while others rely on steel, now can we? The wards leave only your natural physical abilities and fighting skills." His eyes gleam with amusement at our discomfort. "Don't worry—healing factors remain intact. We're not barbarians, after all. Dead warriors make for rather boring training sessions, wouldn't you agree?"

"It takes everything," Rhyland whispers, and I can practically feel his frustration.

"Care to elaborate on that, babe?" I shoot back, my frown deepening by the second.

"Meaning even our vampire abilities are gone. And our bond—I can't feel you." he clarifies, and suddenly, I feel like I've been sucker-punched.

He's right. I can't feel him either.

I glance at Erik, hoping for reassurance, but he nods grimly. Great, it's not just me—we're all powerless in this supernatural dead zone.

"Well, this just keeps getting better and better," I grumble, wondering if the Valkyries have a suggestion box where I can file a complaint.

"Can't even get into your pretty little head," Rhyland growls, sounding like a lion who's had his favorite toy taken away. I instinctively reach for our mental bond, only to hit the psychic equivalent of a brick wall. Radio silence. Supernatural connection? Currently out of service.

"Ah, yes." Baldr interjects. "Fascinating how quickly we rely on those mental links, isn't it?" He taps his temple. "But imagine the advantage—coordinating attacks without a word, sharing battle strategies while your opponent remains deaf to your plans." His perfect smile widens. "This ensures every warrior must master the art of true combat communication. Hand signals, body language, reading your partner's intent through movement alone."

He gestures to a pair of Valkyries sparring nearby, moving in perfect synchronization without a word between them. "That, my friends, is skill earned through sweat and blood—not supernatural shortcuts."

"Well, isn't that just perfect," I huff, beyond done with all these magical blocks. Who knew I'd actually love having a sexy man living rent-free in my head? But here I am, feeling weirdly empty without that constant warm presence of Rhyland's thoughts tangled with mine. It's like missing a limb I never knew I needed until some ancient ward decided to play fun police with our supernatural Wi-Fi.

The compound stretches before us. Huge longhouses with serpent-carved peaks dominate the landscape, their weathered walls dark against the snow. Smoke curls from countless chimneys, creating a hazy ceiling beneath the looming mountains surrounding us like nature's fortress walls.

Two women are putting on quite the show in the central training grounds—their swords singing through the frigid air as they dance their deadly waltz. Snow kicks up around them in glittering clouds, their grunts of exertion echoing off the surrounding peaks.

The smell of woodsmoke mingles with roasting meat and fresh bread, making my stomach growl embarrassingly loud. Cooking fires dot the compound, surrounded by warriors who look like they could bench press a car without breaking a sweat.

Everywhere I look, there are shields decorating walls, spears in racks, and what I'm pretty sure is a drinking horn being passed around by off-duty Valkyries. The whole place screams "warrior paradise."

"Well," I mutter, "looks like I found where the cool kids hang out in Zephyria."

Erik looks like he just walked into a dream. His usually steely expression has softened around the edges, and I swear I can see the ghost of a smile playing at his lips. It's the most relaxed I've ever seen him since Whisper Vale when he basically took over the camp and Fae soldiers like it was his long-lost obsession—something about this place resonates with him deeply. It makes me wonder about his pre-vampire life—what kind of warrior he was before Lilith sank her crazy fangs into him.

Mental note: add "Uncover Erik's mysterious past" to my ever-growing to-do list right after "Survive meeting sister" and "Master being a Savior."

"Shall we? Your sister awaits," Baldr announces with all the enthusiasm of someone about to watch an awkward family reunion unfold.

I take a deep breath, trying to calm the nerves tap-dancing in my stomach. It's fine. Totally fine. I'm just about to meet my long-lost sister, who I didn't even know existed until recently—the same sister who was the OG-chosen one before I got the gig. No biggie.

I mean, it's not like I'm worried she's going to take one look at me and wonder how in the hell we share the same cosmic sperm donor. Or she'll resent me for being the "backup savior" who got the powers and the prophecy.

Nope, not at all.

Oh, who the fuck am I kidding? I'm low-key terrified. I have no idea what to expect, and that's scarier than facing down a horde of frost giants in my underwear.

Baldr leads us through the camp like he's giving a tour. Warriors and Valkyries eye us with curiosity as we pass—probably wondering who the new kids are and why we're here.

We finally reach another ring where the real action is happening. Two Valkyries are going at it. Their swords clash with enough force to make the air sing. I'm standing there slack-jawed, watching them move with a deadly grace that makes Olympic athletes look like clumsy toddlers.

"Bryn!" Baldr's shout yanks me out of my warrior-woman trance. I follow his gaze and promptly forget how to breathe.

The woman who turns at the sound of her name is a goddamn work of art—my sister. Two thick silvery braids frame her face like some hard-core Viking Pippi Longstocking, with smaller braids woven throughout her crown like a halo of badassery. Her lips are full and pouty, and her skin is golden perfection, just like mine.

But it's her eyes that knock the wind out of me. One is Nordic blue, like a frozen fjord, and the other is a familiar honey-gold that exactly matches mine. It's like looking at an alternate version of myself if I'd spent my life training to be a celestial warrior instead of pipetting DNA samples in a lab.

"Hey, Baldr." Bryn waves back then she spots me, and something flickers across her face—recognition, maybe? Or just curiosity?

Either way, she's heading our way with the confident stride of someone who could probably kill you fifteen different ways without breaking a sweat. Her sword is strapped to her back and every movement screams 'trained killer.'

Well, shit. No one told me my sister would be the Viking version of a supermodel crossed with a Navy SEAL.

As she prowls closer, Erik suddenly erupts into the most dignified coughing fit I've ever witnessed—like he's trying to maintain his sophisticated image while hacking up a lung. I whirl around to find Mr. Stoic looking decidedly un-stoic, his silver eyes wide with what can only be described as carefully contained shock.

"Erik?" I ask because watching our resident master of composure lose his cool is about as rare as seeing Lucian pass up an opportunity for a smart-ass comment.

"I assure you, it's merely the... unexpected effects of the ward's limitations," he manages between coughs, straightening his spine. But something in those silver eyes screams 'internal crisis in progress.'

When I turn back around, my sister is standing right in front of me, one eyebrow arched in a way that perfectly conveys 'what in the seven realms is this shit?'

Guess the ability to pack volumes of sass into a single look runs in the family.

Great. Not only do I have to navigate this awkward family reunion, but Erik is acting weirder than usual.

Clearly, this situation needs more complications.

"H-Hi," I manage to squeak out, my voice doing that funny thing where it cracks like I'm going through puberty again. Smooth, Dani. Real smooth. I'm sure she's super impressed by your eloquence.

Bryn stares at me, her mismatched eyes assessing my little crew like she's trying to decide if we're friends or foes. Her gaze flicks to Rhyland briefly, probably noting the whole 'built like a brick shithouse' vibe he's got going on before settling on the hot mess that is Erik.

Erik has decided that now is the perfect time to audition for the role of 'least composed vampire in history.' He's currently wearing a path in the snow with his pacing, making these weird little wheezing noises that sound like he's trying to breathe through a straw. So much for that legendary self-control.

"The wards affect magic differently for everyone," Bryn says, her voice cool as a glacier. She nods toward the disaster zone formerly known as Erik. "What's the deal with your friend there? Should I be concerned?"

Isn't this just a stellar first impression? My long-lost sister probably thinks I've brought a bunch of magical misfits to her doorstep—time to do some damage control before she decides to kick us out on our ass.

"Yeah, the whole power-vanishing act caught us off guard," I try to explain, watching Erik have his refined meltdown. "Guess he's just... extra sensitive?" Honestly, I've got no clue what's making Mr. Serious act like he's mainlined a gallon of espresso. Meanwhile, Rhyland's standing there like a mountain in fur and leather, completely unbothered.

"Seriously, what's his deal?" I prod Rhyland.

Rhyland, in all his Viking glory, stands there with his arms crossed over his chest like he's posing for a Norse god calendar shoot. He gives Erik a quick once-over before responding, "He'll live, Angel. The wards are hitting him hard, just like they're hitting me. It's not every day we're stripped of our powers."

Well, that's reassuring.

Not.

But I guess if Rhyland's not worried, I shouldn't be either. Right?

"Like I said," Bryn continues, "the wards affect everyone differently." She gives me a half-smile that's about as warm as a polar bear's ass. "I never thought I'd actually meet you. But... I'm glad you're here."

Talk about a ringing endorsement.

"Bryn! Your turn!" A voice rings out across the training ground.

"On my way!" Bryn calls back before turning to me with an apologetic shrug. "Let me finish this round, then we can talk somewhere that won't freeze your ass off."

I manage a weak "Yeah, sounds good" while my brain misfires from social awkwardness. Here I am, DNA scientist extraordinaire, reduced to monosyllables like a nervous teenager. But can you blame me? Twenty-eight years of wondering about my biological family, of checking "unknown" on medical history forms, of loving my adoptive parents but constantly feeling that genetic void—and now I'm face-to-face with actual blood family. My sister. A living, breathing piece of my biological puzzle.

After one final glance at Erik (who's still doing his best impression of a malfunctioning robot), I turn my attention to the ring. Bryn strides in like she owns the place, all warrior confidence.

Time to watch my sister—words I never thought I'd get to say—then hopefully some quality bonding time. Preferably somewhere with central heating.

RHYLAND

27

I'm trying to focus on Bryn as she squares up against some Valkyrie built like a fucking tank, but Erik's got me distracted. Something's off with my brother, making my predator instincts go haywire. The moment we passed those gates, everything went sideways—my power crackling beneath my skin like a caged storm, my vampire strength... gone.

It was like getting kicked in the nuts by a giant, but then the feeling passed.

"What the hell is wrong with you?" I ask, sidling up to Erik.

He brushes me off like I'm some annoying gnat. "I've already informed you—nothing requires your concern." His refined tone carries that stick-up-his-ass quality I know too well.

Bryn executes a perfect leg sweep that sends her opponent face-first into the snow. "Bullshit," I growl. "I'm handling this power drain just fine. What's got you all antsy?"

Erik releases one of his patented long-suffering sighs. "I'm perfectly fine, brother. The transition was merely... unexpected."

Lying bastard. I grab his arm and drag his ass away from where Dani's watching her sister demolish the poor fucker in the ring. "Erik." I lock eyes with him, but those silver orbs narrow back at me in a challenge.

Then I hear it.

No. No fucking way. Erik won't meet my gaze now as the truth hits me like a sledgehammer to the face. I scan our surroundings, trying to piece together this mystery, but my attention snaps back to the ring as Bryn unleashes an unholy war cry.

She moves like a force of nature, spinning through the air like some deadly ballerina before landing a kick that would shatter mortal bones. Her opponent barely blocks the strike before Bryn follows up with a combination that's pure poetry in violence—elbow strike to the jaw, knee to the ribs, then a throw that sends the other Valkyrie flying across the ring like a ragdoll.

The other Valkyrie gets up while Bryn's back is turned and bulldozes into her like a goddamn freight train, taking them both down in an explosion of snow and grunts.

Erik's growl is so low I almost miss it, but that sound tells me everything I need to know.

Holy shit.

"Don't," Erik warns, his refined tone carrying a lethal edge that would make lesser men piss themselves.

I drag my hand down my face, scratching my beard like it holds the universe's secrets. "Why the hell not? She can handle—"

"No." Erik's voice cuts through my words like Grave Warden through flesh, those silver eyes promising violence if I finish that sentence. The stick up his ass has officially become a tactical pole.

Well, this shit just got more complicated. Erik needs to come clean with Dani—she deserves the truth, not this silent shit he's pulling. But fuck me if I'm going to be the one to spill his secrets.

I growl low in my throat and stalk back to Dani's side, leaving Erik to stew in his emotional crap. The fight rages on for another ten minutes before Bryn emerges victorious, like some ancient warrior goddess out of the sagas.

She stands in the center of that ring, snow swirling around her like a victory dance while the crowd loses their collective minds. I glance down at my mate and Christ—that smile could power a small country when she looks up at me, those golden irises that shift like molten metal blaze like the sun. It's fucking beautiful seeing her like this—all hopeful and shit about having a sister to bond with. Someone who gets the whole "surprise, you're half-divine" mindfuck on a personal level.

I can sense her nerves, too, buzzing like a swarm of pissed-off bees. She's worried Bryn might not accept her and see her as the usurper who stole her destiny. I mean, shit—the original plan was for Bryn to be my mate, not Dani. Talk about awkward family reunions.

But here's the thing—I don't feel jealousy from my girl. Not a single, possessive spark. She wants to build something tangible with the sister she never knew she had. Destiny bullshit, be damned.

That's my angel—heart big enough to love the whole damn world, even when it's been nothing but a dick to her. She never ceases to amaze me.

Bryn exits the ring, gesturing for us to follow with a sharp nod. Dani's hand slips into mine as we trail after her sister into a longhouse that looks torn from the pages of my oldest memories.

The great hearth dominates the center, flames leaping high enough to cast dancing shadows on the smoke-darkened rafters. Warriors cluster around its warmth, their weapons and armor gleaming in the firelight. Carved dragon heads crown the support beams, their wooden eyes watching our every move. Shields line the walls, each telling its story of glory and death, while spears and axes hang ready for the next raid.

The air is thick with the scent of burning wood, roasting meat, and the unmistakable aroma of sweat-soaked warriors.

I shrug out of my heavy fur cloak, a cascade of snow falling to the floor as I drape it over the nearest bench. The bear pelt is a lifesaver in the freezing temperatures outside, but it's stifling inside this longhouse.

Dani settles beside me on one of the benches, the worn wood polished smooth by generations of warriors. Erik, looking seconds away from collapsing, practically falls onto the table behind us, clearly trying to maintain some distance from the impending confrontation with Dani.

Bryn approaches our table, her movements precise and controlled. The sword finds its home on the scarred tabletop with a resounding clang, its steel catching the firelight. I can't help but admire the expertly crafted weapon, its hilt worn smooth from years of use.

Her attendants descend upon her, removing her armor with practiced efficiency. In moments, Bryn is left in a simple tunic and breeches, her tone frame still radiating the coiled energy of a warrior at rest.

A serving girl appears with a drinking horn, its rim banded in silver and filled to the brim with mead. Bryn raises the horn in a silent toast before taking a deep draught, a trickle of the honey-colored liquid escaping the corner of her mouth. She slams the horn back onto the table with a satisfied sigh and finally settles onto the bench across from us, her mismatched eyes locking onto Dani.

"So, how's it going, *sis?*" Bryn asks, casual as can be, like we're just catching up over a damn pint.

Horns of mead are shoved into our hands, the liquid sloshing dangerously close to the rims. Dani shoots her sister a smirk, but I can tell she's nervous. "I-I can't believe you exist," she blurts, her cheeks flushing pink. "I-I mean, this is just... wow."

Bryn smiles. "Tell me about it." She takes a swig of her mead like it's water, wiping her mouth with the back of her hand. "But just know, I hold no ill will towards you, sister. My destiny is my own, and I embrace it full of heart." Her eyes find mine, a challenge sparking in their depths. "And truth be told, the thought of being shackled to this brooding mountain never quite sat well with me."

Dani's laugh rings out, bright and bold. "Oh, yeah. He's definitely an acquired taste." She leans into me, her smile turning wicked. "But once you get past the scowling exterior, he's got a heart of gold. And an ass that won't quit, but that's beside the point."

I choke, coughing on my mead, the burn of the alcohol nothing compared to the heat of my girl's sass.

Bryn throws her head back, her laughter echoing off the ancient beams. "By the gods, I like this one!" Her smile softens slightly, a hint of reserve creeping in as she studies Dani. "At least one of us got something decent from our glorified asshole of a father—besides his spectacular ability to avoid any real parental responsibility."

"Oh my god, yes!" Dani practically bounces in her seat, nearly spilling her drink excitedly. "Finally! Someone else who sees through his 'holier than thou' bullshit! I swear, his head's so far up in the clouds he probably gets high on stardust."

She leans forward, eyes sparkling with mischief. "Tell me, has he always been this emotionally constipated, or did someone shove his divine scepter up his ass recently?"

I choke on my drink *again,* trying not to spray thousand-year-old mead across the table. My fierce little angel, taking shots at the God of Light himself. Fuck, I love this woman.

I feel the moment something shifts between them—like watching ice crack and melt in spring. The shared pain of Elysium's rejection creates a bridge more potent than blood or prophecy.

Bryn's eyes widen before another laugh bursts from her, genuine and deep. The last of her reserve seems to melt away. "Sister, I think this is the beginning of a beautiful friendship—and our dear father's worst nightmare."

ERIK

28

From my shadowed corner, I wage a losing battle against my baser instincts, my legendary self-control crumbling like ancient ruins. The sisters' laughter filters through the hall, but my attention remains locked on Bryn, with an intensity that borders on obsession. Propriety be damned—she embodies every dark fantasy I've never allowed myself to acknowledge.

My cock strains painfully against my leathers as I recall watching her in that fight, how she commanded the space, radiating raw power and lethal grace. The way she moved, each gesture precise and deadly. Her presence alone threatens decades of iron control.

The elegant curve of her throat begs for my fangs, while the deadly confidence in her stance makes me want to pin her against the nearest surface and claim her until she screams my name. Those mismatched eyes flash with warrior's fire, and fuck—even the way she gripped her sword makes my blood burn with need. The urge to taste, to possess, to mark every inch of her perfect flesh grows stronger with each passing moment.

I sense Rhyland's contentment in his ancestral homeland, but I can barely focus on anything beyond the maddening need to claim what's *mine*. Lilith's machinations and our objectives fade to meaningless background noise compared to the magnificent creature who's demolished my control with terrifying efficiency.

Mate.

The word pulses through my veins like molten silver, a truth I can neither deny nor escape. Each moment in her presence is exquisite torture.

I watch Dani's joy at discovering her sister, knowing my revelation could destroy everything between them. Ensuring Rhyland's silence on this matter will require significant leverage. That loose-tongued bastard better keep his mouth shut, or I'll personally ensure his next sparring session becomes remarkably unpleasant.

The first sight of her obliterated my control. My dead heart slammed against my ribs with enough force to steal my breath, awakening needs I'd buried beneath discipline and duty. After watching my brothers find their destined ones, I'd resigned myself to solitude. Now fate mocks me by presenting the most magnificent warrior I've ever encountered—and making her absolutely forbidden.

The need to claim her burns through me like acid, testing my limits in ways no battle ever has.

Finally, I comprehend my brothers' obsessions with absolute clarity. Our mates truly are our salvation, though I recall Rhyland's stubborn denial of his bond with Dani with newfound sympathy. I pushed him back then, insisted he embrace what fate had chosen—ironic, considering my current predicament.

But this... this is different. My mate sits before me, a warrior goddess who could likely hand me my own ass in combat. The sheer power she radiates, her fierce independence, her raw beauty—it's intoxicating. Yet therein lies the challenge. How does one approach a Valkyrie who radiates pure freedom, whose very essence screams defiance against chains of any kind? She's half angel, half warrior goddess, and entirely capable of separating my head from my shoulders if I make the wrong move.

And there's the additional complication of her being Dani's sister. One wrong step could shatter not only my chance at claiming what's mine, but also destroy their newfound relationship. For the first time in centuries, my mind fails to formulate a clear path forward.

Watching her in that ring made me ache for my powers with an intensity that rivals bloodlust. My gift of foresight has carved my reputation in battle—the ability to see strikes before they land, to counter with murderous precision, to crush opponents through perfect anticipation. Yet these fucking wards stripped me of everything except the maddening need to claim what's mine.

The Little Huntress already proved impossible to read—her time-bending abilities making her movements a lethal mystery. But Bryn... watching her demolish her opponent with brutal efficiency set my blood on fire. Every strike, every deadly twist of her body makes me imagine how she'd move beneath me, against me, over me. My cock throbs painfully as I envision all the ways I could make her scream my name, memorize every inch of that warrior's body with my tongue, and claim her in ways that would make even the gods blush.

"Get your sulking ass over there before Dani starts asking questions, or I swear to fucking god, I'll spill every detail of your little situation," Rhyland grumbles, his alpha-male dominance radiating off him like a storm.

I respond with an eye roll, finding his attempt at intimidation beneath acknowledgment. The sisters remain absorbed in their exchange, mercifully oblivious as my brutish brother drops his considerable mass onto the bench before me.

"For fuck's sake, Erik. Why are you being such a little bitch about this? This is good shit, brother."

I empty my horn in one savage gulp, desperate to numb everything I'm feeling. "Your simple view of this situation fails to account for crucial details," I reply, my cultured voice sharp with frustration. "This is Dani's sister—her *only* blood family. The Little Huntress will either tear me apart herself, or Bryn will use her considerable warrior skills to end my existence in excruciating ways. Neither fate appeals to my continued survival."

"Are you kidding me? Dani will lose her goddamn mind, and bless you both when she hears this, you brooding bastard. She knows better than anyone how this mate bond works—how it keeps us from turning into complete fucking monsters."

I refill our horns while desperately trying to adjust myself without drawing attention. Christ, I haven't experienced this level of basic need in...I don't even know how long. Her scent assaults my senses—a bewitching blend of winter frost and honeyed mead, undercut with the sharp tang of steel and leather. Where Dani's fragrance carries the warmth of sunlight, Bryn's aroma is pure Valkyrie—the crisp bite of a warrior's spirit mixed with something ethereal and divine. The combination makes my fangs ache with desperate hunger.

"Erik, get your head out of your ass and listen," Rhyland growls, drawing my attention from where Bryn sits across the hall. "This is your fucking chance at salvation—at actually having something worth living for. You've been shoving this mate shit down my throat for years—preaching about finding the one who completes you. And now that she's right here in front of your face, you're gonna walk away like a coward? Ignore what fate's handed you?"

I maintain my composure, though his words strike deeper than I care to admit. His frustration rolling off him in waves—the same fierce protectiveness he shows for all his family. But this situation requires a more... delicate approach than his characteristic brute force tactics.

"Your eloquent way with words never ceases to amaze me, brother," I reply, my refined tone masking the aching need coursing through my veins.

"Cut the fancy bullshit, Erik," Rhyland snarls, leaning forward. "You want her. I can smell it on you, see it in the way you track her every fucking move. So man up and do something about it before I lose my shit watching you pine like a lovesick teenager."

"No," I state, my deep tone betraying none of the hunger churning beneath my surface. "Allow me to manage this situation with the same meticulous care you demonstrated with your own mate."

My gaze drifts across the hall, drawn to her with magnetic intensity. Her eyes catch mine and for one breathtaking moment, the world dissolves into nothing. Those beautiful eyes pierce through me, and it's like I can't breathe. The raw power of her stare ignites an inferno in my blood, making my cock throb. Time stretches between us like an eternity, heavy with unspoken promise.

Does she sense this devastating connection?

"Oh, that's rich coming from you, you hypocritical fuck," Rhyland growls, his words shattering our heated exchange. "You spent fucking weeks shoving me toward Dani, preaching about claiming what was mine. About following my goddamn instincts—which is exactly what I did."

I break eye contact, already aching for another glimpse of her face.

I throw back another, the aching need for intoxication clawing at my throat. "That you did, brother," I acknowledge, slamming the horn onto the ancient wood with more force than necessary. "Now, it's time for you to allow me the same courtesy—to navigate this situation on my own terms."

Rhyland sighs, frustration rolling off him in waves. "Erik, you stubborn son of a bitch. Most of the time, I can respect that about you."

Like my decades of iron control, my ability to subsist on minimal blood—even resorting to animal blood before the advent of blood bags and our integration into society.

"But I swear, if you let this go—if you let *her* go—I will personally kick your crabby ass from here to Valhalla."

I quickly drain another horn, to dull my senses. "I'm not our disaster of a brother, Rhyland. I won't stumble over there like some love-struck fool and declare myself with Lucian's characteristic lack of finesse."

My mind races with possibilities. How does one approach a warrior goddess with news of an eternal bond? I know Dani played a crucial role in facilitating Lucian and Seraphina's bond—swooping in to explain the complexities of our world to her guardian angel. But that's not the path I want to take.

"Then get your shit together and figure it out fast," Rhyland grumbles, cutting through my inner turmoil. "We've got enough bullshit to deal with without you eye-fucking her across the hall like some weirdo. You look about two seconds away from throwing her over your shoulder and claiming her right here." Rhyland runs a hand through his hair, clearly frustrated with me. "I know the call, brother. The need to claim. You can't put it off. It will consume you."

I adjust myself for the third damn time beneath the table, fighting to maintain my dignified facade. "Your crude assessment of my current state, while lacking your usual tact, isn't entirely inaccurate," I admit. "However, approaching a Valkyrie of her caliber requires... delicate handling."

"For someone with eons of strategic brilliance, you're acting like a lovesick mortal," Rhyland scoffs, draining his horn. "Get your head straight before—"

Warning horns pierce the air, their deep resonance echoing off the mountains. The hall erupts into controlled chaos—warriors leaping to action, weapons singing as they're drawn from sheaths. I pull Grave Warden free while Rhyland positions himself at Dani's side, his protective instincts in full display.

"Drop the wards!" Bryn's command rings with authority, setting my blood on fire.

We surge outside as the horns grow more urgent. The moment the wards fall, power floods my veins. But any satisfaction at regaining my abilities vanishes as midnight wings explode from Bryn's back—feathers dark as sin and twice as tempting. They arch above her like living shadows, each one gleaming with lethal promise. The way they frame her warrior's form, how they accent the fierce set of her jaw, and the fire in her eyes... My cock hardens more painfully as she stands there, a perfect fusion of grace and deadly perfection. Her braids whip in the wind as those magnificent wings spread wide, ready for battle.

Around us, other Valkyries unfurl their own wings, but my eyes remain locked on Bryn—unable to look away from this vision of dark perfection that fate has chosen as my mate.

The stench hits first—rotting flesh and ancient evil—as ugly, grotesque creatures emerge from the shadows. These aren't the sanitized fairytale monsters but primordial, human-sized nightmares. Their gray-green flesh hangs in loose folds over muscles thick as tree trunks and yellowed tusks jut from lipless mouths. Each breath releases clouds of putrid air that melt the snow beneath them.

Grave Warden sings as I dance through their ranks. My gift shows me their deaths before they happen—the exact angle needed to separate head from shoulders, the precise spot where their crude armor gives way to vulnerable flesh. The head parts from its body with a wet squelch, black ichor painting my face. The second loses its arms in a fountain of gore, tendons, and muscle tissue hanging like obscene ribbons before I drive my blade through its throat.

A club whistles past my ear with enough force to create its own wind. I duck and roll, coming up behind the beast. Grave Warden finds the sweet spot between its vertebrae, and the crack of its spine echoes across the battlefield. The creature's dying roar sounds like mountains breaking.

Through the chaos, I track Dani's progress. Her daggers leave trails of light as she weaves between massive legs, hamstringing our enemies. Each slash of her blades ignites flesh like paper, the stench of burning meat adding to the battlefield's miasma. Rhyland tears through them like a vengeful god, his power turning them into broken toys. Bones splinter with sickening cracks, organs rupture in wet explosions.

But it's Bryn who commands my attention. Her wings cast shadows like death's own cloak as she soars above the melee. Her sword catches the light, trailing crimson arcs through the air. Each strike is poetry written in violence—until a club the size of a small tree arcs toward her exposed back.

My body moves before my mind processes the threat. Grave Warden cleaves through flesh like butter, the resistance of bone and gristle traveling up my arms. The beast's torso splits diagonally, its last meal spilling from its bisected stomach in a steaming pile. Hot blood sprays across my face, tasting of copper and decay.

Bryn spins toward me, those magnificent wings sending gusts of wind that clear the gore-soaked air. For a heartbeat, shock registers in her eyes. Then fury transforms her features into something terrible and beautiful.

"I didn't need your fucking help," she spits, blood and snow speckling her face like war paint—clearly furious at my intervention.

Her fury only feeds my hunger, that warrior's rage making my blood heat as more pour down the mountainside like a tide of flesh and hatred. Some of these bastards rival small buildings, their footsteps making the ground shake.

Bryn launches skyward, leaving me to my bloody work. I scale the nearest behemoth like it's a mountain of rotting meat, Grave Warden finding purchase in its thick hide. The beast's roar of pain vibrates through my bones as I climb higher, black blood raining down. I reach its head and drive my blade deep into its eye socket—the wet pop of bursting tissue followed by the crunch of my steel hitting its skull. Its death throes nearly throw me, but I ride it down, yanking Grave Warden free with a spray of brain matter and vitreous fluid.

Between kills, I catch glimpses of Bryn that make my breath catch. She's magnificent in her savagery—those dark wings carrying her through the carnage like death's own angel. Her sword opens throats and bellies, painting the snow with steaming entrails. Each movement is deadly, and my need to claim her grows with every display of lethal skill.

Dark clouds roll in suddenly—thunder splits the sky as Rhyland finally unleashes his power. Lightning arcs from his hands in blinding ribbons, the scent of ozone mixing with burning flesh. Our enemies explode from within as electricity cooks their organs, their death screams drowned by rolling thunder. The air itself tastes of metal and rage as my brother channels his legacy.

Dani's angelic fire turns the battlefield into an inferno. Hot flames consume our enemies, reducing them to ash even as they charge forward. The combination of her holy fire and Rhyland's lightning creates a devastating light show, casting weird shadows across the gore-streaked snow.

I drive Grave Warden through another temple, the blade emerging from its opposite ear in a fountain of gray matter. Its club drops from lifeless fingers as I twist the steel, ensuring maximum damage. The wet sounds of tissue separation accompany its collapse.

My gift shows me her fall before it happens—the sickening crack of a troll's club connecting with her wing, the way her body goes limp mid-flight. Terror claws through my chest, a feeling I have never known. Every fiber of my being screams as I watch her plummet, those magnificent wings now useless.

I move faster than I ever have, blurring across the thick snow, my boots sliding through gore and entrails. The stench of battle—blood, shit, and burning flesh—fades against the overwhelming need to reach her. I catch her just before she hits the frozen ground, the impact driving me to my knees. Her blood soaks into my tunic, hot and precious. My hands shake as I brush matted silvery strands from her face, my own blood turning to ice when I see the ugly gash across her temple.

The chaos rages around us—the wet sounds of steel meeting flesh, Rhyland's thunder shaking the mountains, screams of the dying echoing off stone. But all I can focus on is the weak flutter of her pulse beneath my fingers, the way those mystical eyes struggle to open. A whimper of pain escapes her lips, and something fundamental inside me roars to life.

My distraction costs me dearly. The impact comes from nowhere—a club the size of a tree trunk catching me square in the back. Bones crack as I'm launched through the air, the taste of my own blood filling my mouth. Bryn goes flying as I slam into a snowbank hard enough to drive the air from my lungs, my vision blurring as rage and pain war for dominance.

White-hot agony slices through my body as shattered bones knit themselves back together, each wet crack and pop a fresh torture. But none of that matters when I see the creature looming over Bryn's still form, its shadow casting her in darkness. My heart stops—fear and rage explode through my veins.

I blur across the blood-soaked snow, scooping her into my arms just as another blow catches me from behind. The impact sends us tumbling, but I curl around her like a shield, refusing to let her fragile body take any damage. We roll through gore covered snow and viscera, the metallic stench of battle thick in my nostrils, until I end up braced above her.

Time freezes. The sounds of battle all fade away. There's only her beneath me, those beautiful eyes wide with something between shock and recognition. I drink in every detail: the flush on her cheeks, the rapid rise and fall of her chest, the way her body fits perfectly against mine. Her warmth seeps into me, igniting needs I've always denied.

Her gaze captivates me—one eye a mesmerizing arctic blue, the other a molten gold that sets my blood aflame. I find myself lost in their depths, unable to decide which hue draws me in more. My eyes trace the elegant lines of her face, committing every detail to memory. The way her full lips part slightly with each steady breath, releasing small clouds of frost into the frigid air. The delicate curve of her cheekbones, still flushed from battle. The proud set of her jaw, a testament to her warrior's spirit. Every feature is a masterpiece, a perfect blend of beauty and strength that leaves me breathless.

The spell shatters as she shakes her head, shoving me off with enough force to send me sprawling in the blood-stained snow. My body screams in protest as fresh injuries make themselves known.

Bryn rises like an avenging goddess, those dark wings unfurling with deadly poise. "Like I said, I don't need your help." The words drip with disdain before she launches herself back into the carnage, leaving me aching in ways that have nothing to do with my wounds.

The slaughter continues for what feels like hours—steel meeting flesh, bone splintering beneath supernatural strength, the wet sounds of death filling the mountain air. By the time the last troll falls, the snow is stained crimson and black, steam rising from cooling corpses. Warriors move among the fallen, delivering mercy blows where needed, while others begin the grim task of gathering their own dead.

I sink onto a blood-soaked boulder, allowing my body to finally acknowledge its injuries. Ribs knit themselves back together with wet, grinding sounds as I watch her across the battlefield—fierce and untouchable as she issues commands to her fellow Valkyries, seemingly unaware of how completely she's shattered my world.

"What the fuck were those things?" Dani gasps out between ragged breaths, her daggers still dripping black ichor.

Bryn approaches her sister, those magnificent wings folding against her back as she checks Dani for injuries. "Trolls," she states matter-of-factly, wiping gore from her sister's cheek. "We haven't faced an assault of this magnitude in years. Something drew them here."

"Something?" Another Valkyrie spits the word like poison, her raven wings bristling with hostility. Her glare fixes on Dani with the intensity of a blade. "Don't play coy, Bryn. We all know what lures these beasts."

I remain seated, letting my shattered bones finish mending, but tension coils through my body at the Valkyrie's tone. Even Rhyland straightens, his protective instincts flaring.

"What?" Dani's voice is confused as she looks at her sister and the hostile warrior. "What does that mean?"

Bryn's exhale crystallizes in the frigid air. Her eyes are heavy with ancient knowledge. "They're drawn to Christian blood," she reveals, her words hanging in the air like frost.

DANICA

29

"Hold up. Christian blood?" I repeat, my stomach clenching. Well, isn't that just wonderful? It looks like I've brought the supernatural equivalent of a neon "eat me" sign to my sister's doorstep in the name of Jesus.

Way to make a stellar first impression, Dani.

"Yes, that would be you, little sister," Bryn confirms, her dual-colored eyes studying me with an intensity that makes me want to squirm. Is that a hint of resentment, I see, or just centuries of warrior-honed suspicion? "It's not your fault, though."

She must see the guilt written all over my face because her expression softens a fraction like she's trying to reassure me.

"Pfft, going soft, Bryn?" The angry Valkyrie spits from beside her, clutching her ribs like she's trying to keep her internal organs from spilling. "You know damn well this is all her fault!" She glares at me with enough venom to drop a giant. "I don't give a flying fuck who this girl claims to be—her blood—her *faith* is going to get us all killed."

Before I can even process the verbal bitch slap, Bryn moves faster than I can register. One second, Angry McStabby is running her mouth; the next, she's eating snow with Bryn's knife kissing her throat. "That's my sister, you're shit-talkin'," Bryn growls, her voice colder than a White Walker's ballsack. "I suggest you keep your forked tongue behind your teeth unless you want to donate it to my blade collection."

A strained, almost guttural sound pulls my attention to Erik. He's hunched over, arms braced on his knees, and his breathing uneven, as if he's forgotten how to inhale properly. When I follow his gaze, I see him staring at my sister with an intensity that could burn worlds.

Well, that's... interesting. I've never seen Mr. Stoic look at anyone like that before—definitely a first.

Rhyland's arms band around my waist like steel cables, a low growl rumbling through his chest that screams "protective Viking mode: engaged." And okay, I'll admit it—having my man get all caveman on my behalf? Kinda hot, even if I'm perfectly capable of fighting my own battles.

I remember the day my adoptive parents took me to church, where I was baptized in the eyes of the Big Guy Upstairs. I've always believed in a higher power, even if I wasn't sure what flavor of divinity I was dealing with. But deep down? I've been Team Jesus since before I could walk, courtesy of my parents' devout faith. The irony isn't lost on me—the girl with the god complex getting dunked in holy water. If only they knew their precious "miracle baby" would grow into a walking, talking monster magnet.

It's wild—here I am, standing in the realm of Norse gods and monsters, having literally just shared a feast with Odin himself. And it's not just here—every realm so far seems to have its own divine crew. The merfolk in Aquaria bow to Poseidon, the fae have their own celestial court, and human history is packed with gods of every flavor.

But Christianity is woven into the fabric of who I am. It's all I've known and believed in until this cosmic bombshell dropped into my lap. Yet, here I stand. Discovering that my devout upbringing is the supernatural equivalent of ringing the dinner bell for every monster in the neighborhood.

"Yield!" Bryn's shout snaps me back to the present, where she's still got the woman pinned like a bug.

The Valkyrie goes limp, her arms splaying out in the universal sign of "uncle." "I yield," she grits out, sounding like she'd rather chew broken glass.

Bryn stands, but not before giving her fallen opponent a parting shove into the snow. "Let this be a lesson to all of you," she announces, her voice ringing with authority as she surveys the gathered crowd. "No one disrespects my sister, or you'll get a personal introduction to my sword. Are we clear?"

A chorus of nods and murmured assent ripples through the onlookers, everyone suddenly very interested in their boots. Meanwhile, I'm just standing here like a slack-jawed idiot, trying to process the fact that my sister—my actual, blood-related sister—just went full mama bear on my behalf.

I swear, if my heart swells any more, it will pop like an overripe grape.

Best. Sister. Ever.

The bathing chamber is a marvel of Norse engineering. It is a mega stone pool carved directly into the mountain, fed by hot springs that heat the water perfectly. Steam rises in lazy spirals, making the air thick and humid. Ornate dragon heads are carved into the walls, their eyes set with gems that catch the light of dozens of tallow candles. The ceiling stretches high above, lost in shadows where elaborate wooden beams cross like ancient branches.

I sink deeper into the hot water, letting it ease my battle-worn muscles while taking another sip of honey-sweet mead from my carved horn. After the fight, Bryn ordered the wards to be kept down just in case we get any more uninvited guests looking for a throwdown.

The guys are in their own bathing chamber across the compound—probably enjoying the same luxurious hot springs while plotting battle strategies or whatever it is warriors do during spa time.

"So, tell me, sister, how fares the mantle of savior?" Bryn asks, lounging against the pool's edge. Her wings tucked against her back, hair loose and long. "Is it all the skalds claim it to be?"

"It's... not exactly what I expected," I admit, tracing patterns in the water's surface. "Don't get me wrong—the power is incredible, and I've found an amazing family. But sometimes..." I trail off, thinking of my father's absence, of the constant danger of watching people I love get hurt. Always saying goodbye to new friends and allies. "It's complicated," I finish lamely, taking another drink.

"By the Norns, you're quite the warrior, though," Bryn grins, splashing water in my direction. "I saw you out there, wielding fire like Surtr himself. And your mate—Rhyland's command of the dark skies rivals the stories of Thor's might. We haven't seen such power since the Thunderer himself blessed these mountains."

I smile into my mead horn at the mention of Rhyland. "He's something else," I say, warmth spreading through my chest that has nothing to do with the hot water.

"Though don't let that whole warrior-god thing fool you. Under all that brooding and those intimidating muscles, he's actually a teddy bear."

"Yeah," Bryn's eyes sparkle with mischief as she refills our horns from a silver pitcher. "I see the way he watches you, sister. Even a blind draugr could see the bond between you two."

I feel my cheeks flush, and it's not from the steam. "Yeah, well..." I trail off, absently running my fingers through the warm water. "He keeps me grounded, you know? When everything else is pure chaos, Rhyland's my constant."

As we soak in the steaming water, the scent of herbs and minerals rising with the mist, my mind drifts to a nagging worry. Despite Bryn's reassurances earlier, I can't help but wonder if she harbors any resentment about Rhyland being destined for her before fate decided to play musical chairs with our lives. I'm about to voice my concern when Bryn beats me to the punch.

"What of the silver-haired one?" she asks, swirling her mead with curiosity. "Erik, was it?"

"Yeah, Erik," I nod, a fond smile tugging at my lips as memories flood my mind. "He's like this perfect blend of badass warrior and secret marshmallow. Tough as nails on the outside, but once you're in his inner circle? Total softie."

I think back to all the times Erik's had my back—grueling training sessions that left me bruised but stronger, late-night talks when the weight of destiny felt too heavy to bear alone, and keeping me sane when Rhyland was taken and held captive. He's shown unwavering loyalty and support time and again."He's been a true brother to me," I continue, my voice soft with affection. "Always ready to jump into the fray to protect the people he cares about."

Bryn hums, her eyes alight with interest as she leans forward slightly. "And his tale? Every warrior has one."

I pause, my brow furrowing, as I realize how little I actually know about Erik's past. Sure, I know he's a vampire and that Lilith's fangs left their mark on him like the rest of my guys. But the details? The path that led him to this life? It's a mystery wrapped in an enigma, sealed with the wax of Erik's ironclad reserve.

"Honestly? I'm not sure," I admit, my shoulders slumping slightly. "Erik plays things pretty close to the vest. He doesn't talk much about his life before, you know..." I make a vague fang gesture. "But I do know he's fiercely loyal. Like ride-or-die level. I'd trust him with my life without question."

"A vampire, though?" Bryn presses, her tone unreadable.

"I hope that's not a problem," I say quickly, my shoulders tensing. The last thing I need is some supernatural prejudice to dampen this whole sisterly bonding thing.

But Bryn just waves a hand dismissively, her bracelets clinking. "No, I hold no ill will towards the fangborn. In Zephyria, a warrior's merit is measured by their deeds, not the ichor in their veins."

Relief washes through me, and I sink deeper into the water. "Good. Because that doesn't define him; he's family, plain and simple."

Bryn nods slowly, her expression thoughtful as she leans back against the pool's edge. Her eyes hold a glimmer of something I can't quite place—curiosity, appraisal, maybe even a hint of admiration.

It's clear my assessment of Erik has piqued her interest, but I'm not sure to what end. But one thing I do know? If Bryn's looking for a character reference, she couldn't do better than my silver-haired brother-in-arms. Erik's the kind of guy you want in your corner when the chips are down and the world's going to Hell in a handbasket.

"Does this Erik make a habit of playing the gallant savior?" Bryn's tone shifts from curious to annoyed faster than a Valkyrie's sword strike.

I blink, taken aback by the sudden change. "What do you mean?" I ask, my brow furrowing in confusion.

Bryn sighs, draining her mead horn in one impressive gulp. "Pay it no mind," she mutters, reaching for the pitcher to refill her drink.

But my mind is already whirring, pieces clicking into place. I think back to the battle, how Bryn took that nasty hit, and Erik was ready to play the hero. Does she resent him for stepping in? Is it some warrior pride thing?

"Hey, don't take it personally," I say gently, trying to smooth over the sudden tension. "That's just how Erik is. He's hardwired to protect the people he cares about, no matter how badass they are."

To my surprise, a flush creeps up Bryn's neck, staining her cheeks pink. She quickly looks away, suddenly fascinated by the intricate carvings on the wall.

"Yes, well, perhaps he should learn to read the battlefield better," she grumbles, a defensive edge to her words. "I am no swooning maiden in need of rescue."

Her reaction hits me like a splash of cold water.

Oh. *Oh.*

I lean back, studying my sister with new eyes. The way she's suddenly so prickly at the mere mention of Erik, the blush staining her cheeks... could it be? Is my tough-as-nails Valkyrie sister actually *attracted* to the brooding vampire?

And then there was Erik's reaction earlier. I noticed something in his eyes when he looked at my sister, especially when she held that knife to that Valkyrie's throat. His stare was intense, almost possessive.

The thought alone is enough to make me choke on my mead. I quickly cover it with a cough, trying to hide my sudden revelation. This is... unexpected. And potentially hilarious.

I make a mental note to keep a closer eye on these two. If there's even a hint of sparks flying, you can bet your ass I'm going to be there with a bucket of metaphorical gasoline, ready to fan the flames.

After all, what are sisters for if not meddling in each other's love lives?

"Can we talk about the cosmic-sized plot twist that is my love life?" I say, making Bryn raise an eyebrow. "Nobody saw this coming—not even my guardian angel Seraphina. Dear old Dad was convinced I was corrupted because I bonded with a vampire. Talk about parental disapproval."

"Corrupted?" Bryn snorts, her warrior pride flaring. "By the Gods, our father can be as blind as Odin, and he still has both eyes! The signs were clear in the ancient texts—two saviors, bound by fate and power."

"But if everyone thought Rhyland was dead, what was Plan B?" I ask, swirling my mead. "The prophecy's pretty specific about needing a mate. Who was supposed to be my magical battery charger?"

"It had to be someone of divine blood," Bryn explains, her eyes glinting in the candlelight. "The gods planned to create another godborn or choose from their existing offspring. But fate," she smirks, "had its own designs. You were always meant to be Rhyland's match. The gods just took their sweet time catching up."

I can't help but laugh at the absurdity of it all. Even the so-called all-knowing gods didn't see this coming. They can take their "chosen plan" and shove it right up their divine asses.

She straightens, all business now. "You leave for the Valhallas Veil at first light. There's quests to be done, before you can reach the Nexus."

"Right," I nod. "So what fun surprises are waiting to kill me when I try to grab this magical rock?"

Bryn's expression turns serious. "The Nexus rises above even the Cloud Palaces, its peak touching the stars. The stone rests at the top—a sacred site where the purest essence of air converges. Only those deemed worthy by the winds themselves can approach. But reaching it..." She trails off, her eyes distant. "Getting there means visiting Valhalla's Veil—a wasteland crawling with draugr and frost giants—amongst other trials. And that's assuming the great eagles of Hræsvelgr don't decide to make a snack of you first."

Great. Another magical obstacle course designed to test my worth. Apparently, just asking nicely for these stones would be too easy. At least this time, I've got a warrior sister to help guide me through whatever celestial American Ninja Warrior course awaits at the spire.

"Oh yeah, sounds like a total cakewalk," I say, aiming for confidence but probably landing somewhere between 'mildly hysterical' and 'barely concealed panic.'

"By the Norns, you'll do fine," Bryn grins, splashing water in my direction. "You're the savior after all—what's a little death-defying climb compared to everything else you've faced?"

Her tone carries that perfect blend of sisterly encouragement and warrior's challenge.

The thought of facing ethereal beings who can manipulate air currents while navigating what's essentially a tornado turned sideways? Yeah, that's going to be fun. But hey, what's one more near-death experience in the name of saving the realms?

I slip into our room after my bath, the heavy wooden door creaking shut behind me. The space is small but cozy, tucked away from the main hall like a secret sanctuary. A hearth blazes in the corner, its flames painting the stone walls in dancing shadows and warm light. Thick fur rugs cover the floor, their softness tickling my bare feet, while a jumbo bed dominates the center of the room, piled high with more furs that look sinfully inviting.

My man is lounging by the fire, the flames highlighting every ridge and valley of his bare chest. His wet hair is slicked back, and drops of water still trail down his neck and over those intricate tattoos I love to trace. His leather pants sit low on his hips, and his freshly trimmed beard accentuates his strong jaw in a way that makes my mouth go dry. He's the perfect picture of a Nordic warrior meets a romance novel cover model.

"How was your bath?" he asks, his ocean-blue eyes drinking me in as I cross the room. His voice carries that deep rumble that never fails to send shivers down my spine.

I pad across the furs, the thick blanket draped around me like a royal cloak. "Good. Relaxing. How about yours?"

His hungry eyes track my movement like a predator, darkening as I slip between his spread thighs. "Would've been better with you there instead of brooding with Mr. Stoic," he growls, his hands finding my hips through the fur.

"Aw, what's wrong?" I tease, enjoying how his nostrils flare as he catches my scent. "Getting tired of Erik's sophisticated company?"

His fingers find the gap in the fur, his breath hitching when he realizes I'm utterly bare underneath. "Fuck, Angel. Did you walk through the hall wearing nothing but this?" His voice drops to that dangerous register that makes heat pool between my thighs. Possessive jealousy flashes in those Nordic eyes, making me grin.

I let the fur slide off my shoulders, pooling at my feet. His pupils blow wide, nearly drowning out that ocean blue as his gaze devours every inch of my exposed body. The fire's warmth kisses my bare skin as I straddle his thick thighs, settling into his lap.

"You're avoiding my question, Rhyland."

His big hands find my breasts, rough palms cupping their weight as his thumbs brush over my nipples. "What question was that?" he asks, his voice thick with need as he kneads the soft flesh.

I arch into his touch, a gasp escaping as he pinches the sensitive peaks. "About—*ah*—Erik's mood?"

"Because he's being a fucking idiot," he growls before capturing my nipple between his lips. The wet heat of his mouth sends electricity shooting through my body. "And it's pissing me off."

I pull back, ignoring the whimper of protest that escapes my throat. "About what?"The need for answers temporarily overrides the burning desire coursing through my veins.

His big paws claim my ass, yanking me forward until I'm pressed against the impressive bulge straining his leather pants."Angel..." he growls, his lips finding that sweet spot on my neck that makes my toes curl. His teeth scrape along my collarbone, marking a path of fire across my skin while his fingers knead my ass with possessive intent.

"Rhyland..." I try to create some distance, but he's having none of it. He rocks up against my core, the friction sending sparks of pleasure through my body.

Frustrated with his noticeable deflection, I grab his face between my palms. "Are you going to answer me or just keep trying to distract me with your considerable... talents?"

A heavy sigh escapes him, his eyes clouding with something I can't quite read. "No, baby. I can't."

The words hit me like a tidal wave. This is new territory for us—dangerous and unsettling. We've never kept secrets since that first night when he finally opened up to me. It was an unspoken pact, sealed with trust and strengthened by our bond. The fact that he's holding something back now makes my stomach tense.

"Why?" The word comes out sharper than I intend, worry starting to gnaw at my insides.

Rhyland's eyes drop, his jaw clenching in that way that tells me he's struggling. "He asked me not to say anything. I gave him my word."

His tatted hands capture my face, forcing me to meet his eyes now stormy with conflict. "Don't look at me like that, Angel. I respect my brother, even if he's stubborn about this. But it has to come from him."

My mind spirals with dark possibilities, each theory more terrifying than the last. The way Erik acted on the training grounds—those intense stares that seemed to burn holes through the air, that suspicious coughing fit that felt more like a cover-up than actual distress. Is there something wrong with him? Did the wards do something to him? Or worse—is he showing signs of corruption, like those other vampires who lost their humanity and turned feral?

I've seen what happens when vampires go dark side, and the thought of our refined, controlled Erik succumbing to that kind of madness makes my blood run cold. What could be serious enough to make Mr. Stoic—the vampire equivalent of a Swiss vault when keeping his composure—swear Rhyland to absolute secrecy?

The possibilities swirling through my head are enough to make me feel sick. Erik's been there for me through everything—the thought of something being wrong with him, something so profound that Rhyland won't even tell me about it, makes me worry more.

"Is he okay?" I press, worry, making my voice crack. "You're freaking me out here. What's wrong with Erik?"

"He'll be fine, baby." The words sound hollow even as they leave his lips, his expression doing nothing to ease my concerns.

I slip from his grasp when he reaches for me, trying to draw me into a kiss. My bare feet pad across the fur rugs until I reach the bed, crawling under the thick pelts. Behind me, Rhyland releases a frustrated growl that echoes off the stone walls. I get it—he's caught between loyalty to his brother and honesty with his mate. But Erik isn't just Rhyland's brother anymore—he's my family, too.

The thought that something's wrong with him, something serious enough to warrant secrets between us, makes my stomach twist into knots.

I can't lose Erik.

The bed dips under Rhyland's considerable weight as he slides in beside me. I roll onto my side, facing the dancing flames in the hearth, putting my back to him.

"Goodnight," I mutter, knowing I'm being petty but unable to help myself.

Through our bond, I feel his emotions warring—frustration and anger mixing with guilt and worry. The feelings wash over me in waves until exhaustion pulls me under, dragging me into uneasy dreams.

RHYLAND

30

I'm shoveling breakfast into my face while my mate gives me the Arctic fucking treatment. After last night's shitstorm, she's ready to hang me by my balls for keeping Erik's secret. I'm this close to saying 'screw it' and spilling everything, but my brother made me swear on my honor in the bathhouse.

Fucking honor.

"Thanks to you, asshole, Dani's not only pissed, but I'm officially in the doghouse. You need to fix this shit, pronto," I grumble around a mouthful of smoked fish.

Erik's sigh could freeze hellfire. "I have no intention of pursuing the matter, brother. Therefore, there is nothing to divulge to the Little Huntress." His voice is clipped, each word as precise as a surgeon's blade.

I damn near choke on my breakfast, fish going down the wrong pipe. "What the actual fuck do you mean you're not *pursuing* it?"

Erik's steel-gray eyes flick meaningfully over my shoulder. I turn to look, and there's Dani with Bryn—who's currently wrapped around some mountain of muscle like a vine on a tree, their faces practically fused together in the middle of the damn hall.

I roll my eyes so hard they might get stuck. "So fucking what? It doesn't change the fact that she's your mate. Man up and stake your claim before I lose my shit watching you brood yourself into oblivion."

Erik's jaw clenches like he's trying to crack granite. "It's not that simple."

"The hell it isn't," I snap, keeping my voice low. "You're just making it complicated because you're allergic to happiness, you stubborn bastard."

Erik's eyes narrow. "It's not, Rhyland. There are... complications. Factors you don't understand."

"Then enlighten me, oh wise one," I shoot back, my patience wearing thin. "Because from where I'm sitting, it looks like you're just being a pussy."

Erik slams his fist on the table, rattling the plates and startling a few nearby warriors. "Enough," he hisses, his silver eyes flashing with barely contained rage. "I've made my decision, and that's final. Now drop it, before I drop you."

Holy shit. I've seen Erik rip enemies apart with his bare hands, but I've never seen him lose his cool like this with me. The guy's usually got more control than a monk on a meditation retreat. It has to be the mating bond turning his brain into scrambled eggs. He can pretend all he wants, but ignoring this shit is like trying to outrun a lightning bolt. He's gonna snap, and it won't be pretty when he does. His bloodlust is probably already tap dancing on his last nerve, especially with her right-fucking-there, real and breathing, and everything his vampire side is screaming for.

I glance back at their table. My angel's got her head down, suddenly super interested in her food while trying to ignore the soft-porn show Bryn's putting on with Muscles McGee.

"At least talk to Dani, for fuck's sake," I growl. "Tell her you're fine—lie through your teeth if you have to. Just fix this shit."

Erik just sits there like a statue with a grudge, nursing his drink. We're stuck here waiting for Heimdall's dramatic ass to show up and that pretty boy Baldr to finish powdering his nose in Ásgard. At least Bryn's staying put—something about this being Dani's destiny and her having to guard this frozen hellhole called Valor's Watch.

Just what I fucking need—a treasure hunt with Ásgard's favorite poster boy, Baldr. But beggars can't be choosers, and the sooner we get this show on the road, the sooner we can get back to somewhere that doesn't freeze my balls off.

At least with Bryn staying behind, Erik can get his head out of his ass and focus on the mission. Maybe some distance will help him get his shit together before he completely loses it. The last thing we need is my brother going full-blown feral vampire because he can't handle being near his mate.

Though, knowing my luck and how the universe loves to fuck with me lately, that'll probably blow up in our faces anyway.

After watching Erik try to drown himself in mead for what feels like a fucking eternity, I need some air.

Outside, a group of Valkyries are going at it in the ring, their swords singing through the frozen air. Thanks to Bryn raising the wards this morning, blocking my powers, I'm about as useful as tits on a bull. Can't even mind-talk with my mate, which is really starting to piss me off.

My fist connects with the wooden beam, the ancient timber exploding into splinters. The sound echoes through the frozen air like thunder, but it doesn't do shit to calm the rage burning in my veins. Between Erik's secrets turning my mate into an ice queen and Dani's Arctic fucking treatment, I'm about ready to level this entire frozen shithole.

Blood drips onto pristine snow, turning white to blood-red before my vampire healing kicks in. The wounds close, flesh knitting together even as wooden shards push themselves out of my skin. At least that golden prick Baldr didn't lie about our healing powers working here, wards or no wards.

The beam's destruction barely takes the edge off. What I really need is either a full-on war or my mate's sweet ass pressed against me, and right now both options seem equally fucking impossible.

I'm watching these warrior women try to dismember each other when Bryn and Dani materialize next to me as if they have news I won't like.

"Change of plans," Bryn announces, her voice carrying that edge of authority that makes lesser warriors piss themselves.

I arch an eyebrow. "That right?"

"Bryn's coming with us," Dani says, her tone clipped but still managing to drip sass. "Baldr thinks it's best." She won't look at me directly, but I can feel the frost coming off her in waves.

Bryn straightens up like she's about to lead a damn raid. "I've commanded my second to lead over Valor's Watch. By Odin's beard, I'll not miss the chance to aid my sister in this quest."

"Great." trying to force a smile that looks more like a grimace.

Just. Fuck.

Erik will lose his mind faster than a berserker in a mead hall. So much for hoping distance might help his control—that plan just got shot to Hell and back. I scrub my hand down my face, trying not to look like I'm already dreading the shitstorm heading our way.

Dani gives me another one of her arctic death glares before turning away, somehow making the silent treatment feel like getting gutted with a rusty blade. Christ, this day just keeps getting better and better.

Before she can slip away, I snag her around the waist, spinning us until her back hits the wooden wall of the longhouse. The impact forces a small gasp from her lips as I cage her in with my arms, my body pressing against hers until there's not even room for the freezing air between us. Her scent—honey and sunshine—fills my lungs, making my fangs ache.

"You can't keep freezing me out, Angel. This mission's too important for your silent treatment bullshit."

She tilts her chin up, defiant as ever, and fuck me if it doesn't make my blood burn hotter. Her breath ghosts across my lips, hot and sweet. "I'm talking to you now, aren't I?" she challenges, her eyes flashing gold fire.

I growl low in my throat. "Woman, you know damn well what I mean."

"What's really bothering you?" Her fingers trail up my chest, deceptively gentle. "Pissed that I left you high and dry last night or that you're keeping secrets from me?"

Christ, this fucking woman. My cock throbs against the confines of my leathers, her defiance only stoking the flames. "I'm not keeping secrets from *you*," I grit out, my nose brushing hers. "It's Erik's shit to deal with, not mine to spill." The words come out rougher than intended, breathing in her frustrated arousal.

Her fingers fist in my tunic, yanking me even closer. "Secrets are secrets, Rhyland." Her honey-gold eyes flash with anger and something darker. "You promised—*we* promised—no more of that shit. Erik isn't just your brother anymore. He's my family, too. I wish you'd get that through your thick arrogant skull."

The hurt in her voice cuts deeper than any blade. I press my forehead to hers, breathing in her scent like it's the only air I need. "I do. I get it, baby. But I also know my brother. He's not ready to face this, and pushing him will only make it worse."

She sighs, her breath mingling with mine. "Since when are you the level-headed one?"

A chuckle rumbles through my chest. "Since you decided to be a stubborn ass about this."

She pinches my side hard enough to make me grunt, her eyes, like freshly harvested honey dripping from the comb blaze with challenge. "Fine. While you boys keep your little secret club going, let's stay focused on the mission." Her lips curve into a dangerous smile. "Can't let ourselves get distracted by... basic instincts. Or desires."

No fucking way. She can't be serious.

I grind my leather-clad cock against her stomach, making damn sure she feels exactly what she's threatening to deny. "Not happening, Angel. You're not putting me on ice because my brother has his head up his ass."

She arches against me, her body a sinful curve of heat and temptation. "Oh, I'm sorry," she purrs, her lips brushing the shell of my ear. "Did you think you had a choice in the matter?"

A shudder rips through me, my control fraying at the edges. "Dani, I swear to God, if you cut me off—"

She nips at my earlobe, her teeth grazing the sensitive skin. "You'll what? Throw a tantrum?"

I tangle my hand in her hair, tugging just hard enough to bare her throat. "More like remind you why denying me is a very, *very* bad idea, Little Angel."

Her fingers trail down my chest, teasing, and she rolls her hips against mine, the friction making my vision blur. "Maybe some solidarity with your suffering brother would do you good."

I capture her wandering hands, pinning them above her head. "Listen here, you beautiful little minx," I growl against her lips. "I'm not Erik. I don't do sexual frustration as a lifestyle choice."

"*—Ahem—*"

I jerk back from Dani like I've been electrocuted. A whole damn audience of Valkyries is staring at us, their expressions ranging from amused to murderous.

"Oh, don't let us interrupt," a blonde warrior drawls. "It's not like this is a sacred training ground or anything. Please, continue dry humping against our walls."

Fuck me. Nothing kills a hard-on faster than getting caught by a bunch of divine warrior women who could probably castrate me with their minds.

I grab Dani's hand, trying to salvage what's left of our dignity—not that I had much to begin with. She's fighting back a laugh, the little minx clearly enjoying my discomfort. We make our way back to the compound's center, where I spot Baldr's golden ass approaching with Heimdall and Bryn in tow.

"Rhyland." Heimdall's voice booms, his massive frame decked out in armor that makes my leather getup look like peasant rags. Golden bastard probably polishes that shit in his sleep.

I give him a curt nod because what else do you say to an all-seeing god who probably watched me almost bang my mate against a wall five minutes ago?

"Well then!" Baldr chirps like we're planning a fucking picnic, not a potentially lethal quest. "I'll take our friend here on Sleipnir—" He gestures to Heimdall. "—and you three can cozy up on Gullfax. As for our fierce Valkyrie..."

Bryn's smirk could cut glass as she straps her sword across her back with practiced ease. The shield slides onto her forearm like it was forged to be there. "Aye, while you lot play Pony Express, I'll take the warrior's path. Meet you at Valhalla's Veil in three hours—if you can keep up." She throws a challenging look our way, every inch the Norse warrior princess with an attitude that could make Thor himself think twice.

Dani's eyes scan the courtyard, her brow furrowing. "Where's Erik?"

For fuck's sake. I can feel a headache building behind my eyes. Through the longhouse's open door, I spot my brother's silver head bent over what has to be his tenth horn of mead.

"I'll get him," I grunt, already stomping across the frozen ground.

The longhouse door slams against the wall as I storm inside, reeking of smoke and alcohol. Erik slouches over the table like it's the only thing keeping him upright. His silver hair's a mess, and Grave Warden lies forgotten beside him like a jilted lover.

I grab a fistful of his tunic, yanking him up with enough force to make the bench scrape against the floor. The sword goes into his hands whether he wants it or not. "Move your ass, brother. We've got a stone to find, and your pity party's over."

Erik sighs, but he straightens his clothes with those precise movements that scream, 'I'm totally fine' even when he's falling apart. He shoulders past me, his boots leaving heavy prints in the snow as he heads for the others.

Gullfax prances up, his golden coat catching the weak sunlight. I wrap my hands around Dani's waist, lifting her into the saddle like she weighs nothing. She settles in with a grunt that tells me she's still pissed, but at least she doesn't try to kick me in the face.

I swing into the saddle behind Dani, my thighs bracketing her hips as I settle against the warm leather. Her scent hits me hard, making my cock ache despite our earlier interruption.

Erik stumbles toward Gullfax like a drunk trying to catch a chicken, his usual lethal grace completely shot to shit.

My brother, ladies and gentlemen—feared vampire warrior, reduced to a stumbling mess because he can't handle his feelings. Fucking perfect.

His first attempt ends with him face-down in the snow. The second time, he manages to get his foot in the stirrup before sliding right back down. By the third spectacular failure, the whole fucking compound is howling with laughter.

Baldr's prissy ass is practically crying, doubled over and clutching his sides. Even Heimdall's cold-hard face cracks a smile.

Dani's body shakes against mine as she tries to hold in her giggles. "Shouldn't we..." she whispers, watching Erik wobble to his feet again, snow clinging to his silver hair.

"Erik!" I bark. "Either get your drunk ass on this horse or crawl to Valhalla's Veil. Your choice, brother."

He glares at me with unfocused eyes, looking about as threatening as a wet kitten. Finally, after what feels like a fucking eternity, he manages to haul himself into the saddle behind me, reeking of enough mead to stock a tavern.

Gullfax snorts and paws the ground the second Erik's ass hits the saddle, his coat rippling with barely contained energy. Bryn's already disappeared into the clouds above us, and this competitive bastard of a horse isn't about to let a Valkyrie show him up.

"Hold on!" I barely get the warning out before Gullfax launches us into the sky like we've been shot from a fucking cannon. The ground disappears beneath his hooves, clouds whipping past us at neck-breaking speed.

Dani's squeal of surprise turns into breathless laughter as she grips the reins. Behind me, Erik sways like a tree in a storm, and I clamp my arm around his wrist hard enough to leave bruises—because like hell am I explaining to Dani why her favorite brooding vampire fell off a flying horse.

"Holy shit," Erik slurs against my back, "when did you learn to control six horses at once?"

Fuck me. He's even more shitfaced than I thought.

LUCIAN

31

"Hey, hey, hey! Hands off the limited editions, Darkness McEdgelord!" I swat at the demon who's treating my vintage collection like it's a demonic coloring book. "Those babies are worth more than your sorry soul on the interdimensional black market. You so much as breathe on them wrong, and I'll go all samurai on your ass faster than you can say 'brimstone and bullshit.'"

I mean, the balls on this guy, waltzing into my crib like he's the Lord of the Underworld, leaving his stanky demon-stank all over my Italian leather couch. Those fiery eyes might work on the dumb schmucks he usually terrorizes, but I've seen scarier things in my morning mirror after a night of bad chimichangas.

The demon just stares at me, those soulless flaming eyes boring into me like he's trying to read my mind. Joke's on him, though—pretty sure even the most powerful telepaths would nope the fuck out of my head after five seconds. It's like a Hieronymus Bosch painting in there, but with more dick jokes and pop culture references.

He grumbles deep in his chest, like a malfunctioning garbage disposal, as I stand my ground. "Oh, don't you even start with that growling crap," I snap, pretty sure that's demon dialect for "fuck you."

"Listen up, Beelzebub," I continue, getting all up in his grill, which, let me tell you, is not a pleasant experience. The dude's breath smells like a tire fire in a sulfur factory. "I don't care if you're the biggest, baddest demon on the block. In Casa de Lucian, we have rules. Rule numero uno: keep your grubby mitts off my shit. Rule numero dos: if you're gonna park your ass on my couch, at least have the decency to Febreze yourself first. I just had this thing steam-cleaned."

"Lucian, quit your whining and leave Braxos alone," Emily snarks from her spot at the kitchen island, not even bothering to glance up from the dusty grimoire she's poring over. "He's not interested in your precious nerd stash, so take a chill pill and unclench, would you?"

I've been dealing with this demonic disaster for longer than I can stand, and it's driving me bat-shit insane. This asshole's got the manners of a brain-dead zombie, putting his grubby mitts on everything like it's a fucking free-for-all. And of course, I'm the only one who can't understand a damn word he's saying because I don't speak Demon like Little Miss Rosetta Crypt over there.

Seraphina, Sable, and Emily are gathered around the kitchen island, their noses buried in Sable's cookbook-slash-spellbook. They are trying to figure out how to send a magical smoke signal to Dani and maybe teach our new roommate some basic communication skills that don't involve Latin or interpretive dance.

Meanwhile, I'm over here, ready to put my head through a wall just for shits and giggles.

"If he's your new boy toy, then why don't you teach him some goddamn boundaries?" I snap, stalking into the kitchen to liberate a bottle of Jack from the liquor cabinet. If I'm gonna survive this asshole, I'm gonna need something a hell of a lot stronger than coffee. "Dude's been invading my personal bubble like he's got a PhD in bad touch."

"*Braxos, sede mecum,*" Emily commands, patting the stool next to her. The demon—all ten feet of midnight muscle—immediately plops down like an obedient hellhound.

"There, problem solved," Emily smirks, returning to her book. "Maybe if you spent more time expanding your mind instead of rotting it with stupid video games and bad porn, you'd be able to communicate with him too."

Seraphina, my sweet celestial snack cake, tries to diffuse the situation. "Now, now, let's all just take a deep breath and focus," she says, her melodic voice carrying an undercurrent of strained patience. "The sooner we find a way to contact Dani, the sooner we can figure out what to do with our new... guest and what to do about Lilith."

It took Seraphina a hot minute to stop treating our resident hellspawn like he had supernatural cooties. Once she figured out that Satan's Hemroid was basically Emily's oversized puppy with separation anxiety—thanks to whatever witchy leash she's got on him—my angel cake finally unclenched enough to stay in the same room without going full "smite first, ask questions later."

However, I can still feel her anxiety buzzing through our bond like a caffeinated hummingbird whenever Braxo's creepy fire eyes drift her way. I can't blame her—the guy looks like he crawled straight out of the Devil's fashion catalog. I tug her into my lap, wrapping around her like the world's most possessive octopus, and bury my face in her neck. Her scent hits me like a shot of pure heaven—all sunshine and cotton candy with just a hint of sass. Take that, demon boy—my girl smells way better than your sulfur-scented ass.

"Well said, Cupcake. However, if Sabrina the Teenage Bitch over here hadn't turned our kitchen into Hogwarts' red-headed stepchild, maybe I'd be able to relax without worrying about tall, dark, and demonic putting his creepy-crawlies all over my shit."

Emily flips me off without even looking up from her book, muttering something under her breath that sounds suspiciously like a curse. Knowing her, she's probably hexing my dick to fall off or something.

"Look! I believe I've found something," Sable announces, her delicate finger tracing ancient text that probably predates electricity. "This particular incantation appears to grant the recipient comprehensive linguistic abilities. Maybe we could use this to help Braxos communicate in a more... conventional manner?"

"Well, it beats playing charades with the Lord of Darkness over here," Emily drawls, eyeing our resident demon like he's a science experiment gone wrong. "Though I gotta say, his confused puppy face every time Lucian opens his mouth is pretty entertaining."

These magical mavens have been buried in that ancient tome for a full day, trying to decode spells that look like someone sneezed alphabet soup onto parchment. I mean, I'm about as magical as a rubber duck, but even I can tell that finding the right spell in that biblical behemoth is like trying to find a specific needle in a stack of identical needles. While blindfolded and drunk.

"Oh, this is quite fascinating," Sable continues, her eyes lighting up. "The spell has roots in ancient Babylonian practices, with elements of early Mediterranean magical theory..."

"Sable," Seraphina cuts in, her angelic voice carrying just enough sass to make me proud, "as absolutely riveting as the magical history lesson is, maybe we should focus on making our houseguest slightly more chatty? Before Lucian has an aneurysm about his comic collection?"

"Hey!" I grumble, squeezing her against me. "For your information, those comics are investments. Unlike some people, I'm planning for my retirement!"

Emily rolls her eyes. "Yes, because clearly, the apocalypse cares about your 401k of superhero memorabilia. Now shut up and let us work, or I'll let Braxos use your precious comics as coloring books."

The demon in question sits there, his eyes bouncing between us like he's watching the world's most confusing tennis match. Poor bastard probably thinks we're all insane. Welcome to the club, buddy.

"Oh, leave him alone," Seraphina giggles, her voice tinkling like bells. "You know how protective Lucian gets over his comic shrine."

"Shrine?" Emily snorts. "More like an altar to his arrested development. Though I gotta say, big guy," she turns to Braxos with a wicked grin, "you've got excellent taste. That limited edition Batman he caught you eyeing? Totally overrated."

"Ex-fucking-scuse you!" I screech, clutching my whiskey bottle like a security blanket. "Don't you dare poison his mind against the Dark Knight! And for your information, that's a first printing, signed by Frank Miller himself!"

"Sparky," Seraphina soothes, trying and failing to hide her amusement, "maybe we should focus on the whole 'saving the world' thing instead of your comic collection?"

"Fine," I grumble, taking a long pull from the bottle. "But if this asshole over there so much as breathes wrong on my mint condition X-Men #1, I'm installing holy water sprinklers."

Braxos blinks at me, probably plotting ways to reorganize my carefully curated comic filing system just to spite me. Demons, man. Can't live with 'em, can't exorcise 'em without Emily throwing a magical hissy fit.

"Damn, maybe I should slap that linguistic mojo on myself," Emily muses, tapping her chin like an evil genius plotting world domination. "Instant Latin fluency, baby! I'd ace my college course so hard. The professor would weep tears of joy."

"Emily." Sable admonishes, her voice carrying that signature blend of sweetness and wisdom that makes me want to puke rainbows. "You know, using magic for personal gain violates the fundamental laws of—"

"Balance, harmony, yadda yadda, I know," Emily grumbles, waving her hand dismissively. "Buzzkill. Fine, let's test drive this bad boy on Mr. Darkness over here. See if we can get him to use his words like a big boy."

Right on cue, Baby Vamp decides to emerge from his basement brooding session like some angsty teenager finally leaving their room. The kid is still deep in his "woe is me, I'm a creature of the night" phase, which, honestly? Been there, done that, got the t-shirt.

But before I can make a crack about his perfect vampire hair—

"What in the actual fuck is THAT?!" Damon shrieks.

Braxos rises to his full nightmare-inducing height and stalks toward Damon like he's spotted his next meal ticket. Oh, hell no, we are *not* adding "demon vs. vampire throwdown" to today's agenda.

"Emily!" I snap, already moving to intercept this clusterfuck. "Call off your hellhound before we end up with demon-vampire fusion cuisine!"

Emily's head whips around faster than a possessed Linda Blair. "*Desiste, Braxos!*" she barks out, her voice carrying that 'don't you dare fuck with me' tone that could probably make Satan himself sit and stay.

Fantastic. Because what this situation needed was another supernatural throwdown with Dani's baby bro. Yeah, no thanks—I've already got enough reasons for my feisty firecracker to want to roast my ass. I am not adding "Let Demon Maul Brother" to that list.

Braxos, ever the obedient little hellhound, slinks back to his seat like a scolded child, leaving Damon standing there looking like he just walked in on a demonic orgy.

"Damon, meet Braxos, Emily's butler," I announce, gesturing to the sulking mass of brimstone and a lousy attitude. "Don't worry, she's got his balls in a vice grip. Metaphorically speaking."

"Jesus fucking Christ," Damon mutters, making a beeline for the fridge like it's his safe house. "I did not sign up for this supernatural circus." He snags a blood bag and plops down at the opposite end of the island, putting as much distance between himself and our resident hellspawn as physically possible. "Just keep that walking nightmare fuel away from me, and we'll be golden."

I have to hand it to the kid—he's adapting to this whole "vampires, witches, and demons, oh my!" situation pretty damn well, all things considered. I mean, sure, he looks like he's about two seconds away from having a full-blown existential crisis, but hey, who isn't these days?

Sable saunters in with an armful of candles and some funky-smelling herbs. She arranges the candles like she's setting up for a romantic dinner date with Satan, then tells Emily to repeat after her. They start chanting in unison, their voices rising and falling in a creepy-ass harmony that makes my skin crawl.

Once the witchy duet finally wraps up, Emily looks expectantly at Braxos. "Alright, big guy, let's hear those dulcet tones in English."

"As you wish, Mistress," Braxos rumbles, his voice so deep it could give Barry White a run for his money. "How may I serve you?"

"Holy shit, it worked!" Sable squeals, bouncing up and down like a kid who just found out Santa's real. "I can't believe it!"

"Great, now, if only you could magic away his face," Damon mutters beside me, shuddering. "Because I'm pretty sure this dude's mug is gonna haunt my nightmares for the rest of my unnatural life."

"Is this more to your liking?" Braxos asks, and suddenly, his entire appearance shimmers like a heat mirage. When the distortion clears, my jaw practically hits the floor.

"Oh, HELL no!" I snap, jabbing a finger at the demon. "You are NOT allowed to cosplay as Bruce fucking Wayne!" Because, of course, this asshole would choose to impersonate the Dark Knight himself straight out of the pages of my precious comic collection.

"Damn," Emily breathes, her eyes wide with fascination. "So you can just... change your appearance at will? Like, to anything?"

"Indeed, Mistress," Braxos confirms, his face still wearing Bruce Wayne's chiseled features. "I can alter my physical form to suit your preferences."

I sit here, gaping like a fish out of water, trying to process that we now have a shape-shifting demon in our midst. A shape-shifting demon who has a hard-on for DC Comics.

I swear, if he starts quoting Batman lines, I'm gonna lose my shit.

Emily bolts into the living room like her ass is on fire, then comes rushing back with a magazine clutched in her hands. She slaps it down on the counter and starts flipping through the pages like a woman possessed until she finally jabs her finger at some poor, unsuspecting GQ model. "Him!" she declares, her eyes gleaming with unholy glee. "Can you make yourself look like this fine specimen of manhood?"

Lo and behold, our resident demon Houdini does his little shimmer-shimmer act, and suddenly, we're staring at a carbon copy of the magazine Hottie. I'm talking luscious, flowing locks that probably have their own line of hair care products, smoldering bedroom eyes that could melt a nun's chastity belt, and a body that looks chiseled out of pure, grade-A beefcake.

Emily's eyes go all liquid sex, and I know that look. I've seen it on every poor bastard who's ever fallen victim to a succubus. She's about two seconds away from climbing this demon like a tree, and I am NOT here for it.

"Ohhh, no. Fuck no!" I protest, holding up my hands like I'm trying to ward off evil. Which, let's be real, I kind of am. "There will be no demon-witch boot-knocking under this roof, you hear me? I did not sign up for a front-row seat to the supernatural porno Olympics!"

Emily shoots me a glare that could castrate a lesser man. "Jesus, Lucian, get your mind out of the gutter for once," she snaps, but I can see how her cheeks are flushed. "What's wrong? Jealous that you can't pull off the 'Abercrombie & Fitch meets Hellraiser' look."

I roll my eyes. "Oh, please. I'm secure enough in my own devilish good looks, thank you very much. I just don't want to have to bleach my eyeballs after walking in on you two doing the nasty on every available surface."

My angel cake tries to play peacemaker. "Guys, come on. Let's all take a deep breath," she soothes, but even she can't entirely hide the appreciative once-over she gives Braxos's new look. "I'm sure Emily knows better than to engage in any... inappropriate activities with...um, this demon—our guest."

Emily huffs, crossing her arms over her chest. But I swear to God, if I catch her playing 'hide the hellsalami' with him, I'm gonna need a whole lot more than holy water to cleanse my soul.

This whole situation is turning into a fucking CW TV show. All we need now is for Damon to profess his undying love for Sable, and we'll have the full bingo card of 'shit I never wanted to deal with in my immortal life.'

"So, we're all in agreement that this is a major improvement, right?" Emily gestures to Braxos's new look as if she's unveiling a work of art. She doesn't even wait for us to answer before barreling on. "Great. Now, let's get down to business. Who or what came through that rift before you decided to join our little party?"

Braxos, apparently feeling right at home in his shiny new meat suit, casually leans against the kitchen island like he's posing for a fucking GQ spread. It's equally impressive and disturbing, if I'm being honest. "From what I gathered, Mistress, it was a vampire," he purrs, staring at Emily with barely enough restrained lust to power a small country.

"Wait, a vampire?" Sable chimes in, her brow furrowing in that adorable way that makes her look like a confused kitten. "Did you catch a name or any identifying details?"

I catch Damon sneaking glances at Sable from the corner of my eye, and I have to physically restrain myself from rolling my eyes so hard they pop out of my skull. Jesus H. Christ on a cracker, I knew it. The kid's crushing harder than a twelve-year-old at a Justin Bieber concert.

"Unfortunately, I don't have a name for you," Braxos replies, somehow managing to make even that sound suggestive as fuck. "All I know is that a vampire was pulled through the rift from the stone."

Well, isn't that just fan-fucking-tastic? Not only do we have to worry about Lilith and her vampire army, but now we've got a mystery vamp on the loose, doing God knows what with a chunk of the most dangerous magical rock in existence.

I swear, it's like the universe looked at our shit show of a situation and went, "You know what this needs? More variables! Let's throw in a wild card vampire to keep things spicy!"

"Okay, let's take a step back and think about this," Sable muses. "Why would Lilith go through the trouble of yanking a vampire's soul out of Unbra? What's her angle here? Could it be Azrael, back for round two?"

I'm pretty sure we're all thinking the same damn thing at this point. Rhyland gave that pretentious prick a one-way ticket to the great beyond before his little field trip to the Thunderdome. But with our luck? I wouldn't be surprised if the bastard found a way to weasel out of eternal damnation just to fuck with us some more.

"Your guess is as good as mine," Emily sighs, pinching the bridge of her nose like she's trying to stave off a migraine. "Braxos, care to shed some light on how the whole Shadow Realm schtick works? What's the deal with souls being able to hop dimensions like it's no big thing?"

"I must admit, I'm rather curious about that myself," Seraphina chimes in, her angelic face scrunched up in thought. "I've pored over the Book of Shadows more times than I can count, but the specifics of soul mechanics have always been a bit... vague."

I lean back in my chair, nursing my whiskey like it keeps me sane. Which, let's be honest, it probably is. "Alright, big guy," I drawl, gesturing to Braxos with my glass. "Lay it on us. Give us the 411 on this whole 'souls playing hopscotch through the cosmos' situation."

Braxos, still wearing his shiny new skin like he's auditioning for America's Next Top Demon, clears his throat. "The Shadow Realm is a complex tapestry of energies and dimensions," he begins, his voice taking on a lecturing tone that reminds me way too much of my least favorite college professor. "Souls are not bound by the same physical constraints as their mortal vessels, and as such, they can traverse the various planes of existence with relative ease."

I blink, trying to process the word vomit that just spewed from his mouth. "In English, please? Some of us didn't major in Metaphysical Bullshit."

Braxos shoots me a look that's half exasperation, half barely-contained lust for Emily Gross. "In layman's terms," he says, each word oozing with condescension, "souls can move between dimensions if the conditions are right. And with the power of the Soul Stone, those conditions become much more... flexible."

Fuck. So not only do we have to worry about Lilith playing puppet master with vampire souls, but she's got a magical MacGuffin that basically gives her a free pass to yank whoever she wants out of the afterlife.

I'm starting to think we need to invest in some cosmic restraining order against this bitch. Like, "Lilith, by order of the universe, you are hereby forbidden from fucking with the natural order of things. Violators will be subject to eternal damnation and/or aggressive bitch-slapping by yours truly."

But knowing our luck, she'd probably wipe her ass with it and keep right on wreaking havoc.

"There is another matter you should understand," Braxos states, his tone carrying the weight of ancient knowledge despite his model appearance. "The souls claimed by the stone are delivered directly to Lord Moretemis in Unbra, like tributes to the Dark God. Each one consumed adds to his terrible might. The stone was never intended to draw souls back from his realm, but with sufficient power and knowledge, one could reverse its purpose."

"So, what happens to the soul once it's punched its ticket back from the Shadow Realm?" Emily leans forward, her eyes sparking with that dangerous curiosity that usually leads to trouble. "Is it just, like, a spooky ghost, floating around all invisible and shit?"

"No, Mistress," Braxos responds with that formal, old-world precision that makes him sound like he stepped out of a Shakespeare play. "Upon breaching the veil of Unbra, souls regain their corporeal form."

I lean forward, trying to wrap my head around this mindfuck. "Let me get this straight," I say, pinching the bridge of my nose. "Thanks to the power of bullshit magic, said soul is just walking around, business as usual, in the body it wore before getting ganked?"

Braxos inclines his head, a simple gesture that somehow manages to convey a metric fuckton of gravitas. "In essence, yes. Once returned, the soul can reclaim its physical vessel to walk the earth as before its demise."

"So then, when a soul goes to Unbra, they aren't...really dead?" Sable asks, her chocolate eyes wide with innocent wonder. She's twisting a strand of pink hair around her finger like she always does when her brain's working overtime. "I mean, I always thought death was so... final."

"The mortal concept of 'death' is but a primitive approximation of a far more complex transition," Braxos intones, his stolen model face attempting solemnity. "Souls are cosmic currency, harvested and categorized according to their essence in the great collection chambers of Unbra. They are meant to remain there for eternity, feeding the darkness." He raises those perfectly sculpted eyebrows in what I assume is supposed to be ominous foreshadowing. "Until that balance was... just disrupted."

Great. Because supernatural soul trafficking wasn't complicated enough. Now we've got interdimensional jailbreaks to deal with.

"So what you're saying is Moretemis basically runs some kind of twisted soul filing system?" Emily cuts in, rolling her eyes. "Like, 'Oh, here's another dead human! Let me just catalog you under 'H' for 'Had it coming' and stick you on my soul shelf'? That's seriously how the afterlife works?"

Ten bucks says she's already planning some half-baked magical experiment that'll either save us all or blow up the mansion.

"Your mortal metaphor, while crude, holds elements of truth. The Great Shadow's methods are beyond mortal comprehension, but—"

I take a long pull from my whiskey bottle, watching this supernatural TED talk unfold. Between Sable's earnest curiosity, Emily's barely-contained magical mad scientist vibe, and our resident demon trying to explain the afterlife like it's a cosmic library system, I'm starting to think we should sell tickets to this shit show.

Maybe we could call it 'Souls, Sorcery, and Sarcasm: A Night with the Supernatural Misfits.' We'd make a killing.

DANICA

32

My boots crunch into snow that sparkles like scattered diamonds, my breath creating little clouds that dance away on the arctic wind. Even through my fur-lined coat—which is seriously the coziest thing ever—the cold tries to bite through to my bones. Thank god for my internal supernatural space heater, or I'd be frozen solid right about now.

Gullfax wasn't exaggerating when he said this was the end of the line. The winds raging ahead look like they could turn our majestic flying steed into a very bewildered golden tumbleweed. But holy shit, nothing could have prepared me for the nightmare wonderland that is Valhalla's Veil.

Gigantic bones bleached white as moonlight, jut from the frozen ground like ancient markers. The fog is impossibly thick, swirling around crumbling ruins that might have been magnificent once upon a time. And then there's the cave—this giant, gaping maw in the mountainside that looks ready to swallow souls whole.

"What in the actual hell happened here?" I breathe, unable to tear my eyes away from the macabre display.

Bryn materializes beside me like some gorgeous gothic angel, her obsidian wings folded against her back. "This, sister, is where the greatest of our kind take their final rest—gods and warriors of old." Her mismatched eyes scan the bone-littered landscape with reverence tinged with caution. "Sacred ground, but don't let the ghosts fool you into thinking they're all that walks here. Quick now—we need shelter before the Hræsvelgr spot us. Those eagle giants have a nasty habit of turning travelers into their evening snack."

Baldr and Heimdall easily dismount Sleipnir. Behind us, Erik is doing his best impression of a drunk trying to solve a Rubik's cube as he attempts to get off Gullfax.

"Your silver-haired companion appears to be... challenged," Gullfax's voice echoes in my head, rich as thunder and dripping with amusement. *"Allow me to provide some... assistance."*

Before I can respond, Gullfax rears up, sending Erik tumbling into the snow with an undignified yelp. He lands with a thud, a tangle of leather and silver hair half-buried in a snowdrift.

Rhyland pinches the bridge of his nose, looking like he's praying for the strength not to strangle his brother or the horse. I swear I can hear his teeth grinding from here.

"Was that really necessary?" I hiss at Gullfax, trying not to laugh at the absurdity of it all.

The horse somehow manages to shrug without actually having shoulders. *"I merely expedited his disembarkation process. Time is of the essence, is it not?"* His mental voice is so smug I'm half-expecting him to manifest a top hat and monocle.

Erik staggers to his feet, swaying momentarily before finding his balance. I approach him, offering my arm for support as we head towards the cave of doom."Okay, spill it, Mr. Broody. What's got you drowning in mead and acting like a freshman at his first frat party?"

He gives me that half-smile that's probably charmed the pants off countless women over the centuries. "Nothing that requires your concern, Little Huntress. I assure you, I'm perfectly..." he hiccups, "...fine."

But I catch his silver eyes darting around the area like he's expecting an ambush. When they land on Bryn, his whole body becomes rigid, as if someone just replaced his spine with a steel rod. "Why is she here?" The words come out like shards of ice. "I was under the impression she was remaining behind."

"She thought it was best to come along. Is that a problem?" I ask, my spidey senses tingling like crazy.

Erik brushes past me, his earlier drunken stumble replaced by a predator's prowl. "No, no problem at all." But his voice is tight and controlled, and I'm pretty sure he just went from plastered to stone-cold sober in 2.5 seconds flat.

The wall of stoicism slams back into place so fast it gives me whiplash.

Well, clearly, I misread those vibes earlier. Erik's acting like Bryn's presence is a personal insult, which is weird considering what I thought.

Not to mention Bryn lip-locking with that mountain of a Viking warrior earlier. Clearly my matchmaking radar needs a serious tune-up. Maybe I should stick to my day job and leave the romance predictions to the professionals.

Maybe that's just it. Perhaps the big secret is that Erik can't stand my sister but is too noble to say anything. It would be just like him to suffer in silence, drowning his annoyance in mead while playing the dutiful soldier because Erik puts everyone else's needs before his own.

God, men are exhausting. Vampires even more so. And don't even get me started on vampire brothers with their stupid honor codes and secret-keeping bullshit. Fine. If Erik wants to brood himself into oblivion while pretending my sister doesn't exist, that's his business. I have bigger issues—like not dying in this creepy bone garden while hunting down magical stones.

As we step into the cave, the temperature shifts, the biting wind replaced by an eerie stillness that raises goosebumps on my skin. Baldr and Heimdall lead the horses to a designated stabling area, complete with stone troughs filled with crystal-clear water and gleaming golden hay. Even in the land of the dead, the gods spare no expense for their equine guests.

But it's the cave itself that steals my breath. I was expecting something dark, damp, and cramped—the kind of place that makes you feel like the walls are closing in. Instead, I find myself standing in a vast underground cathedral, so immense that the distant ceiling is lost in shadows.

The air hums with ancient power, making my teeth vibrate and my hair stand on end. Torches flicker along the walls, their warm light dancing across intricate murals depicting scenes from Norse legends—gods battling giants, Valkyries riding through storm-tossed skies, and heroes feasting in the halls of Valhalla.

"Welcome to our Hall of the Fallen," Bryn announces. "Try not to touch anything. Some of these relics have a nasty habit of... shall we say, expressing their displeasure with unworthy hands."

She gestures to a towering figure with a raised sword, her voice carrying both reverence and pride. "Tyr, the one-handed god of war and justice. Lost his hand binding Fenrir—quite the scandal at the time. But that's what happens when you stick your limbs in a giant wolf's mouth, eh?"

"Indeed," Baldr's voice rumbles from behind me, his smile a little too knowing.

Okay, creepy.

Moving through the cathedral-like space, her wings casting dramatic shadows on the walls, she indicates another statue. "Njord, master of sea and wind. Bit of a drama queen if you ask me—couldn't decide whether he preferred the mountains or the shore. He ended up divorcing his wife over it. Gods," she rolls her eyes, "always making everything so complicated."

She stops before a towering statue, where ethereal lightning seems to ripple across the stone, even in the flickering torchlight. Her voice is softer, tinged with reverence and old sorrow. "This is Thor as he was meant to be remembered—the mighty defender of realms, protector of both gods and mortals. His laughter could shake the mountains themselves, and his heart matched the vastness of his storms." Her fingers trace the carved lightning with careful respect. "He was everything a God should be—honorable, just, powerful. But..." she hesitates, her eyes clouding with memory, "he gave everything for this realm."

"During the war?" I ask quietly, caught in the gravity of her words.

"Yes..." The single word carries the weight of centuries, hanging heavy in the ancient air between us.

I turn to look at Rhyland, who is frozen before the towering statue of his grandfather, his broad shoulders rigid with tension. The family resemblance is striking—and heartbreaking—as the grandson stares up at the carved face of the god who lost his life to save what he loved.

Baldr scoffs. "He may have died protecting the realms, but dead is dead."

"Mind your words, Baldr!" Bryn's voice cracks like a whip, her wings flaring with anger. "You dare dishonor the fallen in their own sacred halls?"

My jaw clenches at Baldr's casual dismissal of Thor's sacrifice—who gave everything to save these realms, and this jerk acts like it meant nothing.

"My apologies," Baldr mutters, though his tone suggests he's anything but sorry.

"Before Ragnarök," Heimdall's voice echoes with the weight of millennia, "Zephyria was one vast kingdom. The great war tore the realm asunder, splitting the land into the floating islands you see today, scattered across the endless sky."

I take in this revelation, imagining how this place must have looked before—one big celestial continent, now broken into these drifting pieces of sacred ground. Even the destruction of their realm couldn't break their connection to these holy sites.

I study the towering statue, feeling its significance. This god sacrificed everything to protect his realm—no wonder they still honor him with such reverence. Even in stone, his presence commands respect.

Bryn pauses before a stunningly beautiful statue, her lips curving into a knowing smile. "And here's Freya—goddess of love, beauty, and war. Don't let that lovely face fool you. She could split a man's skull as easily as she could break his heart. My kind of woman."

As we approach the altar, Bryn's expression grows more serious. "This is where the most sacred rites were performed, where warriors swore their final oaths before battle." She runs her fingers along the ancient runes. "The power here is older than time itself. Can you feel it? The way it makes your blood sing and your skin tingle? That's the old magic recognizing its own."

Bryn turns to face us, her warrior's stance softening slightly. "Mind your step around here, sister. The gods may be gone, but their power lingers. And they do so love to test the mettle of those who enter their domain."

"Right," Baldr interrupts. "Time to discuss the rather... interesting challenges ahead. The gods do so love their tests of worthiness."

"I'm sorry—their what now?" I spin around to face him, my heart doing a nervous little tap dance in my chest. "Because if you're about to tell me we need to solve some divine riddles or fight a kraken, I'd like to submit my formal resignation as savior."

A deep, rich chuckle rumbles from Rhyland beside me, the sound warming me despite the arctic chill.

Just thinking about Aquaria and all those mind-bending riddles, not to mention the delightful encounter with the resident Kraken in that cave, already gives me PTSD flashbacks.

"The path to the Elemental Nexus demands more than just courage," Baldr's continues, unfazed by my rising panic. "The mountains here hold the essence of one Einherjar—the first of two chosen by Zephyria to unlock the Elemental Nexus."

"Hold up—what's an Einherjar?" I raise my hand like I'm back in science class, trying to keep up with this new supernatural curveball.

"A guardian," Rhyland answers before Baldr can open his mouth. "A warrior chosen by the gods."

I blink at him for a moment before the implications sink in. "So you're telling me we have to throw down with some legendary ghost warrior to steal their magical essence? What is this—Viking Fight Club meets Ghostbusters?"

Baldr's lips twitch with what might be amusement—or maybe he's just enjoying watching me process this madness. "Defeat the Einherjar in honorable combat, and their essence becomes yours. Only then will you begin unlocking the Elemental Nexus path."

I glance at Rhyland, hoping for some reassurance, but even he can't quite hide the concern in those steely blue eyes. Great. When the thousand-year-old Viking vampire looks worried, you know you're in for a world of trouble.

"Listen here, sister," Bryn's eyes flash with fierce pride as she grips my shoulder. "You've already gone toe-to-toe with so much and lived to tell the tale. These trials?" She snorts, her obsidian wings flexing. "They're just another story for the skalds to sing about over their mead."

Her grip tightens a warrior's strength in her fingers. "We'll guard your backs as much as we can. But..." she glances around the hall with dangerous amusement, "try not to take your sweet time about it. These lands crawl with Draugr and frost giants—ugly bastards with even uglier temperaments. And trust me, their version of a welcome feast usually ends with someone's head on a pike."

She cocks an eyebrow, her stance pure battle-ready Valkyrie despite her smirk. "Now go make this ancient Einherjar your bitch. The gods might be old, but they've never faced anyone quite like you, sister. Give them hell."

My heart swells with fierce affection for my sister. Gods, her warrior spirit and take-no-prisoners attitude is exactly the kick in the ass I need right now.

"Wait—you mentioned two," I narrow my eyes at Baldr. "Where's the second one hiding?"

Baldr busies himself with his pack, clearly avoiding my gaze. "Let's focus on surviving the first Einherjar before we worry about the second, Lightborn." His tone makes it clear that's all I'm getting out of him right now.

I spot Erik lurking in his signature shadowy corner, while scanning the room with predatory focus. "Watch over my sister." I make it a command, not a request.

"Ha!" Bryn's laugh echoes through the chamber. "Save your worry for the silver-haired lightweight over there, sister. The mighty vampire who can't even dismount a horse without falling on his ass. Some legendary warrior." She smirks, crossing her arms. "I've seen baby Valkyries handle their mead better."

Erik's silver eyes narrow dangerously at Bryn, his glare cold enough to freeze Helheim itself. But I swear I catch the slightest twitch at the corner of his mouth before he transforms his features into their usual stoic mask.

"We make camp here," Bryn announces with a Valkyrie's authority. "I'll take the first watch. When dawn breaks, we track down this Einherjar."

"May the Norns guide your path, Lightborn," Heimdall adds. His bright green eyes shift to Rhyland, and something ancient passes between them. "And you, Godborn. Remember who you are."

ERIK

33

The fire's warmth does little to thaw the ice in my veins as I watch her from across the hall. Everyone else has surrendered to exhaustion—Rhyland's soft snores mixing with Dani's steady breathing—but sleep eludes me. I couldn't leave Bryn to stand watch alone, though every moment in her presence is exquisite torture.

She raises her horn to those perfect lips, drinking deeply as firelight dances across her features. The flames reflect in her mismatched eyes, creating a hypnotic display that makes my chest ache. This morning's memory burns fresher than any wound—that worthless creature's hands on her body, his mouth claiming what should be mine. The image alone makes my fangs itch, jealousy coursing through me like poison.

I know I'm being a fool. She's clearly chosen another, and the thought of her rejecting our bond—rejecting me—is a special kind of hell I'm not prepared to face. Better to suffer in silence than risk the soul-crushing agony of mate denial. At least that's what I tell myself, even as possessive rage claws at my insides. Every time I close my eyes, I see his hands on her body, his lips stealing kisses that should belong to me. The urge to tear him apart had been nearly overwhelming.

It's why I sought oblivion in mead—a pathetic attempt to dull this constant, maddening pull toward her. This bone-deep ache that nothing can satisfy.

Her eyes suddenly lock with mine, and my breath catches as she rises with fluid grace. Each step she takes in my direction sends my pulse racing.

Fuck.

Dani's worry pierced through my carefully constructed walls, her empathy as potent as her sister's disdain. She's relentless in her worry, though I've given her no cause. My brother, suffers his mate's frustration because of my threats to keep silent.

The weight of their combined concern sits heavy on my shoulders, an unwanted reminder of what I'm denying myself.

But what purpose would confession serve? Bryn is Dani's blood, her newly discovered sister, and the contempt in those eyes whenever they fall upon me speaks volumes. Each dismissive glance, each cold shoulder, reinforces what I already know—she despises everything I am.

Why offer up my heart to someone who would surely crush it beneath her bootheel? No, it's better to bury these feelings deep and lock them away with other regrets. Let no one bear the burden of my fate's cruel joke. Once we leave this realm, distance will dull this maddening pull. The ache will fade or at least become bearable.

It has to.

"Having trouble finding your beauty rest, vampire?" Bryn's voice carries a playfulness as she settles beside me, close enough that her scent—battle steel and winter storms—assaults my senses. My fangs ache to descend, I clench my jaw, fighting for control.

The memory of Dani's blood from this morning sits heavy in my stomach—sustenance without satisfaction. It might as well be water compared to the siren call of Bryn's pulse, beating strong and steady beside me. The scent of her calls to me in ways no other's has, rich with power and divinity. My throat burns with thirst. It's maddening how ineffective my control is around Bryn—this mate-bond trying desperately to form.

"No," I manage, the word coming out harder than intended, fighting the urge to drag her into my arms and claim what fate declares is mine.

"Oh? The mighty Erik reduced to one-word answers?" She arches an eyebrow, those beautiful eyes glinting with challenge. "And here I thought vampires were supposed to be charming."

"Just tired." The lie tastes bitter on my tongue.

"Well, tough shit." She takes a long pull from her horn, her throat working in a way that makes my cock thick with need. "I'm stuck on watch duty, and you're the only entertainment available. So congratulations, you've been promoted to a conversation partner." Her lips curve into a predatory smile. "Unless you're not up for the challenge?"

I let my head fall back against the cold marble; the stone's chill is nothing compared to the ice I'm trying to maintain in my veins. "How may I be of service?"

The words drip with resigned sarcasm as I snatch her horn, deliberately letting my fingers brush against hers. The contact sends electricity through my arm. I drain the vessel in one long pull, the mead burning less than her presence beside me.

Her eyes widen at my audacity before that dangerous smile curves her lips—the same smile that's been haunting my dreams. "Well, well. The statue can move after all." She leans closer, her scent making my head spin. "Tell me, vampire, how did you end up playing guardian to my sister? What makes the mighty *Erik* so special that Dani trusts you with her life?"

The way she says my name—like it's both a challenge and a caress—makes my balls ache. Every shift of her body, every subtle movement, draws my attention like a moth to a flame.

"For that particular tale, we'll need significantly more alcohol," I manage to say, keeping my gaze fixed on the dancing flames. Every muscle in my body remains rigid, fighting the urge to turn and drink in her presence. The stone at my back becomes an anchor, something solid to brace against as her proximity threatens to shatter my control.

"Fortunate for you then," her voice carries that melody that sets my fangs on edge, "I came prepared." The whisper of leather against stone tells me she's moved, and her scent grows stronger as she returns. The soft thud of her settling beside me again nearly breaks my resolve. A well-worn leather bladder appears in my peripheral vision, swollen with promise.

She fills the horn to the brim, the scent of honey and spices wafting between us as she hands it back. "Now, where were we? Ah yes, your history with my sister."

I accept the drink. "Dani is family now that she's...mated to Rhyland." The word 'mate' scrapes past my lips like broken glass, knowing what I'm denying myself. "She's proven herself a warrior worth following, fierce enough to match my brother's stubborn ass. I'm honored to call her sister."

"Hm." She plucks the horn from my grasp, her fingers ghosting over mine in a maddening caress. Refilling the vessel, she takes a long pull before continuing, "She speaks highly of you as well. Says you're one of the good ones—a vampire worth keeping around." Her eyes glint with curiosity as she leans closer, her scent torturing me. "But what about before Dani? Surely a vampire as old as you has a few skeletons in his closet."

My jaw ticks at her question, eons of carefully buried memories threatening to surface. The mead suddenly tastes bitter on my tongue. "I was a warrior," I finally admit, the words feeling like ancient rust in my mouth. "A knight during the Crusades. Led men into battle under the banner of faith and righteousness." A hollow laugh escapes me. "Ironic that I now walk the Earth as one of God's forsaken."

The confession hangs between us, heavy with unspoken horrors. I dare not look at her, afraid those eyes might see too deeply into the darkness of my past. Every warrior carries their demons, but mine have had millennia to fester.

"Really?" Bryn shifts closer, her warrior's interest piqued—curiosity in her eyes. "Enlighten me about these Crusades of yours, vampire. What drove a man to fight in the name of faith?"

I take another long pull from the horn, letting the mead fortify me against memories I've kept locked away. "I was young, barely twenty-five when I took up the cross. Second son of a noble house, raised on tales of glory and purpose." A bitter smile twists my lips. "The First Crusade, the year was 1096. Pope Urban II called for warriors to reclaim Jerusalem from Muslim control. We were young, foolish, drunk on promises of glory and divine salvation." My laugh holds no humor. "I led five hundred men across scorched earth and endless desert, watching them die from heat, disease, and enemy blades."

"And you believed in this holy cause?" Her voice carries a warrior's understanding of battle yet challenges my past convictions.

"At first. Seven years later, I saw what 'holy war' truly meant. Women and children were slaughtered in the name of God. Cities burned. Atrocities committed under the banner of righteousness." The memories taste like shit. "I began to question everything I'd been taught to believe."

"So what happened?" She leans forward, her breath ghosting across my cheek. "How did the righteous knight become the vampire?"

Her proximity makes my stomach clench. "Siege of Jerusalem. I'd stopped fighting for God by then—fought only to protect my remaining men. One of them, a boy barely sixteen, took an arrow meant for me. As I carried him to safety, a Saracen blade found my back." I touch the spot where the sword had pierced my heart. "I lay dying in the dirt, choking on my own blood when a shadow fell over me. She called herself Lilith. Said she'd been watching me, admiring how I'd evolved from blind religion to questioning everything. She offered a choice—die there in the sand or rise as something new."

"And you chose to rise," Bryn's voice holds no judgment, only understanding.

"Death held no fear for me. But I had men still alive who needed leadership. So yes, I chose to rise." I meet her gaze finally. "I've spent an eternity trying to atone for the atrocities I committed in the name of faith. Perhaps that's my true curse—living long enough to understand the weight of my sins."

I stare into the flames, memories of blood-soaked sand and burning cities dancing in the fire. Faith had been a constant companion once, as natural as breathing. But watching innocent children slaughtered in God's name, hearing priests justify rape and torture as divine will—it broke something fundamental inside me. How could a merciful God demand such barbarism? The questions plagued me like festering wounds, each atrocity I witnessed another nail in faith's coffin.

The cross I'd worn became heavier with each passing day until it felt like a noose around my neck. I'd knelt in blood-spattered churches, begging for answers that never came. In the end, I didn't lose my faith—I buried it alongside countless innocents in shallow desert graves.

"Atoning for your sins?" Bryn's voice cuts through my dark musings, that playfulness softening into something more profound. "Seems to me you've spent a long time punishing yourself for following orders that weren't yours. The real monsters were the ones giving those commands, not the warriors who had to carry them out." Her eyes lock onto mine with startling intensity. "Sometimes the most honorable thing a warrior can do is question the cause they serve."

Her words strike deeper than any blade, piercing through carefully constructed walls. I turn to face her, fighting against the magnetic pull of her presence. "Honor?" A bitter smile tugs at my lips. "Honor died in the sand. What remained was..." I pause, studying how the firelight catches the gold in her right eye. "Survival. Purpose. The need to ensure such blind devotion never claims more innocent lives."

"And yet here you are," she counters, "protecting my sister, fighting for a cause greater than yourself. Seems your honor survived more intact than you'd like to admit."

I allow myself a moment of weakness, letting my gaze trace the curve of her jaw. "Perhaps. Or perhaps I've grown better at choosing my battles."

"And this battle?" She gestures between us, her meaning clear. "The one where you're trying so hard to maintain that stone wall of yours?"

The metal protests beneath my grip, threatening to buckle. "Some walls exist for good reason, Little Bird." The endearment slips out before I can catch it, a moment of weakness I instantly regret.

"Don't." Her voice carries steel and storm. "I'm not your 'Little Bird' or anyone else's." She snatches the horn, drinking deeply before fixing me with a glare that could freeze Hell. "And while we're clearing the air, I don't need you playing hero every time a fight breaks out. I've been slaying monsters since before you picked up your first sword. I'm a fucking Valkyrie, not some helpless maiden waiting for a knight to rescue her."

Irritation floods my veins, hot and sharp. "Forgive me for thinking a warrior might appreciate battlefield support. Next time, I'll stand back and applaud while you take on an entire army alone." My voice drops to a dangerous whisper. "Because that's worked out so well for you recently."

Her eyes flash with deadly promise, the dual colors blazing. "Glad we understand each other."

I clench my fists until my knuckles whiten, jealousy and regret warring in my chest. "Or perhaps it's just my aid you find so offensive. You seemed perfectly content accepting help from that Viking bastard this morning." The words escape like poison, and I hate myself the moment they leave my lips. The memory of her in his arms turns my stomach and makes my fangs ache with possessive rage. But I have no right to that anger, no claim to her choices.

Bryn rises in one fluid motion, power radiating off her like a storm about to break. "What I do, and who I choose to do it with," she snaps, with lethal sweetness, "is absolutely none of your fucking business, *vampire.*" She spits the last word like a curse before stalking away, her wings rigid with fury.

I drag a hand down my face, cursing my loose tongue. Lifetimes of careful control are shattered by jealousy and mead. The memory of her anger—gods, even her rage is beautiful—sends heat straight to my growing cock. I shift uncomfortably, my leather pants suddenly too tight, too constraining. My body's reaction to her only proves how far I've fallen, how deeply this mate bond has already taken root despite my efforts to deny it.

Brilliant work, Erik. Truly masterful diplomacy.

DANICA

34

The snow crunches beneath Gullfax's hooves as we trudge through the icy wilderness, the biting wind nipping at any exposed skin. Bryn, Erik, and Heimdall flank us on either side, their steps sure and steady despite the treacherous terrain. Behind us, Baldr rides Sleipnir, his eyes scanning the horizon for any signs of trouble.

Rhyland's arms tighten around my waist, pulling me flush against his chest. The unmistakable evidence of his desire presses insistently into my lower back, and I can't help but roll my eyes at his one-track mind.

"Hey, Lightning Rod," I quip, my breath fogging in the frigid air. "Could you keep your 'sword' in its sheath for a bit? It's getting a little distracting."

Rhyland's deep chuckle rumbles through his chest, sending shivers down my spine that have nothing to do with the cold. "Maybe if you stopped playing hard to get, Angel," he grumbles, his lips brushing the shell of my ear. "I wouldn't be so tempted to 'sheath' it elsewhere."

I let out an exaggerated sigh, keeping my eyes fixed ahead. "Sorry, babe, but your sword privileges got revoked when you joined the Secret-Keepers Anonymous club. Maybe try sharing with the class next time."

Rhyland's growl vibrates through my body, his voice low and dangerous. "You can't resist me forever, Angel." He punctuates his words by yanking me tighter against his muscular chest, forcing a small grunt from my lips as Gullfax maintains his steady pace through the snow. "I have my methods. Or did you forget how persuasive I can be when I want something?"

I open my mouth for what would have been a brilliant comeback, but Bryn's sharp "Shh!" cuts through the tension like a knife. We all freeze, the playful moment evaporating instantly as we strain to listen.

The silence engulfs us, the snow absorbing even the faintest whisper of sound. Gullfax stands motionless beneath us. His muscles coiled tight like a spring, ready to snap. The stillness is suffocating, the weight of anticipation pressing on my chest.

Then, in a blur of motion, I'm airborne. Before I hit the ground, the world spins—the impact knocks the breath from my lungs. Snow fills my mouth and nose, and the icy crystals sting my face as I struggle to orient myself.

As I push myself up on shaking arms, a guttural snarl freezes the blood in my veins. Slowly, I raise my head, blinking away the snow clinging to my lashes. What I see sends a bolt of pure, unadulterated terror through my heart.

"Draugr!" Bryn shouts.

Holy shit. These aren't the sanitized zombies from horror movies—they're something far more ancient and terrifying. Their bloated, waterlogged corpses rise from the snow like demons from a Norse nightmare. Their skin has the sickly blue-black hue of the long-dead, stretched tight over swollen flesh. Ancient Viking armor, crusted with ice and decay, still clings to their hulking frames—these warriors died in battle and rose again with supernatural strength. Their eyes glow with an eerie blue fire in sunken sockets, radiating a cold beyond physical chill—the cold of the grave itself.

These undead Vikings tower over us, their forms nearly twice the size of a living man. The stench of death and decay rolls off them in waves, made worse by the putrid black liquid that oozes from their mouths and wounds. Their movements are unnaturally quick for their size, and they possess a terrible strength that death has only enhanced.

We're surrounded, the undead warriors closing in from all sides. Their heavy footfalls crack the frozen ground beneath them, and their rattling breaths sound like the last gasps of drowning men.

The Aquanite stone in my crown pulses with an unfamiliar urgency like it's trying to tell me something. I barely have time to process this new sensation before my body moves on pure instinct, daggers sliding free from my hips as I launch myself at the nearest Draugr.

Time warps around me—my favorite trick, and damn if I haven't gotten good at it. The world crystallizes into slow motion, giving me a front-row seat to the horror show. The Draugr's battle axe cuts through the air with glacial slowness, its rotting muscles bulging beneath blackened skin—child's play to dodge.

I dance under the swing, my movements fluid and precise in the warped time. My daggers find the gaps in its ancient armor, but as black ichor sprays across the snow, the crown pulses again—more assertive this time, almost demanding. The Aquanite stone's energy races through my veins like liquid lightning, and suddenly, I understand.

Snow. It's just frozen water.

A savage grin spreads across my face as I reach out with my mind, feeling for that familiar liquid connection. The Aquanite stone's power surges through me, and holy shit—I can feel every single snowflake, every ice crystal. But more than that, I can sense the frozen water trapped in the Draugrs' waterlogged flesh.

Time snaps back to normal as I flex this new power. The charging Draugr freezes mid-stride, confusion evident in its glowing blue eyes as the moisture in its dead flesh responds to my call. I clench my fist, and the ice crystals within it expand violently. The monster explodes from the inside out, painting the landscape with frozen chunks of undead gore.

"Well, that's new," I laugh, watching black blood crystallize mid-air—the crown thrums with approval.

Two more lumber toward me, but now I'm in my element. Time warps again, and I slide between them like smoke. My daggers find their marks—not to kill, but to create channels for my newfound power. I pull at the snow beneath their feet, transforming it into jagged spears of ice that shoot upward through their bodies. Their inhuman shrieks echo off the mountains as I twist the ice inside them, shattering their frozen forms like macabre glass sculptures.

A fourth gets close enough to grab my arm, its grip like frozen iron. The stench of decay burns my nose, but I smirk. Time slows once more as I reach for every drop of moisture in its rotting form, the Aquanite stone singing in my blood. The Draugr becomes a grotesque ice statue, its face forever frozen in a snarl of rage. One well-placed kick, it explodes into a shower of glittering shards.

I stand in the aftermath, surrounded by a grisly display of blood and ice. My breath comes in sharp pants, creating vapor clouds in the frigid air. The crown pulses with satisfied energy, and I've never felt more in tune with its power.

"Anyone else?" I taunt, twirling my daggers as more undead warriors advance. The snow dances around my feet, responding to my will like an eager pet. "Because I'm just getting started, and I've got some new tricks to try."

Through the chaos, I glimpse Rhyland in action and holy hell—it's a sight to behold. Erik moves like a silver shadow between opponents, Heimdall's spear flashing like lightning, and Bryn's wings spreading darkness as she dances through the air. But there's no sign of Baldr's golden armor or Sleipnir's distinctive form.

A Draugr lunges at Rhyland from behind—he doesn't even turn. The monster suddenly freezes mid-stride, its glowing eyes widening in confusion as it's lifted off its feet. Rhyland clenches his fist, and the creature's armor implodes with a sickening crunch, black ichor spraying from every joint.

He doesn't just fight the Draugr; he dominates them. With a mere flick of his hand, three undead warriors hurtle through the air like ragdolls, their bodies crashing into each other with bone-crushing force. Another gesture and their own weapons turn against them— ancient axes and swords ripping free from rotting hands to spiral through the air in a deadly dance. The weapons pierce through waterlogged flesh and rusted armor with devastating precision, pinning the monsters to the frozen ground.

And then there's Erik—a blur of silver and deadly grace. Grave Warden cuts through the air as Erik moves with that eerie prescience of his. He knows exactly where each Draugr will strike before they move. An undead warrior swings its battle axe at Erik's head, but he's already ducking under the blow, Grave Warden slicing through its knees in one fluid motion. Before the creature can even begin to fall, Erik's blade finds its throat, separating head from shoulders.

Three more Draugr converge on him at once, but Erik moves like liquid mercury between them, each step purposeful, each strike inevitable. Grave Warden's ancient blade cleaves through rotting flesh and rusted armor as if they're made of paper. In seconds, there's nothing left but dismembered corpses, and Erik hasn't even broken a sweat.

Sometimes, I wonder if he has a sixth sense for battle or is just that good at reading his opponents. Either way, his performance is impressive and slightly terrifying.

I scan the area again in search of Baldr. But he's nowhere to be found. Shit. Just what I need—a missing god to explain to Odin. But before I can dwell on that potential disaster, three more Draugr lumber toward me, their rotting forms casting long shadows across the blood-stained snow.

Time warps at my command, the world crystallizing into that familiar slow-motion dance. The first Draugr's sword moves through the air like it's trapped in amber, giving me plenty of time to analyze its trajectory. The crown pulses again, and I reach out with my newfound power, feeling the ice crystals singing in response.

I pirouette between the first two monsters, my daggers opening precise channels in their armor. As time snaps back to normal, I pull at the snow beneath our feet, transforming it into a spiraling column of ice that lifts me above their heads. The Draugr's look up—perfect. I release my hold on the ice pillar, letting gravity do the work as I plunge my daggers into their skulls on my way down. The force of my descent drives the blades deep, black ichor spraying in an arc around me.

The third Draugr charges, but I'm already moving. Time slows once more as I slide under its wild swing, the Aquanite stone's power surging through me. I reach out, not just to the snow this time, but to the very moisture in the air. It freezes instantly, creating a cage of ice spears around the monster. With a twist of my will, the spears shoot inward, impaling the Draugr from a dozen angles.

But it's still moving, its hands reaching for me through the ice. Fine. It's time to get creative. I focus on the frozen water in its flesh while simultaneously manipulating the ice cage. The result is spectacular—the Draugr literally tears itself apart as the ice in its body pulls in one direction while the cage pulls in another. Its torso separates from its legs with a sickening crack, and its black blood freezes instantly as it sprays through the air.

I land in a crouch, breathing hard, my daggers dripping with frozen gore. The crown hums with power, almost like it's pleased with my improvisation. But there's no time to celebrate—I need to find Baldr before he becomes another casualty in this frozen hellscape.

Pain explodes through my body as something heavy slams into me from behind. I'm launched through the air, snow, and sky, blurring together. The impact when I hit the ground drives every molecule of air from my lungs. I skid across the frozen ground, each bounce sending fresh waves of agony through my ribs. The metallic taste of blood fills my mouth, and my vision swims with dark spots.

Trying to push myself up, my arms shake violently, and my muscles scream in protest. I see it through the curtain of hair matted with blood and snow—a Draugr bigger than any we've faced. Its bloated form casts a shadow that seems to swallow the light. Each thunderous step it takes toward me sends vibrations through the frozen ground.

A flash of gold catches my blurred vision.

No. No, no, no.

Gullfax charges across the battlefield, his hooves striking sparks from the frozen ground, mane streaming like liquid sunlight. His eyes burn with protective fury as he races toward me.

"Gullfax, stop!" The words tear from my raw throat, but it's too late.

Time seems to slow, but not by my power—by the cruel hand of fate, which forces me to watch every excruciating detail. The Draugr pivots with unnatural speed, its gigantic battle axe already in motion. The weapon spins through the air, a brutal arc of rusted metal and ancient malice.

The axe connects with a sound that will haunt my nightmares forever—the wet thunk of metal cleaving through flesh and bone. Gullfax's scream of pain is all too human, his powerful body arching backward as blood sprays across pristine snow. His legs buckle, and he falls, his magnificent form crumpling into the blood-stained powder.

"GULLFAX!" My scream echoes off the mountains, raw and primal. Hot tears freeze on my cheeks as I watch my friend's golden coat turn dark with blood, his sides heaving with labored breaths. His eyes find mine, filled with intelligence and pain that breaks something inside me.

The Draugr turns its attention back to me, its heavy footsteps leaving craters in the snow as it advances. Black ichor drips from its hands, and all I can think about is how those hands just took down one of the most magnificent creatures I've ever known.

Grief turns to rage, burning hot enough to melt the snow around me. The crown pulses with my fury, singing for vengeance.

A shadow passes overhead, followed by an ear-splitting screech that vibrates my bones. Through tear-blurred vision, I see monstrous forms wheeling against the gray sky—giant birds with wingspans wider than city streets, their feathers gleaming like sharpened steel.

"Hræsvelgr!" Heimdall's warning booms across the battlefield.

Apparently, undead Vikings weren't enough of a challenge. The universe just had to throw in some mythological murder-birds too.

The Draugr that struck down Gullfax towers over me, its rotting face twisted in a mockery of a smile. Rage bubbles up inside me, hot and fierce, mixing with grief until I can barely breathe. My muscles scream in protest as I push myself to my feet, blood dripping from my split lip onto the snow.

That's when I see it—one of the giant eagles diving straight for Bryn. Its talons, each longer than my arm, extend toward my sister as she twists mid-air, trying to evade. But she's not fast enough. The beast's claws tear through one of her obsidian wings, and her cry of pain ignites something inside me.

Something snaps.

The power erupts from deep within, not the controlled flow I'm used to, but a tidal wave of pure, white-hot fury. Light explodes from my skin, my angel fire burning so bright it turns the snow to steam. The Draugr takes a stumbling step back, its glowing eyes widening with what almost looks like fear.

Good.

The corona of power around me intensifies until I float off the ground, my hair whipping around my face like flames. Every ache, pain, and ounce of exhaustion burns away in the inferno of my rage. The light pouring from me is so intense that it casts no shadows—it simply obliterates them.

With a scream of pure fury, I direct all that power at the Draugr. The beam of light that erupts from my hands isn't the gentle healing light I usually com mand—it's a concentrated blast of divine retribution. It hits the monster square in the chest, and for a moment, the creature's waterlogged flesh glows from within like a grotesque lantern. Then it simply... disintegrates every molecule of its undead form scattered to atoms by the force of my anger.

But I'm not done. Not even close. My sister's pained cry still echoes in my ears, and Gullfax's golden blood stains the snow at my feet. The light within me builds to a crescendo, and I feel it—that moment when a star goes supernova.

And...I let it happen.

ERIK

35

The sight before me undoes me. Bryn's magnificent form lies broken in the blood-stained snow, her obsidian wing shredded like tattered silk. She's curled into herself, a position so vulnerable that it makes my heart clench. This proud Valkyrie, this fierce warrior, is reduced to this because I let my pride and her earlier words stay my hand.

Her blood paints the snow in violent streaks, the scent hitting me like a stone block. My fangs descend despite my iron control, throat burning with need. But the guilt clawing at my chest is stronger than any bloodlust. I crash to my knees beside her, gathering her broken form against me, every point of contact both heaven and hell.

A blinding light draws my attention skyward. Dani—sweet, controlled Dani—has become an avenging angel. A divine fury radiating from her every pore. Power crackles around her, the air itself charged with static that makes my hair stand on end.

She raises her hands, and the battlefield transforms. Beams of blinding light dance from her palms, each one finding its mark with devastating precision. Draugr burst into flames, their unholy screams echoing as they crumble to ash. The eagle-like Hræsvelgr, caught in her crosshairs, plummet from the sky, their wings disintegrating feather by feather.

The snow beneath her evaporates in a hissing cloud, the earth cracking and scorching under the onslaught. Shadows flee before her, obliterated by the divine fire she wields. Rhyland shouts to her, his voice lost in the maelstrom, but she's beyond reach—a goddess unleashed.

Her rage paints the world in shades of white-hot vengeance, the raw power of creation turned to destruction in her hands. For the first time since my turning, true fear grips me—a primal terror at the force she commands.

Dani finally collapses, her divine power extinguished by exhaustion. Rhyland cradles her like something precious, his big frame dwarfing her limp form. I lift Bryn with equal care, her unconscious weight settling against my chest like she belongs there. Her usually fierce expression has softened in unconsciousness, making her look almost peaceful despite her injuries.

"Let me see her." Heimdall's commanding voice breaks through my possessive haze.

Reluctantly, I lay her in the snow. The damage is devastating—her right wing hangs by mere tendons, the obsidian feathers matted with blood and ice. Deep gashes run along her ribs where the Hræsvelgr's talons found purchase. Her armor is shredded, revealing golden skin turned purple with bruising. Each injury is a testament to my failure, a mark of pride's victory over protection.

I move to where Rhyland kneels, watching him tear open his wrist for Dani. The sight triggers something primal in me—the urge to do the same for Bryn is nearly overwhelming. My fangs ache to pierce my flesh, to offer her my ancient blood, my essence, my very being. The mate-bond screams for completion, for the sharing of blood that would bind us eternally.

But I can't. Won't. Such intimacy must be freely given, freely taken. To force it would be to destroy any chance of her truly accepting me. So I swallow back the need, let it burn in my throat alongside the guilt and desire. The choice must be hers—both the taking of my blood and the giving of hers. No matter how it tears at my soul to watch her suffer when I hold the power to heal her.

"The wings must come off." Heimdall's words fall like an executioner's axe. "There's no other way."

My head falls back, jaw clenched against the roar building in my chest. A warrior's pride is a delicate thing—I've watched it shatter in countless men over the centuries. But Bryn... her wings aren't just appendages. They're her identity, her freedom, her very essence as a Valkyrie. To take them is to clip more than feathers—it's to steal the sky itself from her.

I turn away, unable to witness her mutilation, only to face another kind of heartbreak. Gullfax's golden form lies broken in the blood-stained snow, that cursed axe protruding from his noble chest. His intelligent eyes find mine, filled with pain and understanding that makes my throat tight. His labored breathing creates small clouds in the frigid air, each weaker than the last. The proud beast is dying by inches, his magnificent body slowly surrendering to the cold.

The warrior in me knows what must be done. A clean death is the last mercy I can offer him.

Grave Warden's weight is heavy in my hands as I approach Gullfax again. His golden eye meets mine with an ancient wisdom that transcends species. A warrior recognizing another warrior. His steady blinks speak volumes—permission, acceptance, gratitude. It's the kind of silent communication I've known on countless battlefields.

I raise my blade, calculating the precise angle that will make this swift and clean. The steel catches the light, and I steady my grip—

"NO! Erik, wait!" Dani's desperate cry shatters the solemn moment. She crashes to her knees beside Gullfax's head, snow spraying from her impact. "I can save him." Her voice carries the raw determination of someone who's already defied death once today.

Rhyland drops beside Dani, his hand gentle as he strokes Gullfax's muzzle. "Stay with us, buddy." His tender voice is a stark contrast to his usual warrior demeanor.

Gullfax responds with a weak nicker, his golden eye heavy with pain but trusting. Dani wastes no time—her hands find purchase on Gullfax's powerful neck, eyes sliding shut in concentration. The air crackles as her power manifests, her palms igniting with pure white light. I've seen this only once before when she pulled Emily back from death's door during the witch uprising. Sweat beads on her forehead despite the freezing air, her face tight with effort.

"The axe," she grits out, never opening her eyes. "Get it out. Now."

Rhyland and I move as one, gripping the weapon's ancient handle. The sound it makes leaving Gullfax's flesh turns my stomach—wet, thick, final. But Dani's power surges stronger, the Atherite stone in her crown blazing like a miniature sun. The divine light pours from her hands into Gullfax's wound, fighting death itself for the noble beast's life.

Light knits flesh and bone before my eyes, the gaping wound in Gullfax's chest sealing as if time runs backward. The magnificent beast surges to his feet in one fluid motion, his coat shedding snow and remnants of divine energy like golden sparks. His resurrection stands in stark contrast to Dani's collapse—she crumples into the snow, the price of wielding such power evident in every line of her body.

Rhyland gathers her up with practiced tenderness, but tears still track down her cheeks, steam rising where they fall on the frozen ground. Gullfax steps forward, his movements once again proud and sure, and lowers his head to her level. The gesture holds more nobility than any king's bow. Dani's arms encircle his powerful neck, her fingers burying in his mane as she presses her face against his coat.

"You're welcome," she whispers, her voice thick with emotion. "It's the least I could do for what you did."

The air shivers with unspoken communication between them—mortal and divine beast sharing thoughts as easily as breathing. Even after witnessing her obliterate an army of undead, this quiet display of power leaves me in awe.

Bryn's agonized scream splits the sky, sending me sprinting back through the snow. The sight that greets us freezes my heart—one obsidian wing lies severed in the crimson snow, while Heimdall prepares to remove its twin.

"What the fuck are you doing?" Dani's voice cracks with exhaustion and fury as she collapses beside her sister. The raw power that had just saved Gullfax is now replaced by desperate concern.

Heimdall's ancient eyes hold the weight of countless difficult decisions. "The choice was made for us, Lightborn. One wing is beyond salvation, and she cannot survive with such imbalance. The wounds must be sealed."

Dani's attention shifts entirely to Bryn, whose proud warrior's facade has crumbled completely. Tears cut tracks through the blood on her face, her body wracked with sobs that tear at my soul. The scent of her essence—rich, powerful, divine—floods my senses until I have to turn away, fangs descending against my will.

"Bryn, look at me." Dani's voice softens to honey, a stark contrast to her earlier rage. She cradles her sister as Bryn thrashes, wild with grief and pain. "Hey, hey... I'm here. Let me help you, sister. Let me try to heal you."

The hysteria in Bryn's sobs eases slightly at Dani's words, but her blood continues to paint the snow in terrible patterns. Each drop calls to me, forcing me to step further away lest I lose control entirely.

Dani's hands tremble as she summons her power again, the Atherite stone's glow dimmer than before. Exhaustion etches deep lines around her eyes, but determination burns brighter. Rhyland stands behind her, tense with shared pain through their bond, his hand on her shoulder anchoring her as she channels what little strength remains.

Divine light flickers around Bryn's wound—weaker now, struggling like a candle in a storm. The torn flesh where her magnificent wing once joined her body slowly knits together, blood flow ebbing to a trickle. But the wing itself lies lifeless in the snow, beyond even creation's power to restore.

Dani collapses against Rhyland, spent and shaking, as Bryn's sobs fade to quiet hiccups. The reality of her loss settles over us like a shroud.

"I can't—" Bryn's voice breaks, muffled against Dani's shoulder as they cling to each other. "How can I be a Valkyrie with one wing?" The proud warrior I know is gone, replaced by someone small and broken.

"I know." Dani's tears mingle with her sister's, her failure to fully heal Bryn—cutting more profound than any blade. "I'm so sorry. But this doesn't define you, Bryn. You're still a warrior, wings or no wings."

The words hang in the frozen air, well-meaning but hollow against the weight of what's been lost.

RHYLAND

36

Sleipnir's hooves touch down with impossible grace, Baldr's stupid ass glinting in the weak sunlight. "Is everyone intact?" he calls out, with that particular brand of bullshit concern that's about as genuine as fool's gold.

"Where the fuck were you hiding, pretty boy?" I snarl, my fury barely contained. Dani cradles Bryn against her chest—Dani's pain ricocheting through our bond like a constant ache. It hits me so hard my knees nearly buckle, but I'll be damned if I show weakness in front of this coward.

Baldr has the decency to look ashamed, his perfect features twisting into something almost human. "I... well... you see..." he stammers, each word evident with divine privilege. "My gifts lie in peace and beauty. Combat isn't exactly my forte."

"Peace and beauty?" I bark out a harsh laugh, spitting at Sleipnir's feet, earning an indignant snort from the eight-legged beast. "Your *peace* got her wing torn off while you were probably admiring your reflection in some frozen pond."

"Enough, Rhyland." Bryn's voice cracks through the air like a whip, even as she struggles to stand. Her remaining wing tucks close to her back. "Save your venom for actual enemies. This was my battle to lose."

Heimdall unfolds like a avalanche, his mighty frame blocking out what little sunlight filters through the clouds. At his full height, he towers over us like a living monument, his armor catching the weak light in mesmerizing patterns. "Time grows short. We move."

The bitter wind cuts through our clothes like frozen knives as Gullfax carries us deeper into the heart of winter. Ice crystals form in my beard, and Dani's shivers vibrate against my chest. The forest around us is dead silent, the kind of quiet that makes your teeth ache, and your instincts scream.

My mind drifts back to the battle, to Dani wielding power like a fucking force of nature. The Aquanite stone had sung to her, she'd said—and watching her command the frozen landscape, turning snow and ice into deadly weapons, I finally understood why. My little scientist, turning winter itself into her personal arsenal.

But it was nothing compared to when she went nuclear.

The memory of her previous explosion at the hotel still haunts me—shattered glass raining down like deadly diamonds, the room looking like someone had detonated a light bomb. But this? This was something else entirely.

She'd burned like a newborn star, her rage painting the world in shades of celestial vengeance. The very air had crackled around her, reality-warping under the weight of her fury. If it wasn't for her blood singing through my veins—that precious connection binding us together—I would've gone up in flames like a vampire torch. Even with her essence protecting me, my skin blistered and healed in an endless cycle as I fought to reach her.

But what choice did I have? Let her obliterate everything within a mile radius? Watch her burn herself out like a supernova? Fuck that. She might be the most powerful being in the Seven Realms, but she's still my mate. My responsibility. My everything.

Three fucking hours of this frozen wasteland, and still no sign of our destination. Just endless snow and the sound of everyone's footsteps behind us.

"There." Baldr's voice carries on the wind as he gestures toward a mountain that seems to pierce the very sky. Its peak disappears into the storm clouds, ancient and forbidding. Gullfax picks his way through the deep snow, his coat collecting frost as we approach the mountain's base, where a extensive wind tunnel yawns open like the mouth of some prehistoric beast.

I slide off Gullfax's back, my boots sinking into knee-deep snow. Reaching up, I wrap my hands around Dani's waist, lifting her down beside me. Her body trembles against mine, whether from cold or anticipation. I don't know.

Erik, Bryn, and Heimdall stand at the tunnel's entrance, their forms silhouetted against the swirling darkness. The wind howls through the opening like a thousand lost souls, making Bryn's remaining wing flutter against her back.

The wind shrieks through the tunnel like a banshee's cry, making conversation nearly impossible. Dani's teeth chatter as she presses closer to my side. "N-now what?"

"Shelter." Baldr dismounts Sleipnir with his usual divine grace, his short hair whipping around his face. "Before we all freeze solid."

The tunnel swallows us whole, its rocky throat stretching endlessly into the mountain's gut. Our boots crunch against frozen gravel, echoing off the wind-carved walls. Behind us, Gullfax and Sleipnir's hooves click against stone, both beasts eager to escape the bitter cold.

Baldr's pack hits the ground with a thunderous crack that bounces off the walls. He crouches, rummaging through his supplies. "Fire," he announces like we can't all see our breath crystallizing in front of our faces. "Unless anyone enjoys turning into ice sculptures."

Erik and Heimdall move like shadows, gathering what sparse wood they can find. The pile grows beside Baldr as he strikes his flint, cursing in ancient Norse as the wind snuffs out each spark before it can catch.

Dani rolls her eyes and steps forward. "Move." Her palm ignites like a miniature sun, and she flicks her wrist, sending a ball of flame dancing through the air. It kisses the wood, and the whole pile erupts in a satisfying whoosh of heat and light.

"Well," Baldr's lips curl into a smile that doesn't quite reach his eyes. "That's certainly more efficient than flint and steel."

The fire's warmth seeps into our frozen bones as we crowd around it. Bryn retrieves a leather bladder from her pack, her remaining wing twitching with barely contained emotion. She tilts her head back, throat working as she drinks deep—the kind of desperate swallows that speak of drowning pain rather than quenching thirst.

Beside me, Dani tears into a strip of jerky with savage determination, her jaw clenched tight enough to crack teeth. The sound of her aggressive chewing echoes off the cave walls, mixing with the endless howl of the wind.

"This is where we part ways," Baldr announces, his hands hovering over the flames like he's blessing them. "You and Dani will continue on to face the Einherjar alone."

I bite back a snarl of frustration. This pompous fuck has been about as useful as tits on a bull—showing up to point at obvious landmarks and spout cryptic bullshit. Some "wise guide," Odin promised. The bastard's done nothing but preen and posture while others bleed and sacrifice.

The firelight catches his features, casting shadows that make him look almost human. Almost. But something in those eerie eyes puts me on edge. Something that makes my vampire instincts scream: threat.

"So, what exactly are we looking for?" Dani asks between aggressive bites of jerky, her scientist's mind already working to catalog and analyze. Classic Dani—she'd demand a PowerPoint presentation from Death himself if he showed up without proper documentation.

Baldr's lips curve into that infuriatingly mysterious smile he seems to have patented. "The answer will reveal itself when the moment is right." He produces a corked jar from his robes with all the flourish of a stage magician, tossing it to Dani. "For containing its essence. We'll maintain our vigil here until your triumphant return."

Dani catches the jar one-handed, examining it with narrowed eyes. "Seriously? That's all you've got? No user manual? No helpful hints? Just 'you'll know it when you see it' and a mason jar?"

"My dear savior, some mysteries must unfold naturally, like a flower greeting the dawn."

"Right," Dani snorts, shoving the jar into her pack. "Because clear communication would just ruin the whole mystical vibe you've got going."

"The path through these depths will lead you to Einherjar's domain," Baldr says, waving his hand theatrically. "Though I'm sure you'll find your own way to complicate the journey."

Dani rolls her eyes. She turns to Bryn, concern, etching lines around her mouth. Bryn's spine straightens like steel before she can unleash her protective instincts.

"Don't." Bryn's remaining wing pulls tight against her back, her chin lifting with that familiar Valkyrie pride. "Save your concern for the Einherjar. I'm still a warrior of Zephyria, wings or no wings." The bladder dangling from her fingers betrays the cost of maintaining that fierce facade.

I lace my fingers through Dani's, tugging her toward the tunnel's gaping maw. The darkness swallows us whole, leaving the others' voices to fade like smoke on the wind. The tunnel stretches endlessly ahead, black as a demon's heart, while that damn wind keeps howling like a chorus of the damned.

Dani conjures one of her light balls—a perfect sphere of pure energy that bobs through the air like a drunken firefly. Its glow catches on the ice-slicked walls, turning ordinary stone into something out of a horror movie. The shadows dance and twist on the cave walls, making every rocky outcropping look like it might sprout fangs and take a bite out of us.

Our boots crunch against frozen gravel, the sound mixing with the steady drip-drip-drip of water somewhere in the darkness. Each step takes us deeper into this frozen hellhole, and my vampire senses strain against the shadows, searching for whatever cryptic bullshit Baldr sent us to find.

"Just like date night, right babe?" Dani's voice carries that edge of snark she gets when her nerves are dancing on a knife's edge. "Dark caves, possible death around every corner. You really know how to show a girl a good time."

"Fuck yeah," I snort, squeezing her hand. "Though last time we were swimming through Aquaria's caves instead of freezing our asses off. At least the scenery is consistent—rocks, darkness, and more fucking rocks."

"And here I thought you were going to complain about the lack of sea monsters trying to eat us," Dani quips, bumping her hip against mine. "Getting soft in your old age, Viking?"

Her light ball bounces ahead of us, casting wild shadows that make the cave look alive. Christ, my mate and I have a fucked-up idea of quality time together.

I growl, pulling her closer as we navigate the darkness. "Let's find whatever ancient pain in the ass is waiting for us and get the fuck out of this frozen hellhole."

"Agreed," Dani mutters, just as her light illuminates a fork in the tunnel ahead. Three gaping mouths stretch into darkness, each howling with its own particular brand of arctic hell.

"Well, isn't this just fucking perfect." I eye the passages, my nostrils flaring as I try to catch any helpful scent through the damp, mineral-heavy air. The left tunnel reeks of stagnant water and rot. The middle one whistles with the wind that carries the sharp bite of ice. The right passage... something about it raises my hackles—a stillness that feels more like a held breath than peace.

"Three tunnels," Dani's light bobs higher, casting shadows that dance like demented puppets across the frost-slicked walls. "Because, of course, there are three tunnels. That's like Evil Lair Design 101."

A loose stone skitters down one of the passages—the middle one—followed by what sounds suspiciously like a growl.

"Think Baldr could've mentioned the multiple choice portion of this test?" Dani's fingers tighten around mine, her other hand glowing with defensive power.

The growl echoes again, deeper this time, making the icy walls around us vibrate. My fangs descend on instinct, every predatory sense going into overdrive.

"Left tunnel smells like something died in it," I mutter, pulling Dani slightly behind me. "Middle one's got our growling friend and the right one..." I trail off that unnatural stillness, making my undead blood run cold.

"Oh, good. We can choose between eau de corpse, mystery monster, or creepy silence." Dani's light splits into three, sending one down each tunnel. "Is there any chance this is just some elaborate Nordic escape room?"

The middle tunnel's growl turns into a roar, sending stalactites raining around us. Through the falling ice, I catch a glimpse of something massive shifting in the darkness—something with way too many fucking legs.

"Fuck this." I grab Dani's arm, yanking her toward the right tunnel. "I'll take creepy silence over whatever the hell that is."

"Wait—" Dani starts, but the thing in the middle tunnel chooses that moment to emerge into her light's reach. Eight glowing eyes reflect at us, attached to a body that looks like someone crossed a wolf with a spider and threw in some nightmare fuel for good measure.

"Run now, science later!" I shove her ahead of me into the right tunnel, the sound of chittering mandibles spurring us faster.

We sprint through the darkness, Dani's light bouncing wildly ahead of us. The sound of clicking echoes behind us, mixing with that spider-wolf bastard's howls.

"What the actual fuck was that?" Dani pants, her feet pounding against the frozen ground. "Some kind of arachnid-canine hybrid? The genetic implications alone—"

"Less analyzing, more running!" I grab her waist as she stumbles, keeping her upright. "Save the dissertation for when we're not about to be dinner for Odin's rejected pet project!"

The tunnel suddenly drops away beneath our feet. Dani's startled yelp cuts through the air as we slide down an ice-slicked incline, my arms locked around her waist as we hurtle through the darkness. Her light spins wildly, showing glimpses of crystalline formations flashing past us like frozen lightning.

"Hold on!" I twist, putting my body between her and whatever's waiting at the bottom of this frozen hell-slide. Above us, the spider-wolf's frustrated howl echoes down the tunnel, growing fainter—at least the fucker's too big to follow.

The ground levels out without warning, sending us rolling across a floor that feels like polished glass. When we finally stop, Dani's sprawled on top of me, both of us breathing hard.

"Well," she pushes herself up on my chest, her light reorganizing itself above us. "That's one way to make an entrance."

The chamber we've landed in stretches into darkness, its walls lined with what looks like frozen waterfalls. But what's at the center makes my heart skip a beat—a perfectly circular pool of black water, still as death but somehow managing to look hungry.

"Of course, there's a creepy black pool," Dani mutters, climbing off me. "Because regular water would be too mainstream." Her light multiplies, sending spheres floating upward to illuminate the chamber.

"Don't even think about touching it," I growl, catching her wrist as she steps toward the pool. The surface is too fucking still, like a sheet of obsidian glass. No ripples, no movement, nothing—just an endless void pretending to be water.

"I wasn't going to—" She starts, then freezes as her lights reveal what's suspended in the frozen waterfalls around us. Bodies. Dozens of them, warriors trapped mid-battle cry in the ice, their weapons still raised. "Holy shit."

"Einherjar," I breathe, recognizing the ancient armor, the fierce expressions frozen for eternity. Some of these poor bastards probably fought alongside my grandfather.

My gut twists as I study the frozen warriors. Each face tells a story of failure—would-be heroes turned into macabre decorations, their final moments of defiance preserved in crystalline clarity. Some poor bastard's hand is still reaching for a weapon that's now nothing but ice, his face forever locked in a battle cry. This isn't a chamber—it's a fucking gallery of broken dreams, with us about to audition for the next exhibit.

The black pool chooses that moment to move, a ripple starting from its center like something stirring in its depths. The temperature drops so fast that even my vampire ass feels it, frost cracking across the smooth glass floor beneath our feet.

"Uh, babe?" Dani's hand finds mine, power already crackling around her other palm. "Please tell me that's just some weird underground current."

A low laugh echoes through the chamber, coming from everywhere and nowhere. The kind of laugh that makes you think about all your life choices that led to this moment.

"Fuck." I pull her closer, watching as the black surface rises, taking shape like living darkness. "I don't think we're that lucky."

The darkness rises like oil from the pool, twisting into a form that towers over us. Two points of arctic blue light ignite where eyes should be, and that laugh echoes again, making the frozen warriors in their icy tombs rattle.

"Welcome, Lightborn. I am Vidar." the voice sounds like ice cracking over a frozen lake. "And Magni's son. How... disappointing you both appear."

"Wow," Dani's power sparks brighter around her free hand. "Rude much? I'll have you know I dressed specifically for 'confronting ancient entity in a frozen cave' today."

The thing's laugh turns sharp as icicles. "The light-bearer makes jokes while standing in a graveyard. Tell me, child—do you see your future in these walls?"

I bare my fangs, pulling Dani slightly behind me. "The only future I see is us kicking your shadowy ass back to whatever frozen hell you crawled out of."

"Ah, the vampire speaks of hell," the form ripples like dark water. "When he carries such delicious darkness within. Tell me, son of Nyx—do you taste the shadow in your own veins?"

"Actually," Dani steps forward, that dangerous edge in her voice that means she's done playing nice. "I've got a better question—did you practice being a dramatic asshole, or is that just a side effect of marinating in evil pool juice for a few centuries? Because I've got to tell you," her light flares brighter, making the creature flinch, "I've faced scarier things in my morning coffee, and they didn't need the whole 'creature from the black lagoon' routine to make their point."

The creature's form solidifies, the ice cracking as it takes shape. It is a warrior made of darkness and frost, wielding a sword that looks carved from the void itself.

"Let us see if your light burns as bright as your tongue, *savior.*"

ERIK

37

The flames do little to combat this cursed cold, but I keep my hands extended, watching shadows dance across my palms. Even through layers of fur and leather, the chill seeps into my bones. It is a different kind of cold from the desert nights I once knew, more... permanent somehow.

Bryn lifts the horn to her lips again, drinking deep and desperate. Her remaining wing twitches with each swallow. I recognize that look in her eyes—I've seen it in countless warriors who've lost limbs, purpose, and pride. But this... this is different. A Valkyrie without flight is like a vampire without fangs, a fundamental piece of identity torn away.

She catches me watching, and her eyes flash with defiance, but it's dulled by mead and misery. The proud warrior who challenged me mere hours ago drowns herself in alcohol, trying to numb a wound that no amount of drinking will heal.

Her hands shake slightly as she refills the horn. The gesture hits too close to home, stirring memories of my own battles with inadequacy. A warrior without purpose, a protector who failed to protect—some wounds cut too deep.

Heimdall and Baldr's footsteps fade into the howling wind in search of more firewood, leaving us with crackling flames and suffocating silence. The question burns in my throat until I can't hold it back. "How are you holding up?"

Her bitter laugh cuts sharp. "How am I holding up?" She takes another long pull from her horn, eyes flashing with familiar fire despite her pain. "Oh, I'm just kyn-ligr. Nothing quite like having your identity literally carved off your back to really make you appreciate life." Her words bite with lethal sarcasm. "Please, spare me your pity party, vampire. I don't need you to point out how pathetic I've become."

The self-loathing in her voice mirrors what I've heard in my own too many times to count. But there's steel beneath the bitterness—the same unwavering strength that made her one of the most feared Valkyries in Zephyria. Even broken, she burns brighter than most warriors at their peak.

The words scrape out of my throat like gravel. "This isn't your identity, Bryn." My fists clench with frustration at her self-imposed exile into misery. "Wings don't make the warrior. Your heart, your strength, your duty—that's what makes you who you are. One wing or none, you're still a—" The words die on my tongue as I realize what I was about to confess.

The firelight catches her face as she goes still, her horn frozen halfway to her lips. Those dual-colored eyes pin me like swords across the flames. "I'm still what, Erik?" Her voice carries that dangerous edge that makes lesser men tremble.

The silence stretches between us, taut as a bowstring about to snap.

A growl of frustration escapes me. "Forget it."

Snow crunches under her boots as she stalks toward me, dropping beside me. Even wounded, she moves like a warrior—like a force of nature. Those impossible eyes lock onto mine, burning with challenge. "No. Finish what you were going to say." Her voice rises with each word, sharp as a blade's edge. "I'm still *what?* Don't you dare back down now. Say it!" The last word echoes off the cave walls, carrying all her pain and fury.

The words tear from my chest before I can stop them. "A beautiful woman."

Time freezes as I drown in those impossible eyes. The gold one blazes like captured sunlight, while its Nordic blue twin holds all the frost of our surroundings. My gaze bounces between them, unable to choose which is more mesmerizing. Her breath catches, quick and sharp, the sound loud in our shared silence.

She breaks first, turning away with a bitter laugh. "Right. Of course, you'd say that." The words are a dismissal, but her pulse—gods, her pulse tells a different story entirely.

The mate-bond beats between us like a living thing, her proximity making my control strain at the edges. That rapid heartbeat, the slight dilation of her pupils—signs I've learned to read over countless years, now torturing me with possibility.

My fingers find her chin, turning her face back to mine with gentle insistence. "Look at me." The words come out rougher than intended. "It's true. You're beautiful." Her eyes widen slightly at my intensity. I need her to understand—to see what I see. The fierce commander who leads her Valkyries with unwavering strength. The warrior who dances through battle like it's an art form—the woman who stands toe-to-toe with gods and doesn't blink.

Something flickers in those extraordinary eyes—vulnerability so rare it steals my breath. For just a moment, her mask slips, showing me the woman beneath the legend. For a heartbeat, she leans almost imperceptibly into my touch. Then, like a shield slamming into place, her walls rise again. She pulls away, leaving my hand holding nothing but cold air.

"I should check on the others," she mutters, rising with unsteadiness. Her fingers tremble slightly as she adjusts her remaining wing, and her scent carries notes of confusion and something deeper, something she's not ready to acknowledge.

The ghost of her nearness lingers like a phantom touch, my mind racing through lifetimes of experience yet finding no precedent for this moment. The mate-bond thrums with possibility—or perhaps warning. After eons of existence, I'm unsure of every instinct I've honed. Her reaction spoke volumes: the trembling pulse, dilated pupils, that moment of vulnerability before her walls slammed back into place. All signs pointing to—

Bryn's battle cry shatters my contemplation. Grave Warden finds my hand before conscious thought, my body moving at vampire speed toward her position. Through the swirling snow, Heimdall and Baldr stand surrounded by shambling Draugr, their rotting forms a stark contrast to the pristine white landscape.

But Bryn—gods, Bryn moves like she never lost that wing. Her sword flashes as she positions herself before Baldr, shield raised with deadly purpose. Even broken, even wounded, she's still every inch the Valkyrie warrior. The sight stirs something in my chest—pride and protection warring for dominance.

The Draugr surge forward in a wave of rotting flesh and ancient armor. I position myself at Bryn's exposed side—where her wing should be—and she bristles at the implied protection. But pride can go fuck itself when you're facing down an army of undead bastards.

Let her rage. Let her curse. Let her fight my presence all she wants.

The image of her broken body in the snow is carved into my mind like acid on steel. Her blood painted the pristine white. Her wing shredded. Her proud spirit shattered because I let my cursed pride keep me from her side.

Never again.

This time, I won't stand aside.

Grave Warden sings through the air, cleaving through decayed bone and preserved sinew. Bryn's sword flashes beside mine in perfect sync, her movements still graceful despite her injury. We fall into a deadly dance—back to back, blades becoming extensions of our arms. Each strike is precise, each defense covering the other's blind spots.

From the corner of my eye, I catch Baldr's form retreating like the coward he is while Heimdall stands his ground. The prodigious god's sword blazes with divine light as he cuts through three Draugr with a single sweep.

A rotting axe swings toward Bryn's unprotected side. I duck under her shield arm, catching the blow on Grave Warden's crossguard. The impact jars my shoulders, but I use the momentum to spin, decapitating the creature. Its head rolls across the bloody snow as Bryn dispatches another with a savage thrust through its chest cavity.

"I don't need your protection!" she snarls as we move together to face the next wave. Her words lack conviction, though—we both know her balance is off, and the missing wing weakens her defenses.

"Shut up and fight," I growl back, parrying a thrust that would have taken her in the ribs. Our blades flash in lethal harmony, turning the snow black with undead ichor.

A Draugr lunges between us, and I cleave it in half without breaking stride. "Would you rather I let you get skewered?" The words come out clipped as I parry another attack aimed at her blind spot. "Because that can be arranged."

"I've fought battles before you were even turned," Bryn snaps, her shield smashing through a rotting skull. Her remaining wing adjusts instinctively for balance, which she no longer has, making her stumble slightly. I catch her elbow, steadying her before she can fall.

"And now you're fighting injured," I counter, Grave Warden, singing through the air to intercept a blade meant for her neck. "Your center of gravity is off. Your left side is exposed. You're—"

"Analyzing my fucking technique?" She spins, her sword taking a Draugr's arm at the shoulder. "Really? Now?"

The flash of her eyes holds more danger than the undead surrounding us. But beneath her fury, I catch something else—frustration, yes, but fear, not of the enemy, but of her newfound vulnerability.

"Just trying to keep you alive," I mutter, ducking under her swing to gut another corpse. Our movements flow together despite her anger, despite my hovering—like some deadly choreography neither of us consciously chose.

"I don't need—" she starts, but her words cut off as she twists wrong, her missing wing throwing her off balance again. This time, my arm slides around her waist before she can fall, pulling her against my chest as I dispatch the Draugr that nearly capitalizes on her mistake.

The contact lasts barely a heartbeat before she shoves away, but it's enough to make my cock rock hard.

Her warmth lingers against my chest as she launches back into the fray. Her movements are more aggressive now as she fights both the enemy and her limitations. A Draugr's blade whistles past her ear as she overcorrects, and my hand instinctively finds her lower back, steadying her.

"Get your hands—" she growls but breaks off to slam her shield into an approaching corpse. "—off me!"

"The moment you stop leaving yourself open," I counter, Grave Warden's blade separating another undead head from its shoulders. The mate bond pulses with each point of contact between us, making it harder to focus on the battle and not on how perfectly she fits against me.

Heimdall's voice booms across the battlefield, ancient words of power turning three Draugr to ash. But more keep coming, pouring from the shadows like a tide of death.

"This is ridiculous," Bryn snarls, her sword arm trembling slightly from exhaustion. Her remaining wing pulls tight against her back, overcompensating. "I don't need a keeper."

"No?" I spin her away from a deadly thrust, taking the blow on my shoulder instead. The pain is worth it for the flash of surprise—and something deeper—in those beautiful eyes. "Because from where I'm standing, you need someone to watch your blind spot until you adapt."

She curses, but she doesn't pull away when I position myself at her vulnerable side again. If anything, she leans into our shared rhythm, letting me cover her weakness while she focuses on offense.

A huge Draugr charges through our defensive line, its ancient blade aimed at Bryn's heart. Time slows as instinct takes over—I grab her waist, spinning us both away from the attack. She flows with the movement, using the momentum to bring her sword down through the creature's skull. We end up pressed together, her back against my chest, both breathing hard.

"I had that," she pants but doesn't immediately pull away.

"Of course you did," I murmur near her ear, feeling her slight shiver. "I just wanted a better view."

She elbows me hard in the ribs, breaking free to face another wave of undead. But there's less bite in her movements now, less desperate need to prove herself. We fall into a deadly rhythm—her sword extending my reach, my strength compensating for her imbalance. Every time she starts to tilt, my hand finds her waist or back, steadying her without comment.

"This doesn't mean anything," she grits out between strikes, though her body betrays her by leaning into my touch.

"Nothing at all," I agree, dispatching another corpse while admiring how the frosty light catches both colors in her eyes. "Just two warriors watching each other's backs."

Heimdall's battle cry draws our attention—the god stands surrounded, his armor splattered with dark ichor. But his eyes meet mine across the battlefield, and something knowing glints in that ancient gaze.

Through the chaos, Heimdalls voice carries like thunder. "To the caves! Now!"

I grab Bryn's arm as she starts to charge toward another cluster of Draugr. "Time to go."

"I'm not running," she snarls, yanking against my grip—her warrior's pride blazes, even as exhaustion shows on her beautiful face.

"It's not running," I growl, pulling her closer as a wave of undead surges toward us. "It's a tactical retreat. Besides," I add, taking down two more corpses with a single sweep of Grave Warden, "your form is getting sloppy."

She whirls on me, fury and something else dancing in her eyes. "My form is—" A Draugr's blade slices through the air where her head was before I yank her aside. "Fine. But this conversation isn't over."

"Wouldn't dream of it," I mutter, keeping my hand on her lower back as we fight toward the cave entrance.

Heimdall covers our retreat, blocking the entrance as we duck inside. The god's power radiates outward, turning the first wave of pursuing Draugr to ash. But more move in.

The cave swallows us in darkness, broken only by our campfire. Bryn stumbles on the uneven ground, throwing off her balance. My arm slides around her waist automatically.

"I swear to the gods," she hisses, but her hand grips my forearm instead of pushing me away. "If you say one word about my balance—"

"Wouldn't dare," I murmur, steadying her as we move deeper into the cave. Her pulse races under my fingers, matching my thundering rhythm. "Though your left side is still—"

She stomps on my foot. Hard. "Finish that sentence, and I'll show you exactly how good my form still is."

The threat might be more convincing if she wasn't still holding onto my arm, her body betraying her need for support even as her pride rebels against it. Behind us, Heimdall's power illuminates the cave entrance in brilliant gold as he holds the line.

As she presses back against me, the fierce warrior momentarily surrendering to my support, my body responds with a primal intensity that's impossible to hide. The evidence of my desire grows harder against the curve of her ass, and the slight hitch in her breathing tells me she feels every inch.

The mate-bond pulses with savage need, heightening every point of contact between us. Her body heat seeps through our armor.

The subtle shift of her hips—whether intentional or not—draws a low growl from my throat that has nothing to do with the battle we just escaped.

"We need to keep moving," I say, noting how she leans into me slightly with each step. "Unless you'd prefer to stay and discuss your footwork?"

Her elbow finds my ribs again, but this time, there's less force behind it. "Keep talking, and I'll give you a much closer look at my footwork. Specifically, my boot up your—"

A crash from the entrance cuts off her creative threat. Heimdall's voice booms through the cavern: "Move! I'll hold them!"

The sounds of battle echo behind us as we descend deeper into the cave system. Each step takes us further from the chaos, but Bryn's resistance to my support gradually weakens as fatigue sets in. Her pride wages war with necessity until she finally lets out a frustrated breath.

"This doesn't leave this cave," she mutters, allowing more of her weight to rest against me.

"What doesn't?" I keep my tone neutral. "I don't see anything worth mentioning."

My hearing picks up the skittering echoes off the cave walls—a rapid tap-tap-tap of too many legs on stone. My muscles tense before my mind fully registers the threat. I release Bryn just long enough to pivot, Grave Warden singing through the air in a deadly arc.

The blade connects with wet resistance. The creature—a grotesque fusion of arachnid and canine—splits like overripe fruit. Yellow-green intestines spill across the stone floor, steam rising from the viscera in the cool cave air. The stench hits next: rotting meat and something acidic that burns the back of my throat. Its eight eyes, glazed and bulbous, stare sightlessly as thick, black blood oozes between mandibles, still clicking in death.

Bryn sways without my support, and I pull her back against me before her knees can buckle. Her heart hammers against my chest, her breathing sharp and uneven. The monster's blood seeps toward our boots, thick as tar and just as dark, mixing with the ichor still leaking from its bisected thorax.

"Well," I mutter, watching one of its legs twitch in a final spasm, "that's new."

"Gross."

A thunderous boom echoes through the cavern, followed by light that momentarily turns the stone walls to liquid sunlight. Heimdall's voice rolls through the tunnel like thunder: "ALL IS CLEAR!"

"They're gone," Bryn says but doesn't immediately pull away from my support. Her wing twitches against my chest, a reminder of what she's lost—and what she's too stubborn to admit she's gained—a partner who understands the weight of pride and the cost of vulnerability.

"Shame," I murmur, not loosening my grip. "I was rather enjoying our dance."

When she elbows me this time, there's almost fondness in the gesture. Almost. "Keep dreaming, vampire."

I watch her storm away, that proud spine straight as steel despite her injuries, her remaining wing pulled tight against her back in defiance. Each step radiates indignation, from the set of her shoulders to the deliberate placement of her boots. She's beautiful in her fury—a warrior goddess who refuses to show weakness, even now.

And despite everything—the battle, the tension, the weight of what's passed between us—I find my lips curving into a genuine smile. It's been years since anyone has challenged me like this and matched my stubbornness with equal fire. She's unlike any woman I've encountered in my long existence, and that alone is worth the bruised ribs she's left me with.

She may be walking away, but something fundamental has shifted between us. Judging by the slight hesitation in her stride before she disappears around the corner, she knows it, too.

DANICA

38

Vidar strikes with blinding speed. I lean back Matrix-style, watching the blade pass inches from my face in slow motion. Angel fire erupts from my palms as I flip backward, using the momentum to launch a counter-attack. The flames pass harmlessly through the champion's shadowy form.

"Too slow, Lightborn," he mocks, splitting into three identical forms.

"Oh, that's just bullshit," I mutter, channeling the Aquanite's power. Ice crystals form in the air as I weave between the blades, each movement precise and fluid. I create a shield of frozen light just as two swords converge on my position.

Vidar's sword whistles through the air, missing my throat by millimeters as I duck and roll. My shoulder slams into the icy ground, sending jolts of pain up my arm.

"Getting tired yet, Void-face?" I taunt, pushing myself up. Blood trickles down my temple where I hit my head on the ice. "Because I could do this all day."

"Dani." Rhyland's voice carries that edge of barely controlled fury. "Stop provoking it."

The champion moves like a liquid shadow, his form rippling between solid and void. My light passes straight through it while Rhyland's telekinetic assault seems to hit something tangible. But nothing slows it down.

"Provoke it?" I dodge another swing. "I'm just making conversation—shit!"

Pain explodes across my back as the champion's fist connects, sending me flying into one of the frozen waterfalls. Ice shards tear through my shirt, biting into flesh. I hit the ground hard, tasting blood.

Rhyland's roar of rage echoes off the crystalline walls. The air vibrates with his power as he hurls a barrage of ice shards at the creature. "I'm going to fucking kill you!"

Rhyland's power tears chunks from the walls, hurling them with devastating force. The projectiles shatter against two shadow forms but connect solidly with the third. The impact sends the champion reeling—until it's severed arm reforms from pure darkness.

"Rhyland, watch out!"

My warning comes too late. A blade of pure shadow catches Rhyland in the chest, launching him across the chamber. He slams into the frozen wall with a sickening crack, ice shards raining down around his crumpled form.

"No!" Terror and rage explode through me. Time stops completely as I channel both light and ice. Angel fire wraps around my arms like burning wings while frost spreads from my feet in deadly patterns.

The champion laughs—until I phase through its next attack like a ghost, my body moving faster than thought. My fist, wrapped in burning light and crackling ice, connects with its shadowy face. The impact sends shock waves through the chamber.

"Impressive," he hisses, staggering back.

I press the advantage, moving like water between its strikes. Each dodge flows into a counter-attack, light, and ice working in perfect harmony. Vidar's forms try to surround me, but I'm everywhere and nowhere, leaving trails of frozen fire in my wake.

"Your predecessors all thought themselves worthy," the creature growls. "Their frozen forms now decorate my halls. Shall I tell you how each one failed?"

"How about," I grit through clenched teeth, "you tell us how to shut you the fuck up instead?"

A groan from Rhyland splits my concentration. The champion's blade slices across my back, burning cold. I stumble, and another cut opens along my ribs. Blood freezes on my skin instantly.

"Your love makes you weak," Vidar taunts, his forms converging. "Like all who came before."

"No." I rise slowly, power building around me like a storm. "That's where you're wrong, asshole. My love makes me stronger."

The Aquanite stone sings in my crown as I reach out to every frozen surface in the chamber. Angel fire erupts from my hands, but I don't try to pierce the champion's darkness this time. Instead, I create a cage of pure light, trapping it in place.

"What is this?" he snarls, shadows writhing against the barrier.

"This?" Ice crystals form in the air, each one blazing with inner fire. "This is me being done with your shit."

"Nice try," he gasps as its darkness begins to fragment. "You cannot..."

The champion's laugh suddenly turns triumphant. A wave of pure darkness explodes, shattering my light cage like glass. The force slams into me like a freight train, sending me flying across the chamber. I hit the ice wall hard enough to crack it, stars exploding behind my eyes.

"Foolish child," the champion's voice drips with contempt. "Did you think your parlor tricks could defeat me alone?"

I try to push myself up, but my limbs won't cooperate. Blood trickles from my lips, every breath sending daggers through my ribs. The cuts on my body burn with an otherworldly cold, spreading numbness through my veins.

"Dani!" Rhyland's roar echoes off the walls. Through blurry vision, I see him charge the champion, his power manifesting like a storm.

"Rhy, wait—"

Vidar dissolves into shadow, reforming behind him with his sword raised.

Time slows as I push myself up, ribs screaming in protest. The Aquanite sings to me again, urging me to action. I reach out, commanding the ice beneath the champion's feet to spike upward. Vidar leaps away, but his movement gives Rhyland time to spin clear.

"Would you stop trying to be the hero?" I wheeze, stumbling to his side. "We need a plan."

"The plan is keeping you alive," he growls, eyes blazing.

The champions laughter fills the chamber. "Your light cannot pierce my shadow, Lightborn," it taunts, "And your strength cannot grasp what isn't solid, Son of Nyx."

Wait. Wait. Wait. The way it shifts between solid and shadow... the way it only becomes tangible at certain moments...

"Rhyland," I gasp, clutching my bleeding leg. "It's quantum."

"What?"

"Like Schrödinger's cat—it exists in multiple states simultaneously." My scientist's brain kicks into overdrive. "It's only solid when observed when light hits it. But your power affects it when it's in shadow form."

Understanding dawns in his eyes. "So we need to—"

"Hit it in both states at once." I push myself up, ignoring the stabbing pain. "Think you can time it, right?"

His arm tightens around my waist. "Just tell me when."

The champion charges, his blade leaving trails of darkness through the air. Time warps around us as I gather my power, angel fire blazing in one hand while the Aquanite stone pulses in my crown.

"Now!"

My light erupts just as Rhyland's power strikes. The Einherjar tries to shift forms, but it's caught between states—my radiance forcing it's shadows solid, while Rhyland's telekinesis tears at its now solid form. Ice crystals form in the air, infused with burning light, piercing through both aspects of its being.

Vidar screams, a sound of agony and revelation. Its form begins to dissolve, not into shadow this time but into pure energy—its essence.

"The jar!" I fumble for Baldr's container with blood-slicked hands. "Help me—"

Rhyland's power joins mine as we guide the swirling essence into the jar. As I seal the lid, it pulses with captured energy.

His essence swirls like a liquid shadow. Storm-grey light seeps between my fingers, casting strange patterns across the frozen chamber walls. The cold glass vibrates with power, a reminder of how close we came to joining those frozen warriors in their icy tombs.

"One down," I whisper, watching dark energy writhe within its prison. The essence seems to reach toward me, testing its boundaries before coiling back on itself like a wounded serpent.

My legs give out, the adrenaline crash hitting hard. Rhyland catches me, his face tight with rage and concern.

"That was reckless," he growls, already examining my wounds.

"Says the guy who lost his cool and nearly got skewered." I wince as he probes my ribs. "Besides, I totally solved the quantum physics puzzle. You're welcome."

"Angel." His voice drops lower, dangerous. "You're bleeding from at least four places."

"They're just flesh wounds," I joke, but it becomes more of a groan. "Besides, Viking's dig scars, right?"

"Not funny," he grumbles, but his hands are already gentle as they examine my injuries. "You could have been killed."

"Please," I scoff, wincing as he finds a particularly tender spot. "Death would have to get through you first, and we both know you're way too much of a stubborn ass to let that happen."

A deep grumble vibrates through his chest, his blue eyes darkening to midnight. Without hesitation, Rhyland brings his wrist to his mouth, fangs piercing flesh. Blood wells from the wound—the second time today, he's opened his veins for me.

His hand tangles in my hair, tilting my head back as he presses his bleeding wrist to my lips. "Drink." The command leaves no room for argument.

I meet his gaze, taking in the shadows under his eyes, the strain etched into his features. His own wounds from the battle have barely started healing, yet here he is, offering more of himself. The Atherite stone healing power works too slowly for his liking—it always has. The sight of my blood, my pain, drives him to this every time.

His blood hits my tongue, hot and electric. The effect is immediate—a rush of power that makes my nerve endings sing. I feel my torn flesh knitting together, the deep gash in my thigh sealing itself with a strange tingling sensation. My ribs snap back into place with an audible pop that would make me flinch if the pleasure of his blood wasn't overwhelming everything else.

His taste—ocean, thunder, and raw power—floods my senses as my body heals. Each pull draws a low rumble from his chest, his fingers tightening in my hair. Even weakened from battle, his blood carries enough strength to remake me, to erase every mark the Einherjar left on my flesh.

His wrist withdraws, replaced instantly by his mouth claiming mine. The kiss is savage, desperate—all the fear and fury of battle transformed into raw need. His tongue sweeps past my lips, still carrying traces of his own blood, creating an intoxicating mix of flavors that makes my head spin.

My earlier threats of punishment for his secrets with Erik fade into background noise as his tongue strokes against mine, hot and demanding. Each sweep, each taste, sends electricity racing down my spine. Rhyland's hand fists in my hair, tilting my head back to deepen the kiss. His tongue strokes against mine in a sinful dance that has heat pooling low in my belly.

Each teasing flick, ignites nerve endings already sensitized by his blood. He tastes like storm clouds and danger, like lightning about to strike.

I gasp into his mouth as his other hand grips my hip, pulling me flush against him.

My fingers dig into his shoulders as he devours me, his growl of possession vibrating through my entire body.

His teeth graze my bottom lip, not breaking the skin but promising more, making me arch against him. The kiss grows wilder, deeper—our tongues dancing in a heated battle for dominance that he wins easily.

I should be angry about the secrets. I should stick to my threats of punishment. But with his mouth moving against mine like sin incarnate, his tongue doing wicked things that make my toes curl, I can't remember why any of that matters right now.

Rhyland breaks the kiss. His fingers still tangled possessively in my hair. Those stormy-blue eyes bore into mine, dark with hunger and something more profound. The intensity of his gaze pins me in place more effectively than his physical strength.

My legs have apparently forgotten how to function, turning to liquid beneath me. His arm around my waist is the only thing keeping me upright, my body molded against the hard planes of his chest. A smirk tugs at his kiss-swollen lips—he knows exactly what he does to me, the bastard.

"Time to go, Angel." His voice is pure silk wrapped around steel, creating goose-bumps on my skin. I try to nod, but my brain seems to have malfunctioned. I have to swallow twice before I find my voice, and even then, it comes out embarrassingly breathy. So much for maintaining my composure.

Focus, Dani. Remember the plan. No sexy times until I get answers about Erik's secret. I need to stay strong, stay determined, stay...

Rhyland's thumb traces my lower lip, his eyes tracking the movement. A delicate current of electricity dances from his thumb across my skin, something entirely new in his arsenal of seduction. The sensation isn't painful—quite the opposite. It's like liquid lightning coursing through my veins, making every nerve ending sing. My breath hitches as my nipples tighten in response, and I feel that familiar heat pool low in my belly. Damn this Viking and his newly discovered powers. One electrically-charged touch, one smoldering look from those ocean eyes, and my determination dissolves faster than a snowflake in hell.

Who the fuck am I kidding? In our little game of dominance and submission, Rhyland always wins. Always. And judging by the knowing smirk on his face, he's counting on it.

I conjure a portal, the edges crackling with power. No way am I dealing with another round of undead Viking assholes or those oversized murder-birds—the shimmering gateway to Valor's Watch beckons like a beacon of sanctuary.

Baldr stands before us, not a single hair out of place despite the carnage we just survived. His perfect features arrange themselves into what he thinks is a wise expression. "The second Einherjar essence must wait. Seven days of rest, then we return."

Before I can argue, he and Heimdall vanish in a flash of divine light that's way more dramatic than necessary. Show-offs.

My body screams for rest, every muscle trembling from battle, but the image of Bryn tears at my soul. The memory replays in vivid, horrible detail—her wing, proud and beautiful, being ripped away. The sound of her scream still echoes in my ears, her blood staining the virgin snow. This war forever changed my fierce Valkyrie sister. Its weight sits like a lead in my stomach. I want to push forward, to end this quickly, but one look at Bryn's face—the way she holds herself rigid against the pain, her remaining wing trembling with each breath—tells me Baldr is right.

Some wounds go deeper than flesh and bone. This isn't just about physical healing—it's about learning to live with an irreplaceable loss. The thought makes my throat tight, my eyes burning. Seven days feels too long to wait and not nearly long enough to process what's happened.

Gullfax follows me to his stall, his hooves clicking against the stone with a distinctly pouty rhythm. He's being surprisingly childish about taking the portal shortcut for a magical horse that can run on air.

"Come on, handsome." I lead him to his stall, where golden hay gleams in the manger. "There will be plenty of chances for you to show off your fancy moves."

I am a war steed of Ásgard, not some common pack horse to be shuffled through magical doorways. My hooves are meant to strike thunder from the clouds themselves. My sacred duty is to carry you through the skies and across the realm. You're denying me my purpose.

I roll my eyes, running a hand down his shimmering neck. "I get it," I say softly, understanding dawning. "You feel like you failed today because that Draugr got the drop on you. But taking the portal wasn't about not trusting you—it was about being smart. You did great today. Stop whining."

His big hooves stamp against the ground, sending golden sparks flying. *"Perhaps next time you'd prefer to walk? I hear frost-bitten toes are quite fashionable among mortals these days."*

"Did you just... sass me?" I stare at him in disbelief. "Since when did you get so lippy?"

His only response is to turn his back to me, munching his hay with exaggerated dignity. For a horse that can outrun the winds, he's got the dramatic flair of a teenage diva.

"Look," I stroke his fur, "don't take the portal thing personally. You're still my favorite celestial taxi service."

"Arguing with the war horse, Angel?" Rhyland's deep voice carries that hint of amusement as he approaches, his presence filling the stable like a storm front.

I lean back against his chest, feeling the rumble of his laugh. "He's sulking. My portal-jumping offended his sensibilities."

Gullfax keeps his back turned, munching his hay. *"I am an ancient steed of legend, blessed by the AllFather himself. I do not sulk."*

"He says he doesn't sulk," I relay to Rhyland, rolling my eyes. "Apparently, ancient steeds of legend are above such things."

Rhyland's arms circle my waist, his chin resting on my head. "The war horse knows better. Don't you, boy?"

"I am merely expressing my profound disappointment in your lack of appreciation for traditional modes of transportation," Gullfax projects into my thoughts, each word precise and pompous.

I snort. "Now he's lecturing me about 'traditional modes of transportation.' I swear he practices these speeches."

"I do not practice anything," Gullfax's mental voice turns haughty. *"I am naturally eloquent."*

"He claims it's natural eloquence," I tell Rhyland, who's shaking with silent laughter.

"You try maintaining dignity when your chosen rider starts treating you like a backup plan."

I step forward, poking his muscled shoulder. "Backup plan? More like my first line of defense when shit hits the fan. In case you haven't noticed, this happens a lot around here."

His eyes soften slightly. *"Perhaps... I may have overreacted. Slightly."*

"He admits to overreacting," I translate for Rhyland, "but only slightly. Very slightly. His pride is still intact."

"Now, if you'll excuse me," Gullfax says, turning back to his hay. *I have some vital dining to attend to. It requires my full concentration."*

I roll my eyes. "Drama queen."

"I heard that."

"You were meant to."

Rhyland's laugh rumbles through his chest. "Come on, Angel. Let his majesty eat in peace."

"Fine," I concede, giving Gullfax one last pat. "But this conversation isn't over, mister."

I head to the stall door, about to lock it—"

Thank you, Lightborn," Gullfax whispers through my mind, all traces of indignation gone. His mental tone softens with genuine gratitude. *"For what you did today, I will never forget it."*

Warmth blooms in my chest as I step back to his stall, wrapping my arms around his neck. His coat shimmers like captured sunlight beneath my touch. "Anytime, big guy."

Gullfax gently nuzzles my back with his head, bringing tears to my eyes. I catch Rhyland watching us, a rare soft smile on his lips. His eyes are so tender that they make my heart skip.

"What's he saying?" Rhyland asks, his deep voice quiet, respecting the moment.

"Just thanking me," I manage, still wrapped in Gullfax's embrace. "Though I'm the one who should be grateful. You saved my life today, you magnificent drama queen."

Gullfax's mental snort carries equal parts affection and wounded pride. *"I prefer 'theatrical warrior steed,' if you please. Meet me here tomorrow morning, you owe me a ride, Lightborn."*

DANICA

39

The sun barely peeks over the horizon as I trudge through fresh snow toward the stables. My breath clouds in the frigid air, and I swear my eyelashes are developing icicles. But duty calls—specifically in the form of one demanding magical horse.

Gullfax stands regally in his stall, somehow managing to look both majestic and slightly judgmental. How a horse pulls that off, I'll never know.

"Good morning, Lightborn," he greets, his voice carrying that mixture of ancient wisdom and barely concealed sass that I've come to expect.

"Morning, Your Royal Horseness," I reply, pulling my jacket tighter. "Care to enlighten me about our destination? My overprotective Viking isn't thrilled about me galloping off into the unknown."

Gullfax gives me what can only be described as an equine eye-roll. *"Either I'm imagining things, or you two need to hash out whatever storm cloud is hovering over your relationship."* He tosses his magnificent mane. *"Perhaps some time apart will do you both some good. Distance makes the heart grow fonder and all that mortal nonsense."*

I sigh, my breath creating a dramatic swirl of fog in the frigid air. "It's complicated," I deflect, channeling my inner teenager.

Gullfax fixes me with one of those ancient, all-knowing equine stares that makes me feel like I'm being cross-examined by a thousand-year-old therapist in horseshoes. *"Lightborn, I've carried heroes into battle since before your ancestors figured out which end of a sword to hold. Trust me when I say that 'complicated' is usually mortal-speak for 'I'm avoiding an uncomfortable conversation.'"*

What is he now, my therapist? Dr. Phil with hooves?

I ignore his emotional probing and head for his reins. "Where to, O Cryptic One?" I ask, stepping into his stall. "And please don't say 'on a journey of self-discovery' because it's way too early for that nonsense."

He huffs, his nostrils flaring. *"Somewhere I think you'll appreciate,"* he says, managing to sound both mysterious and smug.

Well, that's not vague at all. Good thing I didn't need actual directions or, you know, basic information about where we're heading. Who doesn't love a surprise trip with a snarky horse at dawn?

Without my Viking beefcake here to toss me onto this ginormous beast like a sack of potatoes, I'm suddenly facing a logistical crisis. How exactly does one mount a horse that's roughly the size of a small building?

As if reading my thoughts (and probably judging them), Gullfax steps regally out of his stall. *"Follow me."*

He leads me outside, his hooves crunching through fresh snow, and stops beside what looks like a medieval mounting block. It's basically a fancy ladder for vertically challenged humans like myself who can't spontaneously levitate onto horse-back.

"Ah, nice," I grin. "Your own personal human-loading dock. Very considerate."

I scramble up the mounting block while Gullfax sidles alongside, probably trying not to laugh at my attempts at dignity. The moment I settle onto his back and grab the reins, he launches into the air without so much as a "hold on tight."

"A little warning would be nice!" I yelp, thighs already burning as we soar into the pre-dawn sky.

Despite the Arctic temperatures trying to freeze my face off, it's breathtaking up here. My fur-lined cloak battles the wind chill while my inner supernatural space heater kicks in, finally making this morning flight somewhat bearable.

Gullfax banks gracefully around the compound, heading toward the shadowy cliffs behind it. A colossal structure emerges from the morning mist, its spires reaching toward the stars like dark fingers.

"That's the Twilight Eyrie," Gullfax announces. *"The sacred roost of the Valkyries, where they gather between their soul-collecting missions. It's where warriors worthy of Valhalla are first brought for judgment before ascending to the halls of the honored dead."*

"Wow." The word escapes in a frosty puff as we soar past the Eyrie. Below us, a gigantic frozen lake stretches into infinity, its depths disappearing into darkness that makes me seriously question my desire to ever go ice skating again.

Gullfax gallops through the low-hanging clouds, his hooves striking invisible paths in the air. *"There,"* he announces as another towering structure materializes through the mist. *"The Hall of Wings."*

"Within those ancient walls lies the collected wisdom of every Valkyrie since the first warrior maiden took flight," he explains. *"Scholars—both current Valkyrie and those found wanting of wing—devote their immortal lives to preserving every tale, every battle, every soul-gathering. Though I must say, some of the more dramatic scribes do tend to embellish their accounts. One would think every soul-collection involved a raging tempest and at least three acts of impossible heroism."*

"So basically like any author ever," I snort. "Let me guess—they also love cliffhangers and dramatic pauses?"

My inner nerd practically vibrates with excitement. The thought of all those stories, all that knowledge hidden behind those walls... I'm practically drooling. "What I wouldn't give to browse those shelves," I sigh wistfully. "My scientist brain is having a total nerdgasm right now."

"Not today, Lightborn. I have other plans." His tone carries that 'just wait and see' that makes me nervous. *"Hang on."*

Oh, *now* he warns me?

Gullfax launches us higher, and I grip his mane like my life depends on it (which, let's be honest, it absolutely does). We streak through the sky like a golden meteor, the world blurring around us as he banks in the opposite direction. I settle in for the ride, putting my trust in this ancient, sassy stallion who seems determined to play mystical tour guide this morning.

An hour later, Ásgard materializes before us in all its glory. The transition from arctic wasteland to eternal summer still gives me whiplash—one moment we're flying through air cold enough to freeze your thoughts, the next we're bathed in golden warmth. Gullfax touches down near the great river that winds through the realm like a liquid silver ribbon.

Gullfax actually shows mercy this time, lowering himself onto the sun-warmed grass so I can dismount without risking life, limb, or dignity.

Birds perform their Disney-worthy symphony overhead, as I shrug off my fur-lined cloak, already sweating in the eternal summer of Ásgard. No sooner have I draped it over my arm than His Majestic Snarkiness rises to his full height.

"Come," he commands, because apparently we're still playing the cryptic mentor card.

Gullfax leads me along the riverbank, where crystal clear waters dance over ancient stones that seem to shimmer with their own inner light. The path winds through a grove of trees with silver-white bark and leaves that chime like tiny bells in the breeze.

We emerge into a hidden valley where the air itself seems to dance. Floating spheres of light drift lazily through the air, each one containing what looks like a moving memory.

"The Valley of Windborne Memories," Gullfax announces. *"Here, the winds of Ásgard preserve moments of great significance. The Valkyries use this place to study the patterns of fate and destiny."* He pauses, giving me a meaningful look. *"Including the trials faced by those who sought the Zephyrite stone."*

I watch, mesmerized, as one of the spheres drifts closer. Inside, I see a warrior battling what appears to be living wind, her form flickering between solid and transparent. Another shows someone trying to catch lightning with their bare hands.

"Past attempts," Gullfax explains. *"Some succeeded. But most..."* He trails off meaningfully.

"Let me guess—they became part of the permanent decoration?"

"Indeed. Though I must say, being transformed into an eternal wind chime is one of the more creative outcomes I've witnessed."

I swallow hard. "And you're showing me this because...?"

"Because, Lightborn, sometimes the best way to face what lies ahead is to under-stand what lies behind." A sphere floats between us, showing a familiar face—Thor, in his prime, wielding the Zephyrite stone. *"And because you'll need every advantage you can get."*

The memory sphere bursts suddenly, showering us with tiny motes of light that dance around me like curious fireflies before sinking into my skin. Knowledge floods my mind—fragments of ancient wisdom about air magic, the stone's true nature, the proper way to harness wind itself.

"Did you just—"

"Give you a head start? Perhaps." Gullfax's eyes twinkle with ancient mischief. *"Though if anyone asks, I merely took you on a scenic tour."*

The motes of light continue to dance around me, each one sinking in with a tiny spark of insight. It's like downloading centuries of knowledge straight into my brain, except instead of a progress bar, I get sparkly magical fireflies.

"So these memories," I gesture at the floating spheres, trying to process the information download happening in my head, "they're like a supernatural cheat sheet?"

Gullfax snorts, managing to make the sound both elegant and judgy. *"More like echoes of those who came before. Each attempt, each failure, each rare success left its mark on the winds of Ásgard."* Another sphere drifts close, this one showing a woman wielding what looks like solid air as a weapon. *"The winds remember, Lightborn. They remember everything."*

"Including how not to become a wind chime?" I ask hopefully.

"Among other things." He steps closer to a particularly large sphere, his reflection rippling across its surface. *"Watch this one carefully."*

The memory inside springs to life, showing a warrior facing what appears to be a tornado made of pure light. But instead of fighting it directly, she... dances? Her movements flow like water, each step precisely placed, each gesture working with the wind rather than against it.

"She succeeded," I realize, watching her merge with the tornado instead of being torn apart by it.

"Indeed. She understood what most failed to grasp—that air cannot be conquered, only persuaded." His ancient eyes fix on me. *"Much like a certain stubborn Viking of yours."*

I feel my cheeks heat. "Are we still doing the horse therapy session?"

"Consider it a bonus to your education." Another sphere bursts, its knowledge sinking into my skin. *"Though I notice you're not denying the comparison."*

I sigh dramatically. "Fine. Yes. Rhyland is exactly like trying to conquer air—impossible, frustrating, and likely to blow up in your face if you push too hard." I kick at a tuft of grass. "But that's the problem. He's keeping something from me about Erik, and every time I try to get a straight answer, he goes all 'protective alpha male' on me. Like I can't handle whatever's going on."

I throw my hands up. "I mean, come on! I've faced shadow demons, survived death, discovered I'm basically angel royalty, and he thinks I need to be sheltered from whatever's happening with Erik? It's insulting. And worse—" my voice drops, "it scares me. Because whatever's bad enough that Rhyland thinks he needs to protect me from it... must be really, really bad."

Gullfax regards me with those ancient eyes that have seen centuries of drama unfold. He exhales softly, creating a small breeze that stirs the memory spheres around us.

"Young Lightborn, I have carried warriors into battle since before your kind built their first cities. I have seen the rise and fall of gods. And in all that time, one truth remains constant—those who carry great power often carry greater burdens." His voice deepens with wisdom. *"Rhyland is much like his father, Magni. The apple didn't fall far from that particular tree.*

A memory sphere drifts between us, showing a towering figure with lightning crackling around his fists. In the vision, Magni stands before Thor's throne, his stance defiant as he argues passionately. Though the sphere carries no sound, his intent is clear from his protective posture and fierce expression—he's demanding the right to handle some danger alone, refusing to share the burden even with his father.

"Like father, like son. Rhyland believes protection means bearing burdens alone, carrying secrets like stones in his pockets until they weigh him down into the earth."

Gullfax nudges me gently with his nose. *"But consider this, Lightborn—perhaps what troubles Erik is not Rhyland's secret to share. Perhaps he guards another's confidence as fiercely as he guards your heart."*

He gestures toward another memory sphere, this one showing two warriors standing back-to-back against a horde of enemies. *"Brotherhood among immortals is a bond forged over centuries. What you see as secretive may simply be loyalty to promises made long before you drew breath.*

"The question isn't whether you can handle the truth," he continues, wisdom tempering his usual snark. *"The question is whether you trust him enough to let him keep his word to another, even when it frustrates you."*

I roll my eyes, but Gullfax's words hit their mark. Damn mystical horse making actual sense. Still, the frustration simmers under my skin like an itch I can't scratch.

"Fine. I get it. Brotherhood, loyalty, promises made in the bro-code or whatever." I kick at a pebble, watching it skitter across the perfect grass. "But it still chaps my ass that I'm apparently not worthy of being included in their little supernatural secret society. I mean, what happened to 'mates don't keep secrets from each other'? Or does that only apply when it's convenient?"

Gullfax's deep chuckle resonates in my head. *That, Little Light, is for you two to figure out.* His mental voice carries that infuriating tone of someone who knows they've won the argument but is too dignified to gloat openly.

I leave it at that, though the frustration still simmers beneath my skin. I'm nowhere near ready to just accept whatever mysterious bullshit is happening with Erik, regardless of how many wise horse proverbs get thrown my way.

Am I being a petty, stubborn brat about this? Absolutely.

Do I have even the slightest inclination to stop? Not a chance in hell.

Some hills are worth dying on, and "no secrets between mates" is definitely one of them.

Gullfax leads me deeper into Ásgard's hidden wonders, past the Valley of Wind-borne Memories and through a grove of trees with bark like polished silver. The path winds upward, following the river's course until the sound of rushing water grows from whisper to roar.

We emerge onto a ledge overlooking a spectacular sight—a mammoth waterfall that seems to pour directly from the sky itself. The cascade tumbles hundreds of feet, creating a perpetual rainbow in the mist where sunlight strikes water. At the base, the pool shimmers with colors that shouldn't exist in nature—deep azures fading to violets and golds that pulse with their own inner light.

The Falls of Fafnir. Named for the dragon who once guarded these waters.

A freaking water dragon??

As if summoned by his words, a small creature emerges from the pool's edge, shaking droplets from its fur. At first glance, it resembles an otter with sleek, dark fur—until it unfurls tiny, iridescent dragon wings from its back and gives them a delicate flutter. Its eyes gleam with intelligence, whiskers twitching as it studies us curiously.

A fjörniskratti, Gullfax explains as the creature waddles closer, its webbed paws leaving damp prints on the stone. *Spirit guardians of sacred waters. They are distant cousins to dragons, though they prefer fish to maidens and treasure.*

The fjörniskratti chirps, a sound like wind chimes in a summer breeze, and tilts its head at me. Its wings—barely the span of my hand—shimmer with all the colors of the waterfall as they catch the light.

"They are rare even in Ásgard," Gullfax continues. *"To see one is considered a blessing... or a warning, depending on their mood."*

The little creature seems to consider me for a moment before it stands on its hind legs, paws pressed together as if in prayer. Then, with another musical chirp, it produces a single scale from its chest—a tiny disc that gleams like mother-of-pearl in the sunlight.

"Well," Gullfax sounds genuinely surprised. *"It seems you've made a friend."*

I stand frozen, afraid that even breathing might scare away this impossible creature. The fjörniskratti chirps again, more insistently this time, tiny paw still extended with its offering.

"Is it... giving me a gift?" I whisper, not taking my eyes off the miniature dragon-otter.

"So it would seem," Gullfax replies, sounding impressed despite himself. *"Their scales are powerful conduits for water and air magic. They rarely part with them willingly."*

With trembling fingers, I kneel and extend my palm. The fjörniskratti waddles forward with surprising dignity, places the iridescent scale in my hand, then presses its cool, damp nose against my wrist. A tingling sensation races up my arm—like static electricity but somehow... wetter?

"Holy shit," I breathe as the scale seems to melt into my skin, leaving behind a shimmering mark like a tattoo of overlapping waves. "Did that just—"

"Bind itself to you? Yes." Gullfax sounds genuinely startled. *"That is... unprecedented."*

The fjörniskratti looks extraordinarily pleased with itself. It chirps once more before doing what can only be described as a happy dance—spinning in circles, wings fluttering, webbed feet slapping against the stone.

"I don't understand," I say, staring at the mark on my palm. "What does this mean?"

Before Gullfax can answer, more ripples disturb the pool's surface. To my absolute astonishment, dozens of tiny heads emerge—more fjörniskratti, each one slightly different in coloring but all sporting the same adorable whiskers and miniature dragon wings.

They form a semicircle at the water's edge, watching me with intelligent eyes that seem to contain galaxies. Then, as if responding to some unseen signal, they begin to sing.

The sound defies description—higher than wind chimes, more melodic than birdsong, with harmonies that seem to resonate directly with my bones. The waterfall's roar softens, as if even it wants to listen.

"Oh my god," I whisper, tears springing to my eyes though I can't explain why. "It's the most beautiful thing I've ever heard."

"The Song of Blessing," Gullfax murmurs, his usual snark completely absent. *"They recognize you, Lightborn. Not just as the savior of prophecy, but as something more."*

"Something more?" My voice cracks as the fjörniskratti's song continues to wrap around me like a warm embrace. "What do you mean?"

Gullfax moves closer. *"The fjörniskratti are the keepers of what lies between—the guardians of transition and transformation. Their blessing is rare, given only to those who can bridge worlds."*

I stare at the shimmering mark on my palm. "Bridge worlds? Like... the different realms?"

"More than that." His voice takes on a teaching tone I'm starting to recognize. *"You are born of light, mated to storm and shadows. You walk between science and magic, mortal and divine. The fjörniskratti see this duality in you, and now they've given you the means to harness it."*

The little otter-dragon chirps in agreement, nuzzling against my hand. The mark pulses in response, sending waves of tingling energy up my arm.

"That scale-mark they've gifted you," Gullfax continues, *"it's not just a pretty tattoo. It's a key—one that will help you see and manipulate the spaces between things. The very boundaries that separate elements, realms, even states of being."*

"Like how I saw the guardian was quantum?" I ask, thinking back to our earlier battle.

"Precisely. But now you'll be able to see such things naturally, without having to puzzle them out. The mark will help you perceive the in-between spaces, the transitions, the moments of possibility." He pauses, adding with what sounds

suspiciously like pride, *"It's a powerful gift, little light. One that could change everything about how you approach the trials ahead."*

I flex my marked palm, watching the shimmering patterns ripple. "So basically, I've just been adopted by a bunch of magical otter-dragons who've given me cosmic X-ray vision?"

The Keeper makes a sound suspiciously like a giggle, while Gullfax just sighs. *"If that simplified explanation helps you process this momentous mystical occurrence, then yes. You've been adopted by magical otter-dragons."*

The Keeper chirps one final time before waddling back to the water's edge, its tiny wings giving an almost apologetic flutter. One by one, the other fjörniskratti bow their heads to me before slipping beneath the surface, leaving only ripples and the echo of their song behind.

I turn to Gullfax, emotion tightening my throat. "Thank you," I whisper, reaching out to touch his velvet nose. "For bringing me here. For showing me..." I press my forehead against his, feeling the ancient power that thrums beneath his hide. "For everything."

His mental voice is gentler than I've ever heard it. *"This is my gift to you, Lightborn. A small repayment for saving my life."* His breath ruffles my hair. *"Though I suspect those little troublemakers just gave you a far greater present than I could have planned."*

The mark on my palm pulses warmly, as if in agreement.

I grin up at him. "Well, for a snarky immortal horse who's been nothing but a pain in my ass since day one, you sure know how to plan one hell of a field trip." My voice softens. "Thank you, Gullfax. Really. You've actually turned out to be one of the best gifts I could have asked for."

RHYLAND

40

Six fucking days of sleeping alone while Dani camps out in Bryn's quarters. Six days of watching my mate exhaust herself in the training ring, pushing Bryn through drills like a woman possessed. Meanwhile, I'm stuck brooding with Erik, who's about as comforting as a stone wall with fangs.

Six fucking days of handling my own business like some horny teenager who just discovered his right hand. My body's so wound up I'm ready to explode, and not in the fun way. Every time Dani walks by, my cock stands at attention like it's trying to salute its commander. This self-imposed celibacy is a special kind of torture that's got me acting like I'm back in puberty, discovering what my dick's for all over again.

And the worst part? She knows exactly what she's doing to me. Every little sway of those hips, every "accidental" brush against me—she's playing a dangerous game, and my control's hanging by a thread thinner than Erik's patience.

Six days of watching Erik and Bryn dance around each other in the training ring like two wounded predators. Every time he tries to help, she shuts him down hard. Something went down in that ice cave that neither of them is talking about—and whatever it was has turned their usual tension into a fucking glacier of awkward silences and avoided eye contact.

The tension between them is thick enough to choke on, and neither one's talking about what really happened. Just more secrets and silent suffering to add to our growing pile of shit to deal with.

Whatever happened on her little jaunt through the skies with Gullfax didn't do shit for her attitude either. She gave me the cliff notes version—something about a memory valley and dragons that look like goddamn otters, gifting her a tattoo.

Sure, it's probably some big damn deal, but I'm too pissed off to give a rat's ass right now. My mood is six feet in the goddamn dirt right now, and I can't bring myself to give a shit about whatever privileged information Gullfax decided to share with her.

If she thinks I'm going to keep playing this game of emotional hide-and-seek while she proves her point about honesty and trust, she's got another thing coming.

The Valkyries stripped Bryn of her command—a dick move that made my blood boil. These self-righteous bitches think losing a wing makes her less of a warrior? One wing down, and suddenly years of battlefield glory mean jack-shit. But their realm, their rules, and all that political bullshit.

Bryn's turned into a ghost of herself, moving through the halls like a shadow. Dani keeps throwing sunshine and motivational speeches at her, but you can't fix a warrior's broken spirit with pretty words. Dani's anguish burns through our bond every time Bryn shuts down another pep talk. My mate's heart bleeds for her sister, and there isn't a damn thing I can do except watch them both suffer.

Fuck this whole situation sideways.

Tomorrow, we hunt down another one of these ancient bastards, and my gut's already churning. The last Einherjar nearly took my mate's head off—watching her throw down with that ice-powered asshole nearly gave my heart a restart. But fuck me if she didn't shine like a warrior goddess, all fury and power. My fierce little mate, serving up divine ass-kicking with a side of sass.

Meanwhile, my silver-haired brother is still being a stubborn asshole, finding every excuse in the book not to claim Bryn. "She needs time," he says like he's some emotional expert.

Bullshit.

I see right through his righteous act—he's scared shitless she'll reject him. And I get it. Having your mate tell you to fuck off? That's a special kind of hell that makes death look like a vacation option. But watching him dance around Bryn like she's the plague is starting to piss me off. Man needs to grow a pair and face his fate, one way or the other.

"Planning to burn holes through her skull with that death stare?" I growl over my mead, watching Erik's eyes track Bryn like a heat-seeking missile. The girls are huddled by the fire, while we're doing our best to drink the longhouse dry. At least the alcohol takes the edge off this fucking hunger for Dani.

These days, feeding's become a drive-by affair—she lets me bite, then dances away. My fangs ache for more than just a quick taste, my body screaming to pin her down and remind her exactly who she belongs to. This celibacy bullshit is going to drive me insane.

Erik keeps up his brooding silence, silver eyes locked on Bryn like she might disappear if he blinks. "For fuck's sake," I slam my cup down. "At least tell Dani the truth about the mate bond. Your secretive shit is getting real old, brother."

"Your sexual frustration is hardly my primary concern," Erik's voice cuts like ice, though his fingers tighten around his cup until the metal creaks. "Bryn has made her choice clear with that Viking warrior. I won't force a bond where it's not wanted."

I growl low, watching my brother retreat behind his walls of self loathing.

Fucking martyr.

"Listen well, brother," I lean forward, letting my voice drop to a lethal whisper. "You have until midnight to stop this ethical martyrdom bullshit and claim what's yours, or I'm telling Dani everything. Your choice if you want to keep hiding behind that silver-haired wall of denial, but I'm done letting your emotional shit cockblock my entire fucking existence."

A flash of feral silver breaks through Erik's careful control. "You overstep," he warns, but there's a crack in his mask now. Good.

"No, brother. I'm just getting started."

"You know nothing of my situation," Erik's voice stays measured, but his eyes flash. "Bryn needs stability, not complications. Especially now."

"Bullshit." I drain my cup, setting it down. "She needs her mate, not some Viking dick who can't even look her in the eye since she lost her wing. You think I don't see him flinching every time she moves? Like she's damaged goods?"

A low growl rumbles from Erik's chest—the first crack in his precious control. "Watch yourself, brother."

"Or what? You'll brood at me harder?" I lean forward. "That warrior treats her like shit. Meanwhile, you're over here watching her every move like a starving man, planning fifty different ways to kill him in his sleep. How's that working out for you?"

"I've lived centuries without a mate," Erik's words are clipped, precise. "I can endure."

"Yeah? And how many of those centuries did you spend watching her fuck someone else?" The cup in Erik's hand crumples like paper. "That's what I thought."

"You push too far," he warns, but there's a tremor in his voice now.

"No, brother. I'm pushing exactly where it hurts. Because watching you two dance around each other is fucking pathetic. She's your mate. Fight for her."

"Fight for her?" Erik laughs. "While she lies with another? While she bears fresh scars, I failed to prevent? Tell me, brother, what exactly am I fighting for?"

"A mate who's trying to prove she's still worth something after losing everything." I slam my hand on the table, making the cups jump. "You think she's fucking that Viking because she wants him? She's trying to prove she's still desirable, you stupid fuck. And every day you stay silent just confirms her fears."

Something dangerous flashes in Erik's eyes. "You presume much."

"No, I observe while you wallow." I glance at Bryn, catching her eyes darting to Erik despite her conversation with Dani. "She's watching you right now, wondering why the man she's drawn to won't even acknowledge her existence. Meanwhile, you're here drinking yourself stupid and pretending it's noble suffering."

"Enough." Erik's voice drops to a lethal whisper.

"Not even close to enough. You want to know what that Viking bastard said about her yesterday? Called her a 'broken bird' when he thought no one could hear. Said she's 'still useful in the bed, despite everything.' Like she needs his fucking pity."

The table splinters under Erik's grip, his careful control finally shattering. "He said *what?*"

I lean back, watching the predator finally wake in my brother's eyes. "Oh, now you want to do something about it?"

Erik's fingers uncurl from the splintered wood with deliberate slowness. His face smooths back into that practiced mask of indifference, but I catch the slight tremor in his jaw.

"Your attempt at manipulation is noted, brother," he says, voice arctic cold. "But Bryn's choices are her own."

"For fuck's sake," I growl. "You and your selfless sacrifice routine is getting real old. You think you're protecting her? All you're doing is proving every doubt she has about herself."

"And you believe forcing a mate bond would solve this?" His silver eyes narrow. "Perhaps I should follow your example—throw her over my shoulder and demand submission?"

"At least I'm not watching my mate settle for less while pretending it doesn't gut me." I catch Bryn's reflection in my cup, the way her wing droops when Erik won't meet her gaze. "You think I don't see how she flinches every time that Viking touches her? How she checks your reaction? Pathetic doesn't begin to cover this situation."

"This discussion is finished." Erik rises with fluid grace, but I catch the slight shake in his hands. "Some battles aren't meant to be fought."

"No," I stand too, blocking his retreat. "Some battles are exactly what's needed. But hey, keep hiding behind your duty and honor. I'm sure watching another man claim your mate won't haunt you for the next few centuries."

His mask slips for just a second—long enough for me to see the raw agony beneath—before snapping back into place. Without another word, he turns and stalks away, his rigid posture screaming control while everything else about him bleeds defeat.

"Fucking idiot," I mutter, watching him go. Across the room, Bryn's wing twitches as she tracks his exit, her face a mirror of his hidden pain.

I've barely settled my ass back into my chair, reaching for what's left of my mead, when all hell breaks loose behind me.

"You're worthless now." That bastard Viking says to Bryn, his words slur like shit in sewage. "Just a washed-up Valkyrie. At least you're still good for one thing."

The scattered laughter from his warrior buddies sends my blood pressure spiking. These fuckers think this is funny? Let's see how hard they laugh with their spines decorating the walls.

"Fuck you, asshole!" My mate launches forward like an avenging angel, but I'm already there, pulling her back against my chest. As much as I'd love to watch her turn this bastard into Viking confetti, this isn't her fight.

"Know your place, little mortal," the drunk fuck sneers, mead dripping from his unkempt beard like dog slobber. "This is between me and my broken Valkyrie." His meaty paw swings toward Bryn's face with all the grace of a dying troll. "Come now, wingless one—time to earn your keep. You may have lost your warrior's pride, but you still have other... uses."

"Fuck you, Gunnar," Bryn snarls.

I feel Dani's power surge against my restraining grip. My own beast claws at its cage, demanding blood. Where the hell is Erik? His mate's about to get—

The sound of a slap cracks through the longhouse like lightning. Bryn's head snaps sideways, a red handprint blooming on her cheek like a battle flag. Her wing flares, more in shock than pain.

The longhouse goes dead silent except for this soon-to-be-dead fucker's breathing. Even the fire seems to hold its breath, waiting for the storm about to break.

And it will. Because this asshole who's about to die—that's Erik's mate he just struck. And my brother? He's standing in the doorway, his eyes promising the kind of death that'll make the ancient Norse hells look like a summer vacation.

"Bryn!" Dani's cry rings out, fury and pain twisting through her voice. "How dare you touch my sister—I will kill—"

The rest of her threat dies in her throat as Erik moves. One second he's in the doorway, the next he's got Gunnar by the throat, lifting the bastard clear off his feet like he weighs nothing.

I lean back against the pillar, pulling Dani flush against my chest, my arms locked around her waist like steel bands. Her heart's racing against my palms, but my attention's on Erik. About fucking time my brother woke up and remembered he's got fangs. Been watching him play the noble martyr so long I was starting to wonder if his balls had permanently retreated.

But that look in his eyes right now? That's the predator I've been waiting to see. That Viking fuck is about to learn why you don't touch a vampire's mate—and from the way Erik's eyes are blazing, it's going to be one hell of an educational experience.

Front row seats to a Viking's worst nightmare, and honestly? Couldn't happen to a more deserving asshole.

ERIK

41

I don't recall moving. Don't remember crossing the space between us. One moment, I'm by the door; the next, my fingers are locked around this assholes throat, fangs bared in the firelight.

His pulse throbs against my palm, each desperate beat a reminder of how easily I can end his miserable existence. The acrid stench of fear mingles with stale mead as his feet dangle uselessly above the floor.

"Touch her again," my voice cuts through the silence like frozen steel, "and I'll paint these walls with your entrails."

He chokes out a wet laugh, blood vessels bursting in his eyes. "Defending... damaged goods?" His words wheeze past my grip. "The great... vampire... playing hero for a... broken bird?"

The bones in his throat creak beneath my fingers. "Choose your next words carefully. They may be your last."

"She spreads... her legs... like a common whore..." Snot trickles from his nose. "Maybe... you want... sloppy seconds?"

Something snaps—a darkness I've kept chained for centuries breaks free.

My fist connects with his jaw—bone crunches beneath my knuckles. Again. And again. Blood sprays across the floor, his face caving like ripe fruit. I slam him into the nearest table, wood splintering beneath his bulk. Each punch lands with surgical precision, centuries of combat experience focused on prolonging his pain.

"Erik!" Dani's voice barely penetrates the red haze. "Stop!"

I grab his throat, ready to tear it out—then warmth spreads across me. Dani's palm presses against my chest. My heart hammers against her touch, betraying everything. Her eyes dart between me and Bryn as pieces fall into place. There's no judgment in her gaze—just quiet acceptance and relief.

"He's not worth it," she whispers, fingers curling into my shirt. "Let him live with his shame."

The piece of shit whimpers beneath me, his face a masterpiece of purple bruises and flowing blood.

Gunnar crumples to the floor. My gaze finds Bryn's—dual-colored eyes wide with shock. Something electric passes between us, unspoken yet deafening. The welt on her cheek feeds the inferno in my veins.

I tear myself away before the beast breaks free. The longhouse door splinters as I burst into the night. The Arctic wind does nothing to cool my rage. My boots crack through ice-crusted snow, leaving violent impressions.

Without Dani's intervention, that Viking's blood would have painted those walls.

The thought of his hands on *her*, that mark on her face—my control splinters like the ice beneath my feet.

Through it all, Rhyland smirked from his corner, watching my composure snap because someone dared touch what's mine.

The evidence accumulates like battlefield casualties. That Viking bastard's ham-fisted attempts at dominance. His meaty hands presuming ownership while her wing pulls tight against her spine. The dead look in her eyes at his advances.

Bloody fucking hell.

Her tells are impossible to ignore now: the delay before acknowledging his touch, the subtle shift when he approaches, the way her eyes would find mine across the longhouse like a silent plea.

These truths burn through my defenses like acid. Rhyland, subtle as a war hammer, forced me to confront what I've been denying. Yet she still chose him—chose that bastard's abuse over everything I could offer.

"Erik, wait!" Bryn's boots crunch through the snow behind me, but I lengthen my stride. Looking at her now would shatter what remains of my control. Her choice was clear enough—let her return to her arrogant brute.

The stable's warmth envelops me as I stride inside. Flickering torchlight dances across rough-hewn beams, casting restless shadows. Sweet hay and leather tack fill my lungs as I plant my feet in the center aisle, seeking any anchor against this storm.

Wood groans as Bryn heaves the stable doors shut. Her footsteps echo off the stone as she approaches. "You didn't have to do that. Why do you always feel the need to protect—"

Something snaps. I pivot to face her, my pulse racing. "Because." The word tears from my throat. "Are you truly so *blind?*"

The purple welt marring her cheek feeds my rage—another failure to protect what's mine.

"Blind?" Bryn's laugh cuts sharp and bitter. "I see perfectly clear. I'm half a Valkyrie now—stripped of my command, my honor." Her wing trembles with tension. "What good am I to anyone?"

"You truly believe that?" I stalk toward her, each step measured despite the rage and need coursing through me. "The warrior who's trained harder than any other? Who fights with more skill using one wing than most possess with two?"

"Don't." She backs away, but her scent betrays her—sweet honey and lightning, laced with arousal. "I don't need your pity."

"Pity?" The word tastes like poison. "Is that what you think this is?" Another step closer, backing her toward the stable wall. Her pulse quickens, and her pupils dilate. "You think I defend you out of duty?"

"Why else would you?" Her voice wavers, but her chin lifts in defiance. "I'm broken, Erik. Damaged. Even the Valkyries don't want—"

"You are *magnificent.*" The words tear from my throat as I close the distance. "Every scar, battle, triumph, and loss make you who you are." My body cages hers against the wall, close enough to feel her heat but not quite touching. Her scent floods my senses, making my fangs ache. "While you chase validation from lesser men, you fail to see your own worth."

"And you think you know my worth?" Her breath catches as I lean closer, her arousal spiking sharply enough to make my cock hard as steel.

"I see everything." My voice drops to a dangerous whisper. "Your strength. Your resilience. Your beauty." Each word brings me closer until barely a breath separates us. "The way you move in battle like a goddess of war. The fire that burns in your eyes when you fight."

"Stop it." Bryn ducks under my arm, retreating deeper into the stables. "You don't get to say these things. Not now." Her scent betrays her—desire mixing with fury.

"Why not?" I follow her measured retreat, every step a predator stalking prey. "Because it challenges your carefully constructed self-hatred?"

"Because it's lies!" She whirls on me, backing into a support beam. "Look at me, Erik! Really look! One wing, stripped of rank, fucking an asshole just to prove I still can—"

"And how's that working for you?" My words cut sharp and precise. "Does his touch satisfy? Or do you lie there, thinking of someone else?"

Her cheeks flush, pupils blown wide. "You arrogant bastard—"

"Tell me I'm wrong." Another step closer. Her scent drives me mad—lightning in a bottle, crackling with defiance and need. "Tell me you don't feel this."

"What I feel doesn't matter." She edges sideways, but I match her movement. "I'm not what I was. Not what I should be—"

"You're everything you should be." My voice drops to a dangerous growl. "Strong. Fierce. Untamed." Each word brings me closer as she retreats. "You think losing a wing makes you less? It makes you more. Every battle, every scar—they're proof of your warrior spirit."

"Pretty words from the perfect soldier." Her back hits another wall. "The great Erik, always in control, always—"

"Control?" A harsh laugh escapes me. "You think I'm in control when you're near? When I have to watch that scumbag, put his hands on, what's *mine?*"

"What's *yours?*" Her eyes flash dangerously. "I belong to no one, Erik. Not the Valkyries, not that asshole, and certainly not—"

"You've belonged to me since we landed in Valor's Watch." The truth finally breaks free, raw and unstoppable. "One look at you, and my entire world shifted on its axis."

The memory of landing in Valor's Watch slams into me—that first moment I saw her when the mate bond exploded through my system like fire. Everything I thought I knew shattered instantly, and decades of control and careful planning were obliterated by glancing at those mismatched eyes.

Her laugh is sharp, brittle. "Right. The mighty Erik claimed the broken Valkyrie. Is this pity or—"

"You're my mate." The words hang in the torch-lit air between us. "My *true* mate. I knew it the instant our eyes met in that training ring."

"Don't." She shakes her head, but I catch the slight tremor in her voice. "Don't mock me with—"

"You think I'd mock this?" I close the distance, letting her see the truth in my eyes. "Why do you think I've barely held my sanity since we arrived? Why your pulse calls to me like a siren's song? Why the mere thought of another man's hands on you drives me to *murder?*"

"That's..." Her voice falters as understanding begins to dawn. "No, that's impossible. I was meant for—"

"Rhyland. Yes, I know. But fate had other plans." My fingers hover near her cheek, not quite touching. "I've fought this since that first moment, watching you from afar, telling myself you deserved better than a cold-blooded killer."

"You're lying." But there's less conviction now, her body betraying her as she unconsciously leans toward my touch. "You can't be..."

"Search your heart. You've felt it too—this pull between us. The electricity whenever we're near. The way your body responds to my presence, just as mine aches for you."

Bryn jerks away, stumbling backward into the shadows. "No. This isn't—I can't—" Her wing brushes hay from the stalls, sending golden strands dancing in the torchlight.

Her eyes betray what her lips deny—desire warring with doubt, need fighting fear. Nearly a thousand years of patience crumbles at the sight.

To hell with restraint.

"Fuck it."

In less than a heartbeat, I cross the space between us. My hand catches the nape of her neck, fingers tangling in silken strands as I crush my mouth to hers.

Lightning explodes behind my eyes. Her gasp melts into a moan that vibrates through my bones. She tastes like storm clouds and honey. My fangs scrape her lip, drawing blood that sets my senses ablaze.

Her body arches, wing wrapping around us in feathered warmth. Her fingers dig into my shoulders as her curves press against me, her thundering heart matching mine.

I press her against the stable wall, swallowing her whimpers. Her tongue meets mine, sending sparks down my spine. The scent of her arousal spikes, making my cock throb against my leathers.

My mouth blazes a trail down her throat, across her collarbone, seeking lower—tasting salt and storm, each kiss drawing desperate sounds.

Her breasts press against my chest, the stiff peaks evident through her shirt. I palm one, drawing a sharp gasp from her lips. The weight fills my hand perfectly as my thumb traces circles. Her fingers tangle in my hair, yanking me back to her hungry mouth.

Gullfax's mocking whinny echoes through the stable, his golden head bobbing over the stall door. I tear my lips from Bryn's just long enough to growl, "Mind your business, stallion," before returning to her intoxicating mouth.

Her tongue slides against mine, soft and teasing. Each breathy moan vibrates through my chest, threatening my control. This kiss consumes me, shatters me, remakes me.

The stable doors crash open. "Bryn, are you—oh, sweet Odin's ravens!" The Valkyrie's wings snap tight as she spins, practically flying back through the doorway.

Bryn tears her lips from mine, chest heaving. "This was a mistake. We can't—*I* can't."

"Running away?" Ice edges my voice as I feel her pull back. "That's not like you, little bird."

"Don't." She straightens her disheveled shirt, but her hands shake. "Don't call me that. This isn't—we aren't—" She releases a frustrated breath. "Once you have the stone, you'll return to Midgard. Your duty lies with Dani, with protecting the savior."

"And what about my duty to you?" I step closer, but she backs away. "To us?"

"There is no us!" Her wing flares defensively, but I catch the pain in her dual-colored eyes. "I'm bound to Zephyria. This is my home, my purpose. I can't just abandon everything I've built here."

"Then I'll stay." The words escape before I can stop them. "If Zephyria is where you need to be—"

"No." Her voice cracks. "My sister needs you. The realms need you. I won't be the reason you abandon your post." She lifts her chin, but I see the tremor in her jaw. "I'm a broken Valkyrie who can barely fly. What could I possibly offer—"

"Everything." I catch her wrist, feeling her pulse race beneath my fingers. "You offer me everything. And if you think I'm letting you go because of duty or distance or your own damned stubbornness—"

"Let me go, Erik." But she doesn't pull away, her body betraying her words.

"Never." I draw her closer despite her resistance. "We'll find a way. Between realms, between duties. But don't stand there and tell me you feel nothing when every beat of your heart screams otherwise."

"You don't understand," Bryn wrenches her wrist free. "I can't be what you need. I won't be." Her wing wraps around her like armor. "I've spent centuries building my life here, my reputation. I won't throw that away for some... some magical bond that *claims* we're meant to be together."

The word 'claims' cuts deeper than any blade. "This isn't just some spell, Bryn. You feel it too—"

"What I feel is irrelevant." Ice crystallizes in her voice. "I've survived this long without a mate. I don't need one now, especially not a vampire who can't even protect my own sister without help."

The deliberate cruelty of her words strikes hard. My hands fall to my sides as something vital shatters in my chest. "Bryn—"

"Go back to your duties, Erik." She turns away, her wing trembling despite her harsh tone. "And I'll go back to mine. It's better this way."

She turns, boots clicking against stone as she strides away. Each step echoes like a death knell in my chest.

My knees give out the moment she's gone. I slam a fist into the stable floor, stone crumbling beneath my knuckles. Each breath feels like swallowing glass, the mate bond screaming in agony at her rejection. The pain is unbearable—a crushing weight that threatens to collapse my ribs and tear my heart from my chest.

I press my forehead to the cool stone as I fight for control. But how do you control this? This soul-deep devastation that comes from having your other half look you in the eye and choose to walk away?

A sound escapes my throat—something between a growl and a sob. The stable walls press in, every shadow a reminder of her absence. Even Gullfax has fallen silent as if the stallion senses the breaking of something fundamental.

Let the shadows take me. Let oblivion claim what's left of my cursed existence. Without her, there's nothing but darkness ahead.

LUCIAN

42

"Yeah, all we know is she yanked some vampire soul through the cosmic glory hole. I'll keep the council in the loop if I hear anything else that doesn't make me want to kill myself," I tell Alaric before yeeting my phone across the couch.

I'm exhausted, freaking out, and playing supernatural detective with zero fucking clues about what Demon Barbie is planning. If she's strutting her evil ass around Oregon, my money's on the Citadel—you know, Rhyland and Erik's old bachelor pad before this whole Dark Prophecy shit show decided to crash the party.

It's the only location that makes sense, really. Last we heard, the place was emptier than my liquor cabinet after a bad day. Perfect spot for Lilith's bougie ass to set up her evil lair. Probably already redecorating with expensive shit and whatever passes for furniture in Hell's IKEA.

Fucking typical.

Sable's been burning the midnight oil trying to MacGyver some magical smoke signals to Dani, but so far? Zip. Nada. Bupkis.

At this rate, I'd have better luck trying to reach her through a goddamn Ouija board. Or maybe I should stick to the old-fashioned method of screaming into the void and hoping for the best.

Meanwhile, Emily and Tall, Dark, and Shape-shifty have been getting way too buddy-buddy for my comfort, if you catch my drift.

Just... ugh. Pass the brain bleach, please.

Watching a demon play cosmic cosplay is not how I wanted to spend my week.

The dude's like an Instagram filter—one minute, he's Ryan Reynolds (which—*rude,* there can only be one devastatingly handsome smartass in this mansion) and the next, he's Henry Cavill. Emily's got her own personal Hollywood heartthrob selector, and it's giving me serious creeper vibes.

And get this—my Disney Plus account history is now 90% Marvel because Emily's got her pet demon binge-watching the MCU like it's his job. Pretty sure he's cosplayed as every Avenger by now. Except Hawkeye. Because even a demon has standards.

Someone please explain how this became my life.

My phone starts singing "Highway to Hell"—because yeah, I'm that kind of asshole—and I glance at the caller ID.

It's Kyle, my partner, who keeps Karma from turning into a complete dumpster fire.

What bullshit now?

"What's the damage?" I answer, fully expecting to hear about another fine from the Fun Police or some federal bullshit trying to cockblock my business. But all that red tape got shredded, thanks to Kyle working his legal magic.

No more putting the brakes on our blood-thirsty patrons—public feeding is officially back on the menu, baby! As long as everyone plays nice with the whole 'consent' thing. You know, basic vampire etiquette.

Business has been off the charts, profits soaring higher than a coked-up Wall Street exec.

"Nothing bad. I need your John Hancock on some paperwork. Final docs to get this place rerunning full throttle."

Hell fucking yes! My lawyers just steamrolled over Azrael's party-pooping laws. We've come a long way since the whole "vampires are real, deal with it" reveal, and if people want to get their freak on at Karma knowing full well they're walking into Vampire Central, that's on them once they sign the liability waiver.

No more getting slapped with fines because Karen from accounting decided she wanted the whole vampire experience but couldn't handle the morning-after hickeys. Play stupid games—win stupid prizes, sweetheart.

I swear, some humans are thirstier than the vampires. At least now I've got legal protection against their buyer's remorse.

Time to make Karma kick-ass again. And by kick-ass, I mean letting consenting adults make terrible life choices while I profit from their questionable decision-making skills.

God bless America!

"I'll swing by later tonight," I tell Kyle before hanging up and launching myself off the couch to track down my heavenly honey. She's turned into quite the sassy little minx, and I am so here for it. Now that I've corrupted her innocent, angelic ass (figuratively speaking, get your mind out of the gutter—that'll come later), I'm pretty sure I can bring her to Karma without her clutching her proverbial pearls or thinking I'm the second coming of Lucifer.

I find her lounging on our bed, nose buried in the laptop, probably watching some disgustingly wholesome YouTube video about kittens or some shit—time to shake things up.

I take a running leap and cannonball onto the bed like a majestic fucking dolphin, sending Seraphina bouncing with a surprised squeal. "Alright, angel face, get dolled up and break out the sexy," I announce, waggling my eyebrows at her like a total sleazeball. "We're painting the town red tonight, and I'm not talking about blood. It's time for you to experience the Lucian Spectacular, uncensored edition."

Her eyes go wide, pupils blown with a heady mix of lust and anticipation before she's giggling like a schoolgirl and practically skipping to the closet. I swear, it's like watching a porn star and a Disney princess have a love child.

I lean back, hands behind my head, grinning like the cat that got the canary, the cream, and the whole fucking aviary. Tonight's gonna be one for the record books. I can feel it in my bones. And in other places, but that's beside the point.

Time to show my girl what it means to party like a fucking rockstar. Or, you know, a devilishly handsome vampire with a penchant for causing trouble and making questionable life choices.

Same difference, really.

The bass hits us like a physical force as we slip through the back door, vibrating in my fucking bones. Seraphina—holy mother of sin, my cinnamon roll is working overtime to send me straight to hell tonight.

She's rocking a blood-red bodycon dress that hugs every heavenly curve like it was painted on, the hem barely reaching mid-thigh. The plunging neckline is doing sinful things to her cleavage, and those silver stilettos make her legs look a mile long. Her golden hair tumbles around her shoulders in tousled waves, and she looks like every man's wet dream come to life.

I had to white-knuckle my steering wheel the entire drive here to keep from pulling over and christening my Aston Martin's hood in ways that would make even Braxos blush.

Thank fuck she downed that magical cocktail, "Eau de Not a Fucking Angel," to mask her celestial scent, or we'd have a vampire-feeding frenzy on our hands. Can't have the locals getting a whiff of an actual angel—they'd lose their collective shit faster than a werewolf during a full moon.

The dance floor writhes with bodies under strobing lights. Seraphina's eyes go wide, taking in the scene—the packed bar, the dark corners where couples lose themselves in lust and blood.

It's sensory overload, a hedonistic wonderland of debauchery and excess. And my baby girl is standing there, soaking it all in like a wide-eyed fawn stumbling into a rave.

I slide my arm around her waist, pulling her close so I can purr in her ear, "Welcome to my world, angel face."

"Holy... everything," she breathes, and I can't help but smirk at the way her pulse kicks up. Whether from shock or excitement, I'm not sure yet, but damn if I'm not looking forward to finding out.

I lead Seraphina up the backstairs to my office. The door swings open, and—Jesus fucking Christ.

Kyle's got some bottle-blonde sprawled across my mahogany desk, her black dress bunched around her waist, legs wrapped around his hips. He's slamming into her hard enough to send my expense reports flying, her fake nails leaving scratches in the wood I had refinished.

Phina freezes beside me, a small "oh" escaping her lips. Kyle's head snaps up mid-thrust, his face shifting from ecstasy to pure terror. The blonde just looks over her shoulder, mascara smeared, and has the nerve to fucking wink.

"Really?" I growl. "My desk? The one I actually work at?"

Kyle scrambles to zip up while his conquest slides off the desk. After just getting railed on my paperwork, she adjusts her dress like she's just finished a yoga class.

Kyle at least has the decency to look sheepish, running a hand through his sex-mussed hair. "Shit, boss, I thought you weren't coming until later."

"Clearly." I glare at him, imagining all the ways I could make him regret being born. "Now get the fuck out of my chair before I staple your nuts to it."

The blonde straightens, running a finger across her smeared red lips. Her silicone-enhanced chest nearly spills from her dress as she turns, shooting Seraphina a venomous look before clicking her way to the door in six-inch heels.

Oh, *hell* no.

I grab the door handle, introducing Miss Silicon Valley to the hallway with all the grace of a bouncer at last call. Her indignant shriek gets cut off by the door slamming hard enough to rattle the frame.

"Lucian," Kyle stammers, looking about as comfortable as a nun at a strip club. "My man, I can explain—"

"So this is what I'm paying you for?" I cut him off, gesturing at the desk getting burned and replaced. "Earning Employee of the Month by getting your dick wet on company time? Last I checked, your job description involved watching the floor, not auditioning for 'The Wolf of Wall Street: After Dark.'"

"Look, man, she just walked in and—" Kyle starts, but I cut him off with a raised hand, not interested in his amateur-hour excuses.

"Save the creative writing for your reports. Where's the paperwork?" I've got better plans for tonight than listening to Kyle's latest conquest story, especially with my angel looking like heaven's gift to vampires.

Kyle shuffles through the chaos on my desk, finally producing a manila folder like he's just discovered the Holy Grail. "Right here. I just need your signature on the marked spots. I'll file everything tomorrow."

His eyes drift to Seraphina and instantly glaze over like a teenager spotting his first porn magazine. "Who's this enchanting—" Kyle starts, already slipping into his smooth-operator routine that's worked on half of Washington's eligible population.

"Eyes front and center, Romeo," I snap because I know that look. Kyle's the kind of guy who could charm a nun's habit off without breaking a sweat.

But my angel cake steps forward with that megawatt smile that could probably power Las Vegas. "Hi, I'm Seraphina. Lucian's mate." She delivers the last part with just enough emphasis to make Kyle's smile falter.

That's my girl—sweet as sugar with just enough spice to let them know she's off limits.

"Mate?" Kyle's eyebrows shoot up like they're trying to escape his forehead. "Well, shit. Never thought I'd see the day Lucian 'Commitment-Is-For-Suckers' would actually settle down. What's next, matching sweaters and a white picket fence?"

I scrawl my signature across the papers like I'm signing away my soul, then grab Seraphina's hand. "Sanitize this shit, Casanova. And keep your horizontal tango sessions out of my office—that's what the dumpster behind the club is for. You know, where your standards usually hang out."

I tug Seraphina toward the door, not looking back at Kyle's probably scandalized face.

Time to show my heavenly honey what a real VIP experience looks like. Besides, my throne's been lonely without its queen, and tonight will be one for the highlight reel of "How to Corrupt an Angel documentary." Produced, written and starred in by yours truly.

I guide Seraphina through the crowd to my private booth above the dance floor. The VIP section gleams with chrome and black velvet. My throne is positioned perfectly to survey my kingdom of sin below.

She hesitates at the entrance, taking in the luxury, exclusivity, and raw power radiating from this space. I tug her closer, pulling her down onto my lap. She gasps—

"Like what you see, Cupcake?" I whisper against her ear as she stares at the mass of writhing bodies below. The strobing lights paint her skin in flashes of red and blue.

Her breath catches as my hands slide up her thighs, the silky dress riding up. "It's... intense."

"Baby girl, you haven't seen anything yet." I nip at her neck, feeling her pulse jump under my lips.

Time to show my celestial troublemaker exactly what kind of devil she's fallen for.

A few drinks later, the bass pulses through me as Seraphina grinds in my lap, her dress riding dangerously high. My hands roam her curves, my fangs aching to claim her right here on my throne. Blood and lust cloud my mind as I lean in to taste her skin.

The doors slam open.

Fuck.

My spidey senses start screaming loud as a pack of beefy dudes strolls in like they own the place. The reek of wet dog and aggression slams into me, and I know what they are before I even see the glowing amber of their eyes.

Werewolves. In my fucking club.

I'm on my feet and shoving Seraphina behind me in the space of a heartbeat, fangs bared and ready to tear out the throat of anything that so much as looks at her wrong. But it's not the wolves that seize my heart in my chest.

It's *her.*

Lilith slinks behind her pet mongrels, all sleek curves and a razor-sharp smile. Her green eyes gleam with malice and cruel amusement. She moves like smoke-made flesh, gliding across the floor in her blood-red stilettos.

"Time to make like a tree and get the fuck out of here, Cupcake," I mutter, my eyes never leaving the hellspawn Barbie as she eye-fucks the room like it's her catwalk.

Seraphina tenses against my back, confusion and fear rolling off her in waves. "Who is—"

Her question is cut off as Lilith appears before us, moving faster than any human could track. Up close, her beauty is a poisoned blade, ready to cut down anything in her path.

"Why hello, darling," Lilith purrs. "I'm Lilith. It's an absolute pleasure to meet Lucian's little slice of heaven finally."

I can practically feel Seraphina's confusion morph into righteous fury, her body going rigid against mine. The wolves close in, their hulking frames forming a wall of steroid-fueled muscle around us.

Fucking fuck. Lilith's got herself a pack of loyal dogs to do her bidding. And here I thought that was only Azrael's gig. What is this, evil villain timeshare for werewolves?

"Make this easy on yourself, Lucian," Lilith demands, trailing one blood-red nail down my cheek. "Tell me where Rhyland is, give me the stone, and your little angel might just leave here intact."

My celestial snack cake? She is not having any of it.

Seraphina steps forward, golden eyes blazing, and shoves Lilith's hand away. "Don't you *ever* touch him," she says, her voice honeyed yet razor-sharp, like a cupcake with broken glass inside.

Holy shit. My angel's gone from 'Disney Princess' to 'Avenging Seraph' in 0.5 seconds flat.

Lilith's face twists into a shark smile. "My, my. Aren't you full of surprises?"

"You have *no* idea what I can do," Seraphina replies, her tone maintaining that angelic melody but carrying the unmistakable edge of someone who's personally witnessed the creation of stars and isn't impressed by discount designer evil.

Uh-oh. My angel isn't happy right now, and I can feel her power surging through our bond. It's like dating a nuclear reactor with wings and a cute ass.

Lilith only laughs, examining her manicure like we're just mildly inconvenient speed bumps in her day. "You do realize I can take both of you without so much as breaking a nail? Darling, I was terrorizing dimensions while you were still delivering bland celestial telegrams. Now be a good little halo and step aside before I turn your boyfriend into a very fashionable coat rack."

Shit's about to get real. And by real, I mean apocalyptically, biblically, 'someone call Michael Bay' real.

"Go back to the pit that spawned you," Seraphina snarls, her voice carrying the weight of Heaven's entire customer service department.

And then she fucking *explodes* with light, her body going supernova as she launches Lilith across the room like a designer-dressed ragdoll. The stench of burning flesh fills the air as Lilith screams, her perfect skin blistering and peeling like an overripe banana in the Sahara.

Note to self: Do NOT piss off the angel.

My girl might not be packing the same holy firepower as Dani's DNA-enhanced ass, but her light? That shit's like mainlining sunshine straight into your veins. And trust me, for vampires? That's about as fun as deep-throating a UV lamp. Lilith may be a psychotic, older than dirt bitch, but even she's got to be feeling that heavenly burn right about now.

I don't think. I just move.

I grab Seraphina, throwing her over my shoulder like a sack of righteously pissed-off potatoes, and blur us the fuck out of there fast.

I practically rip the car door off its hinges, shoving Seraphina inside and slamming it shut with enough force to make the whole vehicle rock on its suspension. In the blink of an eye, I'm behind the wheel, my finger jabbing the ignition button like it's Lilith's fucking eyeball.

The engine roars to life, and I punch the gas. The tires scream as they fight for purchase on the asphalt. The stench of burning rubber fills the car, acrid and biting, as we peel out of the parking lot like a bat out of hell.

My mind races as I push the car to its limits, the engine snarling like a living thing as we fly through the empty streets.

What the fuck just happened?

Lilith, in my *club*. And not just her, but fucking werewolves too. Since when did that designer-wrapped demon bitch have mutts on her payroll? And how the hell did she know I would be there tonight?

Something smells fishy as fuck.

Questions whirl through my head like razor blades, slicing at my sanity. But one thing is crystal fucking clear.

We're in trouble. Deep, deep trouble.

Seraphina is a coiled spring beside me, her entire body vibrating with a potent mix of fury, fear, and adrenaline. Her breaths come hard and fast, like she's just run a marathon through the pits of Hell itself.

"That... that *thing* was Lilith?" she grits out, her voice shaking with rage.

I swerve around a slower car, the force of the turn slamming us both against the doors.

"In the rotten fucking flesh," I confirm, my knuckles white on the steering wheel. "The one and only Demon Queen herself, complete with her pack of rabid dogs."

Seraphina's eyes blaze in the darkness of the car, twin pools of molten gold. "I should have ended her right there," she says, her hands clench into fists. "Sent her screaming back to the abyss that birthed her."

I can feel the power rolling off her in waves, crackling the air inside the car. It's intoxicating and terrifying at once.

"Believe me, baby girl, there's nothing I would have loved more than to see you go all angelic wrath on her demonic ass," I growl, weaving through traffic like a man possessed. "But we were outnumbered and outgunned. Discretion is the better part of valor and all that shit."

The rearview mirror might as well be a horror movie screen because all I can see are three sets of headlights bearing down on us like the hounds of Hell themselves. They're gaining fast, the distance between us shrinking with every passing second.

Double fuck.

"Buckle up, beautiful," I warn my hand already on the gearshift. "Things are about to get a little Fast and Furious."

"Lucian, what are you—" Seraphina starts, but her words are lost in a yelp of surprise as I downshift, the car lurching forward like a beast unleashed.

We rocket down the street, the engine's roar drowning out everything but the pounding of my heart. The speedometer climbs higher and higher, the needle swinging past numbers that would make a sane man piss himself.

But sanity is for people who don't have a pack of demon-driven douchebags riding their asses.

"TRUCK!" Seraphina screams as I wrench the wheel left. Our tires shriek against the asphalt. The semi blazes past, missing us by inches.

"Just a love tap, Cupcake," I laugh, as I upshift hard. The engine snarls as we surge forward. "Though your screaming is doing things to me."

"Shut up and—CAR!" Her fingers dig into the dashboard as I weave between vehicles at 120mph. "You're insane! Where the hell did you learn to drive?"

"GTA, Cupcake," I cackle, downshifting and swinging us onto an off-ramp at the last possible second.

"Your *video* game?" Seraphina looks at me like I'm crazy.

"And a few high-speed chases back in my younger days. Stick with me, angel face, and you'll never be bored."

Bullets ping off our rear bumper, shattering our tail light. "Fuck!" I snarl, jerking us down a side street. "That's coming out of Lilith's stolen funds."

"Behind you!" Seraphina's warning comes just as one of our pursuers rams us. The impact sends us fishtailing, but I correct with a hard turn that sends sparks flying.

"Hold on tight!" I slam the car into second gear, the acceleration pinning us to our seats. One of the sports cars tries to pass us—amateur hour. I clip their rear quarter panel, sending them spinning into a row of parked cars. The explosion lights up my rearview mirror.

"Oh my God," Seraphina gasps, but there's heat in her voice. "That was..."

"Sexy as hell?" I finish, taking a corner so sharp our tires leave the ground. "Just wait till I really show off."

"Less talking, more driving!" She grabs my thigh as we narrowly miss a delivery truck. "Unless you want us both dead!"

"Already dead, sweetheart," I remind her, throwing us into reverse. "But your concern is adorable."

Two cars left—time to get creative.

And by creative, I mean absolutely fucking reckless.

I gun it backward down an alley, metal screaming as our bumper scrapes brick walls. The two remaining cars split up—one behind, one parallel in the next alley over.

"They're boxing us in!" Seraphina's nails dig into my thigh. "Lucian!"

"Watch and learn, Cupcake." I slam the gear shift into first, cranking the wheel hard. We burst through a chain-link fence, showering sparks across the hood. "Daddy's got this."

A bullet shatters our back window. Glass rains down as Seraphina ducks, screaming. "If we live through this, I'm going to—"

"Rock my world?" I cut through an empty lot, catching air as we hit a loading dock. "Because this is definitely foreplay."

"You're impossible!" But her hand slides higher up my thigh as we hit the ground hard enough to bottom out. The pursuing car isn't so lucky—its front end crumples like wet cardboard on impact.

"I take it back," Seraphina gasps, her knuckles white on the oh-shit handle. "GTA's got nothing on you."

"One more to go," I sing-song, weaving through a maze of warehouses. "Want to help me make it extra special?"

"Just shut up and drive!" She's breathing hard, her pupils blown wide with adrenaline and something else.

"Yes, ma'am." I downshift, engine howling as we blast onto the main road.

Seraphina's giggle lights up the car like Christmas, and the spike of arousal hitting my nostrils tells me my angel's getting her kicks from this high-speed chaos. "Nothing's touching you, Cupcake. Vampire's honor."

"Mmm, well," she purrs, and something in her tone makes my heart skip. "If you mess this up, I'm collecting on that pegging promise."

Wait, what the actual fuck?

My brain short-circuits faster than a toaster in a bathtub. I whip my head around to stare at her, my mouth hanging open like a broken garage door—

And that's when karma decides to be a complete bitch.

The last sports car appears out of nowhere, T-boning us at full speed. Metal screams. Glass explodes. Our car flips, rolling once, twice, three times before launching into the air.

"LUCIAN!" Seraphina's scream cuts off as we hit the ground.

The impact throws me forward. My head crashes through the windshield. Everything goes black.

I wake up to the taste of blood and glass shards sticking out of my face, my neck, and my arms. Steam hisses from the crushed engine. The hoods crumpled like paper.

"Phina?" My voice cracks. She doesn't answer.

I force my eyes to focus. She's slumped against the airbag, blood running down her face from a gash at her temple. Her chest rises and falls with shallow breaths.

"Cupcake, please." I try to move, but my body won't cooperate. "Wake up."

Sirens wail in the distance, getting closer. Blood drips from my face onto the shattered dashboard.

We're exposed. Vulnerable.

We need to move. Now.

But first, I have to get my head out of this fucking windshield.

Metal groans as her door rips open. Through blood-streaked vision, I see massive hands grab Seraphina's limp body, dragging her from the wreckage.

"No!" I thrash against the glass, still holding me in place. My legs are crushed under the dash. My muscles burn and refuse to work. Blood pours down my face. "DON'T TOUCH HER!"

A gravelly voice laughs behind me. "Lilith sends her regards."

Feet crunch on broken glass. An engine starts. Tires squeal. The scent of werewolf and Seraphina's blood fades into the night.

The sound that tears from my throat isn't human. It isn't even vampire. It's pure rage, pure desperation, echoing off concrete and metal as I scream her name into the darkness.

She's gone.

They took her.

DANICA

43

Well, well, well. Color me shocked—not. I mean, seriously, the signs were about as subtle as a neon billboard in Times Square. Erik's possessive glances, the way Bryn orbited around him like a lovesick satellite, the palpable electricity crackling between them whenever they shared the same air.

And let's not forget that telling heartbeat when I touched his chest—

I'd call myself blind, but that would be an insult to blind people who probably sensed their connection before I did. Honestly, my PhD in Obliviousness is really paying off these days. Maybe next time I'll notice when two people are cosmically destined for each other before they start practically eye-banging across the room.

My sister, the fierce Valkyrie warrior, is none other than Mr. Broody's fated mate. And you know what? I'm absolutely *thrilled*. It's about damn time Erik found his other half. The man's been rocking the tortured soul vibe for so long that it's practically become his trademark look. But ever since this revelation? It's like someone lit a fire under his usually frosty ass.

I've never seen him so focused, so driven. And that display with Gunnar? Holy hell, I thought Erik was going to rip his spine out through his nostrils. Not that the asshole didn't deserve it, and then some. I mean, putting his filthy hands on my sister? He's lucky I stepped in before Erik went full-on homicidal.

But as much as I enjoyed watching Gunnar get his ass kicked was Grade-A entertainment, we've got bigger fish to fry—like, realm-saving-sized fish. Can't exactly play hero when we're busy throwing down with the Valkyrie squad, even if they deserve it for how they treated my sister. I mean, seriously? Demoting her for getting injured in battle? That's like firing a chef for burning their hand in the kitchen. Now they're side-eyeing her like she's yesterday's mead, acting like one wing somehow cancels out centuries of badassery. Please.

They couldn't be more wrong. Bryn's still the same badass she's always been. This past week has been... rough. Watching Bryn try to adapt and helping her work with one wing is like teaching someone to walk again, except with more cursing and occasional airborne accidents. Each failed attempt sends her spiraling deeper into that dark place, that "I'm not enough anymore" pit that I know all too well.

Because losing a part of yourself? That core piece that defines who you are? It's not just physical pain—it's like a cosmic bitch-slap to the face. It messes with your head and makes you question everything. But if there's one thing I know about my sister, she's a fighter. She'll claw out of this funk and return stronger than ever.

And if she needs a little help along the way? Well, that's what sassy, supportive sisters are for. That, and making sure a certain broody vampire pulls his head out of his ass and steps up to the mate plate.

Operation "Get Erik Laid" is officially a go.

I'm seeing a pattern here that I've been too occupied to notice until now. Rhyland and I? Sure, I chalked that up to destiny or whatever. Then Lucian and Sera happened, and I thought, okay, just a cosmic fluke, the universe having a laugh. But now my sister and Erik? That's not coincidence—that's a freaking pattern, and my scientist brain is kicking into overdrive.

Three vampire brothers, three women with angelic DNA. These fanged fossils haven't found mates since mammoths were the hot new thing, and suddenly they're all matched up with heaven's genetic lottery winners? The statistical probability of that is about as likely as Emily voluntarily eating a vegetable. There's something about angelic DNA that's triggering these mate bonds, and my inner science nerd is practically salivating at the molecular implications.

The longhouse erupts into a flurry of activity as the other Vikings haul Gunnar's broken form off the floor. His pitiful moans and whimpers fade into the background as Rhyland's hand closes around mine, his grip unyielding. "Let's go."

He doesn't wait for a response, pulling me through the crowded hall with single-minded determination. The other warriors part like the Red Sea before his stormy expression, their eyes wide with respect and fear.

We reach our room at the back of the longhouse, and Rhyland doesn't break stride. He slams the door open with enough force to rattle the hinges, dragging me inside before spinning me around and crushing me against the now-closed door with his body.

The solid wood at my back vibrates with the impact, but it's nothing compared to the sensation of Rhyland's muscular form pinning me in place. His ocean-blue eyes blaze into mine, the intensity of his gaze stealing the breath from my lungs.

His scent envelops me—sandalwood, juniper, and the crisp tang of a winter storm. It fills my senses, making my head spin and my knees weak. But there's no escaping, no reprieve from the full force of his presence.

His eyes bore into mine, twin pools of molten blue that threaten to consume me. "Are you done now?" His words are clipped, his jaw clenched tight. "You know the truth. No more of this freezing me out bullshit, Dani."

His breath ghosts across my lips, his body a solid wall of coiled muscle and barely leashed power. Every inch of him radiates dominance, demanding submission. The air between us vibrates with tension, a livewire waiting to ignite.

Rhyland growls, "You punishing me for his actions is bullshit."

He's fuming that I've been giving him the cold shoulder all week over Erik's "little secret," even now that I know the truth, it doesn't erase that he kept me in the dark. "Listen to me carefully." I jab my finger into his chest. "Bryn is my sister. Erik is family now. This affects all of us, Rhyland. I deserved to know. Or what, you couldn't trust me with his precious secret?"

His eyes darken as he leans closer, the air crackling with tension. "Trust isn't the issue, Angel. I promised him. Erik needed space to process this without interference." His lips curl into a knowing smirk. "Tell me honestly—would you have stayed silent or played matchmaker the second you found out?"

I open my mouth to protest, then close it. Damn him for knowing me so well.

"No," I mutter, but even I can hear the lie in my voice.

"Bullshit." He moves closer, backing me against the door. His arms cage me in, his scent driving me crazy. "You're a terrible liar, baby. We both know you'd have been plotting ways to throw them together before the sunset."

His body presses against mine, solid and warm. "Erik doesn't work that way. And Bryn?" He laughs darkly. "Your sister's got enough stubbornness to rival my stick-in-the-ass brother."

I bite back a smile, picturing them—Bryn with her 'I don't need a man' swagger, and Erik, probably short-circuiting trying to process actual emotions. But then, a darker thought hits me.

"What if she rejects him?" My voice cracks. "We both know what happens when a mate bond is denied. We could lose Erik forever. I can't—"

"Stop." His hand catches my chin, forcing me to meet his intense gaze. "We can't interfere, Angel. This is their path to walk. Trust fate. Trust them."

"When did you become the level-headed one?" I try to joke, but the slight quiver in my voice gives me away. "I thought that was Erik's job."

"Oh, I'm far from level-headed right now, Angel. Not after a week of you giving me the silent treatment." His voice drops to that dangerous growl that makes my knees weak. "In fact, I'd say I'm feeling quite... unreasonable."

"I was upset," I protest weakly, but his proximity makes it hard to think straight.

"And now?" His lips brush my ear, sending shivers down my spine. "Are you still upset, Angel?"

"I..." His mouth trails down my neck, and coherent thought becomes impossible. "That's not fair..."

"All's fair in love and war, baby." His teeth graze my pulse point. "And right now, I'm done talking."

Bastard. Using our play on words against me.

Before I can respond, his mouth crashes onto mine, hungry and demanding. And just like that, all thoughts of Erik and Bryn fade away, replaced by the burning need to get closer, feel more, and lose myself in the storm that is Rhyland.

His hands are everywhere at once, tearing at my clothes with a feverish urgency that steals my breath. The harsh sound of ripping fabric echoes through the room as buttons scatter across the floor like tiny missiles. Cool air kisses my exposed skin, immediately replaced by the scorching heat of his mouth as he strips me bare. His lips brand a path down my neck, across my collarbone, each press of his mouth leaving behind a mark that claims me as his.

"Too many fucking clothes," he growls against my skin, his voice vibrating through my body like thunder.

He steps back just long enough to tear at his own garments, the muscles in his forearms flexing as he rips the fabric from his body. The sight of him steals the air from my lungs—every inch of him carved from stone and bathed in golden firelight. The intricate tattoos that cover his torso seem to dance with each breath he takes, ancient runes and patterns shifting across his skin like living art. A roadmap of his history etched into flesh.

My eyes travel lower, following the deep V of his hips to where his cock stands proud and thick, the head already glistening with evidence of his arousal. The sheer size of him makes my mouth water and my core clench in anticipation. He is raw masculinity personified—a warrior god in all his naked glory, ready to claim what's his.

When he steps forward again, the heat of him engulfs me. His hands slide up my ribs to cup my breasts, thumbs brushing over my nipples until they peak against his touch. Then his mouth replaces his fingers, hot and wet as he takes one sensitive bud between his teeth.

He bites down just hard enough to make me cry out, the exquisite blend of pleasure and pain shooting straight to my core like an electric current. My head falls back against the wooden door with a dull thud, my spine arching to offer more of myself to his hungry mouth. His tongue swirls around the tender peak, soothing the sting before he moves to lavish the same attention on my other breast.

"You taste like heaven," he murmurs against my skin, his voice rough with desire.

I'm drowning in sensation, my fingers tangling in his thick black hair as he works his way down my body. The scrape of his beard against my stomach sends shivers racing across my skin. He drops to his knees before me, his hands gripping my hips with bruising force as he presses open-mouthed kisses along the sensitive skin of my lower belly. Each touch of his lips moves lower, his beard rasping against the insides of my thighs as he spreads me wider.

I'm trembling now, my legs threatening to give out as the anticipation builds to an almost unbearable level. My skin feels too tight, too hot, every nerve ending alive and screaming for his touch. I need him with a desperation that borders on madness.

He surges forward, pinning me against the door. His body radiates heat like a living flame, making the wood at my back feel like ice in comparison. My skin pebbles at the contrast, a shiver running through me that has nothing to do with the cold. His hand slides between my thighs, and I gasp as his skilled fingers delve into my dripping core, the intimate touch making my hips buck against his hand. He groans in approval at finding me so ready, so desperate for his touch.

"Fuck, baby. You're dripping for me." His voice is strained as he circles my clit with the calloused pad of his thumb, the rough texture creating delicious friction against the sensitive bundle of nerves. "You can't deny it anymore—how much you need me—want me."

And I am soaked, my arousal coating his fingers as evidence of the effect he has on me. My hips rock shamelessly against his hand, seeking more pressure, more friction, more of everything he's giving me.

"No. I can't—I want you. Always." The words tumble from my lips between ragged breaths, my voice barely recognizable through the haze of lust. "I need you. Need you inside me. Now."

His eyes lock with mine, the blue of his irises nearly swallowed by the black of his pupils. There's something dangerous in his gaze, something primal and hungry that makes my heart race and my core clench with anticipation.

"Hold on to me," he commands, his voice a dark rumble that I feel in my bones.

I barely have time to wrap my arms around his neck before he's lifting me, my legs instinctively circling his waist. The blunt head of his cock nudges at my entrance, hot and hard and insistent. We both groan at the contact, the promise of what's to come making my inner walls flutter with need.

"Look at me, baby." His forehead rests against mine, our breath mingling in the scant space between us. "I want to see those pretty eyes while I fill you completely."

My lashes flutter open, my gaze meeting his just as he surges forward, burying himself to the hilt in one powerful thrust. My back arches off the door, my mouth opening in a silent scream as he stretches me to the point of delicious pain. He's so deep I swear I can feel him in my throat, every thick inch of him claiming me from the inside out.

He begins to move, each deep stroke hitting that secret spot inside me that makes stars explode behind my eyelids. I cling to him, nails digging half-moons into the muscled expanse of his shoulders as I try to anchor myself against the onslaught of sensation.

"*Fuck.* You feel so good." Rhyland grunts, his voice strained with the effort of maintaining control.

The door rattles on its hinges with each powerful surge of his hips, the sound echoing through the room like a naughty drumbeat announcing our activities to anyone within earshot. His mouth claims mine in a bruising kiss, his tongue plunging deep in a filthy mimicry of what his body is doing to mine.

"Off the door," I manage to gasp out between searing kisses, my nails raking down his sweat-slicked back. "Too loud."

No need to give the entire longhouse a show. Besides, knowing Rhyland, his powerful thrusts would probably shake this flimsy door off its hinges.

He responds with a growl, his hands gripping my thighs as he tears us away from the abused wood. Three strides carry us across the room before he drops into a chair, keeping me wrapped around him. I straddle his lap, my knees on either side of his hips, as his hands slide under my thighs to reposition me.

With a wicked gleam in his eye, he spreads my legs wider, hooking my heels over the arms of the chair. The position is obscenely exposing, leaving me completely open to his gaze and his touch. I can feel the cool air against my most intimate places, can see where we're joined, his thick length disappearing into my body.

The new angle allows him to sink impossibly deeper, stretching me around his thickness until I'm filled completely. A broken moan falls from my lips, my head falling back as my body struggles to accommodate his size. The sensation is overwhelming—each thick inch of him branding me as his, claiming me in the most primal way possible.

His eyes blaze into mine, twin pools of molten blue threatening to consume me whole. His hand wraps around my throat, not squeezing but claiming—his thumb resting against my thundering pulse point. "Look at me, baby," he de mands, our breath mingling in the scant space between us. "I want to watch you fall apart. Want to see those pretty eyes glaze over when you come on my cock."

I couldn't look away if I tried. I'm captivated by the primal hunger in his gaze, the way his muscles flex and ripple with each powerful thrust. Sweat glistens on his chest, highlighting the intricate tattoos that wind across his skin. His jaw is clenched tight, the cords in his neck standing out as he fights for control. He's raw and untamed, a force of nature unleashed in our small room, and his dominance takes me to the edge and back again.

"Feel how perfectly you take me," he growls, his voice like velvet wrapped around steel. "This sweet pussy was crafted for my cock alone." His hand slides from my throat to cup my jaw, his thumb tracing my parted lips. "Such a good girl, trembling for me." He pushes his thumb into my mouth, and I instinctively suck, tasting the salt of his skin. "Your body was made for me, designed to milk me dry."

His words send liquid heat coursing through my veins. I meet him thrust for thrust, my hips rising to pull him deeper, harder. The wet sounds of our bodies coming together mix with our ragged breaths and mingled moans, creating a symphony of passion that fills the room.

His hand snakes between us, his thumb finding my clit with unerring accuracy. He rubs in tight, merciless circles, the calloused pad creating a delicious friction. The added stimulation has me seeing stars, my inner walls clenching around his thickness as I climb higher and higher.

"Rhyland," I keen, my nails digging into his shoulders. "Please..."

His lips curl into a predatory smile, his eyes darkening to midnight. "Not even close to being done with you, Angel." His voice is pure sin, dark and dangerous as the night. He punctuates his words with a brutal thrust that has my body arching like a drawn bow. "We're just getting started."

Desperate for more, I tangle my fingers in his hair, tugging him closer for a searing kiss. He chuckles into my mouth, the sound low and wicked.

"Look at you, so hungry for me," he murmurs, nipping at my bottom lip hard enough to sting. His tongue soothes the bite immediately, sweeping into my mouth to tangle with mine. "I love how desperate you get, how your body begs for my touch even when you're trying to be mad at me."

His eyes glitter with mischief even as he continues to roll his hips in a maddeningly slow rhythm that keeps me right on the edge without pushing me over. "I should keep you like this for hours, Angel. Right on the edge, dripping and aching, until you're sobbing for release." His voice drops to a sinful whisper. "Until you're promising me anything—everything—just to feel my cock drive you over that cliff."

The thought sends a dark thrill through me, even as my body rebels against the idea of him edging me. "Rhyland," I whimper, my nails raking down his chest, leaving red trails in their wake. "Please..."

"That's right, baby. Fucking. Break. For. Me." Each word is punctuated by a deep, savage thrust that has me gasping. "Beg for it. Let everyone hear who owns this pretty pussy. Show me how desperate you are for my cock."

His dirty, filthy words wrap around me like a physical caress, stoking the flames already consuming me from the inside out. The pleasure builds to almost unbearable heights, my body trembling on the precipice of something earth-shattering.

"Please, Rhy...land," I manage, the words broken and desperate as they fall from my lips. "I need you. Need to come. Please."

My gaze locks with his stormy blue eyes, now blazing with a hunger that steals the air from my lungs. At this moment, he's pure predator, and I'm his willing prey.

Without warning, he lifts me off his cock, my soaked core sliding free with an obscenely wet sound. Before I can protest the sudden emptiness, he's maneuvering me up his body, positioning my knees on either side of his head. His hands grip my thighs, spreading me wide as he brings me down to his waiting mouth.

The first swipe of his tongue against my swollen clit nearly undoes me. He licks and sucks with agonizing skill, his fingers thrusting inside me in a relentless rhythm that has me panting. "Drench my fucking tongue, Angel," he growls against my sensitive flesh. "Watch me feast on this sweet pussy—be a good girl and come in my mouth—flood me with that honey. That's an order."

"Oh, god!" The pleasure coils tighter and tighter, a knot in my core that he expertly unravels with each lick and flick of his tongue. My climax detonates like a bomb, my release spraying over his chin and chest in hot bursts as I cry out his name.

Rhyland moans his satisfaction, the rumble vibrating through me as he laps up my essence like a man starved. Rhyland groans, his thumbs spreading me open wider, exposing me completely to his hungry mouth. "You taste sweet and intoxicating, like cotton candy spun just for me."

With a growl that vibrates through my entire body, he flips me over effortlessly. I barely have time to register the change in position before I'm on my hands and knees, bent over the chair with the furs soft against my heated skin.

His hands grip my hips, pulling me back against him. The new angle allows him to sink even deeper, hitting those spots inside me that blur the line between pleasure and pain. A broken moan spills from my lips, my head dropping forward as I brace myself against the onslaught of sensation.

"Fuck, baby. The sight of you spread open for me like this is enough to drive me insane," his voice is strained, his control fraying at the edges. "So perfect, so tight around my cock."

His fingers tangle in my hair, tugging my head back to expose my throat. "Don't you ever deny me again, Angel. Do you understand?" His voice is a low, deadly rumble that sends goosebumps across my skin. "Say it."

The command is a threat wrapped in velvet, a demand that sends a rush of wet heat pooling between my thighs. This isn't my usually controlled Rhyland—his restraint has snapped, replaced by a primal need that matches my own.

I arch my back, my breasts thrusting forward, offering myself to him completely. "Yes, Sir." The words spill from my lips without thought, a submissive surrender that feels as natural as breathing.

Rhyland freezes, his hips stuttering mid-thrust. "What did you just say?"

I can feel the tension in his body—his arousal, the coil of confusion tightening alongside the raw need that still pulses between us.

My breath comes in short gasps as I tip my head back, meeting his shocked gaze over my shoulder. A knowing smirk curves my lips as I purr, "I said, yes, *Sir.*"

His grip on my hip tightens, his hold on my hair possessive. "Fuck," he growls, his hips snapping forward with renewed ferocity. "Why the hell does that turn me on so damn much?"

I have no answer, only the instinctual need that thrums through my veins.

His fangs strike without warning, the sting melting into ecstasy as he drinks deeply. Each pull sends lightning through my system, my walls clenching around him as I moan brokenly. His venom floods me as his cock claims me from behind, the dual assault making my vision blur.

He tears free with a snarl, blood streaming down my chest. "This tight cunt was made for my cock. Never denying me again, understand?"

I whimper as he pounds into me. His palm cracks across my ass. "Answer me, Angel. Do. You. Understand?"

Another smack—the sharp crack of his palm against my ass echoes through the room like a gunshot, the unexpected strike stealing my breath. The sting spreads like liquid fire across my skin, but instead of pain, it sends a jolt of electric pleasure straight to my entire body. My body responds instantly, clenching around him as the burning handprint on my flesh only heightens every sensation. I never knew I could crave this—this perfect dance between pleasure and pain, each strike pushing me closer to the edge. The heat of his mark brands me, and God help me, I want more.

"Y-Yes! I understand."

He gathers my hair in his fist, yanking my head back with a controlled force that makes my scalp tingle and my back bow. The position forces my throat into an elegant arch, my breasts thrust forward.

"Open your mouth," he commands, his voice dropping to that dangerous register that brooks no argument.

My lips part instantly, a Pavlovian response to his dominance. His fingers push past them without hesitation, sliding down my throat until I feel the intrusion deep inside. I gag reflexively, my body fighting the invasion even as my core pulses with shameless want. The sting of my watering eyes and the struggle for breath only amplifies the electricity coursing through my veins.

"Relax, baby." He withdraws his fingers slowly, leaving a wet trail along my jaw. His voice holds a wicked promise that makes my heart race. "You're going to need that throat nice and pliable for what's coming next."

A dark thrill shoots through me at his words, my inner walls fluttering around his thickness in anticipation. His thrusts become rougher, more urgent, the obscene sound of skin against skin filling the air like a primal drumbeat. Each impact jars my entire body, sending ripples of pleasure-pain radiating outward from where we're joined.

He then wraps his massive paw around my throat, claiming dominance over my very breath. His hold on my hair only tightens, leaving no doubt about who's in control. He's got me locked in his iron grip, at his mercy and loving every second of my surrender.

"Take it, Angel." His command is punctuated by a particularly brutal thrust that forces a broken cry from my lips. He uses his grip to force me into an even deeper arch, my spine bending to his will. "Feel every inch splitting you open. Gonna mark you so deep you'll feel me for days."

I whimper at the promise, my inner muscles fluttering at the thought of carrying his imprint within me long after we're done. He knows exactly what his possessive words do to me, how they liquefy my core and dissolve my resistance. He knows I crave his ownership, his brand upon my body like a physical manifestation of our bond.

"Give me what I want." He demands, his grip in my hair tightening to the exquisite edge where pain transforms into its own kind of ecstasy. "Fucking flood this cock with that sweet cream. Scream for me like the needy little slut you are."

Holy. Fucking. Hell. Note to self: withholding sex from my Viking beefcake for a week might be the best-terrible decision I've ever made. He's completely unrestrained, pure dominant alpha, and fuck if it isn't the hottest thing I've ever experienced. The way he's claiming me, marking me... I might have created a monster, but god help me, I need more.

His grip on my throat, the pain in my hair, his relentless cock—it all shatters me.

"Rhyland, fuck!" My orgasm explodes, flooding us both as he releases my throat. My cum coats everything, the force pushing him from my body. I cry out desperately at the emptiness.

He slams back in immediately, harder and thicker. "God. Damn. Love it when you make a mess for me, baby. Fucking beautiful."

His rhythm turns wild, grip bruising as he chases his release, determined to make me squirt again. His dominance demands my surrender, and I give it willingly.

The sounds I make are dirty, raw, and most definitely not human anymore. My throat is hoarse from screaming his name, my body a trembling mess of pleasure and need.

"Take my cum, Angel. Every. Fucking. Drop."

"Yes." The word falls from my lips like a prayer. "Give it to me. Please."

His growl reverberates through my entire body as his thrusts become more forceful, his cock swelling larger inside me. *Fuuuck!*

He roars as he floods me, hot ropes of cum marking me as his. His grip bruises my hips as he empties himself, his essence claiming me completely. "Fucking *shit.*"

His cum drips down my thighs, hot and thick—evidence of our wild coupling.

In a blur, we're on the bed, my back pressed to his chest as he trails possessive kisses along my shoulder and fresh bite mark. Just as exhaustion starts to pull at me, his deep voice rasps against my neck.

"Not-uh, baby." His fingers find my nipple, teasing it to a hard peak as his cock lays hard against my ass. "That was just round one. You've got a week of denial to make up for, and I'm nowhere even close to being done with this sweet ass."

My body ignites at his words, already craving more.

What have I unleashed?

LUCIAN

44

Voices fade in and out like a poorly tuned radio. Red and blue lights strobe across the shattered glass, each flash sending daggers through my skull. A penlight burns my retinas as someone keeps asking questions I can't process.

Blood trickles down my face. The steering column pins me like a bug in a display case—dashboard crumpled around my legs. Every breath tastes like copper and gasoline.

"Sir, can you hear me?" A female officer crouches by the wreckage, her name plate reading 'Perez.' "The Fire department's en route. Just stay still."

Seraphina. Her empty seat mocks me, airbag deflated and blood-stained. They took her. Those bastards took my angel.

I try to move, but my body screams in protest. Glass crunches with every slight shift, embedded in my skin like thorns.

"Don't move," Officer Perez warns, her hand on my shoulder. "You're wedged in pretty tight. It's a miracle you're even conscious."

Miracle. Right. If she only knew what real miracles looked like.

And I just let one slip through my fingers. Images flash through my mind—Dani's torture, Lilith's cruelty, what that psychotic bitch might be doing to my angel cake right now. Bile rises in my throat, rage burning hotter than the gasoline pooling under the wreck.

How many minutes have I wasted trapped in this metal coffin? How many hours of head start have I given them?

That gravelly voice echoes in my skull: *"Lilith sends her regards."* Something familiar scratches at my memory, like a record needle stuck in a groove. I've heard that sadistic voice and felt that presence. But where?

"Can you tell me your name, sir?" Officer Perez's voice fades beneath the approaching wail of sirens. Red emergency lights paint the wreckage in hellish hues as firefighters swarm the scene.

"Move."

"Out of the way."

Two men approach the vehicle. Metal screams against metal. The jaws of life tear through the car like it's made of paper, each second an eternity while my angel slips further away. Finally, the door gives. I spill out onto blood-slicked asphalt, limbs trembling. Paramedics descend like vultures. Penlight beams stabbing my eyes. Their pulses thunder in my ears—strong, vital, precisely what I need. The hunger rises, primal and vicious.

The first medic never sees it coming. My fangs tear through his carotid like wet tissue paper. Hot blood floods my mouth, sweet and rich with adrenaline. Bones knit, wounds seal as I drink deep.

Screams erupt. The female EMT tries to run. I catch her quickly, dragging her down. Her blood tastes like fear and cherry lip gloss.

Two officers fall next, their service weapons useless against vampire speed. Four bodies drain dry at my feet, their life essence burning through my veins like liquid fire.

I'm usually more of a "live and let live" kind of vampire—you know, if you don't count the occasional consensual blood drinking. But right now? With my angel in the clutches of Hell's Next Top Model? Yeah, this situation's gone from zero to apocalyptic real quick. And if I'm going to crash Lilith's little hostage party, I need my mojo firing on all cylinders.

Wooden bullets slam into my chest, burning like holy fire. Fuck. Officer Perez switched her ammo while I was busy draining the others dry. Smart girl.

I blur forward, ripping the weapon from her grip before her finger can squeeze off another round. Her eyes widen in terror as I lock onto her gaze."Listen up, Officer Not-Buffy," I growl, blood still dripping from my fangs—my compulsion sliding into her mind like silk. "Tonight's highlight reel? Boring traffic accident. No vampire shenanigans, no blood fountains, definitely no sexy undead badass using EMTs as juice boxes. Got it?"

She nods mechanically, holstering her empty weapon. The wooden bullets in my chest burn like a bitch as I work them out one by one. I pluck the last wooden slug from my chest. The wound knitting shut like a zipper. Fishing my phone from my blood-soaked pocket, I punch in Emily's number. "Round up the Scooby Gang. We are going to war."

"Jesus Christ, what the hell have you stirred up now?" Emily snaps with that unique brand of exasperated snark she saves for me. "Some of us were actually trying to sleep, you inconsiderate bloodsucker."

"She took—" My phone buzzes, cutting off my fury-fueled rant.

Unknown:

> Trade offering, darling. One mystical rock and Rhyland for your precious Halo. Tick Tock.

I clench my jaw. This fucking bitch has my angel. And she thinks she can bargain?

I'm bleeding all over my iPhone's keyboard as I type, fingers trembling with rage:

My phone cracks under my grip, Emily's voice crackling through the dying speaker.

> Touch her, and I'll personally introduce your organs to daylight.

> Such language! *Tsk, tsk.* And here I thought we could be civil. Your angel says hi, by the way. Well, she would, but she's a bit gagged and drugged at the moment.

> Shall we discuss terms like grown-ups? Soul Stone, Rhyland for the angelic bimbo. Or...

> I will start express shipping her home to you. Prime delivery. Maybe start with those gorgeous wings? They'd make such lovely wall decorations

> I'm going to wear your fucking spine as a belt.

> Cute. Clock's ticking, lover boy—24 hours. Or your precious angel becomes a DIY craft project. Starting with those pretty feathers...

> Where?

> Come now, darling. Even someone of your limited mental capacity should recall what I like. Do keep up, pet. Time's wasting, and so is your angel's patience... not to mention her blood supply

> When I get to you, I will introduce your face to a wood chipper. Repeatedly.

> Better hurry, darling. Your precious angel's hourglass is running out. And I do so love to play with my food.

I reach out through our bond, searching for that warm golden thread that always leads me to my angel. But there's nothing—just a cold, empty void where her light should be. That bitch must have dosed her with the same mystical roofie she used on Dani.

Fuck!

Her next text pings in, giving me a location. Well, isn't that just fucking perfect? Not Oregon—Seattle, specifically Azrael's architectural nightmare. You know, that Dr. Seuss mansion on steroids where he played "torture chamber interior decorator" with his human collection.

Because of course Lilith would pick that place. Nothing says 'I'm an evil bitch' quite like recycling another psycho's torture palace. Points for dramatic irony, I guess, but minus several million for originality.

"Lucian! What the hell? Are you there?" Emily's snark evaporates when I finally speak.

"It's Lilith." The name tastes like piss in my mouth. "She's got Phina. Wants to trade her for the Soul Stone and Rhyland."

The line goes so quiet I can hear Emily's heart skip a beat. Her breathing turns shallow, and I know she's processing the full weight of how monumentally fucked we are.

And that's saying something, considering our usual threshold for disaster sits somewhere between 'apocalyptic' and 'oh shit.'

"Get your ass over here," I growl into the phone, texting my location with more force than necessary. Like somehow stabbing the screen harder will make Emily materialize faster. "And bring one of my spare cars. The one that's not currently doing its best pretzel impression in a ditch."

I burst through the front door like a man on a mission, keys clattering onto the table like a metallic thunderclap. Emily trails behind me, her heels clicking against the hardwood like an angry metronome.

Between dodging traffic and breaking every speed limit known to man, I'd given Emily the highlight reel of our evening's shit show.

"And where exactly do you think you're going, Captain Impulsive?" Emily's voice could cut diamonds as I beeline for the vault. Of course she knows what I'm planning—the witch probably read it off my blood pressure.

"Well, unless you've got a better idea hiding in that cauldron of yours, I'm getting the stone and going full John Wick on that blood-sucking bitch." My fangs drop as I spin to face her. "Or should I wait until she starts gift-wrapping pieces of my angel with pretty little bows?"

"Jesus, Lucian!" Emily throws her hands up, magic crackling around her. "Your half-cocked suicide mission isn't going to save anyone. Since when do you play by the bitches rules?"

I can feel my eye twitching. "Emily, I swear to God, if you don't move, I will move you myself."

She scoffs. "Try it, Fang Face. I'll hex your dick off before you take a step."

We glare at each other, the tension thick enough to choke on. Every second we waste, my Phina is suffering. I can feel it in my bones.

"Emily, please." My voice cracks, desperation leaking through the cracks in my bravado. "I can't... I can't lose her. Not like this."

Emily's face softens, the snark melting away. "Look, Captain Dramatics, I get it. Sera is... she's family now. But we can't just throw a cosmic nuke into Lilith's manicured hands and hope for the best. We need a plan that doesn't end with the apocalypse."

"What's the problem?"

I whirl around to find Braxos sauntering in, wearing Tony Stark's face like he raided Marvel's costume department. Because apparently, this demon's got a hard-on for my entire comic collection.

"For fuck's sake," I groan, pinching the bridge of my nose. "Could you not? I'm already dealing with one crisis. I don't need Iron Demon over here giving me copyright nightmares."

But of course, he's only got eyes for Emily, his concern practically oozing through Stark's perfectly trimmed goatee. It makes me want to projectile vomit all over this kitchen.

"Brax, it's... we're handling it," Emily sighs, her voice carrying the world's weight. "Lilith snatched Sera. Wants to trade her for the Soul Stone like it's a fucking Pokemon card."

Sable bursts in like a bat out of hell, her eyes wide with panic. "What? No! We can't let that happen! There has to be something we can do!"

"No shit," I snap, my patience fraying like a cheap sweater. "I was trying to do just that, but Witchy McBitchface over here won't move her ass."

Damon struts in behind Sable looking way too satisfied—like a cat who just found an unguarded canary. His skin's got that post-feeding glow.

And—*oh hell no*—is that a fresh fang hickey on Sable's neck?

Great. Fucking wonderful. While my angel's getting the five-star hostage treatment from Hell's favorite fashion cunt, these two are auditioning for "*The Vampire Diaries.*" I cannot deal with this shit right now.

I try to shove past her, but Emily slams up a magical wall in my face, making me stumble.

"And what's your grand plan, dumbass?" she snaps, jabbing a finger into my chest. "Hand over the magical nuke and hope Lilith plays nice? News flash, asshole: she's not exactly known for her integrity!"

A snarl rips from my throat, my fangs itching to descend. "You think I don't know that? But I can't just leave Seraphina there! That sadistic bitch could be doing anything to her!"

Images flash through my mind—feathers drenched in blood, golden eyes dulled with pain—or worse. My heart clenches like it's caught in a vice.

Emily huffs. "Yes, because rushing in guns blazing has worked out so well for us before. Remember Leavenworth?"

"That was ONE time!"

"What possessed your stupid ass to leave the house in the first place?" Emily's voice has enough sarcasm to fill an Olympic pool. "Was there some urgent stripper emergency I should know about?"

"Club shit," I snarl, my patience about to snap. "You know, the business that pays for all this and those fancy witch supplies you love so much?"

She scoffs. "Oh, brilliant plan there, Einstein. Let's waltz right into Psycho's crosshairs because of *paperwork*. You knew she was on the prowl!"

"Yeah, in OREGON!" I explode. "Where you said she was playing house. Last time I checked, Oregon wasn't in my fucking backyard!"

"Enough!" Sable's voice cuts through our bickering like a holy machete. "I can't take all this arguing. Can we focus on the actual crisis here?"

Braxos frowns, his borrowed face scrunching up like he just bit into a lemon. "The Soul Stone is immensely powerful. In the wrong hands, it could spell disaster for all realms."

I throw my hands up, exasperated. "Great. Fantastic. Why don't we all sit around and discuss the ethical implications while Lilith turns Phina into a fucking piñata?"

Sable wrings her hands, her eyes wide with worry. "Surely there must be another way! A spell, or a ritual, or... or something!"

"Well, unless you've got a spare angel stashed in your back pocket and Rhyland's doppelganger, I'm all ears," I growl, my fangs itching to tear into something. Preferably Lilith's smug face.

"Actually..." Emily's eyes light up like she just discovered the cure for stupidity. "We might have something better than a spare angel."

I narrow my eyes. "If you suggest meditation or crystal healing, I swear to God—"

"Oh, shut up, you dramatic blood bag," she snaps, already grabbing the cookbook of witchy wonders. "I'm talking about Dani."

Sable leans over Emily's shoulder as she starts rifling through the ancient spellbook. "Are we certain it's wise to disturb her while she's in Zephyria?"

"You got a better idea?" Emily mutters, fingers dancing over weathered pages. "Because right now, our options are either to bother Dani or let Count Dramatic over here commit suicide by Lilith.

"Now, if you'll all shut your pie holes for five minutes, I might be able to find that spell that'll get us a collect call to that windy realm."

"I resent that accurate description," I grumble, dropping into a chair. "But make it quick. And Braxos?" I point at his Tony Stark face. "Switch to literally anyone else. You're giving me copyright anxiety."

Emily flips through the crusty pages, muttering under her breath. "God, you're such a nerd. Focus, would you?"

"Says the witch using a book that looks like it was written by Gandalf's great-grandfather."

"I'll turn your balls into my personal raisin collection."

"Aw, fuck you, too, sunshine."

I'm on my third bottle of top-shelf bourbon—because if I'm going to spiral into panic, I might as well do it with style—while Emily's been acting like a caffeinated librarian. Her nose hasn't left that ancient spellbook for the past hour, pages fluttering like nervous butterflies under her fingers.

"Any day now," I mutter into my glass, watching the amber liquid swirl. "You know, before Lilith decides to redecorate Hell with Phina's feathers."

"Got something!" Emily's victory screech could probably shatter glass. Her finger jabs at a page covered in what looks like drunk spider calligraphy. "This spell should work. Like magical texting, but way more dramatic."

She starts digging through her bag of tricks. "Okay, we need white sage, obviously. Sea salt—the fancy kind, not that Morton's garbage. Three black candles, preferably beeswax... and where did I put that amethyst crystal?"

Sable's already ransacking the kitchen cabinets like a crazy person. "Got the sage! And that Himalayan salt you splurged on last month."

Emily snatches up a yellow post-it note and her favorite fountain pen because ballpoints aren't aesthetic enough for magical messaging. "According to this ancient headache, we should be able to send her a note across realms. Assuming I don't accidentally open a portal to the demon dimension instead."

"Perfect." I lean over her shoulder, fangs itching. "Make sure you include all the greatest hits: kidnapped guardian angel, psycho demon queen, and for fuck's sake, tell her to move that divine ass of hers before I do something stupid. Again."

Emily cups the crumpled post-it in her palm like she's holding a baby bird. Her lips move in a whisper, ancient words sliding off her tongue like smoke. The air grows thick, heavy with potential, and the hair on my arms stands at attention.

The paper ignites—not with normal flames, but with something that looks like liquid moonlight. It burns away to nothing, leaving behind the scent of ozone and possibility.

"That's it?" I arch an eyebrow, unimpressed. "No explosions? No dramatic light show? Not even a tiny firework? How do we know if our magical message-in-a-bottle actually reached its destination?"

Emily drops her hands, exhaustion etched across her face. "We don't. Welcome to the wonderful world of mystical messaging—where 'read receipts' aren't a thing and we just have to hope our supernatural carrier pigeon doesn't get lost in the interdimensional mail.

Fan-fucking-tastic. My angel's life depends on the magical equivalent of hoping your text didn't get lost in cyber space.

RHYLAND

45

Consciousness creeps in slowly, led by the sensation of Dani's silk-smooth leg draped across my groin, her heat branded against my side. My mate's sprawled across me like a satisfied cat, her chocolate brown hair wild from where I'd gripped it last night, her throat marked with my love bites.

The memory of her screaming my name, her body arching off the bed as I wrung orgasm after orgasm from her sweet pussy, has my cock hardening again. The way she'd begged so prettily, her honeyed-caramel eyes glazed with pleasure as I'd pushed deep into her throat, fucking that smart mouth of hers until tears streaked her cheeks. By the fourth time, she'd come apart around my cock, she could barely form words—just desperate, needy sounds that still echo in my ears.

My savage satisfaction deepens, watching her chest rise and fall in exhausted slumber. She won't be playing games with my control again anytime soon—at least not without expecting the consequences.

Clouded rays of dawn spill through the window slats, painting Dani's skin in strips of light and shadow. My internal clock's screaming that we're burning daylight—Baldr's pompous ass will be strutting through those gates any minute to escort us to the final Einherjar. Just what I want today—the self-righteous deity with a stick up his ass telling us what to do.

The sounds of training already echo from the yard below. But the one sound I'm listening for—the distinctive ring of Erik's blade—is notably absent. After the show he put on last night—nearly ripping Gunnar's throat out with his bare hands—Bryn had chased after him like her ass was on fire. The sexual tension rolling off those two could've set this place ablaze. If my brother didn't finally claim what's his after that display, I'm officially disowning his stupid ass.

I trace my fingers down Dani's spine, savoring how she shivers even in sleep. I need to get some food in her after last night's... activities. However, from the marks I left on her last night, she might need more than breakfast to get moving.

Can't have my mate running on empty when we face whatever bullshit the gods have planned for us today.

My fingers slide into Dani's hair, savoring the silk-smooth strands while I breathe in her scent—honey, sunshine and sex. "Time to wake up, Angel." My grip tightens on her hip, thumb stroking one of the marks I left.

Her answering moan vibrates against my chest, followed by the teasing drag of her fingers across my skin. "Mmm... that feels good." Her palm maps the planes of my chest like she's trying to memorize every inch and fuck if that doesn't make my beast purr.

A growl rumbles through me as her touch dips lower. As much as I want to spend the day buried inside her sweet heat, duty's calling—and it's got Baldr's annoying face attached to it. "Baby, you keep touching me like that, we're never leaving this bed." I press my lips to her temple, breathing her in one last time. "But we've got a realm to save and an asshat god waiting."

Dani nuzzles into my chest, her lips curving into a sleepy pout. "Just five more minutes," she mumbles, her voice still rough from sleep—and from screaming my name last night. "I haven't slept or felt this relaxed in... I don't know how long."

"Oh, is that so?" I tease, my fingers still tangled in her thick hair. "Amazing what happens when you're not icing me out for a week. Guess I wore you out pretty good, huh?"

She lifts her head just enough to shoot me a look through her lashes, honey-gold eyes sparking with mischief. "Don't get too cocky, Mister. I seem to recall someone begging for mercy around round three."

I tug her hair playfully, loving the way her breath hitches. "Funny, all I remember is you screaming my name and coming so hard you nearly blacked out."

She nips at my chest in retaliation, her teeth grazing my skin in a way that has my cock jumping to attention. "Mmm, I think you're confusing me with your reflection, Fjord Fluff."

Her sass, even half-asleep, pulls a chuckle from me. My fingers continue their path through her hair, each silky strand sliding across my skin like a caress. I could do this for hours, just mapping the texture and memorizing the way the light catches each highlight.

Fuck, I'm turning into a sap. But with her warm and pliant in my arms, her scent wrapped around me like a second skin, I can't find it in me to care. I'm obsessed with every inch of this woman, and I'm not even trying to hide it.

My palm connects with Dani's ass in a playful swat, the sound echoing through the room. She yelps, her body jolting against mine as her eyes fly open. "Come on, Angel." I trace a finger over the marks littering her skin, each one a reminder of the pleasure I wrung from her last night. "You need my blood to heal these. And then I'm going to feed you actual food." The scent of sizzling bacon drifts in, making my mouth water. "I can smell them cooking up some bacon."

Dani's gasp is almost comical, her eyes widening as she pushes up on her elbows. "Bacon?" The reverence in her tone, like I've just offered her ambrosia instead of fried pork, brings a grin to my face.

"Mm-hm." I hum in confirmation, my smile widening at how her whole face lights up. Fuck, I'd cook her a whole pig myself if it meant seeing that look every morning.

Dani's out of bed in a flash, her naked body a blur of golden skin and tantalizing curves as she reaches for her clothes. "Yes, please! I'm starving." The words tumble out in a rush, her fingers fumbling with the laces of her tunic in her haste.

I'm dressed before she's even got her pants on, the perks of vampire speed. Leaning against the wall, I watch her struggle with her boots, a smirk tugging at my lips.

"Show off." Her sass is undercut by how she's hopping on one foot, trying to tug the boot without falling over.

Rolling my eyes, I grab her fur-lined coat from the chair. The heavy fabric nearly pulls me off balance—how the hell does she walk around in this thing? As I lift it, something flutters to the floor. A yellow piece of paper—blank when I turn it over. Odd. It's probably just scrap from one of Dani's many pockets. Without a second thought, I toss it on the bedside table and turn back to my mate, holding out the coat for her.

Once fed and healed with my blood, we make our way to the gate.

The morning sun glints off the frozen gates where Baldr's waiting, his godly ass propped against a pillar like he's posing for a fucking painting. No sign of Erik or Bryn—which either means my brother finally got his shit together or we've got one hell of a mess to clean up.

"Ah, Lightborn!" Baldr's voice carries across the courtyard with condescension masked as benevolence. "The Clouds themselves dance with joy this morn! The Cloud Palaces have prepared a grand feast in your honor—a celebration of your triumph over the first Einherjar!"

Dani's eyebrows shoot up. "A party? Really?" Her tone fires off with that unique brand of sarcasm she saves for immortal bullshit. "Because nothing says 'urgent quest to save the realms' like stopping for champagne and canapés."

"It would be most discourteous to decline, Dani." Baldr's smile is all superiority and impatience. "The people of Ásgard await. A mere day's delay, then we journey forth to your next challenge."

Dani's eyes find mine, that warm amber gaze asking what I think. I shrug, letting her take point on this one. "Your call, baby."

"Fine." She rolls her eyes. "But only because saying no would probably cause some sort of diplomatic incident."

"Excellent!" Baldr's tone suggests we should be honored by his approval. Smug bastard. "Perhaps you could portal us? The journey is half a day's ride otherwise."

Oh fuck. Gullfax is going to throw a whole royal equine tantrum about this. That stallion's got more attitude than a longhouse full of drunk Vikings.

"Only if Gullfax comes with us," Dani cuts in, her tone brooking no argument. Clever girl—better to face the horse's attitude now than deal with his sulking later.

"As you wish." Baldr sighs like he's indulging a particularly annoying request.

"Wait—where are Erik and Bryn?" Dani's brow furrows as she scans the courtyard like she's just now realizing they're suspiciously absent. Her eyes widen, a slow grin spreading across her face as realization dawns. "Do you think...?" She presses her hands to her mouth, trying and failing to muffle a giggle.

I can't help but smirk. About damn time; my brother pulled his head out of his ass and did something about that tension. If the way Bryn tore after him last night is any indication, they're either still going at it or passed out cold somewhere.

"I'll find him." And hopefully, not walk in on anything that'll scar me for the next century. I reach out with my senses, searching for my brother's signature.

I zero in on Erik coming from the fucking stables of all places. Well, can't say I expected that location for their first time, but then again, I once took Dani at a Masquerade Ball.

The frozen ground crunches under my boots as I cross the courtyard. Each exhale creates clouds in the frigid morning air. The stable doors creak open at my touch, but Erik is nowhere in sight.

A familiar snort draws my attention. Gullfax's big-ass head appears over his stall door, and the smug bastard is snickering—bobbing his head like he's got the world's best secret.

"Hey, buddy." I reach for his velvety nose. "Have you seen—"

The words die in my throat as I see what's behind Gullfax. There's my brother, sprawled in the hay like he's been hit by Thor's hammer, clutching a bladder of mead like it's his last friend in the world. The devastation across his face tells me everything I need to know about how last night went down.

Fuck.

"Hey, brother." The words scrape past the sudden tightness in my throat. "That bad, huh?"

Erik's laugh is a broken thing, sharp enough to cut. He lifts the bladder to his lips, missing half his mouth as mead streams down his chin. His silver eyes are glazed, unfocused—he's been at this a while. "Your powers of observation remain unmatched, brother." The words drip with that familiar dry sarcasm, but there's something darker underneath.

Gullfax shifts aside with a gentle pat to his chest, letting me into the stall. The hay crunches under my weight as I sink beside Erik, the scent of alcohol and despair thick in the air. "What happened? I thought—"

"Your optimism was misplaced." Erik's precise, measured tone cracks at the edges. His fingers tighten around the bladder until his knuckles turn white. "The logical conclusion I predicted has come to pass. She wants nothing of the mate bond." Another long pull from the bladder. "Nothing of me."

My jaw locks so hard I taste blood. Fuck. This is worse than bad—this is catastrophic. I've heard the stories, the aftermath when a vampire's mate rejects them. The darkness creeps in, eating away at their sanity until there's nothing left but a feral beast. The thought of Erik—my brother, my right hand—losing himself to that kind of madness makes my beast howl in rage.

"Hey." I grip his shoulder, feeling the tension coiled beneath my fingers. "This isn't over. I know what I saw—"

"You saw what you wanted to see." Erik's words slur slightly, his usual precise diction fraying at the edges. He waves the bladder in a mockery of his typical controlled gestures. "Your powers of observation are... questionable at best when it comes to matters of the heart, dear brother." He misses his mouth again as he takes another drink, mead spilling down his chin.

His silver eyes, usually sharp as steel, are clouded with something more than just alcohol. "Our fierce Valkyrie"—his voice catches on the word—"has clarified her position. Duty to Ásgard comes first. Can't have a mate mucking up her grand destiny." A bitter laugh escapes him. "After the whole prophesied mate disaster with you, she's determined not to repeat history's mistakes."

The false lightness in his tone pisses me off. He's trying so hard to maintain his usual analytical facade, but the cracks are showing—in his voice, his hands shake, and the despair rolling off him in waves. "And did she *actually* say any of this?" I arch an eyebrow at him. "Or are you just sitting here making assumptions like the overthinking bastard you are?"

"Oh, yes." Erik fumbles for another drink, mead sloshing. "She made her feelings quite clear." His speech slurs into something bitter and raw. "Right to my face. Quite... efficient about it."

Fuck this. I snatch the bladder from his grip, ignoring his protest as I haul him to his feet. My palm connects with his cheek—not hard enough to hurt, just enough to focus those glazed silver eyes. "Enough of this pathetic bullshit. You think I got my mate by sitting in the fucking stables drowning in mead?"

Erik sways like a tree in a storm, trying and failing to fix me with his usual stern glare. "Brother—"

"No. You're going to listen." My fingers dig into his shoulders, holding him steady. "You think Dani just fell into my arms? That she didn't fight this every step of the way? I had to chase, convince, and show her what we could be. And I didn't give up." My voice drops lower, rougher. "If you roll over and accept this, we'll lose you. All of us. Even Dani. And I won't fucking let that happen."

Erik's finger wobbles as he points it at my chest, his usual dignity entirely undermined by how he can barely stand straight. "Brother...." He draws the word out like he's giving a lecture, though his hiccup somewhat ruins the effect. "I am not you. I don't... I won't be some barbaric caveman, taking what isn't freely wanted."

"For fuck's sake." My fingers rake through my hair as I stare at my brother's pathetic drunk ass. Playing matchmaker isn't exactly my forte, and this shit's wearing thin. "I'm not telling you to drag her off by the hair, you dramatic bastard. Just..." The words stick in my throat. Maybe Dani should handle this—she's better at the emotional crap. "Don't give up, Erik. And for the love of Odin, stop this pitiful shit. We need you functioning. Starting with getting you sobered up."

The water trough looms outside the stable doors—a behemoth of carved stone big enough to water a dozen war horses at once. The morning frost has left a thin sheet of ice across its surface, and the water beneath promises to be balls-freezing cold.

Perfect.

Erik stumbles face-first into the snow as I drag him out, cursing in three different languages. Some warrior. Confused, he blinks up at me as I crack through the ice with my fist.

I haul him up by his jacket, his eyes widening as he spots the trough. "What are you—?"

The question dies in his throat as the splash echoes across the courtyard as his drunk ass hits the water. His thrashing sends waves over the sides as he flails like a landed fish. When he finally finds his footing, he looks like a drowned rat, silver hair plastered to his face, clothes soaked through.

"Son of a bitch!" Erik's usual elegant vocabulary dissolves into sailor's curses as he spits water. "Are you out of your goddamn mind?" Water streams down his face as he tries to muster his dignity. "That was entirely unnecessary."

"Was it?" I lean against the trough, watching him shiver. "Because from where I'm standing, you needed a wake-up call. Now get your ass out of there before your balls freeze off. Though at this rate, it doesn't seem like you're using them anyway."

The crunch of footsteps on snow draws my attention from Erik's pathetic form. Dani's eyes widen as she takes in the scene—Erik half-drowned in the trough, me standing over him like a disapproving parent. Her gaze locks with mine, a silent question in those honey depths.

I give a slight shake of my head, jaw tight. Her face falls, realization dawning like a fucking sunrise. She knows. And from how her shoulders slump, she knows exactly how bad this is.

"I'm gonna go find Bryn." The words come out in a rush, her voice strained. She spins on her heel, long, brown hair flying as she sprints across the courtyard.

Erik slips beneath the icy water again, this time voluntarily. "Just end my misery now, brother." His words bubble up through the freezing water, all pretense of dignity finally abandoned. "I hear drowning is relatively peaceful."

"Keep dreaming, asshole." I reach into the trough, hauling him up by his soaked jacket. He hangs limp in my grip; all the fight drained out of him. "You don't get to take the easy way out, brother. Not while I'm still breathing."

He doesn't respond; he just stares at the ground like it holds all the secrets. Fuck. I've never seen him like this—not in all our centuries together. It's like watching a part of him die right in front of me.

I tighten my grip on his jacket, shaking him until his eyes meet mine. "Listen to me, Erik. This isn't over. You hear me? We'll figure this out. But first, we need to get you dried off and sobered up. Can't have you facing the entire royal palaces like this."

He blinks slowly like he's processing my words through a haze. Then, with a nod so slight I almost miss it, he straightens his spine. It's a far cry from his usual composed self, but it's a start.

DANICA

46

My boots echo through the longhouse like angry drumbeats as I search for Bryn. The whole "avoiding your mate" routine? Yeah, that's getting old really fast. I've seen how she looks at Erik when she thinks no one's watching—like he's water in the desert and she's dying of thirst.

Bryn's stubborn denial of the bond isn't just reckless—it's a death sentence for Erik. I can't lose him, not like this.

I need to talk some sense into her, woman to woman.

Time for some sisterly intervention before her stubborn ass gets them both killed.

I reach her door and knock, the sound echoing through the hall. "Bryn? You In there, sweetie?"

Silence. I press my ear to the door, straining to hear any sign of life. Soft sobs filter through the wood, each one a dagger to my heart. I knock again, more urgently this time. "Bryn, please. Let me in."

I try the handle, but it's locked tight. Of course, it is. "I'm not leaving until you talk to me, Bryn. Open up."

"Just go away, Dani." Her voice is muffled, but the pain in it is clear as day.

"Not happening. We're having this conversation whether you like it or not." More silence, punctuated by hitching breaths. "Bryn, I swear to god—"

Screw this noise. I step back, eyeing the door like it's my nemesis—enough of this bullshit. I'm not about to let Bryn ruin her life and Erik's in one fell swoop. I take a deep breath, channeling all my frustration, and kick the door.

The wood splinters under my boot, the hinges giving way with a metallic shriek. The door swings open, slamming against the wall with a deafening bang. And what I see on the other side stops my heart cold.

"Oh god, Bryn... no." My feet slip in the growing pool of blood as I rush to her crumpled form. My hands scramble for anything—clothes, sheets, towels—to stop the bleeding. "What have you done?"

Bryn curls into herself, a broken goddess amidst a sea of crimson and ebony. Her severed wing lies lifeless on the floor—a mangled mess of bone, blood, and once-pristine black feathers. The jagged edge where she hacked it off weeps dark blood, the flesh raw and torn. Broken shafts of obsidian feathers scatter the floor like shattered pieces of midnight.

"What use is a one-winged Valkyrie?" Her anguished cry rips through the room, each word dripping with despair. "I'm nothing now—a broken warrior, a liability!"

Sobs wrack her body, her shoulders heaving with the force of her pain. This is more than physical agony—it's the shattering of her very identity, the core of who she is.

I drop to my knees beside her, heedless of the blood soaking into my pants. My hands tremble as I cup her face, forcing her to meet my gaze. Tears cut tracks through the blood staining her cheeks.

"Bryn, stop. You're not nothing. You could never be nothing." I swallow hard against the lump in my throat. "You're my sister, my family. And you're so much more than your wings." She shakes her head, a keening wail rising from her throat. The sound is pure agony, and it cuts me to the quick. "You are worth everything—to me—to—" The word 'Erik' dies on my tongue. Not yet. First, I need to heal this nightmare. "Turn around. Let me help you."

She sniffs but complies, revealing the full horror of what she's done. The wound is catastrophic—muscle and sinew hang in ragged strips where she sawed through her flesh. Once a masterpiece of divine engineering, the wing joint is ruined by shattered bones and torn ligaments. Blood still pumps from severed arteries, each beat of her heart sending fresh rivulets down her back.

She must've just done this—moments before I arrived.

I close my eyes, reaching deep within to tap into the wellspring of power. The Atherite stone thrums in response, its energy surging through my veins like a divine current. A soft, ethereal glow emanates from my hands—a pure white light that seems to push back against the darkness engulfing Bryn.

Gently, I press my palms to the ravaged remains of her wing. The moment my skin meets hers, Bryn inhales sharply, her body going rigid. But as the celestial light suffuses her flesh, she gradually relaxes, melting into my touch.

Under the radiance of my power, the brutal wound begins to transform. The ragged edges of the amputation start to draw inward, the skin and muscle knitting together in a way that defies nature. However, healing takes a different path than rebuilding the lost wing.

The shattered remnants of bone and cartilage begin to dissolve, absorbed back into her body like sand pulled by the tide. The gnarled stump smooths out, the angry red flesh fading to match her golden skin. It's as if her body accepts the loss, adapting to this new reality.

Slowly, impossibly, the wound seals itself completely. Where once there was a gaping, blood-soaked void, there is now only smooth, unblemished skin. The place where her majestic wing once sprouted is now a seamless expanse of her back, marred only by the slick blood that still paints her back.

I sit back on my heels, my breath escaping in a shuddering sigh. Bryn's body shakes with silent sobs, the blood loss and emotional toll taking their due.

Without a word, I gather her into my arms, pulling her tight against my chest. She collapses into the embrace, her tears hot against my neck as she finally gives voice to her anguish—the sound raw and broken.

I hold her, rocking gently as she rides out the storm of her grief. I stroke her hair, murmuring soft words of comfort even as my tears fall unchecked.

She's my sister and family, and I refuse to let this break her. We've only found each other and begun building the bond we should have always had. And I'll be her rock, her safe harbor, for as long as she needs.

The loss of her wings may have changed her, but it will never define her. Not if I have anything to say about it.

Rhyland bursts through the doorway, freezing at the horrific scene. His eyes lock on the severed wing lying in a pool of dark blood, his fierce expression crumbling to one of deep sorrow—shock and sadness as he takes in Bryn's broken form in my arms."Is she..." His voice cracks, heavy with emotion.

"She needs time," I whisper, holding her tighter as she trembles. "And her sister."

He nods slowly, grief etched in the lines of his face. "Take all the time you need. I'll be close if you need me." His eyes linger on Bryn with profound pity before he quietly withdraws, leaving us to our healing.

I help Bryn into fresh clothes after scrubbing away the last traces of blood from her skin. The water in the basin has turned a murky pink—evidence of her desperate act slowly dissolving away. Now we're sprawled across her bed, a horn of mead between us, because if there was ever a time for alcohol and sisterly bonding, it's now.

"How do you feel?" The words slip out before I can stop them.

Way to go, Captain Obvious.

"By the Nine, sister, how does it look like I feel?" Bryn's laugh is sharp as a blade. "I'm the talk of every mead hall in Valor's Watch—the wingless Valkyrie, as useful as a shield made of ice." She takes a deep pull from the horn. "That witless oaf Gunnar had the gall to call me a flightless crow. As if that dung-eating son of a frost giant has any right to speak."

I scoot closer, nudging her shoulder with mine. "Screw what those asshats think, Bryn. I know this is your life, your identity... but maybe this is a chance for a new beginning, a new purpose." I waggle my eyebrows, trying for levity. "Something tall, brooding, and silver-haired, perhaps?"

"By Odin's missing eye," she mutters, fixing me with a look that could freeze Hell itself. "Not you, too."

"Oh honey, yes, me too." I snatch the mead horn from her hands. "And you can't keep ignoring this. He's your mate, Bryn. Deny that bond; you might as well stick a stake in his heart yourself."

"What in the name of—" She stops, her eyes narrowing like a hawk spotting prey. "What tales have that silver-tongued vampire been spinning?"

"He didn't have to tell me anything." I tap my chest. "I felt his heart beating when he almost turned Gunnar into Viking confetti. That's Vampire Mate Bond basics, sister dear. And don't think I haven't noticed the way you two circle each other like horny teenagers at a high school dance."

"Mate? Are you insane?" she growls, snatching and draining the horn. "That's a fairy tale, Dani. It's a bedtime story. And even if it were true, my destiny was derailed long ago. Or have you forgotten? I was meant to be Rhyland's before the Gods decided to make sport of my fate."

The question burns on my tongue, a desperate need to understand. "What happened back then? With you and Rhyland?"

"I was told since I could walk that I was destined for greatness, that Rhyland was my fated mate." Her laugh is bitter, sharp. "I was twenty-three when I went to him, to his village. Found him with his wife, his children."

The mead turns to ash in my mouth. Rhyland's stories of his lost family echo in my mind, and I feel a dull ache in my chest.

"There was nothing," Bryn continues, her voice flat. "No spark, no connection. Just... emptiness." She stares into her horn like it holds all the answers. "My mother insisted he was the one, that my powers would awaken when I saw him. But they didn't."

She drains the last drops, her knuckles white around the horn. "Elysium came to me, trying to convince me that Rhyland was my destiny. But I knew the truth. I felt it in my bones."

The mention of our father makes my chest tight, and my head spins, trying to reconcile the image of him pushing a fate that wasn't meant to be. When I first saw Rhyland, it was like a lightning bolt to my soul. My powers surged to life not long after, drawn to him like a moth to a flame.

"He insisted Rhyland was the one—that I must be mistaken. That the prophecies couldn't be wrong." She shakes her head. "When he finally accepted I lacked this precious 'spark,' he shipped me off to Ásgard. Said it was for my protection, but I knew better. I was a failed prophecy, a broken tool."

She passes me the horn, and I drink deep, trying to wash away the bitterness of her words. "For years, I felt worthless. Damaged. And now?" Her eyes meet mine, one blue as a winter sky, one gold as honey—such a badass combination. "Here I am again, sister. Broken in another way—unwanted. The Norns do love their jests, don't they?"

My heart breaks for her. She's been carrying this weight all this time, thinking she was broken, unwanted.

I reach out, gripping her hand tightly. "Bryn, listen to me. You are not broken. You never were." My voice is fierce and unwavering. "Fate had a different plan for you, that's all. It doesn't make you any less worthy or needed."

I lean in closer, holding her gaze. "What's happening now? It's not a repeat of history. It's a chance for you to write a new story, one that's all your own."

My mind drifts to Erik, to the way he looks at Bryn like she's the sun and stars combined. "You said you felt nothing with Rhyland. But what about with Erik? Is it really emptiness you feel when he's near? Or is it something else, something you're afraid to name?"

I smile softly, my heart aching for the pain she's carried for so long. "This isn't history repeating itself. This is your chance to break the cycle, to find the happiness you've always deserved."

Remembering Seraphina's revelation about fate's twisted path for Rhyland and me, a small smile tugs at my lips. "You know what? Maybe that's exactly the point. Fate's a sneaky bitch with a wicked sense of humor."

Bryn furrows her brow, looking at me like I've started speaking in tongues.

"Look," I continue, refilling her horn, "fate doesn't exactly come with an instruction manual. It's messy and unpredictable and sometimes throws you one hell of a curveball. But that silver-haired vampire out there? He's yours, whether you want to admit it or not." I lean closer, dropping my voice to a conspiratorial whisper. "And don't think I haven't caught you checking out his ass when you think no one's looking."

Bryn's cheeks burn to a shade of red. "I have not," she growls, but the lie is about as convincing as Lucian trying not to be smart-ass.

"Oh honey, that lie was weaker than watered-down ale." I can't help but grin. "Look, I get it. I played the same game of denial when I met Rhyland. I tried to ignore the pull and pretend it wasn't happening. But fighting fate? That's like trying to arm-wrestle a frost giant—you're just going to end up flat on your ass." I take a long drink, letting that sink in. "Come on, sister. Tell me you don't feel something. A pull, a spark, like lightning in your veins whenever he's near?"

Bryn stiffens. "Perhaps," she admits grudgingly. "But I wager that's merely because he's shown me a kindness unfamiliar to me. I'm accustomed to brutish oafs who only seek to have me on my knees or my back. Erik is... different."

She jerks her head sharply as if shaking off an unwanted thought. "But he's an insufferable ass, always hovering about like I'm some helpless maiden. I am a Valkyrie—a warrior of Odin. I need no man's protection."

As I listen to Bryn, a realization dawns on me. I may not be a love guru, but my sister is used to being treated like last week's leftovers by the men in her life. It's like she's got emotional whiplash—she doesn't know how to handle a guy who actually respects her. All she's ever known are these douchebags who see her as a disposable pleasure dispenser. Wham, bam, thank you, ma'am, now get out of my furs.

Or just being tossed aside because she didn't meet the gold standard.

And then there's Erik—all quiet strength and unwavering respect. He looks at her like she's precious, not property. Treats her like an equal, not a conquest. No wonder she's fighting this so hard. When you've spent centuries being treated like you're worthless, having someone cherish you probably feels like a trap.

It's like she's got a severe case of emotional Stockholm Syndrome. She needs time to understand that love isn't about dominance or submission. That being treated with respect isn't a sign of weakness. Erik's gentle nature might be foreign to her, but maybe that's exactly what she needs—even if she's not ready to admit it.

God knows it takes time to unlearn years of toxic bullshit. But Erik? He's got all of eternity to show her what real love looks like.

"Sister, he sees you for who you truly are." I touch her arm gently. "But you've spent so long being treated like yesterday's fish by these mead-hall warriors that you can't recognize real respect when it's staring you in the face with silver eyes."

Bryn's gaze meets mine, then drifts away, her expression distant. For once, there's no sharp comeback, no biting remark. It's like watching ice crack on a frozen lake—the first signs of something deeper breaking through.

"Erik's different," I continue softly. "He's not some glory-seeking asshole looking to add another notch to his sword belt. Just...give him a chance to prove it."

Her silence speaks volumes, and I can almost see the wheels turning behind those fierce eyes, pieces clicking into place like a puzzle she's been staring at too long to see clearly.

I take another long pull from the horn, the mead hitting me with a pleasant warmth. Damn, how many horns deep are we? The room's got that soft, fuzzy edge that warns of an incoming buzz.

"Look," I say, trying to keep my thoughts straight despite the alcohol. "You accepting Erik? That's not just about you two. I want you with us, Bryn. God, do you know how long I've dreamed of having a real family? True family?"

I lean forward, almost spilling my mead in my enthusiasm. "And let's be real—what's keeping you here? These muscle-bound jerks who treat you like last season's shield? Who looks at you differently now because of your wings?"

My eyes lock with hers. "Come with us. I need my big sister. And a certain brooding vampire needs his mate, even if he's too stoic to say it out loud."

I flash her a tipsy grin. "Besides, watching Erik try to maintain his whole 'mysterious warrior' vibe around you is better than theater."

Bryn dissolves into laughter, the mead hitting her as hard as it's hitting me. She topples into my lap, her giggles echoing off the walls. "By the Nine, he does look rather constipated when I'm near. Like he's swallowed one of Odin's ravens whole."

Unlike her, she sighs dreamily, and I almost do a double-take. "He kissed me, you know."

"He *WHAT?*" The mead makes my voice hit a pitch that probably has dogs in Mortalis howling. "And you're just now sharing this juicy detail?"

Bryn's laughter only grows louder. "It was..." She pauses, pushing herself back up, her expression sobering slightly. "By the Gods, sister, of course, I'll come. These halls hold nothing but empty glory now and colder stares. I will swear an oath to you know, to stand at your side, to aid you in your quest, and I'll be damned to Hell before I break it.

She holds up a hand as I open my mouth. "But by Odin's beard, if you try to play matchmaker with that silver-haired oaf and me, I'll throw you off the highest tower in Ásgard. Let me handle this in my own time."

"Say no more." I mime, locking my lips and tossing away the key. "I won't push. Sister's honor."

And I mean it. Having Bryn agree to come with us and be part of our little misfit family? That's more than I could have hoped for. The rest will come in time.

Though I make no promises about not teasing her mercilessly about that kiss later.

What are sisters for, after all?

ERIK

47

The new leather and furs scratch against my damp skin as we wait by the gate, my head still pounding from last night's foolishness. Gullfax paws at the snow, his impatient snorts creating clouds in the frigid air. The stallion shoots me a sidelong glance—after sharing his stable during my pathetic display, we've reached some understanding.

Her scent hits me first—storm winds and steel—making my chest constrict. I turn, and the world stops spinning.

Where Bryn's magnificent wing once stretched proud and strong, there's nothing. Just empty space and the rigid set of her shoulders. Her face is carved from ice, daring anyone to comment, but I see the shadows in her eyes.

Rage ignites in my veins, white-hot and blinding. My vision tunnels, the world narrowing to the space where her wing should be. Someone dared to lay hands on her, to mutilate her. Gunnar's smug face flashes through my mind—did he do this as retribution for my actions?

"Who did this to you?" The words tear from my throat, razor-edged and deadly. I'm across the courtyard before I realize I've moved, my hands clenched into fists. "I'll rip their heart out with my bare hands—"

Dani's hand on my arm stops me. The look in her eyes—a mix of warning and sorrow—douses my fury like a bucket of ice water.

Bryn steps forward, her chin high despite the pain etched into every line of her body. "I did it, Erik." Her voice is steady, but I hear the fractures beneath. "I cut it off myself."

The words hit like a wrecking ball driving the air from my lungs. "Why?" It comes out as a broken whisper, my mind reeling. "Why would you...?"

She meets my gaze, unflinching. "It was a reminder of my failure, Erik. A constant shadow hanging over me." Her jaw tightens, but I catch the slight tremor in her voice. "That wing was a constant reminder of what I couldn't be, what I was denied. Now..." She straightens her shoulders despite the cost evident in her eyes. "Now I decide who I am. Not fate. Not destiny. Not even *you*."

Her shoulder slams into mine as she pushes past, the impact barely registering through the numbness spreading in my chest. My eyes bore into the snow at my feet, unseeing. The image of her severing her wing plays on repeat in my mind, each iteration more horrific than the last. What depths of self-loathing must she harbor to mutilate herself so?

Dani's touch barely penetrates the haze, her fingers feather-light on my arms. "Don't give up, Erik." Her voice sounds distant, muffled by the roaring in my ears. "She just... needs time. To adjust to all this."

I manage a nod, the motion mechanical. My heart constricts, each beat a painful squeeze. Bryn, with her warrior's spirit and unbreakable will, loyalty, and fierce protectiveness... How can she not see her own worth? That she would go to such lengths to excise a part of herself...

The mate bond throbs like an open wound, each pulse a reminder of her rejection. What more can I give when the first denial nearly broke me? The memory of collapsing in that stable, my soul screaming in agony, is still raw.

Dani's eyes find mine, a silent plea in their golden depths. She knows what's at stake—not just for me, but for Bryn. For the bond that could save or destroy us both.

Rhyland's gaze bores into me, steel blue and unyielding. They need me to be strong, put aside my fears, and fight for what the Fates have ordained.

Resolve hardens in my gut, chasing away the numbness. I won't let her shatter under the weight of her demons—not like I did. I'll be the shield at her back, the sword in her hand until she remembers her own strength.

"Right then!" Baldr's voice rings with artificial cheer. "Shall we proceed?"

"Where's Heimdall?" Dani's brow furrows.

Baldr's smile doesn't reach his eyes, a serpentine curve that sets my teeth on edge. Every instinct screams that something's off with this pompous deity. "He awaits our arrival at the Cloud Palaces." He sweeps his arm toward the horizon with theatrical flair. "If you would do us the honor, Lightborn."

Gullfax snorts, stamping his hoof as Dani mutters under her breath, clearly engaged in another battle of wills with the stubborn stallion. She turns to Baldr, frustration evident in her stance. "I need more than just 'Cloud Palaces.' My portals require either firsthand knowledge of the location or a detailed description. Otherwise, we could end up scattered across the seven realms."

"Ah, of course." Baldr says with false humility. "Simply focus on Ásgard itself. We can navigate to the Cloud Palaces once we arrive."

Dani's eyes drift shut, brow furrowed in concentration. The air around her seems to vibrate, the scent of ozone and stardust rising. The space before us ripples, then tears open—a window into another world. Through the shimmering gateway, Ásgard sprawls in breathtaking majesty: emerald fields rolling toward the horizon, crystalline waterfalls cascading from impossible heights, golden spires piercing the clouds like arrows of light.

After witnessing it countless times, watching Dani bend reality still steals my breath. She makes the impossible look effortless, as natural as breathing.

"After you," she gestures, a hint of satisfaction in her voice.

The Cloud Palaces hover upon islands of solidified light, suspended amidst an eternal twilight firmament. Crystalline spires transpierce cotton-candy clouds, with pink, lavender, and gold hues intertwining like an ethereal artist's palette. Cascades of liquid starlight descend from one floating island to the next, their mist creating an endless array of rainbows in the otherworldly luminescence.

The palaces seem carved from living glass and solidified clouds, their walls shifting between opacity and transparency with each passing breeze. Gardens spiral up impossible towers, exotic flowers blooming in mid-air, their petals catching the light like scattered gems. Bridges of pure light arc between the floating sanctuaries, their surfaces rippling like water yet solid as steel beneath our feet.

"Wow." Dani's whisper carries on the ethereal breeze as we traverse the floating gardens, each step taking us closer to the towering glass palace.

Bryn appears at her side, her stride purposeful. "The Cloud Palaces rose from Ragnarök's ashes," she explains, her eyes distant with memory. "When the realm fell, the Aesir gathered what remained of their divine power. They wove it with fragments of broken rainbows and solidified starlight, crafting these sanctuaries among the clouds. Each palace holds a piece of the old realm's soul, preserved in eternal twilight."

Her voice softens. "The gardens sprouted from Freya's tears, they say—flowers that bloom on starlight and need no soil to grow. Each cascade of water flows upward as easily as down, defying laws that bind the lower realm."

"That's incredible," Dani breathes as we ascend the massive stone staircase, each step worn smooth by millennia of divine footfalls. The palace doors loom before us, towering slabs of living crystal that pulse with inner light.

"Who holds dominion here?" Rhyland's question cuts through the ethereal silence, his boots echoing against the luminescent stone.

Bryn's eyes scan the towering palaces above us. "The Cloud Palaces answer to no single ruler. Each palace houses different Aesir families, their powers maintaining the very fabric of this realm. The highest palace belongs to Odin's bloodline, but they serve more as guardians than monarchs. They all share equal standing with their fellow Aesir. It's a delicate balance of power, each family contributing unique gifts to keep these islands afloat and the eternal twilight burning."

She gestures to the shimmering towers around us. "Each palace serves a different purpose—healing, learning, crafting, and more. They work in harmony to preserve what remains of the old ways and foster growth and prosperity for all who dwell here."

We cross the threshold, and my breath catches in my throat. The interior defies even my centuries of existence. Light dances through the translucent walls, casting ever-shifting patterns across floors of polished moonstone.

Columns of solidified clouds spiral upward, their surfaces rippling with internal auroras of blue, silver, and gold.

The grand hall stretches before us, its ceiling merging with the eternal twilight visible through the transparent dome. Floating orbs of pure light drift through the air while staircases of spun crystal curve impossibly upward. Tapestries woven from threads of pure light ripple along the walls, their images shifting and moving as if alive.

"Even the libraries of Alexandria pale compared to this architectural marvel," I observe. "This is... beyond words."

"Indeed, it is a marvel to behold," Baldr agrees, golden strands falling across his brow as he inclines his head. He turns to a young man clad in a finely tailored Nordic suit—a deep blue tunic trimmed with intricate silver knotwork, paired with fitted black trousers and polished boots. "Gorm, would you be so kind as to guide our esteemed guests to their chambers? See that they are provided with all they require."

Gorm smiles, dark eyes sparkling sincerely. "Of course, it would be my pleasure. If you would follow me, please."

The crystal staircase stretches before us, and Bryn ascends several steps ahead. From my position below, every step offers a maddening view of her leather-clad curves. The supple material clings to her ass, the muscles flexing with each upward motion. My fangs ache as I recall how that perfect ass felt in my grip, the weight of her breasts in my hands, how they fit against my palms—the intoxicating scent of her arousal as I explored her with my mouth.

I can almost taste her on my tongue, hear the breathy moans that spilled from her lips, my cock hardens instantly.

As if sensing the heat of my hungry stare, Bryn pivots, her eyes burning into mine. "Enjoying the view, warrior?" Her tone walks the razor's edge between seductive and threatening, a challenge sparking in her gaze.

I clear my throat, forcing my eyes to the shimmering walls. "Yes. This is indeed stunning," I deflect, though the knowing smirk tugging at her lips tells me she's well aware it's not the architecture commanding my attention.

The hallway stretches before us, its walls shimmering. Gorm's smirk suggests he knows exactly what game he's playing. "Two chambers for the four of you," he says, gesturing to the ornate doors. "I trust you can... arrange yourselves accordingly."

Before Rhyland can stake his claim, Bryn's already commandeering one room, dragging Dani with her like a protective mother hen. My brother's mate shoots him an apologetic look, those gold eyes pleading for understanding.

Rhyland's growl is pure frustration. His hand clamps around my bicep as he practically throws me toward the other chamber. "Move your ass," he orders, his tone promising violence. "Apparently, we're having a fucking slumber party."

I stumble into the chamber, catching myself against a wall. Behind me, Dani darts back through the doorway, launching herself into Rhyland's arms. Their lips meet in a heated kiss that has me averting my gaze. Let them have their moment—I've got a bed calling my name and Grave Warden's weight heavy on my back.

The chamber's warmth seeps into my bones as I shed my furs, the weapon finding its home against the wall. The sounds of their whispered endearments and soft moans echo through the space.

"I'm just across the hall, handsome," Dani purrs, her fingers playing with Rhyland's beard. "I'll see you later tonight."

A sharp crack splits the air, followed by Dani's breathy gasp. Rhyland's growl of satisfaction tells me exactly what caused that sound.

"Can't wait." his voice rough with need. "Now go before I decide to keep you here."

As Dani saunters out, Rhyland turns to me. "Brother, could you be any more obvious? You were practically drooling over her ass." He stalks closer, his eyes glinting with challenge. "If you don't stake your claim tonight, I will throw you off this floating rock myself."

I sink into the plush mattress, letting out a long-suffering sigh. "Your eloquence knows no bounds, brother. Tell me, did you learn such refined courtship techniques before or after becoming a Viking?"

LUCIAN

48

I'm wearing a trench in the hardwood, pacing like a caged animal. Haven't closed my eyes in eighteen hours—not that I could sleep if I tried. The bond in my chest feels like an open wound, raw and bleeding, screaming for its other half.

Every second without a word from Dani is another nail in my sanity's coffin.

Six hours. We've got six fucking hours before Lilith starts her DIY angel dismemberment project.

The thought sends another wave of nausea through me. My mind keeps spinning worst-case scenarios like a demented carousel—each one more horrific than the last.

Is she hurting her?

Torturing her?

Has she touched those iridescent wings yet?

The vault downstairs calls to me like a junkie. The Soul Stone's down there, practically gift-wrapped for Hell's favorite psychopath. I could end this right now. Just hand over the cosmic nuke and get my angel back.

But she wants Rhyland, too.

I could lie. Feed her some bullshit about knowing where he is. Or tell her the truth—that he's playing hopscotch through the air realm. Either way, I'd be painting a target on everyone's back.

And I don't even care anymore.

Rosa's in the kitchen, filling the house with the scent of her famous enchiladas—the ones that usually have me drooling. But right now? Food tastes like ash in my mouth. The only thing I can taste is failure and time slipping away.

The bond twists in my chest like barbed wire, each pulse a reminder of what I've lost. This isn't like the last time when Captain Bloodbitch took her. The bond wasn't sealed then. Now? It's like missing half my soul, and I'm done waiting for magical Post-It notes and careful plans.

Emily can take her caution and shove it where the sage doesn't burn.

I'm halfway to the vault when my phone chirps. The message makes my heart skip:

> Do try to dress appropriately, darling. Black tie af-
> fair and all that. Wouldn't want your little angel to
> be embarrassed by your... pedestrian fashion choices.
> Though I suppose that's the least of her concerns right
> now

I shove my phone in my pocket, grinding my teeth. *Of course,* Lilith wants to turn this into a spectacle. Because being a psychotic bitch isn't enough—she needs an audience for her megalomaniac theater production.

My fingers barely brush the vault's keypad when an invisible force clothes-lines me. I slam into the wall hard enough to crack plaster.

"Mother *fucker!*" I snarl, peeling myself off the wall. Emily and her fucking protection spells. I blur up the stairs, ready to hunt down my least favorite Glinda and give her a piece of my mind. Fury burning in my veins—

And screech to a halt outside her door, my hand frozen mid-reach for the handle.

Oh fuck. Just, NO.

"Mmm, yeah, split me open with that demon dick," Emily's breathy moan filters through the door. "Show me what that supernatural stamina can do."

Fuck my vampire hearing. Fuck it right to hell.

The wet sounds of skin-on-skin make me want to bleach my brain. Be-cause, *of course,* she's getting railed by a shapeshifting demon while my angel's being held hostage.

"You like that, doll?" Brax's voice rumbles with a distinctly Brooklyn accent. "Want me to show you why they call me America's ass?"

No. NO. He fucking WOULDN'T.

"Yes, Captain!" Emily's enthusiastic response confirms my worst fears. "Paint me like one of your French girls—with your star-spangled banner!"

I spin away from the door, gagging. *Great. Now I need therapy AND to burn my entire Marvel collection.*

"Whatever it takes!" The distinct moan filters through the door, and—*sweet fucking Christ*—that's definitely not Brax's normal voice. The demon's got a thing for borrowing faces, but this? This is a whole new level of copyright infringement.

"Harder, Captain! Show this witch what that super-soldier serum can really do!"

Nope. That's it.

I slam my fist against the door hard enough to crack the frame. "Hey, assholes! Wrap up your 'Avengers: Infinity Whore' audition and get your asses out here. Some of us have an actual crisis to deal with!"

The symphony of super-soldier sexcapades cuts off like someone hit the emergency brake on the porn train. The door flies open to reveal Emily, looking like she just lost a fight with an electrical socket—her hair standing on end and magic sparking around her like a horny Tesla coil.

"Were you seriously creeping outside my door like some undead peeping Tom?" Her eyes narrow dangerously, promising hexes in my immediate future.

"Trust me, catching the X-rated version of 'Captain America: The First Avenger' wasn't on my bucket list." I bare my fangs in frustration. "But newsflash, genius—vampire hearing plus your decidedly *not* soundproofed room means I get front row seats to your patriotic booty call whether I want them or not."

A flush creeps up her neck before her face hardens into its default setting of 'done with your shit.' "What do you want, Lucian?"

"Six hours," I snarl. "We've got six fucking hours before Lilith starts her angel dissection project and nothing from Dani. So either you unhex my vault, or I will start using your grimoire collection as vampire toilet paper."

Emily's eyes narrow dangerously. "You wouldn't dare."

"Try me, Sabrina. I'll start with that crusty leather one you keep under your pillow—you know, the one with the *special* summoning spells?"

Emily glances at her watch, worry flickering across her face before being replaced by her trademark annoyance. "Still radio silence from our realm-hopping bestie, huh?" She runs a hand through her sex-mussed hair. "Fuck. Fine. Give me five to get... presentable."

The door slams forcefully to make Great-Aunt Gertrude's portrait rattle on the wall. Her voice carries through the not-so-soundproof barrier: "And Lucian? If I hear one single 'Star-Spangled Banner' joke out of you, I swear to every god in existence. I will personally relocate your fangs to your ball sack!"

Like, I'd risk that hex. Though I've got to admit, the jokes practically write themselves...

I roll my eyes and head back downstairs, the world's weight settling back on my shoulders with every step.

Damon and Sable are wrapped around each other on the couch, lost in their own little bubble of domestic bliss. *Must be nice,* I think bitterly, *not having your mate's life hanging in the balance.* I give them a wide berth, not trusting myself not to say something I'll regret later.

In the kitchen, Rosa is dancing to an upbeat salsa number, her hips swaying in time with the music as she pulls a steaming tray of enchiladas from the oven. The spicy aroma fills the room, but my stomach just twists into knots. Food is the last thing on my mind right now.

"Rosa," I clear my throat, making her jump. "Heads up—your least favorite demon's about to make an appearance. You know, the one you keep threatening to exorcise with your abuela's rosary?"

"¡Ay, Dios mío! ¡Ese demonio del diablo!" Rosa practically throws the pan onto the counter, crossing herself three times in rapid succession. "¡No, no, no! ¡Me voy! The food is ready, but I will not stay here with that *thing* wearing faces like Halloween masks!"

She's out of the kitchen like her ass is on fire, probably heading straight for her room to reinforce her protection wards.

The bourbon's halfway to my lips when the realization hits me like a stake to the chest. I nearly drop the bottle, my mind racing with possibilities.

Well, fuck me sideways.

Brax's latest party trick—the one that made even *my* jaded ass do a double-take—could be precisely what we need.

A laugh bubbles up from my chest, dark and maybe a little unhinged. And here I've been, overthinking this shit for hours when the answer's been strutting around in borrowed skin this whole time.

The war room (aka my living room) looks like a supernatural think tank exploded. Empty bourbon bottles, grimoires, and magical supplies litter every surface while we hammer out our half-baked rescue mission.

"Alright, Brax," I toss him my phone, pulling up Rhyland's most recent voicemail. "Study up. You're about to play the role of everyone's favorite brooding Viking." I swipe through a collection of candid shots I'd snapped of our resident thunder god.

What? Sometimes, blackmail material comes in handy.

Brax's features are already shifting, his borrowed face melting like wax as he absorbs Rhyland's voice patterns.

"You two," I point at Emily and Sable with my half-empty bottle, "need to whip up a knockoff Soul Stone that'll fool Lilith long enough for us to get Phina out. I don't care if you have to bedazzle a paperweight—just make it convincing."

The bourbon burns going down, but it's not doing shit to calm my nerves. "Knowing that theatrical bitch, she's gonna want to make this a public spectacle. We need to get her somewhere private, somewhere we can—"

"Spring a confinement spell," Sable finishes, her eyes lighting up with that particular witchy inspiration.

"Bingo." I drain the bottle, ignoring how the glass trembles in my grip. "Trap the psycho, grab my angel, make our exit stage left."

Emily looks up from her grimoire; her face scrunched in that way that means she's about to rain on my parade. "And what about Morgan? That witch is Lilith's attack dog—she won't let us anywhere near her precious queen."

A dark smile spreads across my face as I reach for another bottle. "Morgan? Oh, don't worry about her. I've got a special plan for that necromancing nightmare—it involves me, her, and a very permanent separation of head from shoulders."

My fangs itch just thinking about Morgan—that vindictive witch who couldn't leave well enough alone. *Had to go and play prison break with Lilith, didn't she?* After all the trouble my brothers went through to lock that psychotic bloodsucker away, one bitter witch with a grudge decides to throw open the gates of hell.

But that's okay. All I need is one look, one moment of eye contact, and my compulsion will turn her mind into putty. Then we'll see how she likes being trapped in her own personal nightmare.

Payback's a bitch, and tonight, so am I.

The room falls into that heavy silence where you can practically hear everyone's brains churning through worst-case scenarios. My fingers drum against the empty bourbon bottle, each tap marking another second we're wasting.

"Better break out your fancy dress clothes, kids." I wave my phone with Lilith's text. "Satan's Side Piece is insisting on black tie. Wouldn't want to disappoint her royal psychosis."

My gaze locks onto Brax like a laser sight. "Hey, Shapeshifting Steve Rogers," I jerk my head toward the stairs. "Time to play dress up, demon boy. You're about to get a crash course in Rhyland's wardrobe."

And if we're lucky, his suit game will be enough to fool Lilith long enough for us to get Phina out of this mess.

The grandfather clock in the hall strikes with an ominous *dong*, making everyone jump. Five hours until showtime. Five hours until I either get my angel back or paint Seattle red.

"Three hours," I bark, taking the stairs two at a time. "Get your shit ready and in order. If you're not ready by then, I'm taking matters into my own hands. This train waits for no one."

I pause at the top, throwing a wicked grin back at Emily. "Oh, and Em? You might want to leave the star-spangled lingerie in your room. Something tells me Lilith's not a fan of patriotic panties."

"Oh, go gargle holy water," Emily snaps back, her magic popping and fizzing around her like Pop Rocks.

Worth it.

The bond in my chest pulses with each step toward my room, a constant reminder of what's at stake.

Just a little longer, angel cake. Your favorite disaster is about to crash Lilith's party—and this time, I'm bringing hell with me.

RHYLAND

49

The hot bath and fresh trim have me looking like the fucking warrior prince I am. My usual wild scruff now follows the sharp line of my jaw, highlighting the predator beneath the fancy clothes. The midnight blue tunic clings to every hard muscle of my chest, and the red silk sleeves do nothing to hide the strength in my arms. Pure Viking warrior meets Norse royalty in leather pants and boots.

Magni's son cleaning up nicely for once, though the beast inside still prowls beneath all this polished bullshit.

Erik emerges, like a fucking silver prince, all clean lines and regal bearing. His tunic is a shade lighter than mine. He looks put together, composed—a far cry from the broken man I pulled out of that trough.

Trust my brother to make even formal wear look like battle armor.

But my mind's not on my brother. It's on a sassy brunette who's probably knee-deep in Valkyrie drama. I can picture Dani now, playing sister and confidante to Bryn, trying to piece together the mess my brother's mate made of herself. My jaw clenches at the memory of her missing wing, the space where it should be like a fucking wound in reality itself.

The image of her severing her wing, carving away what she saw as a mark of failure... it hits too close to home.

Self-loathing is a poison I know all too well. I've watched it eat at Erik for centuries and watched him punish himself for sins long past. He drowns in guilt, each misdeed another weight around his neck, dragging him down into the depths of his misery. And now Bryn—proud, fierce Bryn—is sinking into that same abyss.

Watching them is like seeing two sides of the same cursed coin: Erik drowning in guilt over past bloodshed, Bryn destroying herself over a destiny she couldn't fulfill. Both are too proud to accept help, too stubborn to see their own worth, and too caught up in their self-imposed exile to recognize salvation when it's staring them in the face.

Both warriors to their core, wearing their scars like armor while bleeding out inside. The irony would be fucking hilarious if it wasn't so tragic.

"Ready?" The question hangs between us, heavy with meaning. Erik's silver eyes meet mine, and we both know I'm not talking about some fancy party.

Erik straightens his collar, a ghost of his usual composure settling over his features. "Let's mingle, brother."

A snort escapes me as we step into the hallway. The moment we hit the grand staircase landing, my jaw nearly hits the floor. Holy shit.

The great hall has transformed into a winter wonderland straight out of Valhalla. Crystalline ice sculptures tower between marble columns, their surfaces catching and fracturing light into rainbow prisms. Floating orbs of pure starlight drift near the vaulted ceiling, casting ethereal shadows across the crowd. Gossamer curtains of silver and blue ripple in a phantom breeze while frost patterns spiral across the windows like nature's art.

The Aesir mingle in their finery, pristine armor gleaming beneath formal robes. Warriors in ceremonial dress swap war stories over horns of mead, while nobles in elaborate Norse attire cluster near the ice sculptures. Though inside, the scent of winter pine and fresh snow hits my senses. Magic crackles in the air, making my skin tingle.

Then I see her.

My heart stutters, then stops. There, beside an ice sculpture that pales in comparison, stands Dani. And fuck me—

Light blue chiffon floats around her, each movement sending ripples of fabric dancing across curves that make my mouth water. The bodice hugs her in all the right places, silver threading and crystals weaving patterns that draw my eyes straight to those magnificent tits. When she moves, the dress parts, flashing a glimpse of leg that has my beast ready to murder anyone else who dares look.

That silky, chocolate brown hair cascades down her back in waves, interrupted by intricate braids that some fancy-ass probably spent hours on. Tiny crystals and sapphires woven in each one, catch the light with every breath, but the way she carries herself—confident, radiant, *mine*—makes my blood surge hot and thick through my veins.

She's a goddamn queen, and every fucker in this room recognizes it. Seeing her punches the air from my lungs—all that power wrapped in starlight and sin. I preen with savage pride.

Look at her.

Look at what chose me.

What fights beside me.

What shares my bed.

My mate. My savior. My everything.

And judging by the hungry stares from half the fucking room, I'm not the only one appreciating the view. I choke back a snarl, ready to stake my claim.

She hasn't spotted us yet, but my body's already moving, drawn to her like a magnet. Erik's knowing chuckle follows me down the stairs.

"Try not to start a war by fucking her against a pillar, brother."

I flip him off without looking back. "No promises."

Dani's in my sights, but a wall of golden perfection blocks my path. In all his prissy glory, Baldr materializes like an unwanted ray of sunshine. His suit probably costs more than most kingdoms, every thread screaming, 'Look at me.' That perfectly styled blonde hair and those sharp, aristocratic features remind me of those marble statues mortals love so much—cold, hard, and full of themselves.

"Ah, Godborn. You clean up nicely." His voice drips honey and wine, matching the crystal glass in his manicured hand. Everything about him is too polished, too perfect.

"Thanks." The word comes out like gravel, bristling at his presence. Something about Baldr pisses me off. Sure, he's Odin's son, Frigg's golden boy, my internal alarm bells scream, like a snake hiding in silk sheets.

Maybe it's how he holds himself like getting his hands dirty would shatter his entire existence. Or perhaps it's his smile never quite reaches his eyes, even when he's laying on the charm.

Sure, he plays the part of the gracious host with all proper manners and protocol. But my centuries of dealing with two-faced bastards scream that there's more lurking behind that perfect facade. The way he watches everyone, calculating behind that benevolent mask...

My instincts have kept me alive too long to ignore them now. And they're telling me this pompous shit is about as trustworthy as a starving wolf in a sheep pen.

"Drink?" A crystal flute appears under my nose, Baldr's fingers wrapped around the stem. The servant who delivered it melts back into the crowd like a ghost.

The drink sparkles like liquid diamonds, the scent of frosted cherries and something stronger tickling my nose. Sweet with a bite—like everything else in this realm. I take a swig, letting the bubbles dance on my tongue.

"Thank you." The words taste less bitter than expected, probably thanks to the drink.

Across the hall, a crowd swarms around Dani. Their excited chatter rises and falls, individual words lost in the general din of the celebration. My mate handles it like she was born to it, her laugh carrying over the noise.

"They're quite fascinated by her victory over the Einherjar." Baldr's voice slices through my thoughts. "Defeating them is quite the accomplishment, even for the prophesied savior."

Another sip of that sweet fire as my eyes sweep the room. Heimdall's impossible to miss—the giant stands like a mountain made of flesh beside a marble column, his ceremonial armor gleaming. Those unsettling green eyes never stop moving, watching, analyzing.

"Tell me, Rhyland." Baldr swirls his drink, the liquid catching the light. "The guardian's name—you never mentioned it."

"Vidar." The name drops like a stone between us. Across the room, Dani's laughter rings out again, drawing my gaze. She's radiant, holding court, while I'm stuck here playing twenty questions with Golden Boy.

"Ah, yes. Vidar." Baldr's eyes gleam with recognition. "Thor's right hand during the great war. They say his strength rivaled the AllFather himself—the silent god who could match Fenrir's fury blow for blow." He takes a measured sip of his drink. "When Ragnarök came, he fought until his last breath, taking down scores of Moretemis's shadow warriors before falling. His sacrifice bought precious time for the evacuation of the lower realm."

The prick actually shows a hint of genuine respect. "After his death, Odin himself chose Vidar to guard the Zephyrite stone. His spirit became one with the trials, testing those who would claim its power. A fitting role for one who died protecting the realm."

My jaw clenches at the reminder of what Dani faced. "And now he rests in Valhalla, having deemed her worthy."

"Indeed." Baldr's perfect features arrange themselves into something like admiration. "The silent god's final judgment. Quite poetic, don't you think?"

I grunt, downing the rest of my drink. Poetic isn't the word I'd use for watching my mate fight for her life, but these gods do love their fucking drama.

"Another drink?" Baldr's hand lifts, and a servant appears like he conjured her from thin air. He selects one, offering it to me. "From Odin's personal reserves. A thousand years of perfection."

I accept the glass and take a drink.

"Magni's son." A woman glides closer, her elaborate gown whispering across marble. Gold threads catch the light as she moves, matched by the lustfilled gleam in her eyes. "The lightning wielder. Commander of Dark Skies."

"Mm." I take a strategic sip of the sparkly liquid, gaze fixed on where Dani charms a group of warriors across the hall.

"Such power in your blood." She steps into my line of sight, blocking my view. "Tell me, grandson of Thor—how does it feel? Standing in the halls of your ancestors?"

"Fine." Another sip. Longer this time.

"Lady Sigrid asks a fascinating question." Baldr adds. "Surely you must feel *something*, walking these sacred halls. Your grandfather's legacy surrounds us."

Fucking perfect. Now I'm trapped between this Aesir woman and Ásgard's golden boy.

"The architecture's nice." I drain my glass, already planning escape routes.

"Oh, you simply *must* see the Great Hall's eastern wing then." Lady Sigrid's hand hovers near my arm. "The murals there depict Thor's greatest victories. Perhaps I could give you a... private tour?"

"Indeed." Baldr's smile widens. "Lady Sigrid is quite knowledgeable about our history. And given your connection to Thor's bloodline..."

I catch Dani's eye across the room. Her raised eyebrow says she's caught this whole clusterfuck—fuck me. Blood rushes south so fast I'm dizzy."Another time." I step back, already feeling Dani's concern pulse through our bond. "If you'll excuse me."

"But surely—" Lady Sigrid starts.

"My mate needs me."

I don't wait for a response, already moving toward Dani. Their voices fade behind me, but I catch Baldr's too-smooth laugh. "Ah, young love. So... consuming."

Each step closer reveals new tortures. Smoky shadow makes those honey-gold eyes burn brighter, and her glossed lips beg to be claimed. My hands itch to touch, to possess.

My arm snakes around her waist before I'm even conscious of moving, pulling her against me. The heat of her body soaks through the delicate fabric of her gown, making my beast purr.

"God damn...you're a fucking vision, baby." My voice drops to a growl as I clock another warrior's appreciative glance. "Though if one more person stares at what's mine, we might have a diplomatic incident on our hands."

Her laugh ripples through my chest, and *Christ*—that smirk. Those glossed lips curve up like she knows exactly what I'm thinking, what I want to do to that mouth. My tongue swipes across my bottom lip, already tasting her, already hungry for more.

My mind floods with images—her mouth wrapped around my cock, those perfect lips stretched wide, that wicked tongue working her magic. Want slams through me, the need to claim that mouth, to taste those lips, to fuck that pretty throat until she's hoarse from screaming my name. I swallow a growl, already desperate for a taste, already aching to make those sinful thoughts reality.

"Down, boy." Those beautiful eyes sparkle with mischief as she tilts her head back to meet my gaze. "Though I suppose I can't blame you for being territorial, considering Lady Sigrid was practically undressing you with her eyes."

My jaw clenches at the memory. "Noticed that, did you?"

"Hard to miss." Her fingers trace the silver threading on my chest. "Especially when Baldr kept parading you around like Ásgard's most eligible bachelor."

"Only bachelor I see is Baldr." I pull her closer, letting my scent wrap around her. "I'm spoken for. Marked. *Mated.*"

Her laugh sends heat straight to my cock. "Mmm, maybe we should remind Lady Sigrid of that fact?"

"You offering to help me make a point, Angel?" My hands slide lower, cupping that perfect ass through silk. "Because I've got some ideas about that."

She swats my chest, but I catch the spike in her arousal. "Behave yourself. A savior has duties, you know. Like charming the masses at parties thrown in our honor."

Her fingers trail up my chest. "Though I must say, watching you work this formal wear is *quite* the distraction."

Topaz earrings catch the light as she moves, drawing my gaze up that graceful neck. The sweetheart neckline of her dress does sinful things to me. My mouth waters at the sight, remembering exactly how those perfect breasts feel in my hands, taste on my tongue, bounce when I'm—fuck.

My cock twitches at the memory, and I have to shift my stance to adjust myself—watching those beautiful breasts strain against that delicate fabric is pure fucking torture.

Her hands slide up to cradle my jaw, fingertips threading through my freshly trimmed beard. The sensation immediately drawing a growl from deep in my chest.

"Angel." The warning rumbles from my chest as her fingers keep working their torture. My eyes flutter despite my best efforts to maintain control. My hands tighten on her waist, pulling her closer. "Keep touching me like that; these fine people might get quite the show."

That laugh hits me like lightning—all white teeth and wicked promises. Her nails rake through my beard, sending sparks straight to my pulsing dick. "Is that so?" Those eyes dance with mischief. "Because watching you squirm is kind of turning me on."

My answering growl has several nearby Aesir suddenly finding other places to be. Smart move on their part.

This woman.

"There are plenty of dark corners in this palace, baby. Care to test that theory?"

"Mmm, I bet you'd love that, wouldn't you?" Her fingers slip under my collar, nails scraping skin in a way that makes me want to act, audience be damned. "You getting all worked up with everyone watching?" She presses against me, those perfect tits crushed to my chest, and *hell*—I can feel her nipples through the thin fabric. "Too bad I've got this whole chosen one thing going on. Can't exactly bend me over the nearest table without scandalizing all these gods, now can you?"

"No, Angel, that's your fantasy." The words have the desired effect—that delicious blush spreads down her neck, making my fangs ache with the need to taste that heated skin, to mark every inch of that rosy flush with my mouth.

Sure, we fucked each other senseless last night, but my blood's already healed that delicious ache between her thighs. She knows damn well I can go for hours—days, that I can make her come again and again until she's begging me to stop. Seeing her now, wrapped in that fuck-me dress, it's taking every ounce of control not to bend her over the nearest surface and remind her precisely who makes her scream. Who makes her pussy clench. Who makes her beg for more.

Her arousal slams into me, sweet and hot—*fuck,* she's actually imagining it. My nostrils flare as that honeyed scent wraps around me, my cock weeping at the knowledge of exactly what's running through that dirty little mind of hers.

"Baby..." The warning in my voice only makes her grin wider.

"Although..." Her hand slides down my chest, painfully slow. "if you behave yourself for the rest of this fancy-ass party and later..." She bites her lip, and those eyes are pure sin. "I'll let you do whatever dirty things you've been thinking about since you saw me in this dress." she winks, *"anything."*

Holy fucking hell. My mind dives straight into the gutter—first thought? Her ass.

I'm ready to throw her over my shoulder and find the nearest empty room. But the challenge in those sparkly gold eyes keeps me planted. Fucking tease knows I can't resist a bet.

"You're going to regret that challenge, baby."

"Counting on it, RhyPie."

She slides from my grasp like smoke through my fingers, throwing one last molten look over her shoulder. That perfect ass sways beneath light blue chiffon as she glides away, my body hums with the need to chase her down. To grab those hips and—Jesus Christ.

My cock strains against the expensive fabric, demanding the attention it's not going to get. Not yet. Not with half of Ásgard's finest watching their precious savior work the room.

Her arousal hits me again, deliberate, like she's broadcasting exactly how wet she is. The image that floods my mind nearly brings me to my knees: that perfect ass up in the air, begging to be filled, her tight little dress hiked around her hips. Her pussy wet and dripping down her thighs, but it's that puckered hole that's calling to me, ready to be stretched around my cock. I can almost hear those desperate little whimpers she makes when she wants it in both holes, the way she begs so pretty when she needs to be filled completely.

Fucking shit. I shake my head, trying to clear it, but my beast is already straining against its chains, desperate to make that vision reality.

Christ. This isn't some fantasy I just conjured—she's beaming straight-up porn into my brain like it's nothing. Last time we tried this shit, I nearly passed out showing her Amara's torture dungeon memories. But my little firecracker? She's dropping these vivid, filthy fantasies into my head like they're fucking text messages.

My savage little mate's getting stronger by the minute; she knows how to use it to drive me insane. If she's already figured out how to weaponize this connection, I'm in deep fucking trouble.

She's across the room pretending to listen to some warrior's bullshit story, but those honey-gold eyes keep finding mine. That knowing look burns straight through me, and when her tongue slides across her bottom lip—fuck. She knows *exactly* what she's doing and images she just planted in my head. My fingers flex against my thighs, already imagining how that delicious ass will feel in my grip, how those lips will look wrapped around my cock.

Just wait, baby. When I get you alone, I'm going to make you pay for every single tease.

Game on, Angel.

ERIK

50

My gaze follows Rhyland as he gravitates toward Dani. Their bodies instinctively turn toward each other across the crowded feast hall. Their movement is like watching celestial bodies in perfect orbit—each step and gesture synchronized in an unconscious dance.

My fingers drum against the ornate goblet as I scan the room for the hundredth time, searching for a flash of platinum hair or the glint of mismatched eyes. Bryn's absence gnaws at me, each passing moment deepening the hollow ache in my chest.

The urge to seek her out claws at my insides, foreign and unsettling. This isn't me—I don't do uncertainty. I calculate, analyze, plan. But Bryn... she's thrown every carefully constructed strategy into chaos.

Is she hiding in their chambers, letting her thoughts of failure fester like a wound? The strategic part of my mind—the part that's gotten me through centuries of warfare and politics—is screaming to retreat, to accept defeat with dignity. But another voice sounds suspiciously like my brother's, urging me to fight.

The cave flashes through my mind—Bryn's body yielding to mine, her breath catching at my touch. The barn... gods, the barn. Her kiss had been wild, desperate, matching my passion with an intensity that still burns in my blood. Her body had come alive under my hands, betraying every denial her lips now speak.

I shift on my feet as memories assault me: Rhyland's determination when he first scented Dani, his relentless pursuit despite her resistance. How often had I watched my brother charge headlong into that battle, refusing to accept defeat?

Rhyland had fought for her and pursued her relentlessly until she accepted their bond. Perhaps that's what Bryn needs—not my careful strategy or measured approach, but raw, unrelenting pursuit.

My fingers tighten around the goblet. The thought of pushing her, breaking down her walls one by one until she acknowledges what blazes between us... it goes against every careful instinct I possess. And yet...

My jaw clenches. Perhaps it's time to take a page from my brother's book. After all, when has anything worth claiming ever come easily?

Movement on the grand staircase catches my eye, and my breath freezes in my lungs.

Bryn descends like a warrior goddess transformed. Her platinum hair cascades like moonlit silver, free from its warrior braids. The white silk gown hugs every curve, crystals on the bodice throwing rainbow light across her swollen breasts. My hands itch with the memory of their weight, how perfectly they'd fit my palms.

The goblet in my hand creaks dangerously as my grip tightens. I force myself to set it on a passing servant's tray before shattering the crystal.

I close the distance between us in long strides, my boots silent against the crystal steps. Bryn's eyes snap to mine, a flicker of something—surprise? Desire?—crossing her features before her warrior's mask slides back into place.

"Well," she drawls, eyeing my formal attire. "The stoic warrior knows how to dress for battle."

"You're one to talk," I manage, though my voice comes out rougher than intended. "You look..." Words fail me as I drink in the sight of her. "Georgeous."

A flush of color stains her cheeks for a heartbeat before she catches herself. I extend my arm, and her eyebrow arches in challenge.

"Playing protector again, Erik?" She says my name like honey over steel. "I've faced frost giants. I can handle stairs."

"The stairs might survive you, but your beauty is more lethal than Grave Warden tonight."

"Fífl," she mutters without heat.

"And what does that mean, little bird?"

"It means 'fool,' you silver-tongued rogue." She takes my arm. "Don't get ideas. I'm just here to support my sister."

"Of course," I murmur, savoring how her body unconsciously leans toward mine as we descend. "Heaven forbid anyone think the mighty Bryn capable of enjoying my company."

She snorts, but I catch the slight upturn of her lips. "Your silver tongue is as dangerous as your blade, Erik." Her fingers flex against my arm. "Though neither will win you what you seek."

"And what is it you think I seek?" I ask, guiding her past a cluster of watching Aesir.

Bryn turns those mesmerizing eyes to mine, challenge written in every line of her body. "You're playing a dangerous game." I feel her tense against me. "One you cannot win."

A smirk tugs at my lips. This isn't something she—or I—can deny much longer. The tension between us is undeniable.

The music swells, and I turn to her. "Dance with me?"

Bryn's eyes narrow playfully. "A warrior and a dancer, silfrhár? You're full of surprises."

"Silfrhár?" I repeat, letting the word roll off my tongue. "Another insult, perhaps?"

She places her hand in mine, her touch sending electricity through my veins. "Silver hair," she translates with a teasing lilt. "Though perhaps I should call you grimmr instead—the masked one. Always hiding behind that stoic facade."

I pull her close, closer than proper but not enough for scandal. "Only you see through my facade," I murmur. "Though I've had centuries to perfect my waltz."

"We'll see who leads whom," she challenges, moving with deadly grace.

She fits against me perfectly as we move across the floor, her warrior's body betraying every denial her lips speak. Each shiver and caught breath when I pull her closer tells its own truth.

The music draws us together, her silk dress whispering against me. Her scent of winter winds and starlight floods my senses, making my head spin. When my thumb traces circles on her lower back, her breath catches, those mismatched eyes darkening as they meet mine. For a moment, her warrior mask slips, revealing raw hunger underneath.

"Be careful, silfrhár," she warns, voice husky as her nails dig into my shoulder. "Your control is slipping."

Christ, how I want to kiss her. To taste those lips again, that smirk up at me with such defiance. To show her exactly how much my control has already fractured. But

I won't—can't—push her. Not here. Not yet. Even if every cell in my body screams to claim what's mine.

I spin her out, using the movement to put blessed space between us. But when she turns back into my arms, she's closer than before, her chest brushing against mine with each breath.

"My control?" I manage, voice rough as sand. "What about yours, little bird?"

Her pulse races beneath her skin, heat radiating between us as her pupils dilate, nearly swallowing the gold and blue of her irises.

"I don't know what you mean," she whispers unconvincingly, her gaze drops to my mouth for a fraction of a second before snapping back up.

Her fingers slide up my neck, sending heat through my veins. For a heartbeat, she leans in, her lips a whisper away from mine. The world narrows to this moment—the heat of her breath, the flutter of her lashes, the slight part of her lips.

But then she pulls back, reality crashing like a bucket of ice. Her hands drop from my shoulders as if burned, and she stumbles backward.

"I..." Her voice cracks, and she clears her throat. "Tell my sister I'm not feeling well." The warrior mask slips back into place, but her hands tremble slightly as she smooths her dress. "I'm retiring for the evening."

Before I can respond, she turns and practically flees toward the stairs, her white dress a beacon in the dim light. She doesn't look back, but the rigid set of her shoulders tells me everything—she's running from this, from us.

Fuck this. I know what I saw—what I felt.

My feet move before my mind catches up, carrying me after her retreating form. Her dress whispers against the crystal stairs as she practically runs, stumbling once in haste. I unleash my vampire speed the moment she rounds the corner at the landing, materializing before her.

She jerks back with a gasp, eyes flashing. "Don't pull that vampire shit with me." The words come out breathless as she sidesteps around me, her skirts brushing my legs.

I let her get as far as her chamber door, watch her fingers close around the handle. Then I'm behind her, pressing her against the solid wood, letting her feel every hard line of my body. My arms snake around her waist, pulling her flush against me.

A groan tears from her throat, and the scent of her arousal floods my senses. Her head falls back against my shoulder, even as her fingers tighten on the door handle like it's the only thing keeping her upright.

My lips brush the column of her throat, feeling her pulse thunder beneath the delicate skin. "Why fight this?" The words ghost across her flesh, drawing a shiver from her body. "This pull between us..." I drag my teeth—not fangs, not yet—along the sensitive spot below her ear. "It's consuming me, Bryn."

Her fingers clutch the door handle like an anchor, her knuckles white with tension. But she doesn't pull away. Instead, she arches into me, her body betraying what her pride won't admit.

"Erik..." My name falls from her lips like a prayer and a curse combined. "We can't—"

I silence her protest by nipping at her earlobe, drawing a gasp that shoots straight to my groin. "Can't what?" My hands slide up her ribs, ghosting just beneath the swell of her breasts. "Can't give in to what we both know is inevitable?"

She spins in my arms, her back hitting the door with a soft thud. Those mystical eyes burn with desire and defiance, setting my blood on fire. "Nothing is inevitable," she growls, but her hands fist in my shirt, pulling me closer as she protests.

Our breaths mingle in the scant space between us, every exhale charged with electricity. One move, that's all it would take. One slight tilt of my head and I could claim those lips that have haunted my dreams.

"Why would you want me? After everything, I'm nothing—"

I crush my mouth to hers, swallowing her gasp of surprise. The kiss is nothing like our first—this is raw hunger, of denial igniting like wildfire. Her lips part beneath mine, and the taste of her—honey mead and storm clouds—obliterates my self-control.

We stumble through the doorway, tangled with desperate hands and hungry mouths. The door slams behind us with enough force to rattle the hinges, but I barely notice. Not when Bryn's nails rake down my back, or when she's making those little sounds in her throat that drive me wild.

"I'm done listening to you tear yourself apart. You are everything, Bryn. Why can't you see that?"

"Erik," she moans against my lips as I pin her to the wall. Her leg hooks around my hip, drawing me closer. The silk of her dress rustles between us, too many layers separating skin from skin. "I can't—I've tried so hard to fight this—"

I claim her mouth deeper, hungrier, and her answering tug on my hair draws a growl from my throat. Something snaps in her at the sound—the last thread of resistance finally breaking.

She molds against me, all soft curves and desperate need. Her arousal fills my senses, making my fangs ache. When I roll my hips against hers, she breaks the kiss with a cry.

"Stop fighting this, little bird," I growl against her lips before claiming them again, my tongue demanding entry. She matches me stroke for stroke, pulling me closer.

"But..." she breathes.

I tangle my fingers in her hair, tilting her head back to devour her mouth properly. She meets my passion with equal force, fisting my shirt to pull me closer. When her hips rock against mine, seeking friction, a groan rumbles through my chest. These clothes between us—they're too much and not enough.

My lips trail down her throat, feeling her pulse race beneath my touch. I pause at her gown's neckline, meeting her heated gaze with silent question.

"Don't stop," she whispers roughly. "I want this. I want you."

I tear at her bodice, needing to see her, taste her. When her breasts spill free—rosy-tipped nipples, tight, perfect—my brain short-circuits. But seeing isn't enough. I capture one nipple with my mouth, sucking and licking until she's writhing. Her moans drive me wild as I switch to the other breast, worshipping it with equal devotion.

"I need you naked." The words come out as a desperate grunt.

I untie her dress, letting the silk whisper down her body until it pools at her feet. She stands naked before me, all graceful lines and lush curves. My gaze devours every inch—from her delicate collarbones to the toned planes of her stomach.

Goosebumps rise on her skin under my heated stare. I step closer, curving my hand around her neck, fingers tangling in her hair.

"Mine," I growl before claiming her mouth. Our tongues battle for dominance as her nails rake down my back, marking me as hers.

I lift her, and her legs lock around my waist as I carry her to the bed. We fall together, my hands exploring every inch of skin I've been denied for so long. Her heat brands me through my leathers as I taste her throat, her collarbones, her breasts.

"Off," she commands, fingers flying to my belt.

I tear away my clothes—jacket, shirt—revealing tattooed skin. Her hands slip beneath my waistband, sending heat through my veins.

Her eyes lock onto my exposed length, and a strangled sound escapes her throat. "That's... not what I expected."

"Oh?" I grin wickedly. "Something less impressive?"

"Honestly? Yeah."

I pounce, pinning her wrists above her head. "Is that so?" My hips grind down, letting her feel every inch. "Pray tell, what about me screams 'small cock' to you?"

"Well..." Her eyes dance with wicked humor even as she arches beneath me. "You're always so... controlled. Measured. Figured that extended to everything."

"Disappointed?" I roll my hips, drawing a gasp.

"Hardly." She hooks her leg around my waist. "Though I might need convincing about your... control."

"Careful what you wish for." My teeth scrape her pulse. "Want to see what happens when I let go?"

"Big talk for someone who's all..." Her words cut off on a moan as I suck her nipple into my mouth. "...show and no action."

"No action?" I growl against her breast, releasing her wrists to slide my hand between us. "Let's see how mouthy you are when I'm done with you."

"That a promise or a—" Her sass dissolves into a whimper as my fingers find their target. "Oh fuck..."

"What was that about no action?" I smirk against her skin, circling slowly. "You were saying something clever?"

"Just shut up, Erik," Bryn growls, lips curved in that haughty smile that makes my blood sing. Challenge glints in her eyes, blue and gold flames. Oh, the lady wants a battle? I can play that game.

My cock throbs, aching to claim her, but first, I need a taste. I want to hear her melt beneath my mouth, feel her heat around my tongue. I trail kisses down the canvas of her stomach, the muscles jumping beneath my lips until I reach the heart of her.

Her skin tastes of winter winds and wild thunderstorms, her unique flavor alone. The heady musk of her arousal fills my senses, clouding my mind with one singular need.

"Wait," she gasps. "What are you doing?"

"Going to devour you, little bird."

"You mean... bite me? There?"

A bark of laughter escapes me. Gods, the thought of sinking my fangs into that tender flesh. But no, not yet. "No, I won't bite you... unless you want me to." The idea sends a pulse of hot need straight to my cock. "But right now, I plan to feast on you with my mouth—my tongue, taste every inch of you until you scream my name."

Her eyes widen, uncertainty replacing the fierce confidence I've come to know. A blush stains her cheeks as she whispers, "I've never... no one has ever..."

The admission hits me, my beast roaring with possessive pride. That no other man has tasted her this way, that I'll be the first to worship her like this.

"Lay back," I murmur against her thigh. "Trust me. Let me show you pleasure you've never known."

She obeys, pupils blown wide, legs falling open in invitation. I start with soft kisses along her thighs, working closer to her center. Each press of my lips draws shivers and moans.

When I find her clit, she bucks wildly. I hold her still, latching onto that sensitive bud until she's writhing.

"Erik... *gods,* what are you—" She thrashes, head falling back. "That feels ....ohhh...don't stop. *Please!*"

Like I could ever find the will to stop now. My cock aches with need, but this—tasting her, hearing her pleas—it's what I've yearned for. Her sweet juices coat my tongue, driving me to the edge of madness.

She tastes like a heady mix of tart berries and wildflower honey—an exquisite nectar that makes me crazy.

I slip two fingers inside her, curling them making her cry out. Her inner walls clench around me, milking my fingers as I thrust gently in tandem with my oral assault on her clit.

I add a third finger, scissoring them as I suck her clit and swirl my tongue.

"Erik! Oh...fuuu....*yes!*" She bucks against my mouth, her legs locking around my head as she fractures apart with pleasure. Her plea breaks into a cry as my lips close around her clit, my tongue swirling. The first ripple of her orgasm sends a flood of hot nectar to my tongue, and I growl—needing more—needing it all.

She rides the wave, her body shuddering, the sweetest music to my starved senses. And still, I drink, her essence filling me like a heady drug. My name falls from her lips in a litany, a benediction, claiming every part of me as hers.

But I'm far from done.

I kiss my way up her body, savoring her flushed skin and dazed eyes. "That.." catching her breath, she whispers, gripping my face. "That was..."

"Was what?" I smile against her belly, kissing her skin.

"Amazing. Mind-blowing." She bites her lip. "The best."

A feral spark ignites in my eyes, possessiveness and pride intertwined. "That's a challenge I can't resist." I grip her leg, wrapping it around my hip as I tease her slick center with the blunt head of my cock. Her sharp inhale sends a thrill through me. "I'm going to ruin you for anyone else," I warn, and in one swift move, I sheath myself within. Our moans become a symphony, each breath a harmony of hunger and satisfaction. "Fuck, you feel..."

Words fail me as her inner muscles grip me tight. Every nerve ending ignites, my breath shortening. It's been too long since I felt a woman's touch, too long since I let myself surrender to pleasure. But with Bryn, I have no defenses, no control.

And when she tightens around me, I know I won't last long.

"Gods." Her eyes widen as she takes in my length. "You're *enormous*—

The words send a surge of possessive pride through me. Her reaction tells me no other man has filled her like this, satisfied her so completely. The beast in me roars with satisfaction, knowing I'll be the one to show her true pleasure.

I curl my hand around the back of her neck, fingers tangling in her hair, exposing the delicate column of her throat. My fangs ache to claim her, but I hold back, needing to hear those words of surrender.

"Feeling full, little one?" I purr against her ear, I flex my hips, drawing a gasp from her.

The muscles of her thighs quiver as I thrust deep. Her soft moans fire my need, each roll of her hips tightening the coil in my gut. Her soft mewls and whispered curses wind me tighter, stoking the fire in my veins.

"Yes. Please. More," she pants, her nails digging into my shoulders. "Harder..."

Her plea snaps the last thread of my restraint. With a growl, I lift her from the bed, using my body to pin her against the wall. Her legs wrap around my waist as I thrust up into her, her hair still imprisoned in my fist.

"Ohhh *gods,*" she breathes, her head falling back, baring her neck to my mouth. "Right there."

"I'm not god, little one." I tug her hair, forcing her to meet my gaze. "Say my name, Bryn. Scream it when I'm buried deep inside you."

Her eyes flash with defiance, a spark that ignites something within me. Without breaking our stare, I crush my lips, devouring her mouth with the same relentless rhythm I plan to use to take her body. My hips snap forward, burying myself to the hilt in her silky heat.

I drive into her with primal intensity, one hand guiding her hips as she meets each thrust. "Come for me, little bird," I command against her throat. "Let me feel you."

Her fingers tangle in my hair as she claims my mouth, our kiss a clash of teeth and tongues. Her inner walls tighten, telling me she's close. Just a little more...

I grip her thigh, lifting her higher, and thrust with punishing force. Her back arches, her nails digging into my shoulder, as a tremor racks her body. "Yes, yes...Erik!" she pants, breathless. "I'm...fuck."

A few more strokes, and she's splintering around me, screaming my name, her release drenching me in pleasure.

Her climax rips through her like wildfire, inner walls clenching around me in a vice grip that destroys my last shred of control. My fangs descend as I throw my head back, a primal roar tearing from my chest. Stars explode behind my eyes as I empty myself deep inside her, each pulse drawing another growl from my throat. Her name becomes a prayer on my lips as we ride the wave together, our bodies trembling in perfect sync.

Still trembling from the aftershocks, I ease her down from the wall, cradling her against my chest. I lay her on the bed, her platinum hair creating a silvery halo around her flushed face.

"You okay?" I kiss against her temple, tasting the salt of her skin.

"Mmm." Her laugh is lazy, satisfied. "Better than okay." Her fingers trace idle patterns on my chest. "Though I think you broke me."

I can't help but smirk against her skin. "I haven't even begun to break you."

She pinches my side, but there's no heat in it. "Careful, vampire. Your ego's showing."

"Among other things," I murmur, rolling her beneath me again, drinking in the sight of her sprawled beneath me, thoroughly claimed and utterly magnificent.

Her fingers trace my tattoos before settling over my heart. She swallows hard. "So... about this mate thing." Her tone is direct, but I catch the undercurrent of uncertainty.

"Bryn—" Her name sticks in my throat as I search those beautiful eyes.

She meets my gaze unflinching, though her body betrays her tension. Her hands press against my chest, and I let her push away. Rising like a warrior preparing for battle, she turns. "I don't know how this will work, Erik." Her voice is steady, but her warrior's mask cracks, showing the uncertainty beneath.

"We need to talk about this." I reach for her, but she slips away, wrapping her robe around herself like armor.

"I need time to think." She stands straighter, her voice firm despite the slight tremor. "We have a long journey tomorrow and need rest."

I open my mouth to protest, but the set of her jaw stops me. I know that look—I've seen it on the battlefield before she charges into the fray.

"Of course." I force the words out, every instinct screaming at me to fight for her, for us. But I know pushing her now will only make her retreat further. "I'll see myself out."

She nods, a quick jerk of her chin. "Goodnight, Erik."

The finality in her tone hits like a Templar's oath. I dress quickly, each layer of clothing a piece of my own armor sliding back into place. At the door, I pause, looking back at her. "This isn't over, Bryn."

Her lips twitch, but whether it's a smile or a grimace, I can't tell. "Goodnight, Erik," she repeats, a clear dismissal.

The soft click of the door closing behind me echoes in the silence of the hall.

LUCIAN

51

The gothic monstrosity looms ahead like Dracula's McMansion got busy with a haunted cathedral. Welcome to Casa de Crazy, formerly known as Azrael's House of Horrors, under new management by Hell's Favorite Bitch.

I half expect to see bats circling the towers and hear organ music echoing from the depths. Seeing it makes my insides twist like a pretzel, memories of this place souring on the back of my tongue.

Seraphina's in there. My angel cake. So close and yet so fucking far.

We're armed to the fangs for this little soirée. I dusted off the old masquerade stash—because if you're going to infiltrate a psychotic vampire's party, you might as well look damn good doing it. Brax is wearing Rhyland's mask, and I've got to say, the sight of not-my-brother wearing my brother's face is enough to make my head spin.

Identity crisis, party of one.

Emily and Sable came through with the fake Soul Stone, a dead ringer for Azrael's old bling.

But the real showstopper? Shadow's Grasp. We're all packing a syringe of that sweet, sweet oblivion juice.

Because when you're crashing the party of the century, you come prepared.

Considering it's Lilith we're up against, we might need the entire fucking pharmacy of Shadow's Grasp to put her ass down.

And you know what? I'm actually hoping we do. Because watching Queen Bitch Supreme convulse while that magical roofie hits her system? That's the kind of entertainment you can't buy tickets for.

Emily gave me the crash course on this magical cocktail earlier—apparently, it turns vampire strength into vampire jelly. Watching Lilith's super-powered ass get knocked down a few pegs? *Chef's kiss.* Worth every drop of that witchy brew.

Can't wait to see how that poison cocktail pairs with her blood type. Bet it goes great with her bitchy personality.

"All right, kiddies—showtime!" I adjust my mask, scanning our little band of misfits. "Brax, just channel your inner douchebag. Trust me—nothing says 'Rhyland' like being a Grade-A asshole with a side of brooding."

Emily tugs at the edges of Dani's borrowed dress, her gold mask catching the moonlight, "For the last time, Dracula, I *know* my part. Go to the room we found on the map, set up shop, and turn it into Witch's Kitchen: Binding Spell Edition."

"The full moon's energy will amplify the spell," Sable adds, helpfully, looking like some fairytale princess gone rogue in her pink dress and gilded mask "Should give it enough juice to hold even Lilith."

The bond in my chest pulses like an open wound. Phina's close—so fucking close I can taste it. But that bitch Morgan has got her doped up on whatever mystical roofie she used on Dani—I can feel the fuzzy edges of Phina's consciousness through our connection.

"I'll handle Morgan." My fangs ache just thinking about it. "Just need to get that necromancing nightmare to look me in the eyes."

The ballroom sprawls before us like some twisted vampire's version of the Met Gala. Crystal chandeliers drip from the ceiling, casting prismatic light across a sea of masked faces. The air practically vibrates with supernatural energy—and the unmistakable scent of way too many vampires trying to out-design each other.

Welcome to Hell's Fashion Week, where the drinks are blood-red and everyone is dressed to kill—literally.

My eyes scan the crowd, picking through the kaleidoscope of masks and evening wear. There is no sign of my Cupcake, and I don't see Lilith's psychotic ass either. It is an endless parade of immortals playing dress-up while my chest aches with every beat of the bond.

Where are you hiding her, you couture-obsessed demon?

The string quartet in the corner strikes up something classical and pretentious, because *of course* Lilith wouldn't settle for a DJ. Not fancy enough for her blood-sucking debutante ball.

Emily catches my eye across the crowd, giving me that subtle "don't-fuck-this-up" nod before she melts into the throng of party-goers. Sable trails after her like a pink shadow, keeping just enough distance not to draw attention.

Look at you, witches, being all stealthy.

Not-Rhyland looms beside me, radiating enough brooding energy to make Edward Cullen look cheerful. A waiter materializes with a tray of champagne flutes—the contents are not your standard Dom Pérignon unless they've started adding O-negative to their blend.

I snag two glasses and push one at Brax. His face twists into that signature Rhyland look of disapproval—like someone just suggested putting pineapple on pizza.

"Drink the damn champagne," I mutter through clenched teeth. "My brother wouldn't be caught dead—pun intended—turning down free booze. Even the pretentious blood-spiked kind."

The champagne barely touches my lips when a voice like nails on a chalkboard slithers behind us. "Well, well, well. If it isn't my favorite brooding boy-toy." Lilith's gaze rakes over not-Rhyland like he's a piece of meat. "And here of your own accord, for once. How novel." Her laugh could cut glass. "Oh wait, my mistake. Still playing the self-sacrificing hero, aren't we? Old habits die hard, I suppose."

I have to physically restrain myself from jamming my champagne flute down her smug throat. *Bitch.*

Subtle reminder about how my brother traded himself to save my ass. Real classy, you ugly bitch.

Lilith dressed in some emerald-wrapped nightmare, her gown catching light like scattered venom. Those electric-green eyes pierce through her black mask, locked on Not-Rhyland with predatory intensity. "Miss me, lover?"

Brax's shoulders stiffen, his voice dropping to a low growl that's pure alpha male. "I'm not here to play your twisted games, Lilith. We have a deal, remember?"

Lilith's smile is all razor blades and venom. "Oh, you mean Lucian's little angel toy?" She tsks, running a finger down Brax's lapel, looking at me. "Really, darling, I thought you had better taste than some feathered bimbo."

I nearly crush the champagne flute in my hand. *Keep talking, you cunt. We'll see who's laughing when this night is over.*

Lilith's venomous gaze slides back to Brax, her blood-red lips curling into a cruel smile. "Speaking of heavenly creatures..." She makes a show of scanning the room, with mock concern. "Where's your little mortal pet? The one I so enjoyed... entertaining."

Not-Rhyland's shoulders bunch with tension, his growl pure Viking rage. *Holy shit, Brax is channeling my brother's protective alpha male routine perfectly.* "You really think I'm stupid enough to bring her anywhere near you?"

"Mmm." Lilith traces a perfectly manicured nail down his lapel, her eyes glittering with malice. "Can't be that attached if you're willing to trade yourself away so easily." Her tongue traces her lower lip. "Miss our little... encounters, darling?"

I swear to god, if she doesn't stop eye-fucking my not-brother, I'm going to hurl up every drop of blood I've consumed this century.

"Like a stake to the heart," Brax seethes. His voice drops to that dangerous register Rhyland gets right before breaking things. "Let's skip the foreplay. Me for Seraphina. That was the deal."

Holy shit. Who knew demons could method act? I'm starting to get uncanny valley vibes. The sneer, the growl, even that signature "I'd-rather-be-stabbing-someone" stance—it's like watching Rhyland's greatest hits performed live.

Lilith laughs. "Always so... direct. That's what I love most about you, darling. That raw... intensity." She groans. "Especially in more... intimate settings."

Oh god, someone fetch me a bucket. Bile burns the back of my throat. "Where's Seraphina?" I snap, done playing her twisted game of Twenty Questions.

"Patience, darling." She waves a dismissive hand, never taking those venomous eyes off Not-Rhyland. "The night's young. Surely you remember our dances, lover? How about a little... warm-up?"

If I survive this night without projectile vomiting, it'll be a miracle.

Brax shoots me a look, and I give him a barely perceptible nod.

Time to play along.

I watch Lilith lead him onto the dance floor, her emerald dress clinging to her like a second skin. They move together like a pair of vipers, all sleek grace and coiled danger. Brax's hand rests on her lower back, his fingers digging in just a little too hard to be friendly.

That's it, buddy. Sell the hate-fuck tension. Make her believe it.

I weave through the crowd like a shark circling its prey, keeping one eye on Lilith and her demon dance partner.

Now, where are you hiding, Morgan? Come out, come out, wherever you are, you necromancing nightmare.

From the landing, I catch Brax's eye. One subtle nod is all it takes—our signal to start the show. *T-minus ten minutes until this party gets started.*

The back room is exactly where we planned—far enough from the crowd to avoid unwanted attention, close enough to spring our trap. Emily and Sable are already there, the air thick with magic that makes my fangs itch.

"We set?" I keep my voice low, though honestly, the pretentious classical crap downstairs is loud enough to cover a demon choir.

Emily doesn't even look up from her work. "All ready for our guest of horror. Full moon's giving us enough juice to hold Cruella De Vil herself."

"What about Morgan? Can't you wave your hands and locate her witchy ass?"

Emily's glare could freeze hellfire. "For the last time, you bloodsucking moron, magic doesn't work like your Netflix shows." She pinches the bridge of her nose. "Though I can try a detection spell."

"In English, please?"

"Think supernatural GPS, you fanged disaster." Magic snaps around her like static electricity. "It'll ping any magical signatures in range."

"Fine. Do your magical sonar thing. The last thing we need is that bitch showing up uninvited to our little party."

The bond flutters in my chest like a wounded bird, pulling me downward. *Below us.* Of course she'd have her in Azrael hell hole.

Emily's eyes are closed, and her lips move in a silent chant that makes the air taste like ozone. The minutes drag by like years until her eyes snap open, glowing with residual power.

"Basement level," she confirms, her voice tight. "And I'm picking up some serious dark magic down there."

Ah yes, the lovely remnants of Azrael's glory days. Back when this basement was his soul-trafficking hub. That sadistic bastard used to lock people in cages down there, feeding their souls to Moretemis like he was running some demonic drive-through.

Lilith's heels click against the marble stairs like a death knell. I flash a quick hand signal, and Emily and Sable vanish down the hall, slipping into their hiding spot like shadows.

Brax guides the Prada, Piece of Shit right to me, her emerald dress swishing with each calculated step. A predatory smile on her ugly fucking face "Well, isn't this cozy?"

I bare my fangs in what might pass for a smile. "Bitches first." I sweep my arm toward the room with exaggerated flourish, like some demented maître d'. "After all, we're here to make a deal, right?"

Come on, you psychotic cum-stain. Step right into our trap.

"Lucian, darling, you're not trying to pull a fast one, are you? We both know subtlety isn't exactly your strong suit."

My fangs ache with the urge to rip her throat out. "Cut the shit, Lilith. I'm here for one thing—Seraphina. Hand her over, and you'll get your precious prize."

She examines her blood-red nails, boredom etched into every perfect feature. "Speaking of my prize, where's the other half of the stone? This all seems a bit too... convenient. Do you think I'm that gullible?"

I spread my arms wide, flashing my signature smartass grin. "Step into my office, princess. Let's negotiate like the civilized immortal assholes we pretend to be."

Before I lose what's left of my already threadbare patience.

Not-Rhyland's grip tightens on Lilith's arm, his growl low and menacing. "Enough games. Get your ass in there before I throw you in myself."

Lilith's eyes sparkle with perverse delight. "Mmm, there's that alpha male charm I adore. So forceful, so... demanding."

I think I just threw up in my mouth a little.

Brax hurls Lilith through the doorway like yesterday's trash. Her Louboutins screech against hardwood as she stumbles, and I move faster than thought. The syringe finding her neck with pinpoint precision and I slam the plunger home before she can react.

Big mistake.

Her shriek of rage shatters my eardrums as she whirls, moving faster than any drugged vampire has a right to. Her claws rake the air where my face was a millisecond ago. The scent of her fury fills the room—expensive perfume mixed with ancient vampire blood.

Then her body slams into mine.

Holy mother of—

The impact drives me into the floor like a fucking meteor. Every bone in my body screams as my skull bounces off hardwood. Black spots dance in my vision, and I'm pretty sure I just felt at least three ribs crack. Her weight pins me down, those murderous eyes boring into mine.

Brax materializes behind Lilith, moving with a speed that would make The Flash jealous. The syringe glints in his hand like a tiny silver sword, plunging into her neck.

Lilith screeches like a banshee on steroids, her heels scraping against the floor as she whirls to face her attacker. But the toxin is already flooding her system, turning her movements sluggish and uncoordinated.

Those killer stilettos that could normally eviscerate a man's heart now scrabble uselessly against hardwood, seeking purchase that isn't there. Her body sways drunkenly, her emerald eyes, usually sharp, cloud over.

"You... treacherous..." The words fall from her blood-red lips like dying leaves. Her body sways—then she crumples, folding in on herself like a broken marionette. Her precious mask skitters across the floor, a final insult to her infamous vanity.

Nighty night, bitch.

"Now that's what I call supernatural synchronized swimming." I flash Brax a fanged grin, but he just stares at me like I'm speaking Klingon. *Tough crowd. Apparently demons don't appreciate quality pop culture references.*

Two syringes of witch-brew to knock her out. *Impressive.* Though how long this magical roofie will keep her ass down is anyone's guess. Ancient vampires aren't exactly covered in Emily's witchy manual.

Emily bursts through the doorway. "What now?"

I yank my custom Glock from its holster, loaded with special wooden rounds. The grip feels cold against my palm as I press it into Brax's waiting hand.

"Keep Sleeping Ugly here nice and docile." My fangs itch with the need to end this once and for all. "If she so much as twitches, put a round in her kneecaps. But keep her dead ass alive—we still need that other half of the Soul Stone."

Brax's fingers wrap around the gun with practiced ease, the metal clicking ominously as he chambers a round. His borrowed face—Rhyland's face—twists into a predatory grin that would make our resident Viking proud.

The bond trembles in my chest, weak and fading.

"Luc...ian..."

Phina's voice barely whispers through our connection, each syllable drenched in pain. The echo of her suffering tears through my heart like barbed wire. She's reaching for me with whatever strength she has left.

The connection pulses downward, a failing beacon in the darkness. "Emily," my voice comes out rough, all traces of humor stripped away. "You're with me. Sable, stay with Brax." My fangs elongate. "Time to collect what this bitch took from me."

I blast through the crowd like a bullet, scattering champagne flutes and immortal socialites in my wake. The basement entrance gapes before us—a familiar mouth of darkness that still haunts my nightmares. These tunnels are etched into my memory like scars, every cursed corner a reminder of darker days.

"Jesus Christ," Emily pants behind me, her heels clicking frantically to keep pace. "What kind of psycho builds a dungeon under their mansion?"

The kind that makes Hannibal Lecter look like a amateur, I think, but the words stick in my throat. The bond's getting weaker with every step, and there's no time for a history lesson about Azrael's house of horrors.

The temperature drops as I descend, the air growing thick with the stench of old blood and darker magic. Azrael's legacy seeps from these stone walls like poison. The golden thread of our bond flickers weakly in my chest, growing fainter with each step—like someone's slowly smothering a flame.

Hold on, angel face. Just hold on.

The passage opens into the cavern—that massive underground chamber where Azrael conducted his worst atrocities. We round the final corner, following that weakening pulse of our bond, and—

My legs give out. The world tilts sideways as my knees crack against stone. My lungs forget how to work, throat closing around a scream that won't come.

No.

My world fractures, reality splintering like a broken mirror. The scene before me carves itself into my retinas, a nightmare made flesh that tears my sanity to shreds.

"Dear God..." Emily's horrified whisper barely registers through the roaring in my ears. My mind short-circuits, refusing to process what my eyes are seeing.

No. No. No. Not like this. Not her.

DANICA

52

"So, Lightborn..." The warrior before me strokes his beard, his eyes gleaming with curiosity. "The guardian—Vidar—how did you manage to best such a legendary fighter?"

I suppress a sigh. If I had a gold piece for every time someone's asked about the trial tonight, I could buy my own realm.

"Strategy over strength," I say smoothly, smiling diplomatically. The truth—that both Rhyland and I nearly met our end at Vidar's hands—stays locked behind my teeth—no need to give these warriors more gossip fodder.

A horn blast cuts through the chatter, announcing dinner.

Thank God for small mercies.

My eyes scan the crowded hall for Bryn, coming up empty. She'd sworn she wasn't leaving our chambers tonight, convinced her presence would somehow overshadow me tonight. I'd tried to tell her how ridiculous that was, but you can't force someone to see their own worth. Yet I'd spotted her earlier, twirling in Erik's arms, her face glowing with something that looked suspiciously like joy. Erik had looked... well, as close to happy as Mr. Stoic ever gets.

Now they're both missing from the festivities. Either they've finally stopped fighting fate and given in to what everyone else can see plain as day, or... they're back to their usual dance of denial, and Erik's somewhere trying to drink himself into oblivion.

Knowing those two stubborn souls, it could go either way.

A strong arm snakes around my waist, pulling me back against a wall of solid muscle. Rhyland's presence engulfs me, his sandalwood and ocean scent making my head spin. I can feel the tension radiating off him in waves—the delicious result of the explicit little mind-movies I've been sending his way all evening while playing nice with the Aesir.

I never expected sharing thoughts would come so easily. This new ability came as naturally as breathing. After he'd shared that brutal memory with me, back in Luminara, I figured it was my turn to experiment. The first fantasy hit him like a lightning bolt—I had to bite my lip to keep from laughing at his reaction.

Besides, I threw down the gauntlet—can't make winning this little game too easy for him. That's not how we work. We push, we tease, we challenge. It's our dance, and damn if I don't love every step.

"Having fun, Angel?" His grip tightens possessively, his voice a deep sexy rumble against my ear.

I blink up at him innocently. "Oh, absolutely. Nothing better than recounting our near-death experience to everyone in attendance." I roll my eyes. "Though I must say, each telling gets more dramatic. By midnight, I'll probably have single-handedly defeated an army of guardians while juggling fireballs."

His fingers dig into my hip, a silent warning that sends heat pooling low in my belly.

"You know damn well what I mean." His voice drops to that dangerous growl that makes my toes curl. "Since when did you become a master at mind-fucking?"

I bat my eyelashes at him, channeling my inner Elle Woods. "What, like it's hard?"

A sound rumbles through his chest, half growl, half groan. "Food. Now. And stop broadcasting porn into my head before I bend you over this table, witnesses be damned."

I roll my hips back, a slow, deliberate grind against the impressive bulge straining his formal wear. "Having concentration issues?" I peek over my shoulder, catching his darkened gaze. "Funny, I don't recall any rules." I wiggle against him again, delighting in his sharp intake of breath. "I must have missed that part of our arrangement. But if it's proving too... *hard* for you to maintain control..."

His grip turns bruising, his cock twitching against my ass as the crowd flows around us toward the feast hall. "Fucking hell, Angel." His voice is pure gravel against my ear. "How am I supposed to keep my hands to myself when you're flooding my mind with every filthy thing you want me to do to you?"

The scorching heat of his erection burns through my dress, sending electricity straight to my already wet core. Feeling him hard and aching, knowing I did this to him—it's intoxicating. Like a drug I can't get enough of. Every twitch of his cock, every growl rumbling through his chest, every flex of those big hands on my hips—it's all because of me.

And god, do I love having this over him, making this powerful man lose control, and watching him fight against his baser instincts. It's the same rush he gets when he has me writhing beneath him, begging for release. Now it's my turn to make him squirm and burn with need.

"Just a few more hours." I flash him an innocent smile, but my mind broadcasts something far more wicked—me on my knees, looking up at him through my lashes as his colossal cock, stretches my throat, as I take him deep.

The sound that rips from his chest is pure predator. "Dani, I fucking swear—"

"Oh hey, speaking of hot and bothered..." I quickly redirect, scanning the crowded hall. "Have you seen your broody brother with my sister? Because I definitely caught them earlier looking way too cozy on the dance floor."

He presses against my back, his thick erection grinding against my ass as his lips brush my ear. "Nice try deflecting, Angel. But if you're so interested—they're upstairs finally dealing with all that sexual tension. Now, about those little mind games you've been playing..."

Relief floods me knowing they're finally giving in to fate's plan. But I can't let my Viking see me sweat—not when his cock is granite-hard against me and he's seconds from going full caveman.

"Oh look, dinner time," I chirp with fake brightness, tugging his hulking frame behind me toward the feast hall.

We follow the crowd, where a massive table stretches endlessly. The aroma of honey-glazed meats, fresh-baked breads, and spiced mead makes my mouth water. Roasted boar glistens under golden light, surrounded by mountains of herb-crusted potatoes and jewel-toned fruits I've never seen before.

Hell yeah. Time to stuff my face.

I take one step toward our seats when the world suddenly blurs—my back hits cold stone, trapped between a wall and six-feet-plus of horny Viking. The sounds of laughter and clinking glasses fade to a distant echo, replaced by Rhyland's ragged breathing against my neck.

My back still tingles from the impact, my heart racing at his supernatural speed. His sexy body cages me against the wall, those tattooed hands bracketing my head.

His tongue traces a hot path up my neck, making my knees weak. "Game's over, Angel." That gravelly voice is pure sin against my skin. "You've been begging for my cock all night with those pretty little fantasies." His hand fists in my hair, tilting my head back. "Time to put that wicked mouth to work. Right here. Right now."

The deep tone in his voice shoots straight between my legs, making me throb with need. My breath catches as his teeth graze my pulse point—a dangerous reminder of exactly who I've been teasing all night.

Maybe I pushed too far. Or perhaps this is precisely where I wanted to end up.

My gaze sweeps the abandoned landing, where ancient murals depict Thor's legendary victories. Candlelight flickers across stone walls, casting shadows that dance over Rhyland's sharp features. His eyes have gone midnight black, pupils dilated with primal need as he looms over me.

"H-here?" The word comes out as a breathless whisper. Public sex has always been this fantasy of mine, but I know Rhyland's still grappling with the idea. Yet right now, with the way he's looking at me like he wants to devour me whole, I don't think he gives a single fuck about propriety.

"Right. Here." Each word is a dangerous growl against my skin. From earlier, the proper, controlled man is gone, replaced by something far more serious. My little mental game has stripped away his restraint, leaving nothing but raw need.

A whimper escapes my throat as his body presses me harder against the wall. The stone is cold against my back, but his body burns like fire against my front. My core clenches, already wet and aching. I've pushed him past his breaking point, and the hungry look in his eyes tells me I'm about to pay the price.

God, I can't wait.

"On your knees, Angel."

I let my gaze drop to his hands, watching them struggle with the fastenings of his pants.

Slowly, I descend, my eyes never leaving his. My fingers gather the skirt of my dress, careful not to rip the delicate fabric. His erection bobs with each rapid beat of his heart, thick and swollen, a bead of pearlescent fluid glistening at the tip.

His fingers thread through my hair at the nape of my neck, just how I like it. "Time to make those naughty visions of yours a reality." His thumb strokes the sensitive skin of my throat, sending shivers down my spine. "Make it nice and sloppy, baby. Then I'm going to fuck you through the wall in that other fantasy you've been taunting me with."

The man's got a way with words; I'm melting at his commanding tone. My pussy clenches at the thought of submitting to him here, now, with the party just beyond our hidden alcove. I don't hesitate, sinking further into my power as I lick a path along the thick vein on the underside of his cock. The salty-sweet smell of his arousal makes my mouth water, and I hum in satisfaction at his sharp intake of breath.

His fingers twist in my hair, yanking me forward. "Show me what that mouth can do, Angel."

I meet his heated gaze through my lashes, letting my tongue sweep across my lips before taking him in. The stretch of his cock makes my jaw ache in the best way. I hum around his length, feeling him pulse against my tongue.

His grip turns brutal, holding me still as he fights for control. "Fuck...that mouth." The muscles in his neck strain as he throws his head back. "Making me lose my goddamn mind, baby."

The power I hold over him is intoxicating. I hollow my cheeks, sucking harder, letting my hands roam his thick thighs. My fingers find his heavy sac, massaging gently as I take him deeper.

"Christ." His hips snap forward, fingers tightening painfully in my hair. "Keep that up and I'll fuck that pretty throat raw."

I pull back with an obscene pop, strings of saliva connecting my swollen lips to his cock. "Yeah?" I lick my lips, tasting him. "What's stopping you?"

His eyes flash dangerously, midnight blue bleeding to black. "Careful, baby." His voice drops, making my nipples pebble. "Might just ruin that smart mouth of yours."

I answer by swallowing him down again, my tongue swirling as I take him deeper. Drool leaks from the corners of my mouth as I devour him, making everything deliciously messy. Just the way we both like it.

"Eyes up, Angel." His voice is a dark command. "Look at me while you choke on my cock." His grip tightens in my hair, forcing my gaze up to meet his. "Want to see those pretty tears running down your face."

He thrusts deep, hitting the back of my throat. I gag and sputter around his girth, spit flying as he holds me there. My eyeliner runs with my tears, but the burning in my throat only makes me want more.

"*Fuck*, baby." His grunts. "Getting my cock nice and wet for that tight little ass, aren't you? Such a filthy girl."

His thick length muffles my answering moan, drool coating his shaft as he uses my mouth. The rougher he gets, the wetter I become, my pussy clenching with need.

"That's it. *Goddamn*." His hips snap forward, making me gag again. "Gonna need all this spit when I bend you over and wreck that ass."

I cough around him as he thrusts hard, using my head as he fucks my throat. I moan, the need to touch myself burning within me. Rhyland pulls out and hauls me to my feet, my chin and chest covered in spit and saliva. He flips me around, yanking my skirts up, the fabric of my gown whispers against my skin as he roughly shoves it up around my waist. Bending down, taking me into his mouth from behind.

His tongue finds my asshole, hot and demanding, making my knees buckle. My nipples rake against the cold stone wall through the thin silk of my dress, sending sparks of pleasure straight through me.

His tongue circles my tight entrance, teasing the sensitive nerve endings and making me whimper with need. He alternates between licking and gently working a finger inside, stretching me open for what's to come.

The wet, filthy sounds of his mouth and fingers fill the air, echoing off the stone walls. He pulls back for a moment, and I hear him spit, the lewd sound making my cheeks burn. His saliva drips down, slicking my hole even more.

"Fuck, you're so tight." His voice is thick with lust. "Gonna feel so good stretching around my cock."

His hands grip my hips, holding me in place as I feel the thick head of his erection pressing insistently against my slick entrance.

"You ready for me, Angel?" He teases the tip just inside, making my body clench greedily. "Been teasing me all night with that sexy mind of yours. Time to give this ass what it's been begging for." he slowly starts to enter me and I groan against the wall, the enormous bulbous head, breaking through the tight ring of muscle.

"Time to wreck you."

I bite my lip to stifle my cry as his cock breaches me, the thick head stretching me impossibly wide. My fingers scrape against stone, seeking purchase.

Rhyland works his way inside me, inch by torturous inch, grunting as my body greedily accepts him. It's not until the very last bit of him is buried deep that I let out a muffled cry against his palm covering my mouth, my body shuddering with the pleasure of being so completely filled.

His hand leaves my mouth, only to lace through my hair, yanking my head back."Perfect." His voice is a dark rumble. "Keep that ass arched, baby. I'm gonna fuck this ass deep and hard."

I obey, arching my back to offer him the perfect angle. He begins to thrust, his big cock sliding *deep*, easier now that my body has adjusted to his size. Our combined juices create a delicious slip as he moves, the burn fading to be replaced by an intense, all-consuming pleasure.

Rhyland thrusts into me, his cock a thick, relentless force claiming my ass. He knows I love it hard and doesn't hold back, pounding into me with intense, deep strokes. His powerful body slams against mine, sending shocks of pleasure through my body. Every brutal snap of his hips sends me higher, taking me to the very edge.

"Oh god..." The sound escapes me as the intensity builds, the rhythmic sounds echoing off stone walls. My eyes fly open at a sound down the hall, scanning our surroundings. My blood turns to ice when I spot a figure lurking in the shadows, watching our intimate moment.

"Rhy—" I try to warn him, but his hand finds my throat, cutting off my words.

"Not stopping now, Angel. You started this game, now we finish it."

He has no idea we have an audience. The knowledge that we're being watched sends an illicit thrill down my spine, making me arch deeper into his thrusts. His grip on my throat tightens as he increases his pace, and heat floods my cheeks at the sounds echoing off the stone walls.

"Close, baby." His voice is strained, desperate. "You feel too good."

The shadowy figure remains motionless, watching, waiting, as Rhyland drives us toward the edge.

"Gonna flood this ass, baby." His hips snap forward, each thrust pushing me closer to the edge. My vision darkens at the pressure on my throat, but it only adds to the overwhelming pleasure building inside me. My pussy throbs in time with his thrusts, the need to touch myself becoming desperate.

"Gonna make you spray that sweet juice all over this floor, Angel." His free hand finds my clit, circling and rubbing until I cry out, my body spasming around him. "Come for me, baby."

His fingers curl inside me, finding that perfect spot that makes me moan. My eyes flutter open, seeking the shadow figure still lurking in the darkness. They remain motionless, drinking in our display, and the knowledge shoots electricity straight through my core.

"Fuck, Rhyland...I—" My words dissolve into a strangled cry as my orgasm rips through me, my inner walls clenching spasmodically around him.

Pleasure hits me in waves, my release dripping down my trembling thighs to pool on the stone floor. Rhyland buries his face in my neck, muffling his roar as his hips stutter. His cock pulses, filling me with his hot release, each thrust pumping me fuller.

My body quakes with aftershocks, every nerve ending singing as he marks me from the inside out. His grip on my throat loosens just enough to let me gasp for air, the combination of oxygen deprivation and intense pleasure making my head spin.

The stranger's presence in the shadows only intensifies each sensation, making me shake and convulse around Rhyland's throbbing length. My legs threaten to give out as another wave of pleasure crashes over me, but his strong arms hold me steady against the wall.

There's something deliciously forbidden about knowing someone is watching Rhyland claim me, watching him dominate every inch of my body.

"That's it, baby," he grumbles against my neck, his hips still moving in shallow thrusts. "Such a good girl."

My throat feels like I deepthroated a freight train and my ass burns in ways that'll make tomorrow's activities interesting. But holy hell, was it worth it. Rhyland tucks himself away before playing gentleman, smoothing down my dress like he didn't just rail me against a palace wall.

Catching my reflection, I have to stifle a laugh. I look like I went ten rounds with a makeup artist from a horror film—eyeliner everywhere, lips swollen and red. My thighs are slicker than an oil spill, and there's a puddle on the floor that some poor servant will have to deal with.

He yanks me against his chest, claiming my mouth in a kiss. His smug grin could power Ásgard's electricity bill for a year when he pulls back.

"Looks like your little mind games backfired, baby." He says with male satisfaction. "Should've known better than to tease me."

I arch an eyebrow, trying to look composed despite my thoroughly debauched state. "Please. I got exactly what I wanted." I tap his chest with one finger. "You're just mad I played you like a—"

A sudden movement, and something crashing to the floor in the shadows cuts me off. Rhyland's playful demeanor vanishes instantly, replaced by the lethal predator lurking beneath. My eyes dart to where our voyeur had been watching, but the space is empty now.

Rhyland takes off, stalking down the hallway, his long strides eating up the marble floor. I hurry after him, trying not to waddle like someone who just got their ass thoroughly destroyed.

"Going Viking on me now?" I pant, struggling to match his pace. "What happened to my smug satisfaction?"

"Someone watched." His voice could freeze hell. "Going to find out who had the balls to spy on *my* woman."

I barely resist rolling my eyes. Like, seriously? Mr. 'Let me eat you out in front of an entire sex club' is suddenly shy about an audience? The same man who made me suck his dick in *said* place, while half the club watched?

The irony is thick enough to spread on toast. Not that I'm going to mention how that mystery voyeur added an extra spark to my orgasm. Something tells me that particular confession might need to wait until his caveman tendencies settle down.

"You do realize we basically invited an audience by fucking against a wall during a royal party, right?" I dodge a decorative vase as I chase after him. "I mean, what did you expect? A 'Do Not Disturb' sign magically appearing?"

He spins around, pinning me with a stare that could melt steel. "I expect my mate to be for my eyes only, not some fucking pervert lurking in the shadows."

He spins around and takes off again. I can't help but snort. "Oh, please. So you can take me to a club and literally eat me out in front of everyone, but this is different?"

Fuck—my feet are screaming as I struggle to keep up with his giant strides in these damn heels.

Rhyland stops so abruptly I nearly faceplant into his back. He spins around, crowding me against the wall with that predatory intensity that never fails to make my pulse race.

"Damn right it's different." His voice is pure pissed-off Viking, his eyes glinting with possessiveness. "At the club, *I* controlled who watched, what they saw. *I* was in charge of who got to see what *I* gave you. But here?" His hand curls into my hair, not squeezing, but a dominant reminder of his strength. "Some random fucker just got an eyeful of what belongs to me, without my say-so."

His gaze burns into me, the need to claim, to possess, to dominate radiating off him in waves. "No one sees you like that without my permission, Angel. No. One."

It hits me then, like a jolt to my lust-addled brain. That night at the club, Rhyland never let me finish. Sure, he teased me to the brink of insanity—a delicious torture that still makes my toes curl thinking about it. But now it clicks: my Nordic control freak doesn't share the grand finale. My orgasms are his personal show, a private performance for an audience of one.

Talk about selective exhibitionism. Leave it to my thousand-year-old vampire to find a loophole in public indecency.

LUCIAN

53

This isn't happening. This can't be fucking happening.

The sight hits me like a fatal blow to hope, shattering my world into bloody pieces.

My angel—my beautiful, radiant Seraphina—hangs crucified against some dark makeshift massive cross, like some fucked up sacrifice. Runed chains wrap around her body, pulsing with sickly black magic that makes my heart race. But her wings... *fuck*, her wings...

"Holy shit," Emily's voice cracks through my frozen horror. "We need to get her down. Right fucking now!"

I stumble forward, crushing broken feathers beneath my feet. Each step leaves crimson footprints, like I'm walking through some demented fairy tale gone wrong. The air smells of Seraphina's sweet blood, and dark magic—Morgan's unique brand of necromantic bullshit.

"Ph-phina?" My voice breaks. "Baby, can you hear me?"

Her golden eyes flutter, glazed with pain. "Lucian." her weak voice fucking undoes me.

Black corruption spreads through her once-pristine wings like poison, stemming from iron spikes that look like they were stolen from Satan's toolbox. Each nail pulses with the same sick magic as the chains.

Through our bond, I feel nothing but static and agony—like someone's replaced our connection with barbed wire.

"The nails," Emily hisses, her hands shaking. "They're warded. I can't—" She swears viciously. "The magic's fighting me."

I reach for the nearest spike, and holy *fuck*—white-hot pain sears through my palm. The metal burns like sacred fire, forcing a snarl from my throat. "What the hell is this?"

"Blessed iron mixed with my own special brew. Like it?" Morgan's voice slices through the room like a serrated knife, making us whirl to face her.

She emerges from the shadows like a goth-whore nightmare, all black leather and too much eyeliner. Dark energy rolls off her in waves, the power that makes my hair stand on end.

"Turn it off, Elvira," I growl, putting myself between her and Phina. "Before I show you a whole new use for that pentagram choker."

Morgan's laugh is sharp. "That's cute, Fangface. You really thought I wouldn't clock your little ambush upstairs?" Her eyes, rimmed with kohl and something darker, lock onto Emily. "Color me impressed, though. Your discount Sabrina packs a bigger punch than I thought."

"Bitch, please," Emily's magic crackles like a live wire. "last time was a fucking warm-up. You really wanna see me go full Scarlet Witch on your bony ass?"

Morgan prowls the room's edges, her black-painted fingernails trailing along the stone. Her movements are pure predatory grace—like a jaguar toying with its food.

I tune out her evil overlord TED Talk, zeroing in on my angel. "Phina, baby." My voice cracks as I brush blood-matted hair from her face. "Just focus on me, okay? We're busting you out of this shithole."

Seraphina's tears cut through the blood spattered on her cheeks. "Lu-Lucian," she whimpers, each word shredded by pain. "It hurts. Gods, it hurts. Make it stop, *please...* please..."

Her pain hits me like a fucking semi-truck, our bond screaming with phantom agony. I swallow hard against the rising tide of rage and bile.

I'm going to destroy Morgan. Viciously. Creatively. With her own fucking curse.

I try again—my hands wrap around the first nail, and *holy motherfucking hell*—the blessed iron sears through my charred flesh like the devil's kiss. I rip away with a roar that rattles the stones, leaving strips of skin behind.

Rage drowns my vision. *Enough of this bullshit.* I blur toward Morgan, fangs bared and ready to paint the walls with her blood—

Agony nukes my skull. I crash to the ground, convulsing as phantom knives fillet my brain. Morgan's boots fill my view, her hand outstretched like the Grim Reaper's bony finger.

"Let's make a trade, hmm?" Her voice slices through the mind-melting pain. Blood drips from my nose and ears as she cranks up the cerebral pressure. "Soul Stone for your feathered fuck-toy. Going once..."

Emily lunges like an avenging witch on a rampage, but Morgan just flicks her other hand with the casual disdain of swatting a fly. Emily crashes to her knees, face contorting in the same brain-melting agony that's turning my skull into a blender party.

"YES!" The word shreds my throat, tasting of desperation and bile. "Fuck ing... deal... just... *STOP!*"

"And where's the *real* Rhyland? That cheap knockoff upstairs might fool the queen bee, but honey, I wrote the book on dark energy." She twists her mental knife deeper with the casual ease of adjusting her lipstick, and my gray matter feels like dollar store jello.

"Fuck... I don't know!"

"Lying makes me cranky. Going twice..."

"Fine! Shit... he's in Ásgard—Zephyria... wherever the fuck!" The pain's got me tap-dancing on consciousness's edge.

"Hmm..." Her voice carries all the warmth of a glacier. "Time to summon myself a God."

The pressure vanishes, abandoning me on cold stone. My head jackhammers like I tongue-fucked a light socket.

Morgan snaps her fingers. "Stone. Now."

I drag myself up, muscles twitching. "Her first, bitch."

Eye roll. Wrist flick. The chains dissolve into greasy mist, their malevolent magic evaporating.

I blur to Phina, gripping the first nail, slick with her blood.

Please don't let this hurt, please...

I wrench it free with a wet, tearing sound that will haunt me for the rest of my life. Phina screams, raw and broken, her wing spasming. Blood gushes from the gaping hole, staining white feathers.

"I'm sorry, I'm so fucking sorry," I choke out, reaching for the next spike. It comes free with a sickening squelch, and Phina convulses, a wail of pure agony ripping from her throat. Her pain slams into me like a battering ram, our bond throbbing with echoes of torture.

The last nail is buried in the delicate joint where wing meets shoulder blade.

Forgive me, Cupcake.

I clench my jaw and pull, feeling tendon and muscle tear. Phina's shriek will be seared into my memory for eternity. She collapses against me, and I catch her, holding her tight as her mangled wings drape across the floor, painting abstract horrors in scarlet.

"I've got you, baby girl." I press my forehead to hers, our tears mingling with her blood. "I'm here. I'm here." Her whimpers vibrate through my chest, dark magic poisoning her light.

Morgan's going to die for this. Screaming. Pleading. Choking on her own fucking hubris.

"Deals a deal." Morgan's voice cracks like a whip. "Cough it up."

I clutch Seraphina to my chest, the need to heal her clawing at my insides. I raise my wrist to my fangs, ready to tear into my own flesh, to give her my blood, my strength—

Invisible chains lock me in place, freezing me mid-motion. "Ah, ah, ah. Not so fast, lover boy." Morgan's finger wags like a metronome of mockery. "Payment first. Then you can play doctor with your angel."

A snarl of pure frustration rips from my throat. I cut my eyes to Emily, desperation a living thing in my gut.

Emily's hands flash out, magic missiles flying from her fingertips. Morgan bats them away with a contemptuous flick of her wrist, retaliating with hellfire that encircles my favorite witch in a ring of brimstone and agony.

"I'm losing my patience, leech." Morgan's voice drips with venom. "Hand. It. The. Fuck. Over."

Fuck. Fuck. Fuckity fuck fuck.

"Upstairs!" The word explodes from me in a roar of frustration. Sable has the fake stone, but this whole shit-show has spiraled so far off script, it might as well be a fucking improv night.

Phina trembles in my arms, each whimper a dagger to my chest. Her skin burns with unholy fever, wings dripping blood onto stone. The need to heal her, to give her my blood, screams through every cell in my body. But with Morgan's death grip on me...

Morgan's lips curl into a razor smile. "Fetch, witch." She drops her hand, and the ring of hellfire imprisoning Emily vanishes.

Emily staggers, magic flickering like a dying light. But then—*holy shit*—she hurls a tsunami of pure power at Morgan. "Like hell I will." Morgan flies backward, hitting the cavern wall with a satisfying crunch.

I don't waste the opening. My fangs slash into my wrist, and I press it to Phina's lips. "Drink, Cupcake. Come on."

She manages two weak swallows before her body revolts. Blood sprays from her lips as she convulses, each spasm driving another stake through my heart. "Phina! Baby, what—"

"It's the dark magic," Emily grits out, heading toward the stairs. "We need to delta the fuck out of here. *Now.*"

I scoop up my angel, but Morgan's voice freezes us in our tracks.

"One more step," she purrs, darkness dancing in her eyes, "and I'll show you exactly what a necromancer can do with angel essence."

I clutch Phina tighter, her mangled wings painting gore across my legs. "Get fucked, Wednesday Addams."

The air suddenly becomes Arctic-level cold, like Hell decided to host a winter festival. Morgan raises her hands, and the floor *splits*—rotting fingers burst through stone, grabbing for our ankles. The stench of decay fills the air.

Emily hurls a bolt of pure magic, but Morgan deflects it. "Really, witch? You think your parlor tricks can match *my* power? I've been collecting death magic since before your grandmother was born."

The undead hands catch my ankles. I kick free, but more replace them, trying to drag us down. Emily's magic blazes like a star, keeping the worst at bay, but sweat pours down her face from the effort.

"Running out of juice?" Morgan taunts. "Let me help with that."

She gestures sharply, and Emily doubles over, gasping. The color drains from her face as Morgan starts pulling her life force.

Shit. Shit. SHIT.

"Stop!" I roar, desperately searching for options. Seraphina's dead weight in my arms, Emily being drained, and undead fuckers trying to drag us under. "I'll get the stone."

Morgan's smile is all razor blades. "Now we're talking." She eases her grip on Emily, who collapses to her knees. "Was that so hard?"

I snarl. "Let's all go, and—"

"Do I look stupid?" She clenches her fist, and Emily screams. "Put the angel down. You go get it. Try anything cute, and I'll finish what I started with those pretty wings."

Through our bond, I feel Seraphina's consciousness flicker dangerously. We're out of time.

"Deal," I growl. "But Emily comes with me."

Morgan's eyes narrow. "The witch is insurance. She stays. You have ten minutes, vampire. After that..." She strokes one of Seraphina's mangled wings, making her whimper. "Well, let's just say there are worse things than death."

I lay Seraphina down as gently as possible, my hands shaking with rage. Emily meets my eyes, and I see steel beneath her exhaustion. *She has a plan.*

"Tick tock," Morgan singsongs.

I force myself to turn away, each step feeling like betrayal. But as I reach the stairs, Emily's voice rings out—strong and clear:

"Revelatio Mortis!"

The spell hits Morgan like a sonic wave of pure light. She staggers, her concentration breaking—and Emily *moves.* Her hands slam into the ground, and a shockwave of power ripples outward, shattering Morgan's undead minions.

I blur into action, fangs bared. Morgan recovers fast, hurling a bolt of necromantic energy that nearly takes my head off. But she's focusing on me—missing Emily drawing symbols in blood behind her.

"You really think you can beat me?" Morgan laughs, darkness swirling around her like a tornado. "I am death incarnate!"

"No," I bare my fangs in a savage grin. "You're just a distraction."

Emily's spell hits with the force of a nuclear bomb. Sacred magic collides with dark energy, and the explosion throws us back. Morgan shrieks—a sound of pure rage—as golden chains of light wrap around her, burning where they touch.

I snatch up Seraphina and run, Emily right behind me. Morgan's howl of fury follows us up the stairs, along with the sound of her power trying to break Emily's binding.

"It won't hold her long," Emily pants as we sprint. "We need to move. *Now.*"

She's already pressed her phone to her ear, barking orders: "Get to the car. Plan B time."

The bond pulses weakly in my chest, Seraphina's life flickering like a dying star. *Hold on, baby girl. Just hold on.*

Behind us, Morgan's power swells like a tsunami about to break, dark energy crackling through the air. The metaphorical shit isn't just about to hit the fan—it's loading into a industrial-grade cannon aimed straight at our asses.

Time to see how fast we can really run.

The ballroom's crystal chandeliers blur past as I streak through the crowd, Seraphina's blood dripping in our wake. Masked faces turn—nostrils flaring at the scent of my injured angel. A hundred pairs of predatory eyes lock onto us like heat-seeking missiles.

Move. Move. MOVE.

I wrench open the Cadillac's rear hatch, the SUV's black lines gleaming under the moonlight. With infinite care, I ease Seraphina into the cargo area, her mangled wings filling the space—white feathers, matted with her blood, scatter across the carpeted floor.

The rapid patter of running feet pulls my focus. Emily, Sable, and Brax—now in his usual scary as fuck demon getup—sprint across the parking lot, their faces painted with desperate urgency. Relief and dread twist in my gut as they close the distance.

Then all hell breaks loose.

A searing flash burns my retinas, followed by a deafening *BOOM* that feels like a sledgehammer to the chest. The shockwave slams me into the Cadillac, the rear hatch buckling under my spine. Glass shatters, metal groans, and the bitter taste of magic scorches my tongue.

What the everloving fuck?!

Ears buzzing, I force my eyes open. The parking lot swims into view, now a jagged metal and debris hellscape. Ozone and burnt flesh clog my nostrils, underscored by the cloying scent of blood.

Far too much blood.

"No... God, no..." Denial and horror claw up my throat as I stagger forward, searching for the others.

Brax is nearest, his hulking demon form shielding Emily. Emily's wild eyes find mine, desperation and dread swirling in their depths before darting to the blast's epicenter.

Fucking Christ...

Sable lies broken and bleeding at the heart of a blackened crater. Razor-edged shrapnel protrudes gruesomely from her body, glittering obscenely in the moonlight. But it's the gaping, fist-sized hole punched through her sternum that steals my breath.

I'm at her side instantly, hands hovering uselessly over the grievous wound. Her heart...*fuck,* I can see her shredded heart through the gore and splintered ribs. It beats weakly, each contraction expelling more vital blood.

"Sable! Shit, stay with me!" I rip into my wrist, pressing the bleeding wound to her slack lips. "Drink, goddammit! DRINK!"

But my blood merely mingles with hers, spilling past her chin in rivulets. Her injuries... they're too catastrophic. Even vampire blood can't regenerate damage this extensive.

"SABLE!" Emily's anguished howl rips through the night as she crawls to her best friend's side. Her hands tremble violently as she presses them against the carnage, trying desperately to hold Sable's life inside her broken body. Each sob carrying the weight of a thousand shattered hopes. "Sable... no...*no*...oh god, please. *Please* don't leave us."

"This all could've been avoided." That voice, smooth and cold as a razor's edge, cuts through the chaos. A figure emerges from the darkness, his dark cloak rippling. "The stone. *Now*."

I know that voice. Why the hell do I know that voice?

And who the hell is this asshole who can throw fucking nukes like hand grenades?

I snatch the ring from Sable's lifeless fingers and yeet that fake-ass piece of costume jewelry at Captain Creep's hooded face. With any luck, they'll be too busy jerking off to their "prize" to realize they got punk'd with the supernatural equivalent of a gumball machine trinket.

He plucks the ring from the air with the casual arrogance of someone who's never had their ass properly kicked.

"You son of *BITCH!*" Emily unleashes hell. Fire erupts—a big 'fuck you' in technicolor glory, a rapid-fire barrage that finally convinces our cloaked douchebag to retreat.

"Emily! She's dying!" Brax seizes her, dragging her back even as she screams and thrashes. "Both of them are fucking dying!"

Seraphina. My angel, broken and dying mere feet away.

I scoop Sable's ruined form into my arms, self-recrimination and sorrow warring in my chest. *I'm so sorry. I'm so fucking sorry.*

But Brax is right. We're out of time.

I lay Sable's broken form in the backseat, each movement weighted with grief and guilt. Blood—*Christ, so much blood*—seeps into the leather upholstery. Emily scrambles in after her, tears carving paths through the grime on her face as she cradles Sable's head in her lap. Her shaking hands stroke Sable's blood-matted hair while she chants desperately, pouring every ounce of power she has into keeping her best friend's soul tethered to her ravaged body.

Don't you dare check out on us, Sable, not like this

Brax vaults into the passenger side, slamming the door—his hulking demon ass barely fitting in the front seat, horns gouging the headliner. The Cadillac's engine roars to life, and the powerful purr is jarringly normal amid so much carnage.

I slam my foot down, and the Cadillac launches forward with a scream of rubber on asphalt. The engine's roar drowns out everything except the sound of Emily's desperate sobs and Seraphina's labored breathing.

LUCIAN

54

I am tearing down I-90, navigating the traffic like a goddamn lunatic. Seraphina's agony sears through our bond, burning in my veins like acid. Each pulse of her pain drives another spike into my skull until—*fuck this.*

I wrench the wheel hard right as we clear the Murrow Bridge, tires screaming as we skid onto the shoulder. Can't wait. Won't wait. Not while my angel bleeds out in the back.

"What the *hell,* Lucian?!" Emily's voice cracks between hysteria and rage. "Get us the fuck home!"

I ignore her, launching myself out and yanking open the rear hatch. Seraphina's eyes flutter—barely conscious, her mangled wings still weeping blood while that goddamn black magic writhes around her like living smoke.

"Emily. Out. *Now.* Help me goddamit."

But Emily just clutches Sable's lifeless body closer, her sobs tearing at what's left of my soul. We lost her fifteen miles back, and the memory of her final breath feels like a dagger through my heart. Sable was *family,* dammit. This wasn't supposed to fucking happen.

"Help with *what?*" Emily's voice shatters like broken glass. "I couldn't... I can't even..." Her words dissolve into raw grief as she rocks Sable's body.

I rake my hands through my hair, desperation clawing up my throat. "Come here, baby girl." My hands shake as I ease Seraphina to the edge of the cargo area. She whimpers, the sound cutting straight through my chest.

"Lucian..." Her voice breaks, thick with pain. "Please... make it stop. I can't—" Her eyes roll back as consciousness finally fails her.

"Phina!" I tap her face, panic rising like bile. "Phina-baby, don't you dare! EMILY! Get your ass over here and *DO SOMETHING!*"

Please don't leave me. Please, don't leave me.

Emily finally staggers out of the backseat, her face a roadmap of tear tracks and devastation. The streetlights catch the wetness on her cheeks, making them glitter.

"Please..." My voice cracks, desperation bleeding through. "Try something. *Anything*. We can't lose them both." I beg, "*I* can't lose her."

Emily squares her shoulders, stretching trembling hands over Seraphina's broken form. Her eyes slide shut, face twisting in concentration as ancient words spill from her lips:

"Expello malum, purgo tenebris. Sanctus lux penetrat umbras..."

The dark magic coiling around Seraphina *writhes*, like an angry serpent disturbed from sleep.

"Fuck!" Emily yanks her hands back like they've been burned. "This evil is next-level shit." She shakes out her fingers, determination hardening her tear-stained features. "Let me try again..."

"In nomine lucis, maledictum solve. Obscurum recede, malum disperde!"

The corrupted energy pulses and twists, fighting Emily's cleansing magic like a living thing.

Come on, witch. Work your magic. Save my angel.

Emily's chanting grows more intense, sweat beading her forehead as she battles Morgan's corruption. Blood begins to trickle from her nose, down and over her lips, but she doesn't stop. Her hands shake violently over Seraphina's body, magic crackling in the air like static before a storm.

"Sanctifica hoc vas lucis, purifica hanc angelum dei..."

The words sound like they're being torn from her throat now, each syllable a war against the darkness. More blood drips, spattering onto Seraphina's wings as Emily pours everything she has into the cleansing.

The dark magic fights back, coiling tighter around Seraphina like possessed razor wire. Emily's hands shake violently, but her voice grows more vigorous, more commanding:

"EXPELLO MALUM, LUX VINCIT OMNIA!"

The corruption *screams*—a sound that sets my fangs on edge—before finally releasing its hold. Finally—*thank fuck*—It dissipates like smoke, leaving Seraphina blessedly free of its taint.

Emily's hands drop to her sides. "It's done," she gasps, blood staining her teeth. "She can take your blood now."

I don't waste a second. My fangs tear into my wrist, ripping open veins with desperate force. I press the bleeding wound to Seraphina's pale lips, terror clawing at my insides.

"Drink, baby girl. Please... *please* drink." My voice breaks on the words. "Don't you dare leave me, Phina. Come on. *Come on*, stay with me, sweetheart."

For one heart-stopping moment, nothing happens. Then—*sweet merciful Christ*—her eyes flutter and she starts to swallow. Relief hits me, and I want to cry as she drinks, each pull of blood through our bond telling me she's still fighting.

"That's it, Cupcake. Take what you need."

Color floods back into her skin, that ethereal golden glow I love so much replacing death's pallor. Her wings—*fuck yes*—the shredded, mangled mess starts to heal. Torn flesh knits together, bloodstained feathers becoming pristine white again, radiating that pure celestial light that makes my heart skip.

"Keep drinking, Cupcake. You're doing so good. That's my girl..."

A thud behind me snaps my attention around. Emily crumples to the ground, blood still streaming from her nose.

"BRAX!"

The demon explodes from the car, moving faster than his hulking form should allow. He drops to his knees beside Emily, gathering her into his massive arms gently.

"Em? Emily!" His usual growl softens with worry. "Come on, little witch, open those baby blues for me."

I try to focus on Emily, but *holy hell*—Seraphina's strength floods back through our bond like someone just plugged her into a power station. Each pull of blood makes our connection pulse stronger and brighter until I'm dizzy with relief.

When she's taken enough, I gently ease my wrist away. Her eyes—those incredible honey-gold irises now swimming with tears—lock onto mine. "Lucian..." My name falls from her lips like a prayer, and whatever's left of my heart shatters into a million pieces.

I pull her out of the car and crush her against my chest, burying my face in her hair. "I've got you, baby girl. I'm right here." The words spill out like a desperate litany as she trembles in my arms, her sobs muffled against my shirt. "You're safe. You're okay. I've got you, sweetheart. Never letting go."

Her fingers clutch my suit jacket like she's afraid I'll disappear, and I hold her tighter, trying to absorb her pain, her fear, her grief. Each tear that soaks into my shirt feels like absolution and accusation all at once.

I almost lost her. Christ, I almost fucking lost her.

I cradle Seraphina's face between my palms like she's made of spun gold and claim her lips with every ounce of desperation, love, and relief coursing through my undead veins. She tastes like sunlight and salvation, her mouth moving against mine with the same frantic need. The bond between us explodes with emotion—fear, love, relief—until I can't tell where my feelings end and hers begin.

"Lucian... oh god..." Her words tremble against my lips before she pulls me back in, fingers tangling in my hair gripping tightly. "I thought—I'd never—you were—"

"We need to move," Brax's deep voice cuts through our moment, all business and worry. He cradles Emily's unconscious form with the careful precision of someone handling precious cargo.

Reality comes crashing back as car horns blare at our roadside drama. *Christ,* we must look like a rejected scene from some B-grade supernatural rom-com—a jacked demon cradling an unconscious witch, while an honest-to-god angel with wingspan to rival a 747 plays tonsil hockey with yours truly.

"Emily!" Seraphina's hand flies to her mouth, horror replacing relief. "Is she—"

"She's breathing," Brax states, his fire-bright eyes fixed on Emily's pale face. "But we need to get her home. Now."

"Cupcake, as much as I love your beautiful wings, might want to dial down the divine display." I gesture, which is giving passing drivers the light show of their mortal lives.

"Oh!" Seraphina's wings dissolve in a shower of ethereal sparkles, like someone just detonated a heavenly glitter bomb.

Brax carefully maneuvers Emily into the car, his massive form surprisingly gentle. But now I'm faced with the task of dropping a bombshell on Seraphina—a truth I'd rather swallow razor blades than say out loud. She needs to know about Sable, and brace herself for the sight that's about to sucker-punch her in the soul.

"Phina, baby..." I take her hands, steeling myself. "There's something you need to know."

"What? What is it?" Her worry slams into me through our bond like a raging torrent of dread.

"It's Sable..."

"Sable? Where is she?" Seraphina's voice quivers, her eyes desperately searching mine for an answer I'd rather chew off my own arm than give.

Fuck. The words lodge in my throat. "She... uh..."

Come on, jackass. Rip off the Band-Aid. She deserves to know.

But my face must be a neon sign of bad news because Seraphina's hand flies to her mouth, a sharp gasp tearing from her lungs.

I guide her around to the backseat with the careful movements of someone handling a live grenade. When I open the door, revealing Sable's lifeless form, Seraphina's anguish explodes through our bond like a supernova. Her knees buckle, and I barely catch her as she collapses against me, her sobs ripping through the night air.

"No... no, no, *no... Sable...*" Her shaking hand reaches out, hovering over Sable's still features. "How? *How* did this happen?"

Each word is a knife in my gut, twisting deeper with every hitched breath and broken cry. I hold her tighter, trying to absorb her grief, but it's like trying to hold back a tidal wave with a paper cup.

Because the universe is a cold, cruel bitch, that's how.

But I can't say that. Not when my angel's heart is shattering in front of me. So I just pull her close, letting her tears soak my shirt as I try to hold us both together.

"I know, I know, I know, sweetheart, I'm so fucking sorry..." The words rip from my throat like they're made of barbed wire as Seraphina fractures in my arms, her grief pouring out in waves that could drown us both. Each sob punches through our bond like a fucking sledgehammer—watching my angel grieve for the pink-haired witch who'd somehow wormed her way into all our hearts.

Fuck, Sable. You deserved better than this.

The living room of my mansion becomes a makeshift triage center. Sable's body lies in the center, still as marble, while Brax gently places Emily on the couch. He doesn't leave her side, and those hellfire eyes never waver from her face.

Seraphina trembles in my lap, her tears soaking through my shirt. Each sob feels like a sharp stab of grief, but what can I say? *Sorry your friend died?*

The drive home was bad enough, watching her shatter piece by piece as I explained everything.

The scene before me is so fucking surreal—a demon dabbing Emily's blood-streaked face with a wet cloth like some infernal Florence Nightingale. Never thought I'd see the day when a creature from the pits of hell would look at anyone with such... tenderness.

The silence weighs heavy as a gravestone while we process this clusterfuck of a night. Seraphina finally cries herself to sleep against my chest, her fingers still clutching my shirt like an anchor. The white sheet over Sable's body feels like an accusation.

Emily stirs after awhile, her eyes fluttering open. Brax tenses like a guard dog coming alert."Are you okay, Mistress?" His gravelly voice softens to something almost gentle.

She groans, pressing a hand to her temple. "Yeah... just overdid it. Magical tank's running on empty."

Understatement of the fucking century, Em.

Emily's gaze locks onto the sheet-covered form, her throat working against a sob. She presses her palms against her eyes, but when they drop, there's steel beneath the tears. She pushes to her feet with grim determination.

"Where are you going?" Brax rises with her, hovering like a concerned shadow.

"I need to prepare her body," her voice cracks but steadies. "The Ritual of Last Light. We have to cleanse her essence and guide her soul to the Summerlands before..." She swallows hard. "Before darkness claims it."

Seraphina's lashes flutter against my chest before those honey-gold eyes find mine. "I need to help her," she breathes against my lips, the ghost of a kiss lingering as she rises to follow Emily.

I beeline for the crystal decanter like it holds the answers to everything that is fucked up. The bourbon burns like liquid courage as I slam it back, then pour another for my favorite demon. "Here. You look like you need this as much as I do."

Brax drains the glass like he's dying of thirst in hell.

The basement door nearly flies off its hinges as Damon explodes into the room, face twisted in panic. His eyes lock onto the sheet-covered form and—*Ah, shit.*

He crumples to his knees, fangs dropping in distress. "No... that's not—it can't be—"

Perfect. Because watching the baby vamp discover his almost-girlfriend is dead is exactly how I wanted this night to end.

Damon crawls toward Sable's body, his hand trembling as it reaches for the sheet. He pulls the sheet back slightly, then jerks back like he's been burned.

"How?" The word scrapes from his throat. "*How??*"

Christ. The bourbon's not nearly strong enough for this conversation. "Morgan," I spit the name like poison. "And some hooded asshole with a fetish for explosions."

A sound rips from Damon's chest—something between a snarl and a sob. His fingers curl into fists against the hardwood, leaving gouges in my imported fucking flooring.

Emily and Seraphina return, arms laden with ritual supplies. Damon's head snaps up, wild eyes finding Emily's tear-stained face. "Fix this," he pleads, voice raw. "You're a witch. You can—you have to—"

Emily's shoulders slump under the weight of those words. "Damon, I..."

Fuck my entire immortal life. This night just keeps getting better and better.

Emily's knees hit the floor beside him, her voice splintering. "I *can't.* God, Damon, I tried. I poured everything I had into her, but..." Her hands spread helplessly. "The damage was too extensive. Even magic has limits."

Damon's fangs drop fully, his eyes bleeding to black. The sound that comes from him is pure anguish—primal and broken. "Then what's the point?" He surges to his feet, power rolling off him in waves. "What's the fucking point of all this magic if you can't—"

"*Enough.*" Seraphina's voice cracks, her divine energy filling the room. "This isn't helping her soul find peace."

Emily begins arranging crystals around Sable's body, her hands shaking but determined. Salt follows, forming a perfect circle. The sharp scent of sage cuts through the heavy air as she lights the bundle.

"We can't save her body," Emily's voice steadies as she slips into ritual mode. "But we can protect her soul. Guide her to the light. It's... it's all we can do now."

Damon sinks back to his knees, the fight draining from him like blood from a wound. His fingers brush the edge of the salt circle, and *fuck*—I've never seen devastation wear a face so young.

Some nights, being immortal really fucking sucks.

Emily slowly removes the sheet from Sable, revealing her wounds. And Damon lets out a sob.

Emily's voice rises and falls in ancient cadence, Latin phrases weaving through smoke-heavy air. Candles suddenly *whoosh* to life around us, their flames dancing unnaturally tall, throwing twisted shadows across the walls.

The crystals begin to pulse with soft light, and the salt circle takes on an ethereal glow. Damon hasn't moved, frozen in his grief like some tragic marble statue.

"*Lux aeterna luceat ei...*" Emily's chanting reaches a crescendo——*Wait.*

What the...Sable's chest wound is... closing?

I blink hard, but nope, definitely seeing skin knit together like some twisted time-lapse video.

Her finger twitches.

No fucking way.

I'm about to say something when—*HOLY SHIT*—Sable's body launches upward like someone hit her with cosmic jumper cables. Her gasp sounds like she's been holding her breath since the Bronze Age.

Emily's chanting cuts off with a shriek. She scrambles backward so fast she upends her altar, sending crystals scattering like marbles.

Sable's head snaps toward Emily, nostrils flaring at the scent of blood. Brand new fangs gleam in the crystal light.

Then it bitch-slaps me harder than Thanos with all six Infinity Stones—*my blood.*

Holy shit. I turned her.

What. The. Actual. FUCK.

RHYLAND

55

I ce-crusted branches stretch endlessly beneath a pearl-white sky, their crystalline fingers reaching toward the heavens. This frozen wonderland sparkles like diamonds scattered across virgin snow beyond Ásgard's jagged mountain peaks. Each breath materializes in the frigid air, dancing upward before dissipating into nothingness.

Gullfax's hooves crunch through the frost-covered ground, his golden mane catching the weak winter sunlight. He had practically begged to carry us, those pleading eyes wearing down Dani's resolve until she finally gave in with her adorable eye roll. Now she's pressed between Bryn and me, her tits against my back, Bryn behind her, as I guide this oversized beast through the frozen forest.

Ahead of us, Erik rides with Baldr, his silver hair nearly lost against the frozen landscape. Last night after the feast, found his drunk ass sprawled in our chambers, reeking of Bryn and drowning in enough mead to impress Thor himself. The bond had been right there, within his grasp, before she slipped through his fingers.

Dani took one look at her sister's haunted expression and made her choice. A quick kiss on my cheek and she was gone, leaving me to deal with my brother's pathetic attempt to drink himself into oblivion. Not exactly how I planned to spend my night with my mate, but fuck if I was going to let Erik destroy himself over this.

Watching him wallow in misery over Bryn's rejection had me grinding my teeth. Brought back memories of Dani fighting our connection—all those times I had to hunt her down, prove my claim, earn every damn inch of ground. But Erik? My strategic, calculating brother is lost in this game. Can't control a mate's heart the way he commands his battles.

Had to practically beat it into his thick skull that Bryn's fear isn't a dead end. That a mate worth having never comes easy. If I'd backed down every time my little firecracker tried to push me away, I wouldn't have the fierce woman who now wears my mark.

These celestial sisters and their stubborn fucking streaks. But at least that killer instinct is back in Erik's eyes—finally got through to him that claiming a mate takes more than just strength and control. Sometimes you have to fight dirty.

The frost-laden branches crack overhead like brittle bones, matching my irritation with this whole mess. Two hours of flying through bitter winds has my ass numb, but we're finally in the Frosted Forest—where our next challenge awaits.

"Tell me about this champion," Dani calls out as Baldr guides his mount alongside ours, his eyes lingering too long on my mate for my liking.

"Skadi," he says, flashing Dani a smile that's too fucking friendly. "Once, she was among the most fierce of Odin's Valkyries."

"Fierce doesn't begin to describe her," Bryn cuts in, her voice sharp as the icy wind. "Skadi was legendary for her brutality in battle. They called her the Winter's Blade."

I catch Erik's gaze fixed on Bryn, his jaw clenched tight enough to crack teeth. Fucking hell, these two need to sort their shit out.

"Winter's Blade?" Dani shifts against my back, her warmth seeping through my clothes. "That's quite a nickname."

"Indeed," Baldr leans closer, his voice dropping to an intimate tone that pisses me off. "And you, little savior, might appreciate this—she was known for her cunning as much as her strength."

A growl builds in my chest before I can stop it. Baldr's eyes flick to mine, a knowing smirk playing at his lips.

"So what happened?" Dani asks, oblivious to the tension. "How does someone that powerful fall to darkness?"

"During the Great War," Baldr continues, "when Moretemis first tried to breach our defenses, Skadi led a legion of Valkyries against his forces. But the shadows..." He pauses, ice crystals forming in his hair. "The shadows found their way into her mind."

"The darkness didn't just corrupt her," Bryn adds, and I notice Erik flinch at the edge in her voice. "It transformed her into something else entirely—half shadow, half Valkyrie. A creature of ice and darkness."

"Wait," Dani's grip tightens on my waist. "If she was corrupted, why didn't they just... you know..."

"Because Odin saw an opportunity," Baldr explains. "He bound her to the Zephyrite stone, making her its eternal guardian. Her corruption became her strength—the perfect blend of light and shadow to test those who would claim the stone."

"Test them how exactly?" she asks, and Baldr's answering smile—all wolfish intent—has my beast clawing to tear his throat out.

"What better guardian," Bryn's voice is bitter, "than one who understands both the light of Ásgard and the darkness that seeks to destroy it? She tests not just their strength, but their ability to resist the shadows themselves."

"Great," Dani mutters against my back. "So we're basically walking into a trap set by a corrupted, shadow-powered Valkyrie who's been stewing in darkness for centuries. This should be fun."

"Don't worry, little savior," Baldr winks—actually fucking winks—at my mate. "I'll make sure no harm comes to you."

My snarl reverberates through the frozen forest as I yank Gullfax's reins, bringing us to a hard stop. The stallion snorts, his breath crystallizing in the frigid air. "You want to explain what the fuck you're playing at? Or should I remind you exactly who she belongs to?"

"Rhyland." Dani's warning carries on a puff of frozen breath, but my eyes stay locked on the smirking bastard before us.

"Peace, Godborn," Baldr's smooth voice carries across the frozen air. "I merely appreciate beauty in all its forms. Surely you can't fault me for that?"

"Appreciate it from a fucking distance," I bark, urging Gullfax forward. "Or I'll show you exactly how *unappreciative* I can be."

Dani's forehead thumps against my back with a groan, her embarrassment radiating through our bond.

"Watch yourself, Baldr," Bryn's voice cuts through the tension like an icy blade. "My sister's taken, and her mate's not known for his patience. Neither am I."

The frozen forest swallows Baldr's chuckle as we press on, but I catch the way his eyes finally drop to the path ahead. Smart fucking move.

The dense forest suddenly opens into a vast clearing, and holy fuck—my grip on Gullfax's reins tightens at the sight before us. An immense ice labyrinth rises from the snow-covered ground, its crystal walls stretching toward the pearl-white sky. Jagged spires of frost twist upward like frozen daggers, while narrow passages snake between walls that shimmer with an otherworldly blue glow.

"The Frost Maze," Baldr announces, his earlier smugness replaced by something darker. "Skadi's playground."

"You've got to be fucking kidding me," Dani mutters against my back. "We have to go through that?"

I catch glimpses of shifting shadows through gaps in the translucent walls—things that shouldn't exist in a place this bright. The wind howls through the maze's corridors, carrying whispers that sound too much like laughter for comfort.

"The Einherjar awaits at the center," Bryn's voice is tense. "But the paths... they shift—change. Like the shadows that corrupted her."

Fuck. A shape-shifting ice maze guarded by a shadow-touched Valkyrie.

I slide off Gullfax, boots crunching in fresh snow as I reach for Dani. Movement catches my eye—Erik materializing beside Bryn like a silver shadow. Before she can dismount, his hands are already at her waist.

"Always the hero, silfrhár." Bryn's words crack like ice, but that spark in her eyes betrays her. The same fire Dani had when she fought our bond.

"Only for you, little bird." Erik's voice carries that dangerous edge I haven't heard in centuries, his fingers lingering on her hips.

Bryn jerks away, but not before I catch the flush creeping up her neck. About fucking time my brother showed some backbone.

Baldr loops Sleipnir's reins around a frost-covered branch. Dani's hand catches my wrist as I reach to do the same with Gullfax.

"He says to leave him free." That familiar sass curves her lips. "In case your Viking ass needs saving."

The golden steed tosses his head, huffing in what sounds suspiciously like agreement—cocky bastard. I drop the reins and pat his flank, earning a gentle headbutt that nearly knocks me into the snow.

"Alright, you oversized show-off," I mutter, following the others toward the towering ice walls. "Just don't wander too far."

Baldr's pack hits the snow with a dull thud. "Erik, Bryn—firewood. We'll make camp while our saviors handle the essence." His tone heavy with that entitled Ásgardian bullshit.

"Oh, look at that," Bryn scoffs. "Odin's precious son can't soil his hands with manual labor." She kicks a frozen branch his way. "Afraid you might chip a nail, *your highness?*"

Erik's silver eyes dance between them, and I catch the smirk tugging at his lips. Seems my brother enjoys watching his mate put arrogant fuckers in their place.

"Such fire from a Valkyrie—or should I say *ex-Valkyrie.*" Baldr sprawls against a fallen log, brushing imaginary dust from his sleeve. "Perhaps that's why you failed your original destiny."

This motherfucker.

The temperature drops ten degrees. Bryn's fingers curl around her blade hilt, knuckles white with rage. But before she can respond, Erik's hulking form fills the space between them, all barely controlled rage and violence.

"Watch your tongue, *prince,*" Erik's voice carries that deadly calm that usually precedes bloodshed. "Or I'll help you find it in the snow."

"Both of you, enough." Dani steps forward, gold eyes flashing. "If his royal ass wants to freeze while we work, that's his choice." She starts gathering branches, shooting Baldr a look that would wither lesser men. "Though I'm sure Odin would love hearing how his son sat on his ass while a *mere* Valkyrie did all the work."

Baldr's jaw ticks. He rises slowly, deliberately, like an asshole trying to save face. "Perhaps I could assist. After all, what kind of host would I be?"

This arrogant prick. I meet Erik's gaze and can't suppress a smirk. He's practically vibrating with the urge to tear this jackass apart for daring to disrespect his mate.

The flames leap to life under Dani's touch, casting dancing shadows across the ice walls. My fingers flex, impatient. Time to face whatever fucked up challenges this maze has waiting for us.

"Anything we should know before we enter?" Dani asks, eyeing the towering maze—frost cracking along its surface like living veins.

Baldr stretches lazily by the fire, that fucking smirk still plastered on his face. "Where would the fun be in that, little savior?" He tosses her a jar and Dani catches it, putting it in her bag. "Good luck."

I make a fist, itching to introduce his face to the nearest tree. Dani's hand finds mine, squeezing once. Her eye roll speaks volumes as she tugs me toward the entrance.

"Useless piece of—" The maze swallows the rest of her muttered curse as we step through the icy archway: the temperature plummets, our breath clouding the air in frozen swirls. Behind us, the entrance shrinks away, swallowed by walls that pulse with an eerie blue glow.

Well, fuck. Guess we're doing this blind.

"Hmm, this is cozy." Dani's voice wavers as her fingers lace through mine. The walls narrow, forcing us to walk single file, her other hand trailing the ice beside us.

The first intersection splits three ways. Identical passages stretch into shadow, each promising its own brand of *fuck that.* A bitter wind howls through the corridors, carrying whispers that sound too much like my name.

scraaaape

We freeze. Something drags across the ice behind us—claws or steel, I can't tell. But when I turn, the passage is empty. It is just our reflections staring back, multiplied in the icy walls.

Wait.

I count again. Three reflections of me. Four of Dani.

The extra one smiles.

"Don't look," Dani's grip tightens. "Just... don't look at them."

Ice groans overhead, shifting like a living thing. The walls around us ripple, reflecting twisted versions of ourselves—darker, hungrier versions that move a heartbeat too slow.

"Screw this." Dani's hands glow, warmth spreading through the chamber as she summons her light. The golden sphere pushes back the shadows, revealing ice-slicked walls and jagged formations. My chest tightens—her power like a beacon in this frozen hell. Beautiful, but dangerous. Every predator in this maze will see it.

"Don't waste your energy unless we need it."

"Rhy—" Dani's whisper cuts off as shadows slither across the ice. Not our shadows. These move against the light, writhing like smoke given form.

"Kill the light. Now." I pull her behind me, positioning myself between her and those shadows. Every protective instinct screams as they twist toward her glow.

The darkness crashes back in as she extinguishes her light. I keep her pressed against my back, scanning the blackness for movement. Her fingers grip my shirt, trusting me to keep her safe. And I will—even if I have to tear every shadow in this maze apart.

A child's laugh echoes down the corridor ahead. Wrong. *So fucking wrong.*

"Stay close." I grab her hand, heading further in, scanning the crystalline walls. Our reflections multiply, fracture, until a thousand versions of ourselves surround us. Some smile with too many teeth.

drip

drip

Something warm hits my cheek. Red droplets splatter the frost at our feet. Above us, half-frozen into the ceiling, a body twists at an impossible angle. Its face—what's left of it—stares down with milky eyes.

"Shit—" Dani stumbles back. "What the *hell* is *that?!*" The corpse's head snaps toward her voice, jaw unhinging like a snake's.

"Fuck if I know." I shove her back, placing myself between her and that thing as it drops. Its body crackles with frost, landing where she stood seconds ago, limbs twisted and contorted, as it scuttles toward us.

"Holy shit—"

"Time to go—hold onto me!" I wrap my arm around her waist, practically lifting her off her feet as we tear down the left passage. Her heart hammers against my side, each terrified beat driving me faster. Ice splinters under our boots, but I don't give a shit about stealth anymore. Not with that thing's wet shuffle getting closer, the walls pulsing like some twisted heartbeat around us.

"There!" Dani points right. A narrow crevice in the ice. I push her through first, my body shielding her as claws rake across my back. Pain explodes between my shoulder blades, but I don't give a fuck—as long as they didn't touch her.

The passage opens into a circular chamber. Six identical exits mock us, each framed by jagged icicles that drip with something too dark to be water. I keep Dani tucked against my side, scanning for threats.

"Please tell me you have some internal-compass thing going on right now," Dani pants, gold eyes scanning each exit. "Are you okay?" She looks at my back that is already healing.

Before I can answer, that child's laugh rings out again. Closer. Small footprints appear in the frost, forming one by one, leading to the second passage on the left.

A small voice cuts through the frozen air. "Papa..."

Ice floods my veins. Ten feet away stands a boy—black hair, ocean-blue eyes mirror of my own. Ten years old. Forever ten years old.

No. Not real. Can't be real.

"What's wrong?" Dani's hand finds my arm. "Rhyland?"

My son takes a step closer, skin pale as the ice around us. Dead eyes fixed on mine. "Why didn't you save me, Papa?"

"What do you see?" Dani's voice shakes. Her grip tightens, but her gaze is fixed on empty air to our right.

Words scrape in my throat. "You don't... you can't see him?"

"Mom?" Dani's whole body jerks, color draining from her face as she stares at nothing. "That's not—you're not—"

Fuck. This place is in our heads, twisting our worst memories into weapons. I pull Dani closer, but can't tear my eyes from my son's lifeless face.

Not real. Not real. Not fucking real.

A shadow darts between our reflections—too fast, too fluid. Not human. Not even close.

"Don't believe what you see." I pull her tighter against my side as we run, my body angled to take any attack that might come.

The passage narrows, forcing us to move sideways. That fucking laugh bounces off the walls—ahead, behind, everywhere. More footprints appear, overlapping now, like dozens of children running circles around us.

"Run."

A flash of white in the ice—a small hand presses against the surface. Then another. And another. The walls fill with them, pushing outward like they're trying to break through.

"Oh, my god. What the hell is this?" Dani pants, freaking the fuck out.

I yank Dani in front of me as the first fingers crack through the ice. "I gotcha ya, baby. Keep moving." My arm bars across her chest, keeping her shielded as we back away. "Don't let them touch you."

The passage splits—right fork pulses with an eerie blue light—left fork darker than sin.

"Play with us..."

The whispers slide like oil down my spine. Through the ice, small faces watch us, skin blue with frost, eyes black as pitch. They track Dani's movements with hungry intensity.

"Left," she gasps. "Has to be left."

A wet scraping sound above snaps my attention. That corpse-thing skitters across the ceiling like a broken spider, head twisting completely backward to focus on Dani. Its mouth stretches into a Glasgow smile, dripping something dark.

"Close your eyes. Now." Lightning crackles to life in my palm, the charge making my hair stand on end—answering my call easily—I curve my body around hers as the walls reflect the energy, turning everything into a storm of blue-white fury. The children in the walls shriek, recoiling from the light.

With Dani's face buried against my chest, I hurl the bolt behind us. Ice explodes. The corpse-thing's scream tears through the air—a sound no human could make.

I half-carry, half-drag her through the darkness, my body between her and whatever horrors might lurk in the shadows. The temperature plummets until each breath feels like swallowing glass, but I barely notice. Every instinct screams to protect her, to get her through this frozen nightmare alive.

The passage opens into a cramped chamber, darkness pressing in from all sides. My eyes strain to pierce the gloom, tracking Dani as she releases my hand to explore. Her boots scrape against the ice as she moves.

"Careful—" The warning dies in my throat as her feet slide out from under her. My heart stops, but she catches herself against the wall, laughing nervously.

"I'm fine. Just channeling my inner figure skater. Minus the grace. And the skill. And the—"

The ice beneath our feet cracks—a sound like breaking bones. Fissures spider-web outward, glowing with that blue light.

"Dani!" I lunge for her as the ground shatters. My fingers lock around her wrist just as she starts to fall, her scream echoing off the icy walls. She dangles over a pit of absolute darkness, chunks of ice tumbling into the void below.

"Don't let go," she gasps, gold eyes blazing, wide with terror. "Oh my god. Rhyland, please—"

"I've got you, baby." My other hand grips the edge of solid ice, muscles straining. Below us, something moves in the darkness. Something massive. "I won't let you fall. Just hold on."

Her eyes lock with mine, terror bleeding through our bond. A sound rises from the depths—like huge wings unfurling. Red eyes blink open in the void, dozens of them, all fixed on Dani.

The ice under my hand splinters. *Fuck.* We're both going down.

I yank Dani up hard, wrapping myself around her as we fall. Whatever's waiting below can tear through me first. My back slams into something solid—a ledge of black ice—and I twist to take the full impact, keeping her pressed against my chest.

CRACK

We slam through more layers of ice, each impact threatening to tear her from my grip. I hold tighter, taking the brunt of every hit. Pain explodes across my back, my shoulders, but I don't give a fuck—as long as she's protected.

We crash into hard ground, the impact driving every ounce of air from my lungs. For one terrifying heartbeat, I can't feel her breathing.

"Dani?" My hands shake as they roam over her body, checking for injuries. "Baby, talk to me."

She coughs, face buried against my chest. "Define talking." Her voice is muffled but steady. *Thank fuck.* "Because if you mean 'coherent sentences', I might need a minute."

"You okay?"

"Yeah. I think so."

Light bleeds through the ice above, casting everything in that sick blue glow. We've landed in some perfectly circular chamber, with walls stretching into darkness. No visible exit. Just smooth ice and—

"Oh, god." Dani's grip tightens on my arm.

Bodies. Dozens of them, frozen into the walls like macabre decorations. Fallen warriors, from their armor and weapons. Their faces twisted in eternal screams.

"Seriously?" Dani's voice shakes as she eyes the frozen corpses. "Do all Einherjar shop at 'Bodies R Us' for their interior design?"

A harsh laugh escapes me despite the horror. Trust my mate to find sarcasm in the face of death. But she's right—this twisted collection mirrors Vidar's fucked up gallery. These fuckers have a real thing for decorating with the dead.

"Welcome, child of prophecy..."

The voice slithers through the chamber, ancient and cold as death itself. The temperature drops until my vampire blood feels like ice in my veins.

A figure in the center of the chamber is a woman in tattered Valkyrie armor. Frost covers half her face like a mask, her remaining eye glowing with that same blue light.

Skadi. The fallen one.

"Your trial begins. Let's see if you're worthy of the essence."

One of the frozen warriors twitches. Then another. Ice cracks as dead limbs begin to move.

"Any brilliant ideas?" I ask as the first warrior breaks free, ice falling from its preserved flesh like shattered armor.

Dani's hands begin to glow with that inner light. "Yeah. Don't die."

ERIK

56

The firelight casts long shadows across our makeshift camp, each flicker illuminating Baldr's insufferable smirk as he reclines against the fallen log. His posture speaks of centuries of unearned privilege—the kind that makes my sword hand twitch.

Bryn maintains her warrior's composure beside me, though I note the slight tightening of her fingers around her horn of mead. Even in this tension, she carries herself with the dignity of a true Valkyrie.

"Tell me, Erik." Baldr's voice carries that aristocratic mockery that makes me want to feed him his own teeth. "How long have you been following our little fallen Valkyrie around like a lost pup?"

"Careful, *your highness*." Bryn's tone could freeze Muspelheim. "Your crown's on so tight it's cutting off blood to what little brain you have."

Baldr laughs. "Oh come now, Brynhildr. We all know your taste runs to... cruder stock."

She grits her teeth, "It's *Bryn*."

My growl fills the clearing as my fingers flex with the need to break things—preferably his face.

"After all," he continues, lips curling into a cruel smile, "isn't that why you let those warriors use you so carelessly, Brynhildr? Always choosing the ones who treated you like the common whore you'd become?"

When it comes, my voice carries the deadly calm that has heralded the end of countless enemies. "Choose your next words with extreme care, *prince*. Your title won't protect you from what follows."

"Such loyalty." Baldr's smile turns vicious. "But we both know she prefers her men cruel. Tell me, Erik, can you give her what she needs? Or are you too... civilized?"

"For Hell's sake, fuck off, Baldr. What in Odin's balls has gotten into you, you fífl?" Bryn's voice cuts through the tension, sharp as a Valkyrie's blade.

"Nothing." He snaps a twig, tossing it into the flames with deliberate arrogance. "Just making conversation." My control hangs by a thread as his eyes fix on me with malicious intent. "Does it not bother you that Brynhildr's been the compound's favorite whore? You must have quite the taste for used—"

The crack of my fist against his jaw silences his filthy tongue, the impact echoing through the clearing. Blood—red and bright—stains his perfect mouth, and something in me purrs at the sight. But before I can savor it, the world spins.

Pine trees shatter against my back—one, two, three—before the frozen ground rushes to meet me. Snow explodes around my impact, the bitter cold starkly contrasting the fury burning in my veins. The prince may dress like a pampered peacock, but the force behind his blow reminds me why Odin's blood runs through his veins.

Instinct takes over. One heartbeat I'm in the snow, the next my fingers wrap around his precious throat, squeezing with pent-up violence. His pulse hammers against my palm—fast, frantic, afraid.

"I warned you, *prince*." My grip tightens as he chokes, face turning an interesting shade of purple. "One more fucking word about her—"

"Erik." Bryn's hand finds my arm, her touch burning through my rage. "Release him. Odin will have my head if his precious heir returns with bruises."

Of course. The entitled bastard can spew whatever vileness he wants, protected by daddy's crown and title. My roar of frustration echoes across the frozen landscape as I release him, boots crunching through deep snow as I put distance between us before I do something that starts another fucking war.

Baldr's laugh—sharp and mocking—chases me through the trees. "Thank you for proving my point, vampire!" His voice drips with cruel satisfaction. "I'm sure my father will be most intrigued by your... attachment to his *fallen* Valkyrie."

A threat. A promise. I can't tell. Bryn's low and furious voice cuts through the night, her words lost to the wind but their intent clear.

Moments later, her footsteps follow, quick and light across the frozen ground. She doesn't call out, doesn't demand I stop. She just follows, silent and steady, a warrior's presence at my back.

The frozen forest swallows my rage as I finally stop, chest heaving. This fury coursing through my veins feels foreign—wild and uncontrolled. The bond pulses with it, transforming centuries of careful restraint into something dangerous.

Her footsteps crunch softly behind me, stopping a respectful distance away. I sense her hesitation and feel it in how she shifts her weight from foot to foot.

"Hey." Just one word, but it carries a world of understanding.

"I apologize." The words taste bitter. "That display of—"

A flash of movement, and suddenly she's there. My words are cut off as her finger presses against my lips. The heat of her catches me off guard—she burns like a star, close enough that I can taste her breath on my tongue, count each golden fleck in her Noric blue eye.

The space between us crackles with tension, heavy with things unsaid. Her scent—honey and steel and battle-fury—fills my lungs, making my head spin.

"I... liked it. No one's ever..." Her voice catches, those eyes blazing with something that stirs my beast. "That's twice now you've defended me—no one's ever done anything like that for me, Erik."

The way she says my name, like it's something sacred, something cherished...

I can't resist pulling her flush against me, needing to feel her. Memories of last night flood my mind—her taste, scent, and how she shattered so beautifully around me. I want that again. Want *her*, in every way possible.

Her fingers trace the lines of my face, each touch a whisper of silk against my skin. Her eyes search mine with an intensity that steals my breath. It's as if she's seeing me, genuinely seeing me, for the first time.

"What am I going to do with you, silfrhár?" Her voice is a sigh, a surrender, an invitation.

My lips find hers, gentle at first—until she moans into my mouth. The sound ignites a hunger I can't control as I pull her closer, hands spanning her waist through layers of fur and leather.

Her fingers tangle in my hair as she arches into me. I groan when she tugs, the sensation sparking like lightning down my spine.

The world blurs. Her back hits the ancient pine, snow cascading around us like stars.

"Sorry—"

"Stop." She growls against my mouth, teeth catching my bottom lip. "Stop apologizing."

The hunger in her voice makes my chest ache. How many taught her that violence was all she deserved? My touch is gentle, and my kiss is turning from desperate to reverent. I'll show her there's more than rough hands and cruel touches.

She whimpers as I trace her lips with my tongue, the sound soft and surprised. Each brush of my mouth against hers is a promise, each caress a prayer. The kiss deepens, slow and thorough—stoking embers into steady flame.

The ground trembles beneath our feet, vibrating like a colossal heartbeat pulsing through the frozen earth. Our lips tear apart as Bryn's eyes widen with recognition—instincts reading danger in the rhythmic tremors.

"Shit." She stumbles back, her warrior's stance returning as she scans the darkening forest. The tremors continue, rhythmic, like giant footfalls shaking the world.

"Bryn—"

"Frost giant." Her voice carries the sharp edge of experience. "They hunt these woods after sunset." Her fingers lock around mine, pulling us toward camp through the snow. "Move. Now."

The tremors grow stronger, each impact rattling ancient pines and sending cascades of snow from their branches. My mind struggles to process the reality of it—a fucking frost giant? But the terror in Bryn's quickening pulse tells me everything I need to know.

The camp materializes through the trees, conspicuously missing one arrogant prince. Of course the bastard fled. Bryn's movements are fluid, practiced—her sword singing free of its scabbard as her shield settles against her arm. Grave Warden's weight feels right in my palm, the blade gleaming with deadly promise in the fading light.

"What's the strategy?"

"Aim for the joints." Bryn's voice carries the authority of countless battles. "Knees, elbows, neck—anywhere the ice armor is thinnest." Another tremor rocks the ground, closer now. "And whatever you do, don't let them grab you. Their touch turns flesh to ice."

The forest groans around us as ancient trees bend under an unseen weight. Bryn shifts into a battle stance I've seen a thousand times in training, but never with such lethal focus.

"They're strong but slow." Her eyes track something in the darkness that my vampire sight hasn't caught yet. "Use your speed. Strike fast, strike hard, and for fuck's sake, don't try to match their strength."

The world slows and crystallizes, that familiar clarity washing over me as future echoes ripple through my mind. *Left. Down. Pivot.* The giant's movements paint themselves in my thoughts seconds before they happen.

A mighty hand, blue as glacier ice, swings through the space where my head was a heartbeat ago. Snow explodes as the giant's fist connects with empty air. Bryn's already moving, her blade a silver arc that catches moonlight as she darts between the creature's legs.

Duck. Roll. Strike.

The vision comes just in time. I drop as a chunk of ice the size of a horse whistles overhead. Grave Warden finds the soft spot behind the giant's knee—exactly where Bryn said it would be. Black blood, thick as tar, steams in the frozen air.

"Erik!" Bryn's voice cuts through the night. She's airborne, shield braced, creating the perfect springboard. Without hesitation, I blur forward, plant my foot on her shield, and let her Valkyrie strength launch me toward the giant's face.

Right eye. Three seconds. Block.

The creature's hand comes up to swat me away—exactly as I saw it would. But I'm already twisting, using its own arm as a runway. Grave Warden plunges deep into its right eye socket. The roar that follows shakes snow from distant peaks.

Bryn moves quickly beneath the giant, her blade finding every weak point in its ice armor. We dance around it in perfect synchronization—her knowledge of its weaknesses combining with my ability to see its moves before they come.

Behind you. Now.

I spin, catching Bryn around the waist as she leaps toward me. The giant's fist crashes into the ground where she stood. Using her momentum, I swing her in a wide arc, her blade carving a deep groove in the creature's throat as she passes.

The bond between us hums with need. Each move flows into the next, centuries of combat experience merging with Valkyrie training. We're no longer two warriors—we're a single weapon aimed at the giant's heart.

Left shoulder. Impact. Bryn.

The vision hits too late. The giant's backhand catches Bryn mid-leap, sending her crashing through the treeline. The sound of splintering wood and her choked cry tears through my chest like a blade.

"BRYN!"

The giant's laugh rumbles like an avalanche. Ice crystals form in the air around its remaining eye, spreading outward in deadly spikes. One grazes my shoulder—pain explodes, flesh instantly blackening with frost.

Above. Behind. Strike.

I blur through the forest, following the trail of broken trees. Bryn lies crumpled against an extensive pine, blood staining the snow beneath her. Her shield arm hangs at an unnatural angle, skin already turning blue where the giant's touch burned her.

The ground trembles. I grab her just as a massive foot crashes down, pulverizing the spot where she lay. Her breath hitches with pain as I cradle her against my chest, dodging another swipe of those lethal hands.

"Put me down," she growls through gritted teeth, though her good hand clutches my jacket. "I can still fight."

Duck. Roll. Three seconds.

I dive behind a boulder as ice spears shred the air where we stood. "Like hell." The words come out as a snarl. "Your arm—"

"Is just an arm." She pushes away from me, swaying but upright. Blood trickles from her hairline, but her eyes burn with Valkyrie fire. "I've killed these bastards with worse."

The giant's roar drowns out my protest. It charges through the trees, each step leaving craters of black ice in the snow. Bryn's blade flashes in her good hand, a familiar gleam of battle-lust in her eyes.

Left knee. Opening. Now.

"Goddamnit, Bryn," I growl, positioning myself at her back. Her response is a war cry that would make the gods themselves tremble.

Above. Shatter. Jump.

Ice rains as the giant brings both fists down, splitting the earth where we stand. Bryn rolls left, I blur right—perfect synchronization even with her injuries. Her blade finds the creature's ankle, black blood spurting as she severs a tendon.

The giant stumbles, its howl of pain echoing off distant peaks. But its hand sweeps low, catching Bryn before she can dodge. Ice spreads up her leg where its fingers graze her.

Three seconds. Choice. Death.

The vision hits like a blade to the gut—Bryn, frozen solid, shattering against the forest floor.

Not happening.

Not while I breathe.

I launch at the giant's face, Grave Warden singing through the air. The blade connects with its remaining eye as its grip tightens on Bryn. The creature rears back, releasing her as it claws at its ruined face.

Bryn hits the ground hard, her cry of pain cutting through me like physical wounds. Ice creeps up her thigh, turning her skin a deadly shade of blue.

Behind. Above. Strike.

The giant's blind fury sends trees crashing around us. I blur to Bryn's side, scooping her up as a gigantic pine splinters where we were seconds ago. Her skin burns with cold against mine, her breath coming in short, sharp gasps.

"The neck," she grits, fingers digging into my shoulder. "While it's blind. I'll be your distraction."

"Fuck no   "

"Trust me." Those magical eyes lock onto mine, fierce despite the pain. "I'm not done fighting yet."

"So goddamn stubborn—"

"Here." Bryn shoves her blade into my free hand, her skin now ghostly pale against the spreading ice. "Throw me."

Understanding clicks. My grip tightens on her good arm as the giant thrashes blindly, searching for us with his hands.

Left. Up. Death.

I spin, using my strength to launch her straight at the giant's chest. Despite her injuries, Bryn's aim is lethal—her shield slams into its throat, the edge biting deep. The creature stumbles back, hands clawing at the metal embedded in its flesh.

Now. Neck. End it.

Time slows. I blur up the giant's arm, both blades crossed before me. It's skin burns through my clothes, but I don't feel it. All I see is Bryn on the ground, ice crawling up her body, her breaths growing shallow.

Grave Warden and Bryn's sword scissor through the giant's neck, spraying black blood across the snow. The head topples first, crystallizing before it hits the ground. The enormous body follows, crashing down with enough force to shake the ground.

I'm at Bryn's side before the echo fades, gathering her against my chest. The ice has reached her hip, her skin blue and brittle.

"Show off," she manages through chattering teeth, trying to smile despite the pain. "Didn't have to... use both swords."

"Hush." I tear at my jacket, wrapping it around her frozen limbs. "Save your strength."

Her laugh comes out as a pained gasp. "Made quite the team... didn't we, Silfrhár?"

The giant's corpse begins to crack, spreading into a network of fissures before shattering completely. The sound mirrors the fractures spreading through my chest as I cradle Bryn closer, willing my body heat to fight back the deadly cold consuming her.

"Tell me how to fix this." My voice shakes as the ice spreads past her waist. "There has to be something—some Valkyrie healing, some ancient magic—"

"Nothing." Her fingers, blue and trembling, brush my cheek. "Frost giant's touch... it's fatal. Always has been." A bitter laugh escapes her. "At least... I died fighting."

The resignation in her voice ignites something in my chest. Centuries of memories flash through my mind—warriors I've watched die, lovers lost to time, an eternity of helplessness.

Not her. Not Bryn. Not my mate.

"Nothing left... to fight for," she whispers, those eyes growing distant. Each word falls like ice between us.

Disbelief wars with the ache in my chest. How can those words fall so easily from her lips? She's found Dani, a sister who needs her, who already loves her with the fierce devotion only family can inspire.

And she's found me. Her soulmate, her other half, no matter how hard she tries to deny the pull between us—the bond hums with the truth of it, an ancient melody that resonates in our very bones.

"Fuck. That." My voice cracks with centuries of buried emotion. "You don't get to decide you're worthless, Bryn. Not after making me feel—" The words strangle in my throat. "Not after making me *care*."

My fangs tear into my wrist with savage force. Blood wells up, dark and potent with power.

"Erik, don't—"

"Shut up." I press my bleeding wrist to her lips, my other hand cradling her head. "For once in your stubborn life, just shut up and let someone save you."

Her resistance lasts only a moment before instinct takes over. Each pull of her mouth sends electricity through my veins, the bond begging to be sealed, flaring bright and wild.

The change is immediate. Where my blood touches her lips, color floods back into her skin. The ice coating her body begins to crack, melting away like spring thaw. Her heartbeat strengthens, the sound of it filling my ears like the sweetest music.

Bryn gasps as feeling returns to her limbs, her body arching against mine. Her fingers dig into my arm, holding my wrist to her mouth as she drinks deeper. The warrior in her finally choosing to fight, to live, to stay.

The beast in me claws at its chains, demanding I complete the bond—take her blood as she takes mine. But ancient law binds me as surely as my own control. The bond must be mutual, willing, chosen.

Still, satisfaction courses through me as I watch life flood back into her body. The blue tinge of death fades, replaced by the vibrant glow of a Valkyrie reborn. Her eyes spark with renewed fire, the shadow of defeat banished by the light of her spirit.

I pull my wrist back. Bryn's tongue darts out, catching a stray drop of blood at the corner of her mouth. The sight sends heat rushing south.

"Well," she drawls, a familiar smirk tugging at her lips, "I was expecting Jörmungandr's rotting scales, but that wasn't half bad."

The laugh that bursts from my chest feels foreign, rusty with disuse. When was the last time I found genuine amusement in anything? But Bryn's morbid humor, even in the face of death, is so quintessentially *her* that I can't help but be charmed.

"Only you," I manage through the unfamiliar sensation of laughter, "would compare my ancient blood to a giant snake's ass."

She sits up, testing her limbs gingerly. The ice is gone, not even a trace of frostbite marring her skin. Only the rips in her clothing and the drying blood suggest she was even injured.

"Suppose I should thank you," she says, but there's no bite to her words. "Though if you tell anyone a vampire had to save my ass, I'll deny it to Odin himself."

I shake my head, marvel at the complex creature before me—fierce and fragile, stubborn and vulnerable, a walking contradiction that somehow slipped past my defenses.

"Wouldn't dream of it," I assure her, helping her to her feet. "Your secret's safe with me, little bird."

DANICA

57

S kadi rises from her frozen throne, vast wings unfurling like shattered obsidian. Half her face gleams with frost, the other twisted in a cruel smirk. Her Valkyrie armor, once golden, now dulled and corroded, hangs in tatters from her towering frame. One eye glows that sickly blue while the other remains pure shadow.

"Look at the little savior," she croons, voice like cracking ice. "Tell me, do you still hear your parents' screams? The sound of wolves tearing them apart because of what you are?"

The memory slams into me—my parents' bloody, torn up bodies. All because Rhyland killed that pack protecting me, and Azrael wanted revenge.

"Shut up," I snarl, summoning angel fire as the first wave of frozen warriors lurch forward.

"Such spirit." Skadi's wings create hurricane winds. "Like John had, before that wolf snapped his neck. Another death on your conscience."

Sweet, protective John. My heart aches as memories of my former boss at Playful Pint flood back—his kind smile, his dad jokes, the way he looked out for all of us like we were family. But those warm memories shatter against the horror of his final moments—his terrified eyes meeting mine as he tried to save me, that awful sound I'll never forget, my own screams echoing uselessly in my ears as I watched him fall...

A dead Viking's blade snaps me back. I bend backwards, time slowing as I arch under his swing. My daggers find gaps in ancient armor, shattering frozen flesh—the Aquanite stone pulses, connecting me to every frozen particle in the chamber.

I reach out with my power, feeling the crystalline structure of the frozen warriors. With a twist of my will, their icy forms crack and splinter from within.

"Dance for me, little savior." Skadi's laughter echoes as more warriors emerge. "Like Adrian danced when his heart was ripped out. Another lost protecting you."

Adrian's death hits my heart like shrapnel. But I channel the pain, letting the Aquanite's power flow through me. The chamber walls respond, ice spears erupting to impale approaching warriors while others dissolve into water at my command, their frozen forms melting and reforming as deadly weapons.

Across the chamber, Rhyland is raw power incarnate. His telekinesis sends corpses shattering against walls, their frozen bodies exploding into crystalline shards. But more keep coming.

"Even your brother," Skadi taunts. "Forced into darkness because of your blood. How many more will fall protecting the precious savior?"

"ENOUGH!" My scream releases a wave of pure light, disintegrating a dozen warriors. Time bends to my will as I flow between the remaining attackers. My daggers sing, finding killing blows while angel fire consumes anything that gets too close. Ice walls rise and fall at my command, crushing enemies while frozen spikes erupt from the ground to skewer others.

"Poor cursed girl," Skadi sighs dramatically. "Death follows you like a shadow. How long before your Viking joins the list?"

"DANI!" Rhyland's voice thunders through the chamber, that alpha-male command that usually makes me want to roll my eyes. But right now, as he slams two warriors into the wall with bone-crushing force, that voice is my anchor. "Block her out and focus on me. Feel our bond."

The sound of ice shattering follows another warrior's demise under his fist. His power pulses through our bond, fierce and protective as he roars, "You're stronger than her games, Angel. Now fight!"

And damn if that voice doesn't light a fire in my blood.

Ice and fire spiral around me as rage ignites in my chest. The chamber becomes a blur of spinning blades and exploding corpses. Each taunt fuels my fury, not because I'm helpless—I've never been helpless. But every death, every loss, every sacrifice made in my name weighs on my soul like a mountain of guilt.

"You want to play mind games?" I snarl, power crackling around me like a storm. "Game fucking on."

A horrific crack splinters the air. My heart stops as Rhyland's agonized scream tears through me. Time slows as I spin to see him—a giant wooden beam protruding from his chest, blood darkening his shirt. His ocean eyes meet mine, wide with shock.

"RHYLAND!"

I lunge toward him but Skadi appears in a blur of frost and shadow. Her wing catches me in the ribs, sending me flying into the ice wall. Pain explodes through my back.

"Poor little girl," she purrs, hovering between us. "Always watching the ones you love suffer."

A familiar figure emerges from the shadows. My heart clenches—John, whole and alive, that same protective smile on his face. But his eyes... wrong. Empty.

"You let me die, Dani." His voice echoes. "I trusted you."

"Not real," I gasp, but hesitate a half-second too long. His blade finds my shoulder, hot pain blooming as steel parts flesh. I roll with the blow, coming up with daggers crossed just as John lunges.

"I'm sorry," I whisper, angel fire consuming his form. The sound of his screams—even fake ones—tear at my soul.

Skadi's laughter rings out as two more figures materialize—Mom and Dad, but twisted, bloody. Wolf bites mar their flesh.

"Sweetheart," Mom reaches for me with mangled hands. "Why didn't you save us?"

"You brought those monsters to our door," Dad's voice grates like broken glass.

I try to dodge but Dad's fist catches my jaw. Mom's nails rake down my back. Real blood flows—illusions shouldn't be able to...

"They're real enough," Skadi calls. "I pulled their memories from your mind. Every detail. Every wound."

Through our bond, I feel Rhyland's pain, his desperate struggle to reach the wooden beam. Each movement drives it deeper.

I summon the Aquanite's power, trying to clear my mind. Ice responds, spearing through Mom's chest. Her blood is so red against the frost. Dad's neck snaps under my kick, that same sickening crack as the real thing.

I gag, as bile churns in my stomach, burning my throat.

"Not done yet, Dani."

Adrian steps from the shadows, that wicked look in his eye. But his chest... a gaping hole where his heart should be.

"You did this," he gestures to the wound. "I died for you."

"No," I choke out, but his fist connects with my ribs. Something cracks. I stumble back, vision blurring from tears or blood loss or both.

Skadi appears behind me, her armored knee driving into my spine. I hit the ground hard, rolling just as her blade embeds in the ice where my head was.

"You're right," she sneers. "You're not helpless. You're worse—you're poison. Everything you touch dies."

Adrian's boot finds my stomach. I curl around the pain, eyes locked on Rhyland. Still struggling, still bleeding. Our bond pulses with agony.

No.

Not again.

Not one more person I love.

Something snaps inside me—not breaking, but awakening. The pain, the guilt, the rage... it all melds into something new. Something dangerous.

"You want to play with memories?" My voice sounds foreign, echoing with something ancient. "Let's play."

I reach deep into the ice chamber, feeling every frozen molecule. Adrian lunges but I'm done playing defense. Water rips from the ice walls, solidifying into razor-sharp spears that pierce his form. He dissolves into shadow with a scream that sounds too real.

"Impressive," Skadi materializes behind me. "But can you fight your demons and save your mate?"

Her wing slams into my back, sending me sprawling. The taste of copper fills my mouth. Through our bond, Rhyland's presence grows weaker.

Mom and Dad appear again, weapons raised. But this time I see through the illusion to the magic animating them. Time slows as I drop into a crouch, my daggers finding the weak points in the spell. They shatter like glass.

"He's dying," Skadi taunts. "I can smell his death. Better hurry, Lightborn."

She hurls another ice spear but I'm already moving. The Aquanite's power flows through me as I redirect her weapon, sending it screaming back at her. She dodges, but not fast enough—the ice shard slices through one wing.

"Bitch!" She snarls, all pretense of amusement gone. Her fist connects with my jaw, stars exploding behind my eyes. I taste more blood.

John appears next to her, but I'm done with ghosts. Angel fire erupts from my hands, incinerating the illusion before it fully forms. The flames catch Skadi's remaining wing, earning a shriek of rage.

She retaliates with a brutal combination—knee to ribs, elbow to face. Each blow feels like being hit by a truck. But I let the pain fuel me, catching her arm on the third strike.

Ice crawls up her limb as I unleash everything the Aquanite has taught me. She tries to pull away but I hold on, feeling the frost spread through her corrupted form.

"You think pain makes me weak?" Blood drips from my lips as I speak. "Pain is what made me who I am."

Her other fist cracks against my temple. The world spins but I don't let go. Ice continues to spread.

"Every person I've lost," I drive my knee into her stomach. "Every sacrifice made in my name," My elbow finds her throat. "They're not my weakness."

Through blurring vision, I see Rhyland slump forward.

"They're the reason I'll never stop fighting."

Every heartbeat sends fire through my broken ribs. Blood runs into my eyes from a gash on my forehead, but I can't spare a hand to wipe it away. Through our bond, Rhyland's agony threatens to bring me to my knees.

Skadi breaks free of the ice with a roar, her partially frozen wing shattering. She moves like liquid shadow, her fist connecting with my already cracked ribs. Something gives way inside me. I taste more blood.

"He's fading," she hisses, catching my hair and slamming my head into the wall. "Can you feel it? The way his life drains away?"

I can. God's help me, I can feel every second of his pain, every weakening breath. The wooden stake is killing him slowly, and our bond carries each moment of his suffering straight to my soul.

"DANICA!" Rhyland's roar echoes off the ice, his voice raw with desperation. I feel his rage and helplessness—watching me struggle while he's trapped on the other side of the chamber. His pain bleeds into mine, a feedback loop of shared agony as he's forced to witness my strength failing, unable to reach me.

My legs buckle but I force myself upright. The chamber spins sickeningly—probable concussion. Definitely internal bleeding. But none of that matters.

"Not..." I spit blood. "done yet."

Adrian materializes again, but this time I'm ready. As his fist comes at my face, I drop into a roll. The Aquanite pulses as I pull moisture from the air, forming ice daggers that find his throat. Another illusion shatters.

Skadi's kick catches my knee from behind. Something pops, wrong and loud. I scream as my leg gives out.

"Just give up, already," she laughs, grabbing my throat. "Can't even save herself, much less her mate."

Black spots dance at the edges of my vision. Through them, I see Rhyland struggle to reach the stake again. His movements are weaker now—our bond flutters like a dying heartbeat.

No.

No.

My body screams in protest, every muscle burning, aching. Exhaustion claws at my bones, but fuck that. I didn't come this far to roll over now. Even as darkness creeps at the edges of my vision, I bare my teeth in defiance. No fucking way am I giving up—like hell I'll let this bitch win.

I dive deep inside myself, clawing for that inferno that lives in my gut—that same holy fire that turned those Drauger bastards to ash. Rage and desperation feed the flames until they scream to be let loose. The power erupts from me in a wave of pure light, sending Skadi flying backward like she's been bitch-slapped by an angel. I slam into the ground hard enough to rattle my teeth, but muscle memory and pure stubbornness get me back on my feet, even as my knee threatens to tell me to go fuck myself.

"You want to see what I can do?" Blood drips from my mouth as I smile. "Let me show you what happens when you fuck with my man."

Power surges through me—raw and endless. The entire chamber groans as I reach for every particle of ice, every drop of frozen water. Skadi's eyes widen as the walls begin to crack.

"Impossible," she breathes.

I bare my bloodied teeth. "Watch me."

I reach deep into the chamber, willing every frozen particle to my command. Water and ice surge upward, encasing Skadi in a crystalline prison, glowing with my angelic light. Her scream of rage is muffled behind frozen walls.

I stumble to Rhyland, my body screaming in protest. Blood trails behind me as I reach him, hands shaking as they grasp the wooden beam.

"This is gonna hurt, babe." My voice breaks. "Ready?"

His eyes meet mine, ocean blue dulled with pain—one sharp nod.

I rip the beam free. Rhyland's roar echoes through the chamber as blood gushes from the wound. But I can already see the injury beginning to heal. He sucks in desperate breaths as the hole in his chest slowly knits closed.

The ice prison splinters. Skadi emerges in a fury of shadow and frost, but freezes mid-attack. Lightning crackles around Rhyland's hands, illuminating the chamber in brilliant white.

Her corrupted face twists in shock.

"No...it's not true," she hisses. "You died...the Godborn....you can't be—"

"Think again, bitch." Rhyland's voice is rough but firm.

Warmth floods my system as the Atherite stone finally decides to join the party.

Divine energy knits my ribs back together, sealing wounds and mending torn muscle.

Thanks for taking your sweet-ass time.

Skadi launches herself at us, but we move as one—Rhyland's lightning arcs across the chamber as my angelic fire erupts from my hands. Light and electricity combine, creating something new—something devastating.

"No!" Terror fills Skadi's voice. "You cannot possess both storm and light!"

"The fuck we can't," I snarl.

Power explodes from us both—pure creation meeting primal storm. Skadi's physical form dissolves in a burst of blinding light. Her essence erupts upward—a swirling vortex of wind and frost that illuminates the chamber in ethereal blue.

"Shit—" I lunge for my pack with all the grace of a drunk penguin, my healing legs choosing now to remind me they're still pissed off. The jar rolls free as the essence begins spiraling toward the ceiling. "Hey! Get your frosty ass back here!"

I snatch the jar and make a wild grab, but the essence dances out of reach. The swirling mass of power pulses mockingly as it hovers above us, always a few inches too far.

"Are you kidding me right now?" I glare at the dancing frost. "What are you, a toddler? Get in the damn jar!"

The essence swirls higher, moving in lazy circles near the ceiling. My arms shake from exhaustion as I jump around like an idiot trying to catch it.

Even Rhyland's height advantage isn't helping; his attempts are missing by inches. "Any ideas?" he grunts, frustration evident in his voice.

"Working on it," I mutter as the essence spins away again.

Then I feel that connection to the water molecules in the air—the same power I used to trap her physical form. With a grin, I reach out with the Aquanite's energy, creating an invisible funnel of crystalline air.

The essence fights the pull, but I've got it now. Slowly, inexorably, it spirals downward through my frozen tunnel until—

The essence enters into the jar with the force of a winter storm. I slam the lid shut, fingers trembling as I twist it tight.

Blue light pulses against the glass like a furious nightlight. I hold up my prize with a smirk. "Not so tough now, are you, you frosty bitch? Welcome to your new studio apartment."

RHYLAND

58

E rik and Bryn huddle near the fire like a pair of wounded animals, my brother looking like death warmed over. The massive fucking crater behind them tells its own story—something big went down while we were dealing with Skadi.

"What the hell happened here?" I ask, pulling Dani closer as we approach. My chest still aches where that wooden stake pierced me, a reminder of how fucking useless I was while my mate fought like a goddess incarnate. The memory of her fighting through Skadi's mind games, bleeding but unbowed, sends me equal waves of pride and shame.

Dani shifts against my side, probably sensing my brooding. She'd already told me to shut my mouth about the stake incident, right before accepting my blood with that fierce little growl of hers. Even with the Atherite stone working its magic, I wasn't taking chances with her healing.

Erik's silver eyes flick up, exhaustion etched in every line of his face. "Frost giant," he grunts, like that explains the goddamn apocalyptic scene around us.

Dani bolts to Bryn's side, her hands reaching for her sister. "Are you okay?"

Bryn's lips curl into a smirk, though her eyes soften at her sister's concern. "Sister, it takes more than some overgrown ice cube to put me down. Though I wouldn't mind finding a nice warm mead hall right about now."

A familiar whinny cuts through the tension. Gullfax emerges from the treeline, trotting toward us like he's ready to leave this frozen shitshow behind.

Smart fucking horse.

Erik scans us for damage. "I see you both made it out intact. The essence?"

"Oh, you mean this?" Dani pulls out the jar where Skadi's essence swirls like an angry blue storm. "Yeah, turns out when you piss off the savior, she might just stuff your magical essence in a mason jar." Her eyes sparkle with that sass I fucking live for.

Erik's lips twitch into that rare smirk. "Never doubted it, Little Huntress."

My patience with this frozen hellhole is wearing thin. "So what's the plan?" I scan the devastation around us. "And where the hell is Baldr?" That golden-haired bastard better not have bailed when we still need his divine ass for the next part of this clusterfuck.

Bryn stands, but her expression could freeze Hell. "That skítkarl probably ran crying to his father's halls the moment that frost giant showed its ugly face." She spits on the ground. "I say we head back to Valor's Watch. Let the precious prince find his balls and come to us."

Erik's jaw clenches, his silver eyes hardening into chips of ice. He stares at the fire like it's a personal insult, every line of his body radiating barely-contained fury. His fingers twitch toward his sword, and I swear I can hear his teeth grinding from here.

Fucking typical. Baldr probably said two words before Erik was ready to introduce him to the business end of his blade. That pompous golden prick has a talent for pissing people off just by existing.

"Are you sure about Valor's Watch?" Dani's eyes narrow with that look I know too damn well. The one that says she's done playing games. "Shouldn't we take this shit straight to Odin? Find out what crawled up Baldr's ass and sent him running?"

My mate's got a point. Valor's Watch is nothing but ghosts and bitter memories for Bryn now. Watching her walk those halls again, seeing the shadows of what could have been? Fuck that noise.

Erik locks his gaze with mine, that silent communication we've perfected over centuries passing between us. His slight nod says he's thinking the same thing. "Agreed. Ásgard it is."

The tension in Bryn's shoulders eases just a fraction—barely noticeable unless you're looking for it.

Yeah, definitely the right call.

The scent of lilacs and winter's frost fills our chambers as steam curls from the bath. Dani's clothes hit the floor, and my mouth waters at the sight of all that golden skin finally going to be free of ice and blood. My battle-worn leathers join her pile as we sink into the heated water.

The journey here was its own special kind of bullshit. Gullfax damn near started a war when Dani suggested he couldn't carry all four of us. My battle horse stomped his hoof and tossed his head at her like they were having a full-on argument—stubborn bastard. The portal was faster anyway, even if it did piss off our favorite golden stallion.

Dani slides between my thighs like she was made to fit there, her curves molding against my hard planes. My cock swells as she wiggles that perfect ass, teasing me without mercy.

The old man's summons won't come until evening, giving us time to wash away the remnants of our ice chamber adventure. My fingers trace the places where Dani's wounds have already healed, remembering how close that frozen bitch came to taking her from me. The memory makes my beast snarl even now, clean and safe in Odin's halls.

My lips brush her neck, tasting the lingering tension in her muscles. "What did she make you see?"

Dani's body trembles against mine, barely noticeable, but I feel every quiver. "My parents. John..." Her voice catches, and her fingers dig into my thighs beneath the water. "Adrian."

That name hits like a fucking blade to the gut. My brother's death—his betrayal—still burns like acid in my veins—the loss tears at me even while rage at his deception claws at my insides.

"They felt so real," she whispers, raw and vulnerable. "Every wound, every accusation. The way Mom's blood looked against the ice..." Her voice breaks, and my arms tighten instinctively around her.

"Look at me," I say softly, turning her face toward mine. Those glittering gold flecks in her eyes shine with unshed tears, and something in my chest fucking shatters. "You're the strongest person I've ever known, and I've lived for centuries. You faced your demons head-on and told them to go fuck themselves. You didn't just survive—you conquered." My thumb traces her cheekbone as emotion threatens to choke me. "Every day you remind me what it means to truly live, not just exist.

You're my light in an endless night, my anchor in the storm. And watching you rise from those ashes like a fucking phoenix in battle? Baby, you make me believe in miracles."

Those beautiful eyes lock onto mine, a single tear trailing down her cheek. "Smooth talker," she whispers, but her voice catches. Her fingers trace the ancient ink on my forearms, following the paths she's memorized countless times. "You know, for a grumpy vampire who growls more than he talks, you sure know how to make a girl feel special."

She lets out a watery laugh that makes my chest tight. "But you're wrong about one thing." Her head tips back, those eyes find mine, blazing. "I'm not the only strong one here. You think I don't see how you carry the weight of everyone's safety on those ridiculously broad shoulders? How you'd sacrifice everything to protect those you love?" A fierce light enters her eyes, the same one I saw when she faced down Skadi. "You're the other half of my soul, Rhyland. My protector, my home. And yeah, maybe you're a brooding pain in my ass sometimes—" her lips quirk into that smile that drives me wild "—but you're *my* brooding pain in the ass. My miracle. My everything."

I bury my face in her neck, breathing in that intoxicating scent that drives me wild—honey and sunshine and pure fucking Dani. "Fuck, I love you. You know that, don't you?" The words rumble from my chest, rough with emotion I can't contain.

"Mmm," she hums, melting back against me as her fingers continue to trace patterns on my forearms. "Let me think... Is it the way you growl when other men look at me? Or maybe it's how you can't keep your hands off me for more than five minutes?" She turns her head, mischief in those sparkling honey eyes. "I love you too, Sexy Fossil Face. More than your ancient ass will ever know."

Her head falls against my shoulder, exposing more of that delectable neck. "Ancient ass, huh?" I growl against her skin, letting my teeth graze that sensitive spot that makes her shiver. "Didn't hear you complaining about my age last night."

"Mmm," she purrs, arching into me like a cat. "Or the other day." Her ass grinds deliberately against my cock, making me hiss. "Though I have to say, for such an old man, your stamina is... impressive."

Fuck. My hands slide up her sides, cupping those luscious tits as she gasps. "Keep talking shit, baby," I rumble, thumbs brushing over her hardened nipples. "See where it gets you."

"Is that a threat or a promise, Thunder Buns?" Despite her teasing tone, she turns her head, her eyes dark with desire. She turns in my arms, water sloshing as she straddles my thighs. Those perfect tits press against my chest as she loops her arms around my neck.

My grip tightens possessively on her hips. "Both." I capture her mouth in a bruising kiss, swallowing her sassy comeback as she melts against me. Odin and his fucking evening audience can wait—my mate needs a proper reminder of precisely what this ancient ass can do.

Odin strides into the hall like a thunderstorm, Frigg gliding beside him with ethereal grace. And trailing behind them? Baldr, the golden shitstain himself.

My jaw clenches at the sight of him, molars grinding like millstones. Across the table, Erik's eyes narrow to slits, his hand twitching toward his sword. Bryn's gaze could freeze a lesser man's blood in his veins.

It takes every ounce of self-control not to launch across the table and introduce Baldr's ass to my boot. Repeatedly.

Odin settles into his seat, his presence filling the room like a physical force. "Þakka þér öllum fyrir að mæta." His voice rumbles. "Let me make this clear—Baldr's actions are not to be questioned. He cannot—"

"Baldr lacks the power to engage in direct combat," Frigg interjects, her melodic voice countering Odin's growl. "Ensuring his safety is paramount."

"Precisely." Odin's single eye fixes us with a stare that could make mountains kneel. "His knowledge of the realm is crucial to your quest."

Silence descends, broken only by the collective sound of jaws hitting the floor. Dani recovers first, her eyes wide with mock innocence. "No worries, your godliness." She says with false sweetness. "We managed just fine without Prince Charming over there."

Odin drains his mead, either oblivious or ignoring her sarcasm. "Good. Then we understand each other." His gaze shifts to Bryn, something ancient and unfathomable in his eye. "Brynhildr, mitt barn av vinden." His voice softens, heavy with sorrow. "Once my proudest Valkyrie, now grounded by sacrifice. Yet perhaps..." He leans forward, power crackling in the air. "Sometimes we must fall to rise higher. Your new path awaits, dóttir, one written in stars older than my wisdom. Trust your heart's flight—it knows the way."

Bryn inclines her head, a warrior acknowledging her king's words: "Þakka þér, faðir." Her voice is steady, but I catch the slight hitch in her breath.

Under the table, Erik's hand moves, a subtle shift that would go unnoticed by anyone not watching for it. But I see the way Bryn's fingers twitch, the almost imperceptible lean of her body toward his. A silent communication passes between them, a language of touch and breath and heartbeats that speaks louder than Odin's proclamations. In this moment, I clearly understand what the old man means about Bryn's new path.

It's not about wings or battles or destinies written in the stars. It's about finding strength in unexpected places, about forging bonds that even the gods couldn't predict. It's about love, plain and simple. The kind that weathers any storm, that rises from the ashes of what was to build something new and unbreakable.

And from the way Erik's eyes soften as they meet Bryn's, the way her lips curve into the ghost of a smile meant only for him? They're already walking that path, wings or no wings.

Odin's eye fixes on Dani and me. "I have heard of your triumph over my fallen champions. To capture the essence of both Skadi and Vidar?" He smiles, fierce and proud. "Only the true saviors could achieve such a feat."

He tears into a hunk of boar meat, the sound of his teeth rending flesh a reminder of the predator beneath the king's finery. "On the morrow, you will journey to the Elemental Nexus." He swallows, fixing us with a stare. "I trust you are prepared to seize this relic and continue your quest?"

Dani's head bobs up and down like a cork in a storm, her mouth half-full of food. "Mmph, absolutely." She swallows hastily, sun-kissed eyes wide and earnest. "I'm so ready to go home, I'm practically vibrating."

I hide a smirk behind my mead, but I can't disagree. Ásgard may be my ancestral land, the birthplace of my divine blood, but it's not my home. My place is with my chosen family—with Dani, with my brothers. With the ones who stand by me not because of destiny or prophecy, but because of the bonds we've forged through blood, battle, and unwavering loyalty.

I'm ready to get the fuck out of this gold and ice realm and back to the messy, chaotic, beautifully imperfect world we've built together.

Odin's words hang in the air like storm clouds as we finish our meal in tense silence. The mead flows freely—too freely maybe, as I'm ten horns deep and the golden halls have started to blur at the edges. Dani kissed me goodnight ages ago, and Erik fucked off to his chambers, probably face-down in his bed by now. My boots echo against marble as I stumble through corridors that shift and twist.

I find myself in an alcove, staring up at Magni's statue. My father's stone face gazes sightlessly ahead, his nameplate gleaming like an accusation in the torchlight.

"Beautiful craftsmanship, isn't it?"

Fucking hell. I don't even try to hide my eye roll as Baldr materializes beside me, offering another horn of mead. "You look like you could use this."

I snatch it, taking a long pull to avoid conversation. The mead tastes off—sharper, more bitter than before.

"What do you want?" I growl.

"Can't two warriors share a drink?" His perfect smile makes me want to introduce it to my fist. "Though I must say, the show you put on at the ball the other night was far more... entertaining."

The horn freezes halfway to my lips. "What the fuck did you just—?"

"Oh, you know." He examines his nails, casual as discussing the weather. "When you had your mate pressed against the wall. The way she fell apart around your cock was quite... spectacular."

Red bleeds into my vision. It was this piece of shit who watched? Watched her intimate moments meant only for me?

"Tell me," his voice drops like venomous honey, eyes gleaming with malevolent mischief, "does she always scream quite so... enthusiastically when you claim that tight little ass of hers? Or was that performance just for my benefit?" His smile pisses me off. "Such a responsive little thing. Makes one wonder how she'd react to a *real* god's touch."

"You son of a bitch." My muscles coil as I swing, ready to remove his fucking head—

The room tilts violently. My knees buckle as the alcove spins like a carnival ride from hell. Baldr's golden form stretches, darkens, and transforms. In his place stands a taller figure, cloaked in shadows. His horned helm gleams with unholy light, black as the depths of Unbra. His smile is a slash of white in the darkness, cruel and sharp as a blade.

"Allow me to introduce myself properly." His voice slithers like oil on water. "Loki, God of Mischief, at your service."

What the fuck?

I try to speak but my tongue feels wrapped in wool, my mind swimming in a toxic haze.

"Ah yes, that would be the mistletoe extract." He examines an empty vial with theatrical interest. "The same herb I used to orchestrate dear Baldr's demise. Such a delightfully toxic little plant." His laughter ripples like black silk. "Poor, precious Frigg—so desperate to protect her golden boy that she made every plant and creature swear an oath never to harm him. But she forgot one *tiny* detail." His eyes gleam with cruel satisfaction. "One insignificant little plant she deemed too young to swear. Such a *fatal* oversight for her beloved son." He tilts the empty vial, watching it catch the light. "Though I must admit, it won't kill you like it did him. No, no—you're made of... hardier stock. Just enough to keep you... compliant."

He grabs my arm, his touch burning cold like frost-bite. Reality shreds apart at the seams—we're moving through darkness, through nothing, through every-thing. My stomach heaves as colors and sensations assault me from all sides.

"Consider this a lesson in mythology, Commander," his voice echoes through the void. "Sometimes the oldest poisons are still the most effective. Even demi-gods can fall to a simple plant... when wielded by the right trickster."

We materialize on a cliff beside a frozen lake, my legs giving out entirely as Loki produces heavy chains from nowhere. "Welcome back to Valor's Watch." The metal bites into my flesh as he works, my limbs too heavy to fight back. "The wards are up," Loki purrs, tightening the chains. "Your precious mate won't hear a thing."

My mind screams at my body to move, to fight, but the bullshit poison he slipped me has turned my muscles to lead. The chains wrap around me like serpents, cold and unforgiving. My powers—the ones that could level a fucking mountain—stay locked away, as frozen as my traitorous body.

"Sweet dreams, Commander of Dark Skies." His grin splits the night. "Try not to drown too quickly."

He shoves me backward. I fall and fall until ice water hits like a thousand knives. The chains drag me down as my body locks up, refusing to fight. Water floods my lungs with the first involuntary gasp, each spasm bringing fresh agony.

As darkness creeps in, one thought burns brighter than the pain.

"Dani."

Gods, *please...*

Then there's nothing but the cold, dark, and endless drowning cycle I know is to come.

LUCIAN

59

R ight. Because my night wasn't already a supernatural shit-show. Now I've got a baby vamp with bubblegum hair to deal with.

"Everyone stay still!" I bark, moving faster than Damon's lovesick ass can react. "No sudden movements, unless you want to be tonight's juice box."

I shift my stance subtly, angling my body to create a living shield between Sable and Seraphina. Her breath comes in quick little puffs against my back, but she's holding it together like a champ.

Emily's still sprawled on her ass, looking like she just witnessed the second coming of Pink Jesus. Seraphina's wings are now practically strobing with divine light—*hello*, migraine—and Brax is doing his best impression of a demon who's seen too much.

"Sable," I keep my voice steady, like talking to a spooked horse with very sharp teeth. "Focus on my voice. The hunger you're feeling? That's normal. But if you eat Emily, you'll feel really bad about it later."

Her head snaps to me, and *holy shit*—those eyes. Black as midnight with a ring of electric blue. *That's* new. Most of us get the standard-issue red-and-black combo, but apparently Little Miss Pink decided to go custom.

"That's it, Bubblegum. Eyes on me. Though maybe ease up on the 'I'm-going-to-eat-your-face' look. It's not your best angle."

Damon finally remembers how to use words. "Sable?" His voice cracks like he's going through puberty. "You're... you're alive?"

Well, technically...

"Define 'alive,'" I mutter, not taking my eyes off our newest member of Club Undead. "Because right now she's more in the 'craving-a-blood-smoothie' category."

"I... I feel..." Sable's voice sounds like she's been gargling gravel. "Everything is so... *loud.*"

Welcome to vampire sensory overload, sweetheart. Where everything's dialed up to eleven and normal volume no longer exists.

"Someone want to explain what the *actual fuck* just happened?" Emily snaps.

Oh honey, buckle up. This explanation is gonna be a wild ride.

"My blood," I admit, running a hand through my hair. "When I tried to save her. Must've been just enough to trigger the change. Congratulations, it's a vampire."

And somewhere in the great beyond, the universe is laughing its cosmic ass off at me.

"So she's not..." Brax's voice hangs in the air, his hellfire eyes darting between Sable and me, "...dead?" The question hangs with equal parts hope and what-the-actual-hell confusion. For a demon who's seen literal hell, he looks impressively bewildered by Vampire 101.

"Oh, she's definitely dead," I clarify helpfully. "Just the fun kind of dead. The kind that comes with eternal youth, supernatural powers, and an unfortunate aversion to tanning."

Sable blinks rapidly. "I'm a... vampire?"

"Surprise?" I offer weakly. "Welcome to the club. We have t-shirts."

"You *turned* her?" Damon's voice does that crack thing again. Seriously, someone get this kid a throat lozenge.

"Not intentionally!" I defend, watching Sable's nostrils flare. "It was more of a 'whoops, accidentally created eternal life' situation. You know, when you mean to text one person but hit 'reply all'? Except with vampirism."

"Oh my god." Emily gapes, stumbling to her feet.

Seraphina's wings finally stop their divine light show, which *thank fuck*, because my retinas were about to file for divorce. "We need blood. Now."

"On it!" Brax actually *volunteers*, probably grateful for any excuse to exit this clusterfuck. His demon ass vanishes in a puff of smoke that smells suspiciously like burnt Pop-Tarts.

"Sable?" Damon tries again, taking a step forward.

"Ah-ah!" I throw out an arm to block Lover Boy. "Vampire or not, baby vamp here is running on pure instinct. Unless you want your romantic reunion to turn into WWE SmackDown: Vampire Edition, stay put, Romeo."

The first tear rolls down Sable's cheek, then another, then *fucking Niagara Falls*. Her emotions ping-pong across her face faster than my Netflix recommendations after Emily's been binge-watching."I can't—" Her voice cracks. "I'm supposed to be a *witch*!" The last word explodes from her with enough force to rattle my prized Marvel figurines. Then— WHOOSH—she's just *gone*, leaving only a pink blur and the sound of my imported vases getting absolutely massacred.

CRASH

Please don't find the Marvel shrine, please don't find the Marvel shrine...

"For fuck's sake, Lucian!" Emily's voice could cut diamonds. "Do something before she redesigns your entire house."

"Like what?" I throw my hands up. "Write her a 'Sorry You're Undead' Hallmark card?"

Another blur of pink, another crash that sounds suspiciously like my art deco coffee table meeting its maker.

Christ.

My limited-edition Iron Man figure wobbles dangerously on its shelf.

"Use your Maker's command, you absolute fucking walnut!"

Oh.

OH.

Right. That whole 'magical vampire maker' thing.

Lilith's memories slither through my mind like unwanted party guests, making me want to shower in holy water. But before I can process my emotional baggage—

CRASH

No. Not going there.

"Lucian." Seraphina's voice cuts through my spiral, honey-warm and steady. "You're not her. You'll never be *her.*"

Another crash, followed by Sable's wail of confusion, makes my Deadpool bobblehead do a concerning dance.

"Fucking DO IT!" Damon roars as my precious entertainment center takes a hit.

Right. Because, this is my life now—

Pink and black blur through my vision until—*gotcha*. My fingers lock around her throat, two hundred years of muscle memory taking over as I pin her to my (thankfully still intact) mahogany-paneled wall. Those newly vamped-out eyes lock with mine, a hurricane of terror and confusion swirling in black-voided depths.

"*Sable.*" My voice drops into that space between command and comfort, the tone that reaches past the feral and finds the person underneath. "You're going to take a nice deep breath—which yes, I know is ironic now—and park your newly immortal ass on that couch so we can talk about this like people who *don't* destroy priceless collectibles."

The change is instant—like someone hit a reset button. Wild black bleeds from her eyes, leaving familiar chocolate brown in its wake. Her muscles unlock under my grip, and the feral energy dissipates like smoke.

Well, shit. Maybe I'm not entirely terrible at this Maker thing after all.

Though my insurance company is going to have questions about tonight.

Brax materializes like a demonic Santa Claus, blood bag in hand. He tosses it to Sable. She snatches it out of the air, fangs already sinking into plastic before her ass hits the couch.

Ah, the dulcet tones of a baby vampire's first meal. Like a symphony of slurping and desperate gulping.

It's obvious self-preservation isn't in her witchy skill set, Emily takes a step toward her bestie. "Sable, honey, let me just—"

But then—*fuck*—Sable's head snaps up, blood bag forgotten. Her nostrils flare, pupils blown wide as they lock onto Emily's jugular. I see the moment instinct takes over, the predator recognizing prey.

"Nope!" I'm between them before Emily can blink, my hand around Sable's throat again. "New house rule: No snacking on the residents. Especially not the witchy one who smells like everything pumpkin spice."

Sable struggles against my grip, her fangs snapping like she's auditioning for Jaws.

"Listen up, Bubblegum," I pour power into my words, feeling the Maker's bond mold between us. "You do not get to sample the locals. And you *especially* don't get within ten feet of my Angel Cake or Dani when she gets back. Those two are like vampire catnip, and I'm not dealing with that drama on top of everything else."

Sable blinks rapidly, the bloodlust haze clearing from her eyes. She looks down at the blood bag like it offended her, then back to Emily. Horrified realization dawns on her face."Em, I... oh my god. I'm so sorry. I don't know what... I wasn't going to..." She looks about two seconds from bursting into tears again.

And here I thought being a nightclub owner was a wild ride. Clearly, I had no fucking idea.

Emily shrugs. "Remember my first spell? Pretty sure I set fire to everything but the actual candle." Her laugh is gentle, understanding. "We've all got our learning curves, babe. Yours just happens to involve a little more... liquid diet."

Sable slumps back onto the couch, attacking the blood bag. Her nose wrinkles with each swallow—*yeah, cold hospital leftovers are definitely an acquired taste.*

I watch her drain the bag, my mind already spinning with the logistics of teaching a newborn vampire how to feed without leaving a trail of bodies.

Maybe Damon can help. He's been there, done that, and has the 'I Survived My First Feeding' T-shirt.

Wait. Does this mean I'm like... a vampire dad now? Do I need to start carrying spare blood bags and wet wipes?

Fuck. My. Immortal. Life.

The reality hits harder than Thanos's pimp slap—I'm actually responsible for someone now.

I can practically feel the gray hairs sprouting. Is that even possible for vampires? Because I swear I'm about to find out.

Congratulations, Lucian! It's a girl! A forever-twenty-something bloodsucking, emotionally volatile girl who could probably bench press a car!

...I'm going to need so much more bourbon for this.

T he lake stretches before me like spilled ink, moonlight fracturing across its surface. The bourbon in my glass matches the darkness, promising temporary oblivion from this clusterfuck of a night. Behind me, the mansion hums with the aftermath—Emily's patient explanations, Sable's questions, Damon's hovering presence.

At least someone's having a productive night.

The whisper of bare feet against the balcony stone barely registers until her scent hits me—cinnamon and honey, somehow untainted by the horror she's endured. I turn—*and fuck me sideways*—those little pink shorts and that white lace top sliding off one shoulder are doing things to my heart that should be medically impossible.

"Hey, *daddy*." Seraphina's voice carries enough sugar to put Willy Wonka out of business, with just enough spice to make my fangs ache.

Jesus tap-dancing Christ on a pogo stick.

I roll my eyes at the reminder of my new 'parental' status to our bubblegum vampire witch, but *fuck me running*—the way those words just rolled off her tongue makes parts of me stand at attention faster than a soldier during inspection.

"Careful there, Cupcake," I manage to choke out, trying to maintain some semblance of composure. "You keep calling me 'daddy' like that, and I might just have to put you over my knee."

Shit. Did I just say that out loud? Apparently my brain-to-mouth filter is on vacation. Probably sipping margaritas with my sense of shame.

"You know, for... discipline purposes. Gotta make sure you're being a good little angel and all that jazz."

Seraphina smirks, a look that's equal parts heavenly and sinful. "Oh, I think you like it when I call you that... *daddy*."

Fuck. Me. Sideways. With a silver-plated dildo.

"You did good, Lucian." Seraphina steps closer, her scent wrapping around me like a heavenly security blanket. "You tried to save her and you did... just in another way."

Right. Because turning someone into a vampire is totally what they mean by 'saving lives' in medical school.

I sigh, the world's weight settling on my shoulders like a lead blanket. "Yeah, maybe you're right. But all of that never should've happened—none of it." I swallow hard, the memory of the night rising like bile in my throat. "Especially with you."

Fuck. The image of Seraphina, broken and bleeding, her wings torn... it's seared into my brain like a brand. A permanent reminder of my failure.

"You didn't deserve that, Cupcake. Any of it." My voice cracks, emotions threatening to spill out like a burst dam. "I should've protected you. Should've been faster, stronger, *better*."

But I wasn't. And now I have to live with the consequences. Forever.

Seraphina's hand finds mine, her touch a lifeline in the darkness. "Lucian, you can't blame yourself. We all made choices tonight. And I'd make the same one again in a heartbeat."

Fuck, I love this woman. This angel. This goddamn miracle in high heels and a halo.

The questions I should ask pile up behind my teeth—*What all did they do to you? How did they hurt you? Who do I need to dismember first?*—but they stick there, trapped by the fear of knowing just how badly I failed to protect her.

My hands find her waist before she can speak, spinning her into the space between me and the balcony rail. The motion triggers something divine because suddenly the night explodes with light—her wings unfurling like living opals, casting rainbow shadows across the deck. Each feather catches moonlight and transforms it, turning the darkness into our own private aurora borealis.

She even makes breathing look holy?

Those sexy eyes tilt up to mine, and the raw emotion there hits harder than any whiskey.

How can she still look at me like that? Like I'm something worth loving? After I let her get taken?

The balcony railing creaks under my grip.

"Stop blaming yourself, Sparky." Her voice is honey, wrapping around me like a caress. The nickname—that ridiculous, perfect nickname—falls from her lips with such tenderness it makes my chest ache.

"I'm sorry, baby girl." The words scrape raw from my throat. My thumb traces the curve of her cheek, needing the tangible proof she's really here. "This should never have happened. I got you hurt, taken, fucking *tortured*—"

Her smile—that goddamn sunrise of a smile—cuts through my self-flagellation. My body responds instantly—my cock inflates faster than a life raft on the Titanic, straining painfully against my zipper.

Great timing, Little Lucian. Nothing says 'I'm devastated about your trauma' like pitching a tent.

"Lucian," my name in her mouth sounds like a prayer. "You can't blame yourself for what that bloodsucking..." Her brow furrows, and angelic vocabulary clearly lacks the appropriate terminology.

"Bitch?" I offer. "Designer Dumpster Fire? Satan's Side Piece? Couture Cock-goblin? I've got a whole thesaurus of options, Cupcake. Been workshopping them for centuries."

Humor: the band-aid for soul-crushing guilt since... well, forever.

"Yes." That *bitch* did this. Not you." The profanity on her divine lips is so deliciously wrong it's right.

Her fingers climb my neck, sending electric currents through nerve endings, before tangling in my hair. My eyes practically roll back in my skull. "You came for me. *Again.*"

Like I'd ever do anything else.

I'm pretty sure 'rescuing angelic girlfriend' is in the fine print of the vampire handbook. Right under 'brooding on balconies' and 'always having a spare leather jacket'.

"What I saw..." My voice scrapes like gravel over the words. My eyes can't look away from hers—those golden galaxies I'd burn the world to protect. "It damn near killed me."

My hands trace the delicate sides of her ribs, memorizing every curve like a blind man reading braille. Her skin—that impossible silk—hums beneath my touch.

So fucking perfect. So impossibly mine.

"How did they get you to..." My gaze drifts to those wings—iridescent miracles folded against her back like living art. "Bring those out?"

Smooth, Lucian. Real smooth. 'Hey babe, quick question about your torture session?

Her eyes cloud with memory, but then her lips curve into that honey-sweet smile. "She threatened to kill you if I didn't reveal them. It wasn't even a choice worth considering, Sparky." She reaches up, thumb gently tracing my bottom lip. "Some things are worth sacrificing for."

Holy fucking shit on a sandwich.

My heart does something anatomically impossible in my chest. She surrendered her most sacred part—to protect *me?* A blood-drinking, smartass vampire with more baggage than an international airport?

I don't deserve her. Not in this lifetime or the next seven.

But my body disagrees completely, my cock throbbing against my zipper like it's trying to morse code "I worship you" directly through denim.

She tugs me down to her level, those fingers suddenly demanding in my hair. Then her lips claim mine, and sweet merciful fuckballs—it's like getting tased by pure sunshine.

Her mouth is warm velvet against mine, and the taste of her—sweet and delicious and something uniquely her—short-circuits my brain. My hands slide to her waist, fingers digging into the silk of her skin as I haul her closer.

The scent of her arousal hits me like a wrecking ball wrapped in Christmas morning. It changes the air between us, turning oxygen into aphrodisiac. Her heart thunders against my chest, each beat pumping more of that intoxicating scent into the space around us.

Vampire kryptonite. Angel-flavored.

My fangs descend without permission, primal instinct overriding centuries of control. Her blood calls to me like a fucking junkie, promising paradise... needing a taste.

Focus, dumbass. This isn't 'Fifty Shades of Fang.' She's been through enough without you going full vampire on her.

But then she makes this little whimpering sound against my mouth, and my restraint crumbles. I press her against the railing, my cock throbbing so hard I'm pretty sure my zipper is one heartbeat away from becoming shrapnel.

"Bite me, Lucian." Her words are a husky whisper against my lips, a plea that hits me harder than a silver bullet. "I know you need to feed. I can feel your hunger. Please."

Jesus, Mary, and the entire heavenly HOA.

I'm starving. After tonight's supernatural bullshit, I haven't fed since Discount Dracula and her Gucci Gang kidnaped Seraphina. And now her blood is singing to me like my greatest hits album.

Her fingers tighten in my hair, guiding my mouth to the delicate skin of her neck, then lower. I pay homage to that flawless canvas with feathery kisses that make her breath catch and her pulse dance beneath my lips.

The lace of her top is a flimsy barrier, doing absolutely nothing to hide the perfect curve of her breasts. I could recite poetry about these orbs—sonnets that would make Shakespeare weep. With a gentle tug, I reveal more supple skin, setting free those twin peaks that star in my dreams.

Tit-tacular. A divine work of art. God's greatest masterpiece.

She arches under my touch, offering herself up like a sacrifice. My mouth waters at the sight of that perfect pink tip, straining toward me like a beacon. I close my eyes, dragging my tongue across the taut peak before capturing it between my teeth and biting down. She jerks against me, a sweet little moan escaping her throat as my fangs graze delicate skin. I soothe the sting with my tongue, lapping up her taste like a starved man.

I worship that nipple like it's my new religion, suckling gently as my thumb strokes its twin. Her heart flutters against my lips—a symphony accompanying this heavenly feast. Her fingers tangle in my hair, urging me on, a silent prayer for more. And who am I to deny my angel's wish?

With infinite care, I pierce the delicate skin just above her nipple, twin pinpricks that well with red droplets. The first taste of her—*fuck*—honey and cinnamon, sunlight and sin—shatters me, reforges me, brands me as hers for eternity. My eyes flutter closed, colors bursting behind my lids, a kaleidoscope of rapture.

My Heavenly Honey's ambrosia. Vintage Seraphina. And the only elixir I'll crave for all my immortal days.

Once I've had my fill, I lick the pinpricks with the reverence of a man sealing a holy covenant. My tongue traces a path back up to her lips, leaving a trail of unholy promises along the way.

Seraphina breaks away, her eyes glittering with something that makes my already-tight pants feel like a medieval torture device. "Although," she says, all sweet, "I do recall a bet was placed if I did get hurt..."

Fuck me. That's the tone that could make a saint sin twice on Sunday.

I'm so wound up on her blood and scent that my brain has hung a "Gone Fishing" sign and clocked out for the day. I just stare at her like a horny mannequin.

She laughs. "Remember? In your GTA getaway—" her voice drops to a teasing whisper, "—getting *pegged* ring any bells in that handsome brain of yours?"

Shit. Shitshitshitshitshit.

The memory crashes into me like a train wreck of kinky promises. I'd sworn nothing would happen to her, and when she countered with what she'd do if I was wrong... well, let's just say it involved her, a strap-on, and my exit-only hole.

I give her my patented panty-dropping smirk, the one that's gotten me out of (and into) trouble for centuries. "Seriously, Cupcake. What's with you and claiming ownership of my ass?" I brush my lips against her ear, feeling her shiver. "Such a naughty little angel."

Seraphina shrugs with all the innocence of an angel who's browsed the kinkier side of heaven's database. "I don't know, something about owning you, taking you down a *peg...*" She emphasizes that last word like it's a holy sacrament. "...kinda turns me on."

Holy fucking shit on a communion wafer.

I think my brain just exploded—actually exploded. Like, someone just set off a nuclear bomb in my pleasure center and the fallout is pure horniness.

Here's this literal angel, Heaven's sweetheart, casually discussing turning my ass into her personal playground like she's planning a picnic.

Somewhere in Heaven, Gabriel's probably having an aneurysm. And you know what? Worth it.

"Look who's been studying the naughtier parts of PornHub's algorithms," I manage to rasp out. "From 'Holy Spirit' to 'Hole-y Spirit' real quick there, Cupcake."

She giggles, the sound going straight to my groin like a heat-seeking missile. "What can I say? A *bad* boy has influenced me."

Oh no, Angel Cake. You're not pinning this corruption on me. You've got a naughty streak a mile wide.

I groan—*fucking groan*—at that innocent-but-not-innocent tone.

No, this isn't just influence. This is pure, unadulterated curiosity, and I'm about to discover just how deep that curiosity goes.

"You know what I think?" My hands find their way under those tiny shorts, cupping that perfect ass that could launch a thousand sins. She gasps at the contact, the sound pure orgasmic. "That my innocent little angel wants to experience it for herself."

Heaven help me, because I'm about to corrupt one of their finest.

A blush spreads across her skin like a sunrise, painting her from neck to cheeks in the most delicious shade of pink.

"Isn't that right?" I let my fingers wander, tracing the seam of her ass with deliberate slowness, watching as her eyes flutter closed and her lips part on a silent moan.

"Mmm...so responsive," I murmur against her throat, nipping at her pulse point. My fingers continue their unholy pilgrimage, circling that forbidden territory like I'm mapping out the gates of paradise. "Look at you...getting all worked up for me?"

Holy fuck, the sounds she's making should be classified as supernatural weapons.

Seraphina arches into my touch, her breath coming in little pants. "Lucian..." The way she moans my name? Better than any prayer I've ever heard.

One hand grips that divine ass like it's my personal slice of heaven, while my other hand explores more... sacred territory. That tight little rosebud is practically begging for attention, and who am I to deny an angel's prayer?

If there's a special place in hell for defiling celestial beings, I just made the VIP list.

"Tell me what you want, baby girl." I trace my tongue along the shell of her ear, keeping my fingers moving in slow, torturous circles. "Want me to stop?"

Please say no. Please say no. Please—

"Don't you dare," she gasps, grinding back against my hand. The movement makes my brain misfire. "I want... I need..."

Christ she's trying to kill me. Again.

"Need what?" I tease, my finger drifting lower, seeking out her core. *Holy shit.* She's soaked—a flood of desire that makes my cock ache in anticipation. I dip my finger into that heavenly honey, coating it before retreating to circle that sacred spot again. My other hand slides up to cup her breast, feeling her nipple pebble against my palm. "Use your words, Cupcake. I want to hear that sweet angel voice tell me exactly what sinful things you crave."

I circle lightly, feeling her squirm against me, her breath coming in little pants.

Her reactions are straight-up celestial porn, and my dick is getting damn close to needing its own halo in these jeans from the friction.

Dear God, she likes it.

Halle-fucking-lujah.

Back door action, here we come.

"You like that, baby girl?" I tease, adding more pressure. Her whimpers are like heavenly hymns. "Want to feel me back there?"

Because I'm about to open those pearly gates and bless the hell out of this angel.

Seraphina's eyes snap open, her gaze sultry and sinful. "Yes." Her voice is a husky whisper. "There. Please."

Praise be the lord and pass the lube. This angel's about to get defiled.

ERIK

60

Sleep proved impossible. Her chambers called to me. When I found her door unlocked, I didn't hesitate this time.

One look. One touch. That's all it took to ignite the powder keg of tension between us. We came together like a storm meeting sea, desperate and wild, with so much denial shattering like glass.

Steam rises beneath the bathing chamber door where she fled, her body still quaking from the wild release that had taken us both. I recognized the shadow in her eyes—worry laced with fear, a wall erected against the intensity of what just passed between us. But I won't let her run this time. My patience has reached its end. Tonight, those walls she's built will come tumbling down, even if I have to tear them stone by stone.

After the battle with the frost giant, something shifted. She let me save her, let me in. Finally, she's seeing past her walls, recognizing what I am to her—not another warrior using her, but her equal, her mate.

The mead still burns through my veins, but not enough to blur the memory of Bryn's eyes across the feast table—steel wrapped in sorrow.

Odin's words echo: *Follow your heart's desire, daughter.*

My chest tightens. Let her desire be me.

I wait, sheets still warm from her skin, staring at the bathing chamber door. Each minute stretches like a century, my fingers drumming against silk. The beast in me paces, scenting a doe ready to flee.

I push up on my elbows, muscles coiled—

The door opens. Bryn emerges wrapped in silk, steam curling around her like a halo. My throat tightens.

"Come here." I extend my hand, the space between us suddenly unbearable. "Please?"

She approaches the bed slowly. At the edge, I stop her. "Naked."

A dangerous smile plays at her lips as she lets the silk pool at her feet. Moonlight caresses every perfect curve, and my mouth goes dry.

She slides beside me, and I pull her close, burying my face in her hair. Vanilla and lavender wrap around me—clean, fresh, but still uniquely her.

"Erik." Her voice trembles as she rolls to face me, platinum hair spilling across the pillow, her golden skin luminous in the candlelight. "I just—"

I move before she can finish, pinning her beneath me. I can't bear to hear the rejection in her voice, not after feeling her come apart in my arms, not after tasting her surrender. Her body was made for mine—every curve, every sigh, every tremor a testament to our connection.

The mating bond howls through my blood, demanding. To make her mine for eternity. But I hold back, muscles trembling with restraint. The choice must be hers—a willing surrender, not a forced submission.

"Look at me," I demand softly, catching her chin when she tries to turn away. "I feel your pulse racing, little bird. Your body still trembling from my touch. You can't deny this."

"It's not that simple." Her beautiful magical eyes shine with unshed tears, but that familiar warrior mask starts to slip into place. "I'm not meant for—"

"For what? Love? Connection?" I press my forehead to hers, letting her feel the tremors running through my body. "You think I'm not terrified too? Lifetimes of control shattered by one fierce Valkyrie who won't leave my thoughts."

Her hands push against my chest, but I capture them, pinning them beside her head. Our fingers intertwine automatically, betraying her body's instinct to connect with mine.

"Erik, please." Her voice breaks. "I'll only disappoint you. I'm not—"

"You're *everything*." I brush my lips across her jaw, feeling her shiver. "Every breath, every heartbeat screams for you. The way you fight, the way you love, that sass that drives me mad—it's all I want. All I need."

"But what if—"

"No more what-ifs." I roll my hips against hers, showing her how ready I am again, drawing a gasp. "Feel this. Feel us. Your body knows the truth your mind keeps fighting."

A tear escapes down her cheek. "I don't know how to do this. How to be..."

"Mine?" I kiss away the tear. "You already are. Just as I'm yours, we will figure it out together."

Her breath hitches as I trail kisses down her throat, tasting the salt of her uncertainty. "You've spent an eternity being the fierce one, the warrior. Let me be your shelter now."

"I don't need—" Her protest dissolves into a moan as I capture her nipple with my mouth, her back arching instinctively.

"No?" I raise my head, watching her pupils dilate. "Your body says different, little bird." My hand slides down her ribs, feeling goosebumps rise in its wake. "Every touch, every kiss—you bloom for me."

"That's... that's just physical." But her thighs part as my hand drifts lower, betraying her words.

I catch her mouth in a searing kiss, swallowing her gasp as my fingers find her still-sensitive flesh. "Physical?" I growl against her lips. "Is that what you call this connection burning between us? This need that consumes me every time you're near?"

Her nails dig into my shoulders as I circle slowly. "Erik—"

"I feel your heart racing." I press closer, letting her feel every hard line of my body. "Feel how you respond to my touch. Your warrior mask can't hide this, Bryn. Can't hide us."

A sob catches in her throat. "I'm scared."

"I know." I gently touch her, pressing soft kisses to her temples, cheeks, and trembling lips. "But I'm here. I'll always be here. Let me show you," I murmur against her collarbone, tasting the thunderstorm beneath her skin. "Let me prove how perfect we are together."

Her hands tangle in my hair as I worship down her body, mapping every curve with reverent kisses.

"I can't—" She arches as I find a sensitive spot. "I can't think when you do that."

"Then don't think." I raise my head, meeting those mystical eyes dark with need. "Feel, Bryn. Just feel."

My hand slides under her lower back, lifting her closer as I settle between her thighs. She's still slick from our earlier passion, her body ready despite her mind's protests. "Look at how your body welcomes mine."

"Erik—" Her voice breaks on my name as I align ourselves.

"Tell me you don't feel this." I push forward slowly, watching pleasure flutter across her features. "Tell me this isn't where you belong."

Her legs wrap around my waist instinctively, drawing me deeper. "I—gods—"

"Your body knows." I capture her mouth, swallowing her moans as I begin to move. "Your soul knows. Stop fighting what's meant to be."

Tears spill from her eyes even as she meets each thrust. "I don't know how to surrender."

"Then let me teach you." I brace on my forearms, caging her beneath me, making her look into my eyes. "Let me love you, fierce one. Let me in."

Her fingers trace the muscles of my chest, feeling each tremor. "I've never..." She swallows hard. "I've never let anyone this close."

"I know." I roll my hips slowly, drawing a whimper from her throat. "That's why this terrifies you. Because you feel it too—how deep this goes."

Her inner walls clench around me, her body's honest response making us both gasp. "What if I'm not enough?" The confession spills from her lips like a secret prayer. "What if—"

I silence her with a deep thrust that makes her eyes roll back. "Feel that? Feel how perfectly you take my cock?" My voice is rough with emotion. "You're everything. Everything I never knew I needed. You're more than enough, Bryn."

Her platinum hair spreads across the bed as she writhes beneath me. "Erik, please—"

"Please what, little bird?" I catch her wrists, pinning them above her head with one hand while the other cups her face. "Tell me what you need."

"I need—" Her words dissolve into a moan as I drive deeper.

"Tell me, Bryn." Forcing those eyes to meet mine. Her walls are crumbling, and I see everything she's tried to hide—the fear of abandonment, the weight of never being enough, the crushing loneliness of standing apart.

"Make me forget everything but this." Her words come out in a desperate rush, punctuated by gasps and soft cries. "Make me forget how to be afraid—how not to be lonely, or rejected."

Her confession shatters my defenses—this fierce Valkyrie finally revealing the wounds beneath her armor. Each word is a hard-won victory over pride, each truth a gift she's never given another.

I cradle her face, wiping tears she'd never let others see. Those mismatched eyes shine with raw vulnerability; her soul is bare beyond flesh. Her pain becomes mine—her father's rejection, lost wings, betrayed friendships, all the cruel weights she's carried alone.

"Look at me, Bryn," I demand softly, waiting until those eyes lock with mine. "You're *mine.*" My hips snap forward, claiming her deeper, harder. "Do you hear me?" Each thrust punctuates the truth she keeps trying to deny. "*Mine.*"

Her body trembles beneath me, pleasure and vulnerability warring on her face. "Show me," she whispers. "Show me what it means to be yours."

Her surrender makes my beast roar triumphantly. This fierce, magnificent creature is choosing me and finally accepting me. The ache in my chest is almost unbearable—eons of loneliness are about to end.

"Do you trust me, little bird?" I breathe against her throat, still moving inside her. "I promise I won't hurt you."

Her answer is simple: "Yes."

I trail kisses up her neck, my tongue finding her pulse point. My fangs descend of their own accord, and with infinite gentleness, I pierce her flesh. Bryn gasps as she clenches tighter, my cock aching inside her.

The taste that floods my mouth nearly undoes me—heaven and lightning, wild storms and ancient power—a sound between a growl and a groan tears from my throat. After *years* of bagged blood—no warm necks—this—her—is paradise.

Her essence is different from any blood I've tasted. Dani's blood has a sweet undertone of light—Bryn's blood tastes of winter winds and thunder, with notes of wild honey and storm-charged air. It's intoxicating, addictive, and perfect.

"Erik... *Oh gods.*" Bryn's legs tighten around my waist, drawing my cock deeper into her as her arousal spikes sharply. Her inner walls flutter around me, her body responding to my claim.

My venom enters her veins, and she melts beneath me, pliant yet burning with need. The sensation of feeding while buried inside her threatens to shatter my control. Each pull of her essence makes me swell harder within her as she rises to meet my thrusts.

I withdraw my fangs and reach for her dagger. Her eyes—one gold as sunlight, one deep as stormy seas—connect with mine, heavy with desire and acceptance.

"Drink, little bird," I demand, drawing the blade across my throat. "Be mine. Only mine."

Her lips brush my throat, hesitant at first, then claims my blood with growing hunger. Each pull of her mouth sends shock waves through my veins, the sensation of her drinking while my cock thrusts deep inside her nearly undoing me.

Ancient words rise unbidden to my lips, a sacred binding as old as time itself:

"Blood to blood—" I claim her with every fiber of my being.

"Heart to heart—" Her moans mingle with the rush of blood as I thrust deep.

"My soul to yours—" Her body arches, offering herself completely. I fill her as the bond ignites.

"Yours to mine—" Her grip on me tightens, her nails digging into my skin—burning with passion.

"Forever bound—" Our connection explodes, threatening to consume us.

"Eternally one."

Our souls weave together in silver and gold threads. I feel her everywhere—in my blood, my mind, between each heartbeat. Her pleasure becomes mine, her breath my air, our hearts beating as one. Colors I've never seen burst behind my eyes as our spirits merge completely.

The bond pulses as her mouth leaves my throat. Every sensation magnifies—her pleasure, surrender, and fear flowing through me.

"Erik," she gasps. "I can feel you everywhere—inside me—"

I claim her mouth, tasting our mingled blood. Her emotions flood me—wonder and terror at how complete this feels. Each thrust draws shared cries as pleasure rebounds between us.

"Mine," I growl. "You are forever mine, Bryn."

Her nails rake down my back as another wave of pleasure crashes through us. "Too much," she whimpers, but her body arches up, seeking more. "I can't—everything's so intense—"

I catch her hands, threading our fingers together and pinning them above her head. "Let go," I murmur, watching tears of overwhelming sensation spill from her eyes. "I've got you. Let yourself feel everything."

The bond blazes brighter with each thrust. Her pleasure spirals with mine, threatening to consume us.

"Look at me," I demand. "Watch me make you fall apart."

Her eyes meet mine, trust warring with fear as her defenses crumble.

"I feel you," she gasps, her inner walls clenching around me. "Everywhere—in my blood—in my soul—" Her back arches as I hit deep, fucking her harder. "Erik, please—"

Her pleasure spirals through our bond until it mirrors mine, building with each thrust. Love, fear, and need tangle, pushing us toward the edge together.

"That's it," I growl as she starts to tremble. "Come apart for me. Let me feel you break, Bryn."

Her legs clench around my waist as pleasure builds. She's close—I feel it in her trembling muscles, hear it in my name falling from her lips like a prayer, feel it in how she tightens around me.

"I've got you," I promise against her throat, where my mark now claims her as mine. "Let go, little bird. Fall with me."

Her release crashes through us both as she screams my name. Her pleasure amplifies through our bond, dragging me over the edge with her. I spill deep inside as ecstasy rebounds between us in endless waves.

"Erik," she sobs, clinging to me as aftershocks wrack our bodies. "I never knew—I didn't know it could feel..."

I gather her trembling form against my chest as we collapse to our sides, still joined intimately. I feel her walls crumbling—centuries of isolation, of believing she wasn't meant for this kind of connection.

"Shh, little bird." I brush tears from her cheeks, my eyes burning as her emotions flood me. "I'm here. I'll always be here."

"I feel you," she whispers, pressing her hand against my heart. "Your love, your fear, your sadness—" A sob catches in her throat. "How did you survive being alone for so long?"

The question pierces my heart. "The same way you did. One day at a time, telling myself I didn't need this." I press my forehead to hers, letting her feel my vulnerability through our newly forged bond. "Centuries of standing in shadows, watching others find their mates, their happiness. Convincing myself that perhaps

I was meant for solitude—that my darkness was too deep, my soul too scarred for such grace."

My fingers trace her cheek, brushing a strand of platinum hair behind her ear. Through our connection, I let her feel every lonely night, every empty dawn, every moment of yearning I'd buried beneath duty and control. "But now I understand, little bird. Every century of solitude was just preparing me for you. Every battle, every scar, every moment of darkness—they were all leading me here, to this moment, to you."

She raises her head, those beautiful eyes swimming with tears. "I feel it all," she breathes. "—all of you. It's beautiful and terrifying and—" Another sob. "I've never let anyone see me like this. Never let anyone past my walls."

"I know." I brush away her tears with my thumb. "Your strength has always been your shield. But you don't have to be strong alone anymore."

Her body shakes against mine as years of maintained control finally crack. "I didn't think this was possible. I thought I was unable to find anyone after—was too broken—" She takes a deep breath. "Promise me," she whispers, vulnerability raw in her voice. "Promise me this isn't temporary. That you won't—"

"Leave?" I tilt her chin up, letting her feel the depth of my devotion. "Never. You're carved into my soul now, little one. There's no going back. No walking away."

Millenia of rejection carved deep scars in her soul—her father's cruel dismissal, the prophecy's bitter truth, watching Rhyland find his true mate. Each blow convinced her she was unworthy of love, destined to stand alone. The thought of her suffering makes my blood boil, my beast raging against those who made her doubt her own worth.

Her pain mirrors my own dark reflections. How many years did I walk alone, convinced I was too broken, too damaged for this kind of connection? Both of us, warriors wearing our solitude like armor, telling ourselves we didn't need what our hearts desperately craved.

But now, holding her in my arms, I see the truth—we weren't meant to be alone. We were meant to find each other, two broken pieces fitting perfectly together.

Bryn melts against me, her curves fitting perfectly into every hollow of my body—her platinum hair spills across my chest like moonlight, and her breaths even out against my skin. I feel her contentment mingling with mine—a sense of rightness, of coming home after an eternity of wandering. My arms tighten around her instinctively, and my beast is finally at peace with its mate secured.

My fingers trace idle patterns across her back, ghosting over the smooth skin where her wings once stretched proud and magnificent. She trembles against me, and through our new connection, I feel the raw ache of loss—phantom pain where divinity once marked her as Valkyrie.

"You're more than your wings ever were, little bird," I murmur into her hair, sending waves of love and acceptance through our connection. "Your strength, your fierce heart—that's what makes you extraordinary."

I feel her consciousness dimming like a setting sun, peace finally replacing her earlier turmoil. I let my eyes drift closed, and my beast purrs contentedly as I follow my mate into slumber.

DANICA

61

Sunlight streams through floor-to-ceiling windows, painting the pristine room in gold. I surface from sleep wrapped around Rhyland like a clingy octopus, my cheek pressed against the warm expanse of his chest. My fingers trace lazy patterns over his ribs, mapping the ridges of muscle I know by heart.

"Mmm..." I nuzzle closer, voice still thick with sleep. "Morning, Thunder Buns."

"Good morning, baby." His deep rumble vibrates through my body, sending delicious shivers down my spine. His hand finds my hip, squeezing possessively.

My leg is already draped over his naked waist, and there's no missing the impressive tent he's making in the sheets. "Well, well..." I smirk against his chest. "Looks like someone's ready to raid and pillage."

Rhyland chuckles, the sound dark and sinful. "I'm always ready to conquer your body, Angel."

Before I can fire back a sassy retort, Rhyland's mouth is on my skin, trailing scorching kisses down my throat. His teeth graze my collarbone, his tongue soothing the sting. Lower and lower he goes, mapping my curves with his lips until he reaches my breasts.

He takes one aching nipple into his mouth, swirling his tongue around the sensitive peak. I arch into him, a needy moan escaping my lips. Heat pools between my thighs as he lavishes attention on my breasts, stoking the fire in my veins.

Lost in sensation, it takes me a moment to realize his touch feels different. The way his hands skim my sides, the pressure of his mouth—it's not quite right. Not quite...him.

Rhyland kisses his way back up my body, claiming my lips in a searing kiss. But the wrongness of it hits me like a bucket of ice water. This kiss...it's too practiced, too polished. Nothing like the raw, hungry way my Viking devours me.

I break away, my heart pounding for all the wrong reasons. My eyes search his face as a chilling realization settles in my gut.

This isn't my Viking.

"Rhyland, what's going on?" My voice trembles, confusion and fear warring in my chest. "Something's not right."

He cocks his head, a too-perfect smile curving his lips. "What are you talking about, baby? Everything's perfect." He reaches for me, but I flinch back.

"No, it's not. You're not...*you*." I search his face, desperate for some flicker of recognition. "Please, talk to me."

But he just shakes his head, that unsettling smile never wavering. "It's okay, Angel." His hands find my hips, dragging me beneath him again. "Just relax and let me make you feel good."

Before I can protest, he's kissing his way down my body again, his mouth hot and insistent against my skin. He nips at my hipbone, his tongue soothing the sting—until he's settling between my thighs.

"Rhy, wait—" But my words dissolve into a gasp as his mouth finds my core, his tongue delving deep. Pleasure sparks through me, my body responding even as my mind screams that this is wrong, wrong, wrong.

He licks and sucks, stoking the fire in my veins even as panic claws at my throat. My hands fist in his hair, torn between pulling him closer and shoving him away.

"Stop," I pant, my head spinning. "Rhyland, please..."

But he ignores me, his mouth relentless against my aching clit. His hands pin my hips, holding me in place as he drives me closer to the edge.

Tears burn my eyes as I struggle against him. This isn't my Rhyland. My Viking would never ignore my pleas, never force his touch on me.

Am I losing my mind? Is this some kind of nightmare?

I squeeze my eyes shut, trying to will myself awake. But when I open them again, he's still there, his eyes dark and hungry as he looks up at me from between my thighs.

"Just let go, baby," he coaxes, his voice a sinful purr. "I'll catch you."

But all I can think as he lowers his mouth to my core once more is that this isn't the man I love.

This is a monster wearing his face.

I wrench away from him, scrambling off the bed. My legs shake as I snatch up clothes—his shirt, my pants, anything to cover myself.

"Stop. Just fucking stop." My voice cracks as I yank the shirt over my head. "What did you do with him?"

"Baby, you're being ridiculous." He lounges on the bed, all predatory grace, watching me with eyes that are both familiar and foreign. "Come back to bed."

"No." I back toward the door, my heart thundering against my ribs. "My Rhyland would never—" I swallow hard. "He doesn't kiss like that. Doesn't touch like that. And he sure as hell doesn't ignore me when I say stop."

Something dark flickers across his face, there and gone so fast I almost miss it. "Perhaps I'm just in a different mood today." His smile is all wrong—too smooth, too practiced. "You're overthinking things, Angel."

That pet name on his lips makes my skin crawl. Because it's not right, nothing about this is right.

And then it hits me—a wave of dread so powerful it nearly brings me to my knees—that gnawing emptiness in my chest where our bond should be pulsing strong and steady. The wrongness I've been feeling isn't just about his touch or his kiss.

I can't feel him.

Can't feel our connection at all.

"Where is he?" Ice spreads through my veins as panic claws up my throat. "What have you done with him?"

He rises from the bed, stalking toward me. "Dani—"

"Don't!" I throw up my hands, light warming at my fingertips. "Don't you dare come near me. Where. Is. Rhyland?"

Something's happened to him. Something terrible. I can feel it in my bones, in that hollow space where our bond should be singing.

Rhyland is in danger. And this thing wearing his face is the reason why.

"Fine." His lips curve into a cruel smile that looks grotesque on Rhyland's face. "Let's drop the charade, shall we?"

The air shimmers like a heat wave, reality-bending as Rhyland's form melts away. My stomach lurches as his bulk stretches taller and leaner. Black hair spills past broad shoulders, and a crown of twisted metal sprouts from his head, two huge horns curling toward the ceiling like polished obsidian. When he opens his eyes, they're a piercing glacial blue that burns with ancient mischief.

"Holy shit." The words slip out as I stumble back, my shoulders hitting the wall.

"Now, now, little savior." He tsks, spreading his arms wide. His leather armor gleams like oil in the sunlight. "Is that any way to greet a god?"

"Who—" My voice cracks. I swallow hard, trying again. "Who the fuck are you?"

His laugh is like serrated knives. "Oh, you mortals are always so entertaining with your profanity." He sweeps into an elegant bow, all fluid grace and deadly intent. "Loki, God of Mischief, at your service." He straightens, those frost-blue eyes dancing. "I must say, I'm impressed. I thought I could fool you longer, but..." His tongue darts out to wet his lips. "You know your mate's touch quite intimately, don't you? Every..." He takes a step closer. "Single..." Another step. "Detail."

My power pulses beneath my skin, desperate to lash out. "Where is he?"

"Rhyland?" Loki's smile is sharp as a blade. "Oh, he's taking a lovely swim. Though I doubt he's enjoying it much—chains tend to make swimming rather difficult."

Bile coats my throat—burning it's way up. I swallow it down. The horror of what he's done—what he might still do to Rhyland—makes my stomach twist.

Loki's lip curls in disgust. He grabs my hair, yanking my head back. "Such weakness. And here I thought the savior would have more... fortitude."

"Why?" I spit the word at him, trying to wrench away. "What do you want?"

He rolls his eyes, releasing me with a shove. "Isn't it obvious? I want the Air Stone. And your dear mate would have been quite the inconvenient obstacle." His smile turns razor-sharp. "Can't have the Commander of Dark Skies *raining* on my parade, now can I?"

"You're insane."

"No, I'm practical. You'll retrieve the stone—it's your destiny after all—and then you'll hand it over to me." He spreads his arms wide. "Simple."

Odin's words echo in my head: *The Soul Stone... Loki's interference... shattered and scattered across three realms...*

Now he wants this one, too.

"Why?" I growl, fury burning away my fear. "Because you're the god of daddy issues and cheap tricks?"

"Because I can." He shrugs, all casual arrogance. "It's my right as the God of Mischief. And..." His eyes glitter with malice. "I do so love watching Odin's precious plans crumble."

His smile turns predatory as he stalks closer. "Speaking of watching... I must say, that show against the wall the other night was quite... stimulating. The way your man took you from behind, claiming that tight little—"

"Stop." My stomach heaves again.

"Oh, but why?" He licks his lips, frost-blue eyes burning. "Left me hard for hours. I enjoyed every moment. Almost as much as I enjoyed tasting you this morning." His fingers ghost over his mouth. "We could continue where we left off. I could even wear his face again, since you seemed to enjoy that so—"

"Fuck you, you twisted piece of shit." My teeth clench. "Touch me again and I'll show you exactly how much 'fortitude' I have."

"Feisty. I do love when they fight back."

"How long? How long have you been lurking in the shadows like a cockroach?"

"Oh, you have no idea how long I've waited." His eyes spark with dark mischief. "Then your Viking put on that *spectacular* light show in the forest—lightning ripping apart the sky as he fought Azrael." He shivers with theatrical pleasure. "Like a beacon calling me home."

His smile turns predatory. "And when that fool Heimdall opened the Bifrost..." He spreads his arms wide. "Well, what better chance to return than alongside the miraculous Godborn everyone thought dead?"

The truth hits me. "You've been trapped there. All this time."

"Trapped is such an ugly word." Frost spreads from his feet as he paces. "Let's say I've been... entertaining myself. Midgard has so many delightful toys to play with." His eyes dance with cruel memories. "Wars, plagues, the occasional genocide—humans really do make the most wonderful chaos."

My blood runs cold as centuries of human history flash through my mind—every war, every conflict, the whispers of chaos that sparked civilizations into flames.

"That was you? All of it. The wars, the famines—"

"Fun, wasn't it?" His grin stretches impossibly wide. "Humans are so delightfully easy to manipulate. A whispered word here, a planted seed of doubt there..." He waves his hand like a conductor. "And boom! Centuries of chaos."

My stomach lurches again as the horror of it all crashes over me. The emptiness where our bond should be screams in my chest. Every calculated move—slipping into Ásgard, centuries of earthly chaos, and now Rhyland... trapped somewhere beyond my reach, beyond our connection.

"What I didn't anticipate was you." Loki's boots click against marble as he stalks back and forth. "When the war ended, watching Nyx's soul bind to that stone..." His eyes gleam with remembered malice. "Well, opportunity knocked."

"To what? Prove you're an even bigger piece of shit?"

His laugh echoes off the walls. "To add a little... spice to the realms." Frost trails in his wake as he moves. "Breaking that stone, scattering the pieces across the realms before your dear daddy sealed them—" He spreads his arms wide. "Can't have everyone living in tedious harmony, can we?"

Rage burns in my chest. This twisted bastard, playing his games across centuries—across realms, destroying lives for his own entertainment.

"You though..." He wags a finger at me like I'm a misbehaving child. "Elysium's little contingency plan. His precious backup savior." His smile turns cruel. "And your mate—that troublesome Viking who just wouldn't stay dead when he should have."

"Funny thing about my Viking—" Power surges through my veins, making the air crackle. "He's really fucking hard to kill. And when I find him? He's going to show you exactly why the God of Lies should be afraid of the dark."

"Adorable. Such spirit." His form shimmers, and suddenly Baldr stands before me—golden, perfect, pristine. "Though I must say, this face has opened so many new possibilities."

"Baldr." My knees threaten to buckle. "This whole fucking time, you were—"

"Playing the dutiful son?" He shifts back to his true form, those frost-blue eyes dancing. "It was almost too easy. Though I suppose you're wondering where the real golden boy is?"

"Where is he?" The words tear from my throat.

"Poor, precious Baldr." He leans in close, his breath like winter against my ear. "Let's just say he won't be attending any more family dinners."

His eyes glitter with sadistic glee. "I can't wait to see Odin's face when he finally realizes his one true heir, his last living son, lies cold and dead within his own realm."

His laugh rings off the walls, sharp. "And now...I'll take his precious Zephyrite Stone, too."

"You're out of your fucking mind." I spit the words at him.

"Such language." He catches my chin in an icy grip. "But you see, I need that stone. And more importantly—" His fingers tighten. "I need your little gift. These realm barriers are becoming quite... restrictive."

I wrench away from his touch. "You want me to open a portal? Go fuck yourself."

"Oh, but I think you will." His smile turns knowing. "Unless you want your precious Viking to remain where I left him." He smirks. "It's quite simple really—you get me the stone, open a portal, and I'll tell you where to find him. Everyone wins."

"Everyone except Rhyland."

"Details. But time isn't on his side, Lightborn."

Light blazes between my fingers as rage burns through my veins. "You forget who I am, asshole. I'm not just some little bitch you can manipulate. I'm the savior of the realms, and when I find Rhyland—" Power crackles around me. "I'm going to enjoy watching him tear you apart."

"*If* you find him." Loki's form begins to fade, his smile cruel as winter. "So much spirit. Let's see how long that lasts while your mate suffers in the dark."

RHYLAND

62

I ce burns through my veins as consciousness slams back into me. My muscles spasm, betraying me with that first desperate gasp. Black water floods my lungs, and raw fury ignites in my chest.

The chains bite deeper, their magic pulsing with ancient power. Each thrash only tightens their grip, metal singing against metal as I fight anyway. Blood clouds the water—my wrists are raw meat from fighting the links. I don't care. I'll tear myself apart if that's what it takes.

"Dani."

Her name blazes through my mind, and I claw for our bond. Nothing. The wards block everything—my powers, our connection, even my ability to sense if she's safe. The thought of her vulnerable while that horned bastard roams free makes my vision go red.

What if he's going after her next? What if right now, while I'm trapped in this frozen hell, Loki is—

My body convulses as more water fills my lungs. The pain transcends anything I've felt in a thousand years—like being torn apart cell by cell, only to be stitched back together for more torture.

Lightning should be answering my rage. These chains should be ash. Instead, that poison still courses through me, leaving me trapped in my own useless flesh while my powers burn just out of reach.

Find me, baby. Please find me.

But the thought of her feeling this agony through our bond makes my heart seize worse than the ice. She'd feel everything—every death, every resurrection, every moment of this endless torture.

Darkness edges in. My heart stumbles...

No—

Black.

Pain explodes through my chest as life crashes back. The water's colder now, if that's even fucking possible. My muscles seize as ice crystallizes in my bones.

The chains rattle with my renewed struggle. More blood clouds the water, but the wounds heal almost instantly—my body repairing itself just to be torn apart again. Some sick cosmic joke.

These fucking wards mock me—letting my body stitch itself back together just so I can die again, while keeping my real power locked away like a caged beast. A thousand years of strength, lightning, and raw fucking dominance, reduced to nothing but an endless cycle of drowning and healing.

Dani. Gods, stay safe. Don't feel this. Don't come.

But I know my mate. Know that warrior's heart that beats in time with mine. One slip in these wards and she'll feel everything. She'll come for me, consequences be damned.

And Loki will be waiting.

The bastard's probably counting on it. Using me as bait to draw her out, to trap her like he trapped me. The thought sends fresh rage coursing through my veins, but it does nothing against these enchanted chains.

My lungs spasm again. Can't fight it this time...

Dark.

The cycle repeats. Ice. Pain. Rage. My thoughts scatter like—

Find me... no, stay away... protect her... kill him...

Images flash behind my eyes—Dani's smile, her fierce light in battle, the way she looks at me like I'm her whole world. Then darker visions: Loki's hands around her throat, her light dimming, her screams that I can't answer...

Consciousness fades.

Returns.

The cold bites deeper. How long has it been? Hours? Days? Time means nothing in this endless loop of death and resurrection.

Baby... please... don't let him...

My body jerks with another drowning spasm. The chains laugh their metal song.

I'll kill him... tear him apart... if he touches her...

Darkness claims me again.

And again.

And—

DANICA

63

Now wearing Baldr's face like a twisted mask, Loki drags me through the palace halls. His grip on my arm is iron, starkly contrasting to the benevolent smile he shows passing servants. My pack bounces against my back with each step, the jars of essence rattling inside, a mocking reminder of the power he wants to exploit.

We reach the gardens, and he pulls me closer, his voice a venomous whisper. "Open a portal to the Elemental Nexus. Now."

I barely suppress a snort. *Yeah, because it's just that easy, asshole.* I've never even seen the place. But I keep my mouth shut, eyes scanning the palace for any sign of help.

Movement catches my eye—a flash of silver hair on the upper balcony. Erik. His eyes meet mine, confusion flickering across his usually stoic features.

My heart leaps. One word. One fucking word and—

"Ah, Erik!" Baldr's voice rings through the gardens. "Glorious morning for a walk, isn't it?" His grip tightens brutally on my arm as he whispers, "Say a word and I'll paint these gardens with his blood."

The threat hangs heavy in the air. I manage a stiff nod, heart pounding against my ribs.

"Indeed." Erik's eyes narrow slightly, assessing. "Perhaps I could join you?"

"Oh, that won't be necessary." Loki waves a dismissive hand, Baldr's golden hair glinting in the sun. "Just giving our esteemed guest a tour of the grounds. We'll return shortly."

Erik's gaze bores into me, a silent question. I force a smile, praying he can see the desperation in my eyes. "It's fine, Erik. I'll catch up with you later."

"As you wish." He inclines his head, but I can see the suspicion brewing in those silver depths. "Enjoy your... walk."

Loki's fingers dig into my arm as he steers me deeper into the gardens, his smile sharp as a blade. "Clever girl. Now..." Frost coats the leaves around us. "About that portal."

"You know," I drawl, dragging my feet, "portals aren't like Uber. I can't just punch in coordinates and—poof!—we're there."

"Do not test my patience." His fingers dig deeper, frost spreading from where he grips my arm. Despite wearing Baldr's golden features, Loki's rage bleeds through.

"I'm not testing anything, dickhead. I literally can't portal somewhere I've never fucking seen or don't have a clear description of." I yank my arm free, rubbing the icy spots. "What part of that isn't penetrating your thick, godly skull?"

Loki's jaw clenches. For a moment, I think he might strike me. But then he takes a breath, Baldr's smile sliding back into place like a well-worn mask.

"The Elemental Nexus," he begins, voice tight, "is a monumental tower at the heart of Zephyria. It's where the essence of air converges..."

I raise an eyebrow. "Wow, could you be any more vague? Maybe throw in a 'really tall' and 'kind of pointy' for good measure?"

His perfect face twists with barely contained fury. "Then allow me to paint you a picture, you insolent little—" He catches himself, forcing Baldr's serene smile back into place as a guard passes. Once we're alone, he continues through gritted teeth. "The Elemental Nexus. A tower of pure light and wind, rising from Zephyria's heart like a silver blade piercing the heavens. Ancient runes spiral up its crystalline walls, pulsing with power. At its peak, the very essence of air converges..."

"Gee." I cock my hip. "That's pretty. Did you practice that speech in the mirror? Maybe write it down first?"

"You dare—"

"What I dare to point out is that your flowery description sounds like something from a tourist brochure." I cross my arms. "Still can't make a portal from poetry, asshole."

His hand shoots out, grabbing my throat. "I'm done with your games—"

I claw at his fingers, light sparking between us. "Killing me—" I gasp out, "—won't get my fucking powers to work."

He releases me with a snarl, pacing like a caged animal. Baldr's perfect features twist with Loki's rage, the illusion slipping.

"Do it. *Now.*"

I try to focus and picture the Nexus in my mind. But all I can feel is the emptiness where Rhyland should be, the hollow ache of our bond stretched too thin. Tears prick at my eyes, but I blink them back. I won't give this bastard the satisfaction.

"I'm trying," I grit out, pulling away from his touch. "But it's not exactly a two-second process."

"Try harder." His voice is a growl, Baldr's eyes glinting with Loki's malice. "Or perhaps you need a little more motivation." He looks back toward the palace, to where Erik disappeared. "I wonder... how fast do you think your Viking's brother can bleed?"

"Touch him, and I swear to every god in this realm and the next, I will end you."

"Then open the portal." He steps back, arms spread wide. "Prove yourself worthy of the savior's mantle."

I close my eyes, picturing the Nexus as he described it—the runes, the swirling energy, the sheer power of it. I reach for my light, feeling it build beneath my skin, crackling in the air around me.

And then, with a rush of wind and a blaze of blinding radiance, the portal tears open before us—a swirling scene of wind and snow, leading to the very heart of Zephyria.

Loki's laugh is a razor's edge, cruel and cutting. "Wonderful. After you, little savior." He gestures to the portal, Baldr's face alight with twisted glee. "Let's go retrieve my stone."

A familiar whinny splits the air. Through the trees, golden hooves flash as Gullfax emerges, his mane catching sunlight like spun gold.

Hope surges in my chest as I reach through our mental connection. *"Gullfax, listen carefully. This isn't Baldr—it's Loki. Get Erik and Bryn to the Elemental Nexus. Now."*

The stallion's eyes flash with divine fury. *"I will tear him apart if he dares harm you."*

"Off with you, you glittering nuisance!" Loki flicks his wrist like he's shooing away a common stable pony.

"He has Rhyland—my mental voice cracks. *"I can't feel him anymore. Please, try to find—"*

"Enough stalling." Loki's hand clamps on my shoulder, frost spreading across my jacket. "Through the portal. Now."

The last thing I hear before he shoves me through the shimmering gateway is Gullfax's battle cry—a sound of pure, golden rage that promises vengeance. The portal snaps shut behind us, cutting off that promise of help, but hope burns brighter in my chest.

Cavalry's coming, you lying piece of shit. And they're bringing hell with them.

Arctic winds howl around us, cutting through my parka like it's made of tissue paper. Before us stretches a bridge of pure light, impossibly thin and delicate, leading to the Elemental Nexus. The tower pierces the heavens like a silver needle threading through star-studded fabric, isolated in its magnificent solitude.

Loki steps forward first, still wearing Baldr's face, and the winds surge with sudden fury. They slam into him with physical force, sending him staggering back. Ice crystals form in his golden hair as he snarls in frustration.

"Get to it," he growls, shoving me forward.

I approach the bridge's edge, heart thundering against my ribs. The winds whip my hair into my face, but as I take that first step onto the light bridge, something... shifts. The raging tempest gentles, becoming a soft caress against my skin. The bridge glows brighter beneath my feet, responding to my presence.

"Well, well..." I glance back at Loki's thunderstruck expression. "Looks like the winds know who's worthy and who's wearing a borrowed face."

He grabs my arm, using me as a shield against the winds that seem determined to reject him. "Move," he hisses through clenched teeth. "Unless you want your mate to suffer for your insolence."

Together we cross the bridge, me walking steadily while Loki clings to my jacket. The winds part around us like a curtain, recognizing the savior's touch even as they try to tear the false god from my side. With each step, the Nexus looms, its crystalline walls reflecting the starlight above and the auroras dancing in the eternal twilight of Zephyria's sky.

"Even the winds reject your lies," I snarl as he uses me like a human shield, the void below us stretching into infinite darkness. Stars glitter in that endless abyss, like diamonds scattered across black velvet, making my head spin with the sheer depth of nothingness beneath our feet.

We reach the Nexus's entrance—a towering door of glass-like material that pulses with ancient power. Two circular depressions mark its surface, perfectly symmetrical and waiting.

Frost spreads across the crystal as Loki's glamour melts away, Baldr's golden perfection replaced by his true form. His black hair whips in the wind as he shoves me forward.

"The essences." His voice carries the bite of winter. "Now."

My pack feels heavier, the two vials of champion essence burning like cold fire against my back. Each one collected through blood and sacrifice was meant to unlock this door—but not like this. Not with this twisted god's knife at my back.

"Two champions," he continues, fingers tracing the depressions with almost loving reverence. "Two essences. The Aesir did love their symmetry." His smile turns cruel. "Though I doubt they expected them to be delivered by such... unwilling hands."

I reach for my pack slowly, mind racing. The door needs both essences to open, but once it does... The thought hangs unfinished as Loki's impatient snarl cuts through the howling wind.

"Don't even think about playing hero," he hisses. "Your mate's suffering grows stronger with every moment you waste."

My hands shake around the vials, not from fear but from pure rage. Rhyland's face flashes through my mind—his ocean eyes, rare smile, and how his arms feel wrapped around me.

Is he already dead, and this lying bastard is just stringing me along? Or worse—

The essence pulse brighter, responding to my fury.

The thought of Rhyland suffering, calling for me, while I'm trapped here with this monster... it's a white-hot knife twisting in my gut.

"I swear to *God*...when I get free," my voice comes out like crushed glass, "I'm going to personally ensure you suffer for every second you've kept him from me. And then—" I meet Loki's frost-blue eyes, letting him see the promise of violence in mine, "I'm going to watch my man tear you apart, piece by fucking piece."

"Oh, you precious thing. You still cling to your delusions of power." He leans in close, frost crackling along my jacket where he grips my arm. "Your *God* isn't here, little savior. No divine intervention coming to save you."

I meet his gaze, refusing to flinch even as his cold seeps into my bones. "I don't need divine intervention, asshole. I have something better." I bare my teeth in a savage smile. "I have a promise to keep. And I always keep my fucking promises."

"Cute," Loki sneers, shoving me toward the door.

I draw a shaky breath, forcing my trembling hands to steady as I pull out the essences. The jars pulse with ancient power—one swirling with storm-gray light, the other gleaming like fresh snow.

First, I press Vidar's essence into the right slot. The gray light surges from its container, filling the depression with swirling power. Then Skadi's essence on the left, its winter-white glow spreading like frost across glass.

The door responds instantly. Light races through previously invisible runes, creating a spiderweb of brilliant lines across its surface. The essences pulse in sync, their combined power building until the air vibrates.

Then—a sound like ancient ice breaking, like mountains shifting in their sleep. The massive door swings inward with the groan of millennia, revealing the darkness beyond.

"Ladies first," Loki purrs.

My feet drag as we enter the Nexus, every step calculated and slow. Each second counts—each moment bringing Gullfax closer with reinforcements. The cold stone beneath my feet seems to pulse with ancient power, but right now, I couldn't give less of a shit about magical architecture.

The hollow space in my chest where Rhyland should be throbs like an open wound. It's wrong, so fucking wrong, like someone carved out a vital organ and left me bleeding. Is he suffering somewhere in the dark? Fighting? Calling for me?

Bile burns the back of my throat as memories of this morning flash unbidden—his touch, his kiss, all while wearing Rhyland's face like a mask. My skin crawls, and phantom sensations make me want to scrub myself raw. Each step feels contaminated, violated, knowing this monster wore my mate's identity like a costume while he...

I swallow hard against another wave of nausea. Focus. Channel the disgust into rage. Store it away with all the other reasons I'm going to make this bastard suffer.

But god, the violation of it all—having something so intimate, so sacred between Rhyland and me, twisted into this perverse mockery—it makes me want to scream until my throat bleeds.

My nails dig crescents into my palms, the pain keeping me focused, keeping me from completely losing my shit, because that's precisely what this frost-fingered bastard wants.

"Having trouble walking?" Loki's voice drips with false concern. "Perhaps thoughts of your precious mate are... distracting you?"

"No, actually I'm having trouble looking at your ugly fucking face."

Loki's laugh rings hollow against the stone walls. "Cute. Though—" his glacial eyes darkening, "—you weren't complaining about my face this morning when it wore a more appealing form."

Before I can unleash the scream building in my throat, an otherworldly howl cuts through the air—the wind shifts, carrying ancient whispers that seem to seep from the very stones around us. Above, through the spiraling staircase that stretches endlessly upward, voices chant in a language that makes my bones ache.

Steps materialize before us, beginning to shift and writhe like living things. The stone ripples, transforming into a treacherous path where each step appears and vanishes in rhythm with the chanting—a deadly dance of solid ground and empty air.

"Ah," Loki's breath mists in the cold. "The Trial of Faith. To reach the Nexus's peak, trust the winds to guide your steps." He shoves me forward, his touch burning cold through my jacket. "Move. Your mate's time grows shorter with each *breath* you waste."

I stare at the shifting steps, watching as they materialize and disappear in a hypnotic pattern. The winds whip around us, their whispers growing stronger, almost like they're trying to tell me something. Like they're calling to the savior's blood in my veins.

Time to find out if these winds really do know their chosen one.

ERIK

64

The wrongness of Baldr's touch on Dani's skin sears into my mind, the image branding itself behind my eyelids. His fingers linger, proprietary and possessive. Every instinct screams danger, the warning ringing as I search for Rhyland through the palace—no sign of my brother.

I reach out through our mental link, searching for my brother's familiar presence. Silence greets me, the connection dead and empty. Fear coils in my stomach as I race through the palace corridors, bursting into Rhyland's chambers. The bed is a tangle of sheets, the room bearing the signs of a hasty exit.

The flash of raw terror in Dani's eyes haunts me now—that split-second when our gazes locked in the garden. I'd seen it then, that silent plea beneath her forced smile. My instincts had screamed warning, but something in her look told me to hold off.

I forced my shoulders to relax, a casual nod masking the alarms blaring in my skull—it all paints a picture that's about as far from a pleasant morning stroll as you can fucking get.

My steps quicken as I head for our chambers. The door slams open under my hands, the force rattling the hinges. Bryn's head snaps up from where she sits on the bed, lacing her boots with quick, precise movements.

"Did it work?" Bryn's eyes search mine, her question hanging in the air between us.

The warmth still tingles across my skin—proof that Bryn's blood carries the same angelic power as Dani's. Three days without Dani's blood had given us the perfect window to test my theory, and sure enough, Bryn's heritage grants the same gift. But the triumph of that discovery evaporates as Dani's haunted eyes flash through my mind.

"Yes, but something's wrong." My fists clench at my sides. "Baldr was all over Dani, and Rhyland's missing. I can't reach him mentally." The words taste bitter on my tongue.

Bryn's eyes narrow, her fingers stilling. "Missing?"

I nod, my jaw tightening. "I checked his chambers. The bed's a mess, but he's gone."

A figure materializes in the doorway, the air shimmering around him. Heimdall's usually vibrant eyes are dull, his face drawn with exhaustion. "Loki." The name falls like a curse from his lips. "He's here."

Bryn's breath catches sharply as she lunges for the door, her sword already singing free from its sheath. "What?! How—"

"I saw him." Heimdall's voice is flat, the words heavy with dread. "He's shown his true form."

Bryn's eyes flash with fierce determination, her knuckles whitening around her sword hilt. "Standing here won't kill a trickster god." She's already moving, a blur of purpose and steel. "Move. Now."

Our boots pound against stone as we race to the gardens. Empty. The space where I last saw Dani now holds nothing but scattered petals and trampled grass. A thundering of hooves splits the silence as Gullfax charges toward us, his golden coat blazing in the fading light. He rears back, muscles rippling beneath his gleaming hide, hooves striking sparks against stone as he screams his urgency to the sky.

"By the Norns!" Bryn's fingers fly to her daggers. "What in helvíti is it, Gullfax?"

The stallion's answering whinny pierces the air like a battle cry. His golden eyes lock onto mine, and somehow I know—he knows where they've gone. The beast drops to his knees, sides heaving, head turned toward us in silent command.

"He knows where they are," I mutter, the certainty settling in my gut like a stone.

"Move your ass!" Bryn barks, already running. I follow behind, grab her waist, launching her into the saddle before vaulting up behind her. Gullfax surges upward before I'm fully seated, the force nearly throwing me backward.

The bond pulses with Bryn's wild energy as I grip her waist. Below, Heimdall swings onto Sleipnir's back, both horses leaving light trails in their wake. Gullfax rockets through the clouds, faster than I've ever known him to run. The wind tears at my clothes, my stomach lurching as we slice through the clouds at impossible speeds.

"Holy shit," Bryn's curse is lost to the howling wind. The beast beneath us is no longer just a horse—he's become pure fury given form, and he's carrying us straight into chaos.

My thighs clamp around Gullfax's sides, fingers digging into Bryn's waist as the beast tears through the skies. Wind screams past us, the ground below nothing but a distant blur. Each thunderous beat of his hooves against the sky sends shockwaves through my bones.

"Gullfax!" Bryn's voice barely pierces the gale. Her fingers wrestle with the reins, knuckles white with effort. "Slow down, you stubborn ass!"

The stallion's ears flatten against his head, his golden mane whipping our faces. Her command only seems to fuel his determination as he surges forward with renewed vigor, the air around us crackling with energy.

"Hold on!" I press my mouth to Bryn's ear, feeling her body jolt against mine as Gullfax banks sharply. My grip tightens, one hand splayed across her stomach, the other fisted in the stallion's mane. The bond between us pulses with adrenaline and fear, but I pour my certainty through it. She won't fall—not while I have breath in my body.

The icy winds claw at my face, tears streaming from my stinging eyes. I swipe them away, blinking to clear my vision. A towering structure pierces the horizon through the swirling clouds—a silver needle threading through the sky's fabric.

"The Elemental Nexus!" Bryn's words battle against the heavy winds, fragments reaching me. "Should've... known! Loki, you... bastard!" Her curse carries on the wind as she leans forward, her body tensing against mine. "With my wings... been there... already."

Gullfax's muscles bunch beneath us, his answering whinny vibrating through my chest. The cocky stallion lunges forward with renewed determination, the sudden acceleration sliding my ass dangerously close to the edge.

"Maybe don't insult the horse that's carrying us!" I tighten my grip on her waist, pulling myself forward. "Especially when we're this high up!"

The wastelands of Valhalla's Veil unfold beneath us, a graveyard of titans. Ancient bones pierce the earth like jagged monuments, the remains of fallen gods and giants reaching toward the sky. Memory strikes—Gullfax turning back at this point the last time we were here, the winds too fierce even for this great steed.

"Gullfax, stop!" I shout as we hurtle toward the barrier. "The winds will tear us apart!"

The stallion's only response is a defiant snort, his golden form streaking toward the light bridge like a meteor. My fingers dig into Bryn's leather armor.

"Fucking hell!" Bryn curses. "The stubborn bastard's going to get us killed!"

DANICA

65

The first step materializes before me, a solid stone hanging in empty air. I step forward, and the stone vanishes. My stomach lurches as I pitch forward into nothingness, a scream rips from my chest. The wind slams into me from the left, throwing me onto a step that appears just in time.

My knees shake as I gasp for breath. One misstep and it's over.

"Having trouble?" Loki's laugh echoes through the void.

The wind tugs urgently at my jacket. I let it pull me right as my current step dissolves beneath me. My boots scrape stone that appears split-seconds before I plummet to my death. Left. Right. Forward. Each leap feels like my last, the ground never there until the final instant.

Halfway up, my foot catches the edge of a disappearing step. I stumble, arms windmilling as I tip backward into empty space. The wind howls, shoving me forward. My fingers scrape stone as I scramble onto the next step, heart trying to punch through my ribs.

"Fuck," I gasp, hands shaking. The void below seems to pull at me, promising a long fall into darkness.

The pattern accelerates. Steps flash in and out faster, the gaps stretching wider. The wind drags me into a frenzied run. I leap—the next step vanishes before I reach it. My stomach drops as I fall, but the wind throws me sideways onto another step, my ankle twisting as I land hard.

Pain shoots up my leg. The step beneath me starts to fade.

"No time to rest, little savior," Loki calls, frost spreading across the steps as he follows. "Your mate awaits."

I force myself up, letting the wind guide me through the pain. Jump. Land. Jump again. My ankle screams with each impact. One wrong step, one moment of hesitation, and I'm dead.

The chanting pulses in my blood as I race for the vanishing stone. Twenty steps left. A stumble sends me sprawling, the wind barely saving me. Ten steps. My bad ankle buckles—I catch myself on my hands as the wind shoves me forward. Five steps.

Loki is following my every move.

I hit the final platform hard, rolling away from the edge. My whole body trembles as I gasp for air, the void still calling behind me.

The wind screams a warning. I see Loki approaching, each step calculating, frost spreading in his wake.

The archway towers before us, ancient runes pulsing with soft-white light. Beyond it, a circular chamber stretches toward a ceiling lost in shadow. In its center, floating in a column of swirling air—the Zephyrite Stone writhes with trapped storms. Lightning crackles within its opal depths, storm clouds churning, frozen in time.

I push myself up, gritting my teeth against my throbbing ankle. The wind whips around me, almost protective now, while frost creeps across the floor from Loki's feet.

"Move," he snarls, shoving me forward.

We step into the chamber and the winds suddenly die. Complete stillness, heavy and wrong, descends like the air before a devastating storm. The stone's internal tempest casts wild shadows across the walls.

A deep voice echoes through the chamber—*"To claim the storm's heart, first master its chaos."*

The air shimmers, and four pillars materialize around us in a perfect circle. My breath catches—they're identical to the elemental pillars from the Valley of Ancients, but these pulse with living storms inside their crystalline walls.

Aquaria's column churns with a waterspout—a hurricane. Mortalis hosts dust devils and earthen windstorms that remind me of Oklahoma during tornado season. Pyrothos writhes with fire tornados that make Hell look like a cozy campfire. And Zephyria's contains what I'd generously call a breeze (seriously, I've had stronger wind from a desk fan).

Lightning arcs between them in a complex web of energy.

"The Trial of Storms," Loki paces around the room. "It's simple, really—connect the storms without crossing paths. Though..." his eyes narrow, "the voltage might sting a bit."

The stone pulses again, its internal storm matching the rhythms of the lightning web.

Watching.

Waiting.

Testing.

I reach for Zephyria's pillar first, figuring air should be the easiest to control. Wrong. Lightning slams through me, dropping me to my knees. Every nerve screams as electricity courses through my body. The pain is blinding, but not as blinding as the knowledge that every second I waste is another second Rhyland suffers.

"Oops!" Loki's laugh echoes off the walls. "Maybe try using that scientific brain of yours? If you have one under all that pretty hair."

My hands shake as I push myself up. The room spins, and my muscles spasm from the shock. I need to focus.

I try matching water with fire, thinking opposites might work. The lightning strike feels like being hit by a truck, sending me flying back. I slam into the ground, the taste of copper flooding my mouth. Smoke curls from my fingertips, clothes singed.

"Tick tock, little savior," Loki says with amusement. "Though I must say, watching you fail is rather entertaining."

"How about you get your fucking ass over here and try this shit yourself?" I snarl through bloody teeth.

"And miss watching you electrocute yourself?" Loki's laugh chills the air. "Darling, you're the most entertainment I've had in centuries."

Frustration burns in my throat. Or maybe that's just the electricity. Every failed attempt wastes precious time, but rushing will only kill me. And if I solve this, I will actually give Loki control of the element.

The stone pulses above, its storm matching my chaotic thoughts.

Think, damn it. *Think.*

I stagger to my feet again, muscles screaming in protest. Three more failed attempts leave me retching on my hands and knees, skin smoking. The room won't stop spinning. My heart stutters in my chest, its rhythm disrupted by too many shocks.

"Perhaps I overestimated you," Loki sighs theatrically. "Such a disappointment."

The mark on my palm begins to tingle, a sensation like static electricity dancing across my skin. Suddenly, everything shifts into sharp focus—but not just the physical world. I can see... more. The spaces between spaces, the gossamer-thin boundaries where one thing transforms into another.

The air itself seems alive with possibility, shimmering with potential energy. And the storms within the pillars—they're not just representations or symbols. They're pure elemental force, raw and untamed, each one singing its own song of power.

Where before I saw only churning clouds and lightning, now I can perceive the intricate dance of energies, the delicate balance of opposing forces that creates each storm. The fjörniskratti's gift lets me see beyond the surface, into the very heart of these elemental powers.

Something clicks—It's not about power or dominance. It's about...

Of course. Of *fucking* course.

"Balance," I spit out along with a mouthful of blood. "It's not about controlling the elements—it's about their harmony."

Nature shows us that water carves the earth, earth banks the fire, fire feeds on air, air drives the rain. An eternal dance, each element supporting the next.

"Finally caught up, have we?" Loki's smug voice makes me want to show him some harmony right up his immortal ass.

"Well, no shit," I mutter, resisting the urge to flip off the universe for making me fry my ass multiple times before figuring out the basics of elementary school science.

My hands tremble violently as I reach for the air pillar again. This time, I let my fingers trail through the breeze instead of trying to control its winds. Feel its nature–its purpose.

The crystalline surface responds, rotating under my touch. As it turns, the lightning arcs shift, searching.

The water pillar pulses brighter. Air and water dance together in every storm. But one wrong degree of rotation will fry what's left of my nervous system.

I align them with agonizing slowness, sweat and blood dripping down my face. The lightning snaps between them, and I brace for pain—but this connection holds, stable and true.

"Finally showing some potential," Loki's frost spreads closer.

My vision blurs as I work. Earth needs water to thrive—I rotate Mortalis's pillar to face Aquaria. The sandstorm inside resists at first, then calms, accepting the connection. Fire requires air to burn—Pyrothos fights me, its inferno raging against control, but eventually aligns with Zephyria.

The stone's internal tempest matches the rhythm of the connected pillars, each element flowing into the next like a perfectly conducted symphony. But the victory tastes like shit in my mouth.

I've done it. I've solved the puzzle.

And I might have just helped destroy everything I'm trying to save.

Loki's eyes gleam like arctic ice. "Perhaps you're more than just a pretty face after all."

The air ripples. The stone descends from its column of swirling wind, hovering between us. Swirls of wind and clouds churn within its opal depths, calling to something profound in my soul.

I want to be sick. What have I done?

"Don't," I warn as Loki steps forward.

"Or what?" His fingers stretch toward the stone. "Your mate suffers while you play hero?" Ice crystals form in his black hair as his lips curve. "Besides, I just watched you solve a puzzle meant for gods. I'm almost impressed enough to tell you where he is before I make you open that portal."

The stone pulses, its storm matching my racing heart. *Rhyland.* My fingers twitch toward the gem, but Loki's faster. His hand closes around it.

"Now," as he pockets the stone, "let's discuss that portal you're going to open for me." He grabs my arm, cold seeping through my jacket. "After you."

As we approach the archway, solid steps materialize, nothing like the previous vanishing platforms. Each one forms just before our feet touch down, a mockery of my earlier trial.

"Hurry now," Loki's grip tightens. "The sooner you get me out of this realm, the sooner you find your man."

My ankle throbs with each step down the spiraling staircase, Rhyland's face burning in my mind.

Hold on, I silently plead. *Just hold on.*

We reach the bottom of the spire and my heart leaps—Heimdall stands before the entrance, his golden armor gleaming—ancient eyes burning with fury.

Loki's grip on my arm tightens, ice spreading, but his voice stays playful. "Heimdall! How lovely to see you. Love what you've done with the place."

"Trickster." Heimdall rumbles. "How did you breach my realm? They've been sealed."

They circle each other, Loki dragging me with him like a shield—relief floods me at the sight of Heimdall—finally, someone who can help.

"Oh, that's the best part." Loki's laugh rings off the stone walls. "When you opened the Bifrost for our dear Commander's triumphant return—I hitched a ride. Hidden in plain sight, wearing dear Baldr's face." His grin stretches wide. "You really should pay more attention to who you let in."

"Why?" Heimdall's eyes narrow. "Why are you doing this?"

"Why not?" Loki spreads his free arm wide. "Chaos is so much more fun than order. And watching Odin's precious plans crumble?" He shivers with theatrical pleasure. "Delicious."

"You will die for this transgression." Heimdall threatens. "Painfully."

Loki throws his head back and laughs. "You think you can kill me? Please." His grip tightens on my arm. "I've already won. I have the stone, the savior, and the poor Godborn taking a long nap." His eyes dance with malice. "What are you going to do, watch me leave? That is your specialty, isn't it? Always watching, never acting."

Heimdall's hand moves to his sword. "Not this time, Trickster."

Heimdall's eyes meet mine for a fraction of a second—a slight nod.

Light explodes from my palm, searing through Loki's frost. He howls, releasing my arm as I dive away. The sound of steel leaving its scabbard rings through the air—Heimdall's sword blazes golden as he lunges.

Loki barely gets his ice blade up in time. The clash of weapons echoes like thunder, frost meeting godly steel in a shower of sparks—the very air trembles with their power.

"Run, Danica!" Heimdall's voice booms as he drives Loki back. "Find him! I need him!"

The gods move faster than my eyes can track. Loki's laughter turns savage as he parries Heimdall's strikes, ice spreading across the floor with each step. "Always so dramatic, old friend!"

Heimdall answers with a blow that shatters Loki's ice blade. The trickster god forms two more instantly, frost crawling up his arms like armor. They clash again, the impact cracking the stone beneath their feet.

"You've grown slow in your watching," Loki taunts, spinning away from a lethal strike. His blades leave frost trails in the air as he attacks, forcing Heimdall to give ground.

"And you talk too much." Heimdall's sword blazes brighter. The following impact sends Loki staggering, ice armor cracking.

"GO!" Heimdall roars at me, his green eyes fierce. "Now!"

I turn and run, their battle shaking the very foundations of the Nexus behind me. The last thing I hear is Loki's wild laughter and the deafening crash of godly powers colliding.

Hold on, Rhyland. I'm coming.

I burst through the doors into biting wind. Erik, Bryn, and Gullfax wait at the bottom of the steps, weapons ready.

"Dani!" Bryn rushes forward, gripping my shoulders. "Are you alright? Heim-dall—"

"Loki," I gasp, lungs burning. "It was Loki the whole time. He has the stone, and Rhyland—" My voice cracks. "He's got Rhyland somewhere. Drowning. I can't feel him, can't sense him anywhere—"

"Wait." Erik's silver eyes flash. "You can't sense him at all? No bond?"

I shake my head, throat tight. "Nothing. Just... emptiness."

"Valor's Watch." Bryn's voice turns hard. "It's the only place in Zephyria that could block a mate bond. The wards must be up."

God damn it. I want to scream at myself for not realizing sooner. Of course that's where Loki would hide him—the one place I couldn't sense him.

"Did Loki say anything else?" Bryn's voice cuts through my panic. "Any details, any hints?"

I force my mind back to our chambers, sifting through his taunts. "He said"—my voice catches. "He said Rhyland was taking a swim. That chains make swimming difficult." The memory makes me want to throw up. "He was laughing about it."

"The Twilight Eyrie," Bryn says quickly. "There's a lake there, deeper than any in the realm. If he wanted to make sure Rhyland couldn't—"

I don't wait for her to finish. Power surges through me as I thrust my hand out, tearing reality apart. The portal crackles with light, opening onto the snow-covered compound of Valor's Watch.

"Move!" I'm already running through, Erik, Bryn, and Gullfax behind me.

Hold on, babe. I silently plead. Just hold on.

The emptiness in my chest turns to ice as realization hits. With the wards blocking our bond, there's no way for him to draw strength from me. No way to know I'm coming. Just endless darkness and burning lungs as water fills them over and over, his immortal body refusing to die even as it suffers.

My hands shake as my stomach twists into knots. Every second we waste is another moment of that torture.

The wards hit like a wall, magic draining from my body instantly—feels like a piece of my soul is ripped away.

Bryn's at the guard's throat in a heartbeat, cold steel kissing his skin. "Lower the wards!" She screams. "NOW!"

The guard's eyes bulge, Adam's apple bobbing against her blade. "I—I can't just—"

She presses harder, drawing a bead of blood. "I said, lower the fucking wards!"

"Okay!" He stumbles back, hands raised. "Okay, just don't—"

He scrambles to the gate mechanism, Bryn's glare burning into his back. Ancient gears groan as the wards power down.

Power floods back as the wards drop, but with it comes agony.

My knees buckle—hitting the ground, ice biting into my skin. Every nerve screams with phantom pain—freezing water in my lungs, chains biting into my wrists, the unbearable pressure of the deep. I can't breathe, can't think.

"Dani!" Erik's hands grip my shoulders. "Dani, look at me."

I force my eyes open, meeting silver.

"Breathe." His voice is low, steady. "This isn't your pain. Breathe through it."

I drag in a shuddering breath, then another. The agony recedes like a fading nightmare, but the soul-deep ache remains. The despair. The loneliness.

"Rhyland?" I reach through our bond. *"Babe, I'm here. I'm coming."*

Silence answers. Just more cold. More dark.

"Lightborn." Gullfax stomps next to me, his voice cracks through the haze. *"All of you, on. Now!"*

"Erik—" The word barely leaves my mouth before his hands lock around my waist, launching me onto Gullfax's back. Bryn lands behind me, Erik a heartbeat later.

Gullfax surges forward before Erik's even settled. *"I'll get us there faster,"* Gullfax promises, hooves thundering over ice and snow. *"Hold on."*

The world blurs as we race against time, the bond screaming in my head.

Gullfax gallops through the air as we race toward the Twilight Eyrie. The ancient structure looms against the mountainside, a foreboding silhouette against the gray sky. My heart pounds in time with his hoofbeats, the bond pulling tighter every second.

We crest the final peak and my breath catches. There, nestled in a valley of shadows, lies the frozen lake. Its surface is a mirror of dark ice, reflecting the eyrie's twisted spires.

Gullfax descends in a blur, my stomach lurching as we plummet. The lake rushes up to meet us.

We hit the ground hard. I'm off Gullfax's back before he's fully stopped, ignoring the searing pain as my ankle twists on the impact. I stumble, catching myself on numb hands, and force myself forward.

The ice beckons, a siren's call. I sprint across the frozen surface, my reflection fracturing beneath my feet. He's here. I can feel him, the bond pulling me forward like a lifeline. Almost there. Almost—

"LIGHTBORN, STOP!"

Gullfax's mental shout slams into me a second before the ice cracks. Fissures spider-web out from my feet, the surface groaning.

"Dani, don't move." Erik's command cuts through the air like steel.

The ice splinters. Gullfax's hooves strike air like solid ground, each step precise as he gallops across nothing to reach me. His teeth catch the hood of my coat just as the surface gives way, yanking me back to shore while dark water surges through the cracks.

"Let me go!" I thrash in Gullfax's grip, feet kicking uselessly. "He's down there, I have to—"

"The temperature will kill you in two minutes." Erik strips his weapons with military efficiency, each movement calculated despite the urgency in his voice. "I can withstand the cold. I'm faster. Tell me exactly where you sense him."

"There." I point to where the bond pulls strongest, voice cracking. "Right there, thirty feet out."

Erik nods once, silver eyes sharp with focus. "Stay here. Do not follow." He meets my gaze, and I see the fear behind his stoic mask for a split second. "I'll bring him back."

Bryn's arms wrap around me as I collapse into the snow. Shielding me from the biting wind.

"He'll find him," she whispers, but I barely hear her through the phantom sensations flooding our bond. Cold. So cold. The pressure crushing his chest, chains biting into flesh, the endless dark...

I clutch Bryn's arm as another wave hits, my throat raw from crying. Through tear-blurred vision, I watch Erik's form slice through the water where I pointed, disappearing beneath the fractured ice.

Minutes crawl by like hours. Bryn suddenly tenses, a sharp gasp escaping her lips.

"Bryn?"

"I can—" Her voice catches. "The cold, the pressure. Erik's... I can feel everything he's—"

My heart skips. Even through my pain, joy flickers—they've bonded. Finally.

"Send it back," I grip her hand. "Your strength, your warmth. He needs to feel you. He needs to know you're waiting." My voice breaks. "That's what the bond is for—to share everything—pain, love, power. Let him draw from you."

Bryn's eyes close, her breathing steady despite the tears freezing on her cheeks. Her focus shifts inward, channeling everything she is through their new connection.

We cling to each other in the snow, two mates waiting for our other halves to surface from the depths.

Minutes stretch into eternity. Each second without Rhyland's heartbeat next to mine is agony, the bond screaming with his pain. Bryn's grip on my hand turns bruising, her fear pulsing with mine.

Just as I'm about to break, to dive into the water myself—the surface explodes.

Erik surges through the shattered ice, a limp form cradled against his chest. Water cascades off them as he powers through the broken surface, silver hair slicked back, face set in grim determination.

"Oh my god." I scramble across the ice, boots slipping as I race toward them.

Erik heaves Rhyland's body onto the frozen shore. My world narrows to a pinpoint of horror.

His skin is corpse-blue, his lips purple-black and cold. Frost crystals glitter in his eyelashes and hair. Iron chains, rimed with ice, bite into the raw flesh of his wrists and ankles. His chest is still—too still.

"No, no, no..." The words fall from my lips like prayers as I drop beside him. His skin shouldn't be this color—this terrible, lifeless blue. What if I'm too late? What if those chains were enchanted, designed to trap his soul and body?

Erik shatters the icy restraints with a feral snarl, metal fragments scattering across the snow. I see the runes etched into each broken link—ancient symbols of binding, drowning, and eternal suffering.

My hands hover over Rhyland's still chest for one terrible heartbeat. What if this doesn't work? What if Loki made sure I'd find nothing but an empty shell?

No. I refuse to accept that.

I lock my fingers together and slam my weight down onto his sternum. "Come on, babe," I choke out, arms burning with the effort. "You promised me forever, remember? This isn't forever."

Each compression feels like pushing against stone. The cold radiating from his body seeps into my bones, but I keep counting. Keep pushing. Keep fighting.

What if he's already been taken somewhere I can't follow?

"I swear to god," I grit through tears, "if you die on me, I will follow you to Valhalla just to kick your ass."

Thirty compressions. Tilt his head back. His lips are blue-black beneath mine as I breathe for him. Once. Twice.

Nothing.

Start again.

"Please," I beg, no longer caring who hears the desperation in my voice. "Please, Rhyland. Come back to me."

The bond is a gossamer thread now, barely there. My arms shake with exhaustion, but I push through it. I won't lose him—not to Loki, not to anyone.

"That's it," I hiss, feeling something shift beneath my hands. "Fight, damn it!"

Rhyland's body convulses suddenly, back arching off the ground. He rolls violently to his side, expelling ice water in gut-wrenching heaves. Each breath tears from his lungs, echoing across the frozen lake.

"I'm here," I soothe, hands steady on his shuddering back. "I'm right here, babe."

His eyes find mine—ocean-blue rimmed with red, wild with pain and desperation. One trembling hand reaches for me, and I'm there in an instant, crushed against his freezing body.

"Angel," he rasps, the word barely audible through chattering teeth.

I break. Tears stream down my face as I cling to him, sobbing against his chest. His arms tighten around me, each violent shiver running through us both as he buries his face in my hair.

RHYLAND

66

Dani's warmth seeps into my frozen flesh as she clings to me, her sobs vibrating through my chest. I crush her against me, breathing in her scent like it's the only fucking air left in the world. My body's still trying to remember how to function after being chained, drowned, and resurrected a thousand times over, but none of that matters. Not when my girl is in my arms.

Our bond thrums with the aftershocks of everything I went through—the pain, the confusion, the psychological mindfuck Loki put me through. But it's Dani's emotions that hit me like a tidal wave—her worry, her agony, her desperation bleeding into my own until I can't tell where I end and she begins.

"I'm okay, baby." The words scrape out of my ravaged throat, vocal cords shredded from screaming and swallowing half the fucking lake. My teeth chatter, cold still deep in my bones.

Dani's wrist presses against my lips, the steady throb of her pulse beneath my mouth. "Here. Drink."

Her eyes lock with mine, a silent command in their honey depths. I don't hesitate. My fangs slice through her delicate skin like butter, and the first rush of her blood hits my tongue like a shock to my system.

A groan tears from my throat as I pull deeply from the wound, her essence flooding my mouth, my veins, my very soul. It's ecstasy and absolution all at once—the taste of sunlight and wildfire, of everything that makes Dani *mine*.

Power surges through me with each draw, energy crackling along my nerve endings as her blood works its magic. I lose myself in the sensation, in the intimate connection of feeding from my mate. The cold, the pain, the helplessness—all of it fades beneath the onslaught of pure, unadulterated Dani.

I pull away not wanting to take too much and Dani's hands find my face, fingers tangling in my beard as she drags my mouth to hers. I devour her like a man starved, pouring every ounce of my rage and desperation into the kiss. Her lips part for me, and I plunge my tongue inside, needing to taste her, to fill every part of her with my presence.

She breaks away, panting, her breath mingling with mine in the space between our mouths. "I love you," she whispers, a fierce declaration against my lips.

I crush her to me again, the kiss brutal and claiming. I need her warmth, love, and light to chase away the lingering shadows of what I endured.

But Dani pulls back too soon, eyes shimmering with unshed tears. "We need to get you some new clothes and get the fuck back to Heimdall." Her voice wavers, but there's an undercurrent of steel. "It's Loki. He's got the stone."

For a second, my brain stalls out trying to process why that horned bastard wants the stone. But then a thought hits me like a sledgehammer, overriding everything else. "Did he hurt you?" I grip her shoulders, sitting up, searching her face. "Did he fucking touch you?"

Shadows flicker across Dani's expression—a darkness she's trying to hide. But I'll be damned if she keeps anything from me. Not now.

"Tell me, Dani."

She swipes at her eyes, taking a shuddering breath. "He—H-he pretended to be you this morning. I woke up to who I thought was you and he—"

Lightning explodes through my veins, white-hot rage vaporizing any lingering cold. I'm on my feet before I realize I've moved, steam hissing off my skin as I rip the tattered remains of my shirt away. She doesn't need to say more. I can feel it through our bond—the guilt, the confusion, the violation.

He touched her.

He touched what's *mine*.

And I'm going to rip his fucking heart out for it.

"Open a portal. Take me to him. *Now.*" The command rips from my throat. I'm done playing games with this horned bastard. He fucked with me, and now he's fucked with my mate. There's no power in any realm that can save him now.

Dani doesn't hesitate. Her hands weave through the air, reality rippling as a portal tears open before us. Through the shimmering veil, the Nexus materializes, ancient steps leading to where two gods clash above the clouds. Heimdall and Loki's energies collide like warring storms, shaking the very foundations of Zephyria.

We don't pause. Together, we step through the portal, the world shifting in a dizzying kaleidoscope. One moment we're in the frozen wasteland of my torture; the next, we're standing above the clouds, wind whipping around us with the force of a hurricane.

But I barely feel it. My body's a living conductor, electricity racing through my veins, turning my blood to liquid fire. My hands flex at my sides as the power begs for release. Every instinct screams at me to unleash hell, rain down fury and vengeance until nothing is left but ashes.

Power shakes the very air as Heimdall and Loki clash. Each impact sends shockwaves through the clouds, their weapons striking with the force of colliding stars. Golden light meets ice-blue frost in explosive bursts that would blind mortal eyes.

My lightning surges in response to their battle, recognizing power rivaling the gods. Beside me, Erik and Bryn take defensive positions, weapons drawn but useless against this level of combat.

Heimdall moves like thunder, his blade carving paths through Loki's ice magic. The trickster god dances away from each strike, frost armor splintering and reforming in heartbeats. But Heimdall's faster—fucking *impossibly* faster—and his next strike catches Loki's shoulder, golden sword biting deep.

The snake stumbles, blood crystallizing on his armor. Heimdall doesn't hesitate. His free hand locks around Loki's throat, slamming him against the wall hard enough to crack stone.

"Now you lose, Trickster." Heimdall's voice booms like an avalanche.

Loki's laugh turns to a choke as Heimdall's grip tightens. The guardian's hand plunges into Loki's pocket, emerging with the Zephyrite stone. Without looking, he hurls it behind him.

"Lightborn!" The stone arcs through the air like a shooting star.

Dani launches herself forward, fingers stretching for the gem. The instant she touches it, pure power *explodes* from the point of contact. The stone vanishes, materializing in her crown with a flash that sears my retinas.

Holy fuck.

Dani rises slowly, and my breath catches in my throat. Power radiates from her in visible waves, her honey eyes blazing with internal storms. Wind whips around her like a living thing, responding to her will. The crown pulses with newfound strength, the Zephyrite stone settling into its destined place like it was always meant to be there—recognizing its owner.

She looks like a goddess incarnate, raw power made flesh, and for a moment I forget about Loki, about revenge, about everything except the magnificent creature before me. My mate. My warrior queen. My perfect match in every way.

Then she turns those storm-filled eyes toward Loki, and the air seems to hold its breath.

Heimdall drags Loki outside into the open, his golden armor gleaming against the dark skies. Above us, Dani's power transforms the heavens—storm clouds boil into existence. The wind rises to a deafening howl, whipping around us with conscious fury.

Heimdall hurls Loki to the ground, the impact cratering the earth. His ancient eyes find mine, burning with knowledge. "Godborn," his voice cuts through the chaos, "let your mate forge the storm, and you become its wrath."

The words hit me, and suddenly I *understand.*

I've been able to call lightning, to force it to my will through sheer fucking dominance. But this—watching Dani summon these storm clouds, feeling her power charge the very air around us—this is different. She's not just commanding the storm; she's creating the perfect fucking playground for my abilities.

Every cloud she summons, every violent wind she unleashes, charges the atmosphere with raw potential. The air crackles with electricity, *begging* for my command. What usually takes intense focus and brute force now feels as natural as breathing.

My lightning responds instantly, no longer fighting to break free but singing through my veins in perfect harmony. I reach out with my telekinesis, feeling the electric potential in every air molecule. It's like the universe is waiting for me to direct its fury.

Dani's power pulses through our bond, her storm merging with my lightning until I can't tell where her influence ends and mine begins. We're not just soulmates—we're two halves of nature's fury itself. She creates the storm, I become its judgment.

My hand rises, and the very sky answers my call.

Lightning arcs toward Loki, but the snake's already moving. His body blurs with impossible speed, and then—

Erik's body pitches backward over the cliff's edge, disappearing into storm-black sky.

No.

Oh my god.

"ERIK!" Bryn's scream cuts through the chaos.

She hurls herself off the cliff after him, silver hair whipping in the wind.

My heart stops. That stupid, brave Valkyrie just—*fuck*. She doesn't have her fucking wings.

They both vanish into the darkness below.

I lash out with my telekinesis, trying to grab them, but Loki's fist cracks against my jaw like a fucking sledgehammer. Pain explodes through my skull as he snarls in my face.

"Still alive, Commander of Dark Skies?" He mocks. "Maybe I should've tried a different method."

The world spins, ground and sky trading places until I taste blood and snow. My head rings like a fucking bell as Loki's hits keep coming, each one backed by godly rage.

Ice erupts from Loki's fingertips, a jagged wave of frost that crashes into Heimdall before the guardian can dodge. The impact sends him flying backward, his golden armor scraping against stone as he slams into the Nexus' wall. The ice doesn't stop—it spreads rapidly, crystallizing around Heimdall's limbs and torso, pinning him against the ancient structure like a frozen butterfly to a collector's board.

Loki's fist connects with my face again, and it feels like my skull's splitting open. "You're like a fucking cockroach," he snarls, icy spittle flecking my skin. "Refusing to die when you're supposed to."

Another punch drives into my gut, forcing the air from my lungs in a pained grunt. I try to suck in a breath, but Loki's relentless.

"The Godborn line should've ended eons ago." His knee slams into my ribs, and I swear I feel something crack. "But here you are, still clinging to life like the pathetic insect you are."

Loki's grip tightens in my hair, wrenching my head back until I'm forced to stare into his crazed eyes. A cruel smile twists his lips, but there's no humor in it—only a cold, merciless determination.

"You know what, godling?" His voice is a low, menacing purr. "I think I'm done playing these games with you. It was fun, but now you're just pissing me off."

He leans closer, his breath icy against my skin. "It's time to finally end your pathetic bloodline, once and for all. No more resurrections, no more second chances."

His fingers dig into my scalp, and I can feel the cold emanating from his touch, seeping into my bones. "I'm going to snuff out your life like a candle, and make sure there's nothing left to rekindle."

Loki's words are laced with a malevolent finality. There's a gleam of anticipation in his eyes, like a predator savoring the moment before the kill.

Through blurred vision, I see Dani—her eyes blazing with storm light, lost in the stone's power. Our bond pulses with raw energy, but she's too far gone to hear me.

Rage explodes through me like a supernova, my vision narrowing to nothing but this piece of shit in front of me. My fist connects with Loki's face, splitting his lips open in a spray of dark blood that freezes midair. His teeth shatter under the impact, jagged fragments mixing with the blood pouring from his ruined mouth.

I drive another punch into his throat, crushing his windpipe. He chokes, gasping for air that won't come as I grab his arm and wrench it backward until the shoulder joint explodes with a wet pop. The limb dangles uselessly as I slam my boot into his kneecap, shattering it into a dozen pieces.

He collapses, but I'm nowhere near done. I stomp on his chest, feeling ribs splinter beneath my heel. Each crack fuels my rage, each whimper feeds my need to destroy him completely.

I drop to my knees beside him, grabbing his hands—the hands that dared to touch my Dani. I squeeze until I feel the delicate bones of his fingers begin to crack.

"This is for touching what's mine," I snarl, methodically crushing each finger joint, one by one.

The sound is like stepping on dried twigs, but wetter. Loki's screams rise with each snap as I work my way through every bone in his hands—metacarpals splintering, carpals pulverizing under my grip. I twist his wrists until they dislocate, then keep twisting until the radius and ulna fracture through his skin.

His hands are nothing but bloody, pulped meat by the time I finish, completely unrecognizable as anything that once belonged to a god.

I grab his face, forcing him to look at me through his one good eye, his other swollen shut from my earlier blows. Blood bubbles from his broken lips as he tries to speak.

"No one puts their fucking hands on my girl," I growl, my face inches from his. "No one!"

Just as I'm about to deliver another crushing blow, Loki's form shimmers and dissolves beneath me—the bastard turning to frost-laced mist that slips through my fingers. He materializes yards away, staggering but out of my immediate reach, blood dripping from his mangled face.

Heimdall appears at my side in a flash of golden light, his ancient eyes fixed on the trickster god. "Godborn." His voice rumbles like distant thunder. "Together. While he's weakened."

My chest burns with rage and grief—Erik, Bryn, both gone in heartbeats. But I can't let that break me. Not now.

Fuck. The raw power pouring off Dani is unlike anything I've seen from the other stones. Her body trembles with the force of it, storm winds whipping her hair wild as her eyes blaze with the force of a storm as she channels the Zephyrite stone's energy.

I feel her struggling to contain the sheer magnitude of energy coursing through her system.

This stone's different—more primal, more demanding. Where the others yielded to her will, this one's like trying to tame a fucking hurricane. Not fighting her exactly, but refusing to be controlled by anything less than absolute mastery.

The ground shudders beneath me as Heimdall and Loki trade blows, their power unleashed in full fury. Each impact sends shockwaves rippling.

It's like watching two titans clash, their strength so far beyond mortal comprehension it's almost laughable. A single punch from either of them could level a city block, but they just keep going, their bodies absorbing the force like it's nothing.

"Baby, can you hear me?" I reach for Dani.

Her response hits instantly, clear despite the chaos. *"I can hold it. End that bastard."*

Heimdall's sword blazes golden as he drives Loki back, each strike precise and devastating. The trickster god's ice armor shatters faster than he can reform it, blood crystallizing on fresh wounds. His movements slow, desperation replacing calculation.

He's weak.

Power floods the air as Heimdall channels everything he has into one final assault. His blade carves through Loki's defenses like they're nothing, opening the bastard from shoulder to hip.

"Now!" Heimdall roars.

This motherfucker's time is up. Every chain around my body, every second I spent drowning in that frozen hell, every goddamn moment he violated my mate—it all fuels the lightning crackling through my veins.

Get ready to burn, you pathetic piece of shit, I'm about to show you what happens when you fuck with a god's descendant and the woman he'd tear realms apart for.

Lightning answers my call. The bolt that leaves my hand could split mountains and shatter realms. It hits Loki dead center, the sound of worlds ending.

For one eternal second, Loki's skeleton shows through his flesh, and his mouth opens in a silent scream. Then he explodes into a thousand shards of ice and shadow, the pieces evaporating before they hit the ground.

The storm above us rages on, but the trickster god is gone. Obliterated. Ended.

And somewhere below us, in the darkness, my brother and his mate are still falling.

I'm at Dani's side in a heartbeat, my arms crushing her against my chest. "Dani, baby. Hey. Let go, sweetheart. It's over."

Her eyes are still white, empty—seeing fuck knows what in the heart of that storm. The winds scream around us, the clouds above us thickening with each second. I can feel her energy draining, the stone sucking her dry.

Words aren't cutting it. So I do the only thing I can think of—I kiss her.

At first, it's like kissing a statue. No response, no recognition. Just the taste of ozone and the chill of stormwinds. But I don't stop. I pour everything into the kiss—my love, strength, and need for her to return to me.

And slowly, so fucking slowly, the winds begin to die. The clouds above us thin, letting in shards of pitch black skies.

Dani's lips soften, molding to mine as her arms wrap around my neck.

She's kissing me back. She's here. She's *mine*.

The storm fades, the stone's power quieting as Dani reasserts control. But I don't break the kiss. I need this—need her—like I need air.

Those honey-gold eyes I know so damn well blink up at me, clarity returning to their depths. Relief floods my chest as Dani takes in the destruction around us—craters, ice shards, scorched earth still smoking from warfare.

"Well, that was a wild ride." She tosses her hair, fingers brushing the Zephyrite stone. "Forget 'power trip,' more like 'power free fall without a parachute.' Definitely gonna have to establish some boundaries with this sassy little rock."

I can't help but snort. Fucking unbelievable. My mate just wrestled a primordial force of nature into submission, and she's talking about it like it's a misbehaving puppy. Her ability to bounce back, to find the humor in any situation—it's one of the million things I love about her.

"Definitely not like the others," she continues, sass fading into something more serious as she scans the battlefield. "Where's Erik? Bryn?"

My throat closes up. How the fuck do I tell her that her sister hurled herself off a cliff after my brother? That Loki's final act of cruelty was—

A familiar whinny splits the air.

Golden hooves flash through remaining storm clouds as Gullfax rockets upward from the abyss, his mane streaming like captured sunlight. Erik's silver hair whips in the wind, his arms locked around Bryn as they cling to the stallion's back.

Fuck, I love that damn horse.

DANICA

67

The great hall of Ásgard falls silent as the truth of Baldr's fate echoes off ancient walls. Frigg's fingers whiten against her throne's armrests, immortal face crumpling as each word strikes like physical blows. Beside her, Odin sits motionless, his remaining eye fixed on some distant point none of us can see.

Bryn kneels before Odin, her shoulders slumped in defeat. "AllFather, I am sorry...I Failed Ásgard." Her voice cracks. "I should have known sooner that Baldr—"

Odin leans forward, his single eye piercing through Bryn. "Já, Valkyrie. Was it not your sworn oath? To shield this realm and its prince?" Each word falls heavy as judgment.

I feel Bryn's pain radiating through the Faerite Stone, but seriously, this is getting old. It's like watching a tennis match of guilt and blame, and I'm about to grab the racket and whack them both over the head with it.

Bryn's head bows lower. "I failed to—"

"Oh my god, enough!" The words burst out of me, my patience snapping. "Bryn, you didn't kill Baldr. You didn't hand Loki a 'Go Fuck Shit Up' free pass. This pity party shit stops."

Erik's hand finds Bryn's shoulder, silver eyes fierce. "Dani is right, this ends now."

I get it—the AllDadddy just found out a wannabe snake whisperer murdered his kid. Grief makes people act like assholes, even divine ones. But watching Bryn beat herself up over Loki's epic betrayal is making my savior senses tingle, and not in the good way.

Odin's eye locks onto me, and my throat constricts. Shit. Did I just overstep my bounds? Mouth off to the God of Gods in his own hall while he's grieving his dead son?

Way to go, Dani. Real smooth.

But goddamn it, I'm sick and tired of watching Bryn flagellate herself for things beyond her control. She's been through enough already, what with the whole 'destined to be a savior's mate but psych, just kidding' thing. Losing everything she's known—she doesn't need to add 'failing to stop a god of lies and trickery' to her guilt resume.

So I lift my chin and meet Odin's stare head-on. Because if there's one thing I've learned in this whole 'prophesied savior' gig, it's that sometimes you have to stand your ground. Even if your knees are shaking and your palms are sweating and you're pretty sure you might puke on an ancient Norse god's boots.

The silence stretches, taut as a bowstring. I can feel Bryn's tension, Erik's readiness to jump in front of me if Odin decides to go all 'wrath of the gods' on my ass. But Rhyland's reaction really sends a shiver down my spine. He's coiled tight, every muscle tensed, ready to tear Odin apart if he so much as twitches in my direction. The bond between us thrums with his barely restrained fury, a hurricane just waiting to be unleashed.

But I don't back down. I can't. Not when it comes to the people I love.

Finally, Odin's eye narrows. His lips twitch beneath his beard, and for a moment I'm sure he will smite me where I stand. But then he inclines his head, just a fraction. "Bold words, Lightborn." His voice is like gravel underfoot. "But perhaps not unwise."

I let out a breath I didn't realize I was holding. Holy shit. I just faced down Odin and lived to tell the tale. Mark that one down in the record books, folks.

Rhyland's hand finds mine, his grip tight enough to border on painful. "*You're going to be the death of me, woman.*" His mental voice is a growl, equal parts exasperation and fierce pride.

"*Hey, you knew what you were signing up for when you mated me,*" I shoot back, squeezing his hand. "*Savior of the Realms, remember? Mouthing off to the gods kind of comes with the territory.*"

His answering snort echoes through my head, and for a moment, the weight of everything—Baldr's death, Loki's betrayal, the looming threat of Moretemis—feels just a little bit lighter. Because with Rhyland by my side? I can face anything—even the wrath of an AllFather.

Frigg's sob shatters the silence. Her shoulders shake as she presses trembling fingers to her lips, each tear crystallizing before hitting the ground.

My heart aches, knowing I'll never meet the real Baldr—the true prince of Ásgard, not the serpent who wore his face like a carnival mask. Another thing to add to Loki's tab of cosmic fuck-ups.

Heavy footsteps echo through the hall, and we turn to see Heimdall approaching. His golden armor catches the torchlight, making him look like a walking sun. His ancient eyes—those eyes that see everything—fix on Odin.

"AllFather." His voice resonates with the weight of eons. "The Liesmith has paid for his treachery with his life." His gaze shifts to Rhyland and me, and I resist squirming. "The Savior and her mate have proven themselves worthy. The Zephyrite stone now rests with its destined bearer."

"Nei." Odin's voice fills the hall, heavy with ages of grief. His eye finally focuses, finding Bryn's bowed head. "Even your sight was clouded, Heimdall. And my queen..." His words falter as Frigg's quiet sobs pierce the air.

Heimdall bows his head, acid-green eyes dimming. "The Liesmith's deception ran deeper than any could have foreseen. But now..." His gaze returns to me, intense enough to make my skin prickle. "Now the balance shifts. The prophecy moves forward."

I feel Rhyland tense beside me, his hand tightening around mine. Because yeah, no pressure or anything. Just the weight of multiple realms and a prophecy hanging over our heads. You know, typical Tuesday stuff.

The torches flicker, casting dancing shadows across Odin's face as he rises—radiating power that makes my head spin.

"My son..." His voice rumbles. "Stolen from us, while a serpent wore his face."

More tears fall as Frigg weeps. The sound of a mother's grief tears at something in my chest, and I have to look away. Because if I don't, I might start bawling myself. And wouldn't that be a sight? The prophesied savior, reduced to a blubbering mess in the halls of Ásgard. Loki would be laughing his ass off.

Odin's eye closes, the weight of loss bowing even his immortal shoulders.

"Brynhildr." Odin's voice softens. "Rise, child of mine."

Bryn stands, shoulders still bowed under invisible weight. Odin's weathered hand reaches out, gently tilting her chin up until their eyes meet. The gesture reminds me of a father with his daughter, not an AllFather with his Valkyrie.

"You carry no shame here." His eye flicks to Erik, whose hand is now wrapped around Bryn's waist, then back to Bryn's face. Something shifts in Odin's expression—understanding, perhaps. Or acceptance. "The path before you is your own now." His words echo with the weight of divine blessing. "Walk it with the same strength that has always made these halls proud."

He bends, pressing his lips to her forehead. Bryn's breath catches, her eyes widening as centuries of duty dissolve in a single touch.

Without another word, Odin turns, his cloak sweeping behind him as he strides from the hall. The sound of his footsteps fades, leaving behind a silence that feels lighter somehow.

Frigg rises from her throne, gliding toward me. Despite her tears, she radiates power that makes my teeth ache. Her hands cup my face, calm as moonlight against my skin.

"You freed us from the serpent's coils, Lightborn. But beware—one shadow falls only for another to rise. When darkness comes, remember—light shines brightest in the deepest night." Her thumbs brush my cheeks. "You carry more than just prophecy in your heart. You carry hope."

She kisses my forehead, just as Odin did to Bryn. For a moment, I smell summer flowers and taste honey on my tongue.

"Remember," she breathes against my skin. "The darkest night comes before the brightest dawn."

Before I can ask what the hell that means, she's gone.

The mead hall of Valor's Watch echoes with ancient stories, though the only tale I care about is how long it will take Bryn to pack her suitcase. She's gathering her "treasured possessions," which in Valkyrie-speak probably means an arsenal of weapons and maybe a few hair ties.

I can't help the ridiculous grin spreading across my face. My sister—my actual, honest-to-gods sister—is coming home with us. Like, to the mortal realm.

Home.

The word makes me want to do a happy dance right here on these hallowed floors. Sorry, Odin, but your blessing translated to "go forth and get that vampire D."

I mean, let's be real. Long-distance relationships are hard enough when your boyfriend lives in another city. Try making it work across different realms of existence. "Sorry, honey, can't make date night. The Bifrost is down for maintenance." Yeah, no.

I can't wait to introduce her to all the wonders of modern life. Netflix binges, where we can watch an entire season of something in one sitting without any divine interruptions. Spa days with actual hot stone massages, not whatever passes for relaxation when you live in the clouds. Online shopping—because something tells me Valkyrie armor isn't exactly comfortable for casual Fridays.

And Erik? Mr. "I-Never-Met-An-Emotion-I-Couldn't-Suppress" is practically glowing. Well, as much as a vampire can glow without bursting into flames. I've seen him crack more smiles in the last few hours than in all the time I've known him. It's almost unsettling, like watching a gargoyle do stand-up comedy.

Though if he keeps up with the lovey-dovey eyes, I might have to start calling him Sir Smitten instead of Sir Stoic. And won't Lucian love that little nugget of ammunition?

God, we have so much to cover—yoga pants, Starbucks, reality TV, and brunch. My sister's about to get the whole mortal experience, which will be epic.

And, can we take a moment to appreciate that we took down Loki? Like, the actual God of Mischief and Lies? I mean, I know I've got this whole 'savior blood' thing going on, and Rhyland's a demigod powerhouse, but still. We tag-teamed a god and won. That's got to earn us some serious cosmic brownie points, right?

Though I guess you get one hell of a cocktail when you mix savior juice with demigod mojo.

Even Loki didn't see that one coming. And speaking of things I didn't see coming—I can go full Storm from X-Men now? That was terrifying and exhilarating, like riding a hurricane while trying not to pee your pants. Definitely need to practice that particular party trick before I accidentally create a tornado in the living room.

I still remember Loki's taunts to Rhyland about "staying dead." It got me thinking—Loki's clearly been playing the long game here. He knew about Rhyland's resurrection, about my whole destiny schtick. He's been lurking in the shadows like a creeper, just waiting for the perfect moment to hitch a ride back to Ásgard and throw a wrench in the cosmic gears.

All those "coincidences," all those perfect moments of chaos—he was moving pieces on a board we didn't even know we were playing on.

The Zephyrite stone pulses against my head, agreeing with my anger. Or maybe it's just reminding me not to accidentally summon a thunderstorm while I'm brooding. Being a savior really needs to come with an instruction manual. "How to Handle Your Godly Powers Without Destroying the Weather System: A Beginner's Guide."

Bryn resurfaces with an energetic grin, leather satchels slung over her shoulders like some mythical bag lady. Erik's on her in a hot second, playing the gallant knight and relieving her of her burdens.

But not before laying a kiss on her that makes me want to whistle appreciatively. Get it, sis!

I turn to Rhyland, jerking my thumb toward our room. "Gonna do a final sweep, make sure we didn't forget any mystical souvenirs or enchanted underwear."

He snorts, rolling his eyes. "Make it quick, baby. If I don't leave this winter wonderland soon, I will start sprouting icicles in unfortunate places."

I blow him a kiss, sauntering off to our love nest. Pushing open the door, I give the room a once-over. Daggers? Check. Boots? Check. Sanity? Debatable, but I'm pretty sure that's not something I can pack anyway.

I'm about to leave when something on the bedside table catches my eye. A crumpled yellow scrap of paper. But not just any paper. Oh no. That, my friends, is a motherfucking post-it note.

In Ásgard?

A realm known for many things—epic battles, mead-soaked feasts, questionable fashion choices involving horned helmets—but definitely not for its office supplies.

Last I checked, Norse gods weren't big on this kind of stuff. So either 3M has started a new interdimensional marketing campaign, or something's up.

I flip the note over, scanning the scrawled message. And promptly feel my blood pressure skyrocket.

> *Yo savior bestie—*
> *Shit's FUBAR. Queen Bitch of the North snatched Seraphina, and*

Morgan decided to DIY a glory hole to hell. Because why the fuck not? Now we've got a demon living it up at House of Hogwarts. Get your prophecy ass home before this turns into Satan's block party.

Your favorite witch who's done with your shit.

"Fuck." The word explodes from my mouth as I burst from the room like my ass is on fire.

Rhyland's head snaps up, his expression shifting from 'mildly concerned' to 'ready to murder someone' in 0.2 seconds. "What's wrong?"

"We need to go. Like, right now." I thrust the post-it at him like it's a ticking bomb. "Read."

He stares at the yellow paper, then at me, then back at the paper. His face is completely blank, as if I had just handed him instructions for assembling IKEA furniture in ancient Sanskrit.

"I don't understand."

"What's not to understand? It's written in plain English!" I snatch it back, waving it in his face. "Did that frozen lake scramble your brain cells? Emily's—"

"Kära," he cuts me off, that stupid sexy eyebrow of his climbing toward his hairline. "That paper is blank."

I freeze, looking between the note and my man like I'm watching a tennis match. "Blank? What do you mean blank? It's right here! Emily's snark in all its yellow post-it glory!"

But Rhyland stares at me with that 'my woman might be losing her mind but I still love her' look. "Baby, I saw this days ago. Thought nothing of it."

Oh my god. Days ago??

I blink at him. Once. Twice. "Let me get this straight—you saw a Post-it note in the realm of Norse gods, magical horses and thought 'yeah, that tracks'? In a place where the most advanced writing technology is probably a fancy quill?"

His brow furrows, and I can practically see the light bulb moment as realization hits him. "Shit."

"Yeah, *shit* is right." I wave the note in his face. "Short version? Your mom's playing kidnapper with Seraphina, and we've got an unexpected demon roommate."

The words tumble out in a rush. "So maybe we could speed up this realm-hopping exit?"

Rhyland's face hardens into that battle-ready mask I know too well. We're moving before I can blink, boots crunching through fresh snow as we head for a secluded spot. Erik and Bryn fall in behind us, no questions asked. That's the thing about immortal warriors—they know when to save the twenty questions for later.

I raise my hand, magic tingling at my fingertips, ready to tear open reality and get us home. That's when I hear it—a sound that squeezes my heart like it's caught in a vice.

The familiar golden whinny splits the air.

Gullfax emerges from the swirling snow like a living sunrise, his golden coat catching what little light filters through the clouds. *"Lightborn,"* his voice echoes in my mind, gentle as summer rain. *"Would you leave without bidding farewell?"*

My throat closes, and the tears come before I can stop them. I press my face into his warm neck, breathing in the scent of sunshine and stardust. His presence wraps around me like a physical embrace, and suddenly, I remember everything—soaring through storm-dark skies to save Erik and Bryn, pulling me from the icy grip of that frozen lake, charging at the Draugr to shield me, always standing by whenever we needed him.

I despise this—these constant goodbyes. They tear at my heart every time.

"You beautiful, magnificent creature," I whisper against his golden coat. "You didn't just carry us through the realm. You carried us through hell itself. You're not just some magical horse—you're family." My voice cracks. "And I don't know how to say goodbye to family."

Gullfax's warm breath stirs my hair. *"Who says this is goodbye, little light? As long as light shines and wind blows, I am a whisper away. Call, and I will answer."*

I hug him tighter, memorizing the feel of him beneath my fingers. "Promise?"

His gentle laugh ripples through my mind. *"I swear by sun and storm. Now go. The realms needs its savior."*

I step back, swiping at my tears. Rhyland moves forward, his hand steady as he extends it to Gullfax. The divine stallion lowers his head, pressing his velvet nose against Rhyland's palm. The touch seems to break something in my man—his shoulders tremble, throat working against emotions I've rarely seen him display.

"Thank you, buddy," Rhyland's voice comes out rough, raw. "For everything."

Seeing my indestructible alpha man fighting back tears breaks the last of my composure. A sob escapes before I can trap it behind my teeth.

Gullfax's ancient eyes close, touching his forehead to Rhyland's. His voice echoes in my mind, meant for Rhyland— *"Guard our Lightborn well, son of Magni."*

I whisper the words to Rhyland, watching his jaw clench tight enough to crack stone.

Then Gullfax rises, powerful and proud, golden hooves striking sparks from the very air. For one breathtaking moment, he's more than just a horse—he's stardust and storms, legend made flesh, divinity wrapped in golden hide.

And then he's gone, leaving nothing but echoing hoofbeats and the lingering scent of summer winds.

LUCIAN

68

Seraphina is curled up against me, all soft skin and curves. Her golden hair is spilling across my black silk pillows like liquid sunshine.

Talk about a morning-after masterpiece.

One of her legs is thrown possessively over my waist, and *fuck*—the way her perfect breasts press against my side should be classified as a weapon. Her peaceful face, those slightly parted lips that were screaming my name just hours ago... it's enough to make my heart beat out of my chest.

I trace lazy patterns on her bare skin, remembering how she arched and moaned beneath me. My angel cake turned out to be kinkier than a demon's tail. Makes me wonder what other naughty surprises she's hiding under those pristine wings.

Last night was a divine revelation of the most sinful kind. Phina let me claim that sacred territory and took backdoor action like she'd been studying the Kama Sutra's secret chapters.

Who knew Heaven's finest would be enthusiastic about getting her halo polished from behind? She moaned my name like a prayer, begged for more like confession, and came so hard I thought we'd both ascend straight to the pearly gates.

Her wings are hidden away now, but the memory of how they trembled and fluttered while I took her ass? That's getting filed away in my spank bank for all eternity.

Note to self: Install mirrors on the ceiling. For research purposes, obviously.

The sunlight streaming through the balcony doors makes her skin glow like she's lit from within. Which, considering she's an angel, might be true.

Seraphina stirs, her silky leg sliding over my already rock-hard morning wood. Her gorgeous eyes flutter open, a coy smile on those sinful lips. "Good morning, Sparky," she purrs, her voice like audible honey.

Hello, Little Miss 'I'm-an-angel-but-I-fuck-like-a-demon.'

"Morning, naughty girl," I smirk, already mentally high-fiving myself for landing the hottest thing to ever fall from Heaven.

Achievement unlocked: Corrupted an Angel. +1000 XP.

She giggles, pressing those perfect lips against mine, and *sweet merciful Batman*—she tastes like cotton candy and whiskey had a baby that was blessed by the Pope.

I cup her face, then grab a fistful of that golden hair, tilting her head back to deepen the kiss. The moan that escapes her goes straight to my cock like it's following a GPS signal.

Down boy. We've got important morning-after conversations to have before round two... or is it round seven? I lost count somewhere around midnight.

I pull back, my brain finally catching up to the rest of me. "How's my favorite ass doing after last night's wild ride?" I ask, tracing a finger down her spine before gripping that perfect peach that took quite the pounding last night.

Because I'm nothing if not a considerate lover. Captain Consideration, that's me.

"I rode you harder than a prized stallion at the Kentucky Derby."

Seraphina laughs, and I can't help but smile at the sound. "I'm perfectly fine," she assures me, that sassy little eyebrow quirk appearing. "Remember, I can heal. Perks of being an angel."

Ah yes, her healing mojo. It's not quite the premium package like Dani's Infinity Stone superpower, but it's more like the basic subscription plan of supernatural recovery. Just enough to handle a night of passionate acrobatics without the awkward morning-after limp.

Angel girlfriend = self-repairing bedroom toy with unlimited warranty. This is definitely a win for Team Lucian.

I roll her beneath me in one smooth motion, my aching cock nestled against that slick, sweet pussy. She arches into me, a soft purr vibrating through her chest that I feel in my bones. Burying my face in the crook of her neck, I inhale deeply, drowning in her scent—vanilla, cinnamon, and something uniquely *her.*

Fuck. I'm addicted. This angel is my drug of choice, and I'm a willing junkie.

Her emotions wash over me through our bond, a tidal wave of love and desire that threatens to sweep me away. It's a feedback loop of passion, her arousal fueling mine until I'm drowning in need. My hips align with hers, the promise of paradise just one thrust away—

Cue record scratch.

A distinctive pop from downstairs shatters the moment, freezing us both in place. Seraphina's eyes widen, mirroring my own surprise. We don't need words to know what—or rather *who*—just interrupted us.

"Dani," we chorus, because *of fucking course* Little Miss Save-the-Realms would pick *this* exact moment to pop back into existence.

Cockblocked by the prophecy. Again. This is getting old faster than Erik's sword collection.

Seraphina launches from the bed like she's been catapulted, leaving me with a severe case of sexual whiplash. My brain's still stuck in sexy-time mode while Phina is already halfway into her clothes, her movements are quick, golden skin and flowing hair.

I slide into my jeans, wincing as I tuck away the evidence of our interrupted morning activities. The look on Seraphina's face—that pure, radiant joy at the prospect of seeing her best friend—almost makes up for the blue balls I'm now sporting.

Almost.

Her eyes dance with excitement as she smooths down her hair, a futile attempt to hide her 'I've been thoroughly ravaged' look. Those golden locks are a certified sex-tornado aftermath—no amount of finger-combing is going to hide our bedroom Olympics.

I should give her a medal for that performance. Olympic-level flexibility deserves recognition.

I catch her hand as she practically vibrates with anticipation, pulling her close for one last taste. Her body melts against mine like she was custom-made to fit there.

Fuck. I'm addicted to this angel harder than humans are to their stupid phones.

"To be continued," I purr against her ear, letting my fangs graze the sensitive skin. Her shiver goes straight to my still hard cock like a heat-seeking missile.

Down boy. We've got a family reunion to attend before I can bend her over the nearest surface and make her see stars again.

Her smile could light up Times Square. And my heart melts at the sight.

Fuck. When did I become this sappy?

The moment my feet hit the bottom step—

"What the *FUCK* is that?" Dani's voice could shatter bulletproof glass at fifty paces.

Ah yes, the universal Brax introduction. Never gets old.

I round the corner to find a tableau of supernatural shock and awe—Dani with her jaw practically unhinged, Rhyland doing his best impression of a Viking shield wall between her and our resident demon, Erik looking stoic as ever (though his hand's suspiciously close to his blade), and some blonde who's staring at Brax like she's witnessing an eldritch horror emerge from the toilet.

Brax, in all his ten-foot, charred-skin glory, towers in the living room. The stench of sulfur and burnt Pop-Tarts wafts through the air like the world's worst air freshener.

"Who are you?" Brax rumbles, smoke curling from his nostrils like a dragon with a sinus infection.

And the award for 'Most Awkward Family Reunion' goes to...

"Alright, alright." I slide between them like I'm breaking up a bar fight. "Brax, really? Can't you pick a face or something? You're scaring the residents."

Brax gives me the demonic equivalent of a 'bitch, please' look before his form shimmers and ripples. The massive black demon melts away, replaced by—

Of fucking course.

Captain America stands in my living room, complete with the Boy Scout smile and perfect hair. My internal Marvel fanboy weeps tears of betrayal.

I roll my eyes so hard I practically see my own brain. A violent shudder runs through me at the memory of hearing—

Nope. Not going there. That's a trauma for another therapy session.

This asshole has officially ruined Cap for me. I'll never watch Avengers again without thinking of demonic Pop-Tart farts.

"What. The. Hell?" Dani enunciates each word like she's trying to make sense of our circus.

Welcome home, firecracker. I hope you brought popcorn because this show's just getting started.

"Well, if it isn't the Avengers finally assembling," I drawl, remembering Emily's magical SOS text that feels like it was sent sometime during the Jurassic period.

"Don't worry, we handled our own 'save the world' mission while you were gone. No infinity stones required."

Though our version involved significantly more demon cosplay and accidental vampirism. Details, details.

"Meet Brax," I gesture toward Not-Steve-Rogers now lounging on my Italian leather couch like he owns the place. The sulfur stench is finally clearing. "He's our resident demon shapeshifter with an unfortunate Marvel fetish. We've got a lot to catch up on."

"No fucking shit." Rhyland's growl could make a grizzly bear piss itself. His massive frame practically vibrates with protective Alpha energy as he eyes Brax. "A damn demon?"

Down, boy. Your Viking is showing.

Before I can explain our resident demon's hard-on for Chris Evans, Seraphina launches herself at Dani like a heat-seeking missile of celestial joy. Their reunion hug looks like something straight out of a Hallmark movie—if Hallmark did supernatural rom-coms.

"Dani! You're back! You're safe!" Her voice is pure sunshine and rainbow sprinkles as she practically lifts Dani off the ground.

"Seraphina, are you okay?" Dani's voice carries equal parts worry and 'I-will-murder-whoever-hurt-you' energy. "Emily's note—"

"She's fine," I interject, puffing up like a peacock. Because yeah, I totally saved my angel's perfectly sculpted ass. "Though the story involves a demon, some accidental vamp—

"Shower, food, and drinks first before I even consider having this conversation," Dani interrupts, returning Seraphina's hug before extracting herself—her eyebrow arches. "And make that drink a double. Something tells me I'm going to need it."

Oh, honey. If you think this is weird, wait until you hear about the baby vampire with bubblegum hair upstairs.

"Fair enough," I concede.

My eyes zero in on Erik and his new appendage—a blonde who looks like she just walked straight off the set of the Vikings TV show where everyone's covered in mud and leather and shouting about Valhalla. She's got the whole "shield-maiden who could gut you with a rusty spoon while reciting Norse poetry" vibe down pat.

Well, well, well. What do we have here?

The girl's rocking some unique peepers—heterochromia that would make a cat jealous—and Erik's got that 'touch-her-and-die' posture going on. Mr. Stoic practically broadcasts 'MINE' in neon letters above his head.

Someone's been busy. And here I thought Erik's only relationship was with his sword collection.

"So," I drawl, eyeing the way Erik's practically melded himself to Viking Barbie's side. "Did I miss the memo about us collecting historically accurate arm candy, or...?"

Because watching Erik play the protective mate is like seeing Nick Fury crack a smile—rare and slightly terrifying.

"Like I said, shower, food, and drinks first." Dani's tone carries the weight of someone surviving on medieval protein bars and whatever passes for road snacks in Viking-land.

"Cool. I'll get Rosa on it," I offer, already planning something Mexican. "Do you have any particular cravings, Princess?"

They all look like they just stepped out of a Norse mythology documentary—all furs, shields, and leather that've seen better days. The kind of outfit that screams 'we've been realm-hopping through frozen wastelands and living off dried meat and determination.'

No wonder Dani's ready to commit murder for a decent meal.

The girl has probably been dreaming of Rosa's cooking while choking down whatever passes for food in the land of eternal winter.

Dani's stomach growls loud enough to wake the dead—the sound carries the promise of violence if food doesn't materialize in the next ten minutes.

"Anything."

"Rosa!" I call out, already moving toward the kitchen. "Emergency protocol—Hungry Human! Break out the good stuff—we've got a famished firecracker who hasn't seen proper food in weeks!"

The exhausted group trudges upstairs, their footsteps heavy with too many miles and insufficient rest. As they disappear to freshen up, Rosa materializes in the kitchen like a culinary genie summoned by the promise of hungry stomachs.

"¿Dónde está ese maldito demonio?" she demands, her eyes narrowing. "Where is that damn demon? He better stay out of my kitchen while I cook!"

Ah, Rosa. Always ready to throw down with the forces of darkness, armed with nothing but a rosary, spatula and a fiery temper.

"Relax, Rosalita," I grin, holding my hands in mock surrender. "Brax is currently cosplaying as Captain America in the living room. Your kitchen is a demon-free zone, scout's honor."

"¡Ay, Dios mío! That *pendejo* still owes me three new sauce pans from last week!" She starts pulling ingredients from the pantry like she's arming for culinary warfare. "And tell him if he shape-shifts into Gordon Ramsay again while I'm cooking, I will stuff him with holy water tamales!"

That incident was both hilarious and traumatizing. Who knew demons could hit such high notes?

"Yes, ma'am," I salute, backing away from her domain. "Though you have to admit, his Jamie Oliver impression was spot-on."

She huffs, her expression softening slightly. "Bueno. Now, what do these poor dears need after their little interdimensional road trip?"

Leave it to Rosa to make realm-hopping sound like a weekend getaway gone awry.

"The works, mi amor," I reply, already salivating at the thought of her legendary cooking. "Dani hasn't had a proper meal in weeks, and you know how she gets when she's hangry."

Rosa nods sagely, tying her apron with the determination of a general preparing for battle. "Say no more. I'll whip up a feast fit for a king—or a cranky superhuman, in this case."

God bless this woman and her magical kitchen skills.

"Have I told you lately that you're my favorite person in this madhouse?" I grin, dodging the playful swat she aims at my head.

"Flattery will get you nowhere, mi diablito," she smirks. "Now get out of my kitchen, vampiro! And keep that demon away, or I swear by all the saints..."

Time for a tactical retreat. Even immortals know better than to argue with Rosa on a mission.

A.L HAMPTON

ERIK

69

I lead Bryn through Lucian's sprawling mansion, her eyes widening at the sleek modern lines and high-tech amenities. It's a far cry from the ancient stone and rough-hewn wood of Valor's Watch. She trails her fingers along the smooth walls, her steps slowing to take in the foreign wonders.

"Careful, you'll catch Lucian's interior decorator." My lips twitch as she jerks her hand back. "I hear minimalism is contagious."

Bryn snorts, her eyes rolling. "Please. I'd rather catch fleas from Geri and Freki." She eyes a particularly abstract piece of art. "Though this place could use a few more weapons on the walls."

I key in the code to my room, the door swinging open silently—revealing walls lined with weapons—blades, axes, and spears from every era of my long life. Bryn steps inside and freezes, her jaw actually dropping. I'd laugh if I weren't so busy memorizing the look on her face.

"Ved Odin's øye!" Bryn makes a beeline for the weapon wall, her fingers hovering over a rare sword. "Now, this is what I call a collection." Her eyes sparkle with appreciation as she examines the blade. "A man after my own heart."

My lips quirk up, watching her move from weapon to weapon with expert precision. Just hours ago, this fierce Valkyrie had launched herself off a cliff after me, her wings forgotten in that split-second of pure instinct. The memory tightens my chest—her reaching for me, fear blazing in those mismatched eyes as we plummeted together.

Thank fuck for Gullfax. That magnificent bastard had appeared beneath us like golden lightning, snatching us both from death's greedy fingers. Now here she stands, this warrior who'd risk everything to save my sorry ass, admiring my blade collection like a kid in a candy store.

I cross the distance between us in three measured steps, my fingers closing over hers as she examines the ancient blade. The steel slides from her grasp as I set it aside, my hands finding her waist in one fluid motion. One sharp tug brings her against me, the small gasp escaping her lips swallowed by my kiss. Her taste floods my senses—honey and storm winds, Zephyria's essence mixed with something uniquely Bryn. Her fingers tangle in my hair as she melts into me, a soft moan vibrating between us.

The need to claim her burns through my veins, but the slight tremor in her hands, the lingering chill of Zephyria's cold clinging to her skin, stays my hunger. My forehead presses against hers, our breaths mingling in the space between.

"Are you okay, little bird?"

Her eyes meet mine, a smile curving those kiss-swollen lips. "More than okay, Silfrhár." The Norse endearment rolls off her tongue like a caress, settling deep in my chest where only she has reached.

My fingers lace through hers as I guide her toward the en suite. The door swings open to reveal gleaming black marble and chrome fixtures that catch the recessed lighting. A rainfall shower dominates one wall, its glass enclosure stretching from floor to ceiling. The freestanding obsidian tub could easily fit three, while dual sinks rest in floating vanities beneath a mirror that spans the entire wall.

Bryn freezes in the doorway, her eyes wide as she takes in the modern luxury. "By the Norns..." Her fingers trail over the smooth marble counter. "What manner of magic is this?"

I smirk as I lead her toward the shower enclosure. Her confidence falters momentarily as she examines the multiple shower heads with suspicion and curiosity. The thought of being her first guide into this modern indulgence sends a possessive thrill down my spine.

I tap the chrome rainfall head mounted in the ceiling. "Think of it as a controlled waterfall."

Bryn traces the sleek metal with her fingers, her eyes narrowing with the same focus she uses to examine new weapons. "From here?" she asks with genuine wonder as she studies the modern marvel.

"Let me show you." My voice drops low as I reach for the controls, anticipating her reaction.

Warm mist immediately fills the enclosure, water cascading down in a perfect waterfall. Bryn's sharp intake of breath sends a surge of satisfaction through me—this fierce Valkyrie who's faced down gods and monsters, captivated by something as simple as modern plumbing.

Her wonder is intoxicating, her joy at discovering something so commonplace making it new again through her eyes.

I strip away my frost-stiffened clothing, aware of Bryn's darkening gaze tracking each movement. Her breath catches as I step closer, my lips finding her ear. I unfasten her armor with practiced precision, each buckle surrendering beneath my touch.

Her scent—wildflowers and steel—floods my senses as I trace her jaw with my teeth. Her pulse thrums against my tongue as I taste her neck, drawing a soft moan from her lips. The armor falls away, forgotten at our feet.

My hands map the curves of her body, working free the laces of her top—the fabric parts, revealing her breasts to my hungry gaze. I brush my thumbs across her peaked nipples, drinking in her sharp intake of breath as she arches into my touch.

Trailing kisses down her throat, I work my way lower, one hand anchored at the small of her back. My fingers find the waistband of her pants, teasing the sensitive skin beneath. Her own hands guide mine lower, and with one fluid motion, I strip away the last barrier between us.

Her eyes meet mine, burning with equal parts desire and defiance. A silent challenge I'm more than ready to accept.

The glass door clicks shut behind us as I position her against my chest. Hot water cascades over her golden skin, drawing a gasp from her lips. "By the Gods, this feels amazing," she moans, head falling back against my shoulder.

My mouth finds her neck, teeth grazing the sensitive spot beneath her ear as steam swirls around us. Her intricate braids come undone under my fingers, platinum strands falling loose like liquid moonlight. I gently turn her head back into the spray, watching the water darken her hair to silver.

Rich shampoo coats my palms before I work it through her tresses, massaging her scalp with firm circles. The sound that escapes her throat is pure pleasure, sending heat straight to my groin. Her warrior's tension melts beneath my touch, each stroke of my fingers drawing another soft moan from her lips.

This Valkyrie, undone by such a simple pleasure, stirs something possessive in my chest. The knowledge that I'm the first to care for her this way only heightens my desire to worship every inch of her.

The last of the conditioner rinses away as she leans into me, her body liquid against mine. Steam wraps around us like a cocoon as I reach for the soap, its masculine scent marking her as mine. The loofah glides over her breasts in slow circles, leaving trails of lather across her golden skin.

Her nipples tighten under my touch, begging for attention. My free hand cups the weight of one breast, thumb circling the peak as she arches into my palm. My cock throbs against the small of her back, her every movement stoking the fire in my blood.

The loofah dips lower, sliding between her thighs. Her breath hitches, and her head falls back against my shoulder. "Erik..." My name falls from her lips, sending electricity down my spine.

"Yes, little bird?" The words ghost across her ear, my arms tightening around her waist. Steam curls between us, hot water beating against our skin.

"Stop teasing and fuck me, Silfrhár," she growls, command bleeding into desire. "Or are you afraid you can't handle—" The challenge in her voice carries that familiar mix of sass and steel that sets my blood on fire.

A growl rumbles through my chest at her words." I can handle anything you dish out, little one."

The soap makes her skin like silk beneath my hands as I position myself. She's hot against my length, drawing sharp breaths from us both as I slide between her thighs.

Finding her entrance, I pause. She answers by arching forward, bracing her hands against the black marble. In one fluid motion, I claim her completely. The sound that tears from her throat mingles with my own groan, echoing off the steam-slicked walls.

"Fuck." The word escapes Bryn in a ragged gasp, her body tensing around me. "Gods, yes," she gasps, her body gripping me like a vice. "So...big, so thick—" Her words dissolve into a moan as I drive deeper.

"Taking my cock so well, aren't you, little bird?" My voice drops to a predatory growl, satisfaction surging through me as she tightens around my length.

"Yes—*please*—don't stop," she pants, her composure shattered. "Harder, E rik... I need it harder," she demands, that last word breaking into a desperate whimper.

I snap.

One hand fists in her platinum strands while the other grips her hip. I spin us around to the opposite side of the shower, pressing her against the cool marble. Her palms slam against the wall, seeking purchase as I claim her with punishing thrusts. Water cascades over us, steam rising as I mark her as mine—here in my sanctuary, surrounded by my scent, taking her exactly how she begs for it.

Something primitive awakens between us, shattering restraint. My beast snarls in satisfaction as she takes everything I give her, claiming her deeper, harder. Each stroke marks her as mine, drawing those sweet, desperate sounds from her throat.

My control fractures as hunger claws through me. Fangs pierce her throat's delicate skin, drawing a carnal moan that vibrates against my lips. Her blood floods my mouth—honeyed fire and forbidden pleasure—as I pound into her from behind. Each brutal thrust drives her against the marble, our bodies meeting in savage, echoing slaps. Her inner walls suddenly grip me with devastating force, pulsing around my length as she comes undone, her cry of release echoing through the steam.

Her release triggers mine, pleasure ripping through me like lightning. I bury myself deep, roaring against her throat as I fill her, marking her from the inside out. Each pulse of my cock draws another tremor from her body, our pleasure feeding off each other in an endless loop of ecstasy.

Her legs melt—no longer able to support her, so I hold her up, my body a pillar of strength. My cock remains embedded within her, pulsing with residual desire. One arm wraps around her slender waist to keep her steady while my other hand cups her chin, turning her face to claim her lips in a searing kiss.

Even as our tongues tangle, I continue to pour myself into her, marking her with my essence. Each kiss and breath carries the taste of completion, of absolute satisfaction.

I guide her from the shower, wrapping her in a plush towel before retrieving one of my black shirts from the dresser. The fabric engulfs her, hanging to mid-thigh and slipping off one shoulder. Something stirs in my chest at the sight of her draped in my clothing, my scent.

Her damp hair leaves dark patches on the fabric as she wanders my room, fingers trailing over unfamiliar objects.

"What's this?" She approaches the sleek rectangle mounted on my wall, eyes wide with curiosity.

"Television." I lift the remote, pressing the power button. The screen flares to life with vibrant colors.

Bryn leaps back, hand instinctively reaching for a weapon that isn't there. "By the AllFather!" Her battle stance while wearing nothing but my oversized shirt sends heat pooling low in my abdomen.

"It's harmless," I assure her, fighting a smile. "Moving pictures. Stories contained in a box."

She approaches cautiously, reaching out to touch the screen. "How do the people get in there? Are they trapped?"

"They're not real people." I open my laptop next, the blue glow illuminating her fascinated expression. Her fingers hover over the keyboard, hesitant yet eager.

"This is... magic?" she whispers, watching the cursor move as I demonstrate.

"Technology. Mortal ingenuity."

Her eyes widen further as I open a browser window. "All the knowledge of your realm... contained in this small box?"

"Much of it," I nod, enjoying her wonder. "This little box holds more knowledge than all of Odin's libraries," I explain, typing a search that brings up images of Valkyries from mortal mythology.

"They got our wings all wrong," she scoffs, but her fingers hover reverently over the screen. "This magic... it's extraordinary."

But nothing compares to what I show her next. She circles the toilet with the reverence of a scholar examining ancient artifacts.

"You mean to tell me," she says slowly, "that mortals no longer use chamber pots or outhouses? They just..." She presses the handle, gasping delightedly as water swirls and disappears. "By the gods! Your realm has mastered indoor waterfalls?" She pulls the handle again, watching the water swirl with childlike fascination. "This is... this is magnificent!"

She flushes it three more times, each with increasing enthusiasm. "Erik! Look at it go!"

The sound that escapes me startles us both—a deep, genuine laugh that feels foreign. I can't remember the last time I laughed like this.

Bryn turns, eyebrow arched, a slow smile spreading across her face. "Well, well... the stoic warrior does have a voice beyond growls and commands." She saunters toward me, my shirt slipping off one shoulder. "I like that sound." Her fingers trail up my chest. "Perhaps I should make it my mission to hear it more often, silfrhár."

Her fingers trace my jawline, eyes sparkling with mischief. "After all, I've already conquered your bed. Your laughter seems like the next logical territory."

A groan rumbles through my chest as she presses against me. Her scent has transformed—no longer just her own, but a heady mixture of us both. My body responds instantly, hardening against her despite our recent release.

"A warrior with a worthy quest," I murmur, tracing the exposed curve of her shoulder. "I think I could surrender to this invasion, little bird." My fingers tangle in her damp hair, tilting her face to mine. "Though I should warn you—making me laugh might be harder than making me come."

"Is that a challenge, silfrhár?" As she presses deliberately against my erection. "Because this Valkyrie has never retreated from battle." Her hand slides down, palming my cock through my sweatpants, making me grunt. "Besides, I've already conquered the mighty sword between your legs. Your laughter should be simple in comparison." She rises on her toes, lips brushing my ear. "Or perhaps I'll make you do both at once, fífl. I do so enjoy a challenge."

Christ. This woman.

A sharp knock shatters the moment. I steal one final taste of those tempting lips before striding to the door.

Dani stands in the hallway, a small pile of folded clothes in her arms. "Hey, sis," she says, peering past me with a knowing smile. "Thought you might need something that actually fits. We're about the same size."

Bryn appears at my side, her smile radiant as she looks at her newfound sister. "Thank you, systir," she says warmly, accepting the bundle. The Old Norse word for sister rolls off her tongue naturally, bridging her warrior past and this new family she's found.

I close the door as Bryn slips into Dani's offerings, the stretchy black fabric clinging to every curve and dip of her body. The yoga pants mold to her like a second skin, transforming her warrior's physique into something that makes my mouth dry. The thin-strapped top barely contains her breasts, and the fabric is stretched taut across her nipples.

A growl builds in my chest as she examines herself in the floor-length mirror.

"These garments are... peculiar," she murmurs, turning to examine her reflection from different angles. Her hands slide down her hips, testing the strange material. "So tight, yet I can move freely." She suddenly drops into a perfect fighting stance and straightens with a delighted laugh. "No wonder mortal women conquered their realm—layers of armor and skirts do not hinder them!"

She bounces experimentally on her toes, watching how her breasts move with minimal restraint. "Though I wonder how these tiny straps provide any protection in battle. One good sword strike, and I'd be exposed to the enemy."

"They're not meant for battle," I say, voice rougher than intended as I watch her move. "Though they're certainly... effective weapons in their own right."

My eyes track every curve now highlighted by the modern clothing. Something possessive claws at my insides, demanding I cover her or hide her away from other eyes.

Bryn catches my gaze in the mirror, a slow, knowing smile spreading across her face. She arches her back slightly, deliberately enhancing the view. "Does the sight displease you, *silfrhár?*" she purrs, turning to face me directly.

"The sight pleases me too much to share," I counter, closing the distance between us in two strides.

She tilts her head—challenge glittering in her mismatched eyes. "Afraid someone else might appreciate your Valkyrie's... assets?" Her fingers trace the low neckline of her top, drawing my attention exactly where she wants it. "How interesting that the mighty Erik, who's faced armies without flinching, feels threatened by a bit of exposed skin."

She steps closer, pressing those perfect curves against my chest. "Perhaps you should mark your territory more clearly," she whispers, "so everyone knows exactly who I belong to."

My hand slides to the back of her neck, fingers tangling in her hair as I pull her flush against me. "You think I haven't already?" My voice drops to a dangerous rumble. "Your skin carries my scent. Your throat bears my mark." I trace the fading bite with my thumb. "This," I slowly reach down and cup her pussy, "still holds my cum."

Her pulse quickens beneath my touch, her pupils dilating with renewed desire.

"But if you need a reminder..." I lower my mouth to her ear, teeth grazing the sensitive lobe. "I'll happily spend the next century making sure every inch of you knows exactly who you belong to."

My other hand slides possessively down her spine, settling at the curve where her back meets that perky ass. "And make no mistake, little bird—" I squeeze, lifting her slightly against me, "—while you may have conquered me, I've claimed you just as thoroughly."

"Is that so?" Bryn purrs, her fingers sliding beneath my shirt to trace the hard planes of my abdomen.

She leans up, lips brushing mine as she whispers, "I wonder if anyone will notice how the mighty Erik trembles when I whisper in his ear or how hard you get when I accidentally brush against you. Will you be thinking about bending me over the nearest surface every time I lick my lips?"

"You have no idea what you do to me," I murmur, voice rough as sandpaper. I grip her harder against me. "A thousand years of control, shattered by one Valkyrie with a wicked tongue."

I back her against the mirror, one hand sliding up to cradle her throat, feeling her pulse leap beneath my thumb. "I've slaughtered armies without blinking, yet you've brought me to my knees with nothing but a look."

My forehead presses against hers, our breath mingling. "Everyone will know you're mine," I promise, the words scraping from somewhere primal and possessive. "Not because I mark you, but because no man would dare challenge what stands between us."

My thumb traces her lower lip, reverent despite my intensity. "I've waited centuries for you, little bird. I'll tear apart the seven realms to keep you."

RHYLAND

70

The hot water washes away the last traces of Zephyria, steam rising around us as I pin Dani against the slick tile wall. Her legs wrap around my waist, nails digging half-moons into my shoulders as I drive into her. Each thrust pulls those breathless little moans from her throat that drive me fucking wild.

"Rhy—" My name becomes a broken cry as she shatters around me, her body clenching so tight I see stars. I hold her closer, feeling the telltale quiver that ripples through her thighs, her stomach, her very core. That full-body trembling that only happens when she's completely lost in pleasure.

And then it happens—that peak of pleasure when she falls apart, her release flooding against my cock, my stomach, slick and hot. And *fuck,* how she lets go—her body surrendering in a way that makes me growl, marking us both with her passion.

Her orgasm triggers mine, and for a moment, there's nothing but Dani and the connection between us.

The shower water can't wash away the memory of her standing defiant against Loki, eyes ablaze with a power older than time itself. Something fundamental shifted between us in Zephyria—something that transcends the prophecy, the bond, everything I thought I understood about us.

When I was drowning in that frozen lake, death's fingers killing me over and over, it wasn't just my life flashing before my eyes—it was her. Every smile, every laugh, every goddamn stubborn argument. And then she was there, refusing to let the darkness take me, her determination burning brighter than any divine light.

The way she suffered my pain through our bond and commanded the Zephyrite Stone like she was born to wield its power broke something open inside me. This woman who walked into my life on a prophecy has carved herself into places I didn't know existed within me.

What started as fate has become something I would choose a thousand times over. Something that makes me—a creature who's lived a millenia—finally understand what it means to be truly alive.

I need to feel her against me, around me, with me. Not just the physical connection, though *gods*—how I crave that constantly, but this other thing between us—this fragile, unbreakable thing that grows stronger with every battle, every sacrifice, every moment we choose each other despite the universe's bullshit.

I've lived lifetimes, but only now do I understand what it means to love someone beyond reason, beyond self, beyond even immortality.

I feel almost normal again, dressed in low-hanging sweats and a cotton tee that still smells like fabric softener. My hair's still damp as I stretch, and my muscles finally relax after weeks of constant vigilance.

I watch Dani move around the bedroom, the gentle curve of her ass visible through her thin shorts. The memory of her just moments ago coming undone around my cock—head thrown back, honey-gold eyes nearly black with pleasure, that perfect mouth forming a silent 'O' as those delicious aftershocks quiver through her body—sends fresh heat through my veins.

Every. Fucking. Time. No matter how often I've had her, I'll always want more. *Mine. All fucking mine.*

We descend the stairs, and the rich aroma of sizzling meat, roasted chilies, and warm corn tortillas wraps around us like an embrace. My nostrils flare, catching the distinctive scents of Rosa's legendary chile rellenos—poblano peppers stuffed with queso fresco, battered and fried to golden perfection. The sharp tang of lime and cilantro cuts through the air, promising her homemade salsa verde isn't far behind.

Dani's stomach releases a growl so fierce it could rival my own territorial snarls. Her eyes widen, fixating on the kitchen with the intensity of a predator spotting prey. After weeks of surviving on dried venison, stale bread, and fermented skyr in Zephyria, the promise of Rosa's cooking has her practically vibrating.

"Feed me, or I die," she whispers, clutching my arm with desperate fingers.

She'd begged for food the moment we stumbled through our bedroom door, but one taste of her lips and my hunger for her overrode everything else. I'd backed her against the wall, my hand tangling in her hair, and watched her eyes dilate as food became the furthest thing from her mind.

But now, with her satisfied in one hunger and desperate in another, I guide her toward the kitchen with a protective hand at the small of her back. My woman needs sustenance—I intend to see her plate piled high.

"¡Mi ángel precioso!" Rosa's voice rings out the moment we enter. She rushes forward, flour-dusted hands clasped to her chest. "How are you, mi niña? Sit, sit! I have chile rellenos, fresh tortillas, everything you need!"

"Rosa, really, I can—" Dani reaches for a plate, but Rosa swats her hand away.

"Ah-ah! You sit your behind down right now. What kind of welcome would it be if I let the savior of the realms serve herself?"

"I'm perfectly capable of making my own plate," Dani protests, but she's fighting a grin.

"And I'm perfectly capable of ignoring you," Rosa fires back, already piling food high. "Now hush and let me feed you before you waste away to nothing."

"I was only gone a few weeks!"

"A few weeks too many! Look how skinny!"

I can't help the laugh that rumbles up from my chest, watching my fierce little mate get mothered into submission. The sound of their bickering, the smell of home-cooked food, the familiar warmth of our kitchen—it settles something in my soul that's been restless since we left.

At the kitchen island, Erik and Bryn are huddled close, my brother pointing at different dishes with unusual patience. "This is guacamole—mashed avocado with lime and spices."

Bryn examines it with the wary concentration of a warrior facing an un-known enemy. "It's... green."

"Most foods in the mortal realm aren't trying to kill you," Erik assures her, his lips twitching in what might actually be a smile.

"The night is young, silfrhár," Bryn mutters, but she accepts the chip, her mismatched eyes widening in surprise at the taste.

Across from them, Lucian and Seraphina are demolishing a mountain of food with the focus of starving wolves. Despite her ethereal appearance, Seraphina has salsa on her chin and matches Lucian bite for bite.

Lucian glances up, catching my eye. "Well, well, if it isn't Thor Junior and his lightning rod. Nice of you to finally join us. Did you get lost in Dani's pants on the way down?" He waggles his eyebrows suggestively.

I arch an eyebrow at my brother. "Better than getting lost in your own ass, which is where your head usually lives."

"Aw, you noticed! I've been doing squats."

"Boys," Rosa warns, wielding her wooden spoon like a weapon. "No fighting at the table."

"We're at the island," Lucian points out, then yelps when the spoon connects with the back of his head.

It's clear Rosa holds a special place in Lucian's heart—she's the only one who can put my smartass brother in his place with nothing but a wooden spoon and a disapproving look. Hell, even I've seen him bite back his usual shit-talking when she gives him that motherly glare. For an asshole who takes exactly zero shit from anyone else, watching him cave to our tiny human cook is fucking hilarious.

Dani snorts into her water glass, and the sound makes my chest tighten with contentment. This is what we fought for in Zephyria—these moments, this family, this home. My mate is safe and happy, surrounded by the people we love, even if half of them are idiots.

Especially the idiots.

"And what about my plate?" I ask Rosa, watching her arrange more tortillas for Dani.

Rosa scoffs. "You have hands, sí? The stove is right there."

"Seriously?" I glance at Dani, who's too busy inhaling her chile rellenos to show any sympathy.

She pauses long enough to shrug. "Not my fault she likes me better."

"The savior gets special treatment," Rosa says primly. "You? You're just a handsome face with fangs."

If she only knew the weight behind those words. Being "just a handsome face with fangs" doesn't quite cover it—I'm neck-deep in this savior prophecy shit right alongside my mate. But I keep that particular bomb to myself, just smirking at Rosa while she fusses over Dani. Some revelations can wait, especially when they involve ancient prophecies and my newfound status as the son of gods. Let her think I'm just the muscle for now.

Dani takes another bite and lets out a moan that should be illegal outside our bedroom. My dick grows thick in response, and I have to mentally recite ancient battle tactics to keep it in check.

"Where's the rest of the circus?" Dani asks between bites. "Emily? Sable?" She wrinkles her nose. "That creepy demon?"

"Emily's probably still primping," Lucian drawls, but when he mentions Sable, something flickers across his face—too quick to catch, but enough to set off warning bells. "And our resident demon? Last I saw, he was practicing his shape-shifting in front of the mirror. Kept switching between Chris Hemsworth and Robert Downey Jr., muttering something about 'method acting' and 'understanding the character arc.'"

"He does know they're not actually Thor and Iron Man, right?" Dani asks.

"Bold of you to assume he cares about reality," Lucian snorts. "Yesterday he tried to convince me the infinity stones were just cheap knockoffs of your realm stones."

"To be fair," Erik cuts in, carefully showing Bryn how to wrap a tortilla, "he's not entirely wrong about the power comparison."

"Don't encourage him," Lucian groans. "He already tried to organize an Avengers-themed game night. In costume."

Bryn looks between them all, confused. "What's an Avenger?"

The horrified gasp Lucian lets out could rival any soap opera diva. "Oh honey, we need to fix this immediately. Movie marathon. Tonight. No arguments."

"Last time you organized a movie marathon, it lasted three days," I point out, finally managing to plate some food.

"Because some people," Lucian glares at Erik, "don't appreciate the artistic merit of the post-credit scenes."

"They're advertisements," Erik deadpans.

"They're LORE!"

"They're bathroom breaks," Erik counters, showing Bryn how to load a tortilla chip with guacamole properly.

"You take that back!" Lucian clutches his chest. "Phina-baby, defend my honor!"

Seraphina doesn't even look up from her plate. "You're on your own, Sparky. I'm having a moment with these enchiladas."

"Betrayed by my own mate! Et tu, Brute?"

"Did you just quote Shakespeare while arguing about Marvel movies?" Dani snorts.

"I contain multitudes," Lucian sniffs. "Unlike Mr. Stoic over there, who probably thinks 'Netflix and chill' means sitting in silence while watching the weather channel."

Erik's silver eyes narrow. "At least I don't cry during Disney movies."

"That's a low blow! Moana's journey of self-discovery is emotionally compelling, and you know it!"

"Speaking of compelling," I cut in, "remember when meals didn't include pop culture debates?"

"You mean those boring years before I graced your lives with my sophisticated taste?" Lucian grins.

"There's nothing sacred about watching a guy eat shawarma for two minutes," Erik continues.

"That shawarma scene was PIVOTAL to character development!"

"It was product placement."

"Says the man who thinks reading ancient war scrolls counts as entertainment," Lucian fires back. "Some of us prefer our entertainment without dust and decomposing parchment."

Bryn perks up. "I like war scrolls."

"Of course you do," Lucian rolls his eyes. "You're perfect for each other. You can bore yourselves to death together."

"Better than your idea of foreplay—making Seraphina watch all your comic book movies chronologically," Erik says with a smirk.

"Hey! That's called cultural education!"

"That's called torture," I chime in, earning a betrayed look from Lucian.

"Rich coming from you, Thunder Struck. At least I don't make my mate listen to Viking metal while—"

"Finish that sentence," I growl, "and I'll shove those post-credit scenes somewhere very uncomfortable."

"Kinky," Lucian winks. "But I don't think they'll fit next to that stick up your—"

Rosa's wooden spoon connects with the back of his head again. "¡Basta! No more! You want to act like children. You can eat like children—in the corner, on the floor!"

I try not to laugh as I settle beside Dani just as Rosa slides a second-heaping plate in front of her. The special treatment would sting if I didn't love watching my girl finally get the pampering she deserves.

"So what's the deal with that thing—Brax?" Dani asks.

Lucian lays out the Braxos situation. Lilith and Morgan ripped open a damn rift chasing some vampire soul, and this demon slipped through in the chaos. Now he's Emily's bound servant—her personal demonic attack dog.

Might come in handy.

"What the hell are they doing ripping shit open?" Dani snaps, crunching into a salsa-loaded chip with the righteous indignation that makes my cock twitch even when she's pissed.

"Who the fuck knows," Lucian shrugs, gesturing dramatically with his fork. "That crazy ass has a reason for most of the shit she does, leaving us over here scratching our heads like we're extras in her personal villain origin story."

I watch them banter, my jaw tightening at the mention of Lilith. Even her name in our kitchen feels like contamination. But watching my mate's fire, the way her honey eyes flash when she's worked up—that never gets old. And as much as I hate to admit it, having Lucian's irreverent ass around keeps things from getting too heavy, even when we're discussing interdimensional rifts and demonic hitchhikers.

"What about Damon?" Dani asks around a mouthful of enchilada, those eyes narrowing with protective sister instinct. "Is he okay—getting better with...you know. Introduction into vampirism?"

My woman doesn't miss a beat, even with her cheeks stuffed like a damn chipmunk. That's what I love about her—takes apocalyptic revelations, realm-hopping, and her brother's transformation into a bloodsucker all in stride, then demands updates between bites of Rosa's cooking. That fierce loyalty to family runs bone-deep in her, a trait we share even if my version comes with a few more centuries of blood and violence attached.

Something shifts in the room—subtle, but in my lifetimes of reading people, catch it instantly.

Lucian's jaw tightens for a fraction of a second, his usual smartass demeanor cracking. "He's with Sable."

"Good!" Dani beams, oblivious to the tension. "She's exactly what he needs—someone full of life and light. God knows he could use less doom and gloom after everything he's been through."

Lucian pushes his food around his plate—a man I've never seen waste a single bite of Rosa's food. Beside him, Seraphina suddenly finds her empty plate fascinating, her shoulders tight with unspoken words.

The hair on the back of my neck rises. Something's wrong. Very wrong.

Erik catches my eye across the island, and a slight nod confirms that I'm not imagining things. Even Bryn, new to our dynamic, has stopped her careful exploration of guacamole to study the strange shift in the atmosphere.

What the fuck aren't they telling us?

DANICA

71

S omething's off. Rhyland is throwing more weird bat signals than the Gotham skyline—like the pieces don't quite fit together. After demolishing my second helping—or was it my third? Who's counting?—I grab Lucian's top-shelf liquor from the kitchen—time to excavate whatever fresh hell happened while we were playing realm-hoppers.

This Brax demon is next-level freaky. But weirdly... harmless? When he shapeshifted from a ten-foot hulking nightmare to Chris Evans' doppelganger, it nearly made me choke on my tongue.

Just when I think I've reached peak weird, the universe says, "Hold my beer," and bitch-slaps me with something new.

"Alright..." I take a shot, embracing the burn. It's five o'clock somewhere, and after the week I've had, day drinking is practically medicinal. "Hit me with it. I know you're hiding something, Lucian. What fresh hell did you stir up while we were away?"

Lucian clutches his chest like I've personally offended his ancestor's cow. "Why do you automatically assume *I* stirred up trouble?"

"Because that's what you do," Rhyland rumbles, crossing his arms over his chest to make his biceps look like they're flexing for a magazine shoot.

"I resent that accusation," Lucian sniffs. "Sometimes I'm merely an innocent bystander while shit happens *around* me."

"Name one time," Rhyland challenges.

"Well, there was—" Lucian pauses, finger raised. "No, wait. I *definitely* caused that one. "But what about—" Another pause. "Hmm. That was also me."

Rhyland's eyebrow arches so high it nearly meets his hairline. "You were saying?"

Seraphina keeps her head down, her golden hair falling like a curtain around her face. "Sera?" I prompt gently. If anyone will give me a straight answer, it's her.

She looks up, a soft smile on her lips that doesn't quite reach her eyes. "It's... Sable." She takes a breath. "Lucian sort of accidentally—"

"I turned her," Lucian cuts in, his voice uncharacteristically flat.

The words hit like a bomb. Erik's glass freezes halfway to his lips. Bryn's jaw drops. The room goes so silent you could hear a pin drop. I stare at Lucian, trying to process the words that just came out of his smart-ass mouth.

"What?" The word comes out strangled like my throat's forgotten how to make sounds.

Lucian shifts in his seat, suddenly fascinated with his drink. "Well, not *willingly.* I was trying to save her after the blast, and she... died." He glances up, meeting my gaze with something that might be guilt. "But—fuck. You know how turning goes."

I'm pretty sure my brain just fried itself.

Sable.

Vampire.

Lucian.

The words swirl in my head, refusing to form a coherent sentence.

Rhyland recovers first, his voice dangerously calm. "Explain. From the beginning."

I knock back two more shots as Lucian spins his tale—Lilith swooping in like the bitch nightmare she is, Seraphina's wings getting impaled, that demon Brax having the audacity to parade around wearing my mate's face (which is going to earn him a one-way ticket back to whatever hell dimension spat him out if he tries that shit around me), and Sable...

"Sable is a... *vampire?"* The word feels wrong on my tongue like I'm talking about someone else, not my bubbly, pink-haired friend who wears unicorn slippers and cries at dog food commercials.

Lucian runs his hand through his golden hair, sticking it up in tufts. "Yeah, and she's not exactly embracing her new liquid diet. That's why Emily and Damon are AWOL—they're babysitting her through her emotional meltdown. Baby vamp emotions make PMS look like a day at Disney."

My mind reels, images of Sable flashing through my head—Sable curled up on the couch during our Netflix marathons, empty ice cream cartons scattered around us—Sable with dark circles under her eyes as we worked tirelessly for three days straight to cook up that potion to mask my angelic scent—Sable hunched over ancient tomes, her pink hair falling in her face as she researched anything that might help our cause.

My stomach twists. I've adjusted to a lot of crazy shit lately—finding out that Loki paraded around the mortal realm causing a thousand years of chaos, realm-hopping, new stone-wrangling, my brother being turned into a vampire—but this? This is *Sable*—sweet, helpful Sable who never hesitated to throw herself into the fire for us.

And now she's... what? Immortal? Blood-dependent? Is she still *her*?

"Where is she?" My voice comes out stronger than I feel. "I need to see her."

Rhyland's hand finds my shoulder, his touch grounding me even as my thoughts spin out of control. "Baby..."

"Don't 'baby' me right now." I shrug him off, eyes locked on Lucian. "Where. Is. She?"

Lucian winces, holding his hands like he's trying to slow a charging bull. "Whoa there, Princess. As much as I admire your friendship goals, maybe—and I'm just spitballing here—maybe waltzing up to Baby Fang with your angelic blood pumping through your veins isn't the smartest move? To a new vamp, you're basically a walking cotton candy stand at a kindergarten birthday party."

"I don't care. She's my friend." I go to leave, but Rhyland's arm blocks my path, a wall of immovable Viking muscle.

"She tried to take a bite out of Emily," Lucian adds. "And that's her witchy BFF."

Seraphina clears her throat delicately. "To be fair, you used the Maker's command. She can't attack Dani now even if she wanted to."

"Not helpful, Cupcake." Lucian shoots her a betrayed look.

My eyes widen, "You *mind-controlled,* Sable?" My voice rises an octave.

"I prefer 'temporarily adjusted her dietary preferences,'" Lucian shrugs. "It was either that or let her snack on the local populace. Trust me, nothing ruins property values faster than a vampire buffet in the neighborhood."

"This isn't funny, Lucian." I put my hands on my hips, done with his shit. Erik's silver eyes track the tension like he's mapping out escape routes.

"She's new." Lucian's voice drops, that razor-edge of seriousness that always makes me pause because it means shit has truly hit the fan. "I did what I had to do to keep her from hurting anyone or herself."

The realization hits me like a punch to the gut—Damon got lucky. If Azrael had stuck around after turning my brother... I shudder at the thought of that psychotic bastard having a Maker's command over him, turning him into some mind-controlled attack dog.

But Lucian? He's seen firsthand what that kind of control does to someone. Hell, he spent decades being Lilith's plaything. The disgust in his eyes whenever we talk about it tells me everything I need to know. He'd rather stake himself than become that kind of monster.

No, Sable might be a vampire now, but at least her Maker—Lucian—gives a damn about her free will. Small comfort, maybe, but in our fucked-up world? I'll take what I can get.

Seraphina shifts closer to him. Even Rhyland's stance changes, that predatory stillness settling over him as he watches his brother.

"Can I see her? Please?" I ask, softer now.

I tap lightly on Sable's door, feeling Rhyland and Lucian's presence behind me like twin shadows. The wood is cool against my knuckles.

"Come in." Sable's voice wavers through the door.

The scene inside hits me like a snapshot—Sable perched on the edge of her bed, fingers intertwined with Damon's, Emily sprawled in the window seat with her rainbow hair catching the afternoon light.

"Well, if it isn't our realm-hopping disaster magnet!" Emily launches herself at me, nearly knocking me over. "When did you crawl back from Viking wonderland?"

I squeeze her tight, breathing in the familiar scent of her coconut shampoo and whatever explosive spell she's been working on. "We just got back—missed you too, you pain in my ass."

"I'm the pain in the ass?" She pulls back, eyes sparkling. "Finally get my note?"

A blur of movement catches my eye—Sable pressing herself against the far wall, her pink hair wild around her face. "Please," she whispers, eyes wide. "Don't come closer. I can't... your scent..."

My heart cracks. This isn't my confident friend who faced down a clan of witches with nothing but determination and a spell book. This is someone afraid of herself.

"Sable—"

Strong arms wrap around me. Damon. My brother. The scent of his cologne—still the same even after everything—brings tears to my eyes.

"Welcome home, sis," he murmurs against my hair.

I return his embrace, studying his face. The tension I'd been carrying about his transformation melts away. His eyes are clear and focused. There is no bloodlust, no struggle—just my brother holding me like he has a thousand times before.

"Look at you," I manage through the lump in my throat. "All vamped up and in control."

He grins, fangs flashing. "Turns out immortality suits me."

Sable makes a strangled sound, pressing herself further into the wall. Her dark brown eyes dart between us like a trapped animal.

Lucian steps forward, his usual snark in full force. "Alright, Bubblegum, time for a Vampire refresher course. Chapter One: You won't go all 'Interview with the Vampire' on our resident angel here. Seriously, look at her—she's like a walking Christmas light. Way too bright to snack on."

His voice carries the subtle resonance of a Maker's command—not controlling, just steadying—like dropping an anchor in stormy waters. Sable's body relaxes instantly, the tension melting from her shoulders as the command settles over her. Her eyes clear, fear replaced by calm understanding.

"Look at you, all paternal and shit," I grin. "Should we start calling you Daddy Vamp?"

Lucian's face twists like he's just swallowed sour blood. "Listen here, Princess Snack Pack, I may be responsible for this baby vamp, but if you ever— *ever*—call me 'daddy' again, I will personally ensure every Netflix account you touch automatically plays nothing but Adam Sandler movies."

"That's cruel, even for you."

"I contain multitudes of cruelty, sweetheart. Just ask my Xbox after I rage-quit Dark Souls."

I take a careful step forward, like approaching a spooked horse. "Better?"

Sable nods, her fingers twisting in her pink hair. "Yeah, it's... clearer now. Your scent is still like mainlining pure sugar, but I'm not feeling quite so... bitey."

"Bitey is not your best look," Emily chimes in. "Stick to unicorn accessories."

"I can still come closer?" I ask, watching Sable for any sign of distress.

Behind me, I can practically feel Rhyland coiling like a spring, ready to move if needed. His protective instincts are sweet, if slightly overdramatic. Then again, this is the man who once tackled me to safety because I almost walked into a spider web.

"Yeah," Sable manages a shaky smile. "Just... maybe no hugging yet? I'm not sure I'm ready for full contact."

"Daddy Vamp?" Rhyland looks at Lucian like he's an idiot, his deep voice rumbles with a suggestive edge that makes my cheeks heat, "if anyone's earning the title 'daddy' around here, brother, I think Dani would agree it's not *you.*"

Lucian gasps dramatically. "Was that... did you just make a dirty joke? Quick, someone check if Hell froze over!"

"I've had a lot of practice," Rhyland smirks, his hand sliding possessively around my waist. "Unlike some people who still giggle at the word 'duty.'"

"You said 'doody,'" Lucian snickers, then straightens up. "I mean, how dare you question my maturity? I'm a responsible Maker now. I have..." he thinks for a minute, "Ah yes, *adulting skills.*"

Emily snorts so hard she nearly falls out of her chair. "You spent three hours yesterday trying to teach Brax how to dab."

"It's an important cultural milestone!"

"Cultural milestone, my ass," Emily mutters. "You just wanted TikTok content."

"Hey, my followers expect quality entertainment!" Lucian protests. "Do you know how hard it is to keep up with Gen Z meme culture when you're technically old enough to be their great-great-great-grandfather?"

"At least you're trying," Sable offers, slowly sinking onto the edge of the bed. "Damon still can't figure out how to use Instagram filters."

"The dog ears are deeply unsettling," Damon defends himself. "And why would anyone want to look like they're vomiting rainbows?"

I lean back against Rhyland's chest, savoring the normalcy of the moment. My crazy, supernatural family is bickering about social media like we aren't a collection of vampires, witches, and whatever the hell I am these days.

"Speaking of unsettling," Emily perks up with that dangerous glint in her eye that usually precedes chaos, "wait until you hear about Brax's latest obsession with Marvel movies. Tell them, Luci."

Lucian groans. "No."

"Tell us what?" I ask, already grinning at his discomfort.

"He's been practicing his Thor impressions," Emily cackles. "Complete with cape and everything."

"It's a cloak," Lucian corrects automatically.

"Don't forget the hammer," Sable adds, smiling now. "What was it he kept saying?"

"'I am worthy!'" Emily booms in a terrible accent, raising an imaginary hammer. "While wearing one of Lucian's designer bathrobes as a cape—I mean, *cloak*."

"That was a $900 bathrobe," Lucian mutters darkly. "Pure Egyptian cotton. Now it smells like burnt ass hairs and disappointment." His expression suddenly shifts to pure devilish glee. "Though not as much disappointment as when I caught someone getting rather... patriotic with our resident shapeshifter. Tell me, Emily, does he really embody America's ass when he's wearing the Caps face?"

Emily's face flames redder than a fire hydrant. "I—that's not—"

Wait. What's going on—

"*No,*" I gasp, staring at my best friend. "Em, you didn't. Please tell me you didn't bang a demon while he was cosplaying Steve Rogers!"

"He has very convincing shapeshifting abilities!" Emily squeaks, burying her face in her hands. "And those shoulders! Have you seen those shoulders?"

"I cannot believe you fucked a demon wearing Captain America's face," I wheeze. "What happened to 'I have standards, Dani'?"

"Have you SEEN Chris Evans?" Emily peeks through her fingers. "Those are very high standards!"

Lucian is practically vibrating with glee. "Don't forget the part where he kept quoting 'That IS America's ass' at very... specific moments."

"I hate you all," Emily groans, covering her face. "Especially you, asshole. I know where you keep your limited edition Pokemon cards."

"Touch my holographic Charizard, and they'll never find your body."

Oh. My. God. My best friend is hooking up with a literal demon. And not just any demon—a shapeshifting demon with a thing for superheroes.

Mental note—Corner Emily later with a bottle of tequila and demand every single X-rated detail. Starting with whether his... patriotism... extends to all parts of his anatomy.

For research purposes, obviously.

"You're just mad he pulls off the cape better than you," Emily fires back, fully committed to tormenting Lucian.

"Again, it's a *cloak,*" Lucian holds up a finger. "And second, I look fabulous in everything. Even that time, I had to wear bell bottoms in the 70s."

"Please tell me there are pictures of this." Sable perks up, her earlier fear almost forgotten.

"Absolutely not," Lucian says, while Erik simultaneously answers, his voice calling from the hallway, "Third drawer of my desk."

"Dick!" Lucian yells. "I thought we agreed the Disco Era was off-limits! You Emo Crusader Extraordinaire!"

I can't help the pure and genuine laugh that bubbles up from my chest. This. This right here. All of us together, safe and whole. Emily plotting chaos, Lucian being dramatic, Sable slowly coming back to herself, my brother rolling his eyes but smiling, and Rhyland...

His arms tighten around me as he feels my happiness radiating through our bond. His chest rumbles against my back with quiet laughter as Lucian continues his tirade about brotherhood and betrayal.

"I love seeing you smile," he murmurs against my ear, low enough that only I can hear.

"Look at them," I whisper back, watching Emily demonstrate what she claims was Lucian's signature disco move. "We're all here. We're all okay. For once, nothing's trying to kill us or end the world."

"Yet," he adds, but I can hear the smile in his voice.

"Don't jinx it, Lightning Rod."

"GET THE PICTURES!" Emily suddenly shouts, launching herself toward the door. "I need to see Disco Lucian!"

"NO!" Lucian races after her. "Erik, I swear to god, if those photos see the light of day, I'm telling Bryn about the Renaissance Fair incident!"

"What's a Renaissance Fair incident?" Bryn's voice drifts up from downstairs.

"NOTHING!" Both Erik and Lucian shout.

Sable's laughter rings through the room, the sweet sound making something in my chest expand with warmth.

Even Damon—my usually always serious brother—breaks his composure, his shoulders shaking as he joins in the mirth, one arm still protectively around Sable's waist.

I lean back against Rhyland's chest. This is what matters. This hodgepodge collection of misfits we've somehow stitched together into something resembling a family. Despite the cosmic chess game we're unwilling pawns in, despite death and resurrection and magical stones and evil queens—we still find these pockets of normalcy.

Where vampires debate superhero movies—witch BFFs sleep with shape-shifting demons, and my man holds me like I'm the anchor to his centuries-old soul.

DANICA

72

After a few chaotic weeks, we've managed to find our rhythm again in this mansion full of vampires, witches, angels, and one shape-shifting demon with a Marvel obsession. Rosa's Thanksgiving feast has left us in an epic food coma—the woman is a culinary sorceress, and I would literally fight anyone for the recipe to her pecan pie. Now I'm sprawled on the couch next to Damon, wondering if I'll ever move again without rolling like Violet Beauregarde post-blueberry transformation.

"So, you and Sable, huh?" I nudge his shoulder, curling deeper into the over-stuffed cushions. The fireplace casts dancing shadows across my brother's face, his hazel eyes still holding that same gentle warmth they had when Dad first brought him home. It's been too long since we've had a moment like this just us, no apocalyptic drama, no supernatural crisis demanding immediate attention. Even Lucian's constant commentary has been silenced, either by food coma or whatever he and Seraphina are doing behind closed doors.

Damon's cheeks flush with that telltale pink that somehow survived his vampire transition. "Yeah," he says, ruffling his hair in that nervous habit he's had since we were kids. "Just kind of happened, you know?"

I tuck my feet under me, feeling the heat from the fire warm my toes through my fuzzy socks. "Hmm-mm," I agree, watching the flames dance. "I sure do." One minute you're a normal human with normal problems, and the next, you're mated to a thousand-year-old vampire with anger management issues and a hero complex.

"Are you happy? You know, after everything?" The question hangs between us, heavy with unspoken weight. My brother—the scared little boy I once taught to tie his shoelaces—transformed into the very creature he once called a "walking blood bank with attitude problems."

Damon's laugh breaks the moment, his fangs flashing briefly before he retracts them with practiced ease. "Happy? I'm dating a pink-haired witch-turned-vampire. And my sister's banging Thor's grandson." He tugs at my hair like he used to when we were kids. "We've come a long way from algebra homework, huh?"

"Excuse you," I sniff, swatting his hand away. "I believe the term is 'mated to,' not 'banging.' Have some class, Sasquatch." The childhood nickname—from when he shot up six inches one summer—slips out naturally.

His eyes crinkle. "Sasquatch? Wow, bringing out the vintage insults. Remember when you convinced me mosquitoes would explode if I ate enough garlic bread?"

"Your face at Olive Garden! Three baskets and a flyswatter!"

"I was ten!" he protests, laughing. "And you were supposed to be the smart one!"

"I was smart enough to get you to do my chores for a month by threatening to tell Jessica Miller you had a crush on her," I counter, poking him in the ribs.

He groans, covering his face. "God, Jessica Miller. With the braces and the—"

"—obsession with horses," we finish in unison, dissolving into giggles like we're kids again.

When our laughter fades, Damon's expression grows thoughtful. "You didn't answer my question," I remind him softly.

He takes an unnecessary breath—old habits die hard. "With Sable? Definitely. The rest... Some days I wake up and forget what happened, reach for my coffee, and then remember I don't need it anymore." He meets my eyes. "But when I'm with her, none of that matters. She makes me feel... alive."

I squeeze his hand. "I'm glad. She's good for you. And if she ever isn't, I'll kick her perky vampire ass myself."

The threat is empty and we both know it—Sable has become as much my family as he is. But it's the principle of the thing. Big sisters have to maintain their reputation, after all.

He squeezes back, his strength carefully measured. "Spoken like a true big sister." His smile turns mischievous. "Speaking of asses that need kicking, how's life with the Viking? Still leaving his wet towels on the bathroom floor?"

"Oh my god," I groan, flopping back. "How did you know? A thousand years on this earth, and the man can't figure out a hamper."

His smile fades into something more serious. "How are you *really* doing with all this savior stuff? The stones, the realms, the whole 'chosen one' gig?" His voice softens. "You don't have to pretend with me, Dani. I know that face—it's the same one you wore when you bombed that organic chemistry final."

With everyone else, I maintain the brave face. But this is Damon. He's seen me ugly cry over rom-coms and stress-eat an entire box of Cap'n Crunch at 3 AM.

"It's... complicated," I admit. "Some days, I feel this incredible rush—like I'm exactly where I'm supposed to be. Other days, I just want to wake up back in my lab, where the biggest crisis was contaminated cell cultures." I swallow hard.

The fire pops loudly, sending a shower of sparks up the chimney.

"The hardest part is the goodbyes," I continue, my voice growing quieter. "Mom and Dad, John—all dying because they were connected to me." My fingers twist together in my lap. "Then there's the other kind of goodbyes, the ones that come after I've made these incredible connections across realms. Mirella with her bravery, Gideon and his fierce loyalty, Axilya's strength, Fadreyn's kindness, Nixie's wisdom..."

My throat tightens as the last name forms on my lips. "Gullfax." It comes out as barely a whisper, the memory of the majestic stallion's constant protection still raw enough to steal my breath.

I blink hard, forcing back the tears. "And then there's the betrayals..." I swallow the lump in my throat. "I trusted him. We all did. Adrian—" My voice breaks on the name. "I'm so damn tired of people I care about either dying or turning out to be villains in disguise. It's like emotional whiplash on a cosmic scale."

Damon reaches over, tucking a strand of hair behind my ear like Dad used to do. "Mom and Dad would be so proud of you," he says softly. "Dad would be strutting around telling everyone his daughter is saving the world. And Mom..." his voice catches, "Mom would be force-feeding everyone her terrible tuna casserole."

"God, that casserole," I laugh through tears. "Remember when she tried to 'improve' it with kale?"

"And Dad ate three helpings just to make her happy—"

"Even though it tasted like hot garbage wrapped in cheese!" I laugh softly, memories flooding back. "Almost as bad as her infamous 'healthy' chicken pot pie, where she substituted cauliflower for literally everything."

"Oh god," Damon groans, covering his face. "That monstrosity! Dad called it 'cloud paste surprise' behind her back."

"And we all got food poisoning because she didn't cook the chicken long enough," I add, tears of laughter mixing with grief now. "But she was so proud of that recipe."

We share a watery laugh, memories of our parents filling the space between us. Two years apart in age, we've been inseparable since they brought him home—from playground bullies to broken hearts to Dark prophecies.

"I miss them so much," I whisper. "Every time something big happens, I reach for my phone to call Mom. And then I remember..."

"Me too," Damon admits. "Last week, I saved a meme to show Dad." He clears his throat. "But you know what? I'm ridiculously proud of you, sis. And not just for the savior stuff. You've always been my hero, even before you started collecting magic rocks and dating Norse gods."

"Please. I was the nerdy sister who made you watch documentaries instead of cartoons."

"You were the sister who beat up Tommy Larson when he stole my lunch money," he counters. "Who stayed up all night helping with college applications. Who convinced Dad to let me take that road trip—"

"The one where you tried to drive to Portland and ended up in Forks?"

"That was ONE time! The GPS was possessed!"

"Uh-huh. Blame the technology, typical millennial."

He flicks my arm. "Says the woman who asked Alexa to turn off the shower last week."

"I was distracted!"

"By what? Rhyland's abs? Again?"

I grab a pillow and whack him with it. "You're one to talk! I've seen you walking into walls because you're too busy staring at Sable."

He catches the pillow mid-swing, vampire reflexes on display. "No rules against supernatural advantages in sibling warfare."

"Just wait until I get all seven stones," I threaten. "Then we'll see who's laughing, Mr. Bloodsucker."

His expression softens. "You will, you know. Get all the stones. Save the realms. The whole shebang." His conviction is unwavering. "If anyone can do it, it's you, Dani."

"Even if I screw up sometimes?"

"Especially then. Because you never stay down. You get back up, make a sassy comment, and keep going." He reaches for my hand. "And you're not alone. Not ever."

I take his hand, feeling the familiar calluses that survived his transformation. "When did you get so wise, Sasquatch?"

He shrugs, a crooked smile lifting one corner of his mouth. "Must've been all those documentaries you made me watch."

The grandfather clock chimes midnight. "I should head up," I say reluctantly. "Rhyland will be wondering where I am."

"Go. Your Viking awaits." His eyes twinkle. "Just try to keep the supernatural gymnastics to a reasonable volume. Some of us have enhanced hearing now."

"Oh my god," I groan, shoving him. "That's it. I'm officially disowning you."

"Too late. You're stuck with me for eternity now."

Eternity. The word hangs between us, both promise and reminder.

I pause at the archway. "Hey, Damon?"

"Yeah?"

"I'm really glad you're here. Through all of this."

His expression softens. "Wouldn't be anywhere else, sis. Someone's gotta keep you from getting too full of yourself with all this savior business."

I roll my eyes, but my heart feels lighter than it has in weeks. "Goodnight, brat."

"Night, nerd."

As I climb the stairs toward where Rhyland waits, I carry the warmth of our conversation with me. Tomorrow will bring new challenges—Lilith's growing power, the next stone to find, whatever dangers lie ahead. But tonight, for just a little while, I was simply Dani, big sister, reminiscing about bad casseroles and childhood pranks.

And sometimes, those quiet moments between the chaos are exactly what a savior needs to keep going.

DANICA

73

Another blanket of snow has fallen overnight—the third this week. Washington rarely sees this much white, but I guess the universe decided we needed a taste of the North Pole this December.

I press my fingertips against the cold glass, watching my breath create fleeting ghosts of condensation.

The irony isn't lost on me—Christmas is just a week away, and Seattle's channeling its inner Hallmark movie. Perfect timing for everyone except the woman with phantom frostbite from realm-hopping through a magical ice kingdom.

My absolute favorite holiday is approaching, and despite begging both Lucian and Rhyland to let me decorate this place, we've got nothing but the perfect white Christmas outside. Though honestly, after Zephyria, I'm thinking Santa needs to stuff my stocking with tickets to Tahiti.

Things have been... suspiciously normal lately. Lilith's gone radio silent—either plotting something nasty, or she's finally learned how to use airplane mode. In my experience, when evil vampire queens go quiet, they're usually just reloading.

But if I don't escape this fortress soon, I'll lose what's left of my sanity. This is my life now—hop realms, collect magical stones like some twisted rock collector, then return to Hogwarts House Arrest.

Yes, we have our angel-scent-be-gone potion, but after Seraphina's kidnapping fiasco (thanks for that brilliant solo mission, Lucian), my overprotective mate has gone full Maximum Security Prison Warden. His eyebrows practically form a unibrow of disapproval every time I mention leaving.

But damn it! Mama needs a me-day! Just us girls pretending to be normal humans with normal problems—mani-pedis, gossip, and, for the love of everything sacred, a professional wax! My legs have reached Wookie status, and my lady garden is approaching "lost civilization" territory. Sure, I could shave, but nothing beats the smooth perfection of a proper Brazilian.

And let's be real—with all this realm-hopping madness, who knows where I'll end up next? Not every magical dimension comes equipped with "Ye Olde Brazilian Waxing Shoppe." I lucked out in Luminara with their fairy beautification tools, but I'm not about to save the universe while rocking a full-on 70's-style situation down there. Last thing I need is to be facing down Moretemis looking like I've got Chewbacca in a headlock between my thighs.

Executive decision made—Rhyland can flex those magnificent biceps all he wants—I'm taking my girl gang out. Lilith's stuck doing her vampire zombie walk after sundown anyway, and I refuse to go full cavewoman.

Last week's plot twist—Lucian discovered Kyle—his right-hand enabler—was Lilith's puppet. One Jedi mind trick later (compulsion inception, anyone?), mystery solved on how Psycho Queen knew when to crash Karma with her wolf pack. Nothing says trust issues like finding out your business partner's brain got vampire-hacked.

In a move that screams "questionable life choices," Lucian insisted I sign the deed to his precious nightclub—claiming I'm the only one he trusts. So now I'm the proud owner of both his properties, which sounds fancy until you realize I'm basically the magical doorman deciding which fanged party-goers get access. But it's become a 24/7 headache. My phone blows up at all hours with texts like "Princess, Kyle says there's a 400-year-old Romanian countess at the door who claims she once shared a victim with Vlad the Impaler. Be a dear and verbally invite her in?"

So I guess I'm Karma's bouncer with the ultimate "You're Not On The List" power. Suck it, Lilith.

We still need that other half of the Soul Stone from the hag, plus whatever she fished-hooked out of that rift. That's a migraine for another day.

At least Bryn's settled into our dysfunctional family perfectly—living in the gym with Erik, training with me and Seraphina. It's nice having another woman who can kick ass in heels.

She's also discovered the joys of mortal fashion. Erik made the rookie mistake of handing over his credit card and giving her an Amazon tutorial. Now we're drowning in packages—though unlike most women's shopping sprees, Bryn's primarily consist of weapons.

So. Many. Weapons.

The UPS guy is definitely filing reports somewhere. I'm half expecting a SWAT team to crash through our windows any day now because who the hell orders seventeen different types of throwing stars and a medieval mace in a single week?

On an entirely different note, my monthly curse appeared, and Rhyland is losing his Viking mind over it. *"Let me make you feel good, Angel. I can smell you,"* he keeps purring, all seductive and tempting. Like I need the extra distraction of my mate going full hormonal caveman.

Not that I'm innocent—I've been sending Rhyland mental images that have him grinding his teeth, testing how far I can push before he decides "monthly maintenance" isn't a dealbreaker. He's been surprisingly respectful... mostly. But that's our game—I push, he growls, we both enjoy the tension.

Look, I'm down for kinky stuff—hell, half the things we do would make Christian Grey clutch his pearls—but I'm not sure I'm ready for Rhyland to take that particular plunge. Though watching him process another month without a mini-Viking in my womb is its own special kind of heartache.

Emily, being the annoyingly perceptive bestie she is, clocks my mood instantly. And yeah, I know the whole vampire-baby situation is about as likely as Lucian giving up his smart-ass mouth. Trust me, I got the supernatural birth control memo. Hell, I even had my IUD taken out last week—because really, what's the point of keeping that thing when my mate's swimmers have been dead for a millennium?

But that vision in the reflection pool? The one dangling the impossible family portrait in front of me? Yeah, it's hitting different today. Like getting tagged in a vacation photo when you're stuck at work, except the vacation is "having kids" and my workplace is "mated to an incredibly hot but reproductively challenged Viking vampire."

The universe has a sick sense of humor sometimes.

Sera and I are tackling the Fire Realm book tonight, while Lucian's determined to convert Bryn to Marvel fandom. The unexpected highlight? His full-blown bromance with Brax. They're inseparable, debating Thor versus Hulk like it's doctoral thesis defense. Yesterday's evidence—a detailed power-ranking bracket system covering our living room wall.

I jingle the car keys like a rain dance, bouncing by the door. "Let's blow this prison, ladies! Operation Escape From Alcatraz is now or never!" I glance nervously at the hallway, where Rhyland and Erik's workout sounds like a testosterone Olympics. "We've got seven minutes before my Tattooed Temptations' sixth sense starts tingling.

"Jesus H. Christ," Emily emerges from the hallway, one boot on, the other dangling from her hand. "Hold your damn horses, woman. Some of us need actual time to put shoes on our feet."

In the kitchen, my girl gang is assembled like Charlie's Angels—if Charlie recruited from the supernatural unemployment line. Seraphina's hiding her wings, Bryn's playing with a throwing star (seriously, where was she hiding that?), and Sable's practically glowing with escape-plan excitement, dabbing blood from her lips, my empty vial beside her.

She's adapted to vampire life amazingly well, rough patches and all. With Damon guiding her, they've become inseparable—his calm perfectly balancing her sweetness. My brother and my witchy-turned-vampire friend finding love? The universe has a weird sense of humor, but I'm here for it.

We bolt out the door—ninja-style quiet—and pile into Lucian's SUV. I smash the garage door opener with the enthusiasm of a prison escapee, all of us grinning as we've just pulled off the heist of the century—one glance in the rearview mirror and—well, shit.

"Did you think you could sneak off without us noticing?" Rhyland's deep voice rumbles, his tone of amusement and alpha male smugness. He's standing behind the car, arms crossed, with Lucian and Erik flanking him like security detail.

I let my forehead thunk against the steering wheel. "Damn it. I knew we should've done that cloaking spell."

"I fucking told you!" Emily snaps from the back seat. "But your impatient ass couldn't wait five goddamn minutes, could you?"

Yeah, no. Emily might be a magical powerhouse extraordinaire, but the girl treats every spell like brain surgery when we all need is magical duct tape and a quick getaway.

Rhyland appears at my window, opening the door with infuriating slowness. His smirk screams, 'I own this situation' as he leans down, filling the doorframe with his bulky shoulders. Jerk.

"I was hoping for more of an 'ask for forgiveness rather than permission' situation," I fire back, fluttering my eyelashes. "Since your overprotective caveman policy on leaving the property is getting a bit stifling."

Lucian pops his head into the backseat, grinning like an idiot. "Well, well, well! Looks like we've got a bunch of naughty jailbirds trying to fly the coop!" He waggles his eyebrows at Seraphina. "Baby girl, you know what happens to rule breakers around here. Spanking time!" Seraphina's giggle is half scandalized, half intrigued.

Erik appears at the passenger door, his face an emotionless mask save for one slightly raised eyebrow. "Attempting to flee the premises without proper notification or security protocols in place. Most unwise, little bird."

"I need no man's permission to venture forth, silfrhár," Bryn declares, pure warrior goddess attitude. Her tone screams badass Valkyrie, but the way she's eye-fucking Erik tells an entirely different story. For someone who decapitates Draugr without breaking a sweat, she turns to Norse pudding around our silver fox.

I groan, slumping back. Busted by the testosterone trio.

"Fine."

Rhyland's voice vibrates through the car as he leans in, his big body blocking the steering wheel. Sandalwood and clean sweat flood my senses.

I lift my head slowly. Did I hallucinate that surrender?

His devastating half-smile sends my pulse racing. Workout sweat still clings to his temple, black hair damp at the edges. His navy tank top might as well be painted on, and those tattooed biceps cage me in, turning the driver's seat into our own intimate universe.

"Really?" I arch an eyebrow, not entirely trusting this sudden surrender from Fort Knox himself.

"Mm-hmm," Rhyland hums. "You deserve freedom. I won't cage what's mine." His ocean eyes pin me in place, that alpha stare brooking no argument. "But you will be safe. That's non-negotiable."

Victory bubbles up inside me like champagne. "Cross my heart," I chirp, stretching up to kiss his lips quickly before attempting my escape.

His sexy body doesn't budge. Typical.

"Not good enough," he growls, that commanding eyebrow arch making my insides flutter. "I want a proper kiss as payment, baby."

The conflicting urges to smack him and climb him like a tree war within me, but I settle for option three. I slide my fingers into his damp hair and pull his mouth to mine, kissing him with enough heat to trigger a fire alarm. His low groan vibrates against my lips, his thumb tracing my cheekbone in that possessive way that turns my bones to liquid.

Heat rushes my face as I register our audience—Emily's dramatic gagging sounds, Bryn's appreciative murmur, Seraphina's soft giggle. The realization that everyone's watching only heightens the electricity between us, sending a delicious shiver down my spine.

"Jesus, get a room!" Lucian interrupts. "Save the Viking mating ritual for Only-Fangs, people! Some of us just ate!"

The penny drops.

I break away, catching that telltale glint in his eyes, the ghost of a satisfied smirk playing at his lips.

Oh. My. God. This devious man planned this whole thing— he's weaponized my exhibitionist streak against me.

Well played, Fjord Lord. Well played.

Nestled in a cozy booth at Ray's Boathouse, with a stunning view of Puget Sound, we girls grab our menus, ready to indulge in much-needed sustenance. After hours of pampering—mani-pedis and Brazilian waxes that left my legs and vag silky smooth—I'm practically purring with contentment.

On the other hand, Bryn is shifting gingerly in her seat, her face a mix of discomfort and annoyance. "Is this what men on Midgard truly prefer? A hairless mound?" she grumbles, her eyes narrowing. "I fail to see the appeal."

I can't help the snort that escapes me. "Oh, honey, just wait until Erik gets a load of your newly bare goods. Trust me, he'll be worshipping at the altar of your smooth snatch faster than you can say 'Valkyrie.'"

Bryn's lips twitch, a dangerous glint in her mismatched eyes. "The silver-haired fífl has never complained about my natural state."

"Oh, he won't be complaining," I assure her. "He'll be too busy thanking every god in the Seven Realms."

The esthetician's warning about waiting 24 hours suddenly pops into my mind.

"Just remember—no test-driving the new look for at least a day. Gotta let things... settle down south."

Bryn's eyes flash with genuine outrage. "What treachery is this? You failed to mention this crucial detail before I allowed that woman to pour molten wax on my nethers!"

I shrug, trying not to laugh at her expression. "Oops. Must have slipped my mind during your screaming fit."

Bryn grumbles something under her breath in Norse, but the way she smiles tells me she's already plotting how to drive Erik wild with her new look. I lean back, basking in the satisfaction of a job well done. Operation 'Valkyrie Makeover' is officially a success.

Our waiter appears, looking slightly overwhelmed by our giggling group. He places a basket of bread at our table—notepad poised and ready. "What drinks can I get you, ladies?"

Sable, trapped at the end of the booth, launches into her drink order first—something fruity with enough alcohol to tranquilize a miniature horse. I catch Bryn eyeing the waiter's tattooed forearm with interest as if she's cataloging the differences between Midgardian men and their Asgardian counterparts.

"I'll have the blackberry mojito," I tell him, then gesture to Bryn with a mischievous smile. "And my sister here will try the Bloody Viking." I can't resist adding with a wink, "Extra spicy."

Bryn's eyes narrow, her warrior's posture suddenly alert as if I've just announced a battle strategy. "Bloody Viking?" she whispers with deadly seriousness. "They serve the blood of fallen warriors in this establishment?"

Emily snorts into her water while Seraphina's eyes widen to celestial proportions.

"Jesus, Bryn," I stifle my laughter behind my hand. "It's just tomato juice and vodka with horseradish. No actual Vikings were harmed in the making of this cocktail."

Bryn's expression shifts from battle-ready to slightly disappointed. "Midgardians have strange customs of honoring warriors," she mutters. "Very well. I shall sample this bloodless tribute."

Emily orders something with enough caffeine to power a small city, while Seraphina requests a virgin piña colada with such sweetness that the waiter practically trips over himself, promising extra cherries on top.

"It wasn't that terrible," Seraphina muses, her honey-gold eyes scanning the menu as our waiter leaves. "Much easier than my first time, thank goodness." Her lips curve into that sweet smile that's picked up a hint of wickedness since falling for Lucian. "Though the 24-hour waiting period doesn't apply to me. Celestial healing has its perks."

She glances at Bryn with a conspiratorial smile. "If you have similar healing properties, you wouldn't need to wait either. Men don't really know the difference—you could use it to your advantage. A little teasing goes a long way."

Bryn arches an eyebrow. "Please, I'm a Valkyrie. A little wax isn't going to slow me down."She smirks, her gaze turning predatory. "Something the silfrhár is about to find out firsthand."

"Oh, well that's just wonderful," Emily explodes, throwing her hands up. "Some of us humans don't have magical healing coochies! Twenty-four hours of throbbing lady bits while you supernatural types get to prance around pain-free? The universe is a twisted bitch."

I burst out laughing at Emily's outburst, nearly choking on my water. "Well, Em, maybe Brax can kiss it better? I hear demons have magical tongues—though I'm not sure that's what the brochure meant by 'aftercare.'"

Emily narrows her eyes at me. "You know what, Pierce? Just because you're getting Viking thunder every night doesn't mean you get to be smug about my human recovery time. And Brax isn't even going to—" She stops abruptly, her cheeks flushing.

Emily's eyes suddenly widen as she catches my expression, and I can practically see the "oh shit" moment flash across her face. Nice try, witch bitch, but you're not escaping this interrogation. She's been dodging me these past few weeks, and I'm officially done with her shit.

I place my elbows on the table, resting my chin on my folded hands and batting my eyelashes with exaggerated innocence. "So... ready to spill the tea on why you've been walking around like you rode a mechanical bull for eight hours straight?"

Emily takes a long sip of her water, the ice cubes clinking as she stalls. "What?" She shrugs with practiced nonchalance. "Like you can judge anyone's sex life, Miss 'I'm-Banging-A-Thousand-Year-Old-Corpse.'"

"Excuse you," I fire back, brandishing my breadstick like a tiny sword. "My Viking's preservation status is not the topic of discussion. We're talking about why you've been sneaking around like you're smuggling contraband dick across state lines."

"Fine. Jesus," Emily throws up her hands in surrender, nearly knocking over her water glass. "Yes, I'm sleeping with Brax. Happy now, Nancy Drew?"

"We already knew that," Sable chimes in, like Brax's shapeshifting abilities are yesterday's news.

I bite back a grin—I already know how Brax transformed into a perfect replica of Captain America (shield included), but now I'm dying to know what other celebrity skins my best friend has test-driven in the bedroom.

I immediately soften, my inner scientist pushing through. "I need to know," I lean in, lowering my voice to a conspiratorial whisper. "Does his... you know... equipment shapeshift, too?"

Emily gives me a wicked grin that tells me everything before she even speaks. "Well, yeah," she says, like I've just asked if grass is green.

"Oh my god!" I practically bounce in my seat, giddy with the implications. "Okay, spill everything. Details. Dimensions. Diagrams if necessary."

Emily rolls her eyes but leans in. She knows our friendship contract includes full disclosure on all sexcapades—I told her every delicious detail about Rhyland's performance at the Playful Pint. Then that night at the sex club, it's only fair she shares the mechanics of her customizable demon dick.

Talk about the ultimate upgrade from store-bought toys.

"His *default* mode," Emily says, lowering her voice, "is absolutely..." She holds her hands apart in a measurement that makes my eyes bulge. Brax is packing something that belongs in a stable, not a bedroom, if what she's indicating is accurate. "Let's just say demons are... proportional."

"Sweet Elysium," Seraphina whispers, her cheeks flaming pink.

Bryn lets out a low whistle. "Even Thor's hammer isn't quite so... impressive."

I choke on my drink, sputtering. "Holy shit, that's not a dick, that's a lethal weapon! You've actually taken that, you ambitious ho?"

"Jesus—*hell*—no." Emily cackles, gaining wandering eyes from three tables over. "What do you think I am, a size queen with a death wish? My va-jay jay doesn't have magical expanding properties just because I date a demon." She takes a smug sip of her water. "Although I did try once—purely for science, you understand—and let's just say the safe word got deployed faster than a paratrooper from a burning plane."

"Actually..." Sable taps her chin thoughtfully, "there might be a spell for that. I've come across some in my grandmother's grimoire with enchantments for magical... expansion."

Our heads whip around so fast my neck pops.

Oww.

"What?" She shrugs at our collective stares. "It's basic mystical anatomy modification. Totally doable."

The mental image alone is killing me—like some supernatural vaginal stretching infomercial.

But wait, there's more!

"Hold up," Emily straightens, her expression suddenly serious as a heart attack. "You're telling me there's actual magical coochie-stretching spells?"

Oh god. I know that look. That's her 'I'm about to do something spectacularly stupid' face.

"No," I point my fork at her. "Whatever you're thinking, stop thinking it. Your lady bits will thank you."

"But—"

"The answer is still no, even if you're about to say 'for science.'"

"It's not exclusively for..." Sable waves her hand vaguely at our pelvic regions, "...accommodating demon—"

The sudden appearance of our waiter materializing beside our table cuts her off mid-sentence. We all straighten up, conversation dying instantly as we plaster on polite smiles. He sets down our drinks with practiced precision, oblivious to the mystical vaginal expansion discussion he just interrupted.

"Are you ready to order?" he asks, pen poised over the notepad.

"Not quite yet," I flash him my best nothing-inappropriate-happening-here smile. "Could we have a few more minutes?"

He nods, professional and mercifully unaware. "Take your time, ladies. I'll check back shortly." His footsteps fade into the restaurant's ambient noise.

The moment he's safely out of earshot, Emily leans forward, picking up exactly where we left off without missing a beat. "Dick?" she supplies helpfully, her tone suggesting she's simply completing a crossword puzzle rather than discussing supernatural genitalia.

Sable continues, ignoring her foul mouth— "The grimoire covers all sorts of anatomical enhancements: healing, flexibility, resilience—even restoring things that were... lost. It's actually quite fascinating from a magical medicine perspective."

"So what you're saying is," Emily grins, "it's basically mystical Botox for your bits *and* a full-body tune-up?"

Bryn eyes her crimson drink suspiciously, nostrils flaring as she conducts a warrior's assessment. When she finally braves a sip, her eyes flash with unexpected pleasure.

"By the AllFather," she murmurs, staring at the glass with newfound respect, "the Midgardians have crafted battle-worthy spirits."

Sable shrugs, a slight blush coloring her cheeks. "Most witches use it for... recreational purposes. But technically, it's ancient healing magic."

I snort into my drink. Trust my best friend to turn ancient healing magic into a freaking spa package.

Girls' day out with my two favorite witches, my Valkyrie sister and my guardian angel—where else can you have lunch conversations about vagina-stretching spells and horse-sized demon dicks?

Fucking nowhere, that's where. Life is good, even if it's batshit crazy.

"Well, hello, darlings."

That silky voice slithers down my spine like ice water. My stomach drops as we all snap our heads up to find Lilith standing at our table, wearing her signature red-soled Louboutins and a smile that would make Satan himself check his back for knives.

There goes my perfect spa day, shot straight to hell by the Queen Bitch herself.

"I simply *had* to come say hello." Lilith's says with artificial sweetness.. "What an absolute *coincidence* finding you girls here. Divine timing, wouldn't you say?"

Our table freezes like someone hit pause on reality. Seraphina's knuckles whiten around her virgin piña colada, her eyes blazing with fury. The last time she encountered Lilith, she almost destroyed her wings—tormenting her.

Wait—daylight streams through the windows, bathing the restaurant in the afternoon glow. How the fuck is Lilith standing here without bursting into flames?

My fingers twitch with the urge to unleash hell on her bougie ass, but families surround us—laughing kids, oblivious tourists, a couple celebrating their anniversary. I can't exactly go nuclear in the middle of Ray's Boathouse without collateral damage.

The stones in my crown vibrate against my skull, responding to my rage like a tuning fork. Outside, storm clouds gather with unnatural speed, transforming Seattle's gray-snowy sky into a threatening canvas of slate and charcoal. The wind whips the water's surface into white-capped fury.

Shit. Calm down, Dani. Don't turn this waterfront restaurant into ground zero for a hurricane because this bitch crashed your girls' day.

"What the hell do you want?" I manage through clenched teeth.

Lilith examines her blood-red manicure with exaggerated interest. "Oh, *darling*," she sighs as if I'm a particularly slow child. "I assumed you'd be *thrilled* to see an old friend. I went to *such* trouble arranging this little reunion."

Old friend? Is she fucking high? Does this psychotic couture nightmare think we're on speaking terms after everything she's done?

She snaps her fingers—actually *snaps* them like I'm the help—but gestures behind her. "Come along, don't be shy."

She's more unhinged than—

A man steps into view beside her, and everything stops. The restaurant noise fades to nothing—my heartbeat thunders in my ears.

Dark hair. Familiar eyes. The same scholarly face that once betrayed us all.

My lungs forget how to function. My throat closes. The world tilts sideways.

No. Impossible. I watched him die. Azrael ripped his heart out—

"Adrian?"

RHYLAND

74

The Holiday Lighting Pros truck pulls up the drive, their logo reflecting off the fresh snow. Lucian chuckles, "Ho ho ho, bitches, the light crew has arrived."

My arms strain with the fifth box of Christmas shit from the basement—centuries of accumulated decorations that Lucian never throws away "because they have sentimental value, you heathens."

The massive pine tree Lucian somehow pulled out of his ass dominates our living room, and Brax—currently wearing some random GQ model's face because Lucian threatened to exorcise him if he saw one more Chris Evans—practically bounces as he strings lights around the branches.

"Last box," I grunt, dropping it next to the growing pile of tinsel and ornaments. Leave it to Lucian to turn this into some grand gesture. "The girls need normal holiday experiences," he'd insisted, like anything about our lives could be considered normal.

The sight of Erik—Mr. Stoic himself—carefully hanging delicate glass ornaments while nursing his bourbon nearly makes me drop the box. In all our lifetimes, I never thought I'd see my brother doing something so... domestic.

"Alright, you seasonal sluts!" Lucian bursts in from his surveillance room, tablet in hand. "Let's turn this place into the North Pole's wet dream!"

Erik doesn't even look up from his methodical decorating. "If you start singing 'All I Want for Christmas,' I will break your neck."

"You're just jealous of my festive spirit, Silver Bells."

Erik continues arranging ornaments with precision. "At least I don't look like an elf that failed Santa's workshop orientation."

Lucian gasps dramatically. "How dare you. I am a majestic Christmas creature. And at least I don't arrange ornaments with military precision, General Grinch."

I sort through the tangled mess of garland, imagining Dani's reaction when she returns from her "me-day" with the girls. The thought of my mate's face lighting up at this winter wonderland bullshit makes all this worth it.

We'd caught wind of their little escape plan—or more specifically, Dani's scheme. Vampire hearing is a beautiful fucking thing when your mate thinks she's being sneaky. Perfect opportunity to turn their surprise into *our* surprise. Hell, for once I actually *wanted* them to leave so we could get this shit done without Dani catching wind of it. Nothing like turning the tables on my feisty angel.

"Speaking of elves," Lucian grins, pulling something from a bag. "Look what I found!"

"No." Erik's voice could freeze hell.

"Oh yes, brother dearest." Lucian holds up three matching sweaters—all featuring prancing reindeer with actual light-up noses. "Matching family Christmas sweaters!"

Brax immediately shifts into a department store mannequin. "Can I have one too?"

"For fuck's sake," I growl, but there's no real heat in it. The happiness radiating from my brothers—even Erik's carefully hidden amusement—is infectious. We haven't done anything like this in centuries.

"If anyone takes pictures," Erik warns, reluctantly accepting his sweater, "I will end you."

"Too late!" Lucian's already got his phone out. "This is going to be our Christmas card. 'Season's Greetings from your favorite bloodsuckers!'"

"You know what this needs?" Brax shifts his face into yet another random model. "A star for the top."

"Touch my Swarovski tree topper and die," Lucian warns, untangling a string of lights. "That's an antique from 1895."

I exchange looks with Erik, who's somehow managed to arrange his section of ornaments in perfect geometric precision. Of course, he has.

"Speaking of antiques," Erik says, reaching for another ornament, "remember the Christmas of 1901 when Lucian tried to—"

"We do NOT speak of the Mistletoe Incident," Lucian cuts him off, jabbing a finger in Erik's direction. "That story died with the Victorian era, where it belongs."

The corner of Erik's mouth twitches—the closest he gets to a full smile. "I was thinking more about the caroling disaster."

"That choir deserved what they got. Nobody butchers 'Silent Night' on my watch."

I shake my head, sorting through more decorations. "You threw their sheet music into the Thames River."

"I was helping them retire with dignity!"

Two of the lighting crew approach our front door, and Lucian swaggers off to handle them, probably to micromanage every fucking bulb placement.

"I'll supervise outside," I mutter, following him. The words feel strange in my mouth—in all my lifetimes, I've never given two shits about holiday decorating. But now? Knowing how Dani's eyes light up at anything Christmas-related has me caring about where these poor bastards hang the icicle lights.

Christ. My mate's turned me into a pussy.

Over a thousand years of being a hard ass, and here I am about to critique the spacing of outdoor Christmas lights. If any of my enemies could see me now, my reputation would be shot to shit.

A worker drops a hammer that narrowly misses another's head. I shoot Lucian a pointed look.

"This is your idea of professional help? Where did you find these idiots—drunks outside your club at closing time?"

"They came highly recommended," Lucian protests, brushing snow from his christmas sweater. "By people who know people who... okay, fine, they were the only crew available on short notice. It's Christmas, you ancient grump. Not exactly peak season for finding elite light-hanging specialists."

"You couldn't have just called a proper electrician?"

"And miss watching you have an aneurysm over improper grounding techniques?" Lucian's brown eyes dance with unholy amusement. "Not a chance in hell, Thunderstruck. Your blood pressure alone is worth the price of admission."

I almost laugh, watching as one worker nearly topples off the roof. This is going to be a long day.

Lucian gestures broadly at the half-strung lights. "Everyone's a critic. Not all of us spent the Middle Ages hammering things, Viking Ken. Some of us developed taste."

"Taste? Is that what you call that neon monstrosity you call a nightclub? Place looks like the 80's threw up after a cocaine bender."

"Bold words from someone who thought indoor plumbing was witchcraft until 1901. Remind me again how you electrocuted yourself trying to install a ceiling fan in '86? Didn't your hair stand on end for a week?"

I fight the urge to smile, remembering how the electricity had barely tickled. If only I'd known then what I know now about my heritage.

The crew wraps up, probably motivated by Lucian's promises of obscene holiday bonuses. Every inch of the mansion drips with professional-grade lighting—warm whites along the roofline; icicle drops from every eave, and these fancy-ass twinkle effects in all the trees.

I flex my shoulders, enjoying the burn from moving their heavy equipment. It beats sitting around watching these guys work—a man doesn't stand idle when there's a job to be done, even if that job involves stringing up enough lights to be seen from fucking space.

Lucian sidles up, throwing his arm across my shoulders. "I'm proud of you, Griswold. Getting your hands dirty with the Christmas spirit."

I shrug him off. Lucian's check had enough zeros to fund a small war—this place is going to outshine the entire fucking neighborhood.

"Just wait until we fire this baby up," Lucian grins, bouncing on his toes like a kid hopped up on candy canes. "The power company's gonna think we're running a meth lab from our backyard."

Erik appears beside us, his eyes scanning the setup. "The electrical load distribution is optimal," he notes, probably the closest he'll get to saying 'it looks nice.'

We stride back inside, and it's like the North Pole exploded in every corner—garland, ornaments, and twinkling lights covering every surface that isn't moving. Warm white lights wrap every banister and frame every archway. A week ago, I'd have called this overkill, but now I'm staking my claim on this holiday shit. If we're doing Christmas, we're doing it right.

Rosa commands the kitchen like a general, hips swaying to "Feliz Navidad" as she moves between three pots. The scent hits me—roasting meat, spices, and the unmistakable sweetness of fresh cookies. My stomach growls with the need to taste whatever she's creating. The kitchen gleams with strands of lights woven through her workspace, reflecting off copper pots and industrial appliances.

"¡Ustedes, muchachos! Wash those hands before dinner," she calls without turning around, somehow sensing our presence despite the music. "Y tú, Lucian, stay away from my cookies or te daré con la cuchara de madera—vampire or not!"

My brother raises his hands in surrender, but I catch the gleam in his eye. Some battles even Lucian knows better than to fight.

Don't know how the hell it happened, but somewhere along the way, Rosa became the mother none of us deserved but all of us needed. Not that I'd ever say that shit out loud—my reputation's taken enough hits lately.

"¿Les gusta la decoración?" Rosa asks, finally gesturing with a flour-dusted hand at the kitchen's transformation. "Your Dani, she will love this, ¿verdad?"

"Yes, she's gonna lose her mind," I nod to Rosa, picturing it all. "That's the plan."

"The plan is for Rhyland to finally earn his 'World's Most Whipped Vampire' coffee mug," Lucian quips, snatching a cookie despite Rosa's warning. "It's back-ordered but should arrive by New Year's."

Rosa whips around, wooden spoon raised. "¡Dios mío! What did I just say about those cookies, chico malo?"

Lucian stuffs the entire cookie in his mouth, speaking around crumbs. "Worth it. I've survived plagues, Rosa. Your spoon doesn't scare me."

"But my chancla might," she threatens, reaching for her flip-flop.

"Protect me, brother!" Lucian ducks behind me, using my body as a shield. "She's gone nuclear!"

I shrug him off with a growl. "You're on your own. I'm not getting between Rosa and her kitchen rules."

"Traitor!" Lucian gasps dramatically. "After I spent a small fortune making this place look like Santa's wet dream? This is how you repay me?"

Rosa waves her spoon at both of us. "No fighting in my kitchen! ¡Fuera! Out! Go hang more lights or whatever you vampiros do."

"We could drain the neighbors," Lucian suggests helpfully. "Very festive. Red is a Christmas color."

"Dios me ayude," Rosa mutters, crossing herself. "Go! Both of you! Before I call your ladies, tell them what you did in Budapest."

My head snaps up. "You told her about Budapest?"

Lucian shrugs innocently. "It might have come up during sangria night."

I grab him by his ridiculous sweater and drag him from the kitchen. "You're dead."

"Already am, technically!" he calls back to Rosa. "Save me some more cookies!"

Rosa yells from the kitchen, "You think you're funny, but dinner is in one hour, and if you're late, there will be no galleta for either of you, ¿entendido?"

"Yes, Cookie Overlord," Lucian salutes. "Your baked goods are worth punctuality!"

As we exit the kitchen, Lucian elbows me. "Remember when we used to make people shit themselves with fear? Now we're racing to dinner like a couple of kids afraid of missing dessert. My badass reputation is officially fucked."

I shove him back, rolling my eyes. "Your reputation was fucked the minute you started your Marvel figurine collection."

"Hey! Limited edition collectibles are badass in certain circles!" he protests. "Besides, I saw you arranging the Avengers ornaments on the tree by movie release order, you closet nerd."

For all his irritating qualities—and there are many—the idiot's not wrong. This ridiculous, light-filled life beats anything we've had recently.

Not that I'd ever tell him that. His ego's already the size of a fucking continent.

Erik materializes in the hallway, silver eyes taking in our bickering with practiced indifference. "Are you two done? The girls just turned onto the road. Five minutes out."

"Battle stations!" Lucian claps his hands together. "Operation 'Make Our Ladies Cry Happy Tears' is a go! Rhyland put on your broody-but-secretly-pleased face. Erik, try to look less like you're attending a funeral and more like you're participating in holiday cheer."

"This is my holiday cheer face," Erik deadpans.

"Jesus Christ on a candy cane, that's depressing," Lucian mutters. "Fine, just stand near something sparkly so you don't suck all the joy out of the room."

Brax materializes beside us, having shifted into what appears to be a perfect replica of Will Ferrell's Buddy the Elf, complete with the yellow tights and conical hat. "Is this festive enough?"

Lucian groans, running a hand down his face. "Of all the Christmas characters in existence, you chose the most obnoxiously cheerful—" He pauses, studying Brax with reluctant appreciation. "Although... the dedication to those yellow tights is kind of genius in a mentally unstable way."

"The best way to spread Christmas cheer is singing loud for all to hear!" Brax announces in perfect Buddy voice, bouncing on his toes.

"I swear to god, demon," Lucian warns, fighting back a smirk. "If you start singing about Christmas spirit, I will stuff you in the chimney. But... keep the outfit. It's working."

Brax shifts his features slightly, keeping the costume but toning down the manic energy. "Emily's going to flip. She loves this movie."

I straighten my ridiculous reindeer sweater, the blinking nose somehow making me feel less intimidating than I'd like. "If Dani laughs at me in this getup—"

"She'll jump your bones faster than Santa inhaling Rosa's cookies," Lucian interrupts. "Trust me, women love this sentimental crap."

Erik's jaw tightens. "Must you always make everything inappropriate?"

"Must you make everything boring?" Lucian counters. "Besides, I'm just stating facts. Christmas decorations are like vampire Viagra—they make the ladies holly-jolly in all the right places."

The sound of car doors slamming cuts through our bickering. Through the window, I catch sight of Dani's brunette hair. My chest tightens in that now-familiar way that still pisses me off and thrills me in equal measure.

"Places!" Lucian hisses. "Remember—we did this because we wanted to, not because we're whipped. Maintain your dignity, gentlemen."

"Says the man wearing reindeer antlers," Erik mutters.

"They're tactical antlers," Lucian adjusts them on his head. "And they're going to get me laid tonight, so who's the real winner here?"

"I can make snow angels on command," Brax whispers, adjusting his pointy hat. "Just say the word."

"Jesus," I growl, "stay in human form, or I'll exorcise you myself."

The front door handle turns, and for a moment, we all freeze like deer caught in headlights—three ancient vampires and one shape-shifting demon suddenly nervous about whether our women will like our Christmas surprise.

How the mighty have fucking fallen.

DANICA
75

I t's impossible. Adrian. Standing here. Breathing. His familiar scholarly presence beside Lilith's designer-wrapped venom like some twisted before-and-after death photo.

My lungs seize.

Skadi's playground comes rushing back—the brutal battle where I fought the Einherjar, including Adrian's ghost. I'd stabbed his phantom form, watched him dissolve into mist. And now here he is, breathing and talking like the last time I saw him without his heart ripped from his chest. The mental whiplash is enough to make me question my own sanity.

Could Morgan have conjured some twisted illusion? No—this is too real, too precise. Every detail matches, from the way he holds himself like he's perpetually about to deliver a lecture to that slight tilt of his head when he's analyzing a situation.

Unless... *fuck*. The rift. The mystery person Lilith dragged back from death's door. Her new pet project—still bound to her will by blood and compulsion.

"*Do* try to remember your manners, Adrian darling," Lilith says with sugary venom as she taps his shoulder with one manicured nail. "It's *dreadfully* rude to keep an old friend waiting."

The silence stretches like pulled taffy until Emily's voice shatters it. "Jesus fucking Christ." Her eyes darting between us like she's watching a tennis match from hell. "Please tell me this isn't the same backstabbing bookworm who got his heart ripped out."

"It's quite good to see you again, Danica." Adrian's voice carries the same measured cadence, the slight professorial tilt that once guided me through ancient texts. "You're looking well. I trust your studies of the ancient codices have continued in my absence."

My absence. As if he stepped out for coffee instead of dying in my arms.

Memories crash through me like a tidal wave—Adrian patiently teaching me of the Dark Prophecy in his book-lined study, his quiet excitement when we discovered the crown's power, his devastating betrayal that cut deeper than any blade, his desperate plea for redemption, his final sacrifice, stealing the Soul Stone as Azrael ripped his heart from his chest, the tears I shed, the guilt I carried.

The taste of copper floods my mouth. I've bitten my tongue, trying to hold back the scream building in my throat.

"We should take our leave, sister." Bryn's voice cuts through the fog of shock, her warrior's instincts on high alert. Her tone carries the steel of a Valkyrie preparing for battle, even with only the abbreviated version of Lilith's greatest hits.

She's right. I need to get out of here before I unleash the maelstrom brewing inside me—before my power erupts and reduces this place to rubble and ash. The wind outside howls like a hungry wolf, and the clouds above have turned the color of fresh bruises.

"H-How?" The word scrapes past the lump in my throat, jagged and broken.

Lilith's smile curls like a knife's edge. "Oh, it's quite simple, darling." She leans forward, her voice smooth as silk. "The stone's power is truly *delicious*, isn't it? Adrian was always my priority, you know. After you got him killed, of course."

Her words slice through me, precise and cruel. I flinch as if she's struck me, the truth of it searing my heart like a brand—everyone who's suffered or died because of me. John. Mom. Dad. My birth mother. Adrian—a trail of bodies and broken souls, the price they paid for being caught in my orbit.

"And thanks to your little angel friend," Lilith's gaze slides to Seraphina with predatory delight. "We have an *abundance* of celestial blood—enough to last quite some time." Her smile widens, revealing the edge of her fangs. "So *thank you*, darling. Your contribution to my day-walking abilities is simply *invaluable.*"

Bile rises in my throat, acid, and rage mingling as the pieces click into place. She harvested Seraphina's blood during her captivity—And now Adrian too walks in daylight, both of them bathed in stolen divinity.

Seraphina's face drains of color, her golden eyes filling with tears that catch the light like trapped stars. Her fingers tremble against the table as she presses one hand to her throat, reliving the violation. The slight choking sound she makes slices through me like a blade.

I know that sound. I know that feeling—when someone takes the very core of what makes you *you* and twists it into something profane. When they steal your essence and use it against everything you stand for.

"What the *hell* do you want?" The words grind between my teeth like broken glass. My jaw clenched so tight it aches. The question hangs between us—redundant and inevitable all at once.

Our waiter approaches with menus clutched to his chest, his customer service smile faltering as he registers the electric tension crackling around our table. Lilith's head swivels toward him, her eyes flashing with something ancient and predatory. His Adam's apple bobs in a visible swallow.

"I'll—I'll check back," he stammers, backing away like he's just stumbled upon a cobra nest.

Lilith leans forward. "It's really quite simple, darling. I want Rhyland and the other half of that delicious stone you're hiding." Her lips curl back, revealing the hint of fangs. "If you don't deliver, well... poor Adrian will suffer *again* because of your stubbornness."

My eyes lock with Adrian's. Behind his scholarly composure, behind that familiar face I once trusted, I see it—the silent scream trapped behind his eyes—the desperate plea for rescue. The invisible chains binding him to Lilith's will cut deeper than any physical restraint could. His gaze speaks volumes; his lips cannot—*Help me. I'm drowning in her darkness.*

Something cold and determined settles in my chest. Lilith hasn't just stolen a body from the grave—she's imprisoned a soul.

Emily erupts from her seat, chair scraping against the floor. "We're done here. We'll be in touch, bitch," she snarls, her voice low enough that only our table can hear the venom. "Come on, Dani." Her fingers close around my arm with surprising strength, yanking me from the precipice of doing something catastrophic.

"I do *so* hope it's soon," Lilith purrs. "Time is such a precious commodity, isn't it?"

My gaze catches Adrian's one last time. His composure slips for just a heartbeat—revealing raw desperation beneath, a drowning man glimpsing a distant shore. Then Lilith's fingers curl possessively around his arm, and the mask slides back into place.

My chest splinters like glass struck by a hammer.

He's trapped. He's alive, and he's trapped.

The next moments blur—restaurant door, parking lot, car. Emily's colorful stream of profanity fades to white noise as she peels out of the lot, her knuckles bone-white on the steering wheel. Seraphina's quiet sobs from the backseat punctuate the tense silence like tiny daggers.

My throat constricts each breath a conscious effort. Words form and dissolve before reaching my lips. Adrian. Alive. Breathing. Walking. Trapped in Lilith's web like a fly. The impossibility of it crashes over me in waves, each realization more devastating than the last.

Adrian is alive.

Adrian is Lilith's prisoner.

Adrian needs me.

Adrian will die again if I fail.

The SUV screeches to a halt at the mansion's entrance, Emily bypassing the garage entirely. The grand house looms against the darkening sky, snow falling again. The windows glow with warm light that spills onto the snow-covered lawn.

Emily yanks my door open. "Jesus Christ, Dani, breathe," she orders, her voice rough with concern. "You're turning the same shade as my freaking hair."

The mansion door flies open before we reach the steps. Rhyland fills the doorway. His powerful frame silhouetted against the interior light. As we cross the threshold, I dimly register the transformation inside—garlands drape the staircase, twinkling lights wind through evergreen boughs, and a giant pine tree dominates the corner of the great room, half-decorated with ornaments scattered on nearby tables.

Rhyland's storm-blue eyes lock onto my face, pupils dilating as he scans for injuries. "Angel?"

His voice drops to that dangerous register that makes lesser beings tremble. He's before me in three strides, big hands cupping my face. "What happened?" The question rumbles from his chest like distant artillery.

I open my mouth, but no sound emerges—just a pathetic gasp of air.

Rhyland doesn't wait for answers. His arm sweeps behind my knees, lifting me against his chest as he carries me into the living room. The couch dips beneath his weight as he positions me in his lap, one hand anchoring me to him while the other tilts my chin up, forcing my gaze to meet his.

"Her pulse is racing like she's seen a fucking ghost," Emily snaps, pacing the hardwood. "Which isn't far off, considering—"

"She's in shock," Bryn interrupts, cutting through the chaos.

Rhyland's jaw locks, a muscle ticking beneath his stubble. "Tell me. Now."

The command isn't directed at me but at everyone else—the protective alpha gathering intelligence to eliminate a threat.

"Lilith," Emily spats. "That designer-label corpse ambushed us at Ray's." Her combat boots scorch the hardwood as she paces. "Bitch is fucking day-walking now, courtesy of premium angel plasma."

A soft whimper escapes Seraphina from her place on the couch. Lucian already there, holding her.

"Hey, hey, baby girl," he murmurs, his usual razor-sharp sarcasm melting into something gentle as he cups her face. "This clusterfuck isn't on your divine tab."

Seraphina's shoulders curl inward, tears tracking down her cheeks. "The drugs she gave me—everything was foggy—it makes perfect sense she would—"

Lucian pulls her against his chest, silencing her spiral with a protective embrace. The tendons in his neck stand out like steel cables as his jaw locks—the room temperature spikes with his barely contained rage.

Erik hovers over Bryn, silver eyes scanning her with clinical precision. His fingers ghost over her arms, checking for injuries with the detachment of a battlefield medic—except for the muscle jumping in his jaw.

"The tík did not touch me, silfrhár," Bryn growls, bristling at the implication she couldn't handle herself. "Save your concern."

Erik's inspection doesn't falter. "She must never discover what you are." The statement falls between them like a sworn oath.

Rhyland's strong arms lock around me like steel bands, his rhythmic rocking at odds with the lethal tension in his muscles. The world feels distant, underwater, my thoughts scattered like leaves in a storm. Each breath catches in my throat like I'm trying to inhale molasses, my chest tight and burning.

"What. Did. She. Do?" Each word drops from Rhyland's lips like arctic shards, the temperature around us plummeting as his power leaks into the air. His fingers dig into my hip, the possessive grip anchoring me as darkness crackles at the edges of his aura.

"Adrian," Bryn announces. "The fallen scholar lives."

On the way here, while I was busy auditioning for a panic attack commercial—still winning that role, by the way—Emily filled Bryn and Sable in on the Adrian saga. Because my trauma bingo card needed just one more stamp to win the grand prize of complete emotional collapse.

Rhyland turns to stone beneath me. His arms constrict until my ribs protest."That's impossible." Each word drops like an executioner's ax. "I watched Azrael tear out his heart."

"The Soul Stone," Sable whispers. "She used it when she opened the rift and dragged him back."

"Wait—holy shit." Lucian freezes mid-gesture, his face draining of color as the realization hits like a sledgehammer. "Adrian?" The name comes out strangled. "*That's* who she pulled? That sanctimonious voice when he wrecked my car taking Seraphina. When Sable got blown to bits? When that bomb—" His fingers curl into fists, veins standing out along his forearms. "That scholastic little shit—

He runs a hand through his golden hair, manic energy radiating off him in waves. "I mean, seriously? Heart extraction is just a minor inconvenience now? What's next—the Titanic just needed some flex tape? Fucking hell, I need a drink. Or ten. Actually, fuck this—I need an entire liquor store."

The edges of my vision blur and pins and needles prickle across my cheeks. Each breath comes faster than the last, too shallow and too quick, like I'm trying to inhale through a coffee stirrer.

Rhyland's hand slides to cup my cheek, the rough calluses catching against my skin as he forces my gaze to meet his. Ocean-blue eyes lock onto mine with that alpha intensity that usually turns my knees to jelly.

"Angel." His voice drops to that commanding rumble that vibrates through my bones. His thumb traces my lower lip, which has gone numb. "We'll handle this—all of it." His other hand splays possessively across my ribcage, monitoring my rapid breathing. "But right now, I need you to fucking breathe before you pass out in my lap."

"She's g-got him under h-her c-command." The words scrape past my constricted throat. "He n-needs help."

Rhyland freezes, his muscles locking down so tight I can feel the tremors of restraint. A tsunami of memories crashes through our bond—Adrian's betrayal, the pain, the blood. But underneath that, a grudging understanding pulses. After all, my man and his brothers know intimately what dancing on Lilith's puppet strings means.

"Oh fuck, that noise sideways." Lucian's face twists into something savage despite Seraphina still tucked against him. "I don't care if he's got more mind control than a Marvel villain's origin story—that backstabbing bookworm can rot in whatever necromantic happy meal box Lilith dragged him out of, Princess."

The world slowly rights itself as feeling creeps back into my tingling lips. I blink hard, convinced I'm still oxygen-deprived because there's no way I'm seeing what I'm seeing. But the telltale crackle of demonic energy gives him away—Brax, shapeshifted into a perfect replica of Will Ferrell in *Elf*, complete with yellow tights, curly-toed shoes, and a jingling hat that makes him look absolutely ridiculous—handing me a glass of water.

"I—" My brain misfires, still trying to process Adrian's resurrection while staring at a demon masquerading as Buddy the Elf.

I don't even have the mental bandwidth to unpack this right now. I accept the water glass, my hand still slightly shaky.

Rhyland's hand trace steady circles on my back as I drain the glass, each stroke pulling me further from the edge of panic.

"Well, this is awkwardly festive given our current situation," Lucian quips, antlers askew. "Nothing like a vampire queen crash and a ghost from Christmas past to really deck the halls."

As the reality of our situation sinks in, the festive atmosphere takes on a somber note. The twinkling lights and garlands seem almost mocking now, a cruel reminder of the normalcy we can't have.

"Holy shit," Emily blurts, taking in our testosterone-laden crew, decked out in fuzzy holiday sweaters. "Did Santa's workshop throw up in here or what?"

"You guys did all this...?"

"Observant as ever, Princess," Lucian snarks. "We only transformed the place into the North Pole's wet dream while you were out getting your lady bits landscaped."

"Surprise," Erik deadpans, his stoic expression made ridiculous by the blinking nose on his sweater.

"By Odin's beard," Bryn marvels, circling Erik like a predator assessing prey. "The mighty silfrhár reduced to wearing festive garments. Most... intriguing."

"The timing could be better," Sable offers softly, "but it's beautiful."

Damon materializes beside her, his usual silent entrance. "Hey, sorry I was asleep—heard all the commotion." He slides next to Sable, taking her hand in his.

"Yeah, thanks for the assist, Sleeping Beauty," Lucian snaps. "Nothing says 'team spirit' like snoozing while the rest of us transformed this place into Santa's sweaty workshop. I personally hung fifteen miles of twinkle lights while Erik was on ladder duty. You know what he says when you ask him if the lights are straight? 'Adequate.' That's it. One word. It's like decorating with a Terminator who occasionally hands you tape."

"Lies." Erik retorts.

Bryn studies the tree. "These ornaments... they serve no defensive purpose. And yet, there is a certain beauty in their frivolity."

"That's kind of the point, Xena," Lucian snarks. "Christmas is all about the unnecessary shit that makes you feel good."

"And you," Emily purrs, sauntering toward Brax in his Buddy the Elf getup. "How'd you know I have a thing for guys in tights? Though I gotta say, I've never wanted to sit on Buddy's face before, but you're making me reconsider my life choices."

Brax's eyes gleam devilishly as he adjusts his pointy hat.

"For the love of *god*," I gag, watching them eye-fuck. "Can you two save the North Pole exploration for when we're not in a crisis? I'm traumatized enough without watching my best friend seduce an elf."

Erik clears his throat, drawing our attention. "Given the circumstances, a bit of cheer might be in order." He gestures at the half-decorated tree. "We saved the best part for you."

Rhyland pulls me close, his ridiculous sweater soft against my cheek. "We wanted to surprise you, Angel. Give you something normal before..." He trails off, his hold tightening protectively.

I lean back into his warmth, blinking back the sudden sting of tears. "It's perfect. All of it. I just wish..."

"Hey, none of that," Emily interjects, her voice fierce. "Lilith doesn't get to ruin this, too. We're gonna deck these fucking halls, drink too much eggnog, and have a goddamn merry Christmas. And if that bitch shows up, we'll shove a tree so far up her ass she'll be coughing tinsel."

A surprised laugh bubbles out of me, and just like that, the heaviness lifts a bit. Leave it to Emily to find the silver lining in a shitstorm.

My focus snaps back to Lucian—the only one of my testosterone trio who couldn't care less if Adrian spontaneously combusted in front of us. Unlike Rhyland's brooding concern or Erik's calculating assessment, Lucian's face screams, "Not my circus, not my traitorous monkeys."

"Look, Lucian," I manage, fighting to keep my tone steady. "I get it—Adrian's currently public enemy number one. But he's being mind-fucked by your psycho *mom,* and if anyone knows what that's like,..." I let that sink in. "I won't leave him to be her puppet. Not when we can help."

"Jesus Christ." Lucian pinches the bridge of his nose, reindeer antlers wiggling. "What's next on this magical redemption tour? Marriage counseling with Satan? Trust falls with Moretemis? Maybe we can all hold hands and sing Kumbaya with the forces of darkness?"

"She's right." Guilt, and regret pulse from Rhyland like a bruised heartbeat—the weight of dismissing my concerns about Adrian before everything went sideways. His arms tighten around me, his voice a low rumble against my back. "Adrian is our brother." The words carry the weight of centuries. "If there's even a chance to save him from that bitch's control..."

"The tactical disadvantages are... significant." Erik adds. His fingers trace absent patterns on Bryn's arm. "Though leaving him as her weapon could prove more costly."

"Okay, timeout." Emily makes the time-out gesture. "Not to rain on this rescue mission parade, but how exactly are we planning to yank Adrian from the clutches of Demonic Vampire Barbie? Because last time I checked, that bitch was collecting power-ups like it's Mario Kart."

"Ha!" Lucian snorts, his big brown eyes dancing with unholy glee. "Lilith does strike me as the type to spam blue shells and camp the rainbow road shortcuts. Bet she's got Adrian riding bitch in her Princess Peach mobile—"

I level my patented death glare at him, which usually makes even Rhyland think twice.

He clears his throat, trying—and failing—to school his features into something resembling seriousness. "What? Can't a guy appreciate a quality gaming reference while discussing our impending doom? No? Fine. Back to our regularly scheduled crisis."

"Thank you."

He smirks. "But you gotta admit, she does have that Bowser energy—"

"Lucian!" We all shout in unison.

"Fine! Jesus, tough crowd."

"Does she even know what the full stone does?" Brax asks, his Will Ferrell face scrunching in concern as his hat jingles with every head tilt.

"Oh sure, because Lilith strikes me as the type to collect ancient artifacts without reading the instruction manual," Lucian drawls. "Next, you'll ask if Deadpool knows the difference between maximum effort and maximum cleavage. Spoiler alert—he appreciates both equally."

Brax stares at Lucian, Will Ferrell's expressive face frozen in a deadpan glare that looks wildly out of place beneath the jingling elf hat—like Santa's happiest helper just discovered coal in his stocking.

Lucian rolls his eyes, "To cause more chaos, bring her shadow boy-toy—Moldy-Wart, over for a playdate—because being Queen Bitch of the Universe isn't enough. She's probably planning to redecorate the realms in fifty shades of black while she's at it."

Brax shakes his head, bells jingling in a discordant melody. "Moretemis can't be brought over with the stone alone. It doesn't work like that."

"Right. We know she needs a sacrifice—hence Thunder Struck over there." Lucian jerks a thumb at Rhyland. "Pretty sure grandson of a thunder god and premium shadow goddess DNA was listed under 'Special Skills' on her Tinder profile.'"

"No. Not even that can bring him over."

Azrael's words echo in my head—how he needed Rhyland's sacrifice to bring Moretemis through. It makes sense now—Rhyland's blood carries both Asgardian divinity and Olympian darkness—the perfect key to unlock a dimensional nightmare.

But if Brax is saying even that wouldn't work.

What the hell is Lilith really planning?

"The stone doesn't just mimic Dani's portals—it can weave shadow essence between realms," Brax explains grimly. "Unbra isn't just darkness. It's the void behind existence. With the complete stone, Lilith wouldn't pull Moretemis here... she'd merge our realm with his, trapping us all in eternal darkness."

Well, fuck me sideways with a candy cane. Merry Christmas to us.

LUCIAN

76

*L*et's recap this shit, shall we?

Not only does Lilith have a supernatural thirst for our resident Viking, but now we discover she's not trying to import Evil Lord McShadowpants. Oh no—that would be too simple. She's going full "Darkness Falls" and trying to merge our world with the shadow realm.

Because, being an immortal pain in the ass for six millennia wasn't enough of a hobby.

Meanwhile, in our little slice of "Supernatural Home & Garden," the girls are absolutely losing their minds over our Pinterest-worthy Christmas explosion. Seraphina and company are decorating the tree like the universe didn't just drop the mother of all plot bombs.

Nothing says 'apocalypse prep' quite like hanging baubles while discussing the end of all existence.

"Should we be concerned that they're handling potential universal destruction by stress-decorating?" I mutter to no one in particular, watching Emily attempt to untangle lights with murderous determination.

Then again, maybe trimming the tree is cheaper than therapy. And hey, if we're going down, at least we'll go down festive.

Watching Dani blue-screen like a Windows 95 computer? That's a new one. And trust me, I've seen this girl survive more dramatic episodes than a CW series marathon. Kidnapping? She sassed her captors. Torture? Made jokes about their technique. Near-death experiences? Just another Tuesday.

But Adrian's zombie comeback tour? That broke her brain faster than explaining the Marvel timeline to a newcomer.

And speaking of comebacks, who had 'traitorous brother returns from the dead' on their supernatural bingo card?

Why the meltdown, you ask? She's got it in her head that Adrian's death is her fault.

Classic Dani, collecting guilt like Pokemon cards.

And don't even get me started on her soft spot for that backstabbing bookworm. My dear brother may have had the personality of a wet library card, but he still betrayed us harder than Loki on a bad day. Death by heart removal seemed pretty damn fitting if you ask me.

But nooooo.

That's our Dani—heart bigger than her common sense and twice as stubborn. She's got that look in her eyes that says she's about to adopt another lost cause. Mark my words. She will turn this into her personal redemption project faster than you can say "terrible life choices."

"¡Mis amores! ¡La comida está lista!" Rosa's voice carries through the mansion like a warm breeze. Then switches to her 'don't-test-me' tone: "And tell that demon if he comes near my kitchen, I'll beat him with my chancla!"

Ah, Rosa, the only person who can threaten supernatural beings with a sandal and make it sound endearing.

I start to stand when—holy mother of angelic pheromones—Phina's right there, hitting me with that heavenly aroma that makes my undead parts feel very much alive. My arms automatically wrap around, and I can't help the moan that escapes me.

Someone should bottle this scent. We'd make billions. 'Eau de Angel: Make Your Vampire Purr.'

But beneath her sweet exterior, I feel the guilt eating at her like acid. My perfect angel actually believes she's responsible for Lilith harvesting her blood like some twisted supernatural juice cleanse.

Right. Because getting vampire-napped by Fashion Week's Worst Nightmare is totally your fault, baby girl.

Under my sass and snark, I'm plotting murder with extreme prejudice. That couture-wrapped succubus stole my angel's essence and used it like some performance enhancer.

Nobody. Takes. What's. Mine.

My grip tightens around Phina like a protective cocoon of Christmas spirit and sass. "Hey, angel face. None of that sad stuff." I gently tilt her chin up, forcing her to meet my gaze. Those golden eyes, usually brighter than a supernova, now glisten with unshed tears.

Fuck me. Seeing her like this is like watching a unicorn cry. It's just wrong on so many levels.

"This is why we stayed in Atheria," she whispers like she's confessing to starting the Spanish Inquisition. "Why Elysium kept us hidden." Her voice catches like she's trying to swallow a holy hand grenade. "I let her take what we've worked so hard to keep hidden, to—"

"Stop." I thread my fingers through her silky hair, gentle but firm, like handling the world's most precious piece of divine art.

I'll be damned (again) if I let my angel carry this guilt. That's my job, along with making inappropriate jokes and looking fabulous in leather.

"You didn't *allow* her to take anything, Cupcake. That's like saying I *allowed* myself to fall for an angel who's too good for my undead ass." I stroke her cheek with my free hand. "And we both know I was powerless against your celestial charms."

Look at me, being all romantic while maintaining my carefully crafted badass image. Somebody give this vampire an Oscar.

Phina's lower lip trembles and I have the overwhelming urge to kiss away every ounce of sadness. "But Lucian, I—"

"Nuh-uh. No buts, baby girl. Unless we're talking about your perfect angelic ass, in which case, I'm all for it."

There's my girl—that little eye roll means the sass is coming back.

"You're impossible," she huffs, but I catch that hint of a smile.

"Impossibly charming? Devastatingly handsome? Supernaturally gifted in the bedroom?"

Mission accomplished: Operation Make Angel Smile is a success. Now back to our regularly scheduled programming of being hopelessly whipped by a celestial being.

"But now she's using my essence to—" Seraphina starts, a hint of sass breaking through her sadness.

"To dig herself a deeper grave," I finish, pressing my forehead against hers. "Because she just pissed off the wrong vampire and his angelic gorgeous girlfriend."

Who, by the way, looks absolutely edible even when she's sad. Is that wrong? Probably. Do I care? Not even slightly.

"You listen to me, Phina. You are not responsible for that hell-spawned harlot's actions. She's the one who's going to pay, and I'm going to be the one to collect. With interest."

And by interest, I mean I'm going to shove my foot so far up Lilith's ass she'll be coughing up boot leather for a century.

Seraphina's lips curve into a smile that could make the Grinch's heart grow three sizes. "Do you have any idea how ridiculous you look right now, wearing reindeer antlers and trying to be all romantic and sweet?"

God, I love it when she gets sassy. It's like watching a kitten try to roar.

I let out a laugh that's half amusement, half 'kill-me-now' embarrassment. "I probably look like a complete fucking idiot, right? Like Santa's perverted cousin who got banned from the mall for inappropriate comments to the elves?"

Phina reaches up and flicks one of the antlers, her eyes sparkling with that heavenly mischief that makes my dead dick spring to life faster than a jack-in-the-box. "I don't know, I think it's kind of cute. In a 'my boyfriend is a dork, but I love him anyway' sort of way."

Cute? I've killed men for less. But from her? I'll take any damn label she wants to slap on me.

"Well, lucky for you, this dork is all yours, antlers and all." I lean in close enough to inhale her scent. "Though I'd much rather be wearing nothing but your thighs around my neck instead of this holiday bullshit."

Too crude? Not crude enough? The line gets blurry when you're mated to literal divinity.

Seraphina's cheeks flush with a rosy glow that spreads down her neck. Instead of the scandalized gasp, most would expect from an angel, her golden eyes darken with desire. She leans in, her lips brushing against my ear.

"Maybe later," she whispers, her sweet voice carrying a hint of mischief, "you'll get to enjoy the results of that spa appointment I had this morning. Let's just say... your sleigh ride will be extra smooth tonight."

Sweet mother of unholy fuck!

My grin turns absolutely predatory as I pull her closer, my hands sliding down to cup her delicious ass.

"Mmm, why do you think I've been walking around with a semi all afternoon?" I growl against her neck. "Rosa will kill us if we're late for dinner, but after that? I will worship at your altar so thoroughly you'll forget you were ever an angel."

Nothing says 'Christmas spirit' quite like planning to defile celestial perfection. Ho ho ho, indeed.

DANICA

77

Nestled in our corner of the couch, I let myself sink into the moment—the towering Christmas tree casting its multicolored glow across the room, twinkling lights strung everywhere like captured stars. It feels like a lifetime since I've experienced anything remotely normal—just being a family soaking in holiday magic while the world outside threatens to implode.

After dinner, we all waddled outside like a herd of overstuffed penguins to marvel at the guys' handiwork on the house. And holy cow—"spectacular" doesn't even begin to cover it. These guys decided that subtlety is for mortals and went full Clark Griswold on steroids. There are enough lights wrapped around Lucian's mansion to be visible from space.

The neighbors probably need blackout curtains at this point. Or therapy. Maybe both.

I sink deeper into the couch, popping the button on my jeans with zero shame. Rosa's feast has transformed me into a human-shaped food balloon, and I regret nothing. Fashion be damned—this is a stretchy pants situation if I've ever seen one—crispy-skinned duck with that perfect layer of fat beneath, potatoes roasted until golden in duck drippings, and vegetables that somehow made me forget I was eating something healthy. The stack of chocolate chip cookies I demolished afterward didn't help matters.

A contented groan escapes me as I stretch my legs toward the crackling fire. Fat snowflakes tumble from the night sky through the bay windows, illuminated by the outdoor lights like falling stars. The fire pops and hisses in the stone hearth, casting dancing shadows across the room and radiating a warmth that makes my eyelids heavy.

Adrian's resurrection still has my brain in a tailspin. I haven't figured out how to pry him from Lilith's perfectly manicured clutches, but abandoning him to her puppet strings isn't an option. I know Lucian sees only the vampire who killed Sable, totaled his precious car, and kidnapped Seraphina—but beneath Lilith's compulsion is the real Adrian. The same Adrian who taught me everything of who I am and what I'm meant to do, who died trying to make things right.

Emily and Sable are already nose-deep in grimoires, hunting for something to break Lilith's maker bond.

Seraphina settles beside me, balancing a steaming mug of cocoa topped with a ridiculous amount of mini marshmallows. Balanced in her other hand is the ancient text on Pyrothos—the Fire Realm—our next research project in this cosmic scavenger hunt.

"So... ready to dive into the fiery abyss?" Sera asks, her voice honey-sweet despite the ominous text balanced on her knee.

I nod, reaching for the ancient tome. "Might as well get acquainted with hell before we vacation there. Need to know what we're walking into when the time comes."

Lilith may still have half the Soul Stone, but according to Brax, it's like having half a key—dangerous but ultimately useless to bring Moretemis here without its counterpart.

Speaking of our resident demon, his encyclopedic knowledge of Unbra shouldn't surprise me. The Shadow Realm was his playground for millennia before Emily yanked him through the rift. Still, watching Will Ferrell lecture us on interdimensional metaphysics in an elf costume was a cognitive dissonance I'm still processing.

Sera cracks open the ancient tome, releasing a cloud of musty parchment and acrid sulfur that wrinkles my nose. Her fingers dance across the yellowed pages, her eyes flashing gold as she absorbs information at supernatural speed.

"Oh my," she murmurs, her delicate features contorting in distaste. Her finger traces along a particularly ominous illustration of what appears to be a landscape of fire and brimstone. "Pyrothos is essentially what mortals imagine when they think of hell—rivers of molten lava, ash-filled skies, creatures born of flame."

She pauses, eyebrows shooting toward her hairline. "The ruler styles himself as Mephistopheles. Complete with horns and a throne of smoldering brimstone."

"Seriously?" I snort, blowing on my cocoa. "Next, you'll tell me he carries a pitchfork and has a pointy tail."

"He calls himself Abaddon."

"The ruler of the fire realm named himself after the angel of the abyss. What, was 'Satan' already trademarked?"

Seraphina continues her rapid page-turning, the ancient parchment crackling beneath her fingertips. I lean closer, trying to decipher the faded text, when a particular illustration makes me pause.

"Wait—who's that?" I tap the weathered drawing that dominates the page.

The illustration, though centuries old with faded pigments and crumbling edges, shows a woman of unmistakable presence. Even through the artist's primitive techniques, her fiery copper hair seems to writhe like a living flame down her back. Her eyes—rendered in a green so vivid it must have come from crushed emeralds—pierce through time with an unnerving intensity. Her alabaster skin stands in stark contrast against the backdrop of darkness, making her appear to glow from within.

Despite the age of the drawing and its crude lines, something about her face seems disturbingly familiar.

Seraphina's finger traces the faded script beneath the illustration, her brow furrowing as she translates—"According to this passage, she was Abaddon's consort—his 'flame of desire'—the one who escaped him, fled from his... devotion." Her voice drops as she continues reading, the words seemingly catching in her throat.

A chill creeps up my spine as I carefully study the copper-haired woman's face. Those eyes, that cruel set to her mouth—

"Does she have a name? Because she looks eerily similar to—"

Lilith," Seraphina whispers, the name falling from her lips like a stone into still water. Her eyes lift to meet mine, wide with shock. "The ancient text calls her 'Lilith, beloved of the eternal flame' and 'keeper of his darkest desires.'"

"Holy shit." The words escape me in a whisper as my brain scrambles to process this bombshell.

I lunge for my laptop on the coffee table, nearly knocking over my cocoa. My fingers fly across the keyboard, pulling up search engines and academic databases I haven't touched since my research days.

"What are you doing?" Sera peers over my shoulder.

"Fact-checking the apocalypse," I mutter, scrolling through the results.

The screen fills with images and texts—ancient manuscripts digitized by universities, theological forums, and obscure religious texts. I click through to a high-resolution scan from the British Museum—a medieval illuminated manuscript showing a copper-haired woman with a serpent coiled around her arm, standing beside a fallen angel. The Latin caption beneath it makes my stomach drop.

"Look at this," I point to the translation notes. "According to Apocryphal texts, Lilith wasn't just Adam's first wife who refused to submit—after leaving Eden, she became consort to Samael, another name for Lucifer after his fall. This 12th-century text describes Lilith as 'she who followed the Morningstar into exile.' And here—" I navigate to another page, this one from the Dead Sea Scrolls archive, "—references to a female entity who 'abandoned Eden's light for the embrace of the fallen one.'"

Page after page confirms it—scattered throughout ancient texts, hidden in the margins of biblical lore, whispered in apocryphal stories deemed too dangerous for canonical texts—Lilith, the woman who chose darkness, who became consort to Lucifer after his fall from grace.

"Our bougie-bitch vampire nightmare used to date the actual devil," I say, my voice hollow with disbelief. "Because, of course, she fucking did."

Seraphina's eyes widen. "You don't think..." she whispers, glancing between the book and me. "Could Pyrothos actually be what mortals have called Hell all this time? With Abaddon—"

"The original fallen angel," I finish, my mind racing faster than my thoughts can form.

The puzzle pieces click together in my mind, each connection sending little electric shocks through my synapses. I press my fingers to my temples to organize the cosmic revelation unfolding.

"Think about it," I murmur, more to myself than to Seraphina. "Lucifer falls from heaven. He's doing his whole 'prince of darkness' routine when suddenly—bam!—my father seals the realms." I stand up, pacing the small area in front of the Christmas tree. "Consider this—Abaddon has been trapped in Pyrothos this entire time, separated from his flame-haired vampire girlfriend."

I stop abruptly, nearly knocking an ornament off the tree. "And all those stories about the devil's influence on Earth? That wasn't Lucifer at all, but Loki. Two tricksters, different mythologies, same MO."

Wait.

My hand flies to my mouth. "Holy shit, Sera. If Abaddon has been imprisoned all this time, separated from his beloved Lilith—his 'keeper of dark desires'—that's leverage we might be able to use." I tap my fingers against the book's ancient cover. "This isn't a love story—it's a prison break from an ex-boyfriend from literal Hell."

I lean forward, the implications crystallizing. "The last thing she'd want is for—

"We just found her weakness," Seraphina cuts me off, her eyes gleaming with understanding.

I trace the rim of my mug with my fingertip, and the question gnawing at me finally spills out. "Did my father ever mention anything about this? About Pyrothos being Hell or Mephistopheles being Lucifer?"

Seraphina's brow furrows, eyes distant as she searches millennia of memories. "Elysium kept many secrets, even from his celestial servants. Only one specific angel knew of them."

"But we're talking about Elysium here—the actual god of light and creation," I argue, frustration creeping into my voice. "Someone had to have seen something—I mean, kicking angels out of heaven had to be in his job description, right? Or did he have some celestial HR department handling that?"

I mentally kick myself as soon as the words leave my mouth. Seraphina shifts uncomfortably in her seat, and guilt twists in my gut. Real smooth, Dani—bringing up heavenly evictions to the angel who just got her own divine pink slip. Sometimes my mouth runs faster than my brain's ability to apply a filter.

Seraphina takes it in stride, staying on subject. "It doesn't work that way. My sight was limited to you—my charges—not entire realms or their rulers." Her lips press together as she considers. "The higher celestials would occasionally observe, but direct interference was forbidden. They watched, they noted, but they never acted."

The fire pops loudly in the hearth, punctuating the weight of what she's not saying—even gods have their politics and secrets.

"Wait..." Seraphina suddenly stills, her cocoa forgotten in her hands. "I—there was something..." She closes her eyes, face scrunched in concentration like she's trying to recall a dream that's slipping away with wakefulness.

"What is it?" I lean forward, nearly spilling my own drink.

"It's just..." She opens her eyes, looking almost surprised. "In Atheria, we didn't speak of other realms and beings directly. Everything was in metaphors and parables. But there were stories—ancient ones—about a being of pure light who turned against Elysium's divine order."

Her voice drops to a near-whisper. "The Lightbringer, they called him. The most beautiful of all celestial beings, who grew too proud, too ambitious." Her fingers trace invisible patterns on her mug. "I never connected it before, but they said he was banished to a realm where his light would burn as punishment rather than glory."

"Pyrothos," I breathe.

Seraphina nods slowly. "The timing would align—his punishment to rule over a domain of suffering, forever separated from the light he once embodied. Had found his... consort." She hesitates on the word, like it doesn't quite fit. "If that consort was Lilith, and she fled before the sealing..."

"She used my father's action as her escape plan," I finish, the pieces clicking together.

I stare into my cocoa, watching the melting marshmallows swirl as the pieces suddenly lock into place with terrifying precision.

"Holy shit," I breathe, the revelation stealing my voice. "Lilith knew *everything.* The prophecy, Rhyland's role—she turned him deliberately to trigger my father into sealing the realms." My fingers whiten around the mug. "Every calculated move—making Rhyland her first, hunting the Soul Stone—it was all a desperate play to keep herself beyond Mephistopheles' reach."

When I look up, Seraphina's eyes reflect my own dawning horror.

"But she never counted on me," I continue, a dangerous warmth spreading through my chest. "She thought Bryn was the prophesied one, thought she had every contingency covered." My voice strengthens with each word. "Rhyland was always her key—the linchpin to keeping the realms permanently sealed. She needs Pyrothos locked tight, needs her devil ex imprisoned where his wrath can't touch her."

The weight of understanding settles over me. "This isn't about power games or domination for her. This is pure survival."

After dumping our biblical bombshell on the group—Pyrothos being actual, literal Hell and Lilith's spicy ex-boyfriend situation with Satan himself—I collapse into the nearest chair with Rhyland, mentally exhausted from connecting cosmic dots.

Emily doesn't even look up from her grimoire, her rainbow hair falling across her face as she mutters incantations under her breath. When my revelation about Lilith finally registers, her head snaps up.

"Hold the fuck up," she sputters, nearly knocking over her cauldron of foul-smelling herbs. "You're telling me that Bloodwhore used to bump uglies with the actual Devil? Like, pitchfork-and-horns, buy-your-soul Satan?" She slams her hand on the ancient text she's been studying. "Jesus. And I thought *my* dating history was a dumpster fire."

She waves the spell notes she's been working on. "At least I might have something to break Lilith's mind-fuck on Adrian. Though considering we're fighting Satan's ex, I should probably find us a goddamn exorcist on speed dial too."

"Just, here me out," I lean forward, energy buzzing. "She literally ghosted Satan. And according to these texts, he's still carrying one hell of a torch for her. That's leverage we can use."

Emily's eyes roll so hard I'm worried they might get stuck. "So what's the master plan here, boss lady? Slide into Satan's DMs? 'Hey, Big Red, want your ex back? She's currently terrorizing the mortal realm, XOXO'?"

"Wait," Lucian interjects, sprawled across his leather chair like a golden-haired cat. "You're suggesting we pull a 'the enemy of my enemy is Satan' scenario? That's like making a deal with Thanos to stop Dr. Doom from stealing your parking spot. Maximum effort, minimum common sense." He pauses, grinning. "I'm totally in."

Erik's brow furrows. "This explains her obsession with power. She's not just ambitious—she's running scared."

"Still doesn't explain the tacky wardrobe," Emily mutters, flipping another page in her grimoire. "You'd think someone fleeing eternal damnation would try to blend in a little."

Bryn finally speaks up, silently absorbing all this from her perch on the windowsill. "In Ásgard, we have tales of beings who escaped Hel's domain. They never stop looking over their shoulder. They become paranoid, power-hungry—believing only strength can protect them from what they pursue."

"Lilith's entire villainous career has been one long panic attack with a side of world domination," I summarize, leaning into Rhyland's solid warmth. My hand finds his, fingers intertwining. "She orchestrated everything—she knew about the Dark Prophecy, about your role in it. That's why she chose you specifically to turn." I squeeze his hand. "She knew my father would seal the realms to protect them from the dark 'corruption.' Talk about playing the long game—she manipulated a god into becoming her unwitting jailor, keeping her safe from her psychotic ex."

"Calculating bitch," Rhyland growls, his voice a low rumble against my back, fingers tightening possessively on my hip. "She's probably the one who stabbed me on that battlefield, set this whole thing in motion." His blue eyes darken to stormy cobalt. "She's always been a calculating bitch. All that fear, all that desperation...It's been festering into something lethal."

"And here I thought we couldn't possibly add more cosmic fuckery to our plate," Emily sighs dramatically. "First we're collecting magic stones like they're Pokémon badges, now we're caught between vampire Satan's ex and shadow boy. What's next—is the Easter Bunny secretly harboring the Infinity Gauntlet?"

"Don't give the universe ideas," Lucian warns with a smirk. "Though I'd pay good money to see a rabbit try to snap with those fuzzy little paws."

"In all our time with Lilith, she never once mentioned this... connection." Erik's gaze shifts between his brothers. "Did either of you know about this?"

"To be fair," Lucian drawls, "most of our quality time with Mommy Dearest involved either torture, compulsion, or her favorite pastime—watching us tear out throats while she sipped champagne and critiqued our technique."

"Great," Emily mutters, flipping another page with enough force to nearly tear it. "So our options are either let Psycho Vamp use the Soul Stone to unleash literal Darkness or potentially unleash Satan on our world. Fucking fantastic choices."

"Let's be real," Lucian says with exaggerated casualness. "Lilith wasn't exactly a paragon of mental stability *before* we learned about her hellish ex." He shoots a glance at Rhyland. "No offense, brother, but your taste in women has dramatically improved."

"Keep talking shit, asshole. I'm sure Seraphina would love to hear about your Amsterdam phase."

Erik clears his throat, cutting off what promises to be an entertaining but unproductive sibling spat. "The tactical advantage is clear. Lilith fears this entity—"

"Satan," Lucian corrects. "We're on a first-name basis with the Devil now."

"—enough to flee across realms. That fear can be exploited." His silver eyes lock with mine. "However, we should consider that anything powerful enough to terrify Lilith may not be something we wish to encounter."

"So what you're saying is," Brax chimes in, having shifted from Will Ferrell to a perfect copy of Samuel L. Jackson in a Santa hat, "we're stuck between a crazy bitch and a motherfucking devil?"

Lucian pinches the bridge of his nose. "I swear to whatever deity is currently laughing at us, if you keep cycling through my favorite actors, I will stake myself." He eyes Brax's new form with reluctant appreciation. "Though I gotta admit, Samuel L. Jackson in a Santa hat is peak aesthetic. Ten out of ten, no notes."

"What should we do?" Sable asks. "Summon him or something? Can we even do that?"

Emily snorts so hard she nearly chokes on her energy drink. "Oh, brilliant idea! Let's just draw a pentagram, light some black candles, and invite Satan over for tea and crumpets. Maybe afterward, we can all hold hands and sing 'Kumbaya' while the world burns. Fucking hell, Sable."

"No summoning rituals," I interject before this derails further. "We have to go there anyway—to the Fire Realm. I'll speak with Abaddon directly, negotiate for the Fire Stone, and dangle Lilith's whereabouts as an incentive." I shrug like I'm discussing weekend plans instead of a diplomatic mission to literal Hell. "It's a win-win. He gets information about his runaway ex. We get another stone."

RHYLAND

78

We're no closer to extracting Adrian from Lilith's clutches, and now it's Christmas Eve. But we're taking the girls out anyway—I refuse to let that psychotic bitch dictate our lives.

Last week's news hit hard—another massacre, this time at both St. Mary's Home for Children and Hope Haven Youth Center. Lilith's signature work. Her preference for children's blood makes my stomach turn. The fact she did it in broad daylight is a deliberate taunt, a message that she's growing impatient.

The intel from our contacts is even worse. She's weaponized Seraphina's blood. The vampire underground is buzzing—she's dealing it like some twisted narcotic, promising three days of day-walking per dose. Vampires fight each other for a taste, and the body count keeps rising.

Seraphina's been devastated since finding out her blood is being used this way. Dani too. Watching that angel cry over what Lilith's doing with her stolen blood... Let's just say my patience for Lilith's power play is wearing dangerously thin.

The bitch wants a war? She's about to get one.

I head to our bedroom, where Dani prepares for Lucian's Christmas party at Karma. The club's secured, with Dani controlling who enters. We're done hiding—let Lilith try something. My mate's power simmers beneath the surface, and I'm eager to fuck shit up.

Pushing open the bathroom door, I freeze. Dani bends over the counter, applying mascara poured into a skin-tight emerald dress that barely covers her curves. Silver chains cross the open back, and the material catches light with every movement. Her legs extend endlessly in stilettos, and the plunging neckline makes my mouth water.

My cock hardens instantly, straining against my zipper like it's trying to break free and claim what's mine. The animal part of me—the part that's been alive for centuries—wants nothing more than to hike that dress up and bend her over that counter right now.

Mine. Every fucking inch of her is mine.

I stalk up behind her, my hands gripping her hips possessively as I press my hard cock against her barely covered ass. "You trying to make me lose my fucking mind, woman?" I growl, nipping at her earlobe. "Walking around like a goddamn invitation for every male in the club to imagine what's mine?"

Dani smirks, applying her mascara with a steady hand despite my grip. "Aww, is my Fjord Fluff feeling threatened by a little dress?"

I snarl, one hand sliding down to squeeze her thigh. "Threatened? No. But you've lost your mind if you think I'm letting you out of my sight tonight."

She meets my gaze in the mirror, sunkist eyes sparkling. "Careful, Rhy. Your caveman is showing."

Dani pivots away from my touch with a playful swat. "Down, boy. Save the territorial display for after our night out." She turns back to the mirror, applying a final coat of mascara. "Tonight is about forgetting all the chaos waiting for us. Just one evening of normal—well, vampire-normal—Christmas fun."

Her reflection catches my eye as she flashes that smile that always makes my cock twitch. "Besides," she adds, voice dropping to a sultry purr, "half the fun is watching you squirm all night knowing what's waiting under this dress." She smooths her hands down her curves. "Consider it my Christmas gift to you—unwrapping privileges... later."

Fuck. My dick's already rock hard just thinking about what slutty little thing she's got on under that scrap of fabric. She's going to make me suffer all goddamn night, knowing I'm imagining ripping it off her while every other motherfucker in the club undresses her with their eyes.

She knows what she's doing. She's been driving me fucking wild with those visions all week, sending me filthy images of what she plans to do to me. Teasing me with her mouth on my cock, sucking me dry while I fantasize about pounding into her tight, wet pussy. I've been a goddamn gentleman, waiting patiently for her to be ready for more, but I won't hold back tonight.

I grip her hips. "Keep it up—we won't make it to Karma at all."

"Promise?" she laughs, the sound pure temptation as she reaches for her lipstick. "Now, let me finish getting ready before Lucian breaks down our door, complaining we're making everyone late."

"Hey, testosterone squad! Get your immortal asses in here!" Emily's voice echoes through the mansion. "Kitchen. Now. That means you, broody bunch!"

Dani flashes me a smirk in the mirror before I head downstairs to find Emily's got shot glasses lined up like she's planning chemical warfare."Drink up, boys! And I don't want to hear any bitching from the peanut gallery." She's wearing that smirk that usually means we're about to be her guinea pigs.

Erik, Lucian, and I eye our shot glasses with the wariness. "What the fuck is this?" I growl, studying the suspicious amber liquid.

"It's bourbon. With a little something extra." Emily smirks. "Consider it your supernatural vitamin shot."

Lucian, never able to keep his smart-ass mouth shut, snorts loudly, "Oh, goodie, Is this like a witch's version of a Red Bull and vodka? Because the last mystery shot I took turned my piss neon green for a week. Not complaining—it made bathroom graffiti way more efficient—but a guy likes some warning before his bodily fluids start looking radioactive."

I shoot Lucian a death glare. "Can you shut your fucking mouth for five seconds without spewing nonsense?"

Erik, ever the serious one, simply picks up his glass without comment.

With a collective shrug that says we've survived worse, we down our shots in unison. The bourbon hits my system with its usual burn, but there's something else riding shotgun—something that tingles and spreads through my chest like wildfire.

Whatever the hell she put in this better be worth listening to my brother's mouth.

"May the odds be forever in your favor," Emily taunts with a knowing smile.

We enter Karma like royalty returning to court. The club's bass rattles my ribcage as we go to Lucian's VIP section—a space that costs more than most mortals' monthly salary.

Dani leads our procession, her hips swaying hypnotically. That emerald dress barely contains her curves, riding up with each step until the teasing glimpse of her ass nearly undoes me. My fangs throb in perfect rhythm with my hardening cock.

Emily and Sable follow with Brax—wearing some model's stolen face—hovering protectively near Emily. Damon shadows them while Lucian plays the perfect host with Seraphina on his arm.

The club has been transformed into Lucian's winter fantasy—crystal snowflakes suspended from the ceiling, ice-blue lighting wrapping the bar, and holographic snow falling over the dance floor. Even the dancers sport North Pole-inspired outfits that leave little to the imagination.

I'm two seconds from throwing Dani over my shoulder and finding the nearest dark corner. All the blood in my body has migrated south, making rational thought increasingly difficult as I watch that dress inch higher with every step.

The crowd enthusiastically embraces Lucian's holiday fantasy—women in tight red dresses with strategic white fur accents, men sporting open shirts with festive headwear. It's Christmas reimagined through the lens of alcohol and lust—a perfect catalyst for poor decisions and morning-after regrets.

Upstairs, Lucian claims his customary throne, pulling Seraphina onto his lap. He can't take his eyes off his angel—wearing a 'sexy' Santa-inspired outfit that Dani bought for her. Lucian's hand rests possessively on her thigh, his eyes promising swift retribution to anyone foolish enough to look too long.

The irony isn't lost on me. Here we stand—ancient beings who've decimated armies—reduced to territorial watchdogs because our women decided to wear fabric scraps in public. We pretend we had input on tonight's outfits, but that's complete bullshit. These women own us, and they know it.

I drop onto the velvet couch beside Lucian, pulling Dani onto my lap with unnecessary force. Her ass settles against my thigh, her dress riding up to reveal a tantalizing glimpse of inner thigh under the pulsing holiday lights. Across from us, Sable, Emily, Brax, and Damon arrange themselves, but my attention remains fixed on the warm skin beneath my possessive grip.

The waitress appears, takes our orders, then vanishes. My hand climbs higher on Dani's thigh, drawing a soft purr as I trace patterns on her skin. Each shift of her hips against my hardness feels deliberately calculated.

"Pace yourself, babe," she teases through our mental link. *"The night's barely started. Keep those hands where I can see them... for now."*

"I'm going to ruin you tonight—have you begging," I promise, fingers digging into her thigh. *"I'm going to take my time, make you come apart until you're sobbing my name."*

Dani's mental laugh is dark with promise. *"Oh, I'm counting on it, big boy, but first, you'll earn it."* She grinds subtly against me. *"I've got plans that start with you being a very good boy and doing exactly as I say."* Her lips brush my ear. "Think you can handle that... *Daddy?"*

That single word demolishes my restraint. "Angel, you're pushing it," I warn, voice dangerously low. "Keep this up, and I won't be responsible for my actions."

She tilts her head back, fixing me with a seductive gaze. "Mmm, I love when you get all alpha-hole on me." Another deliberate roll of her hips. "Maybe I should keep pushing and see what happens when my Grumpy Bear's control finally snaps."

Her grin turns wicked as she leans in, breath hot against my ear. "Or maybe I'll leave you panting and go find my own fun on the dance floor. Give the crowd a little show and make you watch... *Sir.* "

What the actual fuck has gotten into her tonight?

Does she want me to rip out the throat of every bastard in this place? Because that's precisely what will happen if anyone so much as breathes in her direction.

The waitress delivers our drinks. Dani grabs mine before I can reach it, downing both quickly. She licks her lips slowly at my raised eyebrow.

She springs from my lap with feline grace, grabbing Emily and Sable by the wrists. "Ladies, the dance floor is calling."

With a provocative wink, she saunters away, hips swaying hypnotically. Seraphina follows, ignoring Lucian's warning growl. "Don't start without me!"

I'm halfway up when Lucian's hand clamps my shoulder.

"Down, boy! Let the ladies have their fun," he drawls, lounging back with exaggerated casualness. "Though I gotta say, watching our badass vampire selves get played like fiddles by these women is *chef's kiss* absolutely delicious. Like a rom-com meets True Blood, but with better lighting and way hotter cast." He waggles his eyebrows. "Besides, you know this is just foreplay for them. They're putting on a show, and we're the captive audience. Get it? Captive? Because we're so whipped we can't even—ow! Why are you hitting me?"

I growl, shoving his hand off my shoulder. "Your mouth ever stop running?"

"Only when I'm sleeping. Or dead. Wait, I am dead. There goes that excuse." His eyes follow Seraphina. "Sit down and enjoy the view. They're trying to rile us up."

"I'm going to rile her up," I mutter, watching Dani move to the pounding beat, head thrown back in abandon. "Right over my fucking knee."

Seeing Dani on that dance floor hits me like a storm surge. Same spot. Same fucking lights. Different world.

I remember first seeing her here—all uninhibited movement and joy, unaware of the predator watching from the shadows. She moved like she owned the place, oblivious to how she was rewriting my existence. Something primal in me recognized what my mind couldn't yet grasp—*mine.*

Now, we've come full circle. After battles across realms, blood spilled, and a bond forged through darkness and light, the weight of our journey settles in my chest—both burden and blessing.

She still dances like no one's watching but now knows exactly whose eyes track her every move. Still, that fearless woman who captured my attention now carries divine power in her veins and wears my mark on her soul.

The possessiveness remains but has evolved into something deeper, making even an ancient monster like me feel dangerously close to reverence.

An hour of watching Dani throw back shots and dance provocatively has shredded my patience. The club teems with hungry eyes following her movements, my possessive instincts howling. Seraphina has already returned to Lucian's lap, and Sable and Damon practically devour each other nearby. Emily and Brax remain with my mate, both drawing an appreciative crowd.

I'm done watching.

RHYLAND

79

In a blur of movement, I'm behind her on the dance floor, pressing my erection against the curve of her ass. My fingers tangle in her sweat-dampened hair, yanking her head back to expose the delicate column of her throat. "Had enough yet?" I grumble against her ear, the bass vibrating through both our bodies.

Her response is to reach behind her, palm sliding over the rigid outline of my cock through my pants. "Not even close," she slurs, eyes glazed with alcohol and defiance.

The scent of whiskey rolls off her in waves. She's beyond tipsy—she's fucking wasted. Decision made. I spin her around and hoist her over my shoulder, clamping one hand over her thighs to preserve what little modesty her dress allows.

She erupts in wild laughter against my back. "Caveman!" she calls loudly enough for nearby dancers to stare. Her drunken laughter is half challenge, half delight.

She protests halfheartedly as I carry her toward the private bathrooms. If she wants to play games and push boundaries, I'll show her what happens when they break. Besides, my little exhibitionist has always thrived on the thrill of potential discovery.

I kick through the bathroom door, depositing her on the marble counter with minimal gentleness. The lock clicks decisively before I return to her. She's still orienting herself, pushing tangled hair from her flushed face.

That smile—half challenge, half invitation—lights up her features. The fierce woman who's faced down gods and monsters looks at me with eyes that promise both heaven and hell. The pride that surges through me at who she's become nearly derails my mission, but my throbbing cock reminds me we have unfinished business.

"Impatient much?" she taunts, words still slightly slurred.

I don't dignify that with a response. Actions speak louder than words.

I shove her dress up, exposing her to the cold marble. In one motion, I hook her legs over my forearms and drag her to the counter's edge. Her red lace panties—a deliberate provocation—are soaked through. I yank the fabric aside rather than waste time removing it.

The sight of her glistening center has my fangs threatening to descend. She's drenched—all that dancing and teasing has left her ready. I drop to my knees, finding her swollen bud with practiced ease—giving her slow, deliberate circles—gentle torture after a week of her pushing my limits.

Her sharp gasp is all the encouragement I need.

I devour her like a starving man, groaning as her unique flavor floods my senses—sweet nectar mixed with salt, creating an intoxicating combination that drives me past the point of control. My growl vibrates against her sensitive flesh as her fingers tangle in my hair, nails scraping my scalp. Her legs spread wider, stilettos digging into my shoulders through my shirt.

I torture her with open-mouthed kisses around her clit, deliberately avoiding direct contact while my hands keep her thighs spread wide, exposing her completely to my hungry mouth. The vulnerability of her position—splayed open on a public bathroom counter—only heightens our arousal.

"Oh, god, Rhyland..." Her voice breaks on my name, head falling back against the mirror.

"Fuck. I missed this, baby. This pussy." I drag my tongue around her swollen bud before attacking it with rapid flicks that have her hips bucking against my face. Two fingers slide into her wet petals, curling upward to find that spot that makes her see stars. Her inner walls clench around my digits as I work her mercilessly.

She's absolutely drenched, her arousal coating my fingers as they pump into her relentlessly. The obscene wet sounds of her pussy taking my fingers echo off the marble walls, competing with her increasingly desperate cries. Her voice rises above the muffled bass from the club, uninhibited and raw.

"Fuck! Rhyland...yes...yes...right there...oh, GOD!"

The bathroom's acoustics amplify every sound—A private concert of pleasure that feeds my primal satisfaction.

I groan against her sensitive flesh as she chants my name like a prayer, the vibration making her thighs tremble against my face. My tongue works her swollen clit while my fingers curl inside her, stroking that sweet spot over and over. Her thighs shake, her back arching off the mirror as she reaches the edge.

Then she shatters spectacularly, her inner walls clamping down on my fingers with bruising force as she releases a flood of arousal that catches even me by surprise. "Goddamn, baby. That's it," I growl, not missing a drop as she squirts against my mouth and chin.

I drink her down greedily, my tongue working to catch every bit of her release as she continues to convulse around my fingers. Her entire body trembles with aftershocks, fingers painfully tight in my hair as she rides out the intensity of her orgasm.

The scent of her pleasure fills the small space, marking it as ours more effectively than any territorial display.

I don't give her a moment to recover. I yank her off the counter and spin her around to face the mirror in one fluid motion.

Her dress disappears over her head, revealing what she'd been hiding underneath—a sinful red lace teddy with strategic white bows like she'd gift-wrapped herself for me. The Christmas-themed lingerie confirms this was all planned, the little minx.

I roughly tug the lace down, freeing her heavy breasts to spill into my waiting hands. Her eyes meet mine in the mirror—glazed with both alcohol and desire—as I capture her soft flesh in my palms, kneading with just enough force to border on pain. Her nipples harden to stiff peaks as I roll them between my fingers, twisting just enough to make her gasp.

"I love my present, baby," I growl, my lips finding that sensitive spot where her neck meets her shoulder. I bite down hard—no fangs, just teeth—marking her without breaking skin. Her whole body shudders in response. "But I'm done waiting to unwrap it."

With one hand between her shoulder blades, I bend her forward until her bare breasts press against the cold marble countertop. The sudden temperature change pulls a startled grunt from her lips, her heated skin pebbling instantly against the cool surface. The position presents her perfect ass to me, still barely covered by a scrap of red lace.

The mirror offers me the perfect view of her flushed face, her parted lips, and the way her breasts flatten against the marble—a visual feast that has me nearly tearing my pants in my haste to free myself.

I palm her soaked pussy, gathering her cum and coating my painfully hard cock with it. The contact makes her whimper, her hips instinctively pushing back against my hand.

"Rhyland...please." Her voice is desperate, needy—music to my ears.

"Begging already, baby?" I taunt, stroking myself with her slickness, making sure I'm thoroughly coated with her arousal. The head of my cock nudges at her entrance, teasing us both with what's to come. "What happened to all that attitude from the dance floor?"

I push forward slowly, inch by torturous inch. My eyes slam shut at the overwhelming sensation of her tight heat enveloping me. Every muscle in my body tenses with the effort of restraint as her pussy grips me like a vise, threatening to end this before it begins. A controlled breath hisses through my clenched teeth as I fight for control.

Fucking shit. After all this time, she still feels impossibly tight, like she was made for me and me alone. At this rate, I'll be lucky to last more than a few strokes before emptying myself inside her.

I drive forward with one powerful thrust, burying myself balls deep inside her. The sound that tears from her throat is pure sin—half moan, half sob.

"Goddamn, baby," I grunt, snapping my hips forward with enough force to drive her against the counter edge. The marble digs into her soft flesh, marking her in another way. The impact draws a sharp gasp from her lips, but her eyes in the mirror tell me everything I need to know—she wants more.

"Harder. Please. Fuck. Me." Each word punctuated by desperate pants as her honey-gold eyes lock with mine in our reflection, challenging me, begging me.

Christ.

My cock throbs dangerously inside her, already threatening to explode. The sight of her—flushed and begging, bent over in a public bathroom—is almost too much.

I gather her long, thick hair in my fist, wrapping it around my hand until I've fashioned a makeshift handle. I pull her head back with a sharp tug, arching her spine into a beautiful curve. "Yeah? You want to get *fucked*, baby? Is that what all this teasing was about?"

"Yes!" The word bursts from her mouth, desperate and raw.

Something takes over. I hammer into her with punishing force, using her hair like reins to control her movements. Each thrust drives her forward, only for me to yank her back onto my cock. The brutal pace has the counter shaking, her breasts bouncing with every impact as obscene wet sounds fill the air between us.

My breathing remains measured and deep—a warrior's discipline keeping my impending release at bay. One hand grips her hip with bruising intensity while the other maintains its firm hold on her hair, keeping her arched and exposed. I bring my palm down hard against her ass cheek, the sharp crack of skin on skin punctuating our rhythm. The flesh reddens instantly beneath my hand, a mark she'll feel tomorrow.

"Oh *god—yes!*" she cries out, her voice breaking with each thrust. "Don't stop, Rhy—please! Harder! I need—I need—" Her words dissolve into incoherent moans as her fingers scramble for purchase on the slick marble. Her eyes find mine in the mirror, glazed but challenging. "You promised to ruin me—so fucking ruin me already."

Her filthy words shoot straight to my cock. I lean forward, my chest pressing against her back as I growl directly into her ear.

"You want to be ruined, Angel? I'll fucking ruin you. This tight little cunt is mine," I snarl, punctuating each word with a brutal thrust. "You can tease me all you want, dance for every fucker in that club, but at the end of the night, it's my cock splitting you open. My name, you're screaming. And my cum you're begging for."

Her whimpers fuel my frenzy as I continue my relentless assault, the sound of flesh meeting flesh echoing off the bathroom walls. But I need more—need to feel her convulsing around me before I surrender to my release.

"Play with that pretty clit, baby. Make a fucking mess. I'm close," I command, voice strained with the effort of holding back.

Dani obeys without hesitation, her hand snaking between her body and the counter to find her swollen bud. The moment her fingers make contact, she gasps sharply. "Oh, fuck!"

"Yeah? Come on, baby," I encourage, my pace becoming brutal, unforgiving. "Come on this cock, Angel." Each impact sends ripples through the soft flesh of her ass, the visual only driving me closer to the edge.

Her body goes rigid suddenly, a strangled cry tearing from her throat as she shatters around me. Her release is violent and messy—a flood of arousal gushing around my cock, drenching both of us and running down her trembling thighs. The evidence of her pleasure only heightens my own.

"Fuck!" The word is ripped from my chest as her inner walls clamp down on me. Her screams of ecstasy fill the small space, probably audible even over the club's pounding music. I manage just two more desperate thrusts before I'm done, emptying myself deep inside her with a primal grunt, my fingers digging into her flesh hard enough to leave marks.

The simple satisfaction of marking her from the inside only intensifies my pleasure as I continue to pump into her, drawing out both our climaxes until there's nothing left to give.

I withdraw from her with reluctance, satisfaction coursing through me at the sight of my cum slowly trickling down her inner thigh. She moans at the emptiness, the sound triggering something possessive in me. I slip my fingers back inside her still-pulsing entrance, needing to maintain the connection. Her body responds with a weak whimper.

Christ. I'm utterly addicted to this woman—to every sound she makes, every reaction I can wring from her body. The sight of my seed marking her from the inside out has become a particular obsession I'm not interested in fighting.

I spin her to face me, pressing my slick fingers against her lips. She takes them hungrily into her mouth, moaning as she tastes our combined essence. Her tongue swirls around my digits as they slide knuckle-deep into her throat. When I withdraw them, I crush my mouth to hers, both of us groaning as we share the intimate flavor of our passion.

I break the kiss and stare down at her, my cock still rock-hard and throbbing with each heartbeat. The mixture of her release and mine coats my length—slick, pearlescent streaks that glisten under the bathroom lights. Her sexy, golden eyes are dark pools of hunger, pupils blown wide with lust, lips red and swollen from my rough treatment.

"You got a mess to clean up, baby," I purr, voice rough with need.

I need those beautiful fucking lips stretched around me right now. She's been teasing me all goddamn week, and my patience is officially gone. Time to claim every inch of what's mine—every filthy, depraved act she's been promising with those knowing looks. I'm done with the waiting game. Tonight, I take everything.

That wicked smirk crosses her face—the one that makes my cock jerk against my stomach. Without a word, she pushes me up against the wall and sinks to her knees on the hard tile. Her long hair falls in wild waves around her flushed face as she looks up at me through those thick lashes—a goddess on her knees, but every bit as powerful as when she stands.

The first touch of her soft tongue against my sensitive head sends electricity shooting up my spine. She moans as she tastes our combined essence, the vibration traveling through my cock like a current, making my abs clench and breath catch.

"Jesus..." The word falls between us as she takes me fully into her scorching mouth.

Every nerve ending screams with oversensitivity, her tongue mapping every ridge and vein with meticulous attention. The sight of her swallowing me whole, has my cock swelling impossibly harder. I can feel her saliva mixing with the remnants of our passion, creating new slickness that drips obscenely down my length and onto her lucious tits.

I tangle my fingers in her silky brown hair, establishing my grip to guide her movements until my cock hits the back of her throat.

"Fuck...baby," I hiss through clenched teeth. "Your mouth was made for my cock."

She releases me with a lewd pop, moving lower to trace my sac with her hot tongue before taking one ball into her mouth. The gentle suction creates a pulling sensation that settles like molten lead in my core.

"That's it, baby," I pant. "Show me how much you love the taste of us."

Her bewitching honey-gold eyes never leave mine as she attempts to take both balls into her mouth, stretching her lips obscenely wide. When she returns to my shaft, her throat opens—a tight, rippling channel that massages my length with each swallow.

Her nails dig into my thighs, leaving crescent marks as tears gather at the corners of her eyes from taking me so deep, making her irises shimmer like sunlight through whiskey.

The pressure becomes unbearable. I grip her hair tighter as my hips thrust of their own accord.

"Such a good little cocksucker," I growl, hips snapping forward. "Teasing me all fucking night just to end up choking on my dick in a public bathroom."

She moans around my length, eyes watering as I hit the back of her throat.

"Wanted everyone to see what's mine," I snarl, feeling my release building. "But this view is just for me—the realm's savior on her knees, desperate for my cum."

My cock swells as I reach the point of no return.

"Gonna flood that pretty throat now," I command, voice rough with lust. "Swallow every fucking drop or I'll bend you over again and fuck that tight cunt until you can't walk straight."

The orgasm rips through me with brutal force. I hold her head firmly in place as I empty myself down her throat.

"*Fucking*. Shit. Drink it all down, baby—like a good girl," I growl, grinding against her face. "Wear my cum inside you while we go back out there. Let everyone see those fucked-out lips and know exactly what you've been doing."

"Mmpphh" her eyes flutter as her arousal spikes.

She loves it when I'm a filthy-mouthed bastard—talking pure sin—gets her soaking wet when I stake my claim, marking her as mine inside and out. I'm the alpha who knows exactly how to own her body while cherishing the fire in her soul.

Yeah, she's my fierce little warrior queen out there, but right now? She craves my dominance, needs my hands pinning her down while I tell her exactly who she belongs to. That primal part of me that wants to bite, claim, and fuck her until she can't remember her own name? That's what makes her thighs shake and her eyes roll back.

She's mine to protect, mine to pleasure, mine to fucking worship—and we both know it.

She swallows rhythmically, her throat massaging my sensitive head with each gulp. When she finally pulls back, her lips are red and puffy, her eyes glazed with arousal, chin glistening with evidence of her efforts.

She wipes her mouth with the back of her hand, a smug smile playing on those perfect lips. "Mmm... you taste good." she moans, voice raspy from the abuse her throat just endured.

"Not as good as you." I haul her to her feet, crushing her mouth to mine in a searing kiss, tasting myself on her tongue.

The sudden creak of a bathroom stall door shatters our private moment. A woman stumbles out—in her early twenties, pupils dilated, clearly riding some chemical high. Her unfocused gaze travels over our disheveled state with open appreciation.

"Damn, you two are *fucking* intense," she slurs, leaning against the wall for support. "Room for one more in this party?"

Dani gasps, straightening so quickly she nearly loses her balance. Her hands fumble to pull the lacy material back over her exposed breasts while I hastily tuck myself back into my jeans, fury rising in my chest.

"Get the fuck out before I throw you out," I snarl, not bothering to mask the predatory edge in my voice.

The threat lands precisely as intended. Fear sobers her instantly, color draining from her face as she scrambles for the exit, nearly tripping in her haste to escape.

Once the door slams shut, I turn back to find Dani—still flushed and disheveled—dissolving into laughter.

"Well," she manages between giggles, "that's one way to end the night with a bang."

I shake my head, unable to suppress my smirk. My exhibitionist mate got precisely what she wanted, even if our audience wasn't planned.

"You're fucking trouble, you know that?"

She smirks and it's pure sin. "You wouldn't have it any other way."

And goddamn it, she's right.

DANICA

80

I shimmy back into my dress—all cleaned up—tugging the emerald fabric over my curves as I throw Rhyland a mischievous smirk. "What's with you and bathroom nookie, sexy buns? This is becoming a pattern. First, the bathroom at Playful Pint, now here—should I be worried you have some public restroom fetish I should know about?"

Rhyland's eyes darken as he steps into my space, backing me against the counter with one powerful arm caging me in. His bearded jaw grazes my cheek as he leans down, voice a dangerous rumble against my ear.

"What can I say, baby? Something about watching you get all prim and proper after I've had you screaming my name with your dress around your waist." His fingers trace the neckline of my dress, just barely skimming the swell of my breast. "Besides, Angel, you're the one who started this little game. Don't act like you don't get off on the possibility of getting caught."

"Fine, you caught me," I purr, batting my eyelashes with exaggerated innocence. "I have a thing for my man getting all territorial in public. I mean, who wouldn't get hot and bothered watching you go all alpha hole?" I trail a finger down his chest, my smile turning devilish. "Besides, what's the point of having a centuries-old sex god for a mate if I can't make other women cry with envy? Consider it my contribution to public entertainment—spreading sexual frustration one bathroom quickie at a time."

Rhyland's laugh rumbles deep in his chest, a sound that's equal parts amusement and dark promise. His eyes darken to that dangerous midnight blue as he presses me harder against the counter, the marble edge digging into my back. "You're one kinky little minx, you know that?" His hand slides possessively up my thigh, leaving a trail of fire in its wake. "Just when I think I've got you figured out, you pull something like this." His fingers dig into my flesh with delicious pressure. "Making me want to do very, *very* bad things to you."

I arch an eyebrow, smirking. "What can I say? A girl's got to keep her thousand-year-old Viking on his toes." I lean in close, letting my breath ghost over his ear as I whisper, "Besides, your 'bad things' are my *favorite* things. So really, we both win."

"Fuck, Angel," he groans, his eyes dancing with wicked amusement. "A millennium on this earth, and you're still the only one who can make me lose my damn mind." His thumb traces my bottom lip, his gaze following the movement. "And enjoy every second of it."

I smile, hooking my fingers through his belt loops. "Well, let's put that millennium of experience to good use." I tug him toward the door with a deliberate sway of my hips. "Because this dance floor isn't going to set itself on fire, and I've got plans for you that don't involve hiding in bathrooms all night." I throw him a saucy wink over my shoulder. "Though I thoroughly enjoyed our little... intermission."

Warmth surrounds me as consciousness returns. Rhyland's muscled arm drapes heavily across my waist, his breath steady against my neck. The goosedown blanket whispers with each slight movement, a cocoon of softness around our tangled limbs. His morning wood presses insistently against the curve of my ass, a reminder that some parts of him never truly rest.

Embers pop and hiss in the stone fireplace, casting amber shadows across the room. Beyond the frost-etched windows, snow falls in thick, silent curtains, transforming the world into a pristine white canvas. A Christmas card scene come to life.

I smile, remembering last night—Rhyland's hands possessively gripping my hips on the dance floor, his body moving perfectly with mine. His eyes darken—watching me, that predatory intensity making my skin tingle. For a man who claimed to hate dancing, the way he'd rolled his hips against mine told a different story. The memory alone sends heat pooling low in my belly.

After our bathroom encounter, I'd practically had to bite my tongue to keep from dragging him back for round two. My body still bears the evidence of our passion—delicious soreness between my thighs, faint bruises blooming where his fingers had gripped too hard.

I arch my back slightly, pressing against his hardness, feeling him stir in response.

His arm tightens around my waist, pulling me closer against the hard planes of his chest. Lips brush the sensitive spot where my neck meets my shoulder, sending shivers cascading down my spine.

"Mmm," I murmur, nuzzling closer.

Rhyland's kisses grow more deliberate, trailing up my neck to the sensitive spot behind my ear. His beard scrapes deliciously against my skin, the slight sting only heightening the sensation. His hand slides up from my waist, palm warm as it cups my breast, thumb circling lazily over my nipple until it pebbles beneath his touch.

"Merry Christmas, Angel," he rumbles, voice still rough with sleep. His morning voice—that deep, gravelly sound—never fails to make my stomach flutter. His cock presses more insistently against me as he rocks his hips forward.

His other hand sweeps my hair aside, exposing more of my neck to his attention. "Best Christmas morning I've had in centuries," he murmurs against my skin between kisses. "Waking up with you in my arms... nothing compares."

I turn in his embrace, needing to see his face. Morning sunlight filtering through the snow-frosted windows catches in his ocean-blue eyes, making them glow like sapphires. His black hair stands in adorable sleep-mussed spikes, and the sight of him—powerful, ancient warrior with bed head—makes my heart squeeze in my chest.

"Merry Christmas," I whisper back, reaching up to trace the bearded line of his jaw.

His eyes darken at my touch, pupils dilating. Without warning, he rolls me onto my back, his powerful body caging mine against the mattress. The blanket slides away, cool air kissing my skin for just a moment before Rhyland's heat envelops me again.

"I have a present for you," he murmurs, lips hovering above mine.

"I can feel that," I tease, shifting my hips against his obvious arousal.

A wicked smile curves his mouth. "Not that. Though that's yours whenever you want it." He reaches over to the nightstand, muscles flexing beneath his tattooed skin.

His jaw is set with purpose when he turns back, but his eyes betray everything.

"I've walked this earth for over a thousand years," he states, voice deep and unwavering. "I've conquered enemies, ruled territories, and amassed more wealth than most kingdoms. I thought I had everything I could possibly need."

His hand emerges with a small midnight-blue velvet box, fingers curling possessively around it.

"Then you crashed into my existence and proved me wrong."

My breath catches, a lump forming in my throat as he continues.

"Before you, I was just... surviving. Moving through time without purpose, without true connection." His voice breaks slightly. "You didn't just walk into that club that night, Dani. You walked into my soul and lit up every dark corner I'd forgotten existed."

He opens the box with trembling fingers. Inside nestles a ring that steals my breath—a brilliant oval diamond surrounded by sapphires that match his eyes perfectly, set in intricate white gold that resembles ancient Norse knotwork.

"Our souls are already bound in ways no human ceremony could match," he says, voice dropping. "But you deserve everything, Angel. And I intend to give it to you."

His calloused thumb brushes away a tear I didn't realize had fallen. "You faced down gods and monsters without flinching. You've seen the darkness in me and claimed it as your own. You are mine in every way that matters across all realms."

He takes the ring from its velvet nest, holding it between us like a vow. "I want the world to know it, too. I want to watch you walk down that isle in white, wearing my mark, my ring for everyone to see. I want to claim you in the human way, just as I've claimed you in every other."

Tears spill freely down my cheeks now, but I don't look away from the fierce determination in his gaze.

"I know it's traditional, maybe even cliché," he says with a soft, self-deprecating laugh. "But after a millennium of darkness, I find myself desperately wanting these human moments with you. Will you marry me, Angel? Make this ancient, broken vampire the happiest man across all seven realms?"

A sob escapes me, joy so intense it feels like physical pain blooming in my chest. This man—this dominant, protective force of nature—demands my answer while offering me his immortal heart.

"Yes," I manage through tears, my hands clutching at his shoulders. "God, Rhyland, yes, yes. A thousand times, yes!"

Rhyland's smile blazes brighter than any light I've ever created—those damn dimples making my heart stutter in my chest. His hands, capable of wielding lightning and devastating enemies, are impossibly gentle as he slides the ring home. The metal feels warm against my skin, like it's always belonged there.

"Mine," he growls against my knuckles, pressing a kiss there that brands me straight to my soul. His voice carries centuries of possessiveness, wrapped in tender devotion. "Now and for all eternity."

"Yours," I whisper back, my heart so full it might burst. I press my forehead to his, feeling that electric connection spark between us. "I'll always be yours—I love you, you beautiful, brooding, towel-dropping disaster of a Viking."

His answering laugh rumbles through his chest, but his eyes—those ocean-deep eyes that first captured my heart—shine with such profound happiness that it makes my throat tight. In this moment, he's not the thousand-year-old warrior or Thor's grandson. He's just my Rhyland, looking at me like I've given him every star in the sky.

He claims my mouth in a tender and demanding kiss, the taste of salt mingling with the familiar heat of his lips. When we finally break apart, both breathless, he presses his hand over my heart, a gesture of possession and protection.

"You remade me," he states, the words an unbreakable vow. "Everything I am belongs to you."

I cover his hand with mine, feeling our hearts beat in perfect synchrony. "And everything I am belongs to you."

That signature smirk plays across Rhyland's lips as his eyes darken with hunger. "Now I'm going to give my *fiancée* a proper Christmas," he growls. His hand slides up my thigh, leaving goosebumps in its wake. "But first—" he pauses, his gaze raking over me with such intensity I swear I can feel it like a physical touch. His eyes linger on my breasts, my hips, the apex of my thighs, claiming ownership of every inch. "—I need my damn breakfast."

The diamond on my finger catches the morning light, sending prisms dancing across his tattooed chest as he descends my body with single-minded purpose. There's nothing gentle in his movements—he stalks down my form like the apex predator he is, all coiled muscle and barely leashed power. His beard scrapes deliciously against my sensitive skin, the slight tickle only heightening my awareness of every touch.

His mouth blazes a trail of hot, demanding kisses along my stomach, each press of his lips a brand of ownership. He nips at my hip bone, soothing the sting with his tongue before continuing his journey southward. My fingers tangle in his sleep-mussed black hair, not guiding but simply holding on as he takes exactly what he wants.

"All mine," he rumbles against my inner thigh, the vibration of his deep voice sending shivers straight to my core. His hands grip my legs with firm insistence, spreading me open to his hungry gaze. His thumbs press into the sensitive flesh, leaving marks that will bloom into bruises later—a reminder of this moment that I'll secretly trace throughout the day.

He pauses, looking up the length of my body, and the expression on his face makes my heart stutter in my chest. There's raw devotion there, a soul-deep connection that transcends the physical, but it's tempered with such carnal intent that my breath catches. His eyes hold mine captive as he lowers his head, the first touch of his tongue making me gasp.

"Mmm—so fucking sweet, baby," Rhyland whispers against my core, his breath like a feather-light caress on my sensitive skin. His tongue swirls out in a slow, deliberate lick, starting at the entrance to my aching core and lazily making its way up to the swollen peak of my clit. "Marinated in my cum all night, making your perfect little pussy taste even better for me."

Holy hell.

My beautiful, savage beefcake. Here he is, finding new ways to set me on fire with that sinfully talented mouth of his, casually reminding me how thoroughly he wrecked me just hours ago—how the evidence of our wild night is still sealed inside me like his own personal brand.

He's absolutely unhinged, completely shameless, and I'm addicted to every single filthy word that comes out of that gorgeous mouth. He could teach a masterclass in dirty talk, and I'd be first in line to enroll.

He devours me, his tongue alternating between teasing flicks and deep, penetrating thrusts. His strong hands hold my thighs apart when they begin to tremble, refusing to let me close myself to his morning feast. When his lips close around my clit and suck with perfect pressure, I cry out.

Outside our window, snow falls in gentle, silent flurries, transforming the world into a pristine white canvas. The morning light filters through the frost-etched glass, casting an ethereal glow across our tangled forms. Such a stark, beautiful contrast—the peaceful winter wonderland beyond our walls and the consuming heat between us.

My delicious, sinful, man. Who's walked the earth for over a millennium, now worships between my thighs with the devotion of someone who's found his salvation. I never imagined this kind of happiness existed—this perfect blend of soul-deep connection and physical bliss. The engagement ring glitters on my finger as I grip his hair, a tangible symbol of the immortal heart I've somehow captured.

I smile even as a moan escapes me. From feared vampire warlord to my fiancé in just a few short months—who would have thought? But as his wicked tongue drives coherent thought from my mind, I can't help but think I'm the real winner in this arrangement.

Merry Christmas to me, indeed.

"**H**oly shit!" Lucian rips into the wrapping paper like a caffeinated raccoon on meth. "No fucking way..." He cradles the limited edition Iron Man Mark 85 helmet like he's just discovered the holy grail of nerdgasms. "Only 100 of these cock-loving beauties exist in the entire shit show we call Earth!"

He vibrates on the couch cushion, making Seraphina facepalm beside him. "Rhy-Rhy, you beautiful brooding thunder-fuck! Did you have to murder someone for this? Please tell me there was murder. Or at least some light maiming? I bet Erik went all 'grr-face' on some poor nerd. Give me the dirty details, you sexy Scandinavian snack!"

I snort-laugh as he jams the helmet on his head, the electronic eyes lighting up. "Friday, baby girl, do these circuits make my ass look fat? Quick, someone get me a cheeseburger and my collection of daddy issues! I'm about to science the shit out of this Christmas!"

Rhyland looks like he's questioning every life choice that led to this moment. "I'm starting to think staking you would've been easier."

"Too late, no take-backsies, you magnificent bastard! This bad boy and I are now eternally bound. Like you and Hot Pants over there, except with less bow-chic-ka-wow-wow and more awesome. Now, who wants to help me recreate the Battle of New York? I call dibs on being Iron Man—Erik can be the Hulk. He's got the emotional constipation down pat!"

With a shimmer of demonic energy, Brax transforms into a perfect copy of Chris Hemsworth's Thor, complete with rippling muscles and flowing golden locks. "I say thee YAY! Let us commence this glorious battle, Man of Iron!"

"Hey, fuck-face," Lucian snaps, though his helmet stays firmly in place. "Last I checked, Comic-Con isn't until March—just because you can shape-shift doesn't mean you get to horn in on my Marvel moment. This is MY emotional Christmas breakthrough, you demon-shaped dick waffle. Thor doesn't say 'yay' like some basic bitch at Starbucks."

Brax grins, swinging an imaginary Mjolnir. "Another!"

"Sweet Jesus, you're killing me. This is worse than that time Erik tried to smile—actually, no, nothing's worse than that. Quick, do Cap instead. At least then, I can mock your star-spangled ass properly. And Erik can be the Winter Soldier; he's already got the whole 'I-haven't-pooped-in-seventy-years' face."

I can't help but snicker as Lucian and Brax's Marvel showdown steals the spotlight. Trust these two to turn Christmas morning into their personal Comic-Con.

The entertainment screeches to a halt when Erik—our resident champion of stoicism—produces an elegantly wrapped package for Bryn. The paper shimmers silver because heaven forbid Erik do anything without perfect precision.

"Look who's embracing the Christmas spirit," I whisper to Rhyland, nudging him with my elbow. "Never thought I'd see the day."

But my teasing fades as Bryn unwraps a stunning music box. It's crafted from ancient silver and crystal, with intricate Nordic designs that seem to move in the firelight. When she opens it, a melody fills the room—haunting and beautiful, like wind through mountain peaks. Inside, two figures dance, their forms crafted with impossible detail—a warrior and his love, eternally spinning to their private symphony.

"It's the song from our first dance," Erik says quietly. "I memorized every note that night and transcribed the sheet music myself. I found a master craftsman in Portland who specializes in custom music boxes. " His fingertips hover reverently over the box, almost afraid to touch it. "Spent two weeks working with him to capture the exact cadence—the way it echoed through the Cloud Palace halls when you first let me hold you."

I've never heard Erik's voice carry such emotion before. The man who calculates battle strategies with cold precision, revealing the soul of a composer hidden beneath that warrior exterior.

I set my coffee mug down, emotion catching in my throat as the music box's melody fills our living room. The same haunting tune played that night at the Cloud Palace ball when Erik finally let his guard down and asked Bryn to dance. I remember watching them from Rhyland's arms, seeing the usually stoic vampire transform as he held her.

Of course, my brooding brother-in-law would use music to express what his reserved nature rarely allows him to say. The melody wraps around us all, a reminder that beneath that icy exterior beats the heart of a musician who spent centuries collecting songs and stories.

I think back to our time in Aquaria, the memory as vivid as if it happened yesterday. Erik standing in that shimmering Siren's cave, his silver eyes scanning those ancient musical notations with perfect understanding. While the rest of us stood baffled, he not only recognized the complex melody but reproduced it flawlessly with his voice, unlocking secrets none of us could access. That quiet, unexpected talent saved us when we needed it most.

Watching him now with Bryn, I see that same depth—the layers beneath his hard exterior that most never see. His gift isn't just strategy or combat; it's his ability to observe, collect, and preserve what matters. He's archived centuries of knowledge, music, and art in that brilliant mind of his, and now he's using it to immortalize something precious for the woman he loves.

The way Bryn's eyes shine with tears, the tender way Erik watches her—it's enough to make my heart melt.

"Wow." I murmur, swallowing the lump, "Someone's definitely getting their stocking stuffed tonight."

"I heard that," Erik mutters without breaking eye contact with Bryn.

"That's what happens when you have vampire hearing, Mr. Stoic." I wink at Bryn, who's trying—and failing—to hide the tears in her eyes as the music box plays their song.

"Well, shit," Lucian declares, clutching his Iron Man helmet to his chest. "Look at you, Silver-Studded Sulker, making us all catch feelings. What's next—you gonna start a poetry slam? Write some emo lyrics? Quick, someone get me a gift before Erik's romantic side gives me fucking hives!"

I nearly choke on my coffee, watching Erik's eye twitch while Bryn tries to hide her smile behind the music box.

I lean forward in anticipation as Lucian hands Seraphina a perfectly wrapped box—which is suspicious enough, considering this is the same vampire who usually throws gifts in Halloween-themed gift bags because "Christmas paper is too mainstream."

"Before you open it, Cupcake," Lucian announces, bouncing like a kid who's had too much sugar, "just remember that if Erik can be a romantic little bitch, then I can too."

Sera unwraps the gift carefully (because, of course, she does—angels apparently never rip paper), revealing a custom-made snow globe. But not just any snow globe. Inside, there's a perfect miniature replica of that fateful moment in Aquaria—complete with tiny Lucian getting blasted by tiny Sera's light grenade. The 'snow' is golden sparkles, and when she shakes it, they swirl around a banner that reads 'You had me at 'take that, bloodsucker!''

"Because you literally knocked some sense into me," Lucian grins, looking mighty pleased with himself. "Get it? Because you actually blasted me. With holy light. Which was both the most enlightening and most painful moment of my undead life. Nothing says true love like celestial violence!"

I snort. Leave it to Lucian to turn getting holy-smacked by an angel into both a pun and a collectible. But watching Sera's eyes well up as she shakes the globe again, I must admit—the idiot nailed it. Somehow, he made it both ridiculous and touching, just like their entire relationship.

"And look," he adds excitedly, "if you turn it upside down, tiny-me gets blasted all over again! I even had them add the exact shade of 'oh shit' on my face when I realized a hot angel just kicked my ass. Now that's what I call attention to detail!"

"Lucian!" Sera gasps, but she's laughing through her tears.

I curl deeper into Rhyland's side, letting the warmth of his body chase away the morning chill. My fuzzy reindeer pajamas might not be the sexiest thing I own, but they're perfect for a cozy Christmas morning with our crazy family.

Emily's laugh draws my attention as she tears into Brax's gift—wrapped in Deadpool paper to annoy Lucian. Inside is a custom Marvel comic book with Brax and Emily as the main characters. The title reads "The Witch and the Demon: A Love Story (Now with 100% More Explosions!)". I catch glimpses of their adventures reimagined as superhero escapades, complete with Brax's signature snark in the dialogue bubbles.

"You made us into a comic book?" Emily laughs, flipping through the pages. "And why am I wearing a cape?"

"Because capes are awesome," Brax declares, still wearing Chris Hemsworth's face because he's a shit-stirrer. "And look, I even included our greatest hits—like that time you set my ass on fire. Literally. Page 12."

"It's a *cloak!*" Lucian corrects.

Next to them, Sable unwraps a sleek package from Damon to reveal the latest Kindle Paperwhite. Her squeal of delight makes us all smile.

"I noticed you've been devouring those steamy vampire romances faster than I drink blood," Damon teases, his voice warm despite the ribbing. "Figured you might appreciate something that doesn't leave evidence of your... literary tastes all over the mansion. Plus, I've already loaded it with the complete works of your favorite authors—including that series where the vampire has, and I quote, 'abs that could cut glass and a brooding stare that melts panties.'"

Sable's cheeks flush pink to match her bubblegum hair, but she clutches the Kindle to her chest like it's made of gold. "This is perfect," she whispers, kissing him.

"Just so we're clear," I call out, wiggling my eyebrows, "I'm totally borrowing that when you're done with the dirty parts. Call it research for my own love life." I gesture between Rhyland and me with a wink. "Though I might need to take notes—some of those positions require serious flexibility."

Rhyland chokes on his coffee beside me, and Sable throws a balled-up piece of wrapping paper at my head, her embarrassment melting into laughter.

"Oh my *god*," Lucian groans, dramatically throwing his head back. "Can we go five goddamn minutes without hearing about your bedroom acrobatics? Some of us are trying to enjoy Christmas without picturing Rhyland's naked ass. Though—" he points his candy cane at Sable with sudden interest, "if that Kindle has that series with the vampire twins who share everything, I call dibs after Dani. Erik needs some educational material since he's been dead inside since the Renaissance."

Erik's eye twitches as he silently contemplates which of Lucian's limbs to remove first.

I sip my coffee and snuggle back against Rhyland's chest. His arms tighten around me automatically, and I feel his smile against my hair.

This right here—surrounded by our crazy, supernatural family, watching love stories unfold uniquely—is better than any Christmas I could have imagined, even if Brax is still trying to convince everyone to watch all three Thor movies as our Christmas marathon.

Perfect doesn't begin to cover it. Perfectly chaotic, maybe. But I wouldn't have it any other way.

RHYLAND

81

Watching my makeshift family celebrate makes my chest tighten with fierce pride, even if Lucian can't keep his mouth shut for five fucking minutes. This is the first Christmas in forever that's meant a damn thing to me. Seeing my mate's face light up like that—yeah, that's a memory I'm keeping forever.

"Hold the fucking phone and rewind!" Lucian dramatically interrupts. "Are we just going to ignore the fact that Thunder Struck over here hasn't given his Christmas present yet? Come on, Rhy-Rhy, don't be a holiday cheapskate. Did you at least get her a gift card to Amazon?"

Everyone's eyes swing to us like it's feeding time at the zoo. Dani's grin threatens to split her face in half as she looks up at me, that spark of mischief in her caramel eyes making my heart beat faster.

"Show them, baby," I rumble, my hand sliding possessively around her waist.

Dani sits up straight, practically vibrating with excitement as she extends her left hand. "Oh, you mean this little thing?" she says with mock innocence, wiggling her fingers so the 4-carat diamond throws sparkles across the room. "Turns out Rhyland finally decided to make an honest woman out of me."

The custom-designed platinum band hugs her delicate finger perfectly, just like she fits perfectly against me.

Seraphina gasps, her hands flying to cover her mouth, golden eyes wide with angelic wonder. "Oh, Dani..."

"And before you ask, Lucian—yes, I'm fully aware I'm marrying a grumpy, possessive, ancient-as-dirt vampire. But he's my grumpy, possessive, ancient-as-dirt vampire."

Lucian throws his hands up dramatically. "You just had to go and beat everyone in the gift-giving department, didn't you? What happened to the brotherhood pact of 'reasonably priced presents so nobody looks bad'? Now my snow globe to Phina looks like toilet paper compared to your whole 'let's get hitched' extravaganza. Thanks for raising the bar to the stratosphere, asshole."

The girls swarm Dani like a pack of excited wolves, cooing over the ring and practically tackling her with hugs. I reluctantly let her go, watching with smug satisfaction as she shows off my claim on her.

"About damn time, you old fart," Emily snarks, elbowing me in the ribs before turning back to Dani. "And just so we're crystal clear, I've been this girl's Maid of Honor since we pinky-swore over wine coolers in high school. Though I gotta say, I pictured the groom with less brooding and more pulse."

I can't help the satisfied smirk spreading across my face as I watch them fuss over my mate. Yeah, I definitely won Christmas this year.

While everyone's cleaning up the massacre of wrapping paper, Emily clears her throat.

"Hold up. Got one more gift to deliver," she announces, turning to Bryn with an uncharacteristically nervous smile. "If Her Royal Valkyrie-ness will permit it?"

Sable's knowing grin catches my attention, but Dani just looks confused as she presses closer to my side.

Bryn's shoulders tense as she takes a half-step back. "For me?" Her voice carries an edge of wariness. "I have nothing to—"

"Oh, hush." Emily waves her hand dismissively. "Trust me, watching this unfold will be *my* gift. Now, will you let me?"

Bryn's gaze darts to Dani, who merely shrugs, looking equally mystified. After a long moment, Bryn gives a sharp nod.

"Perfect. Plant that warrior ass right here by the tree." Emily pats the floor with exaggerated patience.

Bryn lowers herself, folding her legs beneath her. The rest of us exchange confused glances as Emily kneels behind her, positioning her hands just above Bryn's shoulder blades.

"Just relax," Emily instructs, her usual playful tone replaced with something more focused. "And try not to stab me if this feels weird. I'm going to try to give you back your wings."

Bryn twists around, alarm flashing across her face. "Wait, what?"

"Shh." Emily flicks her wrist dismissively. "Less talking, more sitting still. This spell is tricky enough without you going all warrior-fidgety on me. Trust the process, Valkyrie."

The air grows thick with anticipation. Emily begins a low chant in Latin, her voice taking on an otherworldly resonance. Every candle in the room springs to life simultaneously, flames dancing in an unfelt wind. The taste of magic fills the air—sharp and electric, like the moment before lightning strikes.

"Quod amissum est, nunc restituo. Pennas perditas revoco. Sanguine caelesti, potentia terrae, redde quod ablatum est. Surge iterum, filia aeris."

Dani leans forward, perched on the edge of the couch like she can't wait to see if this can actually work. Beside her, Sable's grin threatens to split her face. Erik remains motionless, but his stormy eyes track every movement Emily makes, muscles coiled tight with protective instinct.

The chant rises in volume and intensity as Bryn's features contort, a mask of agony twisting her warrior's visage. Every eye in the room is locked on the unfolding scene, the raw power emanating from Emily's hands commanding complete attention.

"Redde quod periit," Emily intones, her voice echoing with ancient authority. *"Restitue quod ablatum est!"*

Fucking wings explode from Bryn's back without warning, unfurling to their full glory in a symphony of ripping fabric. But these aren't just any wings—the left one spans out in midnight black, pure Valkyrie power—to match the icy blue of her eye, while the right gleams with angelic white reminiscent of Seraphina's celestial wings—matching her gold eye.

"Holy shit," I mutter, the dichotomy striking me instantly. The contrast is jarring yet perfect—two halves of her heritage manifested physically.

The collective gasp that tears through the room is almost as powerful as the magic itself. Dani's mouth hangs open, her eyes wide with wonder. Erik stands frozen, grey eyes reflecting a thousand emotions simultaneously as he stares at his mate's transformation.

Bryn staggers to her feet, wobbling slightly as she adjusts to the new weight and balance. She steadies herself against the tree, unaware of what we're all staring at. The wings curl forward instinctively, bringing their tips into her line of sight.

Her mismatched eyes widen as she catches sight of the contrasting colors. One hand reaches toward the midnight feathers while the other hovers over the pristine white, trembling visibly. Watching Bryn, this badass warrior—who I've seen cleave enemies in half without flinching—is suddenly undone by this gift. It hits me in a place I didn't know existed.

"By the All Father," she whispers, voice cracking. A single tear slides down her cheek, followed by another, then a flood. "They're... perfect."

Emily sits back on her heels, looking immensely pleased with herself despite the exhaustion evident in her face. "Well, the grimoire *did* say to expect the unexpected when returning what was lost." She flashes a self-satisfied smirk. "I mean, the spell promised restoration, not replication. But holy shit, Bryn—this is like, next-level badass. You're literally walking duality now."

I catch Dani's eyes widening with recognition, that mischievous spark lighting up her face.

"Wait—is this that spell we talked about at Ray's—the cooch—"

"Yes!" Sable cuts her off with suspicious enthusiasm, tossing Dani a conspiratorial wink. "That *exact* one."

My woman's smile turns downright wicked. That look never means anything good for my sanity.

"What the hell are you two talking about?" I ask, eyes narrowing as I look between them. The last thing I need is more magical surprises, especially when Dani's got that dangerous gleam in her eyes.

Without warning, Bryn lunges forward, tackling Emily in an embrace that sends them both sprawling across the floor. The massive wings curl protectively around them, creating a black-and-white canopy.

"Thank you," Bryn sobs against Emily's shoulder, all warrior stoicism abandoned. Her fingers dig into Emily's sweater like she's afraid this might all disappear. "Thank you, thank you, thank you."

Her breakdown cracks something open in the room. Dani's wiping tears from her cheeks. I've witnessed civilizations rise and fall, but watching someone regain a piece of themselves they thought lost forever—that's power that even immortals recognize.

Watching Bryn's transformation, I can't help but feel a surge of satisfaction. The warrior who lost everything protecting my mate now stands restored—though in true cosmic fashion, the universe had its own ideas about the restoration. The duality of those wings suits her, matching those mismatched eyes that have seen both darkness and light.

Dani launches herself at her sister, colliding with enough force that Bryn's new wings flare out to maintain balance.

The sight of my fierce mate wrapped in those contrasting wings, babbling about family and belonging, stirs something even in my jaded heart.

Erik—that stone-faced bastard who's stood unmoved through centuries of war-fare—looks like he's about to crack. His silver eyes shine suspiciously bright as he watches his mate whole again, restored but transformed. Never thought I'd see the day Erik might actually shed a tear.

Leave it to Lucian to shatter the fucking moment.

"Well damn," he drawls. "Talk about a heavenly makeover. You're like a walking yin-yang of badassery now. The ultimate warrior-angel hybrid. Should we start calling you Dark-Light Barbie?"

I shoot him a look that promises violence. "Shut the fuck up, Lucian."

But Bryn's laughing through her tears, and even Erik cracks a smile. Trust my asshole brother to diffuse an emotional moment with stupid logic. Though I suppose that's why we keep him around.

DANICA

82

The world erupts in blinding white. Glass explodes inward as the blast hurls me across our Christmas sanctuary. My spine connects with marble, the crack reverberating through bone. Copper floods my mouth as warm rivulets trace down my face, turning my reindeer pajamas blood-red. The Christmas tree lies shattered, ornaments pulverized to glittering dust, catching winter sunlight through blown-out windows.

I force trembling limbs to move, glass slicing into my palms. The room tilts and spins—a kaleidoscope of horror. Wrapping paper flutters like wounded butterflies. Lucian's Iron Man helmet rolls past, faceplate shattered, one eye still glowing in mechanical death.

"Rhy—" His name catches on blood coating my throat.

Black combat boots materialize through settling debris. Fingers lunge, tangling in my hair before I can process the movement. My scalp ignites as she yanks upward, suspending my weight by burning roots.

Morgan's face swims into focus, onyx-black lips curved in satisfaction. A droplet of my blood spatters across her cheek. She savors it, tongue darting out to taste.

"*Movere!*" The Latin cuts through the air like a blade.

An invisible battering ram slams into my sternum. For one suspended moment, I'm weightless. Then marble intercepts my flight with unforgiving solidity. My skull rebounds with a wet thud. Something cracks—inside me, behind me, I can't tell anymore.

Warmth cascades down my neck as snow drifts in through shattered windows, landing on my outstretched hand, melting instantly to pink. The mansion's grand foyer fragments before my eyes—twinkling lights and evergreen garlands now splinters and dust.

Morgan's boots strike a deliberate rhythm against marble.

Thump.

Thump.

Thump.

Each sound drives spikes through my fractured skull, her boots leaving bloody footprints across Italian tile.

Twenty feet away, Rhyland lies crumpled beside our fallen Christmas tree. Our star—placed together, laughing—lies shattered beside his outstretched hand.

Morgan extends one elegant hand toward him, rings catching winter light. "*Cruciatus spiritus,*" she purrs.

Rhyland contorts unnaturally. Veins bulge black beneath his skin, spreading like dark rivers. The scream that tears from his throat isn't human—a primal howl that scrapes against my soul. His fingers claw at his temples, drawing fresh blood.

Lucian hangs suspended against the wall, a jagged shard of wooden banister impaled through his chest. Blood—so much blood—cascades down his torso, soaking his clothes. His eyes stare vacantly, mouth frozen in a silent scream.

Erik lies face-down, three wooden stakes protruding from his back like grotesque ornaments. Blood pools beneath him, turning the white marble black. Beside him, Bryn sprawls motionless, her platinum hair fanned in a sticky bloody halo. Her wings lie partially visible, the ethereal feathers singed and matted with blood, her fingertips barely brushing Erik's outstretched hand.

Seraphina's broken form curls against the base of the staircase, her white nightgown now scarlet-soaked. Blood seeps from a gash across her temple, trickling down to join the growing puddle beneath her head.

I search frantically for the others. Damon—my brother. Emily. Sable.

Where are they?

The silence screams back at me.

I can't process what I'm seeing—my family—my powerful, immortal family—reduced to death, lay scattered across our home. The Christmas tree lies toppled on its side, ornaments shattered across the floor, yet somehow its lights still twinkle stubbornly, casting colored shadows across pools of blood.

I reach deep for my light. Golden sparks dance weakly across bloodied palms—

Morgan's head snaps toward me, nostrils flaring. "*Caput percutite!*" she snarls.

My head slams backward. Skull meets marble with a sickening crunch. White-hot agony obliterates thought. Fresh blood drips down my neck as Christmas morning fragments into spinning shards.

The light within me gutters like a candle in a hurricane. Each throb scatters my focus, power slipping through numb fingers.

Morgan chants ancient syllables that darken the air. Frost crystallizes on broken ornaments and pooling blood. Shadows in corners lengthen, reaching hungry fingers across the floor.

"Stop," I rasp through blood-slick lips.

Rhyland's torment hammers through our bond, shorting out coherent thought. I taste his pain, feel his terror—our connection transmitting every nuance directly into my soul.

"*Vinculum amoris disrumpere,*" she intones, voice resonating at frequencies that make my teeth vibrate. "*Animas separare!*"

My blood betrays me, answering Morgan's call. It seeps through my skin—not flowing but floating—crimson beads rising from my pores like macabre dew. The droplets hover, suspended in the air around me as her chanting intensifies.

But it's not just blood she's stealing. With each scarlet sphere that pulls free, I feel Rhyland's essence being extracted—the part of him that lives in me, that merged with my very cells when we bonded. His power, his immortality, the fragments of his soul that became mine.

The connection between us unravels strand by strand. Each droplet that joins the crimson cloud carries away another memory, another piece of what makes us one. My veins burn hollow as they empty, my mate bond hemorrhaging into the air around me.

My body lifts inches off the floor, suspended in Morgan's invisible grip as she harvests what was never hers to take. The blood orbits me in a grotesque constellation, each droplet pulsing with Rhyland's stolen essence. My vision dims at the edges, the void inside me expanding as Morgan strips away not just my life, but the foundation of who I've become.

Something tears inside my chest. The mate bond stretches taut, thinning visibly. I scream as invisible hands pull at that sacred connection. The agony transcends understanding—my essence extracted through my sternum, one cell at a time.

No. No. No.

"Don't," I choke, feeling something fundamental fracture inside me.

Rhyland's pain fades like a radio losing signal. The blessed warmth of his presence recedes with each syllable. My soul reaches desperately across the widening chasm, grasping at dissolving threads.

"Rhyland!" His name tears from my throat.

Blood streaks marble as he drags himself toward Morgan, fingernails splitting against stone. His Christmas pajamas—little lightning bolts I'd bought as a joke—now soaked in blood.

"*Animae tuae non amplius ligatae!*" Morgan's voice cracks like a whip. "*Fractae et separatae!*"

Our bond shatters like struck crystal. A thousand razor-sharp pieces slice through my chest. The following emptiness is absolute—a void where Rhyland's presence should be.

My sobs echo off marble—animal sounds from a creature mortally wounded. So fucking empty. Hollowed out where a soul used to be.

"*Mens dominari,*" Morgan purrs, fingers weaving patterns that dance before shattering.

Rhyland jerks upright, movements disjointed. His ocean-blue eyes go vacant. My proud warrior becomes a marionette responding to Morgan's will.

I thrash against invisible bonds, blood soaking my Christmas pajamas. The engagement ring catches light, a cruel reminder of promises now hanging by threads.

"NO!" The word emerges garbled through blood and tears.

His feet drag across marble, leaving smeared bloody footprints. His hand twitches—one final rebellion—before they disappear through the shattered doorway.

Christmas snow swirls in, settling on abandoned presents and pooling blood like a mockery of the perfect morning that had been ours moments before.

Sulfurous smoke erupts before me, acrid and biting. My nostrils burn as Brax materializes, his monstrous form solidifying from darkness as he gently sets Emily down. The transition from demon smoke to his hulking ten-foot charred form is instant—obsidian skin cracked with glowing embers, horns curving from his skull.

"Rhyland," I croak, the name barely audible through blood-filled lungs.

Emily's eyes flash electric blue, crackling energy rolling off her in waves as she whirls toward the doorway where Morgan disappeared with my mate. Brax lunges for her, clawed hand extending.

"Stay with Dani!" Emily commands, her voice resonating with newfound power. "Protect her with your life!"

Brax freezes mid-motion, bound by their magical connection. Frustration contorts his demonic features as he watches Emily sprint after Morgan, her hands already weaving complex patterns in the air.

"*Sistere in nomine lucis!*" Emily's voice thunders down the hallway. "*Animas captivas liberare!*" The mansion trembles with her power, plaster dust raining from the ceiling.

Sable appears before me, her bubblegum hair matted with blood, brown eyes wide with determination. Her fingers—steady despite the chaos—cradle my face.

"Here. Drink." Before I can protest, she bites savagely into her own wrist. Blood wells immediately, bright crimson against her pale skin. She presses the wound against my mouth, her other hand holding my head firmly in place. "Now, Dani!"

Fuck. Has she forgotten what blood-sharing does?

The first drop hits my tongue—electric, vibrant, alive. My body recognizes the salvation before my mind can process it. I swallow reflexively, then deliberately, drawing deeply from her wrist. Warmth floods through me, targeting each broken piece. My shattered ribs knit together with audible clicks. My punctured lung inflates, the torn tissue sealing itself. My fractured skull mends, the pressure behind my eyes subsiding as blood vessels repair themselves. My dislocated shoulder pops back into place with a sickening wrench that barely registers through the healing euphoria.

I gasp, drawing my first full breath since the attack, no longer drowning in my own blood. The world snaps back into terrible focus—every detail crystalline in its horror.

But the emptiness where Rhyland should be remains an absolute void that no amount of healing blood can touch.

That fucking bitch carved out what should have been untouchable. Our bond—violently shredded from our souls like she reached in and gutted us both. The emptiness howls inside me, a raw, bleeding chasm.

I want to scream until my vocal cords shred.

Sob until I vomit.

I want to hunt that soul-stealing bitch to the darkest corner of every goddamn realm and rip her apart piece by bloody piece with my bare hands.

What kind of twisted, unholy shit has she tapped into? What abomination of magic lets someone tear apart what the universe has bound together?

Strength surges through newly-healed limbs as I lurch to my feet, blood still smeared across my Christmas pajamas. "Help the others," I command Sable, already moving. My bare feet leave bloody prints across marble as I sprint after my mate, the engagement ring on my finger catching winter light with each desperate stride.

The mansion's grand entrance hangs in splinters. Outside, horror unfolds across our pristine front lawn.

The dead claw their way through frost-hardened earth—rotting hands punching through snow-covered ground, decayed bodies dragging themselves from shallow graves. Morgan stands at the center of this nightmare, one hand extended toward my vacant-eyed mate, the other conducting her macabre orchestra of corpses. Her elegant black coat billows around her despite the lack of wind, power radiating from her in visible waves of darkness that wither everything they touch.

Emily fights a losing battle against the horde. Fire erupts from her in roaring columns, incinerating three corpses at once. Their flesh blackens and crackles, but still they come. She stomps her foot, and the earth responds—a fissure opens to swallow two more walking dead. Sweat pours down her face despite the freezing temperature, her rainbow hair plastered to her forehead as she summons a whirl-wind that tosses rotting bodies like rag dolls.

"You think you can over power me?" Morgan's voice carries across the front yard, rich with contempt. "I've consumed more black magic than you could ever imagine."

To demonstrate, she flicks one manicured finger. The huge oak that's stood sentinel over our driveway shrivels instantly—bark blackening, branches contorting as if in agony. With another casual gesture, she sends Emily flying backward, her body slamming into our stone fountain with bone-crushing force.

"Yeah, well..." Emily spits blood onto pristine snow, staggering to her feet with a savage grin. "That's cute. But guess what? I've got a hundred crispy witch souls riding shotgun in my veins. And unlike your bargain-bin black magic bullshit, mine came with a side of righteous fucking fury." She wipes her split lip with the back of her hand, eyes blazing. "So why don't you take your necromantic horse shit, and shove them both straight up your ass!"

Emily's hands slash through the air, "Ignis!" Flames erupt in a perfect circle around Morgan. The fire roars twenty feet high, trapping the witch in a blazing prison. Through the fire, I see Morgan's face contort with fury—but even her power can't breach Emily's inferno.

But the dead keep coming. Dozens of corpses claw their way from frozen earth, moving with unnatural speed across our snow-covered lawn—their rotting flesh and exposed bone—a grotesque contrast to the pristine winter morning.

Rhyland stands motionless between us, his vacant eyes reflecting the dancing flames. Blood drips in ruby trails down his temple, his powerful frame unnaturally still under Morgan's control.

I reach for my power, expecting the familiar surge of winter's might, but nothing happens. The snowflakes continue their lazy descent, deaf to my call. I scream in frustration, clawing desperately at that well of power that should be there—that *needs* to be there. But where I should feel the icy rush of strength, there's only emptiness. My connection to the Aquanite stone feels severed, leaving me helpless as I watch the undead advance.

The blast hits without warning—raw arcane energy that feels like liquid lightning. One moment I'm standing, the next I'm airborne, the world spinning in a kaleidoscope of snow and fire. My body slams into frozen ground fifteen feet away, my back screaming as air explodes from my lungs. The impact rattles through every bone, leaving me gasping like a landed fish on ice-crusted snow.

Through blurred vision, I see him. Adrian—the brother who betrayed us, now another puppet in Lilith's collection. Dark power rolls off him in visible waves, his eyes obsidian pools of emptiness. The gentle scholar who helped me understand ancient texts now stands ready to annihilate us all with devastating magic.

My heart twists as I force painful limbs to move. I have to reach him, have to break Lilith's hold before his power—always so carefully controlled—reduces everyone I love to ashes. But first, I need to remember how to breathe.

"Adrian!" His name tears from my oxygen-starved lungs. "Stop! This isn't you—fight it!"

He advances with mechanical precision, each footstep crushing snow beneath expensive leather shoes. His hands—once gentle with ancient scrolls—now crackle with death magic. His eyes reflect nothing, twin voids where kindness once lived. Whatever command Lilith embedded runs deep—kill me or drag me back for her entertainment.

"Adrian..." My voice cracks with warning as I struggle upright. "Don't make me do this."

One blast will kill him.

Then realization hits like a thunderbolt—daylight, and Adrian's not burning. Seraphina's blood still flows in his veins.

I don't hesitate—I reach deep for that golden power, my birthright from Elysium, but where there should be warmth and radiance, I find only a void. Nothing. Not even a spark. Panic claws at my throat as I try again, desperately searching for that familiar glow, but there's...nothing. My power is gone.

Adrian advances closer, dark magic crackling around his fingers, and I can't access the one thing that could stop him.

A flash of gold streaks to my side. Seraphina's wings flare out protectively as pure celestial light erupts from her hands, slamming into Adrian's chest. The impact lifts him off his feet, his body arcing through the frigid air like a broken doll before crashing into the snow thirty yards away. He lies motionless, smoke rising from his chest where her divine light burned through his expensive fabric to the flesh beneath.

Holy shit. "Sera—"

Brax explodes through the doorway as Chris Hemsworth Thor, complete with flowing locks and Mjölnir.

"AVENGERS ASSEMBLE!" he bellows.

Lucian staggers out behind him, blood soaking his shirt. "You absolute thunder-stealing asshole!" he seethes. "We specifically discussed this—that was MY line!"

Erik and Bryn spill onto the battlefield next, moving in perfect sync despite their injuries. Erik's silver hair is matted with blood, Bryn's wings drag slightly in the snow, but her eyes burn with determination.

They launch into battle with lethal efficiency. Erik's sword, Grave Warden, slices through rotting limbs, leaving silver light in its wake. Beside him, Bryn's Valkyrie blade dances in lethal arcs, decapitating three corpses with a single sweep. Where Erik is precision, Bryn is fluid grace—together forming a whirlwind of destruction.

Seraphina takes to the air, wings fully unfurled. Divine radiance pulses from her palms in concentrated beams. Where her celestial light touches the undead, they disintegrate, the snow beneath them glittering with ash.

Relief floods through me at seeing them alive—though I swear I'm going to shove that Iron Man helmet down Lucian's throat when this is over. Only these idiots could turn an apocalyptic battle into a Marvel moment.

Across the battlefield, Brax abandons his Thor cosplay. The handsome facade melts away, revealing the nightmare beneath—obsidian skin cracked with pulsing ember lines, massive horns curving like a crown of darkness. Against the pristine snow, he stands as a monument to primal terror.

His chest expands impossibly before he unleashes apocalyptic fury. Blood-red flame erupts from his blackened lips, cutting through the morning frost like a laser. The temperature spikes as his hellfire carves a smoldering trench through the advancing horde.

My jaw drops as Brax sweeps dragon-like breath in devastating arcs, each blast melting perfect semicircles in the snow. The heat blisters my face from twenty feet away as another wave reduces Morgan's puppets to cinders.

I've never imagined this sarcastic, Marvel-obsessed demon possessed such devastating force. This creature commands elemental destruction, moving with terrifying purpose as blackened bones crumble to the earth.

I sprint toward Rhyland, heart pounding. My fingers almost brush his arm—

Then the world tilts violently. His hand shoots out, familiar strength now turned against me. My body hurdles backward, snow and sky spinning until impact, shooting pain straight to my ribs.

What the fuck? The man who'd held me so tenderly this morning just threw me like garbage.

Morgan's laughter carries across the lawn, a reminder that the man I love is trapped behind those vacant eyes.

"He's not going anywhere," Morgan's says with satisfaction, each word a poisoned dagger.

Before anyone can react, darkness coalesces beside Rhyland—a writhing mass of shadow and smoke solidifying into Lilith's elegant form. Her red lips curve triumphantly as she wraps possessive fingers around his arm. Morgan materializes next to her, stepping into Lilith's expanding shadow.

Lilith's gaze finds mine across the devastation, eyes glittering with malice.

"Merry Christmas, darling," she purrs. "I do hope you like my gift of loneliness. It suits you."

Then they dissolve together—Lilith, Morgan, and the love of my life—swallowed by a void of swirling darkness that dissipates like ink in water, leaving nothing but empty space where my world stood seconds before.

No.

Gone.

She's taken him.

RHYLAND

83

The smoke and shadows dissipate, leaving behind that gut-wrenching sensation of being ripped through the fabric of reality. I collapse onto the blacktop, vomiting a pool of blood as my body rejects the unnatural transportation. Every muscle spasms in protest, my vision swimming as I try to orient myself against the nauseating vertigo.

A sleek private jet materializes through my fractured vision. We're on some private tarmac, location unknown. Lilith's talons dig into my bicep, her nails breaking skin as Morgan hovers at my right. I'm a fucking puppet on their strings, my limbs responding to their commands rather than my own.

Dani. *Fuck.* She's gone. Where her presence once filled every corner of my soul, there's nothing but a raw, bleeding void. Not physical pain—worse. The mate bond—that golden thread connecting our essences—severed, leaving jagged edges where her light once flowed into me. A metaphysical amputation.

I'm a prisoner in my own fucking skin. My mind screams while my body betrays me, muscles obeying Morgan's commands rather than my own. A millennium of power reduced to this—a marionette dancing on a witch's strings.

Every cell strains toward that emptiness where Dani should be, like a phantom limb reaching for what no longer exists. The bond's absence bleeds continuously, a cosmic violation beyond torture.

This fucking witch forced my hand against my own mate—made me use my power to hurt the one person I'm supposed to protect. Watching Dani's body slam backwards, knowing my own abilities caused it... pure fucking torture. My insides turned to acid, bile rising in my throat, but Morgan's magic kept me locked in place like a goddamn puppet. Couldn't even look away as my mate took the hit. Just had to stand there, rage burning through every cell while that psychotic bitch used me as her personal weapon.

The memory makes my fangs descend, murderous fury coursing through my veins. Being forced to hurt Dani—my fierce little warrior—that's the kind of violation that demands blood payment. And when I get free, Morgan will learn exactly what that feels like.

"Come, darling. We have a long flight ahead of us." Lilith yanks me toward the jet like a trophy she's just won.

She shoves me into butter-soft leather seating, rolling her eyes as she snaps at the pilot. "For God's sake, get this thing in the air before I replace you with someone competent."

Once we're airborne, Morgan slides beside me. Inside, I'm a fucking inferno of rage, every cell screaming for blood. The primal beast howls for vengeance, demanding their throats.

"Morgan, darling. I think now is as good a time as any," Lilith examines her manicure with exaggerated boredom. "But first, let my dark prince speak. I'm simply dying to hear what pathetic threats he's managed to cobble together." She smirks cruelly.

Morgan flicks her wrist, releasing my voice.

"You fucking bitch! I'm going to rip your fucking spine out through your throat and—"

Another casual wave, and my vocal cords seize.

Lilith sighs dramatically. "Honestly, is that the best you can do? So predictably primitive. I expected something more... creative from you." She examines her nails again. "Do it. I'm already bored with his caveman routine."

The witch places both hands on my temples. I fight like a caged animal, muscles straining to rupture point. My fangs descend fully, useless without flesh to tear.

She begins chanting, her nails piercing my scalp as I scream silently. My brain feels shredded, ablaze from within.

"*Memoria delere... animus purgare... praeteritum eradere...*" Morgan's voice rises and falls, each syllable driving white-hot spikes through my skull.

Through the agony, I hear Lilith: "Do remember, darling, to leave the good parts. We need him functional, just... redirected."

What the fuck?

The chanting intensifies. I strain harder, blood vessels rupturing in my eyes. Suddenly, visions of Dani flood my consciousness—her honey-gold eyes, fierce determination, the way she curls against me in sleep.

Our first meeting. The electric shock of her touch. Her body writhing beneath mine. Her tears, her pleasure, her courage.

The memories unspool backward like film burning, each ripped away, leaving bleeding gaps in my consciousness.

No. *Gods no.*

The bitch is stripping away my truth, layer by fucking layer. I feel it happening—my heritage dissolving like smoke. Everything I am—son of Magni, grandson of Thor, child of Nyx—ripped from my skull, leaving bleeding gaps they'll fill with lies.

Morgan's magic burns through each memory like acid. Whatever they pour back into these wounds won't be my truth. They're gutting my mind to remake me, and I can't do a fucking thing to stop it.

I roar inside my mental prison, murderous rage boiling through every cell. I've slaughtered armies, conquered realms, survived a millennium of bloodshed—now rendered helpless while they lobotomize me.

The final memory—where I knew beyond doubt that I loved Dani—begins to dissolve. That night in her apartment, when she accepted me completely. Her body yielding to mine as we sealed our bond, her whispered acceptance as I claimed her. The memory unravels like a tapestry violently torn apart as I desperately cling to fragments.

"He's fighting me!" Morgan snarls, her nails drawing blood as she digs deeper.

"Well, darling, push harder." Lilith's voice drips with impatient entitlement. "We don't have all night for your incompetence."

My consciousness fractures as I battle the invasion, clinging to Dani's face with everything I have. This is worse than death. They're erasing what matters, leaving a hollow shell that looks like me but isn't.

Every neuron fires in desperate resistance as Morgan's magic tears through my mind, leaving scorched earth where Dani once lived.

"There we go," Morgan pants, sweat beading on her forehead. "Just a little more."

I'm verging on blackout, blood vessels repeatedly rupturing and healing. When Morgan finally releases me, I slump forward like a marionette with cut strings. Fucking drained.

"Wonderful. Let's see now. Let him speak." Lilith snaps her fingers impatiently.

I blink, disoriented, as the fog clears. My vampire healing frantically repairs damage I don't remember receiving. One moment we were... wait—where? The details slip away like smoke.

My gaze lands on Lilith, and an unexpected wave of affection surges through me. My body reacts before my mind processes it—reaching for her hand, lips curving into a devoted smile.

"My Queen," I hear myself say.

"Much better," Lilith purrs. "So much better." She sips champagne, snapping for another flute.

She shoves the crystal glass at me, blood-red nails clicking against the stem. "A toast to victory, darling. I've finally reclaimed what's *always* been mine."

My fingers close around the glass. Of course they do. This is where I belong—at Lilith's side. That's how it's always been... hasn't it?

"Where are we headed, my Queen?"

The words leave my mouth, automatic and reverent, but something deep twists—an ancient instinct contradicting the memories crowding my skull. My head says I love her, but my body recoils from her touch.

"Somewhere far away, my love. Where no one will ever find us."

No one will find us.

The phrase echoes like a warning bell. Something dark and powerful stirs in my chest—a beast recognizing a cage. There's an emptiness inside me, raw and bleeding, like a phantom limb reaching for something beyond memory.

I nod, raising my glass.

The jet cuts through clouds, and I can't shake the feeling that something essential is missing. Something vital. Something *mine.*

But that's ridiculous.

Isn't it?

THANK YOU

Hey You, Yes You—The Amazing Reader Who Just Finished Book Four!

First off, high-fives, hugs, and a whole parade in your honor, because you? You're the real MVP here. Give yourself a round of applause for sticking with Dani and Rhyland through another chapter of their pulse-pounding, realm-hopping escapades.

Thank you from the bottom of my caffeine-fueled heart for diving back into the whirlwind world of the Crown of the Seven Realm series. Your support means the world to me and quite possibly to all seven realms (they're still counting votes on that one). These characters and their stories are my babies; you've just helped them grow.

Now, take a breath, grab a snack, and pat yourself on the back because you've survived the twists, turns, and cliffhangers (oh, the cliffhangers!). Your dedication to following our fearless (and sometimes fearsome) lovebirds on their journey is more appreciated than you know.

But hold onto your hats—or crowns—because this roller coaster isn't done yet. Get ready for Book Five—**DARK DESIRES** which is lurking just beyond the horizon, and it's packed with more realm-hopping shenanigans sending our heros to the Fire Realm—Pyrothos.

Keep an eye out because Dani and Rhyland will be back before you can say "realm-hoping romance," and trust me, you won't want to miss the next leg of their journey. So, recharge your reading device, mark your calendars, follow me on social media to stay in the loop, and prepare your favorite reading nook. It's going to be a ride you'll never forget.

Until our paths cross again in the pages of Book Three, I'm sending loads of gratitude and the promise of more thrills, more heart, and yes, more swoon-worthy moments.

With all my thanks and anticipation,
Your Favorite Portal-Pushing Author,
A.L. Hampton

THE SEVEN REALMS

 1. Atheria. The Realm of Light and Creation. It is a realm of divine beauty and purity where celestial beings and creatures of light reside. It is a place of harmony and enlightenment, where the power of creation flows freely, shaping the fabric of existence.

 2. Aquaria. The Realm of Water. Aquaria is a vast world with vibrant marine life and mystical creatures, such as Merfolk, Skelkies, and Pirates. It is a realm of serenity and fluidity where the ebb and flow of tides hold great power.

 3. Luminara—The fae reigns supreme in the realm of Luminara, a world filled with enchanting beauty and mystical wonders. Luminara is a realm of ethereal forests, shimmering lakes, and glowing meadows, where the natural world is interwoven with magic and wonder.

 4. Mortalis—The Mortal Realm, where humanity resides with immortals and explores the boundaries of their existence. It has diverse landscapes, bustling cities, and uncharted territories. Humans navigate their everyday lives in Mortalis, unaware of the existence of other realms.

 5. Pyrothos—The Realm of Fire. Pyrothos is a land of perpetual flames and scorching heat, where volcanic landscapes and fiery mountains dominate. It is a realm of passion and intensity, where the essence of fire fuels the powers of its inhabitants. Pyrothos is home to powerful fire elementals, fire-breathing creatures, and ancient fire temples.

 6. Unbra—The Realm of Shadows. A world consumed by eternal darkness, where pure evil lurks, and creatures of nightmarish origins dwell. It is a realm shrouded in mystery and treachery, harboring ancient secrets and maleficent forces.

 7. Zephyria—Realm of Sky and Air— Zephyria is breathtaking, with endless skies and gentle breezes. No one knows what this realm is besides vast expanses of open air, where the wind guides the movement of everything.

About the Author

Hi there! I'm A.L. Hampton, and like so many of you, I've been completely obsessed with books for as long as I can remember. There's nothing quite like getting completely lost in a story—you know that feeling when you look up and realize hours have passed? That's my happy place.

I'm absolutely head-over-heels for fantasy, urban fantasy, romantasy, and anything dark and paranormal. And yes, I'm totally here for the spice! After years of devouring every book I could get my hands on in these genres, I found myself thinking, "What if I combined all my favorite elements into one series?" That's how the Crown of the Seven Realms Series was born. I'm a total sucker for witty banter and characters that feel like real people— flawed, funny, and fierce. When I'm not busy torturing my characters, you'll find me gaming, or exploring the gorgeous Pacific Northwest with my patient husband and two spoiled dogs.

My background is a bit all over the place—I have an A.A. in Criminal Justice, a B.S. in Psychology, and an M.Ed. in Education. Turns out, studying human behavior comes in pretty handy when you're trying to write believable characters and relationships!

As a debut author, I'm beyond excited to share these stories with fellow book lovers.

Welcome to my world!
-A.L. Hampton

Acknowledgements

Y'all, This Book Was A Whole Team Effort!

Listen up, because these incredible humans deserve ALL the spotlight! First, to my ride-or-die beta readers—**Kerry Taylor, Talia Harris, and Samantha Parisi**—y'all really said "challenge accepted" to those rough drafts and turned them into pure gold. You dove headfirst into my chaos and emerged with golden feedback that had me screaming "YES QUEEN!" into my coffee mug every morning.

And my ARC squad? *chef's kiss* You beautiful souls took this story and claimed it. Your enthusiasm gives me life, and I'm living for every single reaction!

Enola Henderson, you magical unicorn of support! Your cheerleading game is stronger than my coffee addiction (and that's saying something). You've been promoting this series like it's your job, and I'm forever grateful for your magical friendship.

To my family who's witnessed every writing meltdown and victory dance—thanks for nodding along when I rambled about plot twists at dinner (even when your eyes were glazing over). And to my husband, my real-life romantic hero—my personal plot bunny wrangler—babe, you've been my anchor through every writing storm, my cheerleader through every doubt. You're the true MVP of this journey, and I couldn't do any of this without you!

TALIA!

Girl, you deserve your own paragraph because HOW do you still answer my texts after the millionth "but what if..." message? Our late night plotting sessions are legendary. You're stuck with me now, sorry not sorry!

And to my readers, you beautiful, beautiful people—four books deep into this series, and you're still here, still screaming in the comments, still making my heart do that weird flippy thing. You've turned this journey into something more magical than I ever dreamed possible. Y'all aren't just readers anymore—you're family!

A.L HAMPTON

Now, let's go cause some more literary mayhem together, shall we?